CLARENCE

broadview editions
series editor: L.W. Conolly

Frontispiece from the 1849 edition of *Clarence*.
Engraved by W.J. Jackman after a portrait of
Catharine Sedgwick by Charles Cromwell Ingham.
Courtesy University of Pennsylvania.

CLARENCE; OR, A TALE OF OUR OWN TIMES

Catharine Maria Sedgwick

edited by
Melissa J. Homestead and Ellen A. Foster

Introduction by Melissa J. Homestead
and
Notes by Ellen A. Foster

broadview editions

Library and Archives Canada Cataloguing in Publication

Sedgwick, Catharine Maria, 1789-1867
    Clarence, or, A tale of our own times / Catharine Maria Sedgwick ; edited by Melissa J. Homestead and Ellen A. Foster ; introduction by Melissa J. Homestead and notes by Ellen A. Foster.

(Broadview editions)
Includes bibliographical references.
ISBN 978-1-55111-861-1

    I. Homestead, Melissa J., 1963- II. Foster, Ellen A. III. Title.
IV. Title: Tale of our own times. V. Series: Broadview editions

PS2798.C53 2011   813'.2   C2011-905203-2

Broadview Editions
The Broadview Editions series represents the ever-changing canon of literature in English by bringing together texts long regarded as classics with valuable lesser-known works.

Advisory editor for this volume: Michel Pharand

Broadview Press is an independent, international publishing house, incorporated in 1985.

We welcome comments and suggestions regarding any aspect of our publications—please feel free to contact us at the addresses below or at broadview@broadviewpress.com.

North America
PO Box 1243, Peterborough, Ontario, Canada K9J 7H5
2215 Kenmore Ave., Buffalo, New York, USA 14207
Tel: (705) 743-8990; Fax: (705) 743-8353
email: customerservice@broadviewpress.com

UK, Europe, Central Asia, Middle East, Africa, India, and Southeast Asia
Eurospan Group, 3 Henrietta St., London WC2E 8LU, United Kingdom
Tel: 44 (0) 1767 604972; Fax: 44 (0) 1767 601640
email: eurospan@turpin-distribution.com

Australia and New Zealand
NewSouth Books
c/o TL Distribution, 15-23 Helles Ave., Moorebank, NSW, Australia 2170
Tel: (02) 8778 9999; Fax: (02) 8778 9944
email: orders@tldistribution.com.au

www.broadviewpress.com

This book is printed on paper containing 100% postconsumer fibre.

Typesetting and assembly: Eileen Eckert, Calgary, Canada.

PRINTED IN CANADA

Contents

Acknowledgements

We have benefitted from the advice and assistance of many scholars in the preparation of this edition. Susan Belasco and Stephen Behrendt gave advice on our original proposal, and Broadview's two anonymous reviewers helped us to sharpen our approach. Audiences at the Catharine Maria Sedgwick Symposium, the Society for Early Americanists, and the Society for the Study of American Women Writers listened attentively to our work in progress and asked productive questions. Librarians at the American Antiquarian Society, Historical Society of Pennsylvania, Library Company of Philadelphia, Van Pelt Library at the University of Pennsylvania, Massachusetts Historical Society, Stockbridge Library Association, Morgan Library, Alderman Library at the University of Virginia, Boston Public Library, British Library, Bodleian Library at Oxford University, and New York Public Library helped us locate and access important materials.

Excerpts from *The Education of the Heart: The Correspondence of Rachel Mordecai Lazarus and Maria Edgeworth* (Appendix A2), edited by Edgar E. McDonald, copyright © 1977 by the University of North Carolina Press are used by permission of the publisher. We also thank the American Antiquarian Society, Massachusetts Historical Society, and the University of Pennsylvania for permission to use images and manuscript excerpts from their collections. A Reese Fellowship in Bibliography and the History of the Book in the Americas funded Melissa Homestead's research in the papers of publishers Carey & Lea at the Historical Society of Pennsylvania. James Green of the Library Company helped her navigate this byzantine archive. Eve Tavor Bannet answered queries about Maria Edgeworth and Rachel Mordecai Lazarus, and Charlene Avallone about Herman Melville in the Berkshires; both also read and provided helpful suggestions about the introduction, as did Patricia Larson Kalayjian. The University of Nebraska-Lincoln English Department funded several semesters of graduate research assistance. Melissa is particularly thankful for two semesters of able and rigorous work by Sarah Weinert Huppert. The UNL English Department also provided a special stipend to fund Shannon McMahon's work as initial translator of French in the novel. Funding from the College of Arts and Sciences and the Department of English at Clarion University supported Ellen's research and conference travel. Clarion University-Venango

Campus funded several semesters of undergraduate research assistance; Ellen especially appreciates the careful work and patient attention to detail that Erin Wincek brought to this project.

Introduction

Melissa J. Homestead

Catharine Sedgwick and the American Novel of Manners

In his preface to his novel of manners *Home as Found* (1838), James Fenimore Cooper repeats what were already commonplaces about American society as the subject matter for fiction. Lamenting "that no attempt to delineate ordinary American life, either on the stage or in the pages of a novel, has been rewarded with success,"[1] he admits *Home as Found* is another such attempt but professes he has "scarcely a hope of success. It would be indeed a desperate undertaking, to think of making anything interesting in the way of a *Roman de Société* [novel of social life] in this country; still, useful glances may possibly be made in that direction."[2] Twentieth-century literary historians largely took Cooper at his word, citing his preface and accepting his judgment that *Home as Found* was the earliest "glance" in the direction of an American novel of manners. Proclaiming that realistic portrayals of social custom were the appropriate province of the early nineteenth-century European novel, but not the American, they argued that antebellum American authors resorted instead to the romance. In this literary historical trajectory, the full flowering of the American novel of manners occurred only late in the century, with the rise of Henry James and Edith Wharton.[3] Taking account of Catharine Maria Sedgwick's *Clarence* (1830) troubles this critical narrative on several grounds.

---

1 James Fenimore Cooper, *Home as Found*, ed. Lewis Leary (New York: Capricorn, 1961), xxvii.

2 Ibid., xxviii.

3 Richard Chace, articulating his influential theory of the American romance, implicitly cites Cooper's preface. See *The American Novel and Its Tradition* (Garden City, NY: Doubleday Anchor, 1957), 158. See also Lionel Trilling, "Manners, Morals, and the Novel," *The Liberal Imagination* (New York: Viking, 1950), 213. James Tuttleton ignores Sedgwick and jumps from Cooper as founding figure to James. See *The Novel of Manners in America* (Chapel Hill: U of North Carolina P, 1972). Gordon Milne includes Cooper and Sedgwick but gives Cooper precedence as "genuine." See *The Sense of Society: A History of the American Novel of Manners* (Rutherford, NJ: Fairleigh Dickinson UP, 1977), 2. Cooper's first novel, *Precaution* (1820), was a novel of manners set entirely in England.

The recent recovery of Sedgwick as an important antebellum American novelist has positioned her primarily in relation to the genre of historical fiction and to New England as a region.[1] *A New-England Tale* (1822), subtitled "Sketches of New-England Character and Manners," is set in early nineteenth-century western Massachusetts, while *Hope Leslie* (1827) addresses white-Indian relations in the Massachusetts Colony in the seventeenth century. *The Linwoods* (1835), subtitled in homage to Walter Scott's influential historical novel *Waverley* "Sixty Years Since," is set in both New York and New England during the American Revolution. *Clarence*, subtitled "A Tale of our Own Times," is set primarily in the New York City of Sedgwick's own day, and in it Sedgwick proves herself to be an astute critic of the social world of the young nation's most cosmopolitan city.

Claims to firstness in literary history are always problematic— Sedgwick's second novel, *Redwood* (1824), set primarily in rural New England, is also arguably a novel of manners. In a review of *Redwood*, poet William Cullen Bryant, Sedgwick's close family friend and colleague, praises her for succeeding at the "hazardous experiment" of writing "a novel founded on domestic incidents" in "our own time,"[2] despite the widely-held conviction that a novel "descriptive of the manners of our countrymen" could not succeed (see Appendix A1). This prevailing wisdom was based on a perception that American culture lacked the hierarchical class structure and leisured elites that featured prominently in British novels of manners. As Bryant writes, the "active and practical" pursuits of Americans and the absence of a moneyed class with leisure to pursue "intrigue, those plottings and counterplottings" left American authors without the raw materials from which British authors formed the plots of their novels of contemporary social life. Sedgwick, Bryant claims, succeeded by varying the formula, focusing instead on "quiet times and familiar manners" that

---

1 For notable exceptions, see Patricia Larson Kalayjian, "Disinterest as Moral Corrective in *Clarence*'s Cultural Critique," *Catharine Maria Sedgwick: Critical Perspectives*, ed. Lucinda Damon-Bach and Victoria Clements (Boston: Northeastern UP, 2003), 104-17, and Charlene Avallone, "Catharine Sedgwick and the Circles of New York," *Legacy* 23.2 (2006): 115-31. Susan K. Harris notes Sedgwick's focus across her *oeuvre* on "manners," and contrasts her approach to Cooper's in *Home as Found*. See "The Limits of Authority: Catharine Maria Sedgwick and the Politics of Resistance," in Damon-Bach and Clements, 272-85.

2 William Cullen Bryant, "Redwood," *North American Review* 20 (April 1825): 246.

transpired in "the most ancient and tranquil parts" of the American nation of her day.

In *Clarence*, however, Sedgwick moved further into the traditional territory of the novel of manners, trumping the priority of Cooper's *Home as Found* on precisely the grounds that mark it as an heir of the British tradition and as a precursor to Wharton and James. Like *Home as Found*, *Clarence* traverses New York City, a country estate, and resort areas. Sedgwick's novel, also like Cooper's, features a marriage plot, British travelers experiencing and critically evaluating American culture, and American characters drawn from urban social elites. Sedgwick does not merely imitate the British novel of manners, however; instead, she revises the genre to fit American culture and corrects perceived excesses of the society that engendered the British literary form.[1]

Clarence originated both in Sedgwick's reading of British novels and in social and epistolary encounters with British authors and travelers. These origins make *Clarence* a key text in the tradition of Anglo-American literary transatlanticism. Sedgwick's novel has significance beyond its distinction as a pioneering American novel of manners, however. As Philip Gould argues, Sedgwick's nationalism in *The Linwoods* is not parochial because she folds people and cultural materials from England and France into her plot and narrative frame of reference to depict the new nation as cosmopolitan.[2] In *Clarence*, Sedgwick does the same, balancing her nationalist critique of British culture with a cosmopolitan embrace of the foreign. Her frame of reference is even broader than in *The Linwoods*, however, encompassing immigrant and traveling characters not only from Europe, but also from Jamaica, Haiti, and Cuba. She thus aligns her novel and the American nation hemispherically as well as transatlantically.

Gertrude Clarence, a young heiress, is the novel's heroine, and its plot revolves around her negotiation of a perilous marriage market in New York City. Rather than plunging directly into the marriage plot, however, Sedgwick embeds her heroine in a decades-long Atlantic family history. In the first chapter, Gertrude

---

1 As Eve Tavor Bannet observes, imitating models was central to writing practices in the long eighteenth century, enabling "variation, correction, amplification, inversion or radical adaption of the model or models in use, to their 'improvement' and creative transformation" rather than sameness. See *Empire of Letters: Letter Manuals and Transatlantic Correspondence, 1688-1820* (Cambridge: Cambridge UP, 2005), xii.

2 Philip Gould, "Catharine Sedgwick's Cosmopolitan Nation," *New England Quarterly* 78.2 (June 2005): 232-58.

is young and her father a clerk of modest means in New York City. Subsequently, other characters recount events occurring back to the 1780s and 1790s in England and Jamaica. When Gertrude enters society, she and her father live in a grand country house in (fictional) Clarenceville, and a crucial series of events transpires at Trenton Falls, the (actual) popular tourist site. The masquerade ball at the novel's climax and the havoc it wreaks cap off a novel replete with cases of mistaken and misrepresented identities. Ultimately, true identities are restored, and Gertrude brings virtue and a genteel republicanism to the city, displacing urban corruption.

This introduction examines the origins of *Clarence*, including its relationship to Sedgwick's earlier career and life experiences, and its composition, publication, and reception, orienting the novel both transatlantically and hemispherically in Atlantic World contexts. In the absence of a modern Sedgwick biography or a complete edition of her letters or journals, the introduction is primarily biographical. I close by considering the 1849 revised edition of the novel, intended to be part of a standard edition of Sedgwick's works, and the revival of her reputation as a major novelist, positioning her 1830 novel of manners as an influence on the flowering of the American fiction in the 1850s.

Clarence in Transatlantic Context: Maria Edgeworth and Captain Basil Hall

As Lawrence Buell observes in "American Literary Emergence as a Postcolonial Phenomenon," early nineteenth-century American authors had to "reckon with" "an extensive discourse of America" produced by Europeans who observed Americans with a kind of "colonial condescension."[1] Writing from within a recently colonial culture and sharing a language with their former rulers, American authors both "anticipat[ed] a transcontinental readership" and "imagin[ed] foreign as well as native opinion" in ways that had "textual consequences."[2] Buell's examples derive exclusively from works of male authors, such as "Cooper's rewriting of the trope

---

1 Lawrence Buell, "American Literary Emergence as a Postcolonial Phenomenon," *American Literary History* 4.3 (March 1992): 417.

2 Ibid., 424, 425. For a critique of the author-centered study of influence and reception in transatlantic literary studies embodied in Buell's work and in Robert Weisbuch's *Atlantic Double-Cross: American Literature and British Influence in the Age of Emerson* (Chicago: U of Chicago P, 1986) , see Susan Manning and Andrew Taylor, "Introduction," *Transatlantic Literary Studies: A Reader* (Baltimore: Johns Hopkins UP, 2007), 6-7.

of the genteel protagonist cum vernacular sidekick in [Sir Walter] Scott's Waverley novels" by making frontiersman Natty Bumppo his hero. While the novelist known as the "American Scott" rewrote *Waverley* and anticipated and actively sought British readers, Sedgwick, the "American Edgeworth," revised *Belinda* (1801), by Anglo-Irish novelist Maria Edgeworth, and sought British readers for it. By arranging a British edition of her novel, Sedgwick simultaneously sought a broad audience in Britain and delivered a pointed rejoinder to the colonial condescension directed at her by Edgeworth and Edgeworth's friend, the British naval officer and travel writer Captain Basil Hall. Writing back to Edgeworth and Hall and their assumptions about the lack of manners, social distinction, and fashion in American society, Sedgwick launched the American novel of manners.

Sedgwick's transatlantic address to Edgeworth and British audiences began eight years earlier at the inception of her career. By dedicating *A New-England Tale*, her first novel, "To Maria Edgeworth, as a slight expression of the writer's sense of her eminent services in the great cause of humanity," Sedgwick signaled that she knew Edgeworth's body of work and modeled her own authorial persona on Edgeworth's. Sedgwick clearly found Edgeworth an admirable model. Born and raised in the western Massachusetts village of Stockbridge, Sedgwick remained single so she could devote her attention to her siblings and their families;[1] similarly, Edgeworth devoted herself to her father and her younger half-siblings on the Edgeworth estate in rural Ireland. The beginning of Sedgwick's career coincided with her conversion from Calvinist-inflected Protestantism to Unitarian Christianity, and Edgeworth's didacticism and promotion of rational morality in her works suited Sedgwick's embrace of an "enlightened, rational, and liberal" faith.[2] Sedgwick and other American read-

---

1 For contrasting views of this choice, see Mary Kelley, "A Woman Alone: Catharine Maria Sedgwick's Spinsterhood in Nineteenth-Century America," *New England Quarterly* 51.2 (June 1978): 209-25, and Marshall Foletta, "'The dearest sacrifice': Catharine Maria Sedgwick and the Celibate Life," *American Nineteenth Century History* 8.1 (March 2007): 51-79.

2 Catharine Maria Sedgwick (CMS) to Susan Higginson Channing (SHC), 12 March 1821, Catharine Maria Sedgwick Papers (CMS Papers), I.7.1, Massachusetts Historical Society (MHS), Boston. Some of the letters cited can be found, often in heavily edited form, in Mary Dewey, ed., *Life and Letters of Catharine M. Sedgwick* (New York: Harper & Brothers, 1871), but I cite the manuscript letters as more authoritative.

ers had easy access to Edgeworth's works because US publishers began reprinting them early in the nineteenth century. In 1814, the Boston firm Wells & Lilly published the first American edition of *Belinda* as part of a collected edition of Edgeworth's works, and S.H. Parker of Boston did the same a decade later (a London collected edition of Edgeworth's works would not appear until 1832).[1] Sedgwick likely first read *Belinda* in Wells & Lilly's edition. A borrowing from *Belinda* in Sedgwick's *The Travellers: A Tale Designed for Young People* (1825) provides evidence of her reading. Reminiscent of Edgeworth's works for children, *The Travellers* embeds as a back story for a minor character a truncated version of a striking subplot from *Belinda*, Clarence Hervey's quixotic plan to raise a young woman as an ideal wife for himself.[2]

By arranging a London edition of *A New-England Tale* with publisher John Miller, Sedgwick increased the likelihood that the novel would find its way into Edgeworth's hands so that she might respond to the dedication addressed to her.[3] Initially, Edgeworth accepted Sedgwick's invitation: by the fall of 1823, Sedgwick had received a letter from Edgeworth (now lost), which circulated among Sedgwick's family and friends. As she wrote to her close friend and frequent correspondent Eliza Lee Cabot (later Follen) with assumed modesty, "I have received a letter from Miss Edgeworth—I had rather have one of your letters but still it is a very gratifying circumstance to such a humble personage as I am."[4] By the time Sedgwick received Edgeworth's letter, composition of her second novel, *Redwood* (which specifically references, emulates,

---

1 Kathryn J. Kirkpatrick, "Select Bibliography," in *Belinda* by Maria Edgeworth (Oxford: Oxford UP, 1994), xxxiii.

2 Edgeworth's subplot was based on an incident in the life of her father's friend Thomas Day. Marilyn Butler, *Maria Edgeworth: A Literary Biography* (Oxford: Clarendon P, 1972), 39n. In Sedgwick's revision, the man loses interest in his intended wife when smallpox scars her. *The Travellers* (New York: E. Bliss and E. White, 1825), 111-12.

3 Her only documented contact with Miller is in relation to the London edition of *Clarence*, but that letter (discussed below) and the timing of Miller's volumes evidence a well-established practice. Miller's edition was based on the second American edition of 1822, and thus appeared very late in the year, accounting for Edgeworth's lateness in responding.

4 CMS to Eliza Lee Cabot (ELC), 12 November 1823, CMS Papers, I.8.2. Jennifer Elmore considers these letters and others documenting the relationship between CMS and Edgeworth in *Sacred Unions: Catharine Sedgwick, Maria Edgeworth, and Domestic-Political Fiction*, Diss. Florida State University, 2002, ch. 1.

and revises Edgeworth's Irish novel *The Absentee* [1812]), was well under way.[1] Once again, Sedgwick arranged a London edition, which appeared not long after the New York edition.

Both Edgeworth and Sedgwick maintained multiple transatlantic correspondences, so one might expect that Edgeworth's 1823 letter would have inaugurated a continuing epistolary relationship in the context of which Edgeworth would have responded to *Redwood*. Instead, she communicated indirectly, recording her response and conveying advice to Sedgwick in a letter to Rachel Mordecai Lazarus, a Jewish schoolteacher in South Carolina. Lazarus—a perfect stranger to Sedgwick—then copied these passages from Edgeworth's letter into her own letter to Sedgwick.[2] Lazarus had initiated her own correspondence with Edgeworth the previous decade, when she wrote to protest Edgeworth's stereotypical portrayal of Jews in her fiction.[3] As their correspondence and long-distance friendship grew, Lazarus sent American books to Edgeworth, and she wrote to Edgeworth in 1824 about reading a positive review of *Redwood* (see Appendix A2 for excerpts from these letters). Several months later, she sent a copy to Edgeworth, along with her enthusiastic praise of it, demurring only against Sedgwick's portrayal of the condition of slaves in Virginia. Edgeworth took advantage of this opening to use Lazarus as an intermediary.

Edgeworth's choice of an indirect address to Sedgwick *via* Lazarus produced a distinctly passive aggressive result. Professing to Lazarus that she enjoyed *Redwood* and was "flattered"

---

1 For *Redwood*'s revision of *The Absentee*, see Elmore ch. 5; Clíona Ó Gallchoir, "*Uncle Tom's Cabin* and the Irish National Tale," in *Transatlantic Stowe: Harriet Beecher Stowe and European Culture*, ed. Denise Kohn, et al. (Iowa City: U of Iowa P, 2006), 24-45; and Juliet Shields, "Pedagogy in the Post-Colony: Documentary Didacticism and the 'Irish Problem'," *Eighteenth-Century Novel* 6-7 (2009): 465-93. My choice of "emulate" over "imitate" draws on Richard Gravil's distinction, in "Nature and *Walden*," in Manning and Taylor, *Transatlantic Literary Studies*, 106.

2 A mutual acquaintance, such as Mary Griffith (see below), would have been a more logical intermediary, but Edgeworth was stung when a Philadelphia newspaper reprinted her letter to Griffith conveying critical comments about Cooper's *The Spy*. See Eve Tavor Bannet, "Maria and Rachel: Transatlantic Identities and the Epistolary Assimilation of Difference," in *New Essays on Maria Edgeworth*, ed. Julie Nash (Burlington, VT: Ashgate, 2006), 31-56.

3 Rachel Mordecai to Maria Edgeworth (ME), 7 August 1815, in *The Education of the Heart: The Correspondence of Rachel Mordecai Lazarus and Maria Edgeworth*, ed. Edgar E. MacDonald (Chapel Hill: U of North Carolina P, 1977), 3-7.

by mentions of her works in the novel,[1] Edgeworth praises the character Deborah Lenox as "first rate, in Scott's best manner, yet not an imitation of Scott." From praise, however, she moves quickly to advice that smacks of colonial condescension. Advising that America, unlike Scotland, has no "tradition" that might be made the subject of historical fiction in the manner of Scott, she advises Sedgwick to write about the present rather than the past.[2] Although the present is also the domain of the novel of manners, she warns Sedgwick against portraying society and fashion, particularly European characters, because "English Criticks" and female readers will pass judgment on misrepresentations of the "shades" and "minute particulars" of fashion that will inevitably elude a "transatlantick writer."

The sting of Lazarus's letter conveying Edgeworth's advice was likely soothed by a letter Sedgwick received virtually simultaneously from her friend Catherine Norton excerpting a letter from British poet Felicia Hemans. "Miss Sedgwick's writings are most honourable to her sex; full of high feeling, of moral beauty," Hemans wrote. Bestowing particular praise on *Redwood*, Hemans opines, "Miss Sedgwick's lofty standard of morality might give an useful lesson to Miss Edgeworth, whose works, though excellent yet appeal far more to worldly prudence than to any nobler motive of action."[3] Bolstered by this transatlantic flattery, Sedgwick responded graciously to Edgeworth's criticism, writing *via* Lazarus that Edgeworth's sentiments rewarded her "past exertion" and would encourage her in the future when she felt inferior to the task of writing. Sedgwick explains that "some of [her] most intelligent friends" believed that America's early history was the best subject matter for fiction, but she seemingly concedes that she lacked the necessary "touch of a magician to body forth the shadows of the past." She further reinforced her ostensible concession by sending Lazarus a copy of *The Deformed Boy* (1826), "a pathetick little story, founded on fact," as Lazarus wrote approvingly to Edgeworth, which Sedgwick had "written for the benefit of a Benevolent Society." Sedgwick claimed to be "much impressed" with Edgeworth's advice. However, her letter (which

---

1 Sedgwick's reference to the *Absentee* in *Redwood* is *not* flattering, and the novel's villain, a fortune-hunting Captain in the British Navy, likely spurred Edgeworth's warning about fashionable British characters.

2 CMS's "The Catholic Iroquois" (published late 1825 in the *Atlantic Souvenir*) was her first historical fiction, but it did not appear in England until Mary Russell Mitford's *Stories of American Life* (1830) anthology.

3 Catherine E. Norton to CMS, 7 August 1826, CMS Papers, II:1:6.

Lazaraus predictably copied and sent to Edgeworth) deployed a pointed irony invisible to Lazarus and Edgeworth, who had no way of knowing that Sedgwick was nearly done writing her first historical novel, *Hope Leslie*, in which she emulated and revised Scott's *Ivanhoe*.[1] Its critical and popular success would prove Edgeworth wrong about American history as rich subject matter for fiction. Edgeworth's condescending "advice" of 1826 became as notorious in Sedgwick's family and social circle as Edgeworth's letter of 1823. Well over a year after she received Lazarus's letter, Catharine referred to it in a letter to her brother Harry, with which she forwarded a letter from Swiss economist and historian Jean Charles Léonard de Sismondi praising *Hope Leslie*: "Such a letter to an obscure unknown individual from a man so distinguished & so occupied in the career of letters is a proof of a most kind & generous disposition—how different from Miss Edgeworth! She certainly belongs to the class of egotists."[2]

In late 1827, Sedgwick was also smarting from an encounter with another British egotist who found American culture "vulgar," Captain Basil Hall. In his American travels of 1827-28 (undertaken with the intention of writing a travel book), Hall, his wife, and young daughter met the Sedgwick family on a visit to Stockbridge.[3] As he described his purpose in the preface to *Travels in North America* (1829), he wanted "to see things with my own eyes, in order to ascertain, by personal inspection, how far the sentiments prevalent in England with respect to that country were correct or otherwise."[4] Despite his posture of open-mindedness, he was, as Alice Hiller points out, a conservative Tory who "slanted his reportage the better to discredit the practice of democracy in

---

1   On CMS's transformation of *Ivanhoe*'s Jewish Rebecca into a Native American Magawisca, see Alide Cagidemetrio, "A Plea for Fictional Histories and Old-Time 'Jewesses'," in *The Invention of Ethnicity*, ed. Werner Sollors (New York: Oxford UP, 1989), 14-43. As Gary Dyer argues, Scott created his "Jewess" out of the Pocahontas legend, making CMS's appropriation of Scott an uncanny return to Scott's source. See "The Transatlantic Pocahontas," *Nineteenth-Century Contexts* 30.4 (2008): 301-22.

2   CMS to Henry Dwight Sedgwick (HDS), 19 December 1827, CMS Papers, III.3.7.

3   Una Pope-Hennessy, ed., *The Aristocratic Journey: Being the Outspoken Letters of Mrs. Basil Hall Written during a Fourteen Months' Sojourn in America, 1827-1828* (New York: G.P. Putnam's Sons, 1931), 39-40, 77-78.

4   Basil Hall, *Travels in North America, in the Years 1827-1828* (Philadelphia: Carey, Lea & Carey, 1829), iii.

the run-up to political reform in England."[1] When, in the course of his travels, Hall complained of the excesses of American democracy and lack of social cultivation he had seen in eastern seaboard cities, his acquaintances exhorted, "Go to our flourishing villages, sir ... and talk to our farmers; there you will see our character—there you will find the high-minded and intelligent citizens of our country" (See Appendix A5).[2] In his account of his visit to Stockbridge, he writes admiringly of "the more wealthy class of the village residents," including "the accomplished author of several admirable works of fancy—'Redwood,' 'Hope Leslie,' and others,"; however, he devotes far more space to lampooning a celebration of the "fourth anniversary of the Agricultural Society."

Despite this flattering published mention of Sedgwick, on the evening of his departure from Stockbridge, Hall sent her a letter cataloging the "vulgarisms" in *Hope Leslie*'s language and criticizing her depiction of immoral characters, scenes and incidents (he particularly objected to the character of Rosa, rejected paramour of Sir Philip Gardiner, who disguises herself as a boy in order to travel with him as his page. (See Appendix A4 for Hall's letter and Sedgwick's response.) Sedgwick responded to his criticism by vigorously defending her American idiom and the morality of her fiction. Significantly, Hall (a Scotsman) was Maria Edgeworth's friend, and he carried letters of introduction from her to Rachel Lazarus (whom he did not meet) and Philadelphia author Mary Griffith (whom he did).[3] Notably, Griffith was both Edgeworth's transatlantic correspondent and Sedgwick's friend. As Sedgwick wrote to her brother Harry in the same letter in which she characterized Edgeworth as an egotist, "I wish you could see [Edgeworth's] letter of introduction for Capt Hall to Mrs. Griffith, & a subsequent one—'Capt H. does me the honor & pleasure to permit me to introduce him to you'—& 'have you seen the Capt?'—'have you heard him talk?—have your friends heard him,' & then quite a rant about his fine powers—Miss E must think the Americans just up to the level of Dr Johnson's requisitions for a

1 Alice Hiller, "The Perverse Tourism of Captain Basil Hall," *Studies in Travel Writing* 3 (1999): 82.
2 The failed quest for the "American gentleman" was a defining characteristic of the British travel account of America. Christopher Mulvey, *Transatlantic Manners: Social Patterns in Nineteenth-Century Anglo-American Travel Literature* (Cambridge: Cambridge UP, 1990), 19, 25.
3 Frances Anne Beaufort Edgeworth, *Memoir of Maria Edgeworth* (London: Joseph Masters, 1867), II:285, and ME to Basil Hall, 9 April 1827, in Ibid., 285-88.

female travelling companion. One would think Hall equal to Mad de Stael & Napoleon."[1]

The Origins and Composition of *Clarence*: Observing American Manners and Revising *Belinda*

Sedgwick left no definitive traces of the origins and composition of *Clarence*, in contrast to the research for and writing of *Redwood*, *Hope Leslie*, and *The Linwoods*, all clearly traceable in her letters and journals. In the late 1820s, her complaints of an inability to write and her brother Harry's descent into mental illness take center stage in family letters, with *Clarence* first referred to in March 1830, when she had already finished writing it.[2] Nevertheless, one can glimpse the seeds of *Clarence* in her letters and journals of 1827, entangled with her encounters with Edgeworth and Hall and the British literary culture they represented. In July 1827, she traveled with family and friends to the fashionable resort of Saratoga Springs (setting for an incident in *Redwood*), staying through August. In her journal entries about this trip (see Appendix A3), she tested her skills in describing and critiquing upper-class American society. Using her journal to record impressions of "the characters that figured on that gay scene," she tries out converting members of the actual American *haut ton* into literary types, simultaneously comparing what she saw to the social atmosphere in similar circles in England. She records the presence of "maneuvering mothers" managing their daughters, but also notes with approval the lack of "debasing arts—the heartlessness, and depravity of the same class described in England." Recognizing that the people at the springs were "our people of fortune our idlers, our Fainéants," she similarly praises the lack of excess, scandal, and maneuvering typical of "fashionable society." Sedgwick did not encounter England in person until 1839, so she necessarily compares the American scene to aristocratic society in England as "described" in literary texts. Indeed, her use of the word "maneuvering" twice (the presence of maneuvering mothers and the relative absence of the social vice) suggests that Sedgwick was thinking of Edgeworth's novella *Manœuvring* from her *Tales of Fashionable Life* series. While professing that American society features fewer distinctions and fashionable excesses, she nevertheless

---

1 CMS to HDS, 19 December 1827, CMS Papers, III.3.7.
2 CMS to Charles Sedgwick (CS), 7 March 1830, CMS Papers, I.1.13.

acerbically anatomizes the "great show of fine faces, fine dancing, fine dresses, and fine jewels."

Soon after her return to Stockbridge, Sedgwick encountered Captain Hall, and her satire of him in *Clarence* confirms that the novel originated in her experiences of 1827. The fictional Mr. Edmund Stuart (like his prototype, proud of his aristocratic ancestry) appears in Clarenceville as part of six months of US travels preliminary to writing a travel book. At every turn, Stuart displays colonial condescension, even though he (like Hall) is a Scotsman and a British provincial (Hall and Edgeworth, despite being provincials, positioned themselves as cosmopolites in relation to Sedgwick as a resident of a former colony). In *Clarence*, Stuart is sure that American-born painter Benjamin West is purely English. "[H]is name is known throughout Europe," he opines, "though it may not have reached America yet, owing probably to the ignorance of the fine arts here" (161). He pontificates about British inheritance law (particularly entail and primogeniture), which "fosters genius by preserving in families the chef d'œuvre of the arts," and laments that the American abolition of these practices "will for ever retard your advance in the sciences, arts, and manners" (161). After this statement, Sedgwick includes a disclaiming footnote: noting the "striking coincidence between the opinions of our traveller and those announced in Captain Basil Hall's travels," she explains that she is not alluding to his writings because "This chapter was written a year before their appearance" (161). If accurate, the footnote dates the composition of the chapter and the completion of the novel's first volume to summer 1828, when Hall's tour was drawing to a close and the American newspapers were widely reporting his movements. Sedgwick's disclaimer fails to disabuse readers of the impression, however, that Sedgwick derived the character and opinions of Mr. Stuart from her in-person encounter with Captain Hall.

In *Clarence*, Sedgwick synthesized elements of her life experiences in the antebellum US, including her encounter with Hall, and her reading of literary works, including Edgeworth's *Belinda*. As Janet Egleson Dunleavy observes in her analysis of *Belinda* as a novel of manners, Edgeworth similarly "synthesized" her "fictional fashionable world ... in part from literary antecedents, in part from observations of real life."[1] By adopting and transforming the name of a significant character in *Belinda*—the given

---

1   Janet Egleson Dunleavy, "Maria Edgeworth and the Novel of Manners," in *Reading and Writing Women's Lives: A Study of the Novel of Manners*, ed.

name of Edgeworth's male protagonist, Clarence Hervey, becomes the surname of Sedgwick's female protagonist, Gertrude Clarence—Sedgwick invites readers to connect the novels and reinforced her reputation as "the American Edgeworth." Sedgwick's novel also employs fictional devices familiar to *Belinda*'s readers and the British novel of manners tradition of which it is a part: the masquerade and disguised and mistaken identities; a heroine negotiating a perilous marriage market; upper-class mothers unable to parent their children; upper-class men who drink, gamble, and duel; and, finally, the potential for redemption through the heroine marrying a man worthy of her goodness and character.

The masquerade ball in *Clarence* finds its precedent in *Belinda* or in any number of eighteenth-century British novels, but also in Sedgwick's attendance at a famous March 1829 masquerade ball celebrating the inauguration of Andrew Jackson as President, the first public masquerade in New York after many years of legal prohibition.[1] Sedgwick also drew on her own experiences to develop the marriage market motif characteristic of the novel of manners. In the fifteen years leading up to writing *Clarence*, Sedgwick declined several marriage proposals. She also watched her older sister Frances suffer as a result of her marriage to the abusive and financially irresponsible Ebenezer Watson and observed her younger brothers, Harry, Charles, and Robert, negotiate the marriage market in Boston and New York. Young Harry and Robert joked often in their correspondence about the desirability of marrying a wealthy woman. They recognized "the native repugnance" their sister Catharine would feel towards financial motives for marriage, but they resolved this conundrum in a way Catharine echoes in the statements of D. Flint, her Yankee lawyer in New York who courts Gertrude Clarence: a man should not marry a woman because of her wealth, but he

---

Bege K. Bowers and Barbara Brothers (Ann Arbor, MI: UMI Research P, 1990), 59.
1 On her attendance (coyly writing about herself in the third person),
    see CMS to Katharine Sedgwick, 24 March 1829, CMS Papers, II.1.7.
    An advertisement for the masquerade appears in Appendix C4. On the
    eighteenth-century literary tradition and masquerade's disruptive potential that drove Americans to such prohibitions, see Terry Castle, *Masquerade and Civilization: The Carnivalesque in Eighteenth-Century Culture and Fiction* (Stanford: Stanford UP, 1986).

should not let a woman's wealth obscure her genuine charms as a romantic partner.[1]

In *Clarence*, however, Sedgwick does not simply repeat family stories, nor does she merely imitate Edgeworth's novel. Instead, *Clarence* qualifies as an American anti-text to Edgeworth's novel, much, as Jenifer Elmore argues, *Redwood* serves as anti-text of Edgeworth's Irish novel the *Absentee*.[2] Sedgwick strikingly revises *Belinda*'s eponymous heroine in Gertrude, whose strong female agency contrasts with Belinda's passivity. And although Edgeworth designed Belinda Portman as a rational heroine who could make informed choices about her own life based on reason rather than sentiment, even the author expressed frustration with her creation. When revising *Belinda* for publication in Hannah Letitia Barbauld's "British Novelists" series, she observed that she was "provoked by the cold tameness of that stick or stone" character.[3] Belinda exerts her influence to reform Lady Delacour, but she seldom acts for herself. In a notable exception, she breaks her engagement to Mr. Vincent, the Jamaica-born son of a planter, but Edgeworth's revision removed all traces of their engagement, further muting Belinda's agency. Although Belinda holds firm to her rational principles and lets them guide her actions, her financial status constrains her agency and mobility: she is virtually penniless, and her aunt, acting as her guardian, sends her to Lady Delacour's house in London so she can marry money. Sedgwick, by making her heroine Gertrude a wealthy heiress, a "prize lady" sought by multiple suitors, reverses these polarities and mobilizes her heroine. Gertrude acts—most often for others, but also for herself. Gertrude's expressions of agency, especially when her aims are benevolent, establish her as a model American heroine, "a fit heroine for the nineteenth century; practical, efficient, direct, & decided—a rational woman—that beau-ideal of all devotees of the ruling spirit of the age—utility" (197).[4]

---

1 See Timothy Kenslea, *The Sedgwicks in Love: Courtship, Engagement, and Marriage in the Early Republic* (Boston: Northeastern UP, 2006), 85-86. Kenslea also narrates the marital fates of all the Sedgwick siblings, including Frances's abusive marriage and Harry's descent into madness.

2 Elmore, *Sacred Unions*, 14.

3 Butler, *Maria Edgeworth*, 494.

4 As Nina Baym observes, Gertrude's strength of character enables her to claim "the conventionally male prerogative of rescue," as well as making her less subject to manipulation than Isabel Archer, the similarly situated heroine of Henry James's late nineteenth-century novel of manners, *The*

Not only does Sedgwick give her heroine more agency than Edgeworth's, her virtuous characters avoid the morally corrupt behaviors of both men and women in European fashionable life. As Sedgwick notes of Gerald Roscoe's friendship with the older and married Mrs. Layton (a friendship paralleling Clarence Hervey's with Lady Delacour), it was "an intimacy, that might have degenerated into a *liaison* of more doubtful nature, in circumstances where moral restraints are less salutary, and severe, and pervading; and the eye of the public less vigilant, than in our fortunate country" (240).While Pedrillo is an outsized villain, Roscoe remains firmly virtuous and moral throughout, unlike Edgeworth's hero, Clarence Hervey. *Clarence* also features no equivalent to *Belinda*'s most outrageous female character, Harriet Freke, who dresses as a man and engages in a duel with Lady Delacour (also cross-dressed for the occasion). Sedgwick revises even her clearest borrowing from Edgeworth, Mrs. Layton (a borrowing so clear that one British reviewer called her a "Transatlantic copy" of Lady Delacour—see Appendix D5). Like Lady Delacour, Mrs. Layton is a middle-aged woman of fashion married to a man she once loved, but whom she now despises. Similarly, she spends her time in the company of a younger single man, while she seems incapable of loving and properly mothering her own children. In both novels, the heroine, on entering metropolitan society for the first time, is put under the (dubious) supervision of this fashionable married woman. Notably, however, Sedgwick, unlike Edgeworth, refuses to redeem her fashionable matron, although at every turn Gertrude provides Mrs. Layton with opportunities to reform.

Sedgwick, *Clarence*, and the Hemispheric Imaginary

Much of the first volume of *Clarence* turns on the discovery and reclamation of an English and West Indian family history and inheritance for Charles Carroll, who becomes Charles Clarence when his title to his father's estate is confirmed. Indeed, by devoting so much space to Gertrude's family history, Sedgwick departs notably from the precedent of *Belinda*, which plunges its heroine into the whirl of London fashion in the first chapter after providing only an "indistinctly sketched domestic background."[1]

Portrait of a Lady. See *Woman's Fiction: A Guide to Novels by and about Women in America, 1820-70* (Ithaca, NY: Cornell UP, 1978), 60.

1 Heather MacFadyen, "Lady Delacour's Library: Maria Edgeworth's *Belinda* and Fashionable Reading," *Nineteenth-Century Literature* 48.4 (March 1994): 427.

Edmund Clarence (Charles's father), the second son of a British aristocrat, must make his own way because the family estate is entailed to his older brother. He chooses Jamaica, Britain's lucrative sugar colony, as a place to make his fortune. Wealth deriving from the slave economy of Jamaica plays a similarly important role in the plot of *Belinda*: the heroine's suitor Mr. Vincent is the son and heir of a wealthy Jamaican planter, who on his deathbed arranges to send him to England to be educated. Through a plot about the fate of West Indian assets, then, Sedgwick tackles the problem of her literary inheritance from Edgeworth's *Belinda*.

By relocating her marriage plot from London to New York City, Sedgwick also reorients her novel's engagements with cultural and economic forces in the Atlantic World. While Jamaica was Britain's transatlantic colony, the US engaged the West Indies through trade, and, as Rodrigo Lazo argues, the Monroe Doctrine of 1823 promoted the idea of the "separation of the Americas as a hemisphere" from the European nations across the Atlantic.[1] Furthermore, New York City, Sedgwick's home for part of the year and the setting of much of *Clarence*, was a major port for hemispheric trade with French and Spanish colonial possessions. Sedgwick's evocations of the West Indies in *Clarence* thus testify to her participation in what Kirsten Silva Gruesz characterizes as a "hemispheric imaginary" that emerged in the early nineteenth-century United States, created by "itineraries of the circulation of texts and persons [and] closely bound to material and political developments."[2] In her earlier novels, Sedgwick also engaged this hemispheric imaginary, although more peripherally: in *A New-England Tale* and *Redwood*, off-stage deaths in the West Indies from climate and disease initiate and resolve key subplots, and villains in *A New-England Tale* and *Hope Leslie* emerge from and escape to careers in West Indian piracy. Not until *Clarence*, however, do hemispheric plots and characters take center stage.

Engaging these Caribbean spaces in the Western hemisphere, Sedgwick drew on both literary precedent and her own experiences and family history. Sedgwick's Puritan ancestors had ties to both the New England colonies and Jamaica. As she wrote in

---

1   Rodrigo Lazo, *Writing to Cuba: Filibustering and Cuban Exiles in the United States* (Chapel Hill: U of North Carolina P, 2005), 5.

2   Kirsten Silva Gruesz, *Ambassadors of Culture: The Transamerican Origins of Latino Writing* (Princeton: Princeton UP, 2002), 37. See also Anna Brickhouse on a "transamerican literary imaginary." *Transamerican Literary Relations and the Nineteenth-Century Public Sphere* (Cambridge: Cambridge UP, 2004), 6.

her 1853 autobiographical narrative addressed to her great niece, "The first of our Sedgwick ancestors of whom I have any tradition was Robert Sedgwick, who was sent by Oliver Cromwell as governor or commissioner ... to the island of Jamaica." Her claim, while only partially accurate, is still telling—a Massachusetts colonist of long standing, Robert Sedgwick led "a military that Cromwell dispatched to fortify the occupation after the English had seized the Island of Jamaica from the Spanish," dying there in 1656.[1] Catharine Sedgwick never traveled to the West Indies, but in both New England and New York she regularly encountered people and goods circulating between the islands and the United States. The US had strong economic and cultural ties to Cuba (still a Spanish colony) in the 1820s[2]—so although "Pedrillo" makes a romantic and exotic spectacle of himself, befuddling the judgment of those he meets, the appearance of wealthy Cubans traveling for pleasure or business was commonplace enough to cause no alarm.

Sedgwick likely encountered Cuban immigrants living in New York through William Cullen Bryant, now a key figure in hemispheric American studies. After Bryant moved to New York to become an editor in the mid-1820s, he boarded with the Salazar family, usually characterized (much like Pedrillo) as "Spanish," but with strong ties to Cuba. The mastery of Spanish Bryant acquired while boarding with them enabled him to translate hispanophone texts, most notably the poetry of Cuban exile poet José María Heredia, and stories he heard from his landlords led to his composition of a gift book tale, "A Story of the Island of Cuba," which Sedgwick read.[3] Before boarding with the Salazars, Bryant boarded with the Evrards, "a French Catholic family that had owned a plantation in Haiti and had escaped the revolution there."[4] On several occasions, Sedgwick's brothers similarly

---

1   Mary Kelley, ed., *Power of Her Sympathy: The Autobiography and Journal of Catharine Maria Sedgwick* (Boston: Massachusetts Historical Society, 1993), 45.

2   On these ties, see Gruesz; Louis A. Pérez, Jr., *Cuba and the United States: Ties of Singular Intimacy* (Athens: U of Georgia P, 1990), ch. 1; and Lazo, *Writing to Cuba*, ch. 1.

3   On Bryant as translator of Heredia, see Gruesz, *Ambassadors*, Chap. 1. On the Cuban-ness of the Salazars and the gift book tale, see Brickhouse, *Transamerican*, Chap. 2. CMS implicitly references Bryant's tale as "the account of the Cuba Indians in one of the annuals." CMS to SHC, 17 March 1829, CMS Papers, I.7.3.

4   Gilbert H. Muller, *William Cullen Bryant: Author of America* (Albany: State U of New York P, 2008), 47.

boarded with "French" families in order to improve their French language skills.[1] Sedgwick's affectionate portrait of the Abéille family in *Clarence*, "French" planter-class refugees from the Haitian revolution who take in lodgers, including "an old bachelor, bitten with the mania of learning French, and a clerk qualifying himself for a supercargo" (172), makes one suspect that her brothers' "French" landlords were similar refugees.

Sedgwick also encountered West Indian travelers in the social world of women of her own class. In an epistolary account of an 1820 visit to Saratoga, she writes of "rival belles of all degrees, kinds, and *colors*, from our fair Northern beauties to the questionable hues of the West Indies. Wealth, you know, is the grand leveling principle, and every body nowadays understands the philosophy of colors too well to give in to a vulgar prejudice against a dark complexion."[2] Knowing that wealthy planters often sent their children to the United States for schooling and that some of those children may have been of fractional African descent, she sought out such children as pupils for her sister-in-law Elizabeth Sedgwick (Mrs. Charles) when Elizabeth decided to open a school for girls in her home in Lenox, Massachusetts in 1827.[3]

Sedgwick became even more closely concerned in the circulation of West Indian children as a consequence of the business and romantic entanglements of the brother of her friend Eliza Lee Cabot. The Cabots were a distinguished Boston merchant family, and during the War of 1812, Stephen Cabot, like many other ocean-going merchants, became an American-sponsored privateer when the war made his normal business impossible.[4] After the war, he continued trading in the West Indies, settling on the Island of St. Thomas. In late 1828 Cabot was accused of benefitting financially from a piratical enterprise, and he fled St. Thomas for his life (piracy—legally distinct from privateering—was a hanging offense). Catharine Sedgwick felt deeply Eliza Cabot's

---

1 Kenslea, *Sedgwicks in Love*, 177-78.
2 CMS to SHC, 10 August 1820, CMS Papers, I.7.1.
3 CMS to Lucy Russell, 24 September 1827, Sedgwick Family Papers, MHS, IV.4.21.
4 The great age of piracy was long over, and privateering highly regulated and, despite Cabot's later troubles, was not the seamy threshold to lawlessness it had been. See Faye Kert, "Cruising in Colonial Waters: the Organization of North American Privateering in the War of 1812," in *Privates and Privateers: New Perspectives on the War on Trade in the Eighteenth and Nineteenth Century*, ed. David J. Starkey, et al. (Exeter UK: Exeter UP, 1997), 141-54.

distress and shame, writing in her journal that "My friend Eliza has been bowed down to the earth" by the news.[1] The Cabots soon received more surprising news from Stephen: he was not alone in Haiti, where he had sought sanctuary, but had with him a family he had never told them about, consisting of Zamie Féche (a native of Port Au Prince), their son, and Zamie's older child, a daughter from a previous relationship. Explaining that he was legally unable to marry Zamie—seemingly because she was a mixed-race Haitian creole—he explained that he had adopted his own son and had also adopted Zamie's daughter.[2] In March 1829, Stephen and Zamie sent their children to his brother Samuel in Boston to be educated. Joseph Cabot remained in Boston, but Eliza and Samuel sought to place Zamie's daughter in a boarding school. In late 1829, as her writing of *Clarence* was nearing its end, Catharine Sedgwick found herself asked to advise whether her sister-in-law Elizabeth should take Eliza's Haitian quasi-niece, a "belle" of "questionable West Indian hue," into her Lenox school. "The only objection that there can be to taking her," she wrote to her brother Charles, "arises from the fear of giving pain to Eliza & her family—but sweet and benevolent as she is, I cannot but think she would be glad that a human being so young and so unfortunate should have such an opportunity in securing her virtue."[3] She discounts, however, the value to Elizabeth and the school of the girl being fluent in French because "It is *Creole* French [and] I do not think that worth any thing." Elizabeth Cabot was ultimately placed in another school, but the incident nevertheless demonstrates that even the most seemingly derivative or fanciful elements of *Clarence*, such as Pedrillo's history of West Indian piracy and Edmund Clarence's interracial family in Jamaica, intersected with Sedgwick's hemispheric reality.

---

1 CMS Journal, 31 December 1828. See also CMS to ECF, 7 December 1828, CMS Papers, I.8.6.
2 On Stephen Cabot, see Vernon L. Briggs, *History and Genealogy of the Cabot Family* (Boston: C.E. Goodspeed, 1927), 598-637, including many letters. The Samuel Cabot Papers (MHS) include letters reproduced in Briggs and additional ones, but Stephen Cabot's letter in which he first disclosed his relationship with Féche and her children and explained fully the basis for his contention that he could not legally marry her is absent from both sources. Although her race remains unspecified in extant letters, no other explanation for the legal prohibition other than African descent seems likely.
3 CMS to CS, 17 December 1829, CMS Papers, I.1.12.

Although *Clarence* is set in the early nineteenth century, Edmund Clarence's Jamaican residence takes place in the 1790s. As Sean Goudie observes in his analysis of the West Indies in American literature and culture of the Early Republic, for the new nation "the West Indies function as a surrogate, a monstrous double for urgent political, cultural and economic crises, not least among these slavery."[1] The islands of the West Indian archipelago remained European colonies through the early nineteenth century, with the notable exception of the French colony of St. Domingue, which became the black republic of Haiti as a result of a successful slave revolt and revolution. The inhabitants of the US and the West Indies shared a status, Goudie argues, as creoles, the native-born descendants of voluntary or forcible emigrants to distant colonies. Making an "unclean break from" its colonial past, the US "labored to repress the inter-American cosmopolitanism of many of its leading citizen-subjects" by claiming "a pure, uncorrupted white creole identity."[2]

In *Clarence*, Sedgwick conjures up the "monstrous double" of British colonial enterprise in Jamaica, including Edmund Clarence's interracial liaison with a free woman of color, 'Eli Clairon, whose father is a white French merchant. Sedgwick's treatment of this history is complex, however. She could have damned the West Indies and claimed the excellence and purity of the American republic in contrast, but her novel's plotting foregrounds rather than represses inter-American cosmopolitanism. Given the opportunity to revise *Belinda*, Maria Edgeworth edited out most traces of serious romance and marriage between Jamaican creoles (whether white or black) and English women that had figured prominently in the novel as first published.[3] The American

---

1   Sean X. Goudie, *Creole America: The West Indies and the Formation of Literature and Culture in the New Republic* (Philadelphia: U of Pennsylvania P, 2006), 10.

2   Ibid., 9.

3   On the significance of ME's revisions, see Suvendrini Perera, *Reaches of Empire: The English Novel from Edgeworth to Dickens* (New York: Columbia UP, 1991), chap. 1; Kathryn Kirkpatrick, "'Gentlemen Have Horrors upon this Subject': West Indian Suitors in Maria Edgeworth's *Belinda*," *Eighteenth-Century Fiction* 5.4 (1993): 331-48; Susan B. Iwanisziw, "Intermarriage in Late-Eighteenth-Century British Literature: Currents in Assimilation and Exclusion," *Eighteenth-Century Life* 31.2 (Spring 2007): 56-82; and Susan C. Greenfield, "'Abroad and at Home': Sexual Ambiguity, Miscegenation, and Colonial Boundaries in Edgeworth's *Belinda*," *PMLA* 112.2 (March 1997): 214-28.

edition of *Belinda* Sedgwick likely read during the decade preceding her own emergence as a novelist, however, was the unrevised original. Given the opportunity to revise *Clarence* in 1849 (see below), Sedgwick kept Edmund Clarence's interracial liaison in Jamaica in place.[1]

Nevertheless, Edmund Clarence's creole mistress and son die, sending a devastated Clarence to the US alone to escape. Although a few unnamed black servants flit through *Clarence* and the Marion family are Virginia planters, no West Indians of African descent make the short ocean crossing to the North American continent. However, the novel's engagements with slavery in the West Indies leave a residue.[2] The fortune that makes Gertrude a "prize lady" on the New York marriage market descends, in part, from her grandfather's Jamaican enterprises. Similarly, Henriques Pedrillo's true identity connects the Cuban slave economy to New England. I leave a full interpretation of Sedgwick's engagements with the Caribbean to future critics, but *Clarence* merits the same attention that Cooper's *Last of the Mohicans* (1826) has received as a novel with a "transamerican" genealogy.[3]

The Publication and Reception of *Clarence* in the United States and Britain

Clarence was Sedgwick's first book published by Carey & Lea of Philadelphia, but her arrangements with Henry Carey (negotiated by her brother Robert) attest to her well-established reputation as a novelist and her market power. In early March, Catharine reported to her brother Charles that she was recopying the first volume of her novel for the printer and that Robert "sold the

---

1 Although the revision supplanted the original in England, Wells & Lilly of Boston used the 1801 first edition for its 1814 edition. S.H. Parker used the 1810 revision for his 1824 edition.

2 On the evolution of Sedgwick's thinking on slavery and abolition, see Karen Woods Weierman, "'A Slave Story I Began and Abandoned': Sedgwick's Antislavery Manuscript," in Damon-Bach and Clements, *Catharine Maria Sedgwick*, 122-38. Charlene Avallone argues Sedgwick's approach to race, slavery, and nation in *The Linwoods* is conservative. See "Catharine Sedgwick's White Nation-Making: Historical Fiction and *The Linwoods*" in *ESQ: A Journal of the American Renaissance* 55.2 (2009): 97-133. Five years earlier, however, Sedgwick had entertained more progressive possibilities.

3 Brickhouse, *Transamerican Literary Relations*, ch. 1. See also Goudie, *Creole America*, Epilogue.

copy right of an edition of 2000 to be printed uniform with Hope Leslie for $1200." She was "quite satisfied" with the pay and the reputation of the publisher, although Carey had argued that "the cheap reprints of popular English novels has reduced the value of copyright productions as much as Hope Leslie has raised the reputation of mine."[1] Notably, Carey published only one other new American novel in 1830, John A. McClung's *Camden: A Tale of the South*, printed in an edition of only 500 copies, while the firm's list is liberally sprinkled with reprints of British fiction. In 1830, *Clarence*'s edition size was respectable and returned to the author a sum in excess of fifty cents per copy, more than half of Carey's $2,188.40 cost for the edition.[2] Despite the large payment and edition size, Sedgwick's experience with Carey was mixed. Carey contracted the printing to a fledgling New York printing firm, and she complained to her brother Harry in mid-May, "I don't know when my book will be out. I am so heartily sick of these printers that I am tired of the whole concern." The printers "loitered admirably" and ignored repeated requests to provide her with proof sheets for revision and correction.[3] Two days later, she hastily sent the last proof sheets back to the printers,[4] and in late May complained to Harry about further unaccountable delays. "Carey was here [in New York City] on Tuesday," she reported, and "He said my book would not be out in less than a fortnight." She suspected that the delay served his interests but would hurt sales of the book.[5]

When the book finally appeared in June, she sent fellow novelist Lydia Maria Child a copy and complained, "I am not just now at all in love with novel-writing," was, indeed, "heart sick" about the "irretrievable errors" in the printed text caused by "a new printer, ignorant & careless workmen" who failed to allow her the proof revisions "essential to the correct printing of a book." Imaginatively putting herself into the scene of the New York promenade that opens her novel, she confided, "I ... feel just now pretty much as I should if I were walking through Broad-way with holes in the

---

1 CMS to CS, 7 March 1830, CMS Papers, I.1.13.
2 David Kaser, ed., *The Cost Books of Carey & Lea, 1825-1838* (Philadelphia: U of Pennsylvania P, 1963), 252, 83. On antebellum edition sizes, see Susan Geary, "The Domestic Novel as Commercial Commodity: Making a Best Seller in the 1850s," *The Papers of the Bibliographical Society of America* 70 (1976): 365-93.
3 CMS to HDS, 12 May 1830, CMS Papers, III.3.11.
4 Kelley, *The Power of Her Sympathy*, 126.
5 CMS to HDS, 24 May 1830, CMS Papers, III.3.11.

heels of my stockings."[1] The 1830 edition of *Clarence* was, indeed, full of careless errors, especially inconsistencies in spelling (see "Note on the Text"). The reviewers, however, did not notice them and responded mostly positively, praising her delineation of character and her venturing into New York City of "the present times" as a setting (see Appendix D).

The difficulties with the Carey edition of *Clarence* also complicated Sedgwick's arrangements for a British edition, which, despite her complaint to her brother about the lack of international copyright, she aggressively pursued. She forwarded proof sheets to John Miller in London, continuing the pattern she established for *A New-England Tale, Redwood, The Travellers,* and *Hope Leslie.* In 1830, the copyright status of works not authored by British subjects was unclear, but the general understanding among publishers (soon confirmed by the courts) was that copyright would protect such works as long as publication in Britain was first or simultaneous with elsewhere.[2] As Miller wrote to her in late June (less than two weeks after US publication), her "new work" had reached him safely, but the "*first* copy of Volume 1" (the proof sheets) never made it to London. Because of this failure of transatlantic communication, he was not "able to dispose of [*Clarence*] for a specific sum because [he could] not convey a copy-right." Nevertheless, he was able to persuade "Messrs Colburn & Bentley— our great Publishers" to "put it to press" and "make [Sedgwick] such a fair compensation as the sale of the work may justify."[3] Colburn & Bentley's London edition appeared on 23 July 1830,[4] and although Miller worried about other London publishers bringing out an edition of *Clarence* when the August "packet ships" arrived carrying "perfect copies from the Booksellers of New York," Colburn & Bentley's was the only London edition published in 1830 (in 1839 and 1846, much less expensive unauthorized editions did appear).[5]

---

1 CMS to Lydia Maria Child, 12 June 1830, Boston Public Library.

2 James J. Barnes, *Authors, Publishers, and Politicians: The Quest for an Anglo-American Copyright Agreement, 1815-1854* (Columbus: Ohio State UP, 1974), 153.

3 John Miller to CMS, 24 June 1830, CMS Papers, III.3.11.

4 Richard Bentley & Son, "Corrigenda et Addenda," University of Illinois at Urbana Champaign, Special Collections Library.

5 In two newspaper format series, *The Novelist: A Collection of the Standard Novels* (London: Foster and Hextall, 1839) and *The Parlour Novelist: A Collection of Works of Fiction by the Most Celebrated Authors* (Belfast: Simms and M'Intyre, 1846).

Sedgwick may have chosen the surname for the novel's central family in part for its resonance with another British genealogy connected to the novel's British West Indian back-story and America's colonial past. In 1789, King George III created the title Duke of Clarence for his son William. In his younger days, naval service transported the future Duke to Jamaica, where he was rumored to have a black mistress, and to New York City, anticipating the geographic trajectory of Sedgwick's Edmund Clarence. Once appointed a peer, the Duke served in the House of Lords, where he vocally opposed the abolition of the slave trade.[1] Sedgwick could not have predicted, however, that her novel would appear in the US and England nearly simultaneously with the death of King George III and the ascension of the Duke to the throne as King William IV. Some British reviewers suspected intentional fraud on the part of publisher, author, or both, an attempt to capitalize on the royal succession. "Who would imagine that 'Clarence, a Tale of our own Time,' was an American story, and the hero, Clarence, a clerk in a Yankee insurance office," protested the *Ladies Museum* on behalf of readers seeking "royalty for a repast" (see Appendix D6).

Sedgwick was less interested in royalties from British editions (she received a modest payment of £20 from Colburn and Bentley for *Clarence*)[2] or positive reviews, however, than in the power to negotiate transatlantic personal relationships conferred by them. While she was disillusioned with Edgeworth and Hall, she used her arrangements for the London edition of *Clarence* as a pretense for introducing herself to another British author, Mary Russell Mitford. In an early June 1830 letter, she addressed Mitford informally as one already a friend because of her sympathetic reading

---

1   On the suspected black mistress, see J.R. Oldfield, *Popular Politics and British Anti-Slavery: The Mobilisation of Public Opinion Against the Slave Trade* (London: Frank Cass, 1998), 173. Young William's time in New York is referenced in Francis Herbert (joint pseud. of William Cullen Bryant and Gulian Verplanck), "Reminiscences of New York," *The Talisman for MDCCCXXIX* [1829] (New York: Elam Bliss, 1828), 320-21. On the collaboration, Muller, *William Cullen Bryant*, 72. See also Michael Brock, "William IV (1765-1837)," *Oxford Dictionary of National Biography*, Oxford UP, Sept 2004, online edition, January 2008; Hugh Thomas, *The Slave Trade: The Story of the Atlantic Slave Trade, 1440-1870* (New York: Simon & Schuster, 1997).

2   General Author's Ledger, vol. 1, Bentley Archives, British Library, in *The Archives of Richard Bentley & Son 1829-1898* (Chadwyck-Healey, 1976), reel 54.

of Mitford's works.[1] Praising Mitford as a benevolent author who had done "great good ... to our race," Sedgwick characterizes herself as "humble artisan" offering a "specimen" of her wares (*Clarence*) to Mitford. Characteristically self-effacing in her description of her new novel, she is also preemptively defensive, suggesting that her encounters with Hall and Edgeworth still rankled: "It is not professedly a delineation of our scenery or manners, but, wherever they are incidentally introduced, I have endeavored to make the portrait accurate, neither exaggerating beauties nor veiling defects."[2] Mitford responded with all of the warmth and approbation missing from Edgeworth's communications of 1826. Although the promised copy of *Clarence* had not yet arrived and thus Mitford had not read it, she let Sedgwick know she had "seen the highest possible character" of Sedgwick's works generally in a respected British magazine and expressed satisfaction "that it is not merely reprinted but published in England, and will contribute, together with the splendid novels of Mr. Cooper, to make the literature and manners of a country so nearly connected with us in language and ways of thinking, known and valued here."[3] Cataloging the popularity and influence of various American authors in England and their equivalence to various British figures, she praises (unaware of the irony) "a lady, whom I need not name, [who] takes her place amongst these great men, as Miss Edgeworth does among our Scotts and Chalmerses."[4]

The friendship that developed out of this initial correspondence satisfied Sedgwick and Mitford for a decade,[5] but the published writings of British travelers who believed American society lacked "manners" briefly produced some friction between them. Captain Basil Hall set the pattern for travelers and travel books after him, but his reputation was eclipsed by Frances Trollope and her *Domestic Manners of the Americans* (1832). Sedgwick, like many Americans, felt compelled to read Trollope's account, and

---

1 CMS to Mary Russell Mitford (MRM), 7 June 1830, in *Friendships of Mary Russell Mitford*, ed. A.G. L'Estrange (New York: Harper & Brothers, 1882), 155-56.
2 Ibid., 156.
3 MRM to CMS, 6 September 1830, in L'Estrange, 116.
4 Ibid., 117.
5 Sedgwick's published account of meeting Mitford in England in *Letters from Abroad to Kindred at Home* (1841) offended Mitford. See W.J. Roberts, *Mary Russell Mitford: The Tragedy of a Blue Stocking* (London: Andrew Melrose, 1913), 303-35 and Vera Watson, *Mary Russell Mitford* (London: Evans Brothers, 1904), 237-79.

she took Trollope's published acknowledgment of her friendship with "Miss Mitford" as a warrant for writing to Mitford about it. While conceding some of the justness of Trollope's criticism of the crudeness of society in the Western frontier settlements, she complained, "she ... has for the most part caricatured till the resemblance is lost." Vigorously defending American culture and presenting English misunderstanding of it as nearly inevitable, she concedes that it is "difficult, almost impossible, for a foreigner to comprehend" class distinctions in the US.[1] After receiving a "very fine account" of Trollope as a person from Mitford, Sedgwick still expressed sensitivity and frustration about British judgments of Americans: "It must be confessed that we are nationally ridiculously sensitive on this matter of opinion. It is a kind of new-small-townish feeling, an anxiety to be known, a determination to be admired when known."[2]

The 1849 Author's Revised Edition of *Clarence* and Its Influence on American Fiction of the 1850s

Sedgwick has often been characterized as self-effacing and unsure of herself as an author and her career after the publication of *The Linwoods* as evidencing a retreat from literary ambition. The "determination to be admired" in her letter to Mitford and her determination to keep her novels in print bely such a characterization, however: until the end of her long career as a publishing author, she continued to think of herself as a novelist and took steps to ensure that the public knew about the scope of her body of work and could purchase copies of her novels. The 1830 *Clarence* was not stereotyped, making it unavailable for purchase not long after publication. Although stereotyping enabled publishers to keep a book in print indefinitely, few routinely undertook the expense for novels until the 1840s.[3] Early in that decade Sedgwick clearly realized that her earlier novels were at a disadvantage, as indicated by her arrangement with Harper & Brothers to stereotype and reissue *Hope Leslie* when they published her *Letters from Abroad to Kindred at Home* (1841).[4] George Palmer Putnam's 1849 edition of *Clarence* marked

---

1   CMS to MRM, 12 December 1832, in L'Estrange, 173.
2   CMS to MRM, 17 May 1833, in Ibid., 178.
3   Michael Winship, "Printing with Pates in the Nineteenth Century United States," *Printing History* 5.2 (1983): 15-26.
4   Contract between CMS and Harper & Brothers, 16 April 1841, Harper Bros MS Collection, Butler Library, Columbia University, New York.

another such moment of reflection and consolidation in Sedgwick's career, as she embarked on an ambitious plan to revise much of her *oeuvre* for a uniform, stereotyped edition of her collected works.

The year before, Putnam created and marketed a standard edition of the works of Washington Irving, notably helping Irving become the first nineteenth-century American author to achieve canonical status while still alive. Indeed, Putnam explicitly modeled his edition of *Clarence*, intended to launch a collected edition of Sedgwick's works, on his edition of Irving (see Appendix E1). In early 1849, he also brought out new editions of Sedgwick's works for children published earlier under his imprint, *Morals of Manners; or, Hints for Young People* (1846) and *Facts and Fancies for School-day Reading* (1848). Two other revised Sedgwick novels followed, *Redwood* in 1850 and *A New-England Tale* (accompanied by selected short stories) in 1852. Simultaneously with his collected edition of Sedgwick's works, Putnam commenced a similar revised author's edition of Cooper's.[1]

In 1830 the subtitle of *Clarence*, "A Tale of Our Own Times," emphasized Sedgwick's shift from historical romance to contemporary novel of manners. By 1849, *Clarence* had itself become a kind of historical fiction. Putnam's earliest advertisements re-christened the novel *Clarence; or, Twenty Years Since* (see Appendix E1), echoing Sedgwick's echoing of Scott in the subtitle of *The Linwoods; or, Sixty Years Since*. Between 1830 and 1849, the United States' posture towards its hemispheric neighbors also shifted significantly. As far back as the founding of the American republic, some suggested that the West Indian islands, and particularly Cuba, should be annexed to the new nation, but no action was taken and these ideas remained muted. The revised *Clarence*, however, came out during the era of the US war with Mexico and filibustering expeditions to the Caribbean and Central America, putting Pedrillo in the company of a host of Cuban characters in pro-imperialist print culture.[2] And although the Duke of Clarence

---

1   See Ezra Greenspan, *George Palmer Putnam: Representative American Publisher* (University Park, PA: Pennsylvania State UP, 2000), 216-31.

2   Goudie, Brickhouse, Lazo, and Gruesz all trace the emergence of US imperial designs in relation to the Caribbean. US designs on the Caribbean were ambiguously imperial in 1830, but shifted to explicitly imperial by 1849. See also Gretchen Murphy, *Hemispheric Imaginings: The Monroe Doctrine and Narratives of U.S. Empire* (Durham: Duke UP, 2005). On Cubans in 1840s popular fiction, see Shelley Streeby, *American Sensations: Class, Empire, and the Construction of Popular Culture* (Berkeley: U of California P, 2002).

had opposed abolition of the slave trade while serving in Parliament, early in his reign as King William IV, Britain abolished slavery in its colonies, including Jamaica.[1]

In preparing *Clarence* for republication, Sedgwick did not reflect on these particular developments, but she did revise her novel significantly and reflect on the distance between New York of the late 1820s and the late 1840s.[2] She added a new preface and a note at the conclusion of chapter one commenting on "the local and notable changes in our city in the nineteen years since." She removed much of the untranslated French, and in response to a review in *The North American Review* that criticized Gertrude's unchaperoned ramble with Gerald Roscoe at Trenton Falls (see Appendix D4), she added a passage excusing Gertrude's behavior. Most notably, rather than closing with Gertrude's letter describing her new domestic arrangements in New York, she cut the letter entirely, concluding the novel instead with Emilie Layton's letter preceding it. The omitted letter implicitly responded to earlier British critiques of American culture (including Basil Hall's) by picturing a cultured social elite that valued place and inheritance. Sedgwick also eliminated the footnote about Basil Hall's travel book, converting Edmund Stuart into a generic type rather than a lampoon of the man who had become her friend during her 1839 English travels.[3] By 1849, it seems, she was ready to let go of her "sensitiv[ity] on this matter of [British] opinion."

As her preface notes, *Clarence* was the first title published in "Miss Sedgwick's Works," but the series was to be comprehensive, including her works for children and didactic novellas in addition to her novels proper. However, in 1849, Harper & Brothers—not Putnam—controlled the stereotype plates and accompanying copyrights for eight Sedgwick titles, including two novels (*Hope Leslie* and *The Linwoods*). A comprehensive "Miss Sedgwick's Works" was economically and legally feasible only with cooperation from Harpers. In April 1849, Sedgwick scrambled to arrange a meeting between Putnam and Fletcher Harper, but by June, she wrote resignedly to Harpers, "I have concluded

---

1 Michael Craton, *Sinews of Empire: A Short History of British Slavery* (Garden City, NH: Anchor/Doubleday, 1974), chap. 5.

2 See Victoria Clements, "Note on the Text," in *A New-England Tale* (New York: Oxford UP, 1995), [xxix]-xxx, for CMS's considerably less substantive revisions to that novel.

3 She defends Hall as "the English bull-dog" who "bark[s] at his neighbour's door" but "will caress you at his own" in *Letters from Abroad* (New York: Harpers, 1841), I:44.

with Mr Putnam our arrangements to publish Clarence and Redwood, which, as they are not included in my contracts with your house, can I presume, be so published without at all interfering with our mutual relations," which she had decided to "leave undisturbed for the present."[1]

Even though reviews of the 1849 *Clarence* were uniformly positive, endorsing the revival and marketing of Sedgwick's *oeuvre* in this way, the splitting of her works between two competing publishers undermined the project of making Sedgwick, like Irving and Cooper, a living "classic" American author. Putnam's financial difficulties in the mid-1850s[2] further undermined these canonizing aims. After printing a second edition of *Clarence* in 1852, he was forced to lease his plates for it, *Redwood*, and *A New-England Tale* to J.C. Derby, who issued one printing of all three in 1854, but failed thereafter to comply with the contractual obligation "to publish, keep on hand, & sell" Sedgwick's novels.[3] Sedgwick tried to control the subsequent disposition of Putnam's plates, badgering him and suggesting to Harpers that they might purchase them and thus offer a "uniform edition" of her works.[4] Putnam briefly regained control of his plates of the three novels in 1856, printing editions from them. However, he went into receivership in 1858,[5] and the plates and the potential they carried of additional printings disappeared.

While the failure of the planned "Miss Sedgwick's Works" and the disappearance of the revised *Clarence* is poignant, it did, for a time, gain the novel a new readership, including authors half a generation or more younger than Sedgwick. In December 1850, a year and a half after the revised *Clarence* had first appeared, Susan Warner's *Wide, Wide World* quietly appeared under Putnam's imprint. Underestimating its potential, he printed only 750 copies,[6] less than half the number of copies of *Clarence* Carey printed twenty years before. An unexpected bestseller,

---

1 CMS to George Palmer Putnam (GPP), 30 April 1849, Miscellaneous MSS, Rare Books and Manuscripts Division, New York Public Library. CMS to Fletcher Harper, 10 June 1849, University of Virginia.
2 Greenspan, *George Palmer Putnam*, 323-34.
3 CMS to Mr. Harper, 20 March 1856, Morgan Library, New York.
4 CMS to GPP, 22 February 1858, Stockbridge Library Association, Stockbridge, MA. CMS to Harper & Brothers, 24 March 1858, Morgan Library.
5 Greenspan, *George Palmer Putnam*, 381-90. Putnam's plates were sold at public auction as a result of the receivership.
6 Greenspan, *George Palmer Putnam*, 253.

The Wide, Wide World inaugurated the boom in women's fiction. Warner lived a wealthy and privileged childhood in New York in the 1820s,[1] in the same social circles as the New York branch of the Sedgwick family. Indeed, the news of Maria Edgeworth's 1823 letter to Catharine Sedgwick circulated in the Warner family. "Catherine [sic]. Sedgwick has received a letter from Miss Edgeworth," Susan's father Henry wrote to his wife in the Spring of 1824; "Think of that."[2] As an orthodox evangelical in desperate economic straits after her family's fall from affluence, Susan Warner contemplated Sedgwick's precedent with ambivalence. As a guest at the Putnam residence on Staten Island while she was reading proofs of *The Wide, Wide World*, she read books she found around their home, including Irving, Cooper, and Sedgwick, undoubtedly in Putnam's collected editions of each. She initially dismissed Sedgwick's works, writing to her sister that *Redwood* and *Clarence* were "dismally poor."[3] Nevertheless, Sedgwick's novels drew her back; she reported to Anna that she "'dilectate[d] with *Redwood*," concluding a few days later, "Miss Sedgwick's novels are *inexpressible*."[4]

Maria Susanna Cummins, whose best-selling first novel the *Lamplighter* (1854) inspired Nathaniel Hawthorne's famous denunciation of the "d——d mob of scribbling women" over-running the American market,[5] was educated at Elizabeth Sedgwick's boarding school. Scholars have suggested that Cummins's contact with Catharine Sedgwick as an adolescent fostered her literary ambitions,[6] but an encounter with Sedgwick's works in print at a later stage of her life would have been equally formative. Surely, she would have read Sedgwick's urban novel of manners in its newly available edition while considering how to depict urban life and manners in *The Lamplighter*.

Carolyn Karcher has argued that Sedgwick influenced Harriet Beecher Stowe, and in particular that *Redwood*'s portrayal of

---

1   Jane Tompkins, "Afterword," *The Wide, Wide World* (New York: Feminist P, 1987), 587-89.

2   Henry Warner to Anna Bartlett Warner, 1824, in Anna Warner, *Susan Warner* (New York: G.P. Putnam's Sons, 1909), 65.

3   Susan Warner to Anna Warner, 2 October 1850, in Ibid., 305.

4   Susan Warner to Anna Warner, 4 and 8 October 1850, in Ibid., 307, 313.

5   Nathaniel Hawthorne to William D. Ticknor, 19 January 1855, in *Letters, 1853-56. The Centenary Edition of the Works of Nathaniel Hawthorne*, vol. 17 (Columbus: Ohio State UP, 1987), 304.

6   Heidi L.M. Jacobs, "Maria Susanna Cummins's London Letters: April 1860," *Legacy*, 19.2 (2002): 242.

the martyrdom of the slave Africk influenced *Uncle Tom's Cabin.*[1] Sedgwick's portrayal of hemispheric characters and West Indian slavery in *Clarence* also echoes in *Uncle Tom's Cabin*, and in both Sedgwick and Stowe, French names predominate in relation to this history. To take just one example, the "Spanish" Pedrillo of *Clarence* has a French-sounding given name, Henriques, that echoes in the name of Henrique St. Clare in *Uncle Tom's Cabin.* The young nephew to Augustine St. Clare, Henrique mercilessly beats an innocent slave and sparks a discussion between Augustine and his brother (Henrique's father) about the Haitian Revolution. These names suggest that Sedgwick's novel contributed to what Anna Brickhouse calls the "Franco-Africanism" of *Uncle Tom's Cabin*, a literary configuration that enables Stowe simultaneously to call up "a partially erased story of racial ambiguities" in the US and displace it onto Haiti and other Francophone regions in the hemisphere.[2]

Sedgwick's readership was never exclusively female, of course, and male authors also encountered her novels in the late 1840s and early 1850s. Shortly after the revised edition of *Clarence* appeared, Nathaniel Hawthorne and Herman Melville spent a year as neighbors in the Berkshires, making Catharine Sedgwick their neighbor as well. What if we were to imagine Melville and Hawthorne reading their neighbor's novel *Clarence* in its new edition, just as her reputation was undergoing a revival?[3] Melville's "Bartleby the Scrivener," serialized in *Putnam's Monthly Magazine* in November and December 1853, depicts its narrator wandering the same lower Manhattan streets that figure prominently in *Clarence* and in Sedgwick's long footnote reflecting on the changes

---

1. Carolyn Karcher, "Catharine Maria Sedgwick in Literary History" in Damon-Bach and Clements, *Catharine Maria Sedgwick*, 8-9, 13. See also Karcher, "Stowe and the Literature of Social Change," *Cambridge Companion to Harriet Beecher Stowe*, ed. Cindy Weinstein (Cambridge: Cambridge UP, 2004), 203-18, and Ó Gallchoir, "*Uncle Tom's Cabin* and the Irish National Tale."

2. Brickhouse, *Transamerican Literary Relations*, 244.

3. Melville critics have largely seen women authors, including CMS, as a target of Melville's parody rather than as an influence. See Charlene Avallone, "The Company of Women Authors," in *A Companion to Herman Melville*, ed. Wyn Kelley (Malden, MA: Blackwell, 2006), 313-26, and "Women Reading Melville/Melville Reading Women," in *Melville and Women*, ed. Elizabeth Schultz and Haskell Springer (Kent, OH: Kent State UP, 2006), 41-59. The latter essay suggests CMS's *The Linwoods* and "The Country Cousin" as intertexts for Melville's *Pierre*.

in that cityscape. *The Blithedale Romance* (1852), Hawthorne's first novel published after his Berkshire years, also suggestively echoes *Clarence*. At the masquerade ball in *Clarence*, Mrs. Layton "personate[s] the Sybil," wearing "a richly wrought white lace veil" over her face (376), while Hawthorne's Veiled Lady is covered from head to foot in a silvery veil, and is also (falsely) "sybilline."[1] Just after her forcible unveiling on stage, Hawthorne shifts the scene to an outdoor masquerade, at which the residents of Blithedale, like the maskers in *Clarence*, have donned boundary-crossing costumes, such as an Indian chief, a "Jim Crow" black man, medieval foresters, a Kentucky woodsman, a Bavarian broom-girl, and a Shaker elder.[2]

The appendices to this edition situate *Clarence* in relation to a variety of nineteenth-century contexts, tracing Sedgwick's sources and influences and documenting responses to her novel and her influence on others. *Clarence*'s nineteenth-century life was cut short by the business failures of her publisher, and it was largely ignored by twentieth-century literary historians, but it is more than a period piece. It is as engaging for twenty-first-century readers as the late nineteenth- and early twentieth-century novels of manners of Henry James and Edith Wharton. Its plot twists and turns the unraveling of mistaken identities still surprise and delight, and Gertrude Clarence's struggles to reconcile moral and economic imperatives in the boom and bust economy of New York City often feel contemporary. By bringing *Clarence* back into print, we seek a place for it in the history of America's literary past, but we also seek to make it live for readers in the present and the future.

---

1 Nathaniel Hawthorne, *The Blithedale Romance*, ed. Seymour Gross and Rosalie Murphy (New York: Norton, 1978), 6, 3.
2 Ibid., 193.

Catharine Maria Sedgwick: A Brief Chronology

1789   Catharine Maria Sedgwick (CMS) born to Theodore and Pamela Dwight Sedgwick in Stockbridge, Massachusetts on 28 December. Siblings include Elizabeth (Eliza), b. 1775; Frances, b. 1778; Theodore, b. 1780; Henry Dwight (Harry), b. 1785; Robert, b. 1787; and Charles, b. 1791.

1802   Spends first winter in New York City, living with sister Frances Watson and family, attending school and first theatrical performance.

1803   Moves to Albany, living with sister Eliza Pomeroy and family; attends Mrs. Bell's School there; in 1803 and 1804, attends Mrs. Payne's school in Boston.

1807   Mother, Pamela Sedgwick, dies.

1808   Father, Theodore Sedgwick, marries Penelope Russell.

1813   Father, Theodore Sedgwick, dies.

1821   Resigns her membership in a Presbyterian church in New York City and joins All Souls Unitarian Church. Summer travel to Niagara Falls and Montreal.

1822   Her first novel, *A New-England Tale*, dedicated to Maria Edgeworth, and *Mary Hollis*, a tale published as a pamphlet by the New York Unitarian Book Society.

1823   Receives letter from Maria Edgeworth.

1824   Her second novel, *Redwood*.

1825   *The Travellers: A Tale Designed for Young People*. "The Catholic Iroquois," the first of many tales and sketches published in gift books, appears in *The Atlantic Souvenir*.

1826   *The Deformed Boy*, a children's tale published by the Unitarian-sponsored Publishing Fund of Boston. Lengthy visit with friends including Eliza Cabot (later Follen) in Boston in the fall.

1827   Her third novel, *Hope Leslie; or, Early Times in the Massachusetts*. Begins contributing to the *Juvenile Miscellany*, edited by Lydia Maria Child. Brother Charles's wife Elizabeth begins conducting a school for girls in their home in Lenox, MA, and CMS is a regular presence there. Brother Harry and wife Jane Minot move from New York to Stockbridge because of a significant decline in his health (June). Thereafter CMS resides with brother Robert and family in New York City most of the year, summering in Stockbridge and Lenox, MA. CMS visits Saratoga Springs, Ballston Spa, and Lake George (July-August). British travel writer Captain Basil Hall visits Stockbridge and meets Sedgwick family (fall). Sister Eliza dies (October).

1829   "Cacoethes Scribendi" in *The Atlantic Souvenir* (1830). Elizabeth Freeman, African-American servant to Sedgwick family CMS considered a foster mother ("Mumbet"), dies.

1830   Her fourth novel, *Clarence; or, A Tale of Our Own Times.* Travels to Philadelphia to visit Mary Griffith and Rebecca Gratz. Initiates a correspondence with Mary Russell Mitford.

1831   Visits Washington, DC, meeting President Jackson (January-February). Brother Harry dies after many years of physical and mental illness (December).

1832   "Le Bossu" in *Tales of Glauber Spa.*

1833   Meets actress Fanny Kemble, initiating a lifelong friendship. Travels to Virginia (June-July).

1834   Meets Harriet Martineau during her American tour (October). Falling out with Lydia Child over her unwillingness to write a story supporting abolition of slavery for a gift book. Sits for portrait by Charles Ingham.

1835   Her fifth novel, *The Linwoods; or, 'Sixty Years Since' in America*; *Home*, her first didactic novella, published in Reverend Henry Ware's series *Scenes and Characters Illustrating Christian Truth*; and *Tales and Sketches*, collecting gift book stories.

1836   Her second didactic novella, *The Poor Rich Man and the Rich Poor Man*; *Memoir of Lucretia Maria Davidson.*

1837   Her third didactic novella, *Live and Let Live; or, Domestic Service Illustrated*; *Love Token for Children*, collecting her children's tales. Meets Anna Jameson, thereafter a lifelong friend.

1838   CMS becomes brother Robert's primary caregiver following his stroke.

1839   *Means and Ends; or, Self-Training.* Travels extensively in Europe (through 1840) with brother Robert and family in an attempt to recover his health.

1840   *Stories for Young Persons.* CMS begins residing in Stockbridge or Lenox, MA, year-round until, in the 1860s, she joins the household of her niece Katherine Sedgwick Minot in West Roxbury, MA.

1841   *Letters from Abroad to Kindred at Home*, drawn from her journals of her European travels in 1839-40. Regular contributor to *Godey's Lady's Book*. Brother Robert dies (September). *[handwritten: popular enough to get published]*

1844   *Tales and Sketches, Second Series*, collecting magazine fiction. Becomes regular contributor to *Graham's Magazine*.

1846   *The Morals of Manners; or, Hints for Our Young People*. Regular contributor to *Columbian Lady's and Gentleman's Magazine*.

1847   Becomes regular contributor to *Sartain's Union Magazine*.

1848   Two children's books, *The Boy of Mount Rhigi* and *Facts and Fancies for School-Day Reading*. Building upon her involvement in prison reform, CMS becomes first directress of the New York Women's Prison Association.

1849   George Palmer Putnam announces the planned publication of a collected edition of "Miss Sedgwick's Works."

1850   *Tales of City Life*.

1853   CMS begins to write an autobiography, intended for her great-niece Alice Minot, a project that continues in 1854 and in 1860.

1854   With brother Charles and his family, travels to the western US, visiting Chicago and St. Paul and cruising portions of the Mississippi from Minnesota to St. Louis.

1857   Her sixth and final novel, *Married or Single?*. *[handwritten: writes romances but never married]*

1858   *Memoir of Joseph Curtis: A Model Man*.

1862   Her last publication, "A Sketch from Life," in *Only Once, Original Papers, by Various Contributors*, for the Benefit of the New York Infirmary for Women and Children.

1867   CMS dies in West Roxbury, MA, on July 31; buried in the Sedgwick family grave plot (the Sedgwick "pie") in Stockbridge, MA.

1871   *Life and Letters of Catharine M. Sedgwick*, edited by Mary E. Dewey.

[handwritten: has an autobiography, popular enough]

A Note on the Text

Clarence was published as a two-volume novel in June 1830 by Carey & Lea of Philadelphia. In October 1849, George Palmer Putnam published an "author's revised edition" of *Clarence* (two volumes bound as one) as part of a planned uniform edition of Sedgwick's works. No manuscript of the novel is extant. Sedgwick made many small and some substantial revisions for the 1849 edition. Nevertheless, we have chosen the 1830 text as copy text because our primary aim is to present the novel in its 1830 context and as growing out of Sedgwick's experiences in the 1820s. Information about and documentation of the 1849 changes can be found in the introduction, in the explanatory notes, and in Appendix E.

We have not attempted to modernize the text, preferring to retain nineteenth-century spelling, punctuation, and other conventions when possible. However, we have corrected obvious printers' errors of spelling, punctuation, and usage and have regularized internal inconsistencies. We have, for instance, regularized possessive forms of proper names across the text (the possessive of "Clarence" is always "Clarence's") and supplied missing accents in French surnames when they are supplied elsewhere. We have retained hyphenated forms of compound nouns, consulting the 1849 edition when necessary. The treatment of foreign words (mostly French) is not consistent across the text, with such words often italicized, but not always. We elected not to regularize italics, except in a few instances in which changes in the 1849 edition suggested that Sedgwick felt such changes were necessary or appropriate. The 1830 edition switches back and forth at random between English and American spellings (e.g., "honour" *versus* "honor"), and we have regularized these spellings across the text, favoring the American spellings, which Sedgwick favored in her letters and journals at the time. Finally, we have not attempted to reproduce the typographical treatment of quotations in the 1830 text, in which a double quotation mark appears at the beginning of every line for a multi-line quotation, favoring instead the modern practice of beginning and end quotation marks, nor have we retained the irregular typographical treatment of epistolary materials (letters), allowing Broadview's typesetters to treat them uniformly.

We have followed similar practices in relation to nineteenth-century printed materials included in the appendices. For manuscript materials, we have elected to present clear reading copies of the originals. Although we have retained nineteenth-century spelling, usage, and punctuation, we have silently expanded many abbreviations adopted in manuscript to conserve space (as opposed to standard contractions, which have been retained). In private manuscript documents, Sedgwick and her contemporaries often used a casual punctuation style, consisting of dashes and marks of various lengths that cannot be accurately reproduced in print. Although some dashes have been retained, clarity dictated the substitution of commas and periods in many instances. In the case of manuscript letters, we have used standardized formatting of information presented at the opening and closing of letters (dates, salutations, signatures, etc.), rather than trying to replicate their widely varying locations on the physical manuscript pages. Finally, when a manuscript author has used underlining for emphasis, we have substituted the print convention of italics. We have followed similar practices when including quotations from manuscript materials in the introduction.

J.R. Cornell

CLARENCE;

OR,

A TALE OF OUR OWN TIMES.

BY THE
AUTHOR OF "HOPE LESLIE," &c. &c.

" Return, return, and in thy heart engraven keep my lore,
The lesser wealth, the lighter load—small blame betides the poor." [1]
BISHOP HEBER.

IN TWO VOLUMES.
VOL. I.

PHILADELPHIA.
CAREY & LEA.—CHESTNUT STREET.
1830.

Courtesy University of Pennsylvania.

---

1 From "Imitation of an Ode by Koodrut, in Hindoostanee" in *Palestine, and Other Poems, with a Memoir of His Life* (1828) by Reginald Heber (English, 1783-1826).

Southern District of New York, to wit.

BE IT REMEMBERED, That on the sixteenth day of March, in the fifty-fourth year of the Independence of the United States of America, A. D. 1830, Cary & Lea, of the said district, have deposited in this office the title of a book, the right whereof they claim as proprietors, in the words following, to wit:

"Clarence; or a Tale of our own Times. By the Author of 'Hope Leslie,' &c. &c.

'Return, return, and in thy heart engraven keep my lore,
The lesser wealth, the lighter load—small blame betides thee poor.'

BISHOP HEBER

In two Volumes."

In conformity to the Act of the Congress of the United States, entitled, "An Act for the encouragement of learning, by securing the copies of Maps, Charts, and Books, to the authors and proprietors of such copies, during the time therein mentioned." And also, to an Act, entitled, "An Act, supplementary to an Act, entitled, An Act for the encouragement of learning, by securing the copies of Maps, Charts, and Books, to the authors and proprietors of such copies, during the time therein mentioned, and extending the benefits thereof to the arts of designing, engraving, and etching historical and other prints."

FREDERICK J. BETTS.
Clerk of the Southern District of New York.

Sleight & Robinson, Printers, New York.

DEDICATION.

To my Brothers—my best friends, the following pages are inscribed, as a tribute of affection, by

THEIR AUTHOR.

PREFACE.

We had intended to affix a precise date to the following narrative, when we seasonably recollected the prudent counsel of my Uncle Toby! "Leave out the date entirely, Trim," quoth my Uncle Toby— "leave it out entirely, Trim, a story passes very well without these niceties, unless one is pretty sure of 'em!" "Sure of 'em!" said the corporal, shaking his head.[1]

The reader will be pleased to suppose the events of our story to have occurred at any period within the present century, and will have the indulgence to pardon sundry anachronisms, particularly the liberty the author has taken in anticipating the masquerade of 1829.[2]

---

1 From *The Life and Opinions of Tristram Shandy, Gentleman* (1759-67) by
   Laurence Sterne (English, 1713-68).
2 Public masquerade balls, held at large venues such as the Park Theater
   and Bowery Theater, were popular entertainments in New York City in
   the winter of 1829.

CHAPTER I.

"Dis moi un peu, ne trouves tu pas, comme moi, quelque chose du ciel, quelque effet du destin, dans l'aventure inopinée de notre connoissance?"[1]
MOLIÈRE.

IT was one of the brightest and most beautiful days of February. Winter had graciously yielded to the melting influence of the soft breezes from the Indian's paradise—the sweet southwest. The atmosphere was a pure transparency, a perfect ether; and *Broadway*, the thronged thoroughfare through which the full tide of human existence pours, the pride of the metropolis of our western world, presented its gayest and most brilliant aspect.

Nature does not often embellish a city; but here, she has her ensigns, her glorious waving pennons in the trees that decorate the park, and the entrance to the hospital, and mantle with filial reverence around St. Paul's and Trinity churches. A sudden change from intense cold to rain, and then again to frost, changes and successions not uncommon in our inconstant climate, had encircled the trees, their branches, and even the slightest twigs that bent and crackled under the little snowbird, with a brilliant incrustation of ice, and hung them with countless crystals—nature's jewels—how poor in the comparison a monarch's regalia!

The chaste drapery of summer is most beautiful; but there was something in all this gorgeousness, this ostentatious brilliancy, that harmonized well with the art and glare of a city. It seemed that nature, for once, touched with the frailty of her sex, and determined to outshine them all, had donned her jewelled robe, and come forth in all her queenly decorations in the very temple of art and fashion; for this is the temple of these divinities, and on certain hours of every auspicious day is abandoned to the rites of their worshippers.

But the day has its successive scenes, as life its seven ages. The morning opens with servants sweeping the pavements—the pale seamstress hastening to her daily toil—the tormented dyspeptic sallying forth to his joyless morning ride—the cry of the brisk

---

1   "Tell me something, don't you find, like I do, something of Heaven, some effect of destiny in our acquaintance's unexpected adventure?" From *Le Malade Imaginaire* (*The Imaginary Invalid* or *The Hypochondriac*), 1673, by Molière (French, 1622-73).

milkman—the jolly baker and the sonorous sweep—the shop-boy fantastically arranging the tempting show, that is to present to the second sight of many a belle her own sweet person, arrayed in Flandin's garnitures,[1] Marquand's jewels, Goguet's flowers, and (oh tempora! oh mores![2]) Manuel's 'ornamental hair work of every description.'[3]

Then comes the business hour—the merchant, full of projects, hopes, and fears, hastening to his counting house—the clerk to his desk—the lawyer to the courts—the children to their schools, and country ladies to their shopping.

Then come forth the gay and idle, and Broadway presents a scene as bustling, as varied, and as brilliant, as an oriental fair. There, are graceful belles, arrayed in the light costume of Paris, playing off their coquetries on their attendant beaux—accurately apparelled Quakers—a knot of dandies, walking pattern-cards, faithful living personifications of their prototypes in the tailor's window—dignified, self-complacent matrons—idle starers at beauties, and beauties willing to be stared at—blanketed Indian chiefs from the Winnebagoes, Choctaws, and Cherokees, walking straight forward, as if they were following an enemy's trail in their own forests—girls and boys escaped from school thraldom—young students with their backs turned on college and professors—merry children clustering round a toy-shop—servants loaded with luxuries for the evening party, jostling milliners' girls with bandboxes—a bare headed Greek boy with a troop of shouting urchins at his heels—a party of jocund sailors from the 'farthest Ind'—a family groupe of Alsace peasants—and, not the least jolly or enviable of all this multifarious multitude, the company of Irish orangemen stationed before St. Paul's, their attention divided between the passers-by, their possible customers, and the national jibes and jokes of their associates.

It was on such a day as we have described, and through such a throng, that one lonely being was threading his way, who felt the desolateness of that deepest of all solitudes—the solitude of a crowd—the loneliness of the tomb amidst abounding life. He was a stranger. No one of all that multitude, high or humble, saluted him; no familiar eye rested on him. He was not old, but

---

1 Apparel, or ornamentation or trim on clothing.
2 Oh the times! Oh the customs!, from *Catilinarian Orations* of Cicero (Roman, 106-43 BCE), philosopher.
3 Sedgwick refers to Flandin, Marquand, and Goguet as "fashionable shopkeepers" in her note to the 1849 edition. See page 56, note 1.

the frosts of age were on his head, and his cheek was indented with furrows of 'long thought and dried up tears.'[1] There was not one of all the gay and reckless, confident in happiness, and secure in prosperity, that could sympathize with the sullen, disappointed, and wretched aspect of the stranger; but the beggar as he passed him forgot his studied attitude and mock misery, and the mourner in her elaborate weeds threw a compassionate glance at him. The stranger neither asked nor looked for compassion. Though his dress indicated poverty, there was that in his demeanour that would have repressed inquiry, and seemed to disdain charity. Something like a scornful smile played on his features, a smile of derision, of hostility with a species that could be thus occupied and amused; such a smile as a show of monkeys might extort.

A knot of ladies stopped his way for a moment. "Was you at Mrs. Layton's last night?" asked one of the fair ones. "Indeed was I—something quite out of the common way, I assure you. Nothing but Italian sung—nothing but waltzes danced." "Do you know poor Mrs. Bruce is just gone?" "Poor thing! is she?—Where did you get your Marabouts?"[2]—"Is not that hat ravishing?"—"Do you know Roscoe's furniture is to be sold to-morrow?"—"Julia, look, what a sweet trimming!"—"My! let that old man pass."—For an instant the gaze of the pretty chatterers was fixed on the ashen countenance of the stranger, and there was something in the expression of his large sunken eye, as its sarcastic glance met theirs, that arrested their attention and steps. But they passed on, and their thoughts reverted to trimmings, parties, and Marabouts.

The stranger pursued his way slowly and pensively as far as Trinity-church, and then crossing Broadway turned into Wall-street, where he eyed the bustling multitude of merchants, merchants' clerks, brokers, and all the servants, ministers, and followers of fortune, with even a more bitter mental satire than the butterfly world of Broadway. As he reached the corner of William-street, his attention was attracted by a beautiful boy who stood at a fruit-stall stationed there, trafficking with an ill-favored old woman for a couple of oranges. The love of childhood is a tie to our species that even misanthropy cannot dissolve. Perhaps it was this bond of nature that strained over the stranger's heart;

---

1 From *Childe Harold's Pilgrimage, Canto III* (1816) by George Gordon, Lord Byron (English, 1788-1824).

2 Marabou, or marabout: plumes of feathers used in trimming hats.

or there might have been something in the aspect of the boy that touched a spring of memory; a faint color tinged his livid cheek, and the veins in his bony forehead swelled. The boy, unconscious of this observation, completed his bargain, and bounded away, and the stranger perceiving that he in turn had become the object of notice to some loiterers about the stall, purchased an apple and passed on. In taking a penny from his pocket, he dropped his handkerchief. The old woman saw it, and unobserved, contrived by a skilful sweep of her cloak to sequester it, and at a convenient opportunity transferred it to her pocket, saying to herself as she did so, "It is as fine as a spider's web, a pretty article for the like of him truly; it's reasonable that my right to it is as good as his," and with this comment entered on the records of conscience, she very quietly appropriated it.

In the mean time the stranger pursued his way down William-street, and the little boy, who, for some reason, had retraced his steps, was running in the same direction, tossing up his oranges, and amusing himself with the effort to keep both in the air at the same moment.

Intent on his sport, he heedlessly ran against the stranger, dropped his oranges, knocked the man's cane from his hand, and nearly occasioned his falling. Something very like a curse rose to his lips. The boy picked up the cane and gently replaced it, saying at the same time, with such unaffected earnestness, "I am *very* sorry, sir," that softened by his manner, and perceiving it was the same child who had before attracted his attention, he replied, "Never mind, boy; pick up your oranges." He did so, and looking again at the stranger, who to his unpractised eye seemed old and poor, he said modestly, "Will you take one, sir?"

"No, no, boy."

"Do take one."

"No, thank ye, child."

"I had much rather you would than not; I don't really want but one myself."

"No, no; God bless ye."

By this time they had reached an old Dutch domicil, with a gable end to the street, one of the few monuments that remain of the original settlers of our good city.

The steps or (to use the vernacular word) the *stoop* had just been nicely scoured: the boy perceiving the stranger breathed painfully, and moved with difficulty, sprang forward to open the door. The sound of the lifted latch brought out an old woman who appeared by the shrill tones of authority and wrath that issued from her lips, at the sight of the boy's muddy footsteps on the clean boards, to be the "executive" of the establishment.

She stood with a scrubbing brush in her uplifted hand, and the boy started back, as if he expected farther and more painful demonstrations of her anger. "Stay, stay, my child," said the stranger, "and sit down on that bench," and then turning to the old woman, "hold your foul tongue," he said, "and let the lad alone."

"Leave him be! It's my own house and my own tongue, and neither you nor any other man can master it."

"God knows that's true," replied the stranger, and without wasting any farther efforts on the confessedly impossible, he very unceremoniously extended his cane, and poked the woman's garments within the door, so as to enable him to shut it in her face, which he effected without delay. Perhaps the boy laughed from instinctive sympathy with the power of the superior sex; he certainly laughed most heartily at its timely demonstration, and shouted again and again, "Cracky! cracky!" an exclamation that the young urchins of our city often send up, equivalent to "a palpable hit, my Lord!"[1]

The saturnine features of the stranger relaxed, and from that moment there was a tacit compact between him and his young friend, who seemed the only link that connected him with his kind. He received even his pity with complacency, for he felt that the pity of a child was tolerable, because 'without any mixture of blame or counsel.'

The boy's father, Mr. Carroll, was clerk in an insurance office opposite the stranger's lodgings. Frank came daily to his father's office, and as he passed and repassed the stranger's door, he stopped with some good humored greeting, or to share with him his fruit, cakes, or candy. His bonbons were received with manifest pleasure, but never eaten, at least in Frank's presence, and when he inquired the reason of this extraordinary abstemiousness, his friend would answer, "I keep them to console me, Frank, when you are away."

Mr. Carroll's desk was stationed at his office-window, and his eye often involuntarily glanced from his books to his boy, whose benevolent friendship for the forlorn stranger, he secretly watched, and promoted, by permitting him to loiter in his society, and by daily largesses of pennies.

What draught is so delicious to a parent as a child's virtue? What spectacle so beautiful to man as the aspect of childhood?

---

1 *Hamlet* V.ii.282 by William Shakespeare (English, 1564-1616).

childhood flushed with health and happiness; its buoyant step, its loud laugh, and joyous shout; its little bark still riding in its secure and guarded haven; its interminable perspective of an ever brightening future? And infancy—who has not looked with prophetic eye on the fair face of infancy, the dawn of never ending existence, and seen in vision the temptations, the struggles, the griefs, the joys, that awaited the unconscious little being? Who has not contemplated the placid minute frame, enveloping such capacities for suffering, and not longed to withhold it from its fearful voyage? Peaceful infancy! must those senses that now convey to thee but the intimations of thy new existence, become the avenues of all good and evil? Must these pulses which now beat so softly, harmoniously, throb with passion? Must this clear eye be dimmed with tears? this soft cheek, this smooth brow be furrowed with care and sorrow? Even so; for the destiny of humanity is thine, with its joys and its triumphs. Enfolded in this minute frame are the capacities of an angel. Go forth then, labor, struggle, and knowledge shall fill thy mind with light of thine own—endure, and resist, and from the fires of temptation shall rise and soar to heaven, the only phœnix—virtue.[1]

---

1 Sedgwick's note in the 1849 edition:

In revising the first chapter of Clarence, I am struck with the local and notable changes in our city in the nineteen years since its publication. The mutations are so constant, and the progress so rapid in our country, that a portrait cannot long have the value of a resemblance. Youth is painted, and the original has become clothed with the attributes of maturity.

The majestic old elms that stood before Trinity Church, in the time of Clarence, have disappeared; the venerable old church itself is razed, and the present magnificent metropolitan edifice has risen in its place. Water has been brought from distant sources and plays in lovely fountains under the shadow of trees not planted nineteen years ago. Then the fashionable residences of the city were below Chambers-street. Now they are more than a mile above it. Then during certain hours of every bright day the west pave of the lower extremity of Broadway resembled the Boulevards of foreign cities—it was filled with the beauty and fashion of the town, with admiring strangers, with observed and observers. The children were arrayed in their best, and turned out there for exhibition. It was a scene of beauty and gaiety.

The old masters of those fine old houses are now quietly inurned, and their residences are converted into warehouses and hotels. The elegant loungers have given place to buyers and sellers, to staring emigrants and mere passengers through the city from boat to boat, all hurrying to and fro, deafened with the rattling of carts, and smothered with the dust of omnibuses—an invention since the time of my dramatis personæ!

CHAPTER II.

"Vous avez de l'argent caché."[1]
L'AVARE.

THE stranger with whom Frank Carroll had contracted so intimate an acquaintance was known to his hostess, and to Frank, and with them only did he appear to have any communication, by the name of Flavel. Frank was satisfied with finding that he was always glad to see him, interested in his little wants, attentive to his prattle, and reluctant to part with him; and his Dutch hostess being regularly paid the pittance of his board, felt no farther curiosity in his conduct or history.

This remarkable exemption of Dame Quackenboss from one of the ruling passions of her sex, was more strikingly illustrated towards another lodger, who had, for ten successive years, rented her miserable garret. All she knew of this man was, that his name was Smith, that he was employed in copying papers for lawyers, that he thus earned his subsistence, that he practised the most rigid economy (as she suspected) and accumulated money. Economy was a cardinal virtue in the eye of Mistress Quackenboss—*the* virtue, par excellence,[2] and she reverenced Smith as its personification. Every one has a beau ideal, and Smith was hers. To him alone was she ever known to defer her own convenience. He was allowed, whenever he wished it, a quiet place in

---

Wall-street has the same class of occupants it had then—the full tide of business existence still ebbs and flows there, but its structures are almost wholly changed. The king of New-York, the *Fire-King*, did his work of devastation there. The burnt district of '35 is now covered with edifices adapted to this great commercial city, and indicating, by their extent and architectural beauty, a rapid progress in wealth and taste. Even in William-street the miscellaneous character of the buildings is changed, and rows of lofty warehouses have taken place of low dwellings and mean shops. One would look in vain now for "an old Dutch home with its gable end to the street."

Where now are the fashionable shopkeepers, the Flandins, Marquands, and Goguets, that supplied the outfit of my heroine? They have passed, and others are in their places. "That which hath been is now, and that which is to be hath already been." (Ecclesiastes 3.15)

1 "You have money hidden somewhere." From *L'Avare* (*The Miser*), 1668, by Molière.

2 Notably.

her chimney-corner, where he was wont to warm his benumbed fingers and toes, while he heated on her coals the contents of a tin cup, that served him for tea-kettle, shaving-cup, gruel-pot, and in short was his only culinary utensil.

The indulgence of a fire in his own apartment was limited to those periods of intense cold when it was essential to the preservation of life, and then it was supported by the faggots and coal-cinders, which in the evening he picked up in the streets. His apparel was in accordance with this severe frugality. For ten years he had worn the same coat, hat, neckcloth, and waistcoat, and he still preserved their whole and decent appearance, from his "prudent way," as his landlady called it, of dispensing with their use altogether when he was in-doors, and substituting in their stead, in summer, a cotton, and in winter, a well patched red baize-gown. Our inventory of his wardrobe extends no farther. He did his own washing within the walls of his little attic, and they told no tales. That they could have betrayed secrets was evident from the extreme caution with which he always locked the door of his apartment, whether he was in or out of it. This was the occasion of a semi-annual altercation with his landlady, who very reluctantly conceded to him his right to an exemption from her house-cleaning. With this exception, he was the subject of her unvarying respect and commendation. "A saving and a thrifty body was John Smit," she was wont to say; "and if there were more like him in our city we should not have to pay for an alms-house and a bridewell, beside having the Dominies preaching the money out of our pockets for an Orphan-Asylum."[1]

She magnified his virtue by contrasting him with Mr. Flavel. "No wonder," she said, "that *he* had come to the fag-end of his money. Every day he left sugar enough in his cup, and victuals on his plate to serve John Smit a week. And such loads of clothes as he put out to wash—a clean Holland shirt every day—it was enough to make a body's heart ache! and clean linen on his bed *twice* a week. True, he paid for it—but she could not abide the waste, how long would his money last at that rate?" Thus she passed in review the common habits of a gentleman, in which Mr. Flavel indulged, though in the main he seemed to observe a strict frugality. She usually concluded her criticisms with a bitter vituperation of Mr. Flavel's and Frank's friendship. "What business had he to bring

---

1   Bridewell: a prison. The Dominies: ministers, particularly of the Dutch Reformed Church in the US, though the term also refers, generally, to any minister.

that rampaging boy there, slamming the door, and tracking the entry; in all the ten years John Smit had lived in the house, he had never had one track after him." She kept up a sort of thinking aloud, an incessant muttering like the low growl of a mastiff in his dreams, and this last remark was repeated for the hundreth time, as she passed by Mr. Flavel's door on her way to Smith's room, and with a harsher emphasis than usual, from her seeing some dark traces of poor Frank's footsteps, and hearing his voice in a merry key in Mr. Flavel's apartment.

Smith had appeared to be declining in health for some months—for several weeks he had rarely left the house, and for the last week Dame Quackenboss had not once seen him. She remembered the last time he came to her kitchen was late in the evening—that he was then trembling excessively,—obliged to sit down for some minutes, and that when she had lighted his lamp for him, he supplicated her, in the quivering voice of a sick or frightened child, to carry it for him as far as his chamber door. She had imputed his agitation to physical exhaustion, and all unused as she was to such manifestations of pity, she had, on the following morning, deposited some soup and herb tea at his door, with the proper intimations of her charity. Smith's emotion was, in truth, owing to a cause known only to himself, and far different from that naturally assigned by Mrs. Quackenboss.

He had come in that night as usual with his little bundle of sticks and shavings, and was groping his way up stairs with his cat-like inaudible tread, when Mr. Flavel with a lighted lamp in his hand, wrapped in his white dressing-gown, and looking more ghastly than usual, passed from his room across the entry to the parlor, and after remaining there for a moment, returned, without perceiving Smith, who remained riveted to the spot where Mr. Flavel had first struck his sight. To Smith's excited imagination, he appeared a spirit from the dead, and a spirit invested with a form and features of all human shapes, to him the most terrible.

From that night he had never left his room, and his landlady deemed it prudent to defer no longer investigating his condition, lest it should be betrayed in the mode Hamlet suggested for the discovery of Polonius.[1] She found his door, as she expected, locked. She knocked and called—there was no answer. She screamed, but

---

1 In Shakespeare's *Hamlet* IV.iii.35-36, Hamlet advises King Claudius regarding the location of Polonius's body: "But if indeed you find him not within this month, / you shall nose him as you go up the stairs into the lobby."

in vain; not the faintest sound, or sign of life, was returned; and concluding the poor man was dead, and with the usual vulgar fear of encountering the spectacle of death alone, she hastily descended the stairs, and communicating her apprehensions to Mr. Flavel, she begged he would stand by, while she forced open the door. He attended her, followed by Frank. The weak fastenings gave way at once to her forcible pressure, and they all entered the apartment so long and so sedulously concealed. Smith was living, but insensible, and apparently in a deep lethargy. Nothing could be more miserable and squalid than the room, its furniture, and tenant. He lay on a cot-bed, tucked so close under the inclining ceiling, that he seemed hardly to have breathing space. There was no linen on his bed, and his coverings were made of shreds and patches, which he had himself sewn together. A little pine-table, with an ink-stand carefully corked, crossed by two pens worn to the stump, and as carefully wiped, stood by his bedside. A broken basin, mug, tea-cup, and plate, bought at a china-shop for a few pennies—a single chair, the bottom of which he had curiously repaired with list,[1] and a small box-stove, comprised his furniture. His thread-bare garments were hanging around the room. A six-penny loaf, half-eaten and mouldy, a dried herring, and a few grains of rice rolled in a paper, and tied, lay on the table.

Quiescent as the landlady's curiosity had hitherto been, it was now called into action by what usually proves a sedative—the means of present gratification. After a glance at the sick man, she made a rapid survey of the room, and holding up both hands, exclaimed, "John Smit's a fool! and that's what I did not take him for—lock his door indeed! he might as well bolt and bar a drum-head—a pretty spot of work, truly, to have to wrench off a good lock to break our way into this tomb, where there's nothing after all but his old carcass!—Ah! what's this?" A new object struck her eye, and stooping down she attempted to draw from beneath the bed an iron box; she could not move it; her predilection was confirmed; her long cherished faith in Smith's worldly wisdom re-established, and looking up with an indescribable expression of satisfaction and triumph, and laughing outright, for the first time for many a year, she exclaimed, "Johny a'n't a fool but!"

Her look appealed to Mr. Flavel. He did not notice it. Frank enforced it by taking hold of his arm, and saying, "See, see, Mr. Flavel!" But Mr. Flavel saw but one object. His eyes were riveted to Smith. For a moment he gazed intently, and then uttered his

---

1 Strips of cloth woven to replace the chair's seat.

thoughts unconsciously and in a half suffocated tone—"Good God!—It cannot be—and yet how like!" He removed the black and matted lock from Smith's forehead. It was wrinkled and furrowed. "Seven and twenty years might do this—No, no, it is impossible."—He turned away and covered his eyes, and then again turned towards the dying man, and exclaimed vehemently, "It is—it is—it must be he!" and putting his lips down to the dull ear, he shrieked in a voice of agony. "Savil! Savil!" The poor wretch made a convulsive struggle, half opened his eyes, and looked mistily on Mr. Flavel. A slight shudder passed over his frame, and he sunk again into his deathlike sleep.

The landlady now interposed, and rudely seizing Mr. Flavel's arm, "Clear out!" she said, "what right have you to be tormenting him?" Mr. Flavel shook her from him, and again bending over Smith, he murmured, "No, no, it cannot be—I was wild to hope it—and if it were—oh God!" He turned away abruptly, and said hastily, "Come, Frank—come down stairs with me." Frank followed him, and when he was again in his own room, he took the boy in his arms, and wept aloud. Frank gazed at him in silence. To a child there is something unnatural and appalling in the tears of a man, but the benignant tenderness of the boy, however, soon surmounted every other feeling. He wiped away Mr. Flavel's tears, and caressed and soothed him; and then whispering, as if he were afraid to speak aloud on a subject that had called forth so much emotion, "had I not best," he asked, "run and beg Dr. Eustace to come and see that man?"

"Dr. Eustace! who is he?"

"Our doctor—mother's doctor—the best doctor in New York!"

"God bless you—yes—why did not I think of it?—tell him I beg him to come instantly. No, say nothing of me—here Frank—say nothing to any one, not to your father even, of what you have seen to-day—but this doctor will not come to this poor devil—what shall we do?—I have money enough to pay him for half a dozen visits—tell him so, Frank."

"Dr. Eustace does not care for the money, sir;" said Frank, as he ran off, with all possible haste, on his benevolent errand.

"Poor boy," thought Mr. Flavel, "you must yet learn that there are no disinterested services in this world!" The doctor arrived in a few moments, but not before Mr. Flavel had disciplined himself into perfect self-command. As the doctor came from Smith's room, Mr. Flavel stopped him in the entry, and inquired if the poor man were still alive. The doctor said "yes," and that he thought it possible he might be revived for a short time, as he had probably fallen into his present state from extreme exhaustion and helplessness.

"You hear what the doctor says," said Mr. Flavel to the landlady, who was also listening to the doctor's report—"do your utmost—if the man dies now, he dies from your neglect."

The landlady put in her protest, and a just one, but Mr. Flavel did not stay to listen to it.

Either his reproach, or the thought of the strong box, which, it had already occurred to dame Quackenboss, might, in default of heirs at law, escheat[1] to the mistress of the tenement, roused all her energies. She prepared a warm bath, and did every thing else the physician required, in the shortest possible time. The warm bath and powerful stimulants produced such an effect on the patient, that the stupor gradually subsided, and when the physician saw him in the evening, he was restored to consciousness. This the doctor told Mr. Flavel, and said at the same time, "the man must have died but for the assistance given him to-day—the discovery of his situation was quite providential."

"Providential!" echoed Mr. Flavel in a sarcastic tone, "the same *Providence* has interposed that left the poor wretch pining in desertion, and exposed to the accidents of starvation and death!"

"Yes, Sir," replied the physician, "the same Providence. I suspect, if we could read this man's history, we should find that he is now enduring the penalty which the wise government of Providence has affixed to certain offences. I infer from all I can learn from your landlady and from my own observation, that this Smith is a miser, and that he is dying of self-inflicted hardships, which have induced a premature old age. I do not believe he is more than fifty."

"Fifty! good God!" exclaimed Mr. Flavel, in a voice so startling that Dr. Eustace turned on him a look of surprise and inquiry; but he instantly recovered his self-possession, and added, "are you skilled? are you accurate, doctor, in your observation of ages?— The man seemed to me much older."

"I am not infallible," replied the doctor, "but my profession naturally leads me to make nice observations on the subject. I perceive in this man indications of vigor quite incompatible with advanced age in his present circumstances. The first thing he did when he recovered a glimmering of consciousness, was to look for a key which was under him in the bed—he grasped it and held it firmly clenched in his hand—so firmly that it would have been

---

1 Default to, or be turned over to.

difficult to have wrested it from him. A painter could hardly have invented a better illustration of miserliness than the apartment of this poor wretch—the iron chest peeping from beneath his bed, and its key still tenaciously held by the famished, dying creature. My blood ran cold as I looked at him. This evening his reason is stronger, and I have persuaded him, as the fear of dropping the key increased his restlessness, to let me attach it to a cord and fasten it around his body."

"Do you think him then quite rational this evening?"

"Perfectly—perfectly himself, I fancy. I proposed to send a nurse to him, but he protested most vehemently against it, repeating again and again that he was a 'poor man—a poor man—nurses were extortionate.' I told him I would defray the expense for a night or two, for I thought I should sleep better if I had not left him to die alone, but he still remonstrated, saying that 'a nurse would burn a light all night; would eat up all he had; would keep a fire;'—and on the whole I thought so violent an interruption of his usual habits might do him more harm than good."

"He is then entirely alone?"

"Yes, but nothing can make any material difference in his condition. This is but a temporary revival. The man must die in the course of a day or two." The conversation was now turned from Smith, but Dr. Eustace still prolonged his visit. He found Mr. Flavel far more stimulating to his curiosity, than the poor mendicant miser. He had a variety of knowledge, a keenness of perception, a lucid and striking mode of expressing his thoughts, and withal, a vein of deep and bitter misanthropy, that indicated a man of marked character and singular experience. The doctor's professional interest, too, was awakened. He saw Mr. Flavel was suffering from severe physical derangement, and he hinted to him the necessity of some medical application, which Mr. Flavel declined, intimating at the same time, his complete infidelity in the science of medicine. The doctor soon after took his leave, with a somewhat abated estimation of his new acquaintance's sagacity. Few men, however liberal, can bear to have their profession disparaged.

At his usual hour Mr. Flavel retired to bed, but not to sleep—the strange and strong emotions of the morning had been soon subdued, and his subsequent reflection had convinced him they must be groundless. These reflections were in daylight, when reason bears sway; but alone, in the stillness, darkness, and deep retirement of the night, his imagination resumed its ascendancy. That face, so well known, so well remembered, so changed, and yet the same, haunted him. The bare possibility that it was the same, had awakened passions that he had believed dead within him. He passed in review the last few weeks of his life. He was himself changed—he no longer 'dwelt in despair.' His soul had revived to kindly influences. The instrument, that he believed broken and ruined, and that had sent forth nothing but discord and wild sounds, had responded music to the touch of nature—to the breath of sympathy. "What was it in this boy, whom he had so recently known, that had melted his frozen affections? what, in his mild tender eye, that pierced to the very depths of his soul?" His thoughts again reverted to the strange agitations of the morning—and again, the electric flash of hope darted athwart his mind. He started from his bed. "Are these the mysterious intimations of Providence?—*Providence!* If such a power exists, it has been to me oppressive—obdurate. Have I not ceased to dread it?—to believe it? Still the web of nursery superstition clings about me. I had dreams last night of the long dead—forgiven—forgotten—forgotten! Singular, that such dreams should be followed by this strange event! Am I doating? I must still this throbbing heart. I will see him again, though the opened wound should bleed to death!" Thus deciding, and obeying an impulse of inextinguishable hope, Mr. Flavel took his lamp, wrapped his dressing gown about him, and cautiously ascended to Smith's apartment. He found the room in darkness. He closed the door after him and advanced to the foot of the bed. The sick man was in a sweet slumber, but the sudden light of the lamp falling directly across his face awakened him. At first he seemed confused, doubtful whether he still dreamed, or whether the apparition before him were a reality or a spectre, but in an instant the blood mounted into his pallid face, and he made an effort to shriek for help. The sound died on his powerless lips—drops of sweat burst out on his forehead—he stretched out his arm as if to repel the figure, and articulated in the lowest whisper—"Not yet! I am not dead yet! oh don't come yet!"

"Fool!—madman!—What do you take me for? I am a living man—speak, speak to me once more." The affrighted wretch was confounded with a mingled horror of the dead, and dread of the living—the terrors of both worlds were before him—his eyes were glued to Mr. Flavel, and his features seemed stiffening in death. "Oh, speak to me!" reiterated Mr. Flavel, agonized with the apprehension that he was already past utterance. "Speak one word—am I deceived?—or are you John Savil?"

"*Clarence!*" murmured the dying man.

Flavel staggered back and sunk into the chair—a deadly faintness came over him, but in one instant more the tide of life rushed back, and he darted to the bed, crying, "Tell me, is he living?"

The poor wretch made an effort to reply, but the accents died on his lips—there was a choaking rattling in his throat—he attempted to sign with his hand, but the weight of death was on it, and he could not move a finger—he fixed his eye on Flavel—its eager glance spoke—but was there life or death in its language?—who should interpret it?

Flavel bent over him in torturing, breathless expectation. The faint hue of life faded from his lips. There was a slight convulsion in his throat, and his eyes closed. Mr. Flavel rushed to the door and called aloud, again and again, for help—no one answered—no one heard him.

Again he returned to the bed and laid his hand on the dying man's heart. It was still feebly beating. "There is yet a spark of life," he thought. "It may be possible once more to revive him." A bottle of spirits of hartshorn[1] was standing on the table; he dashed it over his face, bosom, and hands. Smith gasped, and unclosed his eyes. Mr. Flavel administered a powerful stimulant—the effect seemed miraculous—the mysterious energies of nature were quickened—consciousness returned—and after repeated efforts, he articulated, "he lives—wait."

Mr. Flavel pressed both his hands on his own heart, which seemed as if it would leap from his bosom; and warned by the effect of his first impetuosity, he attempted to be calm, and to say deliberately, "Savil, I'll forgive you every thing, if you'll rouse your powers to tell me all you know." He again offered the medicinal draught.

The dying man received it passively, and shortly after said, "I am too far gone to tell it!"

"God help me!" exclaimed Flavel, in utter despair.

"It is all written," murmured Smith.

"Written!—where?"

"Oh! do not speak so loud to me. It is all written; when I'm gone, you'll find it."

"Where?—tell me where!"

"In my iron box."

What the physician had said of the box and key flashed upon Mr. Flavel's mind; he instantly dragged the box from beneath the bed, threw open the blankets, and tore the key from the skeleton body.

---

1 A solution containing ammonia; smelling salts.

The ruling passion, strong in death, nerved Smith with supernatural strength. He raised himself in the bed—"Oh, don't take my money," he cried—"there is not much—'tis but such a little while I want it—it is my all. Oh, there's somebody coming—they'll see it—they'll see it—Oh, shut the box!"

Mr. Flavel did not hear him; he heard nothing, saw nothing but a manuscript, which he seized, and dropping the lid and turning the key, he threw it on the bed, and left the apartment, without seeing the tears of joy that streamed from the miser's eyes, as, sinking back, he breathed out his last breath, muttering, "My money is safe!"

CHAPTER III.

"Come and sit down by me!
My solitude is solitude no more."[1]
MANFRED.

"WHO is this Mr. Flavel, Frank, that you make such an ado about?" asked Mrs. Carroll, as she was adjusting a napkin over a cold partridge which her son had begged for his friend.

"Who? why, mother, you know—the person who lives in William-street."

"Ah, that I know very well; but he is only a lodger there: where does he come from?"

"I am sure, mother, I do not know."

"What countryman is he? You must know that, Frank."

"An American, I believe; he speaks just as we do;—no, I guess he's English; he speaks shorter, and cuts off his words just in that crusty way that father says is English."

"Does he never say any thing about himself?"

"No, never. Oh, yes! I remember the day I carried him some of those superb peaches cousin Anne sent us, he said I was the only person in the world that ever thought of him; and he said it in a choking kind of way, as if he could scarcely help crying."

"Does he seem extremely poor?"

"Yes—oh, no; not so very poor—I never think of his being poor when I am with him, any more than if he were a gentleman."

"Is he well looking?"

---

1   From Byron's "Manfred: A Dramatic Poem" (1817).

"Yes, mother; at least I like his looks very much now; but when I first saw him, I thought him such a fright! He has very large black eyes, and they are so sunken in his head, that they looked all black to me; his hair is a dark brown, like father's excepting where it is gray; and his skin looks like some of the old shrivelled parchment in father's office; and he is very tall, and so thin that it seems as if his bones might rattle; and he has turns of breathing like a cracked whistle. But for all, mother, I like his looks; and one thing I know, I had rather be with him, than with any body else."

Making all due allowance for the juvenile superlatives of Frank's description, Mrs. Carroll was at a loss to understand what attraction there could be in the stranger to counteract the first impression of such a figure as her son had depicted. After a moment's pause, "Does Mr. Flavel give you any thing, Frank?" she asked.

"Mother! he has nothing in the world to give; that he very often says to me."

"What can make you like him so much, Frank?"

"Because I do, mother. Now don't say that's no reason; just give me the partridge, and let me go."

"Not quite so fast, if you please, Mr. Frank? You surely can tell me, if you will, what it is that attaches you to this stranger? Does he talk to you,—does he tell you stories?"

"Not very often. He has told me of some ship-wrecks, and of the Obi men in the West Indies."[1]

"It's extremely odd you should care so much about him; what can the charm be?"

"I am sure I do not know, mother; only he is always glad to see me, and he seems to love me, and he has not any body else to care for him."

Mrs. Carroll smiled, kissed her boy, and added to the partridge she had arranged, a small jar of jelly, and Frank ran off, happy in the indulgence of his affection, without being compelled to give a reason for it. When he arrived at the little Dutch domicil, a hackney coach was standing before the door; and as Frank put his hand on the latch, the coachman called after him, "Here, my lad, tell the folks in there to make haste; it's bad enough to wait for my betters, without being kept standing for the alms-house gentry."

---

1   Obi, also Obeah: West Indian slave religion synthesizing practices from various African locations. English colonists in Jamaica believed that obeah fomented slave revolts and therefore attempted to suppress it. West Indies: most common nineteenth-century geographical designation for the Caribbean islands.

The sound of Frank's first step in the entry was usually greeted by a welcoming call from Mr. Flavel; but no kind tone saluted him now, and alarmed by an unusual turmoil in his friend's apartment, he hastened forward to his door, which stood a little ajar, and there he remained riveted to the threshold, by the scene that presented itself. Mr. Flavel lay extended on the bed, his eyes closed, and his head awkwardly propped with chairs and pillows; his hostess was bustling about him, and at the moment arranging a neckcloth around his throat, while two strapping blacks stood at the foot of the bed awaiting the conclusion of her operations to convey him to the coach. He appeared entirely unconscious, till an involuntary exclamation of "Oh, dear!" burst from little Frank's lips. He then languidly opened his eyes, and attempted to speak; but failing, he made a violent muscular effort, and succeeded in beckoning the child to him, took his hand, and laid it first on his heart, and then to his lips. Frank burst into tears. "Stand away, boy," cried Mrs. Quackenboss, rudely pushing Frank, "stand away, the men can't wait."

Frank maintained his ground: "Wait for what? what are you going to do with Mr. Flavel?"

"What am I going to do with him! send him to the alms-house, to be sure."

"Oh! don't send him to the alms-house."

"And what for not to the alms-house?"

"Because—because he is so very sick, and the alms-house is such a strange place for him to go to. Oh don't—don't send him there."

"Pshaw, boy! stand away—I tell you there's no time to be lost."

"Let him stay one minute then, while I can run over the way, and speak to my father about him."

"No, no, child, what's the use?" replied the old woman. But when Mr. Flavel again attempted to speak and failed, and tears gushed from his eyes, still intently fixed on Frank, her obduracy was softened and perhaps a superstitious feeling awakened. "It's an ugly sight to see the like of him this way," she said, "go but, boy, and be quickly back again."

Frank ran, found his father, and touched his heart with the communication of his benevolent grief. "Well, my son," he said, "what do you wish me to do?"

Frank hesitated; his instinct taught him that the proposition his heart dictated was rather quixotic, but his father's moistened eye and sweet smile encouraged him, and when Mr. Carroll added, "speak out, Frank, what shall I do?" he boldly answered, "take him home, to our house, sir."

"My dear boy! you do not consider."

"No, father, I know it—there's no time to consider; the men are waiting to take him to the alms-house. The alms-house is not fit for Mr. Flavel, father; and besides, I can never go there to see him. Oh, don't consider—do come and look at him."

Nature inspired the truth of philosophy, the senses are the most direct avenues to the heart, and Frank Carroll felt that the sight of his friend would best plead his cause; and he deemed it half gained when his father took up his hat and returned with him. As they entered the apartment together, Mr. Flavel, whose eye, ever since Frank left the room, had been turned towards the door in eager expectation, rose almost upright on the bed, stretched his hand out to Mr. Carroll, drew him to the bed-side, and perused his face with an expression of intelligent and most mysterious earnestness. He then sunk back quite exhausted, and articulated a few words, but so faintly that they were not audible.

Mr. Carroll was confounded. He first thought the stranger must be delirious; but after a moment's more consideration he was assured of his sanity, and he felt that there was something in his appearance that accounted for Frank's interest, and justified it. It was the ruin of a noble temple. Humiliating as the circumstances were that surrounded him, there was still an air of refinement about him that confirmed Frank's opinion that the alms-house "was not a fit place for him," and when, a moment after, the old man fondly laid his hand on Frank's head, and the tears again gushed from his eyes, the boy turned to his father as if the appeal were irresistible, saying, "There, sir, you will take him home with us, won't you?"

To tell the truth, Mr. Carroll's heart was scarcely less susceptible than his son's, and he only hesitated from dread of a certain domestic tribunal, before which some justification of an extraordinary and inconvenient charity would be necessary. Therefore, while the hackman was hallooing at the door, the blacks were muttering their impatience, and the old woman kept a sort of under barking, he proceeded to make an investigation of the subject.

He took the old woman aside: "Who is this Mr. Flavel?" he asked.

"The Lord knows."

"How long has he lodged here?"

"Six weeks."

"Has he paid you his board regularly?"

"What for should I keep him if he had not?"

"Then I am to understand he has?"

"Yes, yes; and in good hard money too; for I can't read their paper trash."

"And how do you know that he has not money to pay any farther expenses you may incur for him?"

"How do I know?—how should I know, but by finding out? When I came in the room to make his fire this morning, he laid in a stiff fit, and I made an overhaul of his pockets and trunk, and nothing could I find but a trifle of change."

"Has he not clothes enough to secure you?"

"Yes, he has lots of clothes; but who wants dead men's clothes to be *spooked* all their lives; and besides, a lone woman, like I am, what should I do with a man's clothes?"

"You can sell them to the pawn-brokers."

"No, no; it's bad luck to meddle or make with *daut* clothes. Come Tony," she continued turning to the black men, "take hold; and Jupe, as you go by the 'ready made coffin' store, call and tell them to send a coffin for Mr. Smit. The body is short, and narrow at the shoulders; let them send an under sized one, that will come at a low price; for poor Mr. Smit would not like waste in his burying.—Come, boys, up with him."

"Oh, father!" exclaimed Frank, in a voice of the most pathetic entreaty.

"Stop, fellows!" cried Mr. Carroll, and then turning again to the surly woman, "keep Mr. Flavel for the present," he said, "spare no attention. I will send a nurse and physician here, and see that all your charges are paid."

"No, no; there's one death in the house already, and he'd soon make another—the place will get a bad name—let him quit."

Mr. Carroll perceived that her dogged resolution was not to be moved, he was disgusted at her brutal coarseness, and not sorry to be in some sort compelled to the decision which his heart first prompted, he asked Mr. Flavel if he thought he could bear to be carried on a litter to Barclay-street. For a moment Mr. Flavel made no sign of reply, but pressed his hand on his head as if his feelings were too intense to be borne. Then again taking Mr. Carroll's hand in both his, he murmured "Yes."

Every expression, every movement heightened Mr. Carroll's interest in Flavel, and strengthened his resolution to serve him. He ordered the blacks to go immediately to the hospital for a litter, and himself hurried home to prepare his wife for the reception of her unexpected and extraordinary guest. This was a delicate business; but he executed it with as much skill as the time admitted. Mrs. Carroll, though kind-hearted and complying to a reasonable degree, never lost sight of the 'appearance of the thing,' nor was she ever insensible to the exactions and sacrifices that render many forms of charity so costly. She heard her husband through, and then exclaimed, "What have you been about, Carroll! You may as well turn the house into an alms-house at once. I don't know what people will think of us! You and Frank are just alike! There's some excuse for him; but really, Carroll, I think you might have some consideration. What are we to do with the man?"

"Whatever you please, my dear Sarah, it can be but for a very little while. If he lives, I will get lodgings for him. I had not the heart to refuse Frank."

"Frank should be a little more considerate; but men and boys are all alike. I never knew one of them have the least consideration. They just determine what they desire must be done, and there's an end of their trouble. A sick *man* is so disagreeable to take care of, and who is to do it here? You surely would not have me nurse him; and as to Barbara and Tempy, they have their hands full already."

"I have already thought of this trouble, my dear wife, and have obviated it. On my way home I met Conolly; he applied to me to recommend him to a place as nurse, or waiter; I have directed him to come immediately here; he is perfectly competent to all the extra labor necessary, and as to the rest, my dear Sarah, no creature beneath your roof will ever suffer for attention or kindness."

Mrs. Carroll smiled, in spite of her vexation, at this well-timed, and in truth, well-deserved compliment; and when Frank at the next moment bounded in, looking beautiful with the flush of exercise and the beaming of his gratified spirit through his lovely face, and springing into his father's arms embraced and thanked him, and kissed his mother, and expressed the joy of his full heart by jumping about the room, clapping his hands, and other noisy demonstrations; Mrs. Carroll went with as much alacrity to make the preparatory arrangements, as if the charity were according to the accepted forms of this virtue, and as if it had originated with herself.

Before an attic room, which was most suitable to the condition of the expected guest, could be prepared, he arrived; and Mrs. Carroll alarmed by his pale and exhausted appearance, which seemed to her to portend immediate death, threw open the door of her neat spare-room and thus instated the poor sick stranger in the possession of the best bed and most luxurious apartment of her frugal establishment.

Mrs. Carroll had a worrying vein, but the serene temper, superior qualities, and affectionate devotion of her husband duly tempered the heat and prevented its rising to the curdling point.

There were a good many annoyances in this benevolent enterprise that none but a housewife as precise as Mrs. Carroll could rightly appreciate. "Any other time," she thought, "she should not have cared about it, but the room was just white-washed and the curtains were so uncommonly white, and though the chimney smoked the least in the world, it did smoke, and every thing would get as yellow as saffron, and it was such a pity to have so much racing over the new stair-carpet—if she only had not given away the old one—and Tempy would get no time for the street-door brasses, and nothing did try her so much as dirty brasses"; and in short, though every inconvenience seemed to her peculiar to this particular case, her good dispositions finally triumphed over them all, and her sick guest was as scrupulously attended as if he had derived his claim from a more imposing source than his wants.

CHAPTER IV.

"'Tis nature's worship—felt—confess'd
Far as the life which warms the breast!—
The sturdy savage midst his clan
The rudest portraiture of man,
In trackless woods and boundless plains,
Where everlasting wildness reigns,
Owns the still throb—the secret start—
The hidden impulse of the heart."[1]
BYRON.

A FEW days of skilful medical attendance from Dr. Eustace, the care of a tolerable nurse, and the kindest devotion of the whole Carroll family, worked miracles on Mr. Flavel's exhausted frame.

He seemed no stranger to the little comforts and modest luxuries he now enjoyed. No 'Christopher Sly'[2] awaking from his

---

1   From "To my Daughter, on the morning of her Birth-Day," attributed to Byron in *The Port Folio, and New-York Monthly Magazine*, II.4, October 1822.

2   Character in Shakespeare's *Taming of the Shrew*, a tinker who is convinced by the illusion of a play within the play that he is a nobleman, only to "awaken" to find that he is not.

dreams, but as if he might have been both 'Honor' and 'Lord' all the days of his life. But, though the refinements of Mrs. Carroll's *spare-room* did not produce any marked sensation, the kindness of the family did; no look or word escaped his notice; never was man more sensible—more alive to the charities of life. Dr. Eustace said he appeared as much changed since the first time he had seen him, as if an evil spirit had been driven from his breast to give place to the ministry of good angels.

"Do you mean to pay a compliment to my children, Doctor?" asked Mr. Carroll, to whom the Doctor had addressed his remark.

"No; not to them exclusively. I think your influence, Carroll, on Mr. Flavel is more striking than theirs—than Frank's even—though he doats on Frank; but I have noticed that you excite an obvious emotion whenever you come into his room; and once or twice I have been feeling his pulse when you were coming up stairs, and feeble as they were, the sound of your approaching footsteps has quickened them even to throbbing."

"It's very odd," said Mrs. Carroll, "if he really feels so much, that he never speaks of it; not that I care about it at all, you know; but I think it is but civil, when one is receiving all sorts of favors, to express some gratitude for them."

"I am sure he feels it, and feels it deeply," replied Doctor Eustace. "He betrayed so much emotion yesterday in speaking of your husband, that I thought it prudent to leave the room; and to-day he begged me, in case he should suddenly lose his speech or faculties, to request Mr. Carroll to keep him under his roof while he lived. He knew, he said, that Carroll's means were too limited to allow him to indulge his generous dispositions, and he wished him to be informed, that he had sufficient funds in the hands of the Barings[1] to indemnify him for any expenses he might incur. He has made some memorandums, to that effect I presume, to be given to you in case of his sudden death."

"That is just what I should have expected," exclaimed Mrs. Carroll, "true John Bull,[2] keeping up a show of independence to the last gasp; as if a few dollars were a compensation for all this trouble in a gentleman's family. Now, my dear husband, don't look so solemn; is it not a little provoking, considering all our trouble, to say nothing of expense?"

"Yes, dear; a *little* provoking."

---

1 The Baring family's companies were significant commodity traders and bankers in England from 1762 until 1995.
2 A typical Englishman.

"Oh! nothing ever provokes you. I should not think any thing of doing it for a friend, but for a stranger it is quite a different affair."

"Few would scruple doing for a friend, Sarah, all you have done for Mr. Flavel, but I know few beside you that would have done it for a stranger."

Mrs. Carroll was mollified by her husband's praise. She knew she in part deserved it, and she was too honest to put in a disclaimer. "I know, Charles," she said, "that I am not half so generous as you are;" that was true; "but I have really done what I could for the old gentleman; gentleman he certainly is; that *is* a satisfaction; poor man, I do feel for him. Yesterday, doctor, after you told me that a recurrence of the fits might carry him off at any moment, I thought it my duty to hint to him the importance of seeing a clergyman, and I proposed to him to send for Mr. Stanhope. He replied very coldly that he wished to avoid all unnecessary excitement. *Unnecessary!* said I. My dear madam, said he, do not give yourself any uneasiness on my account. I must take my chance. Quackery cannot help me."

"He has, no doubt, had a singular experience," said Mr. Carroll, "and has probably peculiar religious views, but I trust, better than these expressions indicate. When I went into his room last evening, Frank was reading the Bible to him, and Gertrude stood ready with her prayer book, to read the prayers for the sick. He had, it seems, requested this. His face was covered with his handkerchief, and I left them to their celestial ministry. Mr. Flavel has probably lived in a corrupt state of society and has become distrustful of religious teachers—has involved them all in a sweeping prejudice against the priestly office. Such a man's devotional feelings would have nothing to resist in the ministry of children. He would yield himself to their simplicity and truth, and feel their accordance with the elements of Christian instruction. I feel an inexpressible interest in him, and I cannot but hope that the light of religion has, with healing on its beams, penetrated his heart."

"That is hoping against hope, Charles; if he has any such feelings as you imagine, why, for pity's sake, does not he express them?"

"There are various modes of expression; his present tranquillity may be one. There are persons so reserved, so fastidious, that they never speak of their religious feelings."

"Well—that's what I call being more nice than wise," replied Mrs. Carroll, "especially when one, like Mr. Flavel, has done with the world."

Mr. Carroll made no reply. His wife's mind was of a different texture from his, and the sensation her remarks sometimes produced was similar to that endured by a person of an exquisite musical ear from a discordant note. He said something of not having seen Mr. Flavel since dinner, and went to his apartment. He was sitting up in his bed and looking better than usual. Frank sat on one side of him, abstracting the skins from a bunch of fine grapes, and giving them to the invalid. His little sister, Gertrude, on the other, reading aloud. "Where did you get your grapes, Frank?" asked his father.

"Cousin Anne Raymond gave them to me, but I would not have taken them if I had not thought to myself, they would be good for Mr. Flavel."

"Why not, my son?"

"Because cousin Anne is such a queer woman. I wish I had not any rich cousins; or, at least, I wish mother would not make me go and see them. I am glad we are not rich, father."

"Riches do not, of course, Frank, make people like your cousin Anne; but how has she offended you?"

"In the first place, I met her in the entry, and without even saying, 'how do you do,' she asked me if I had scraped my shoes."

"There was surely no harm in that."

"I know that, sir; but then she might have looked first, as you would have done. Mother told me before I left home, about cousin Anne's famous carpets, and charged me to scrape my feet, and I had. Blame her new carpets! I wish I had soiled them."

"My son!"

"Well father, I was too provoked with her; there was ever so much fine company in the parlor, and I went to get myself a chair, and they were all looking at me, and I stumbled, I don't know how, but at any rate I broke the leg of the chair, and cousin Anne laughed out loud, and said to one of the gentlemen, 'I expected it,' and then she whispered to me, 'always wait for a servant to hand you a chair, my dear;' and then she ordered the man to give me some cake—I was determined I would not take any if I died for it, and one of the ladies said, the young man is quite right, it is too *rich* for him."

Mr. Carroll laughed at the boy's simplicity. "Frank," he said, "she meant too *rich* to be wholesome."

"I don't know what she meant, sir, but I hate the very word rich. Soon after, when most of her visiters were gone, she said, 'so Frank, your mother has a famous new hat—where did she get it?'

I told her it was a present from aunt Selden; 'I thought so,' said she, 'I thought she would hardly buy such an expensive hat.' I hope mother will never wear it again—I wish she would not wear any fine presents."

"I wish so too, Frank; but was this all that our cousin said?"

"No, not all; but I will tell you the rest some other time, sir." The rest, which Frank's delicacy suppressed, was in relation to his father's singular guest. Mrs. Raymond made many inquiries about him; said 'it was absurd to take in a man of that sort. It was making an alms-house of your house at once; and beside, it was an enormous expense; but, as to that, it seemed to her, that poor people never thought of expense; to be sure, benevolence, and sentiment, and all that, were very fine things, but for her part, she did not see how people that had but fifteen hundred dollars a year could afford to indulge them.' This scornful railing was not, of course, addressed to Frank, but spoken, as if he had neither ears nor understanding, to another rich supercilious cousin. This, conspiring with the mortifying incidents of the morning visit, filled the generous boy's bosom with a contempt of riches that all the stoicism of all the schools could not have inspired. When he, afterwards, related this supplement to his cousin's conversation, Mr. Carroll's only reply was, "It is true, my dear boy, that our income admits few luxuries—but the luxury of giving shall be the last that we deny ourselves."

But we must return to the little circle around the invalid's bed, which was soon enlarged, by the addition of Mrs. Carroll, and the following conversation ensued, and seemed naturally to arise from what had preceded.

"Suppose for a moment, Frank," said Mr. Flavel, "that one of the good genii of your fairy tales were to offer to make your father rich, would you accept the offer?"

"No, no; not if he must be like other rich people."

"What say you, my little Gertrude?"

"Not if he were to be at all different from what he is."

"I am not in much danger," said the delighted father, "of sighing after fortune while I possess you, my children."

"Then," said Mr. Flavel, whose countenance seemed to have caught the illumination of Carroll's, "you do not desire fortune?"

"No, I do not; at least I have no desire for it that in the least impairs my contentment. Every day's observation strengthens my conviction that mediocrity of fortune is most favorable to virtue, and of course to happiness."

"And you would not accept of fortune if it were offered to you?"

"Ah, that I do not say; money is the representative of power—of the most enviable of all power, that of doing good. I have my castles in the air as well as other men—my dreams of the possible happiness to be derived from using and dispensing wealth."

"And you flatter yourself that with the acquisition of wealth you should retain the dispositions that spring naturally from the bosom of virtuous mediocrity?"

"Surely, Mr. Flavel, some men have resisted the corrupting influence of money, and have used it for high and beneficent purposes. At any rate, if I flatter myself, the delusion is quite innocent, and in no danger of being dispelled. It is scarcely among the possible casualties of life, that I should possess wealth; my decent clerkship only affords moderate compensation to constant labor. I have not a known relative in the world, and I never gamble in lotteries"—

"Life is a lottery, my dear friend," replied Mr. Flavel; "your virtue may yet be proved."

"Heaven grant it!" sighed Mrs. Carroll.

"Then you do not share your husband's philosophic indifference to wealth, Mrs. Carroll?"

"Wealth, that is out of the question; I do not care for wealth, but I confess that I should like a competency—I should like a little more than we have; my husband works from morning till night for a mere pittance."

"Why should not I? Labor is no evil."

"Pshaw! Mr. Carroll, I know that; but then one does like to get some compensation for it. You seem to forget the children are growing up, and want the advantages of education—"

"Pardon me, that I never forget; but the essentials of a good education are within our reach, and as to accomplishments, they are luxuries that may be dispensed with, and for which I, certainly, would not sacrifice the moral influences of our modest competence."

"I do not see, Charles, that moral influences need to be sacrificed. If you were as rich as Crœsus,[1] you would be careful to instil good principles into your children."

"Perhaps so; but I have more confidence in the influence of circumstances favorable to the formation of character, than in direct instruction. The most energetic, self-denying, and disinterested persons I have ever known, have been made so by the force

---

1 A very rich person, after a king of Lydia (Greece).

of necessity. Mr. Flavel, you must have seen a good deal of the world—are you not of my opinion?"

"My opinions," replied Mr. Flavel, with a sigh, "have been moulded by peculiar circumstances, and scarcely admit of any general application. Mrs. Carroll has given honorable reasons for coveting more ample means; she may have others equally strong"—he looked inquiringly at Mrs. Carroll, as if anxious she should speak her whole mind on the subject, and she frankly replied, "Certainly, I have other reasons; I should like to be able to live in a better house—to have more servants and furniture—in short, to live genteelly." Mr. Flavel's countenance for a moment resumed its sarcastic expression, and Mr. Carroll rose and walked to the window; but Mrs. Carroll, without observing either, continued, "By living genteelly, I mean merely, being able to move in good society, on equal terms."

"Is cousin Anne *good society*?" asked little Frank.

"Yes, my son," replied his father; "all your mother's connections are good society."

If there was satire in the tone of Mr. Carroll's voice, it passed unnoticed by his wife, who said, with the most perfect self-complacency, "Yes, that's true; my family has always been in the very first society, and it is natural that I should wish my children to associate with my relatives."

"Perfectly natural, my dear wife, but perfectly impossible, since wealth is the only passport to this good society, at least, the only means of procuring a family ticket of admission."

"Well, that's just what I say, just what I desire riches for; but then," she continued, with a little petulance in her manner, "if you had not been so particular, Mr. Carroll, we might have kept on visiting terms with some of our connections. We have been repeatedly invited to uncle Henry's and cousin William's."

"Yes, we might have been guests on sufferance, and have gone to weddings and funerals at sundry other uncles and cousins, but I was too proud, Sarah, to permit you to receive your rights as favors."

"There is such a thing, Mr. Carroll, as being too proud for one's own interest; and for our dear children's interest, I think we should sacrifice a little of our pride."

"It can never be for the interest of our children," replied Mr. Carroll, with decision, "that they should sacrifice their independence of character for the sake of associating with those to whom the mere accidents of life have assigned a superior—no, I am wrong—a different station. I have no ambition that my children should move in fashionable society; I do not believe that in any country it includes the most elevated and virtuous class; certainly not in our city, where the aristocracy of wealth is the only efficient aristocracy. No, I thank God that there is a barrier between us and the fashionable world; that we cannot approach it near enough to be dazzled by its glare: for like the reptile that fascinates its victims by the emission of a brilliant mist, so the polite world is encircled by a halo fatally dazzling to common senses." Mr. Carroll spoke with less qualification, and more earnestness than was warranted by his more deliberate opinion; but he was particularly annoyed at this moment by the display of his wife's ruling passion.

"It does not signify talking, Mr. Carroll," she replied; "you and I can never agree on this subject."

"Not exactly, perhaps, but we do not materially disagree. Indeed, if the old rule hold good, and actions speak louder than words, you have already given the strongest opinion on my side, by allying yourself to a poor dog, who you well knew could not sustain you in the fashionable world."

Mrs. Carroll felt awkwardly, and was glad to be relieved by a summons to the parlor, where she found the 'cousin Anne,' from whose gossiping scrutiny the insignificance of her humble condition did not exempt her. While Mrs. Carroll was parrying her ingenious cross-examination relative to her guest, her husband continued the conversation with him: "Fortunately in our country," he said, "there are no real, no permanent distinctions, but those that are created by talent, education, and virtue. These fashionable people, who most pride themselves on their prerogative of exclusiveness, feel the extreme precariousness of the tenure by which they hold their privileges. A sudden reverse of fortune, one of the most common accidents of a commercial city, plunges them into irretrievable obscurity and insignificance; for to them all that portion of the world that is not shone upon by the sun of fashion, is a region of shadows and darkness. Perhaps I overrate the disadvantages and temptations that follow in the train of wealth; but if my estimate of them increases my own fund of contentment, my mistake is at least useful to myself. The fox was the true philosopher; it is better to believe that the grapes which we cannot reach are sour, than to disrelish our own food by dwelling on their sweetness.[1] But, Mr. Flavel, I beg ten thousand pardons for my prosing. I have wearied you with all this common-place on the commonest of all moral topics."

---

1 Reference to "The Fox and the Grapes," one of Aesop's fables.

"No, not in the least; it is a common topic, because one of universal interest. No, my dear friend, your sentiments delight me. I find myself in a new region. I feel like one awakened from a confused, distressful dream. Life has been a dream to me; strange, eventful, suffering."

His voice faltered, and Conolly, his nurse, entering at the moment, and observing his agitation, whispered to Mr. Carroll that he had best remove the children, for he believed the old gentleman was going in his fits. The children were accordingly dismissed, and a cordial administered, though Mr. Flavel protested it was unnecessary, for he felt stronger than he had done for some time, and lowering his voice, he requested Mr. Carroll to send Conolly away, and direct him to remain below till called for. "I must be alone with you," he said, "I must not, I cannot delay this longer."

Conolly was dismissed and not recalled till after the lapse of an hour, when the bell was rung repeatedly and so violently that the whole family, in excessive alarm, ran up to the sick chamber. Mr. Flavel was in violent convulsions in Mr. Carroll's arms, who was himself bereft of all presence of mind. He gave hurried and contradictory orders. He sent for Dr. Eustace, and on his appearing, appealed to him, as if happiness and life itself were at stake, to use all his art to restore Mr. Flavel to consciousness. For twenty-four hours he never left his bed-side—scarcely turned his eyes from him; but at the first intimation that he was recovering his senses, he quitted him, retired to his own room for a few moments, then came out and took some refreshment, and returned with a calm exterior to his bed-side. Still the unsubdued and intense emotions of his mind were evident in his knit brow, flushed cheek, and trembling nerves. He could not be persuaded to leave Mr. Flavel for a moment, day nor night. He would not suffer any one else to render him the slightest service, and he watched him with a mother's devotion—a devotion that triumphs over all the wants and weakness of nature.

CHAPTER V.

"When just is seized some valued prize,
And duties press, and tender ties
Forbid the soul from earth to rise,
How awful then it is to die!"[1]
MRS. BARBAULD.

WEARY days and nights succeeded. To all Mr. Carroll's family it seemed as if he were spell-bound. His color faded, his eye was red and heavy; he had forgotten his business, his family, every thing but one single object of intense anxiety and care. His altered deportment gave rise to strange and perplexed conjectures; but curious glances and obscure intimations alike passed by him as if he were deaf and blind. Dr. Eustace said in reply to his anxious demand of his medical opinion, "If Mr. Flavel has quieted his mind by the communication he has made to you, he may again have an interval of consciousness. The mind has an inexplicable influence on the body, even when to us it appears perfectly inert." Mr. Carroll made no answer. Nor, when Conolly's curiosity flashed out in such exclamations as that "Sure, and it's well for him, any way, that he's made a clear breast of it," did he reply word or look to the insinuation. He persevered in his obstinate silence even when Mrs. Carroll, impatient at this new exclusion from conjugal confidence, said, "I am sure I don't wish any one to tell me any thing about it; but your silence, Charles, does wear my spirits out; where there is mystery, there is always something wrong. I had misgivings from the first; you must do me the justice to remember that. A great risk it was to take in such a singular stranger. I always thought so, you know. We could not tell but he had committed some great crime. Dear! it makes my blood run cold to think what sort of a person we may have been harboring." All this was said, and passively endured, while Mr. Carroll was swallowing his hasty breakfast. He moved abruptly from the table, and, as usual, hurried to Mr. Flavel's apartment.

Frank was startled by his mother's suggestions. He dropped his knife and fork, and signed to his sister to follow him out of the room. "Oh, Gertrude," he said, "do you believe Mr. Flavel is a bad man!"

"No, Frank, I know he is not."

---

1   From "A Thought on Death: November, 1814," by Anna Lætitia Barbauld (English, 1743-1824).

"How do you know it?"

"Why perfectly well. He does not seem so."

Gertrude certainly had given an insufficient reason for the faith that was in her; and it had little effect in allaying Frank's apprehensions; and impelled by them he ventured, though he knew it was forbidden ground, to steal into Mr. Flavel's room. His father was at his constant station at the bed-side. Frank drew near softly, took Mr. Flavel's hand, looked at him intently, and then hiding his face on his father's breast, he sobbed out, "He has not committed any crime, has he, father?"

Mr. Carroll disengaged himself from his son, and locked the door. "My dear child," he said, "I am fearful, but I must trust you. While the breath of life is in him you shall know."

"Know what, father? Oh, don't stop."

"You shall know whom you have brought to me." He stopped, almost choked by his emotion.

"Oh! tell me—tell me, sir."

"My father!"

Frank was confounded; he scarcely comprehended the words; his mind was still fixed on his first inquiry. "But has he committed any crime?" he repeated.

"My dear boy, I do not know; I only know he is my father."

"Father—father," repeated Frank, as if the words did not yet convey a distinct idea to his mind, but as he uttered them they penetrated Mr. Flavel's dull sense, he languidly unclosed his eyes, and looked up with something like returning intelligence, but it seemed the mere glimmering of the dying spark; his eyelids fell, and he was again perfectly unconscious.

Mr. Carroll shuddered at his own imprudence. He knew that Mr. Flavel's life hung by a single thread. Till now he had resolutely acted on this conviction, and had now been betrayed by a coercive sympathy with his child. He summoned Conolly, and taking Frank into his own apartment, impressed on him the importance of keeping the secret for the present, and Frank's subsequent discretion proved what self-government even a child may attain.

Doctor Eustace, at his next visit, announced a slight improvement in his patient, which was followed by a gradual amendment. This, the Doctor said, could not last; the powers of nature were exhausted. Of this, Mr. Flavel was himself perfectly aware, and said, with his characteristic firmness, "if it is in the power of your art, Doctor, suspend the last stroke for a little time."

Medical skill did its utmost; happy circumstances shed their balmy influence on the hurt mind; and the mercy of Heaven interposed to protract the flickering flame of life. Mr. Flavel's countenance assumed an expression of serenity, and when his eye met Carroll's, it beamed forth a bright and tender intelligence, that seemed almost supernatural. As his strength permitted, he had short and private interviews with him, during which he communicated his history. We shall recount it in his own words, without specifying each particular interruption.

"Do not expect, my son," he said, "minute particulars. I scarcely dare to think of past events. I dare not recall the feelings they excited; you will sufficiently comprehend them by their ravages.

"My father was a gentleman of Pembrokeshire, in England. At his death his whole property, a large entailed estate, went to my eldest and only brother—Francis Clarence.—We never loved each other; he had no magnanimity of temper to reconcile me to the injustice of fortune. He was a calculating sensualist, governed by one object and motive, his own interest. I was naturally of a generous and open temper. Our paths diverged. He entered the fashionable and political world. I drudged contentedly in mercantile business for an humble living. He married a woman of rank and fortune. I a beautiful unportioned girl. Her name was Mary Temple. It is now almost thirty years since I have pronounced that name, save in my dreams. She was your mother. I have forgiven her.

"You were born at a cottage near Clifton. When I first took you in my arms, I was conscious of a controlling religious emotion; I fell on my knees and dedicated you to Heaven; I now believe my prayer was heard.

"I must not stir the embers of unholy passions; an evil spirit entered my paradise; I was persuaded that it was imbecile and ignoble passively to bear the yoke of a lowly fortune; and to permit my lovely wife to remain in obscurity. Favor and patronage were offered, and a road to certain wealth opened to me in a lucrative business in the West Indies. My wife and child could not be exposed to a tropical climate, they were to be left to my *brother's protection*. My *brother* was my tempter. Oh! the folly of foregoing the certain enjoyment of the best gifts of Heaven in pursuit of riches—at best a perilous possession, and when the foundations of human happiness are gone, virtue and domestic affection, a scourge, a curse! Two years passed; my wife's letters, the only solace of my exile, became infrequent. Some rumors reached my ear. I embarked for England. My brother and wife were in France!——Be calm, my son—I can bear no agitation—I followed them—I found them living in luxury in Paris. I broke into their apartment; I aimed a loaded pistol at my wife; my brother wrested it from me; we fought; I left him dying; returned to England, got possession of you, and re-embarked for Jamaica."[1]

Here, in spite of the force Carroll had put on his feelings, "My mother?" escaped from his lips.

"Your mother; she died long since in misery and penitence."

"In penitence; thank God for that."

"I returned with a desperate vigor to my business; by degrees, my son, you won me back to life; but I had horrid passions; passions, that never slumbered nor slept, tormenting my soul, and I was not to be trusted with the training of a spirit destined for heaven. When you were five years old, your health drooped. The physicians prescribed a change of climate. I had a clerk, John Savil, a patient, and as I thought faithful drudge. He was going to England on business for me, and was to return directly. I intrusted you to his care, and also a large sum of money to be remitted to England. This money was the price of the sordid wretch's virtue. While the English ship in which he was embarked lay in the harbor, awaiting the serving of the tide, he escaped with you, in a small boat, to an American vessel. During the night a hurricane arose. All night, wild with apprehension, I paced the beach. The morning dawned; the sun shone out, but I could neither be persuaded nor compelled from the shore, till the news was brought in by a pilot-boat, that the English ship was capsized and that every soul on board had perished.

"I was then first seized with epileptic fits; the effect of exposure to a vertical sun, combined with my grief and despair. This malady has since recurred at every violent excitement of my feelings. The wretch who robbed me of my only treasure was the same whom I discovered at my lodgings in William-street; the miser. In my trunk you will find a manuscript I obtained from him. It contains the particulars and explanation of his crime, and the fullest proof that you are my son. This discovery brought on a return of my disease, which had well nigh ended my suffering life, when Frank brought you to me. God only knows how I survived that moment of intense joy.

"But I must return to those years which have worn so deep their furrows. Time seared, without healing my wounds. I resumed my business; all other interests were now merged in a passion for the acquisition of property. I seemed endued with a magic that turned all I touched to gold. I never mistook this success for happiness;

---

1 Jamaica was then a British colony with a large African slave population that labored on lucrative sugar plantations.

no, the sweet fountains of happiness were converted to bitterness. Memory was cursed and hope blasted; I was not sordid, but I loved the excitement of a great game, it was a relief to my feverish mind.

"After a while, I formed one of those liaisons common in those islands, where man is as careless of the moral as the physical rights of his fellow-creatures. 'Eli Clairon was the daughter of a French merchant; she had been educated in France, and added to rare beauty and the fascinations of a versatile character, the refinements of polished life. Though tinged with African blood, I would have married her, but I was then still bound by legal ties. Her mother, whose ruling passion was a love of expense, to which I gave unlimited indulgence, connived at our intimacy, till the arrival of 'Eli's father from France. He had contracted there an advantageous matrimonial alliance for her. I was absent from her in the upper country. She was forced on board a vessel, in spite of her pleadings and protestations. The first accounts from the ship brought the intelligence that she had refused all sustenance, and thrown herself into the sea.

"O my son, did not the curse of Heaven fall on every thing I loved? I believed so. 'Eli left a son; I resolved never again to see him—never again to bind myself with cords which I had a too just presentiment would be torn away, to leave bleeding, festering wounds. I supplied the child's pecuniary wants, through his grandmother. She contrived afterwards to introduce him, without exciting my suspicion, among the slaves of my family. He was a creature of rare talent, and soon insinuated himself into my affections. It was his custom to sit on a cushion at my feet after dinner, and sing me to sleep. There was a Spaniard, a villain, whom I had detected, and held up to public scorn. The wretch found his way to my apartment when I was taking my evening repose. I was awakened by a scream from Marcelline. He threw himself on my bosom, and received through his shoulder the thrust of the Spaniard's dirk. The assassin escaped. I folded the boy in my arms; I believed him to be dying; he believed it too, and fondly clinging to me, exclaimed, 'I am glad of it—I am glad of it—I have saved my *father's* life!'

"From that moment he recovered the rights of nature, and became the object of my doating fondness; but no flower could spring up in my path but a blight was on it. My temper was poisoned; I had become jealous and distrustful. Poor Marcelline was facile in his temper, and was sometimes the tool of his sordid grandmother, to extract money from me. I was often unjust to the boy. Oh! how bitterly I cursed the wealth, that made me uncertain of the truth of my boy's affection!

"Marcelline was passionate in his attachments, guileless, unsuspicious, the easy victim of the artifices of bolder minds. At sixteen, he was seduced into an affair in which his reputation and life were at hazard. He believed he owed his salvation to the interference of a young Englishman. In the excess of his gratitude, and at the risk of disgrace with me, he disclosed the whole affair to me, and claimed my favor for the stranger, who proved to be my nephew, Winstead Clarence. My soul recoiled from him; he was the image of my brother: but for Marcelline's sake, I stifled my feelings, permitted Winstead to become a member of my family, and thus was myself the passive instrument of my poor boy's destruction.

"I have not strength for further details. Young Clarence was no doubt moved to his infernal machinations by the hope of ruining Marcelline in my favor, and, as my heir at law, succeeding to my fortune. My broken constitution stimulated his cupidity. Practised as I was in the world, his arts deceived me. My poor boy was a far easier victim. He destroyed our mutual confidence. While, to me, he appeared the mentor of my son, he was decoying him into scenes of dissipation and vice; and while, to Marcelline, he seemed his friend and advocate, he magnified the poor fellow's real faults, and imputed to him duplicity and deliberate ingratitude. Incited by Winstead, Marcelline gamed deeply; and on the brink of ruin, he confessed to me his losses, and entreated pardon and relief. I spurned him from me. He was stung to the heart. Winstead seized the favorable moment, to aggravate his resentment and despair. He retired to his own apartment, and inflicted on himself a mortal wound. I heard the report of the pistol, and flew to him. He survived a few hours. We passed them in mutual explanations, and mutual forgiveness. Thus did I trample under my feet the sweet flower that had shed a transient fragrance in my desolate path!

"I once again saw Winstead Clarence; I invoked curses on his head. I now most solemnly revoke those curses.

"As soon as I could adjust my affairs, I left the West Indies for ever, execrating them as the peculiar temple of that sordid divinity, on whose altar, from their discovery to the present day, whatever is most precious, youth, health, and virtue, have been sacrificed.

"My brother was dead; but Winstead Clarence had returned to England: and I abjured my native land, and came to the United States, where I was soon known to be a man of great riches, and precarious health. I was, or fancied myself to be, the object of sordid attentions, a natural prey to be hunted down by mean spirits. My petulance was patiently endured; my misanthropy forgiven; I was told I was quite too young to abandon the thoughts of marriage, and scores of discreet widows and estimable maidens were commended to my favor. Literary institutions were recommended to my patronage, and emissaries from benevolent societies opened their channels to my meritorious gifts. Wearied with solicitations, and disgusted with interested attentions, I determined to come to New York, where I was yet unknown.

"Scorning the consequence of wealth, and indifferent to its luxuries, I assumed the exterior of poverty; and the better to secure my incognito, I hired a lodging at the old Dutch woman's, where I remained in unviolated solitude till my meeting with Frank stimulated once more to action, that inextinguishable thirst of happiness which can alone be obtained through the ministry of the affections. Frank's striking resemblance to you at the period when I lost you revived my parental love—a deathless affection. He seemed to me an angel moving on the troubled waters of my life. I sedulously concealed my real condition from him, even after I had determined to bestow on him the perilous gift of my fortune. I distrusted myself—I dreaded awaking those horrid jealousies that had embittered my life—I wished to be sure that he loved me for myself alone.

"You may now conceive my emotion when I discovered that my son lived—was near me—was the father of Frank Carroll—when you saved me from being sent to the alms-house, an accident to which I had exposed myself by my carelessness in not preparing for the exigency that occurred. But you cannot comprehend—who can, but He who breathed into me this sentient spirit, who knows the whole train of events that have borne it to the brink of eternal ruin—who but He, the All-Seeing One, can comprehend my feelings when I found myself beneath my child's roof: when I found what I believed did not exist—a disinterested man, and him my son! when I received disinterested kindness, and from my children!

"Forgive me, my son, for so long concealing the truth from you; it was not merely to strengthen my convictions of your worth, but I deferred emotions that I doubted my strength to endure. When I am gone, you will find yourself the heir of a rich inheritance; it may make you a more useful—I fear it will not a happier man.

"In my wrongs and sufferings, my son, you must find the solution, I do not say the expiation, of my doubts of an overruling Providence—my disbelief of the immortality of that nature which seemed to me abandoned to contend with the elements of sin and suffering, finally to be wrecked on a shoreless ocean. Believe me, human life, without religious faith, *is* a deep mystery."

"But, my dear father," said Mr. Carroll "you have now the light of that faith; you now look back on the dark passages of life without distrust, and forward with hope?"

"Yes, yes, my son; my griefs had their appointed mission; the furnace was kindled to purify; it was my sin if it consumed. But how shall I express my sense of that mercy that guided me to this hour of peace and joy, by those dark passages through which I blindly blundered! My son, there is an exaltation of feeling in this full trust, this tranquil resignation, this deep gratitude, that bears to the depths of my soul the assurance of immortality. I now for the first time feel a capacity of happiness, over which death has no power—it is itself immortal life, and I long to pass the boundary of that world whence these glorious intimations come.

"My beloved son, do not wish to protract my exhausted being. I should but linger, not live; to-morrow, if I am permitted to survive till then, I will press your children to my bosom and give them my farewell blessing. Kneel by me, my son, and let us send up together an offering of faith and thanksgiving to God."

During the following evening, Mr. Carroll communicated the secret to Dr. Eustace and his family. The doctor commended his prudence in so long withholding it, sympathized with his sorrow, and congratulated him on his prospects. Mr. Carroll shrunk from his congratulations. The wealth that had been attended by such misery to Mr. Flavel, and must come to him by the death of his parent, seemed to him a doubtful good.

Nothing could be more confused than Mrs. Carroll's sensations. She was half resentful that the precious secret had so long been detained from her; and quite overjoyed to find it what it was. She was afraid some attention to Mr. Flavel might have been omitted, and from the first he had appeared to her such an interesting person!—such a perfect gentleman!—and then there was a deep, unhinted feeling of relief at finding out at last that her husband—her dear husband, was of genteel extraction.

From his children Mr. Carroll received the solace of true sympathy. "Is Mr. Flavel our grandfather?" said Gertrude, "and must he die?" Frank remained constantly in a closet adjoining the sick room, listening and looking, when he might look, without being perceived. Doctor Eustace made his morning visit at an earlier hour than usual. He found his patient had declined so rapidly during the night, that life was nearly extinct.

"Tell me truly, my good friend," he said to the doctor, "how long you think I may live?"

"Your life is fast ebbing, my dear sir."

"Then, my son, call your wife and children: let me call them mine before I die."

They were summoned, and came immediately. Mrs. Carroll's heart was really touched; she said nothing, but knelt at the bedside. The children did not restrain their sorrow; Frank sprang on the bed, kissed Mr. Flavel's cheek, and poured his tears over it. Mr. Carroll would have removed him, but his father signed to him to let him remain. "Frank, my sweet child," he said, "God sent you to me; you saved me from dying alone, unknown, and in ignorance of my treasures—you brought me to my long lost son!"

Here Conolly, the Irish nurse, who was sitting behind Mr. Flavel supporting him in an upright position, gave involuntary expression to his pleasure at the solution of the riddle that had wrought his curiosity to the highest pitch. "Sure," he said, "and it's what I thought, he's his own son's father, sure is he!"

This exclamation was unheeded by the parties in the strong excitement of the moment, but afterwards they had ample reason to recall it.

"My children, my children;" continued Mr. Flavel, "live to God; I have lived without Him; the world has been a desert to me; I die with the hope of his forgiveness; God bless you, my children; kiss me, my son; where are you, Frank? I see you; farewell!" His voice had become fainter at every sentence, and died away at the last word. Still his eye, bright and intelligent, dwelt on his son, till after a few moments he closed it for ever.

A deep silence ensued; Mr. Carroll remained kneeling beside his father; his eyes were raised, and his lips quivering. But who can give utterance to the thoughts that crowd on the mind at the death of the beloved;—when aching memory flashes her light over the past, and faith pours on the soul her glorious revelations; when the spirit from its high station surveys and feels the whole of human destiny!

CHAPTER VI.

"That there is falsehood in his looks
I must and will deny:
They say their master is a knave,
And sure they do not lie."[1]
BURNS.

"AT this moment I must think for you," said Dr. Eustace to Mr. Carroll, after the family had withdrawn from the chamber of death; "of course you will wish to avoid for the present the public disclosure of the circumstance recently developed?"

"Certainly."

"Then lay what restrictions you please on Mrs. Carroll and the children, I will take care that Conolly does not gossip." Accordingly the funeral rites were performed in a private and quiet manner. The clergyman, and the few necessary assistants were struck with the grief of the family being disproportioned to the event; 'but,' said they, 'death is always an affecting circumstance, and the Carrolls are tender-hearted.'

On the morning after the funeral Mrs. Carroll was washing the breakfast-things, her head busy with various thoughts. To some she gave utterance and suppressed others, pretty much after the following manner: "Charles, my dear, I think we had best give Conolly Mr. Flavel's—la! how can I always forget—our dear father's clothes; I believe it is customary in England for people of fortune to do so."

"Give Conolly what consideration you please, Sarah, but leave my father's personal effects undisturbed."

Mrs. Carroll nodded assent, "I do wonder," she continued, "what cousin Anne will say now! she did ridicule our taking in a *pauper*, as she called him, beyond every thing"—to herself, "I did keep it as secret as possible, but we shall be rewarded openly! what a mercy Charles never suspected his riches; if he had, he would just have sent him to lodgings;" aloud, "Only think, dear, the children the other day in Mr. Flavel's—how can I!—our father's room, asked me to send them to dancing school; I told them I could not afford it; he smiled, I little thought for what—dear souls! they shall go now as soon as it is proper"—to herself, "*can't afford it*—thank heaven, I have done for ever with that hateful, vulgar phrase." "By

---

1 From "On Hearing It Asserted Falsehood is expressed in the Rev. Dr. Babington's very looks" (1794) by Robert Burns (Scottish, 1759-96).

the way, Charles, I saw in the Evening Post, that the Roscoes' house is to be sold next week; it would just suit us."

"The Roscoes' house; my dear wife, the Roscoes have been my best, at one time, my only friends; I could not be happy where I was continually reminded of their reverse of fortune."

"Oh, well; I do not care about that house in particular; there are others that would suit me quite as well; but I hope you will attend to it at once; this house is so excessively small and inconvenient." Mr. Carroll assured his wife that she must suppress her new-born sensibility to the discomforts of her dwelling; "for his own part," he said, "he had no heart for immediate change." His mind was occupied with sad reflections, softened, he trusted, by gratitude for singular mercies. Besides, it was necessary, and he rejoiced it was so, before he could receive any portion of his father's property, that his claim to it should be admitted in England, where it was vested; he wished, therefore, that Mrs. Carroll would not at present make the slightest variation in their mode of life. She submitted, but not without betraying her reluctance, by saying, she wondered what forms of business were for, they were too provoking, too stupid, and so utterly unnecessary!

Mr. Carroll made no farther secret of the change in his prospects. He assumed the name of Clarence, and forwarded the necessary documents to England. In other respects he kept on the even tenor of his way.

About six months after a certain John Rider, Esq., a lawyer better known for his professional success in the mayor's court than for his distinction before any higher tribunal, joined a knot of Irishmen who were hovering round a grocery-door, and earnestly debating some question that had kindled their combustible passions. It appeared they were at the moment particularly jealous of the interference of an officer of the law, for one and all darted at him looks of impatient inquiry and fierce defiance. The leader of the gang advanced with a half articulated curse. He was pulled back by one of his companions. "Be civil, man," he said, "it's his honor, Lawyer Rider; he'll ne'er be the one to scald his mouth with other folks' broth."

"Ah, Conolly, is that you?"

"Indeed is it, your honor; was it me your honor was wanting?"

"Yes; I have been to your house, and Biddy told me I should probably find you here."

"And what for was she sending your honor to the grocer's? She might better have guided you any way else to find me."

"To seek you, may be, Conolly, but not to find you."

"Ah, your honor's caught me there; but I'll tache the old woman."

Rider perceived from Conolly's flushed cheek, that he was in a humor to demonstrate some domestic problems that might not be agreeable to a spectator, and therefore instead of accompanying him to his own room, to transact some private business he had with him, he proposed to him to walk up the street. Conolly assented, saying to his companions as he left them, "Stay a bit, lads, and I'll spake to Lawyer Rider about it."

"About what is that, Conolly?"

"Is it that your honor has not heard about Jemmy McBride and Dr. Eustace?" The doctor's name was followed by an imprecation that expressed but too plainly, 'Jemmy and the whole Irish nation versus the doctor.'

"I have heard something of this unlucky affair, but you may tell me more, Conolly."

"Indeed can I; for wasn't I there while his knife was yet red with the blood of him? and wasn't Jem my father's own brother's son?"

"But Conolly, you do not believe the doctor had any thing to do with McBride's death?"

"That I do not say. But I believe, by my soul I do, the doctors have more to do with death than life, the heretics in particular, saving your honor's presence. Any way, Jemmy McBride died in his hands, and the very time he had said the poor fellow was mending; but that was all to keep the priest away. Never a confession did Jem make; never a bit prayer was said over him, nor the holy sign put on him; nor, Mr. Rider, as true as my name's Pat Conolly, was there a light lighted for his soul to pass by. The next night the doctor told Jemmy's wife, a poor innocent cratur that knew no better, that he was going to examine the body to look after the disease a bit; and so she, God forgive her, gives him a light, and he goes in the room and makes fast the door. But you see, the old woman, Jem's wife's mother, looked through the key-hole, and she saw him at his devil's work, and she ran, wild-like, to the neighbors, and there were a dozen of us at Roy McPhelan's, that were thinking to keep poor Jemmy's wake that night, and we made a rush of it, and forced the door, and there stood he over poor Jem, and such cutting and slashing, och! my heart bleeds to think of it; indeed does it, and poor Jemmy's soul tormented the while; for it's sure, your honor, his soul was there looking on his body handled that way by a heretic. Roy seized his knife, and would have had the life of him, but Jem's wife set up such a howling, and she held Roy's arm, and made us all stand back while she said the doctor had shown kindness to her and hers, and we should first kill her before a hair of him should be the worse for it. And then he calls to me, and he says, 'Conolly,' for he knew me, it's six months past when I was nurse to one Flavel, and he says, 'Conolly, my friend,' (the devil a bit friend to the like of him!) 'Conolly,' he says, 'you'll get yourselves into trouble at this mad rate. Go, like honest men, and make your complaint of me, and let the law take its course.' And there was one McInster among us, who is but half an Irishman, for his grandmother was full Scotch, and he's always for keeping the sword in the scabbard, and he would be for persuading us to the law, and while we were all giving our advice, in a breath like, Jemmy's wife whips the doctor through a side door, down a back passage; and once at the street-door, he made a bird's flight of it. But we'll have our revenge. A hundred oaths are sworn to it."

"Don't be rash, Conolly. Have you consulted a lawyer?"

"That have we, Mr. Rider, and he says there's no law for us, and sure is it the laws are made for cowards, and we'll stand by ourselves."

"Listen to my advice, Conolly, you know I am a friend to the Irish—you know how hard I worked for you all in Billy McGill's business."

"Ay, your honor, sure you did make black white there. Did not I say you was a lawyer, every hair of you?"

Rider was compelled to swallow Conolly's compliment, equivocal as it was, and he replied, "I do indeed know something of the law, and believe me, it will be the worse for you all if you take any violent measures. The doctor, though a young man, is well known, and has many friends in the city. That Mr. Carroll, or Clarence as he calls himself, at whose house you first knew him, is ready to uphold him in every thing. You have not heard, perhaps, Conolly, that the old man you nursed left a grand fortune?"

"Lord help us! no. I have been out of the city ever since the old gentleman's funeral, till Easter Sunday, the very day poor Jemmy died."

"I suppose you know that this Carroll claims to be son to the old gentleman?"

"Ay, sure, did not I hear him with my own ears call him so?"

"Just state to me, Conolly, precisely what you recollect about this matter."

"Some other time, your honor, the fellows are waiting for me now."

"Heaven and earth, man! you must not put it off; it's a matter of the first importance, and here's something to make all right with your friends."

Conolly pocketed the douceur,[1] smirking, and saying, "Sure I'll do my best to pleasure you, Mr. Rider; but my head's all in a snarl with Jemmy and this d——d doctor."

"Begin and you will soon get it clear—you were some time at Carroll's?"

"That was I, and for a time it was all plain sailing, though the old gentleman used to mutter so in his sleep, and look at Mr. Carroll so through and through like, that I thought there was more on his mind than we knew of; and, I was sure from the first he was no poor body, for he had the ways of a gentleman entirely, and you know they are as different as fish and flesh."

"Yes, yes, Conolly, go on, we all know he was a gentleman."

"And you know too, may be, that he had epileptics. Well one day after they had had a long nonsense talk about riches, Mr. Carroll sent us all out of the room to stay till he rung, and sure he did ring, distracted like; when we came in the room the old gentleman was in fits, and Mr. Carroll was not much better; and from that time he was an altered man; he had been kind before, but now it was quite entirely a different thing. It was plain, his life was bound up in the old gentleman's. I had nothing worth speaking of to do any more, he gave him all his medicines, and his eyes was never off him day or night, and they would often be alone together. I had my own thoughts, for there was something in their looks, I need not describe it to ye, Mr. Rider, for if you've had either father or son you know what it is."

For an instant the current of Rider's feelings turned, it was but an instant, and he said, "Yes, I understand you, go on."

"I have not far to go, for the fire burned too bright to burn long. It was but two or three days after that he found himself to be just on the launch, and he told Mr. Carroll to call in the family, and then it all came out just as I expected, your honor. He called them all his children, and Mr. Carroll 'my son' again and again, and talked to the child, that's Frank Carroll, about being his grandfather. I could tell you just the words if you please."

"No, they are of no consequence."

"Then, your honor, there's not much more to tell. They all cried of course you know, and I cried too, and that's what I have not done before, since I quitted home. He spoke but few words, but they were rightly said as if he'd had them from the priest's lips, and then he just sunk away like an infant falling asleep."

---

1 Bribe.

Rider hesitated for a few moments; Conolly's statement was particularly hostile to his wishes, and the course to be pursued required some deliberation; "These epileptic fits," he said, "are very apt to derange the mind—the doctors tell me they always weaken it."

"Sure they lie then;" and here followed an execration of the whole faculty; "I've seen men die, many a one, both at home and here in America, and never did I see one behave himself to the very last, in a more discreet, regular, gentale-like manner, than this Mr. Flavel; I don't know how he lived, but he died like a gentleman, any way."

"I must strike another key," thought Rider; "Conolly," he said, "it is not worth while to dilly-dally about this matter any longer; I know I may confide in you. This Mr. Flavel, or rather Clarence, had an own brother's son in England, whom he hated, and had wronged. If he died without children, and without a will, his nephew would, of course, be his natural heir. Now, is it not possible, that, feeling very grateful to this Carroll, he might consent to pass him off for his son; just to call him so, you know?"

"No, no, Mr. Rider; he did not die like a man that was going off with a lie in his mouth."

"Perhaps you don't consider the whole, Conolly; it was an innocent deceit—stop, hear me out—Carroll, who, besides getting the fortune, would gladly wipe off the disgrace of having been an alms-house slip, might beguile him on; Eustace combined with him, at least I suspect so, and," he added, cautiously looking about him, "if he keeps the fortune, one thing is sure, the doctor will have a good slice of it; he will swear through thick and thin, every thing Carroll wants."

"Och! the villain! what will he swear?"

"That the man was of perfect and sound mind; Conolly, this is a hard case and we must try every expedient—every way to get justice done; now if you will stand by us—my client is generous, and he has authorized me to spare neither pains nor money to get witnesses for him—name a particular sum, my good fellow."

"For what? tell me what I am to do just."

"Why, in the first place, you are to right your cause with this doctor; he's more than suspected already of leaguing with Carroll, and if your testimony goes against his, he can't live in the city."

"Ah; that would pleasure me!"

"And if three or four hundred dollars—?"

"Three, or four! *four!* I have one hundred already, and that would just make up the sum, and fetch them all over; the old man, and Peggy, and Roy, and Davy, and Pat, and just set them down gentalely in New York—but tell me how deep in, it is you want me to go?"

"That we must consider; if we could prove the old gentleman was not in his right mind."

"No, no, Mr. Rider, I would not like that; it's ill luck dishonoring the dead that way."

Rider, like a careful angler, had prepared various baits for his hook. One refused, he tried another; "Well, my good fellow, if you cannot on your conscience say, that you think the old gentleman was a little out, may you not have been mistaken in thinking you heard those words, grandfather, son, father? hey, Conolly?"

"You mane, Mr. Rider," said Conolly with an indescribable leer, "whether I can't quite entirely forget them; that is to say, swear I never heard them at all?"

Rider, hardened as he was, felt his cheeks tingle at this sudden and clear exposition of his meaning; "Why, Conolly, on my honor," he said, "I believe that my client has the right of the case, and we are sometimes forced, you know, to go a crooked path to get to the right spot. Those words might have dropped from the old man accidentally, just as he was going out of the world, and then Carroll and the doctor between them might have contrived the rest. The doctor is as cunning as the devil himself; you know how he hoodwinked your cousin's wife—a scandalous affair that was—and yet I don't know how you are to right yourselves; we have no law for you, Conolly, and you know our people don't like club-law."

"D—n the law; the law was made for villains; I beg your pardon, Mr. Rider. It's true I can't sleep till we're revenged on the doctor—four hundred dollars ye say, Mr. Rider? It would be heaven's mercy to the poor souls that's starving at home. What is it ye'll have me forget?" Conolly's conscience had by this time become as confused as his mind. The opportunity of gratifying his resentments against the doctor, and of obtaining the means of bringing to this land of plenty, this full sheaf, his lean and famished brethren at home, overpowered his weak principles, and his real good feeling, and he listened to Rider's lucid and impressive instructions in relation to the testimony he was to deliver, with strict attention and with reiterated promises to abide by them. Rider did not forget to make Conolly fully sensible of the importance of keeping the purport of their interview a profound secret, and then giving him a farther earnest of future favors, he bade him good night. As Conolly's 'God bless his honor,' and 'long life to him,' died away on the lawyer's ear, he was entering a plea in arrest of judgment before the tribunal of conscience. 'After all,' he thought, 'if I have saved Eustace's life from these violent devils, I have done more good than harm; another man might have let them go on; certain it is, Eustace once out of the way, the property would have been ours;' his thoughts diverged a little—'ours?—yes, I may say *ours;* five thousand pounds if I gain it; one should work hard for such a fee!'

Mr. Rider's client had found a fit instrument to manage his cause; a most unworthy member of that profession which from Cicero's day to our own times, has called forth the genius, the ardor, the self-sacrificing zeal of the noblest minds of every age.

CHAPTER VII.

"Are you good men and true?"[1]
MUCH ADO ABOUT NOTHING.

MR. CLARENCE, (we shall hereafter call this gentleman by his rightful name,) as has been stated, transmitted to his deceased father's agents in England, such documents as he deemed necessary to establish his claim. They were admitted as sufficient, and satisfactory, and the property, amounting to about ninety thousand pounds sterling, was transferred to his account, and transmitted to him.

Mr. Winstead Clarence was, at the same time, apprized of the death of his uncle, and of the fact that the property, which in case of his uncle's death without a will, devolved on him as his nearest blood-relative, was intercepted by an American, claiming to be Edmund Clarence's son. This, Mr. Winstead Clarence declared, and perhaps believed to be, an incredible story. His lawyer examined the papers, and was of opinion that the claim might be contested, but as the ability of the English agents to respond for so large an amount of property was doubtful, he advised that the suit should be commenced against the pretended heir, and prosecuted in the American courts. Accordingly, Mr. Winstead Clarence wrote to John Rider, Esq., to institute a suit, and instructed him to rest its merits on the ground of collusion between Mr. Carroll and the doctor; and to procure *adequate testimony at any cost.* As a sort of insurance on the cause, he promised Rider, in case of success,

---

1 Shakespeare's *Much Ado About Nothing* III.iii.1.

five thousand pounds. He had formerly had some acquaintance with Rider in the West Indies, and had had occasion to admire the professional ingenuity with which he had there managed a very suspicious business.

Whatever confidence Rider might have had in his own talent, he was too well aware of his questionable standing at the bar, to assume the exclusive conduct of the suit; he therefore associated with himself a counsellor of the highest reputation for integrity as well as talent; taking care, of course, in his statement of the case to this gentleman, to represent Conolly as a *bona fide* witness.

The facility with which lawyers persuade themselves of the righteousness of a cause in which they have embarked, is often alleged as a proof of the tendency of the profession to obscure a man's original perception of right and wrong. Perhaps no class of men have a deeper sense, or a more ardent love of justice, but they are of all men best acquainted with the uncertainty of human testimony, and most conversant with the dark phases of human character. In the case in question, the honorable counsellor was persuaded that Mr. Clarence had been guilty of deliberate villany. Had he not been so, nothing would have tempted him to attack and undermine, by the power of his eloquence, the character of an innocent and high-minded man.

The cause produced a considerable sensation. It not only involved a large amount of property, but the reputation of individuals which had been hitherto unquestioned. Mrs. Clarence's relationship with some of the most distinguished families in the city, was, at the dawn of her prosperity, remembered, and the cause became a topic in fashionable circles. The trial before one of the Judges of the Supreme Court, then holding The Sittings, was announced in the morning papers. At an early hour the court room was crowded to overflowing, and notwithstanding the opinion of certain of our English friends, that the decorum of judicial proceedings can only be secured by the necromantic presence of gowns and wigs, the most silent and respectful attention was given to the proceedings. Mr. Clarence sustained himself through the whole cause with unvarying dignity. Nor even when it assumed an unexpected and most threatening aspect, did he manifest any emotion. His manly calmness contrasted well with the disinterested enthusiasm of a young friend, who never quitted his side during the trial. This youth, Gerald Roscoe, with the fervid feeling of fifteen, confident in his friend's right, and indignant that it should be contested or delayed, expressed his feelings with the unreservedness natural to his age; sometimes by involuntary exclamations, and then as unequivocally by the flashings of one of the darkest and most brilliant eyes through which the soul ever spoke.

Rider's assistant counsel opened the cause for the plaintiff, and in his behalf appealed to the jury, as the natural guardians of the rights of a stranger, a foreigner, and an absent party. He then proceeded to state, that he rested the cause of his client on two points, which he expected to establish: first, that in default of heirs of the body, he was heir at law and next of kin to the late Edmund Clarence, Esquire, who had died intestate; and secondly, he pledged himself to prove fraud on the part of the defendant, a collusion between him and his witnesses, by which he had obtained possession of, and still illegally detained the property which by the verdict of the jury could alone be restored to the rightful claimant. He should state what he could support by adequate testimony if necessary, but what he presumed would not be controverted, viz. that the deceased, Edmund Clarence, after having resided in a sister city for some months, and his condition having been well known there, had come to the city of New York, where, for reasons irrelevant to the present case, he had assumed the name of Flavel, concealed his real consequence and fortune under the garb of poverty, and lived in mean and obscure lodgings. That during this time he had made an accidental acquaintance with the child of the defendant; that their acquaintance and intercourse had been watched and promoted by the defendant; that all this time Mr. Clarence's health was manifestly declining, under the encroachments of a most threatening malady; that during a frightful attack of this constitutional malady, he was removed to the house of the defendant, still personally an utter stranger to him; that there, with seeming good reason, but certainly most unfortunately for the cause of his client, he was secluded from the observation of all but the family of the defendant, his family physician, (a most intimate friend,) and a *male nurse*.

That Mr. Clarence survived his removal to the house of the defendant about three weeks; that immediately after his decease, the defendant had forwarded to England documents containing evidence of his consanguinity and claim to the property of the deceased. The evidence of this newly discovered relationship was supported by a written declaration, assumed to have been wrested from a dying miser by Mr. Clarence, and by him given to the defendant—by the testimony of the child of the defendant—and by the dying declaration of Mr. Clarence, attested by Dr. Eustace.

He then proceeded to say he should rest the cause of his client on the powerful, and to him he must confess irresistible deduction from circumstances, and on the direct testimony of a single witness. This witness was the nurse to whom he had already alluded. In the documents sent to England no mention had been made of this man, though he presumed it would not be denied that he was present when the deceased gave utterance to those startling declarations, which Dr. Eustace had so fully vouched. This nurse had gone from the defendant's service to his own humble walk of life, and had never received any communication from the defendant; and had first heard of the present controversy when summoned by the plaintiff's counsel to appear as a witness on the trial. He therefore begged the gentlemen would listen attentively to his testimony, and would give it the weight it deserved, as coming from a man who could not possibly have any motive for disguising, or perverting, or withholding the truth.

Nothing could exceed the astonishment of Mr. Carroll, his counsel, and his friends, when Conolly was named as a witness on the part of the plaintiff; they exchanged looks of inquiry and alarm, and as Conolly brushed past them to take his station at the witness's stand, Doctor Eustace, who had a grudge against his whole nation, half ejaculated, "The d——d Irishman!" The words reached Conolly's ear, and nerved his half-shrinking resolution; and once having girded on the battle-sword, he was determined with true blood to fight out the cause, right or wrong.

After some prefatory and unimportant interrogatories, the counsel for the plaintiff asked Conolly to state how he came into the service of the deceased Mr. Clarence. "You see, gentlemen," he said, "I was just leaving service next door to Mr. Carroll's, a big house it is, where they keep more servants than they pay; and so they were going to hold back my dues, and I thought to myself I could not go astray to take a bit of advice of Mr. Carroll; and said he to me, 'Conolly, is it that you're going to leave the place?' Indeed, sir, and that am I not, said I, for I've left it already. And he seemed right glad of it, and said he'd a bit of a job for me—a sick man to nurse—and if I would come straight away to his house, he would spake to my employer, and he was a very fine gentleman, and sure he was he would pay me. 'Och! Mr. Carroll,' said I, 'it takes more nor a gentleman to know a gentleman. They don't scruple showing their hands dirty to us servants—God forgive me, for myself calling me so here in America.'"

Conolly was interrupted, and told to go straight to the point. "Well, your honor, I did go straight to the gentleman's chamber; for gentleman I saw he was, and no poor body, with the first glance of my eye."

"How long did he live?"

"Somewhere between three and four weeks, your honor; but that was nothing to signify, for Mr. Carroll paid me the full month's wages, like a free-hearted gentleman as he is, any way."

"How was Mr. Clarence treated by Mr. Carroll and his family?"

"Trated, your honor! As a good subject would trate the king, or a good Christian the Pope. He'd every thing that money could buy for him, and all that hands could do for him, and Mr. Carroll and his boy, that's Frank Carroll, were by his bed both day and night, sure were they."

"Did Mr. Clarence, a short time previous to his death, have a confidential, that is to say, a private conversation with Mr. Carroll?"

"Yes, your honor, that did he, and I don't belie him in saying so. It was just three days before he died, and the family had all been about him, and they'd had a flummery talk about riches, and Mr. Carroll spoke as if he cared nothing at all about them, and by the same token ye may know he's neither rich nor poor, for it's they that have got more than they want that set store by riches, and we that's poor that are tempted to sell our souls for them—God forgive us!"

"Spare your reflections, my good friend, and tell us what happened after this private conversation?"

"Well, your honor, when the bell rang distracted-like we all ran up together; the poor old gentleman was in his fits again, and he'd been making a clean breast of it, and it seemed a heavy unloading he'd had—it had like to have brought him to his death struggle."

"But he revived, and was himself again after this?"

"Yes was he, but weak and death-like."

"Did you perceive any change in Mr. Carroll's manner?"

"That did we; as the doctor will remember for he said to me, 'Conolly,' said he, 'I am afraid Mr. Carroll will go astray of his reason, for he's quite entirely an altered man,' and so was he—his eye was down-cast, and his cheek flame-like, and I thought it was watching and wearying with the old gentleman, and I tried to get him to take rest, but not a word would he hear of it; he never left him for one minute day nor night, and for the most time he kept us all clear of the room, till the morning the doctor told the old gentleman he'd but scant breathing-time left, and he asked to see the family, and especially the boy, that's Frank Carroll, to thank them for all their kindness to him; and they all come in, and the boy was on the bed by him and kissed the poor old gentleman and cried over him, and then he took the hand of each of them and he gave his blessing to each and all, and he says to me, 'God bless you Pat,' said he; and that was the last word he spoke. I think, your honor, he called me Pat for shortness' sake, and knowing it was all one to me; for when I first came to his service, Conolly bothered him, and I told him if it plased him better, he might call me Pat McCormic, for McCormic was my father's name and Pat my godfather gave me; but McCormic bothered him still worse than Conolly, and then I told him if it were asier, to call me 'Pat Ford,' for that was my grandfather's name, that rared me, and the boys at home called me that just, and it's only since I came to America that I took the name of my mother's brother, which is Conolly."

Here Conolly was interrupted, and told that the court had no concern whatever with his cognomens.

Conolly's excursiveness was doubtless partly owing to his natural garrulity, but quite as much to his desire to get through his testimony as to the last scene with the least possible quantum of lying. He had a common superstitious feeling about the superior obligation to tell the truth of the dying, and he would have preferred traducing Mr. Clarence's whole life to misrepresenting his death-bed.—In reply to some farther questions that were put to him, as to Mr. Carroll's deportment after Clarence's death, he testified to his having been closeted a long time with the doctor.

The plaintiff's counsel then having signified, with an air of complete satisfaction and even triumph, that they had completed their examination, Mr. Carroll's counsel cross-examined the witness, acutely and ingeniously, but without eliciting the truth. There was a strange mixture in Conolly's mind, of malignant resentment towards the doctor, and good will to Mr. Clarence; of determination to secure the price of his falsehood, and of desire not to aggravate the injury he inflicted; a compound of good-heartedness and absence of all principle, and that mixture of simplicity and cunning, that characterizes his excitable and imaginative nation.

During his cross-examination he was questioned in relation to his exclamation when the fact of Mr. Clarence's relationship to the Carrolls first flashed across his mind. He denied it entirely; denied ever having heard a word indicating such a fact from any person whatever, till he was summoned to the trial.

Mr. Carroll's counsel then ably stated his grounds of defence, which, as they are already well known, it will not be necessary to recapitulate.

Doctor Eustace, as witness in behalf of the defendant, was next examined. His calm philosophic countenance, strongly contrasted with the sanguine complexion, large open lips, low forehead, bushy hair, and little, keen, restless gray eye of Conolly, at another time would have commanded respect and confidence.

But now, watchful and distrustful eyes were fixed on him, and by some he was even regarded as deposing in his own cause. Next to the misery of conscious guilt, to a delicate mind, is the suffering of being suspected by honorable persons. Doctor Eustace was embarrassed; there was neither simplicity nor clearness in his testimony, and though he never contradicted himself, yet there was a want of directness, and of self-possession, that darkened the cloud gathering over him and his friend.

Frank Carroll was the next witness offered in behalf of the defendant. His face was the very mirror of truth. Her seal was stamped on his clear, open brow. His whole aspect was beautiful, artless, and engaging, and after a single glance at him, the plaintiff's counsel objected to the admission of his testimony. He contended that a child of eleven years was too young to be disenthralled from his father's authority—certainly was too flexible a material to resist his influence—that he would be merely the passive medium of his dictations. His objections were strenuously opposed by the opposite counsel, and overruled by the court, and Frank was directed to take his station. He was intimidated by a discussion which he did not perfectly comprehend, and not aware of the import of his evidence to his father, and occupied only with a wish to shrink from public notice, he entreated Mr. Clarence, so loud as to be overheard, to excuse him, and permit him to go home. His father endeavoured to inspirit him, but finding his efforts ineffectual, he sternly bade him go to the assigned stand. He obeyed with trembling and hesitation.

After a few unimportant preliminary questions, to which he replied in scarcely audible monosyllables, he was asked to state all that he could recollect of Mr. Clarence's death-bed scene. It requires far more presence of mind to tell a story than to answer questions. Poor Frank was abashed. His manly spirit quailed; he tried to gather courage; he looked up and looked around; every eye was fixed on him, and it seemed to him as if every man were an Argus.[1] His lips quivered, his crimsoned cheeks deepened to fever heat, and when the judge in a voice of solemn authority bade him proceed, he burst into tears.

His father now interposed, and sternly commanded him to speak. The voice of his offended father was more terrible than

---

1   In Greek mythology, Argus was a giant with a hundred eyes, hence a very vigilant person.

even the eyes and ears of the staring and listening crowd, and he at last told his story, but with down-cast eyes, hesitation, and blundering.

He was asked to relate all he remembered of Mr. Clarence's visit to the miser's room, when he (Frank) was with him. He did so; but he could not be sure of any particulars. He was sure Mr. Clarence was very much agitated; but when cross-examined, he was not at all sure but it might have been the expression of sympathy at the extreme misery of the famished, dying old man. He thought he recollected Mr. Clarence pronouncing the name of Savil; but on the cross-examination he was not sure he had not first heard that name from his father. On the whole his testimony appeared, even to Mr. Carroll's firmest friends, confused and suspicious. A fatality seemed to attend his cause. When it was opened, there was not, on the part of the defendant's friends, a doubt of its favorable issue; but the most confident among them now began to fear the result, and many there were who secretly asked themselves if it were not possible they had been deceived in him. His counsel, in this threatening position of affairs, offered to bring forward any number of witnesses to the hitherto unimpeached integrity of his, and of Doctor Eustace's character. The plaintiff's counsel said they would concede that point to the fullest extent it could be required.

Nothing then remained but to present before the court the miser's manuscript. This was objected to as an isolated, unattested document, and, of course, null and impotent in the present cause. The judge, however, remarked that it might throw some light on the impeached testimony of the defendant's witnesses, and he overruled the objections of the plaintiff's counsel.

The document was accordingly read as follows:

"I, Guy Seymour,[1] formerly of England, since an inhabitant of Jamaica, and now of the city of New York, United States, do declare that this writing contains the truth and nothing but the truth, so help me God. Twenty-seven years ago this 5th day of August, A. D. 181-, I was sent from the island of Jamaica by Edmund Clarence, Esq. with the sum of $10,000, which by me was to be remitted to England; and with his only son, Charles Clarence, who was sent on the voyage for the benefit of his health. The devil tempted me to abscond with the money. I took the child too to guard against

---

1 The 1849 edition corrects this error, replacing "Seymour" with "Savil," the name otherwise used consistently in the 1830 edition.

discovery. I left the vessel in which I had embarked in the evening, hoping I should not be missed till it was at sea, and they would believe I had returned to shore with my charge. I got on board an American vessel. When I arrived in New York I heard the English vessel was lost. Therefore no inquiry was made about me. I put the child to a decent lodging. The woman imposed on me, and made me pay a cruel price for his board, charges for washing besides. On the 25th day of the following January, being A. D. 181-, I took him to the city alms-house. He was then five years old. I marked his age and the name I had given him, Charles Carroll, on a card, and sewed it to his sleeve. I did not lose sight of the boy. One year after he was taken from the alms-house by one Roscoe, and has since got well up in the world. I now declare, that when I die he shall be heir to all I possess: eight thousand dollars in my strong box, besides one half-jo, one Spanish dollar, three English pennies, and a silver sixpence, all contained in my knit purse, which my grandmother (a saving body she was, God bless her!) knit for me when I was eight years old. When she gave it to me, 'Johnny, son'y,' said she, 'mind ye well these words I have knit into your purse, and ye'll live to be a rich man.' The words are there yet, 'a penny saved is a penny gained,'—betimes I think the devil branded them on my soul. I put my ten thousand dollars in different banks and insurance companies. They all failed! I lost all! all but my luck-penny, my silver sixpence. What I have now, I've earned, and I've saved all I earned. I have always meant it should go to Mr. Clarence's son when I am dead and gone, and I pray he prove no spendthrift of my hard-gotten gains. All I have got now I've come by honestly. I never was guilty of but the one crime, and I was sore—sore tempted. It is my intention, before I die, to employ an attorney to draw my will; but it's a great cost, and for fear of accidents, I have written this paper, and hereunto I put my name and seal.

"John Savil.
"August, 5th, 181-."

All the evidence in the case was now before the court. The defendant's counsel rose to sum up. He contended that the evidence, on the part of his client, deemed sufficient in England, where it was necessary to overcome the universal and strong feeling against alienating property, still remained in full force. He insisted that it was overthrowing the basis of human confidence, to withdraw their faith from men of the age and unimpeached integrity of his client and his witnesses, and transfer it to an ignorant unprincipled foreigner, who had no name and no stake in society. There were thousands of such men in the city, they could be picked up any where, from the swarms about the cathedral, to the dens of Catharine-lane; men who for a few dollars or *shillings*, would swear whatever pleased their purchasers. Was the property and reputation of our best citizens to be put in jeopardy by such testimony? 'One of the plaintiff's counsel,' (and he glanced his eye with honest scorn at Rider,) 'was a man familiar with the use of such instruments; he had been long suspected of practices which should exile him from the society of honest men; which should banish him from this honorable tribunal, and that by their own official sentence.' The counsel was interrupted, and reminded that such vituperation was irrelevant and not admissable.

He contended that it was in order, and a necessary defence against a secret and criminal proceeding, which could only be exposed by unmasking the true character of the chief agent, who had sheltered himself from suspicion behind the unspotted shield of his able and upright associate. Testimony brought forward under the auspices of this gentleman would receive a false value. Advantage had been taken of his client's conscious integrity, and his just confidence in the sufficiency of the testimony he had adduced to support his cause. Conolly was absent from the city at the time his client prepared the documents to be sent to England, and deeming his testimony superfluous, he had taken no pains to obtain it. For the same reason, and because he had not before adduced it, he had omitted to bring him forward on the present occasion. His client had been betrayed by his confidence in the truth of his cause. He had not anticipated that the instrument he thought worthless, could be whetted to his destruction; he would not believe it could be so; it would recoil from the armour of honesty, the 'panoply divine,' in which his client was encased. There had been a dark conspiracy to defraud and ruin, but 'even-handed justice' would return the ingredients of the poisoned chalice, to the lips that had dictated, and had borne false witness. He declared that the evidence for his client, which he luminously and forcibly recapitulated, could not be overthrown by a thousand such witnesses as Conolly. He begged that the jury would not permit their minds to be warped by the train of singular circumstances that had led his client to the discovery of his parent. He admitted they had been correctly stated by the opposing counsel; but what then? was not the remark as true as it was trite, that the romance of real life exceeded the most ingenious contrivances of fiction? Who should prescribe, who should limit the mysterious modes by which Providence brought to light the secret iniquities of men? He intreated that gentlemen would allow due weight to that circumstance which ought to govern their decision—the character of his client. The opposite counsel, coerced by his own sense of justice, had paid it involuntary tribute, when he conceded all testimony on that point to be superfluous. The same just homage had been rendered to the witness, Doctor Eustace, a man of whom he might say what had once been as truly said of the political integrity of an honorable citizen: 'The king of England was not rich enough to buy him.'[1] He then adverted to the testimony of the child, and asked if it were credible that the father should be the corrupter of his son—the destroyer of his innocence?

All these and other arguments were urged at length, and so ably, that when the counsel finished, the current seemed to have set in Mr. Carroll's favor. Animated whispers of encouragement were heard from his friends, and Rider, who had hitherto been forward and officious, was quite silent and crest-fallen, and slunk away as far as possible from observation.

The counsel for the plaintiff now rose to make his closing argument. He began by expressing his deep and unaffected regret that he must be the instrument of justice in exposing to dishonor and scorn, the character of two gentlemen who had been held in esteem by the community. It had become his painful duty to array circumstances in such a light that it could no longer be doubted that the defendant's integrity had been too deeply infected with human infirmity to resist the solicitations of temptation, temptation double-faced, alluring him with offers of fortune, and of rank.

It might seem strange—it was most strange that man should barter virtue for money. But had not this base instrument slain its thousands and its tens of thousands? He would refer those who questioned whether it were of all agents most powerful in vanquishing human virtue, to the daily occurrences of their commercial city, to the records of their courts, to their own observation, to the page of history, to its darkest, most affecting page—the story of thirty pieces of silver.[2]

He would not magnify the crime it was his duty to unveil. He wished that all the indulgence might be extended to the defendant which human frailty claimed; for the sins of our common nature should be viewed in sorrow rather than in anger.

---

1 A quotation attributed to Joseph Reed (1741-85) in response to a proffered bribe to give up his allegiance to the cause of the American Revolution.
2 The money received by Judas for betraying Christ. See Matthew 27 and Luke 22.

He should endeavor to show how the unhappy man had been led astray; how temptation had at first suggested but a slight departure from the straight path; but *that* once left, how her victim had been darkened, entangled, and lost.

He adverted to Frank Carroll's first accidental meeting with the deceased. He dwelt on his father not only having permitted, but encouraged the child's intercourse with the repulsive stranger.

Subsequently when he was seized with a frightful disease, and apparently near death, the defendant, instead of suffering him to receive relief through the appropriate and adequate channels of public charity—or, even like a Howard or a man of Ross,[1] maintaining him in a private lodging suited to his apparently humble condition—had removed him to his own house, placed him, not in some attic room, or homely apartment suited to a mendicant, but in the best apartment of his house, with a nurse, an expensive male nurse, especially provided for him, and the luxury of medical attendance twice and thrice a day. It must be remembered that the defendant was a man, not of wasteful, nor even of free expenditure, but of very limited means, and living carefully within his means. It had not been pretended that the defendant had been led on by the mysterious instinct of nature—no, the circumstances remained unexplained, unadverted to by the defendant's sagacious counsel. Where then was the key to this extraordinary, this romantic charity? Was it not possible that the defendant was previously acquainted with the real condition of his pensionary? His person was well known in a sister-city—his immense wealth and peculiarities had been a topic of common conversation there. The supposition that the defendant was in possession of this knowledge, and kept it secret, furnished a complete, and the only solution to the riddle. He saw a lone old man, on the verge of life, divorced from his species, without apparent heirs. Why should he not take innocent measures to attract his notice, and secure his favor?

It certainly was not an unnatural nor extravagant hope, that the old man's will, made under the impression of recent kindness, should render an equivalent for that kindness. Thus far the defendant's fraud was not of a deep dye, and probably would not offend against the standard of most men's virtue.

---

1 John Howard (English, 1726-90), philanthropist and social reformer, particularly of prisons; John Kyrle, referred to as "the man of Ross" in *An Essay on Man*, Epistle III, "Of the Use of Riches" (1734), by Alexander Pope (English, 1688-1744).

"The instruments of darkness
Win us with honest trifles to betray us
In deepest consequence."[1]

It is a presumptuous self-confidence that hopes to set limits to an aberration from the strict rule of integrity. Had a voice of prophecy disclosed the dark future to the still innocent man, would he not have shrunk with horror from the revelation? But temptation, fit opportunity, convenient time, assailed him, and he fell!

He now begged the particular attention of the jury to a most important circumstance in the testimony, the private interview which occurred between the defendant and the deceased, three days before his death.

The late Mr. Clarence, as the defendant's counsel had admitted, then disclosed to him the particulars of his life. The effort of recalling past events, and living over far-gone griefs, brought on a recurrence of his disease.

He had revealed, among other events of a clouded life, one which naturally struck the imagination of the defendant.

The old man, seven and twenty years before, had lost a child at sea. The defendant, about the same time, had been abandoned at the gate of our city alms-house!

He did not allude to the circumstance as a reproach to the defendant. He did not unnecessarily present it before the public; but he would ask what feeling was more natural, more universal, than a desire of honorable parentage? He could almost forgive the defendant for grasping an opportunity to wash this stain from his family escutcheon. His family escutcheon! alas, it was a blank! He dated his existence from the moment when, a deserted, shivering, half-starved, half-clad child, he was received under the shelter of public charity!

Is it strange that the project being once conceived by evil inspiration, of ingrafting himself on the stock of an honorable family, his invention should have been quickened to fertility in producing and maturing the means? The old miser's singular and solitary death was remembered. The documents in question might be forged; who should disprove its authenticity? It might be pretended that it was received through the hands of the deceased Mr. Clarence!

Still it was an unattested and insufficient document; and other testimony must be provided—where was it to be obtained?

---

1 Shakespeare's *Macbeth* I.iii.124-26.

Where!—Did the enemy of our souls ever fail to present fit agents to execute a plotted mischief?

He would only remind the jury of the protracted and secret interview between the defendant and the physician, immediately after Mr. Clarence's death.

He could not raise the protecting curtain of secrecy; he could not paint the first shrinking of the confederate—he could not calculate the amount of the bribe—it had been enough for the price of integrity, but not enough to stifle the voice of conscience, as they had all witnessed in the consequences of her violated law, the blundering and confusion of the testimony given by a man, on all ordinary occasions, clear-headed and self-possessed. Much had been said by the opposite counsel on the superior claims of this medical gentleman to their confidence, over the humble witness of his client. Did he hear this argument brought forward in a country of boasted equal rights? A new privileged class! a new aristocracy was this! that was to monopolize esteem and confidence, and to disqualify and disfranchise the poor and humble. Thank God, truth and virtue grow most sturdily in the lowly bosom of humility! The opposite counsel had adopted a plausible explanation of what he no doubt felt to be a very suspicious circumstance—the neglect of the defendant to take the testimony of Conolly. He would suggest the obvious explanation; it had probably already occurred to them. The defendant had not anticipated a legal investigation in this country. He had calculated wisely the amount of proof necessary for the agents in England. It was certainly prudent to have as few instruments as possible in a conspiracy of this dark nature. Conolly, as was apparent, was of that frank, sociable, communicative disposition, which characterizes his amiable nation. If it had been possible to corrupt him, he might, in some convivial moment, disclose a secret which neither involved his fortune nor reputation. Fortune, poor fellow! he had none; and reputation, alas! it had been seen at what a rate the reputation of a poor Irishman was valued.

He begged the jury would not be misled by the relative standing of the witnesses, but in their verdict would imitate that holy tribunal, that was 'no respecter of persons.'

He had now come to the last point of the evidence. He would willingly pass it over; he would for humanity's sake efface it from their memories. But his duty to his client forbade this exercise of mercy. He need not tell them he alluded to the testimony of the child. Surely the unhappy father must have stifled the voice of nature—must have 'stopp'd up the access and passage to remorse,'[1]

---

1   Shakespeare's *Macbeth* I.v.44.

before he practised on this innocent boy—before he effaced or blotted the handwriting of the Creator, still fresh on his beautiful work. But he had not effaced it. All had witnessed the struggles of Heaven and truth in that little heart against falsehood, fear, and authority. All had seen him yield at last with tears and sobbings to the stern parental command.

He begged the jury would mark by what apparently feeble instruments Heaven had thwarted a well-contrived plot; and finally, he resigned the cause to them, confident, that guided by the light which Providence had thrown across their path, their verdict would establish his client's right.

We have given an imperfect abstract of a powerful argument, but inadequate as it is, it may show how ably men may reason on false premises; how honestly good men may pervert public opinion; and how hard it is to adjust the balance of human judgment.

The Judge then proceeded to charge the jury. He told them that the question before them was one of fact, to be decided by them alone; that they must perceive that the testimony of the Irishman was utterly irreconcileable with the truth of the defendant's witnesses. It was for them to estimate the credibility of his apparently honest testimony. A great array of circumstances, favorable to the plaintiff's claim, had been presented before them. It was for them to decide what weight should be allowed to them. On the other hand, they must determine how much consideration should be accorded to the hitherto unassailed reputation of the defendant and his witnesses. Their good faith established, the defendant's right to the property was incontestible. Thus he dismissed them with the unadjusted balance in their hands; and the court was adjourned to the following morning.

CHAPTER VIII.

"Dead! art thou dead? alack! my child is dead;
And with my child, my joys are buried!"[1]
ROMEO AND JULIET.

MR. CLARENCE returned to his home at a late hour in the afternoon, in a state of mind in which there was nothing to be envied but a consciousness of rectitude. For six months his righteous claim had been suspended, and by the interposition of Winstead

---

1 Shakespeare's *Romeo and Juliet* IV.v.63-64.

Clarence, that man, who, of all the world ought not to have prof-ited by the fortune of his injured relative; and now, when Mr. Clarence had flattered himself that all uncertainty was about to end, his reputation had become involved with his fortune, and both were in jeopardy. He had never coveted riches; neither his day nor his night dreams had been visited with the sordid vision of wealth. He had had the good sense and firmness never to attempt to conceal, or forget, or cause to be forgotten, the degraded con-dition of his childhood; and he now thought there was a species of injustice, a peculiar hardship in his suffering the reproach and consequences of these vulgar passions, and disquietudes. It was true, that since he had known himself to be the heir of wealth, the exemptions and privileges of fortune had obtained a new value in his eyes. His usual occupations and pleasures had lost their inter-est in the anticipation of elegant leisure, refined pursuits, and the application of adequate means to high objects.

There was a feeling too, not uncommon when any thing ex-traordinary and peculiar occurs in our own experience; a feeling of the interposition of Heaven in our behalf; a communication with Providence; an intimate revelation of his will, and his concur-rence in our strongest and secret wishes. Mr. Clarence's ruling sentiment was his parental affection; his children appeared to him, and really were, highly gifted. His boy had been the instrument, as far as human agency was concerned, of the singular turn in the tide of his fortunes, and he had regarded him as distinguished by the signal favor of Heaven, and destined to gratify his honorable ambition. These had been his high and happy visions; but he had been harassed by suspense and delay, and he was now beset with unexpected dangers, and tormented with unforeseen anxieties.

After the adjournment of the court, he had passed some hours with his lawyers in balancing the chances for and against him, and had pretty well ascertained their opinion of the desperateness of his cause. As he entered his house he met his little girl, Gertrude, in the entry. She bounded towards him, exclaiming, "Good news! good news! dear father!"

"What news? what have you heard, Gertrude?"

"I have received the first prize in my class," and glowing with the emotion she expected to excite, she drew from beneath her apron a prize-book, bright in new morocco and gilding.

"Pshaw!" exclaimed her father, "I thought you"—had heard some news from the jury, he was going to add; but he suppressed the last half of the sentence, half-amused and half-vexed at his own weakness. He then, almost unconsciously, kissed the little girl, and turning from her, paced the room with an air of abstraction and anxiety.

"You don't seem at all delighted, father," said the disappointed child, "I am sure I don't know the reason why; you used to seem so pleased when I only got the medal."

Her father made no reply, and a few moments after Frank came limping into the room. Mr. Clarence turned short on him, "A pretty piece of blundering work you made of it in court, Mr. Frank, how came you to disgrace yourself and me in that manner?"

"Oh, father, I was so horribly frightened, and besides, sir, you know I felt sick."

"Sick! what ailed you?"

"Father, have you forgotten that I run a nail into my foot yesterday?—I have not been well since."

"My dear boy, I beg your pardon; but I have had concerns of so much more moment on my hands. If your foot still pains you, go and ask your mother to poultice it."

"Mother has gone to Brooklyn. She said she should get a nervous fever, if she staid at home waiting for the decision of the cause."

"Well, go to Tempy; she will do it as well."

"Tempy has gone to Greenwich, to speak to her brother about coming to live with us, for mother says we must have a man-servant immediately after we get the cause."

"Have a little patience, Frank, I am going to Doctor Eustace's, and I will ask him to step over and look at your wound." Mr. Clarence snatched up his hat and went to Doctor Eustace's; but in his deep interest in discussing the occurrences of the day with his friend, he forgot the apparently trifling malady of his boy.

"Gertrude," said Frank, as his father shut the door, "don't you wish our grandfather had not left father any money?"

"No, indeed, I don't wish any such thing. But why do you ask me, Frank? I am sure it is all the same, since he has not got it."

"No, it is not all the same, by a great deal, Gertrude. Don't you see how different father has been ever since: he does not play to us and talk to us as he used to; he never helps me with my lessons; he always seems to be thinking, and every body is talking to him about the cause; and mother, too, she seems more different than father."

"How do you mean, Frank?"

"Why, she always used to be at home, and had something pleasant for us when we came from school, and so forth; but now she is always talking about how we are going to live, and what she is going to buy when we get the cause."

"Oh, but Frank, we shall have such pleasant times then; mother says so. She says we shall be richer than cousin Anne! and I shall have a piano; and we shall keep a carriage of our own; and we shall have every thing we wish—and that will be like having Aladdin's lamp at once, you know."

"Oh, dear me! all I should wish if I had Aladdin's lamp, would be for somebody to cure my foot. Can't you be my good Genius, Gertrude?" said the poor boy, with a forced smile.

"Yes, Frank. Just stretch your leg out on the sofa, and lay your head in my lap, and I will read to you a beautiful Arabian tale out of my prize-book. You will forget the pain in a few minutes."

The sweet oblivious draught administered by his sister's soothing voice, operated like a charm. Frank's attention was rivetted, and though he now and then startled Gertrude with a groan, he would exclaim in the next breath, "Go on—go on!" She continued to read till he fell asleep. Neither his father nor mother returned till a late hour in the evening.

Early next morning it was known to all persons interested in the cause, that the jury were still in solemn conclave, and it was rumored that they were nearly unanimous in favor of the plaintiff. Those who understood the coercive power of watching and fasting over unanimity of opinion, predicted that the verdict would be forthcoming at the opening of the court.

It is an admitted fact, that notwithstanding the precautions that are taken to maintain the secresy of a jury's deliberations; notwithstanding the officer who attends them, and who is their sentinel, locks them in their apartment, and is sworn neither to hold nor permit communication with them; the state of their opinions does marvellously get abroad. What is the satisfactory solution of this mystery to those who believe that the nobler sex scorn the interchange of curiosity and communication?

At the opening of the court, the court-room was crowded as if a judicial sentence were about to be passed upon a capital offender, but by a different and higher class of persons. Some were attracted by the desire to see how Mr. Clarence would receive the annunciation of the ruin of his hopes; how he and his friend Dr. Eustace would endure the consequent dishonor. These were disappointed, for neither of these gentlemen were any where to be seen. Gerald Roscoe too was absent—he who the day before had so boldly scorned every opinion unfavorable to Mr. Clarence. There could be no *coup de theatre*[1] without the presence of these parties. The

---

1 Dramatic turn of events.

general conclusion was, that they were too well apprised of the probable result to meet it in the public eye.

The proper officer announced that the jury were ready to present their verdict. They were accordingly conducted to their box, and the foreman arose to pronounce their verdict for the plaintiff, when he was interrupted by a noise and altercation at the door, and Gerald Roscoe entered, and pressed impatiently forward. He was followed in the lane he made by an old woman, who seemed utterly regardless of the dignity of the presence she was in, looked neither to the right nor left, and elbowed her way as if she had been in a market-house. The young man cast one anxious glance back to see she followed, and then sprang forward and whispered to Mr. Clarence's counsel. This gentleman was electrified by the communication; but he was anxious not to betray his sensations, and he rose, and with great coolness begged the suspension of the verdict, and the indulgence of the court for a moment. His young friend, Mr. Gerald Roscoe, he said, had found a witness whose testimony might have an important bearing on the case.

Rider interrupted him. He was astonished at such an application. The gentleman must be aware that it was utterly inadmissible; he seemed to have forgotten all legal rules, and all his judicial experience. Had he taken counsel of the unfledged youth who was certainly a most extraordinary volunteer in the defendant's cause? The young man's impertinent obtrusion of his sympathies on the preceding day had deserved reproof; he trusted his honor the Judge would not pass by this gross violation of the decorum of that tribunal.

Roscoe's boyish, slightly-knit frame seemed to dilate into the stature of manhood, as he cast an indignant glance at Rider, whose eye fell before him, and then turning to the court, he said, "I pray the Judge to inflict on me any penalty I may have incurred even in that man's opinion," pointing to Rider, "by my unrepressed sympathy with integrity; but I entreat that my fault may not prejudice Mr. Clarence's cause."

"It shall not," said Rider's associate counsel, willing to humor what he considered the impotent zeal of the youth. "I pray your honor that the new witness may be heard. In the present state of our cause, we have nothing to fear from the machinations of this young counsellor—our beardless brother will scarcely untie our Gordian knot."

The Judge interposed. "This is somewhat irregular, but as the counsel on both sides consent, let the witness be sworn." She was so.

"Be good enough to tell us your name, Mistress," said Mr. Clarence's counsel.

"Olida Quackenboss."

"You keep a lodging-house in William-street, Mrs. Quackenboss?"

"You may call it what you like; it's my own house, and I take in a decent body or two now and then, as sarves my own convenience."

"Did a man, calling himself Smith, die at your house last April?"

"No, he died there the thirtieth day of March;" then, in an under voice, and counting on her fingers, 'Thirty days hath September,' and so on—"No, no but, it was the thirty-first of March."

"That is immaterial, good woman."

"What for did you ask me then?"

"Because I wanted to ask you further, if you knew any thing of a certain purse, which this man, calling himself Smith, died possessed of?"

"Yes, do I; and the lad there," pointing, or rather jerking her elbow, towards Gerald Roscoe, "laid down ten dollars to answer for it, if any of you wronged me out of it; and that would not be as good as the purse, for it's got Smit's luck-penny in it."

"How came you by it, Mrs. Quackenboss?"

"Honestly, man."

"No doubt; but did Smith give it to you?"

The old woman grinned a horrible smile. "Are you a born-fool, man, to think Smit, a sensible body, would give away money like your thriftless spend-all trash, that's flashing up and down Broadway? Why look here, man;" and she thrust her arm to the almost fathomless abyss of her pocket, and brought up an old sometime snuff-box, which she opened, took from it the purse, undrew the string, and piece by piece dropped into her hand, the half jo, the Spanish dollar, the English pennies, and the lucky sixpence, specified in Smith's document. "All this was in it, good money as ever rung on a counter."

"Then it was paid to you as due from Smith, was it?"

"Not that neither; Smit paid his own dues; all but a week's hire of the place, that run up against him, poor man, while he lay sick and arning nothing. But leave me be; I'll just tell you how it was. You see, the man that they call the public administrator came to take Smit's strong box, and he said the money was all to go into the public chist; and right glad was I it was to be locked up, and not go to any heirs, to be blown away with a blast like the leaves that's been all summer a growing. And so when this man that they call the administrator came, I helped him fetch the box from the garret, and he looked round poor Smit's room upon his clothes that were hanging about as if they were but so many cobwebs dangling there, and he said to me, 'You may keep these duds—they'll serve you for dusting cloths.' I asked him, 'Do you mean I shall keep them, and all that's in them?' and he said 'Yes;' and to make sure, I called in a witness, and he said 'Yes' again. And then I shut and locked the door after us; for I knew of the purse, that Smit once showed me in his life-time, and I went straight back and got it, and it has not seen the light since till the lad came this morning; and now no man, nor lawyer either, dare to take from me what's honestly mine own. And now ye may take one look at it; it's just as good as when his granny knit it for him, with them words in it—next to a gospel verse are they—'*a penny saved is a penny gained;*' and if ye'd all hare to it, especially yon gay-looking younkers, ye'd have mighty less need of your courts, and your judges, and your lawyers, and your jails. Now you have my word and my counsel, ye may let me go."

"Stop one moment, Mrs. Quackenboss. Who apprised the public administrator that Smith had left the money?"

"He told me one Mr. Carroll had sent him there."

The truth of the miser's document was now attested, and the evidence, of course, conclusive in Mr. Clarence's favor. All, who had watched the progress of the trial, remembered that he might have rested a claim to the miser's money, on the declaration of his manuscript; and his delicacy and disinterestedness in avoiding to do so swelled the tide that was setting in his favor. Murmurs of honest joy, at the triumph of innocence, ran through the court-room. The counsel for the plaintiff rose; 'he had nothing,' he said, 'to allege in answer to the last witness. He was himself convinced,' he magnanimously added, 'of the validity of the defendant's claim to the name and fortune of the late Edmund Clarence, Esquire.'

"Ye're right, your honor, ye're right," cried a voice that made breathless every other in the court-room, "and didn't I tell ye, Lawyer Rider, didn't I tell ye that I heard Clarence that's dead tell him that's living, that he was his own father's son; didn't I tell ye so, Lawyer Rider?—spake, man."

But Rider did not speak. He had no portion of the warm-heartedness of the poor misguided Irishman. He could not throw himself on the wave of generous sympathy, and forget it might engulf him.

Both the offenders were ordered into custody, and both subsequently punished. Rider with the heaviest, Conolly the most lenient infliction the law permitted.

Nothing now remained but for the jury to make out their formal verdict. As soon as this was done, Gerald Roscoe, to whose thought and ingenuity the happy issue of the cause was owing, rushed from the court-room to be the bearer of the happy tidings to Mr. Clarence. He ran breathless to Barclay-street. His glad impatience could not brook the usual formalities. The street door was open. He entered—he flung open the parlor-door; no one was there. He heard footsteps in the room above; he sprang up stairs, threw wide open the door, and the joyful words seemed of themselves to leap from his lips, "It's yours—it's yours, Mr. Clarence!"

Not a sound replied—not an eye was lifted. Silence, and despair, and death, were there; and the words fell as if they had been uttered at the mouth of the tomb. Where were now all the hopes, and fears, and calculations, and projects, that a few hours before agitated those beating hearts?

Where was that restless, biting anxiety, that awaited the decision of the cause as if it involved life and happiness? Gone—forgotten; or if it for a moment darted through the memory, it was as the lightning flashes through the tempest, to disclose and make more vivid all its desolation!

What was wealth? what all the honor the world could render to that father on whose breast his only beloved son was breathing out his last sigh? What to the mother who was gazing on the glazed, motionless, death-stricken eye of her boy? What to the poor little girl whose burning cheek was laid to the marble face of her brother, whose arms were clasped around him as if their grasp would have detained the spirit within the bound of that precious body?

The flushed cheek of the messenger faded. His arms that a moment before had been extended with joy, fell unstrung beside him; and he remained awe-struck and mute till the physician who stood bending over the foot of the bed, watching the sufferer for whom his art was impotent, moved round to his side, and bending over him, uttered those soul-piercing words, "*he is gone!*"

Gerald Roscoe closed the door, and with slow footsteps, and a beating heart, returned to the bustling court-room.

CHAPTER IX.

"The graceful foliage storms may reave,
The noble stem they cannot grieve."[1]
SCOTT.

OUR readers must allow us to take a liberty with time, the tyrant
that takes such liberties with us all, and passing over the three
years that followed the events of the last chapter, introduce them
into the library of Gerald Roscoe's mother, now a widow. The
apartment was in a dismantled condition. A centre-table was covered with files of papers. The book-cases were emptied of their
precious contents. The walls stained with marks of pictures just
taken down. The centre-lamp removed from its hangings, vases
from their stands, and busts from their pedestals, and the floor
encumbered with packages, labelled with various names, and
marked 'sold.'

Mrs. Roscoe was sitting on a sofa beside her son, and leaning her head on his shoulder. Their faces in this accidental position, had the very beauty and expression that a painter might have
selected to illustrate the son and mother—the widowed mother.
The meek brow on which the fair hair, unharmed by time, was
parted, and just appeared in plain rich folds from beneath the
mourning-cap; the tender, vigilant, *mother's* eye; the complexion,
soft, and fair, and colorless, as a young infant's; and the slender
form, which, though it had lost all beauty but grace and delicacy,
retained those eminently; were all contrasted as they should be
with the firmly knit frame and manly stature of her son; with the
dark complexion, flushed with the glow of health; a profusion of
wavy jet black hair; the full lustrous eye of genius; an expression
of masculine vigor and untamed hope, softened by the play of
the kind affections of one of the most feeling hearts, and happiest
temperaments in the world. One could not look at him without
thinking that he would like to take the journey of life with him;
would select him for a *compagnon du voyage*,[2] sure that he would
resolutely surmount the steeps, smooth the roughnesses, and
double the pleasures of the way. And who to look at the mother
would not have been content to have travelled the path of life with
her, 'heaven born and heaven bound,' as she was, unencumbered

---

1 From "The Lady of the Lake" (1810) by Sir Walter Scott (Scottish,
  1771-1832).
2 Traveling companion.

with the burden of life, and unsullied with any thing earthly? She bore the traces of grief, deep and recent, but endured with such filial trust that it had not disturbed the holy tranquillity of her soul. There was such feminine delicacy in her appearance, her voice was so sweet and low-toned, her manners so gentle, that she seemed made to be loved, cherished, caressed, and defended from the storms of life. But she was overtaken by them, the severest, and she endured them with a courage and fortitude, not derived from the uncertain springs of earth but from that fountain that infuses its own celestial quality into the virtue it sustains.

"This has been a precious hour of rest, my dear Gerald," said his mother, "but we must not prolong it. We have still some matters to arrange before we leave the house."

"No, I believe all is finished. I have just given your last inventory and directions to the auctioneer."

"Then nothing remains but to dismiss Agrippa. I had determined to have no *feelings*, but I am not quite equal to this task. You must do it for me, Gerald."

"I have already arranged that business. Agrippa would not be dismissed. He says he is spoiled for new masters and mistresses; and to tell you the truth, my gentle mother, Agrippa is half right, your servants are not fit for the usage of common families."

"I certainly would retain Agrippa, Gerald, if we had any right to such a luxury as the indulgence of our feelings. But my annuity will hardly stretch to the maintenance of a servant, and you, my dear boy, have yet to learn how hard it is to earn your own subsistence."

"That's true, mother; but it will be only a little harder to earn Agrippa's too; and I shall work with a lighter heart, if I toil for something beside my own rations. Thank heaven! in our plentiful country there is many an extra cover at nature's board, and those who earn a place there, have a right to dispense them. Agrippa, poor fellow, would follow our fortunes even though 'he died for lack of a dinner.'[1] When I asked him where he meant to go when we left the house, he drew up with the greatest dignity, and said, 'With *the family*, to be sure. Who could ever think of madam and Mr. Gerald living without a servant?'"

"Well, Gerald, if the fancy that his services confer grandeur or benefit on us, makes him happier, we will not destroy the illusion. Your exertions to support the old man will give me more pleasure than a thousand servants. My mind has, of late, been so occupied

---

1 Shakespeare's *As You Like It* II.vi.15-16.

with inventories, that I have thought of making a list of my compensations for the loss of fortune. I should place first the power of adversity to elicit the energies of a young man of eighteen."

"Pass over the *mother's* compensations, if you please, and specify some other particulars. For instance, is adversity the touchstone of friendship?"

"No, I think not—that is the common notion; but it seems to me that the misanthropic complaints of human nature, with which most persons embitter their adversity, result from accidental connections and ill-assorted unions. In prosperity intimacies are formed, not so much from sympathy of taste and feeling, as from similarity of condition. We associate with those who live in a certain style, and when this bond is dissolved, why should not the friendship be?"

"Friendship! mother?"

"True, Gerald, it is an absurd misnomer. We fancy the shadow is a substance, and when the light enters complain that it vanishes. Those who are not intoxicated by fortune, nor duped by vanity, do not need adversity to prove their friends. I have been disappointed in one instance only, and there the fault is my own. I humbly confess I was blinded by his flattery. I ought always to have known there was nothing in Stephen Morley to deserve our friendship."

"Stephen Morley! the poor scoundrel, he does not deserve a thought from you, my dear mother."

"But we must bestow a few thoughts upon him just now, Gerald. Run your eye over that power of attorney," she added, giving him a paper, "and if you find it correct, send it to Denham." The paper authorized Denham, Mrs. Roscoe's lawyer, to convert a certain property into money, and therewith to pay a debt due to Stephen Morley from the late Edward Roscoe, Esquire.

"This is superfluous," said Gerald, "Morley's debt is already provided for in the assignment."

"True, but Morley is dissatisfied and impatient."

"Good heaven! does the fellow dare to say so?"

"Read his note, Gerald, and you will think with me that a release from even the shadow of an obligation to Mr. Morley is worth a sacrifice." Gerald read the following note:

"My dear Madam—A severe pressure of public business (private concerns I should have put aside) has prevented my expressing in person, the deep sympathy I feel in your late bereavement. The loss of a husband, and *such* a husband is indeed a calamity; but we must all bow to the dispensations of an all-wise Providence.

"It is painful to intrude on you, my dear madam, at *such* a moment a business concern, and nothing but an *imperative* sense of duty to my family, would compel me to do it. I understand you have assumed the settlement of my late friend's affairs—a task, suffer me to say, my dearest madam, en parenthése, ill-suited to one of your delicate sensibilities.

"I hesitate to allude to my late friend's debt to me—a debt, I am bound in justice to myself to say, contracted under *peculiar* circumstances; still I should not refer to them as a reason for an earlier settlement of my claim than is provided for by your assignments, (which Denham has exhibited to me,) was I not constrained by that *stern* necessity that knows *no* law, to intreat you to make arrangements for an *immediate* payment.

"Believe me, my dear madam, with the sincerest condolence and respect,

"Your very humble, and

"devoted Servant

"STEPHEN MORLEY."

Gerald threw down the note; "the sycophantic, selfish rascal!" he exclaimed, "yes, pay him, my dear mother—if it were the pound of flesh, I would pay him—'*peculiar circumstances*,' peculiar enough, Heaven knows! The only requital he ever made for loans from my father that saved him, time after time, from a jail—'peculiar,' peculiar indeed, that after our house has been a home to him he should be the only one of all the creditors dissatisfied. Pay him! Yes, mother, pay him instantly."

A servant opened the door "Mr. Morley, madam! He asks if he can see you alone."

"Show Mr. Morley up—leave me, Gerald."

Gerald paused at the door: "Let me see him, mother," he said earnestly; "he does not deserve"—his sentence was broken off by Morley's entrance. Gerald looked as if he longed to give him the intimation the Frenchman received who said of the gentleman who kicked him down stairs, 'he intimated he did not like his company.' Morley seized his hand, gave it a pressure, and said in a voice accurately depressed to the key of condolence, "My dear Gerald!" and then elongating his visage to its utmost stretch of wofulness he advanced towards Mrs. Roscoe. She baffled all his preparations by meeting him with a composure that made him feel his total insignificance in her eyes. The bidden tear that welled to his eye was congealed there, and the thrice conned speech died away on his lips. "You have business with me, Mr.

Morley," she said in a manner that excluded every other ground of intercourse.

"Yes, my dear madam, I have a small matter of business; but it *is* particularly painful to intrude it at this moment. I am really quite overwhelmed with seeing preparations for an auction in *this* house. God bless me, my dear Julia, was it not possible to avoid this consummation of your misfortunes? And now, when the details of business must be so extremely trying to you?"

"On the contrary, Mr. Morley, they are of service to me."

"Ah! I fear you are overtaxing yourself—an unnatural excitement, depend on it. I fear too—suffer me to be frank—my deep interest in you must be my apology—I fear you have been ill-advised. In your peculiar circumstances, nothing would have been easier than a favorable compromise with the majority of your creditors—certain debts, of course, to be excepted."

"Fortunately, Mr. Morley, there was no necessity for exceptions; I have the means to pay them all."

"Undoubtedly, madam; but by the surrender of your private fortune—to that my friend's creditors had no claim; of course I except those debts in which my friend's *honor* was involved."

"You must pardon me, Mr. Morley; as a woman, I am ignorant of the nice distinctions of men of business. Gerald has not yet learned an artificial code of morals; and we both thought all honest debts honorable."

"Undoubtedly, madam, in one sense; you have high notions on these subjects; the misfortune is, they do not accord with the actual state of things; such sacrifices are not required by the sense of the public."

"Perhaps not, Mr. Morley, but we were governed by our own moral sense."

"Fanciful, my dear madam; and suffer me to say that whatever right you may have to indulge your romantic self-sacrifice, you seem to me to have overlooked your duty to Gerald."

"A mother," replied Mrs. Roscoe, with a faint smile, "is not in much danger of overlooking such duties to an only son. Had our misfortunes occurred at an earlier period of Gerald's life, the surrender of my fortune would have been more difficult. But Gerald has already had, and availed himself worthily, of every advantage of education that our country affords. His talents, zeal, and industry—I speak somewhat proudly, Mr. Morley—are his present means, and adequate to his wants. His agency for Mr. Clarence, and another honorable employment he has been so fortunate as to obtain, will furnish him a respectable support without encroaching on his professional studies."

"Very fortunate, very respectable, undoubtedly, my dear madam; but then my friend Gerald is so very promising—such an uncommonly elegant young man—he would have come into life under such advantages. Why, there are the Vincents, Mrs. Roscoe. Who are more sought and visited than the Vincents? Mrs. V. was left in circumstances precisely analogous to yours. She had, I may say, if not an able, a fortunate adviser at least. We called the creditors together, and exhibited rather a desperate state of affairs. She was, you know, at that time a remarkably pretty woman, and looked uncommonly interesting in her widow's weeds; her children were assembled around her in their deep mourning—it was quite a scene. I assure you the creditors were touched; they signed a most favorable compromise—compounded for ten per cent. I think. Mrs. Vincent lived in great retirement while her daughters were being educated—spared no expense—and now they have come out in the very first style, I assure you. Nobody has a more extensively fashionable acquaintance—nobody entertains in better style, than my friend Mrs. Vincent."

"I believe I must remind you that you have business with me, Mr. Morley."

Morley bit his nails; but after a moment he recovered his self-possession, and reverted from the natural tone into which he had fallen, to that of sentimental sympathy. "Yes, my dear madam, I have business; but really my own concerns were quite put out of my head, by seeing this house, in which I have passed so many pleasant hours, in preparation for an auction! I hardly know how to proceed; I could not fully explain myself in my note. It is too delicate an affair to commit to paper—I was particularly solicitous not to excite your feelings." Mrs. Roscoe listened with that quiet attention, that said, as plainly as words could speak it, *You* cannot excite my feelings, Mr. Morley. She was however mistaken. Morley proceeded: "I perceive, by the exhibit of your affairs, that you have placed me on the same footing with the other creditors of my late friend; I know it is your intention they shall all be fully paid, principal and interest—but permit me to say this is a fallacious hope—a case that rarely occurs; there are invariably great losses in the settlement of estates—if the creditors get fifty per cent., they esteem themselves fortunate. I am compelled to say, though reluctantly, that there is something a little peculiar in this debt to me, which renders its immediate and entire payment very important—important, I mean, to the memory of my late friend."

"Will you have the goodness, Mr. Morley, to explain to me the peculiar circumstances attending this debt?"

"Excuse me, my dear madam; it would be too painful a task; take my assurance that my friend's honor is implicated. I beg," he added, lowering his voice, "that you will not communicate to Gerald what I am going to say. He is hot-headed, and might be rash. An exposure of the circumstances attending the loan would be most unfortunate; I could not avert the consequences to my friend's reputation. The dishonor, I am sorry to say it, would be great, and the disadvantage to your son, inestimable. It is therefore on his account, far more than my own, that I urge immediate payment."

"Let me understand you distinctly, Mr. Morley; do you mean that there were circumstances attending the borrowing of that money dishonorable to my husband?"

"I grieve to say there were, madam."

"And those circumstances must transpire if the money is not immediately refunded?"

"This is the unhappy state of the case."

"Will you run your eye over that power of attorney, Mr. Morley?" Morley did so, and felt a mingled sensation of joy, at finding himself so secure of immediate possession of the total amount of his debt, and of vexation that he had taken so much superfluous trouble; however, the pleasure preponderated and sparkled in his eyes, as he said, "This is perfectly satisfactory, my dear madam, entirely so; it wants nothing but your signature."

"And my signature, sir, it never will receive." Morley's face fell. He looked as if he felt much as a fox might be supposed to feel, who sees the trap-door fall upon him, just as he is in the act of grasping his prey. "Mr. Morley," continued Mrs. Roscoe, "that instrument will convince you how solicitous I was to escape from a pecuniary obligation to you—galling as it is, I will continue to endure it, to show you that neither your broad assertions, nor malignant insinuations, can excite one fear for the honor of my husband's memory. I shall *not* communicate what you have said to my son, for he might not be able to restrain his indignation against a man who has slandered his father, to his mother's ear. Our business is now, sir, at an end." Mrs. Roscoe rang the bell. Morley fumbled with his hat and uttered some broken sentences, half remonstrating, and half apologizing. The servant appeared. "Agrippa, open the street-door for Mr. Morley." Mr. Morley was compelled to follow Agrippa, with the mortifying consciousness of having been penetrated, baffled, and put down, by a woman.

It may appear incomprehensible to our readers, that Stephen Morley should ever have been honored with the friendship of the Roscoes, but they must remember we have shown him without his mask.—"The art of pleasing," says Chesterfield, "is the art of rising in the world," and one of the grossest but surest arts of pleasing is the art of flattery.[1] Morley flattered women for their love; men for their favor, and the people for their suffrages.[2] From the first he received all grace, from the second, consideration, and from the last, office and political distinction. When the Roscoes were affluent and distinguished, Morley was as obsequious to them as an oriental slave to his master. But when a sudden turn in the tide of fortune changed the aspect of their affairs, and cloud after cloud gathered over them, Mr. Stephen Morley, who resembled the feline race in their antipathy to storms, as well as in some other respects, shook the damps from his coat, and slunk away from the side of his friends.

The Roscoes, occupied with deep sorrows and difficult duties, had almost forgotten him, when he consummated his meanness by the conduct we have related.

CHAPTER X.

"By my troth, we that have good wits have much to answer for."
AS YOU LIKE IT.[3]

THE following letter was addressed by Mrs. Layton, whom we take the liberty thus unceremoniously to present to our readers, to Gerald Roscoe, Esq.

"Upton's-purchase, June, 18—.
"Tell me, my dear friend, if you love the country, (to borrow your legal phrase,) *per se?* Here I am surrounded by magnificent scenery, in the midst of 'bowery summer,' in the month of flowers, and singing-birds, the leafy month of June, and yet I am sighing for New York. It is Madame de Staël, I think, who says that 'love and religion only can enable us to enjoy nature.'[4] The first, alas! alas! is (for *is* read *ought to be,*) passé to me; and the last I have exclusively associated with the sick-chamber and other forms of gloom and misery.

---

1 Philip Dormer Stanhope, Fourth Earl of Chesterfield (English, 1694-1773), Letter LXXV, 27 May 1753, in *Letters written by Lord Chesterfield to his Son* (1774).

2 Vote, or right or privilege of voting.

3 Shakespeare's *As You Like It*, V.i.11-12.

4 Madame Germaine de Staël (French-Swiss, 1766-1817).

"I honestly confess, I do love the town; I prefer a walk on a clean flagging to draggling my flounces and wetting my feet in these green fields. I had rather be waked in the morning, (if waked I must be) by the chimney-sweeps' cry, than by the chattering of martins. I prefer the expressive hum of my own species to the hum of insects, and I had rather see a few japonicas, geraniums, and jasmines, peeping from a parlor-window, than all these acres of wheat, corn, and potatoes.

"Oh, for the luxury of my own sofa, with the morning-paper or the 'last new novel' from Goodrich:[1] with the blinds closed, and the sweet security of a 'not at home' order to faithful servants. Country people have such a passion for *prospects*, as if there were no picture in life but a *paysage*;[2] and for light too, they are all Persians—worshippers of the sun.[3] My friends here do not even know the elements of the arts of life. They have not yet learned that nothing but infancy or such a complexion as Emilie's can endure the revelations of broad sunshine. It would be difficult, my dear Roscoe, to give you an idea of the varieties of misery to which I am exposed. My friends pride themselves on their hospitality—on their devotion to their guests. They know nothing of the art of 'letting alone.' I must ride, or walk, or sail. We must have this friend to dine, or that 'charming girl to *pass the day*.' My old school-mate, Harriet Upton, whom in an evil hour I came thus far to see, was in her girlhood quite an inoffensive little negative. She is now a positive wife—a positive house-wife—a positive mother—and Mrs. Balwhidder, the busiest of bees, nay, all the bees of Mount Hymettus[4] are not half so busy as Harriet Upton. She has the best dinners, pies, cake, sweetmeats, in the country—her house is in the most exact order, and no servants—or next to none—a house full of children too, and no nursery! She is an incessant talker, and no topic but husband and children and house-affairs.

"She is an *economist* too, and like most female sages in that line, that I have had the misfortune to encounter, she loses all recollection of the end in her eternal bustle about the means. Every thing she wears is a *bargain*. All her furniture has been bought

---

1 Samuel Griswold Goodrich (American, 1793-1860), Boston publisher and author.
2 Landscape.
3 Reference to Mithraism, the worship of the sun god Mithra in pre-600 BCE, in what is now Iran.
4 Mrs. Balwhidder: character in *Annals of the Parish* (1821) by John Galt (Scottish, 1779-1839). Hymettus is a mountain range near Athens, Greece, famous for its honey.

at auctions. She tells me with infinite naïveté (*me* of all subjects for such a boast) that she always makes her visits to town in the spring, when families are breaking up, and merchants are breaking down—when to every tenth house is appended that prettiest of ensigns, in her eyes, a *red* flag, and half the shop-windows are eloquent with that talismanic sentence, 'selling off at cost.' Oh Roscoe! would that you could see her look, half incredulous and half contemptuous, when I tell her that my maid, Justine, does all my shopping, and confess my ignorance of the price of every article of my dress.

what a dick →

"But even Dame Upton, a mass of insipidities as she is, is as much more tolerable than her husband, as a busy, scratching, fluttering, clucking motherly hen, than a solemn turkey-cock. He, I fancy, from the pomp and circumstance with which he enounces his common-places is Sir Oracle among his neighbors. He is a man of great affairs, president of an agricultural society, colonel of a regiment, justice of the peace, director of a bank—in short, he fills all departments, military, civil, and financial, and may be best summed up in our friend D.'s pithy sentence—'he is all-sufficient, self-sufficient, and insufficient.'

"I am vexed at myself for having been the dupe of a school-day friendship. You, Roscoe, are partly in fault for having kept alive my youthful sentimentalities. What a different story would Emilie tell you, were she to write! Every thing is *couleur de rose*[1] to her; but that is the hue of seventeen—and besides, from having been brought up in a tame way with her aunt, common pleasures are novelties to her. From the moment we left New York, she had a succession of ecstacies. The palisades were 'grand;' the highlands 'Alps;' and the Caatskills 'Chimborazo,' and 'Himlaya.'[2] She could have lived and died at West Point, and found a paradise at any of those pretty places on the Hudson. Albany, that little Dutch furnace, was classic ground to her, and she dragged me round at day-light to search among the stately modern buildings for the old Dutch rookeries that the alchymy of Irving's pen[3] has, in her imagination, transmuted to antique gems. Even in traversing

---

1 Rose-colored.
2 These New York State landscapes and sites, such as the Catskills, West Point, the Hudson River Valley, and Albany, are compared to famous European, South American, and Asian mountain ranges. Chimborazo is an inactive volcano in Ecuador, believed the highest summit in the world until the early nineteenth century.
3 Washington Irving (American, 1783-1859), author of the humorous *History of New-York* (1809) about the city's early Dutch settlers.

the pine and sandy wilderness from Albany to Schenectady, she exclaimed, 'how beautiful!' and when I, half vexed, asked 'what is beautiful?' she pointed to the few spireas and sweetbriars by the road-side. Alas for her poor mother! the kaleidescope of her imagination was broken long ago, and trifles will never again assume beautiful forms and hues to her vision. There are pleasures, however, for which I have still an exquisite relish—a letter from you, my dear Gerald, would be a 'diamond fountain' in this desert.

"By the way, what do you know of the Clarences of Clarenceville? They called on us a few days since; the father, daughter, and a young man by the name of Seton, an artist, who resides in the family and teaches the young lady painting. She, if one may judge from the poor fellow's blue eye and sunken cheek, has already drawn lines on his heart, that it will take a more cunning art than his to efface. He seems to regard her as a poet does his muse, or a hero his inspiring genius, as something to be worshipped and obeyed, but not approached. She appears a comely little body, amiable, and rather clever—at least she looked so: she scarcely spoke while she was here; once I fancied she blushed—and at what, do you think? Your name, Gerald. The father was very curious about you. He is a 'melancholy Jacques'[1] of a man, but he is a dyspeptic, which accounts for all moral maladies. They are evidently the lions of this part of the world. Harriet Upton has a constitutional deference for whatever is *distingué* in any way; and she was in evident trepidation lest Mr. Clarence, who, she took care to tell me, was 'very particular,' should not accord his suffrage to her friend. I was piqued, and determined to show her there was more in woman's power than was dreamt of in her philosophy.[2] I succeeded so well that she kindly assured me she had never seen Mr. Clarence 'take so to a stranger,' and 'husband said so too.' 'Husband says,' in Harriet Upton's mouth, is equivalent to 'scripture says' from an orthodox divine.

"Mr. Clarence betrayed some surprise at my particular knowledge of you, and your affairs; for to confess the truth, I was a little ostentatious of the flattering fact of our intimacy. I cannot account for his curiosity about you, but on the—*feminine* supposition, you will call it—that he has designs, or rather hopes, in relation to you; and on some accounts the thing would do remarkably well. But then there is your genuine antipathy to rich alliances to be

---

1   Character in Shakespeare's *As You Like It*, a satiric and skeptical lord attendant on Duke Senior in his banishment to the forest of Arden.

2   Play on Hamlet's line to Horatio: "There are more things in heaven and earth, Horatio, / Than are dreamt of in your philosophy." I.v.167-68.

overcome; and, Gerald, you are such a devotee to beauty, that this young lady would shock your beau-ideal; and besides, to a young man who is a romantic visionary in affairs of the heart, there is something chilling and revolting in the sort of exemplary, mathematical character that I take Miss Clarence to be; and finally—and thank Heaven for it—you are not a marrying man, Gerald.

"I wonder that any man—that is, any man of society—should trammel himself with matrimony, till it becomes a refuge from old-bachelorhood. An old bachelor is certainly the poorest creature in existence. An old maid has a conventual asylum in the obscurity of domestic life; and besides, it is *possible* that her singleness is involuntary, and then you feel more of pity than contempt for her; but an old bachelor, whether he be a fidgety, cynical churl, or a good-natured tool who runs of errands for the mamas, dances with the youngest girls in company, (a sure sign of dotage,) and feeds the children with sugar-plums; an old bachelor is a link dropped from the universal chain, not missed, and soon forgotten.

"But to the Clarences once more. Miss Clarence and Emilie have taken a mutual liking, and Emilie has accepted an invitation, received to-day, and expressed in the kindest manner, to pass a week at Clarenceville. The invitation to the Uptons and me is limited to a dinner. If Miss Clarence were a woman of the world, she would not care to bring herself into such close comparison with such exquisite beauty as Emilie's. Is it not strange that Emilie, Hebe[1] as she is, should have so little influence over the imagination. She is a great deal more like Layton than like her poor mother. By the way, will you tell Layton he must remit us some money, and also that I shall conform to *his* wishes in respect to going to Trenton,[2] and shall of course expect the necessary funds. Be kind enough to say I should have written to him if I had had time.

"Oh, that my friend would write—not a book—heaven forefend! but a letter. Do gratify my curiosity about the Clarences. I mean in relation to any particular interest they may have in you. I know generally the history of Mr. C.'s discovery of his father, and his law-suit.

"Adieu, dear Gerald. Believe me with as much sentiment as a wife and matron may indulge,

"Yours,

"GRACE LAYTON."

---

1 Hebe was the Greek goddess of youth. In the 1849 edition, Sedgwick revises this phrase, writing "Emilie, young and beautiful as she is."

2 Trenton Falls, New York, then a fashionable destination for nineteenth-century tourists.

"Gerald Roscoe to Mrs. Layton.

"*New York, June, 18—*.

"My dear Madam—It is I believe canonical to answer first the conclusion of a lady's letter. My reply to your queries about the Clarences will account for Mr. C.'s interest in me, without involving any reason so flattering as that you have suggested. My uncle, Gerald Roscoe, was one of that unlucky brotherhood that have fallen under your lash, and so far from being a 'dropped link, not missed, and soon forgotten,' he had that warmth and susceptibility of heart, that activity and benevolence of disposition, that strengthen and brighten the chain that binds man to man, and earth to heaven. Blessed be his memory! I never see an old bachelor that my heart does not warm to him for his sake. But to my story. My uncle—a Howard in his charities—(you touched a nerve, my dear Mrs. Layton, when you satarised old bachelors)—my uncle, on a visit to our city alms-house, espied a little boy, who, to use his own phrase, had a *certain something* about him that took his heart. This certain something, by the way, he saw in whoever needed his kindness. The boy too, at the first glance was attracted to my uncle. Children are the keenest physiognomists—never at fault in their *first loves*. It suddenly occurred to my uncle, that an errand-boy was indispensable to him. The child was removed to my grandfather's, and soon made such rapid advances in his patron's affections that he sent him to the best schools in the city, and promoted him to the parlor, where, universal sufferance being the rule of my grandfather's house, he was soon as firmly established as if he had equal rights with the children of the family. This child was then, as you probably know, called Charles Carroll. He was just graduated with the first honors of Columbia College, when, within a few days of each other, my grandfather and uncle died, and the house of Roscoe & Son proved to be insolvent. Young Carroll, of course, was cast on his own energies. He would have preferred the profession of law, but he had fallen desperately in love with a Miss Lynford, who lived in dependence in her uncle's family. He could not brook the humiliations which, I suspect, he felt more keenly than the subject of them, and he married, and was compelled, by the actual necessities of existence, to renounce distant advantages for the humble but certain gains of a clerkship. These particulars I had from my mother. You may not have heard that at the moment of his accession of property he suffered a calamity in the death of an only son, which deprived him of all relish, almost of all consciousness, of his prosperity. He would gladly have filled the boy's yawning grave with the wealth which seemed to fall into his hands at that moment, to mock him with its impotence. The boy was a rare gem. I knew him and loved him, and happened to witness his death; and being then at the impressible season of life, it sunk deeply into my heart. It was a sudden, and for a long time, a total eclipse to the poor father. The shock was aggravated by a bitter self-reproach, for having, in his engrossing anxiety for the result of his pending lawsuit, neglected the child's malady while it was yet curable.

"He was plunged into an abyss of melancholy. His health was ruined, and his mind a prey to hypochondriac despondency. He languished for a year without one effort to retrieve his spirits.

"His physician prescribed entire change of scene, as the only remedy, and a voyage to Europe was decided on. His daughter was sent to Madame Rivardi's in Philadelphia,[1] where, by the way, if she had been of a polishable texture, she would now be something very different from the unembellished little person you describe. Mrs. Clarence went abroad with her husband. My mother, who is a sagacious observer of her own sex, says she was a weak and worldly-minded woman, quite unfit to manage, and certainly to rectify, so delicate an instrument as her husband's mind. They had been in Europe about eighteen months, when Mr. Clarence received the news of my father's death, the last, and bitterest of our family misfortunes. This event roused Mr. Clarence's generous sympathies. It gave him a motive for return and exertion. He came home to proffer assistance in every form to my mother. He found that she had heroically surmounted difficulties with which few spirits would have struggled; that she had declined a compromise with my father's creditors, and had succeeded in paying off all his debts; and that we were living independently, but with a severe frugality almost unparalleled in our bountiful country. I mention these particulars in justice to Mr. Clarence, and to do honor to my mother. My mother! I never write or speak her name without a thrill through my heart. A thousand times have I blessed the adversity that brought forth her virtue in such sweet and beautiful manifestations. It was there, like the perfume in the flower, latent under the meridian sun, but exhaled by the beating tempest.

"I should not care my wife should honor my memory by mausoleums, cherished grief, and moping melancholy, and their

---

1 Madame Rivardi's Seminary for Young Ladies, established in 1801 and closed in 1815, was widely considered to offer the finest female education in the US; its students included daughters of the American elite as well as young refugees, often French, escaping the Napoleonic wars or Caribbean uprisings.

ostentatious ensigns. Deep and even *unchanging* weeds, do not excite my imagination; but the tender, cheerful fortitude with which my mother endured pecuniary reverses; the unblenching resolution with which she met all the perplexing details of business, never faltering till my father's interrupted purposes were effected, and till his memory was blessed, even by his creditors; this is the honor that would make my ghost trip lightly through elysium—shame on my heathenism!—that would enhance the happiness of heaven.

"But to return to Mr. Clarence. He insisted that he owed a debt to my father's family, and that my mother ought not to withhold from him the right as he had now the opportunity to cancel it.

"My mother, with the scrupulousness which, if it is an infirmity, is the infirmity of a noble mind, recoiled from a pecuniary obligation. Mr. Clarence, however, was not to be baffled. Inspired with confidence in me, as he said, by the ability with which I had assisted my mother in the management of our private disastrous affairs, he made me his man of business, and paid me a salary that relieved us at once from our most pressing necessities. I soon after entered on my profession, and from that time have received a series of kindnesses, which, in the temper of his noble nature, he has bestowed as my dues, rather than as his favors. It is now five years since I have seen him. His daughter I have never seen since her childhood; though far less striking than her brother, she was then interesting. I am mortified, on her father's account, that she should have turned out such an ordinary concern. But it is a common case; the fruit rarely verifies the promise of the bud. However, I fancy her father has his consolations. I infer from his letters that she is exemplary in her filial duties. They have resided at Clarenceville ever since her mother's death, when Miss C. was withdrawn from school. It is certainly a merit in a girl of her brilliant expectations to remain contentedly buried alive in the country—a merit to point a moral, not adorn a tale. Is it natural depravity, my dear Mrs. Layton, or artificial perversity, that makes us during the romantic period of life so insensible to useful home-bred virtues? 'A comely little body—amiable and rather clever!' Heavens! such a picture would give Cupid an ague-fit.[1] The words raise the long forgotten dead in my memory and carry me back to good Parson Peabody's, in Connecticut, where I was sent to learn Latin and Greek, and where, even then, my wicked heart revolted from 'a comely little body—amiable and rather clever,' a Miss Eunice Peabody—a pattern damsel. I see her now knitting the parson's long blue yarn-stockings, and at the same

---

1 Chills, sweating, or shaking accompanying a severe fever.

time dutifully reading Rollin, Smollett, (his history!) and Russell's Modern Europe[1]—knitting, and reading by the mark. Many a time in my boyish mischief I have slipped back her mark, and seen her faithfully and unspectingly retrace the pages, though once, when I had ventured to repeat the experiment on the same portion of the book, she very sagely remarked to the admiring parson 'that there was considerable repetition in Rollin.' However, I beg Miss Clarence's pardon, and really take shame to myself for any disrespect to one so nearly and dearly allied to my excellent friend, her father. The truth is, I have been a good deal vexed by having her seriously proposed to me as a most worthy matrimonial enterprise, by several of my friends, who flatter me by saying, it would be an acceptable alliance to the father, and that I want nothing but fortune to make a figure in life. Now that is just what I do not want. I have my own ambition, but, thank God, it does not run in that vulgar channel. I honor my profession, among other reasons, because it does not hold forth the lure of wealth. I would press on in the noble career before me, my eye fixed on such men as Emmet and Wells,[2] and if I attain eminence it shall be as they have attained it, by the noblest means—the achievements of the mind; and the eminence shall be too, like that 'holy hill of the Lord, to which none shall ascend but those that wash their hands in innocency.'[3] If you have the common prejudices against my profession, you may think this holy hill as inaccessible to lawyers, as the promised land was to the poor sinning Israelites. But allow me, by way of an apt illustration of my own ideas, to repeat to you a compliment I received from Agrippa, an old negro-servant of my father. He came into my office and looking round with great complacency, said, 'Well, Master Gerald, you've raly got to be a squire.'

"'Yes, Grip; but I hope you do not think that lawyers cannot be good men.'

"'No, that I don't sir; clean hands must do a great deal of dirty work in this world.'

---

1 Charles Rollin (French, 1661-1741), educator and author of histories including *Ancient History* (1730-38); Tobias George Smollett (Scottish, 1721-71), author of works including *A Complete History of England* (1757-58); William Russell (Scottish, 1741-93), author of *The History of Modern Europe* (1779-84).

2 Thomas Addis Emmet (American, 1795-1827) and John Wells (American, 1770-1823) were well-known and greatly respected lawyers in New York in the early nineteenth century. Emmet also served as New York State Attorney General in 1812 and 1813.

3 Paraphrase of Psalm 26.

"I shall never undertake a doubtful cause—a necessity which I believe the best ethics include among our legal duties—without consoling myself with Agrippa's apothegm. But enough, and too much, of egotism. One word as to your womanly fancy that Miss Clarence blushed at the mention of my name; I never knew a woman that had not a gift for seeing blushes and tears. Poor Miss Clarence! Never was there a more gratuitous fancy than this.

"And now, my dear madam, for a more agreeable topic. When do you return to the city? I am becoming desperate. My dear mother has been at Schooley's mountain[1] for the last four weeks; and since your parting 'God bless you,' I have not exchanged one word with 'Heaven's last, best work.'[2] My condition reminds me of a play, written by a friend of mine, which was returned to him by the manager, with this comment, 'It will not do, sir. Why there is not a woman in it; and if your men were heroes or angels, they must be damned without women.' Now I am far enough from being hero or angel; but there is no paradise to me without women—without you, my dear madam—and—my mother. I put her in, not so much for duty's, as for truth's sake. Commend me to Miss Emilie; it is no wonder she should love the country—all that is sweet, beautiful, and inspiring in nature, is allied to her.

"My temper was put to the test the other day on her account; or more on yours, than hers. Tom Reynolds joined me on the Battery. 'So,' said he, 'your friend Mrs. Layton has made a grand match for her peerless daughter!'

"'How? to what do you allude?'

"'Bless me! you have not heard that Emilie Layton is engaged to the rich Spaniard, Pedrillo?'

"'Pshaw! that is too absurd. Pedrillo is a foreigner, unknown, and twice Miss Layton's age.'

"'Mere bagatelles,[3] my dear sir. He is rich; and put what you please in the other scale, and it kicks the beam, that is, if fathers and mothers are to strike the balance.'

"'Upon my word, you do them great honor; but in this case I fancy Miss Layton's own inclinations will be consulted.'

---

1 Popular destination for early nineteenth-century tourists seeking its reportedly healing waters, located near present-day Hackettstown, New Jersey.
2 Reference to Pope's "Epistle to a Lady," lines 271-72: "Heav'n, when it strives to polish all it can / Its last best work, but forms a softer Man."
3 Trifles.

"'*Tant mieux.*[1] Pedrillo is a devilish genteel fellow, handsome enough, and has a very insinuating address. What more can a girl ask for?'

"I was not, as you may suppose, my dear madam, fool enough to throw away any sentiment on a man destitute of the first principles on which sentiment is founded. So we parted; but I was indignant that rumor should for a moment class you with persons who are degraded far below the level of those pagan parents who abandon their children to the elements, or sacrifice them to their divinities. Of all the mortifying spectacles of civilized life, I know none so revolting as a parent—a *mother*—who is governed by mercenary motives in controlling the connubial destiny of a daughter! But why this to you, who are independent, to a fault, (I should say, if the *queen* could do wrong,) of all pecuniary considerations?

"But my letter is so long, that my moral has little chance of being read; so here is an end of it. Return, I beseech you, my dear Mrs. Layton; nothing has any tendency to fill the vacancy you make in the life of your devoted friend and servant,

"GERALD ROSCOE."

CHAPTER XI.

"Rural recreations abroad, and books at home, are the innocent pleasures of a man who is early wise, and gives fortune no more hold of him than of necessity he must."[2]
DRYDEN.

THE sentiment of Dryden, which we have prefixed to this chapter, accorded with Mr. Clarence's views, and will in part explain his preference of a rural life. But he had other reasons—reasons that neither began nor terminated with himself. The formation of Gertrude's character was the first object of his life, and he wished, while it was flexible, to secure for it the happiest external influences. He believed that direct instruction, the most careful inculcation of wise precepts, and the constant vigilance of a single individual, (even though that individual be a parent,) are insignificant, compared with the indirect influences that cannot be controlled, or with what has been so happily called the 'education of circumstances.' He

---

1 So much the better.
2 From the Dedication of *Pastorals of Virgil* (1697) by John Dryden (English, 1631-1700).

wished to inspire his child with moderation and humility. She was
surrounded by the indulgencies of a luxurious town-establishment,
and exposed to the flatteries of the frivolous and foolish. He wished
to give her a knowledge and right estimate of the just uses and
responsibilities of the fortune of which she was to be the dispenser.
His lessons would be counteracted in a society where wealth was
made the basis of aristocracy and fashion. He wished to infuse
a taste for rational and intellectual pursuits. How was this to be
achieved amidst the 'dear five hundred friends' she had inherited
from her mother—the flippant idlers of fashionable life?

Mr. Clarence was too much of a philosopher to condemn *en
masse*[1] the class of fashionable society. He knew there were individual exceptions to its general character, but he regarded them as
the golden sands borne on the current, not giving it a new direction. He esteemed the devotees to morning visits and evening parties as the mere foam on the fountain of life—as having no part in
its serious uses or purposes. He felt a benevolent compassion for
them; they seemed to him like the uninstructed deaf and dumb,
beings unconscious of the rich faculties slumbering within them;
faculties, that if awakened and active, and directed to the ends
for which they were designed by their beneficent Creator, would
change the aspect of society.

Mr. Clarence was not disappointed in many of the benefits he
expected from his daughter passing the noviciate of her life in the
country. She learned to love nature from an acquaintance and
familiarity with its sublimest forms, and most touching aspects.[2]
Those glorious revelations of their Author refined her taste, and
elevated her imagination and her affections to an habitual communion with Him.

In a simple state of society, she felt the power of her wealth
only in its wise and benevolent uses. She learned to view people
and things as they are, without the false glare of artificial society. Her domestic energies were called forth by the necessities of
a country-establishment, which, with all the facilities of wealth,
does, it must be confessed, sometimes require from the lady of the
ménage[3] the skill of an actual operator.

---

1 As a body or group, wholesale.
2 In the 1849 edition, Sedgwick replaces this sentence with: Gertrude
   Clarence had a poetic element in her nature, and an early acquaintance
   and familiarity with the lovely forms and changing aspects of the external
   world nurtured that mysterious sympathy which exists between the spirit
   of man and the spirit ever present in the works of God.
3 Household.

In this education of circumstances, there was one which had a paramount influence on the character of Gertrude Clarence—her intercourse with her father. Gibbon has said, that the affection subsisting between a brother and sister is the only Platonic love.[1] Has not that sentiment that binds a father to his daughter, the same generosity and tenderness arising from the distinction of sexes, and with that something higher and holier?

A parent stands, as it were, on the verge of two worlds, and blends the fears and hopes of both. He feels those anxieties and dreads that arise from an experience of the uncertainties of this life, and that inexpressible tenderness, and those illimitable desires, that extend to the eternal hereafter.

Mr. Clarence had perhaps an undue anxiety in regard to the possible evils of the present life. His mind never quite recovered from the melancholy infused into it by the relation of his father's history. The shocking death of his son nearly destroyed for the time his mental faculties, and permanently impaired his health. He timidly shrunk from every form of evil that might assail his child, not considering that she had the unabated ardor, and the elastic spirit that are necessary to sustain the burden of life. Gertrude's character, originally of a firm texture, was strengthened by her father's timidity. Her resolution and cheerfulness were always equal to his demands, and these were sometimes unreasonable. His solicitude sometimes degenerated to weakness, and his sensibility to petulance. To these Gertrude opposed a resoluteness, and equanimity, that to a careless and superficial observer might seem coldness; but such know not how carefully the fire that is used only for holy purposes is concealed and guarded.

But our fair readers may be curious to know whether Gertrude's rustication was to be perpetual? whether the matrimonial opportunities of a rich heiress, were to be circumscribed to the few chances of a country-lottery? and whether she had arrived at the age of nineteen without any pretenders to her exclusive favor? Certainly not. The spirit of enterprise, in every form, is too alert in our country to permit the hand of an heiress to remain unsolicited, and Gertrude Clarence was addressed by suitors of every quality and degree. Clergymen, doctors, lawyers, and *forwarding merchants*, addressed, we should perhaps say approached her, for they soon found something in the atmosphere of Clarenceville that chilled and nipped

---

1 From *Memoirs of My Life and Writings* (1796, published posthumously) by Edward Gibbon (English, 1737-94), author of *The History of the Decline and Fall of the Roman Empire* (1776, 1781, 1788).

their young hopes—they soon felt, all but the most obtuse, that Gertrude Clarence was no game for the mere fortune-hunter.

But, ask my fair young readers, did she pass the most susceptible years of her life without any of those emotions and visions that disturb all our imaginations? She had her dreams, her beau-ideal. Her memory had retained the image of a certain youth who had appeared to her in all the graces of dawning manhood when she was a very young and unobserved child. In her memory he had been associated with her brother, so fondly loved, so long and deeply lamented. In her hopes—no, her thoughts did not take so definite a form—in her visions, there was one personification of all that to her imagination was noble, graceful, and captivating. Her father unwittingly cherished this preposession.

His debt to the Roscoe family, and his love to its departed members, inspired, naturally, a very strong interest in Gerald, now its sole representative. Gerald's personal merit confirmed this interest. Mr. Clarence delighted to talk of him to Gertrude, to dwell on and magnify his rare qualities. He maintained a constant correspondence with Mr. Clarence, and his graceful and spirited letters seemed to impart to her acquaintance with his character, the vividness of personal intercourse.

It was natural that Mr. Clarence, in looking forward to the probable contingency of Gertrude's marriage, should in his own mind fix on Gerald Roscoe, as the only person to whom he would willingly resign her; but it certainly was not prudent to infuse a predilection into her mind, and to nourish that predilection without calculating all the chances against its gratification, and that fatal but unthought of chance, that her sentiment might not be reciprocated.

But we are in danger of anticipating, and we proceed to give a day at Clarenceville which will enable our readers to judge of our heroine's character, from its developement in action, a mode as much more satisfactory than mere description, as a book than its table of contents.

Mr. Clarence's house was no 'shingle palace,' but a well built, spacious, and commodious modern edifice, standing on a gentle slope on the northeast shore of one of the beautiful lakes in the western part of the state of New York. The position of the house was judiciously selected to economize sunshine, and soft breezes, the luxuries of a climate where winter reigns for six months. Literally, the monarch of all he surveyed, Mr. Clarence's right of property had enabled him to save from the relentless axe of the settler, a fine extent of forest trees that sheltered him from the biting north winds, and rising in strait and lofty columns, a 'lonely depth of unpierced woods'[1] offered a tempting retreat to the romantic and the contemplative; or to those more apt to seek its 'lonely depths,' the sportsman and deer-hunter. Between the house and the lake, not a tree had been suffered to remain to intercept the view of the clear sparkling sheet of water, the soul of the scene.

The lawn was circular, and surrounded with shrubs and flowers, which Gertrude loved better than any thing, not of human kind.

Sweet-briars, corcoruses, passion-flowers, and honey-suckles, wreathed the pillars of the piazza; and the garden which was a little on the right of the house, and filled with fruit-trees, and arranged in terraces, covered with grapes, tempered the bolder features of the scene with an air of civilization, refinement, and even luxury. The opposite shore of the lake, was mountainous, wild, and rugged, and enriched with many an Indian tradition. The lake was not a barren sheet of water, but dotted with islands, some without a tree or shrub, green, fresh, and smooth, looking as if they might have been the cast-off mantles of the sylvan deities; others were embowered with trees, and overgrown with native grape-vines, that had leaped from branch to branch, and hung their leafy draperies on every bough.

Less romantic, but not less agreeable objects terminated the perspective; a thriving village, with its churches, academy, and court-house, and all the insignia of an advancing, busy population.

The day we have mentioned was that appointed for Mrs. Layton and the Uptons to dine at Clarenceville. Any interruption of his customary occupations was apt, before breakfast, to disturb Mr. Clarence's serenity. The demon of dyspepsia was then lord of the ascendant. When he entered the breakfast parlor, Gertrude and Mr. Seton only were there. "Where is the breakfast, Gertrude?" he asked. "I hope you do not mean to wait for Miss Emilie. Young ladies should really learn that good manners require them to rise at the family hours."

"Emilie was up with the birds, papa, and has gone to walk."

"To walk! my dear child, how could you permit her to expose herself to the morning air?"

"I was asleep."

"Asleep! Nothing is more fatal to health than sleeping in the morning. I have mentioned to you the anecdote of Lord Mansfield, Gertrude?"

---

1   From "A Summer Evening's Meditation" (1773) by Barbauld.

"O yes, papa." And Gertrude could scarcely repress a smile, when she recollected how many times it had been mentioned to her.

"I presume, Gertrude, it is not necessary to wait breakfast for Miss Layton."

"Not at all, sir; I have ordered it already."

Mr. Clarence walked to the window, and unhappily espied his favorite riding-horse. "What a stupid scoundrel John is!" he exclaimed, "to leave Ranger in the sun."

Seton started from his seat: "It was not John, sir; I have been riding, and I took it for granted that John would see the horse."

"I beg your pardon, Mr. Seton; but really, sir, it is not agreeable—it is not the thing to use a horse in this way." Poor Seton went with all possible haste to repair his fault, while Mr. Clarence continued, "Such imbecility is really too bad; twenty good shades within as many yards. He 'took it for granted John would see the horse;' this 'taking it for granted' is just the difference between those that get along in the world, and those that slump through. Do you know why Sarah does not bring the breakfast, Gertrude?"

"I hear her coming, sir."

"What are you looking at, Gertrude? Oh, I see—Ranger has got away from Louis; I expected it. Sarah, send John instantly here." Mr. Clarence threw up the sash, and would have expressed his impatient displeasure to Seton, but Gertrude laid her hand on his arm:

"My dear father! Louis is not well this morning."

Mr. Clarence put down the window, walked once or twice across the room, and asked for the Edinburgh-Review. Gertrude looked on the tables, on the book-shelves, on the piano, on every thing that could support a book; but the London Quarterly, the North American, the Literary Gazette, New Monthly, Ladies' Magazine, the Analectic, Eclectic, every thing but the Edinburgh, was forthcoming—*that* had vanished.[1]

"There is no use in looking, Gertrude; it's gone of course; it's of no consequence; the breakfast is here." They sat down; but here a new series of trials commenced. The coffee was burned too much, and Mr. Clarence made his daily remark, that he believed all the difficulty might be remedied, if people would say *roast* coffee, instead of *burnt* coffee. Then the dyspeptic bread had been forgotten, and the family bread was underbaked; the fish was cold, and

---

1 These periodicals suggest that the Clarences subscribed to the top American and English magazines of their day.

the eggs were stale. Sarah was inquired of, 'why fresh eggs had not been gotten from John Smith's.'

"Mr. Smith don't calculate to part with any more till after Independence."

"I dare say; it is all independence to our farming gentry! Has Mrs. Carter brought the fowls for dinner, Sarah?"

"No, sir; she has concluded not to."

"What is the meaning of that?"

"Why, sir, she says poor Billy reared them, and she don't love to spare them."

"Nonsense! tell John to go down and tell her I must have them."

"I have another errand for John to do at the same time," whispered Miss Clarence to the girl; "tell him to wait till after breakfast."

While these domestic inquiries had been making, Miss Clarence had prepared some remarkably fine black tea, just received from New York—the gardener had sent in a basket of strawberries, the first product of the season—and the cook had found a mislaid loaf of the favorite bread; and when Miss Emilie Layton returned from her walk, all radiant and glowing with beauty, health, and spirits, Mr. Clarence was in the best humor possible. "Up rose the sun, and up rose Emilie!"[1] he exclaimed. "Pardon me, my dear little girl, I do not often quote, even prose; but you look so like the spirit of the jocund morning"—he drew her chair close to himself, kissed her white dimpled hand—"the privilege of an old man, Miss Emilie—don't look cast-down, Louis; every dog must have his day."

"What delightful spirits you are in, Mr. Clarence!" said the young lady.

"Spirits! ah my dear Miss Emilie, bless your stars that you did not see me half an hour sooner. I have been tormenting poor Gertrude and Louis; but I can't help it—I believe spirits, sensibility, every thing, as a friend of mine says, depend on the state of the stomach. Don't eat that egg—take some of these strawberries, Miss Layton; they are delicious *haut bois*."[2]

"I prefer the egg, sir; I am very hungry."

"Stop, my dear girl! don't you know you should always open an egg at the obtuse end, and if it is perfectly full to the shell, it is fresh; I have tried the experiment all summer, and I have not found half a dozen good ones."

---

1 From "The Knight's Tale," *The Canterbury Tales* (1387-1400), line 193, by Geoffrey Chaucer (English, c. 1343-1400), describing young Emelye.
2 Wild as opposed to garden-grown.

"And I have broken all mine in the middle, and never found a poor one," said Miss Layton, dashing hers out, and proceeding to eat it with the keen relish of a youthful and stimulated appetite.

"I like that—I like that, Miss Emilie; that makes all the difference in life, the difference between such a poor fidgetty creature as I am, and such a happy spirit as yours. Go on, my dear child, and break your eggs in the middle for ever; but excuse me, I have an errand that must be done immediately," and he rose to leave the room.

"Are you going to the widow Carter's?" asked Gertrude, with a very significant smile.

"Yes," and though Mr. Clarence bit his lip, he smiled in return.

"It is unnecessary. John was directed not to do the errand till after breakfast."

"There it is—see there, Miss Emilie—My good Gertrude has saved me from playing Blue Beard on a poor widow's chickens this morning. The brood of a Heaven-forsaken boy of hers who has been drowned in the lake this summer—the only good thing the graceless little dog ever did, was to rear these chickens. It would have been a worse case than that of the widow's cow, immortalized by Fenelon[1]—all the poultry in Christendom would not have made up the loss to her, and she would have sent them, poor soul! she would have surrendered her life, if either Gertrude or I had required it."

Mr. Clarence had resumed his seat, and taken up a newspaper, when a servant entered with letters from the post-office; they were distributed according to their different directions. Miss Layton looked conscious and disturbed, and retreated to her apartment. Mr. Clarence broke the seal of his, saying it was a short business-letter, and that he had left his spectacles in the library; he asked Gertrude to read it to him. She accordingly leaned over his shoulder, and read as follows: "I have thought over and over again what I told you the day we parted. I am right—It is all fudge— there is no lion in the way. I tell you again, make hay while the sun shines—strike while the iron is hot—clench the nail"—Louis started from his seat, but Miss Clarence without observing him, read on, "straws show which way the wind blows. If I have eyes, it sets from the right quarter—delays are dangerous. A certain

---

1 François de Salignac de la Mothe-Fénelon (French, 1651-1715), writer and Catholic bishop. This anecdote is included in *Selections from the Writings of Fenelon, with a Memoir of His Life* (1829), collected by Sedgwick's friend Eliza Cabot Follen (American, 1787-1860).

person's life hangs by a thread, and when he's gone, she's off to the city, and snapped up by the dandies—three hundred thousand—"

"Stop, for God's sake!" cried Seton, and snatching the letter, flushed and trembling, he instantly disappeared. Mr. Clarence closed the door after him, and turning to Gertrude, asked her what could be the meaning of this. Gertrude was in tears; for a moment she could not reply, but taking up a letter Seton had dropped, and, glancing at it and looking at the signature, "It is so," she said; "the letters are both from that vulgar brother of Seton—they were misdirected—this was meant for you."

The letter designed for Mr. Clarence's eye, was as follows:

"Respected Sir—I take the liberty, by return of mail, to tender my sincere thanks to you and Miss Clarence, for your politeness to me during my late visit to my esteemed brother. It was very gratifying to me to find your health so much improved, and my brother so pleasantly situated in your valued family. I think I may say Louis deserves his good fortune—he has always been a remarkably correct young man, Louis has. It was a disappointment to my father, after giving him a liberal education, that he should take such a turn for painting; but Allston, our great painter, says he has a remarkable talent that way, so that there is a good prospect, if he should go to foreign countries, that he may, at some future day, become as celebrated as Sir Benjamin West;[1] but I for one should be perfectly content to have him settle down in the country, and only handle the brush for his amusement. My wife would be very glad to accept Miss Gertrude's invitation, as she is remarkably fond of Louis, as indeed we all are. The rose for Miss Gertrude, and the calliflower for yourself, I shall do myself the pleasure to send by the first opportunity. Till then believe me, sir, with much respect and esteem, and gratitude, to you and to Miss Gertrude,

"Your very obedient,
"humble servant,
"WILLIAM SETON."

"It is too bad," said Mr. Clarence, "to be expected to be the dupe of such a vulgar, grovelling wretch. Is it possible, Gertrude, that Louis has any thing in common with this base fellow?"

"Nothing, my dear father, nothing."

---

1 Washington Allston (American, 1779-1843), painter of the Romantic movement, had studied under painter Benjamin West (American, 1738-1820), President of the Royal Academy in London, England, from 1792 to 1820.

"Has he in any way indicated an intention of addressing you?"
"Never."

Mr. Clarence paused for a moment, and then added, "Pardon me, my dear child, for catechising you a little further: have you any reason to think that Louis loves you?"

"I believe he does."

Gertrude's tears dropped fast on the letter which she still held in her hand, folding and refolding it. Mr. Clarence walked up and down the room, till suddenly stopping, he said; "Seton is not all I could have wished for you, my dear Gertrude—his delicate health—the nervous, susceptible constitution of his mind, are, according to my view of things, great evils—but he is pure, and disinterested, and talented. I reverence a sentiment of genuine affection. It is cruel to disappoint or trifle with it. I see your emotion, Gertrude, your wishes shall govern mine."

Miss Clarence subdued her agitation—"You misunderstand my emotion, sir," she said; "I was grieved that Mr. Seton should have been so outraged, insulted, that I should myself have dragged forth feelings that he has never betrayed but involuntarily—my dear father, my only wish is to live and die with you."

"Do you mean deliberately to abjure matrimony, Gertrude?" asked her father, reassured, and animated by discovering the real state of his daughter's heart.

"No; that would be ridiculous; but I am sure, very sure, I shall never marry."

"Oh! that is all. That resolution and feeling will last, Gertrude, till you see some one worthy to vanquish it; but that it exists now is proof enough that you are yet fancy free. But what is to be done for poor Seton? one thing is certain, he must leave us."

"Do not say so. We certainly can convince him how deeply we feel the injustice his brother has done him—he is sick—at present incapable of the labor of his profession—he has no refuge but the house of his sordid brother. From you, my dear father, I would not hide a shade of feeling—I do love Louis Seton—with sisterly affection"—(Mr. Clarence smiled)—"you are incredulous—I could voluntarily confess to Louis all I feel for him—can that be love?"

"No; but how soon may it become so?"

"Never—I am confident of that—I have involuntarily robbed Louis of his happiness—I know the exquisite sensitiveness of his mind—If he were to leave us now he might never recover the shock and mortification of his brother's disclosure. If he remains, I think we may by degrees restore his self-respect, his self-confidence, and his serenity. At least let us try."

"Do as you please, my noble-minded girl. I am satisfied to trust every thing to you, superior as you are to the heartless coquetries and pruderies of your sex; but remember we are handling edged tools."

"But not playing with them," replied Gertrude with a faint smile; and then kissing her father, and thanking him for his compliance, she left him and went to a difficult task. She met a servant in the entry; "Have you seen Mr. Seton?" she asked.

"Yes ma'am; and Miss Clarence," he added, drawing closer to her, and lowering his voice, "there's something the matter with Mr. Seton—he just called me to pack his clothes, and he was all in a flutter, and just walked about the room without doing the least thing for himself."

"Mr. Seton is ill, John, and insists on leaving us; but we must prevent him. You would all be willing to nurse him, would you not, John?"

"Indeed, that would we, Miss Clarence—a nice, quiet young man is Mr. Louis."

"Then I will try to persuade him to stay. Tell him, John, I wish to speak with him in the library." Miss Clarence having thus adroitly averted the gossiping suspicions of the inferior departments of the family, repaired to the library. Seton soon followed her. He had an expression of self-command and offended pride, bordering on haughtiness, and so foreign to his customary, gentle, and sentimental demeanor, that Gertrude forgot her prepared speech and said, "You are not offended, Louis?"

"Offended, Miss Clarence!—I am misunderstood—defamed—disgraced!"

"Louis, you are unjust to yourself, and unjust to us; do you think that my father or I would give a second thought to that silly letter?"

Seton was soothed. He fixed his eye on Gertrude, and she proceeded. "It is essential to our happiness that we should understand one another perfectly. Have we not in two years too firmly established our mutual confidence and friendship to have them shaken by the accidents of this morning?" She paused for a moment, and proceeded with more emotion. "Louis, you know I lost my only brother. It is long ago that he died, and I was very young at the time, but I perfectly remember the tenderness I felt for him—remember! I still feel it. The chasm made by his death has never been filled. You know my father is all that a father can be to me, but for perfect sympathy there must be similar age, pursuits, and hopes." While Gertrude dwelt in generals, she could talk with the coolness of a philosopher; but as she again approached particulars, her voice became tremulous.

"I can, I *do* feel for you, Louis, the sentiments of a sister—a sister's solicitude for your honor and happiness. I would select you from all the world to supply poor Frank's place to me. You will not permit false delicacy, fastidious scruples, to deprive me of the brother of my election? Forget the past." Seton made no reply. "You do not mean to reject me, Louis?" she added, playfully extending her hand to him. He turned away from her.

"Oh Gertrude! Gertrude! why should I deceive you? why rather should I suffer you to delude yourself? You might as well hope to distil gentle dews from consuming fire, as to convert the sentiment I feel for you into the tranquil, peaceful, fearless, satisfied love of a brother. Mine was no common love—it subsisted without hope or expectation—a self-sustaining passion—the light of my existence—the essence of my life—a pure flame in the inmost, secret sanctuary of my heart—that sanctuary has been violated. I betrayed, and another has dishonored it. '*Forget the past!*' forget that my thoughts of you have been linked with sordid expectations and base projects. God knows I never, in one presumptuous moment aspired to you, but not because you were rich. In my eyes, your fortune is your meanest attribute—my poverty makes no part of my humility.

"You must not interrupt me, Gertrude. I know your generosity—I know all you would say; but hear me out, now, while I have courage to speak of myself. I have been injured, and the worm trodden on, you know, will turn."

"I must interrupt you, Louis; I cannot bear to hear you speak of yourself in these unworthy, degrading terms."

"You misunderstand me. I do not mean to degrade but rather to justify myself, by making you acquainted with the short, sad history of my mind. I know I am weak and pusillanimous. Nature and circumstances have been allied against me. I was born with a constitutional, nervous susceptibility that none of my family understood or regarded. I was a timid, sensitive boy. My brothers were bold and bustling. They were steel-clad in health and hardihood, while I shrunk, as if my nerves were bare, from every breath. This, in their estimation, was inferiority, and so it became in mine. I was humbled and depressed; my life was an aching void. I rose in the morning, as poor Cowper says he did, 'like an infernal frog out of Acheron, covered with the ooze and mud of melancholy,'[1] and my days flowed like a half-stagnant and turbid stream, that gives

---

1   William Cowper (English, 1731-1800), author, hymn-writer, and translator. From Letter LXXXVI, to William Hayley, 5 October 1793, in *The Life and Posthumous Writings of William Cowper* (1803). The River Acheron (Greece) was believed to flow to Hades (Hell), a "river of woe."

back no image of the bright heaven above it, and takes no hue from the pleasant objects past which it obscurely crawls. My spirit was crushed; I felt myself to be a useless weed in creation, and when I first discovered that I possessed one talent—one redeeming talent—my heart beat with the ecstasy that an idiot may feel when his mind is released from its physical thraldom, and throbs with the first pulse of intellectual life. That talent introduced me to you, Gertrude, gave me estimation in your eyes, was the medium of our daily intercourse, and I cherished and cultivated it as if it were, as it in truth was, the principle of life to me. The exercise of this talent, and the secret indulgence of my love for you, were happiness enough. I expected nothing more: I did not look into the future—I forgot the past. I was satisfied with the full, pervading sense of present bliss. But you are wearied, Miss Clarence, and I am intrusive."

"No, no, Mr. Seton," replied Gertrude, raising her head, and removing from her face the handkerchief that had hidden from Seton the deep emotion with which she listened to him. "No, Louis," she continued in the kindest and firmest tone, "but such disclosures are useless—they may be worse than useless."

"Gertrude, I have no terms to keep with consequences, and I pray you to hear me out. My tranquillity vanished like a dream, when, last week, I betrayed my passion to you. Your calmness and gentle forbearance soothed me, but it was not, it is not in your power to restore the self-confidence I felt while my passion was unknown. A fever is preying on my life; my spirits are disordered. This cruel letter of my brother will shorten the term of my insupportable existence—for this I thank him. Nothing now remains but to pray you to render me justice with your father; and to beg you, Gertrude, to bear me kindly in your memory." He took her hand and pressed it to his burning lips.

Gertrude was agitated with the conflicting suggestions of her own mind. She had sought the interview with a definite and decided purpose. That purpose was now nearly subdued by seeing the strength of a sentiment which she had hoped to modify or change. She shrunk with instinctive delicacy from the manifestation of a passion that had no corresponding sentiment in her own heart. Her first and strongest impulse was to escape from the sight of misery which she could not relieve. But 'were not these selfish suggestions?'—'Could she not mitigate it?'—'At least,' she thought, as the current of generous purpose flowed back through her heart, 'at least I will try what persevering efforts may do,' and bodying her thoughts in words, "Louis," she said, "I will not part with you; you must stay with us. If I have power over you, it shall be exercised for some better purpose than to nourish a sentiment which I can never return. It may be because I am inferior to you—certainly not superior—that was the suggestion of your excessive humility, arising from circumstances to which you have already alluded. You have erred, by your own confession, you have all your life erred in distrusting and undervaluing your own powers. You have now only to put forth your strength to subdue all of your feelings that should be subdued." *repression isn't good advice, Gertie*

"Do you believe this, Gertrude?"

"Believe it! I am sure of it. The frankness of our explanation has dissolved all mystery. Hobgoblins vanish in the light. Your feelings have been aggravated by concealment. They are too intense for any earthly object. Louis, let me use a sister's liberty and give you sisterly counsel; let me remind you of one of the safest passages of a book that you have read and admired perhaps too much for your own happiness. 'Se rendre digne de l'immortalité est le seul but de l'existence—bonheur—souffrance-tout est moyen pour ce but.'"[1]

Seton caught one moment of inspiration, from the sweet tone of assurance in which Gertrude spoke. 'There is a medicament for my wounded spirit,' he thought; but the light was faint and transient, like the passing gleam reflected by a dark and distant object. "Ah, Gertrude," he said, "you are happy, and have the energy and hope of the happy; but for me there are no bright realities in life; it is stripped of its illusions. Oh, most miserable is he who survives the illusions of life! I am yet in my youth, Gertrude, and I look forward with the dim, disconsolate eye of age. Life is a dreary desert to me, beset with frightful forms, and inevitable perils. I am sick, and steeped in melancholy; why should I drag my body of death along your bright path?"

"You shall not, Louis; we will drive out the foul fiend, and court the spirit of health and cheerfulness. You know I have had all my life to contend with the demons of disease in my father. Practice has given me some skill in detecting and expelling them. I will be your leech;[2] and you shall promise to be docile and obedient. I

---

1 "To become worthy of immortality is the only purpose of life. Happiness, suffering—everything is a means to this purpose." From de Staël, *Corinne, ou l'Italie* (1807).

2 Physician, or healer. The medical practice of leeching uses live leeches to start bleeding, either to restore blood flow or to remove blood from the body.

shall lock up your easel for the present. My father has proposed a jaunt to Trenton. We will go there. Beautiful scenery should 'minister to the mind diseased'[1] of a painter. Shall I tell papa that I have your consent to go with us?"

"Do what you will with me. You will be blessed in your ministry, if I am not."

This conference, which had been long enough, was now broken off by the entrance of Becky, an old and privileged domestic. "I should think, Mr. Seton," she said, "you might have consideration enough to put off your lessons to-day, when there is but every thing for Miss Gertrude to see to." Seton tacitly acquiesced in the reprimand, and left the apartment.

Gertrude was alarmed and oppressed with the depth of poor Seton's sorrow; and though, to him, she had assumed a tone of firmness and serenity, his despondency had infected her, and as he left the room, she sunk back in her chair, her mind abstracted from every thing around her, and filled with gloomy and just presentiments.

"Miss Gertrude," said Becky.

Gertrude made no reply, she did not even hear Becky, shrill and impatient as her tone was. Her vacant eye accidently rested on a fine game-piece Seton had recently finished, which was standing before her on the library-table. Becky gave her own interpretation to her mistress' gaze.

"It's well enough done to be sure, but," she added with professional scorn, "it's a shame and a silliness to take the *creaters*' lives in midsummer, just to draw their pictures, when they'd make such a relishing dish in the fall. But come, Miss Gertrude, I should be glad you would tell me what we are to do?"

"Do, do about what, Becky?"

"Did not Amandy tell you?"

"Tell me what?"

"Why Miss Gertrude; I never saw you so with your thoughts at the end of the world, when sure we had never more need of them; but you will have to make up your mind to it, for the dinner has fallen through—the whole—entirely."

This was indeed an alarming annunciation to the mistress of an establishment, who expected invited company to dinner, and who, like Gertrude, considered a strict surveillance of her domestic concerns as among the first of woman's temporal duties. She therefore recalled her thoughts from their wanderings, and roused

---

1 Shakespeare's *Macbeth* V.iii.41.

all her powers, to avert the shower of grievances which she saw lowering on Becky's clouded brow.

We advise all those who have not experienced the complicated embarrassments of giving a dinner-party in a country-town, unprovided with a market and other facilities, to skip the ensuing conversation, for they will have no sympathy with the trials that beset rural hospitality—trials that, like woes, cluster and sometimes so thick and heavily, that their poor victim wishes, but wishes in vain for the bottle which the good little man in the fairy legend gave to Mick, that did its duty so handsomely, and spread the poor fellow's table so daintily.[1] But alas, among all our *settlers*, we have none of these kind-hearted little people—they are the true patriots and never emigrate, and unassisted human female ingenuity is put to its utmost stretch. Fortunately Miss Clarence was not often, and certainly not on the present occasion, of a temper to be daunted by the minor miseries of human life; and she now demanded of her domestic, with an air of philosophy which Becky deemed quite inappropriate, what was the matter?

"Matter, Miss Gertrude! matter enough to turn a body's hair gray; and to cap all, Judge Upton has just sent down word that he shall bring a grand English gentleman with him."

"Oh, is that all, Becky? Then I have nothing to do but to order John to lay an additional plate."

"An additional plate, indeed! I think, ma'am, you had better order something to put on it."

"I ordered the dinner yesterday," said Miss Clarence, with faint voice and faint heart; for she well knew that the result of ordering a dinner, bore a not very faint resemblance to that of 'calling spirits from the vasty deep.'[2]

"Yes, ma'am, I know you ordered it; but I told Amandy to let you know that the butcher did not come down from the village this morning, and we've neither lamb nor veal in the house."

"But we have Neale's fine mutton?"

"Not a pound of it. He came up yesterday to say his fat sheep had all strayed away."

"Why did not you tell me?"

"You were riding out, ma'am, and I sent John to Hilson for a roaster."

---

1   Refers to the Irish folktale "The Legend of Bottle Hill" in which Farmer Mick exchanges a cow for a magic bottle that instantly provides lavish meals.

2   Shakespeare's *Henry IV, Part I*, III.i.51. Vasty deep: the underworld.

"Oh, spare me, Becky; a roaster, you know, is papa's aversion, and mine too."

"I know that, Miss Gertrude, but then I thought to myself, it's no time to be notional when there's company invited, and not a pound of *fresh* to be had for love or money; but as ill luck would have it, Hilson had engaged the whole nine for the Independence dinner, a delightsome sight they'll be, all standing on their feet with each an ear of corn in his mouth. But thinking of them," added Becky,—mentally reproaching herself for this gush of professional enthusiasm,—"Thinking of them won't fill our dishes; and so, Miss Gertrude, I want you to send word to the Widow Carter, you must have her fowls, whether or no. To be sure they'll be rather tough, killed at this time of day."

"Yes, Becky, since we know why she refuses them, they would be too tough eating for any of us. No, I had rather give our friends a dinner of strawberries and cream."

"Cream! the thunder turned all that last evening."

"The elements against us too!"

"Elements! ice creams, you mean. No, ma'am, they were mixed last night; but Malviny says she can't stay to freeze them. She must go down to the village to Mrs. Smith's funeral. She says the general expects it."

"It is a hard case, Becky; but we must make the best of it. You must not let this Englishman spy out the nakedness of our land. Your fingers and brains never failed me yet, Becky. Now let us think what we have to count upon."

"There's as good a ham as ever came from Virginia."

"Yes, or Westphalia[1] either, and as beautiful lettuces as ever grew. Ham and salad is a dinner for a prince, Becky; and then you can make up a dish from the veal of yesterday with currie—bouillie a tongue—prepare a dish of maccaroni—see that the vermicelli soup is of your very best, Becky—papa says nobody makes it better—and the trout, you forgot the trout, here comes old Frank up the avenue with them now—bless the old soul, he never disappoints us—boil, stew, fry the trout; every body likes fresh trout. As to the ice-creams, tell Malvina she shall go down to the village to every funeral for a year to come, if she will give up the general's lady. The dinner will turn out well yet, Becky. As you often say, 'it's always darkest just before day.'"

"And you beat all, Miss Gertrude, for making day-light come," replied Becky, pleased with her mistress' compliment, and relieved

---

1 Region of what is now Germany, known for its fine hams.

by her ready ingenuity. "There's few ladies use what little sense they have got to any purpose. If there were more of them had your head-work, the house-business would not get so tangled, and that's what John and I often say." Thus mutually satisfied, mistress and servant parted.

Miss Clarence's thoughts reverted to Seton; and she repaired to her own apartment, happy in the consciousness of a firm resolve to make every effort to secure his tranquillity. Alas, that human judgment should be so blind and weak, that its best wisdom often leads to the most fearful consequences!

When Gertrude entered her own apartment, she found Emilie Layton sitting at a writing-desk, busily employed in answering her letters. Her face was drenched in tears, but so unruffled that it seemed as if no accident could disturb its sweet harmonies. "You put me in mind, Emilie," said Gertrude, kissing her cheek, "you put me in mind of a shower when the sun is shining."

Emilie dashed off her tears. "I will not be miserable any longer; would you, Gertrude?"

"No, I never would be miserable if I could help it, Emilie."

"It is too disagreeable," replied Emilie, with perfect naïveté, "it makes one feel too bad; but I really have enough to make me miserable. If I dared, I would show you all these letters; but, dear Gertrude, you can advise me without knowing what the real state of the case is, only that papa and mama want me to do something that I hate to do—that I would rather die than do. Now would you do it if you were I?"

Gertrude did not need second sight to conjecture what the nature of this parental requisition might be. "It is difficult to answer your question, Emilie; but there are things that it is not right to do, even in compliance with parental authority. This may be one of them."

"Oh, it is, I am sure. You have divined it most certainly, Gertrude; but I have not told you a word, you know. Mama charges me not in her letter. I am so glad you think as I do; but I am afraid mama will persuade me. She suffers so much when any thing crosses her. If she could only be persuaded to think as I do about it. I have written a letter to a certain person who has great influence over her. You may read it, Gertrude. You cannot understand it, though he will. Read it aloud, for I want to hear how it sounds."

Gertrude read aloud, "To my mother's best and dearest friend."—"Your father, of course?" she said, looking up a little perplexed at Emilie. *what?*

Miss Layton blushed, and there was an expression of acute pain passed over her face, as she said with quivering lips, "Oh no, Gertrude, I wish it were so; but perhaps you think I have addressed it improperly—if you do, just run the pen through that line." Gertrude did so, and read on, "As mama has told me, Mr. Roscoe, that you already know all about a certain affair, I trust I am not doing wrong in begging you to intercede with my dear mother in my behalf. Do convince her that it is not my duty to sacrifice my happiness to my father's wishes. It is very hard to make one's self miserable for life, and is it not an odd way to make one's parents happy? Papa says there is no use in being romantic. I am sure I am not so. I would as lief marry a rich man as a poor one, if I loved him. Any person, however romantic, might love Miss Clarence, in spite of her fortune. Therefore it is *not*, as my father says, an absurd, girlish notion about 'love in a cottage,'[1] that gives me such an antipathy to ———. Do intercede for me, if I have not made an improper request, and if I have, forget it, and remember only your friend, E. L." Gertrude laid down the letter without comment. "It is a very poor letter, I know," said Emilie, "and poorly written, for I blotted the words with my tears as fast as I wrote them."

Gertrude smiled at her simplicity. "No, Emilie, it is a very good letter, for it is true; and truth from such a heart as yours is always good. But would it not be best to burn the letter? It seems to me you may trust to your own representations to your mother. No intercessor can be so powerful as her tenderness for you."

"Oh, Gertrude, you do not know mama. She can talk me out of my five senses, and she says nobody in the world has such influence over her as Mr. Roscoe." On second thoughts, Gertrude believed that Emilie might need a sturdier support than her own yielding temper, and she acquiesced in the letter being sent; and Emilie despatched it, and drove from her heart every feeling of sorrow almost as easily as she removed its traces from her heart's bright and beautiful mirror.

---

1 Marriage based on mutual love rather than wealth, usually suggesting that love alone will not overcome insufficient means.

CHAPTER XII.

"I will tell thee a similitude, Esdras. As when thou asketh the earth, it shall say unto thee that it giveth much mould whereof earthen vessels are made, but little dust that gold cometh of; even so is the course of this present world."[1]
ESDRAS.

MADAME ROLAND[2] has left it on record—let any woman who fancies she may soar above the natural sphere of her sex, remember who it is that makes this boast—that she never neglected the details of housewifery, and she adds, that though at one period of her life she had been at the head of a laborious and frugal establishment, and at another, of an expensive and complicated one, she had never found it necessary to devote more than two hours of the twenty-four to household cares. While we have this illustrious woman before us, as evidence in the case, we would venture to intimate, in opposition to the vulgar and perhaps too lightly received opinion, that talents are as efficient in housewifery as in every other department of life; and that, cæteris paribus,[3] she who has most mind will best administer her domestic affairs, whether her condition obliges her, like the pattern Jewish matron, to 'rise early and work diligently with her own hands,' or merely to appoint the labors of others.[4]

If our opinion be not heresy, we would commend it to the consideration of scholars, and men of genius, and all that privileged class, (privileged in every thing else,) who have been supposed to be condemned by their own elevation to choose an humble, grubbing companion for the journey of life, at best not superior to Johnson's beau-ideal of a female travelling companion.[5]

But to return to our heroine. Her happy genius had rode out the storm threatened in the morning, by her trusty Becky, and she saw the dinner hour draw nigh with a tranquillity that can only

---

1   2 Esdras, Chapter 8, of the Apocrypha, King James Bible, also known as 4 Ezra.
2   Madame Roland (Marie-Jeanne Philipon) (French, 1754-93), writer.
3   Other things being equal (Latin).
4   Refers to Proverbs 31.10-31: "Who can find a virtuous woman? for her price is far above rubies" (King James Version). In the 1849 edition, 'Jewish matron' is 'Jewish maiden.'
5   Perhaps a reference to the discussions of marriage and human happiness in *The History of Rasselas, Prince of Abyssinia* (1759) by Samuel Johnson (English, 1709-84).

be inspired by the delightful certainty that, to use the technical phrase, *all is going on well*. She was in the parlor with Miss Layton, and awaiting her guests, when Judge Upton, who, true as a lover to his mistress, never broke 'the thousandth part of a minute in the affair'[1] of a dinner, arrived. After the most precise salutations to each and all, he expressed his great satisfaction in being punctual. 'He had done, what indeed he seldom did, risked a failure in this point. He must own, that with a certain divine, he held punctuality to be the next virtue to godliness; but it had been impossible for him to dispense with attending the funeral of general Smith's lady. The general expected it; such a respectable person's feelings should not be aggravated on so afflicting an occasion. He must own he had been uncommonly gratified; the general behaved so well; he bore his loss like a general.'

Miss Clarence suppressed, as nearly as she might, a smile at the conjugal heroism of a 'training-day' general, and asked Mrs. Upton why Mrs. Layton was not with her.

Mrs. Upton's volubility, which had emitted in low rumblings such tokens of her presence, as are heard from a bottle of beer before the ejection of the cork gives full vent to the thin potation, now overflowed.

"Oh my dear," said she, "Mrs. Layton chose to come on horseback with Mr. Edmund Stuart, our English visiter. Don't be frightened, Emilie, dear, husband's horses are remarkably gentle; indeed he never keeps any others, for he thinks dangerous horses very unsafe. Oh, Mr. Clarence, by the way, do you know we must change our terms. Mr. Stuart says that it is quite vulgar in England to say, we *ride*, when we go in a carriage. We must call a ride a *drive*—only think! He says we cannot conceive how disagreeable Americanisms are to English ears."[2]

"My dear madam," replied Mr. Clarence, who was rather sensitive on the subject of Anglo-criticism, "do let us remember that in America we speak to American ears, and if any terms peculiar to us have as much intrinsic propriety as the English, let us have the independence to retain them."

"Oh! certainly, certainly," said the good lady, who had no thought of adventuring in the thorny path of philological discus-

---

1 Shakespeare's *As You Like It* IV.i.44.

2 Sedgwick's niece Maria Banyer Sedgwick, in a letter to her father Theodore, records a similar anecdote in connection to the visit of Captain Basil Hall and a conversation about the differences in English and American expressions (Maria Banyer Sedgwick to Theodore Sedgwick II, 5 February 1828, Sedgwick Family Papers, MHS).

sion, "husband says he don't see why *ride* is not as proper as drive, especially for those who don't drive. But girls, I must tell you before Mr. Stuart comes, that he is remarkably genteel even for an Englishman. He is the son of Sir William Stuart, and, of course, you know, will be a lord himself." Our republican matron was not learned in the laws that regulate the descent of titles; but, in blessed unconsciousness of her ignorance, she proceeded: "I was determined he should see Clarenceville, for, as husband says, it is all important he should form favorable opinions of our country."

"Why important?" asked Mr. Clarence, in one of those cold and posing tones that would have checked a less determined garrulity than Mrs. Upton's. But her impetus was too strong to be resisted, and on she blundered. "Oh, I don't know exactly, but it is, you know. He is to pass six months in the United States, and he is determined to see every thing. He has already been from Charleston to Boston. Only think, as husband says, what a perfect knowledge he will have of the country."

"Does he propose," asked Mr. Clarence, "to enlighten the public with his observations?"

"Write a book of travels, you mean, sir? Oh, I have no doubt of it, and that made me in such a fever to have him see the girls. Girls, you must be on the *qui vive*.[1] The dinner party will be described at full length. Your dinners, Gertrude, are always in such superb style. Husband told Mr. Stuart he did not believe they were surpassed in England." Gertrude blushed when she thought of the disasters of the larder, and the miscellaneous dinner preceded by such a silly flourish of trumpets. "Oh, don't be alarmed, Gertrude, dear," continued the good lady, "I am sure it will be just the thing, and then you know a beauty and a fortune," glancing her little glassy eye, with ineffable gratulation from Emilie, to Gertrude, "a beauty and a fortune will give the party such eclat![2] Oh, I should have given up, if any thing had happened to prevent our coming. The children gave me such a fright this morning! Thomas Jefferson fell down stairs; but he is a peculiar child about falling, always comes on his feet, like a cat. Benjamin Franklin is very different. He has never had but one fall in his life, so husband calls it 'Ben's fall,' like 'Adam's fall,' you know; very good, is not it?" That solemn, responsible person, 'husband,' whose sententious sayings were expanded like a drop of water into a volume of steam, by that wonderful engine, his wife's tongue, was solemnly parading

---

1 On the alert.
2 Brilliance.

the piazza, his watch in his hand, and his eye fixed on the avenue, while with lengthening visage he groaned in spirit under that misery for which few country gentlemen have one drop of patience in their souls—a deferred dinner.

"Oh, there they come!" he was the first to announce, and after the slight bustle of dismounting, &c., and a whisper from Mrs. Upton of 'do your prettiest, girls,' Mrs. Layton entered the drawing-room, her arm in Mr. Stuart's, who with his hat under his other arm, his stiff neckcloth, and starched demeanor, looked the son of an English baronet at least. His stately perpendicularity was the more striking, contrasted with the grace and elasticity of Mrs. Layton's movements. This lady deserves more than a transient glance.

Mrs. Layton was somewhere on that most disagreeable stage of the journey of life, between thirty and forty—most disagreeable to a woman who has once enjoyed the dominion of personal beauty; for at that period she is most conscious of its diminution. If ever woman might, Mrs. Layton could have dispensed with beauty, for she had, when she pleased to command them, graceful manners, spirited conversation, and those little feminine engaging ways, that though they can scarcely be defined or described, are irresistibly attractive. But never were the arts that prolong beauty more sedulously studied than by this lady. She owed much to the forbearance of nature, who seemed to shrink from spoiling what she had so exquisitely made. Her eyes retained the clearness and sparkling brilliancy of her freshest youth. Her own profuse, dark hair was artfully arranged to shelter and display her fine intellectual brow, and the rose on her cheek, if too mutable for nature, claimed indulgence for the exquisite art of its imitation. She was yet within the customary term of deep mourning for a sister, and as she was not of a temper to crusade against any of the forms of society, her crape and bombasin were in accordance with its sternest requisitions; but their sombre and heavy effect was skilfully relieved by brilliant and becoming ornaments. Like the Grecian beauty who sacrificed her tresses at her sister's tomb, she took care that the pious offering should not diminish the effect of her charms. Mrs. Layton resembled a Parisian artificial flower, so perfect in its form, coloring, and arrangement, that it seems as if nothing could be more beautiful, unless perchance the eye falls on a natural rose, and beholds His superior and divine art whose 'pencil' paints it, and 'whose breath perfumes.'[1] Such a contrast was Emilie Layton

---

1   From "The Botanic Garden: A Poem, Part II: The Loves of the Plants, Canto 1" (1789-91) by Erasmus Darwin (English, 1731-1802),

to her mother. There was an unstudied, child-like grace in every attitude and movement, the dew of youth was on her bright lip, and her round cheek was tinged with every passing feeling.

Mrs. Layton presented her English acquaintance to Miss Clarence and her father, and returned their salutations with an air of graceful self-possession that showed she was far too experienced to feel a sensation from entering a country drawing-room. Her brow contracted for an instant as she kissed her daughter, and whispered, "I see you are going to be my own dear girl, Emilie." Emilie turned away, and her mother's scrutiny was averted by the outbreaking of Mrs. Upton's ever ready loquacity. "Would you think, Mr. Clarence," she asked, "that Grace Layton and I were girls together. I don't deny I have a trifling advantage of you, Grace, dear; but, as husband says, when I die, you will shake in your shoes."

"Do, Miss Clarence," interposed Mrs. Layton, "convince our friend Mrs. Upton, that such familiarity with time is quite rustic and barbarous. Time is as obsolete in civilized life as his grim personification in the primer.[1] We never talk of time in good society, Mrs. Upton."

"Not talk of time!" retorted her good-natured contemporary, "that's odd for a married woman. Old maids are always particular about their ages, but it's no object for us; besides, as husband says, children are a kind of mile-stones that measure the distance you have travelled. That was quite clever of husband—was not it? Husband," she continued, stretching her neck out of the window, and addressing her better half, "when was it you made that smart comparison, of children to mile-stones?"

"Children to mile-stones! what are you talking about, my dear?"

"Oh, I remember, it was not you—it was"—but on drawing in her head she perceived no one was listening to her. Mrs. Layton, unable as she confessed, any longer to endure the odious flapping of time's wings, had adroitly turned the conversation. "What are those pictures you are studying, Mr. Stuart?" she asked.

The gentleman colored deeply, and replied, "Some *American* representations of naval engagements, madam."

---

naturalist, father of Charles Darwin. William Erasmus Darwin, eldest son of Charles, and Sarah Ashburner Sedgwick, Sedgwick's great-niece, married in 1879. The anemone, not the rose, is the subject of these lines in Darwin's poem.

1 Refers to the depiction of time (for the letter "T") in *The New England Primer*, a schoolbook published c. 1683-90 and in use through the 1790s): "Time cuts down all / Both great and small."

"And if the British lion were the painter he would have reversed the victory?" said the lady archly.

Miss Clarence felt that the rites of hospitality demanded the interposition of her shield: "That picture," she said, "does not harmonize well with our rural scenery, but my father values it on account of the artist, who is his particular friend."

"An *ingenious* young person, no doubt," replied the traveller, with an equivocal emphasis on the word ingenious, and a supercilious curl of his lip.

"Oh, remarkably ingenious," exclaimed Mrs. Upton, "by the way, Gertrude, dear, where is Louis Seton to-day?"

"Confined to his room by indisposition," replied Miss Clarence, without hesitation, or blushing.

"Hem—hem—hem"—thrice repeated the vulgar little lady, who like other vulgar people thought the intimation of something particular between any marriageable parties always agreeable to a young lady. Miss Clarence looked deaf, and Mrs. Upton was baffled; but she good-humoredly continued "I do wish, Mr. Stuart, you could have seen the young gentleman who painted that picture. Husband thinks him an uncommon genius, almost equal to that celebrated American who is such a famous painter—I forget his name—I do believe husband is right, and I am losing my memory; but at any rate I remember the interesting anecdote about him—I forget exactly who told it to me, but I believe it was husband—however, that is of no consequence—yet it is so provoking to forget—if I could only remember when I heard it."

"Oh, never mind when," exclaimed Mrs. Layton, "tell the story, Mrs. Upton. We shall never forget *when* we heard it."

"Well, he was born—oh, where was he born? you remember, Gertrude, dear?"

"If you mean West, I believe he was born in Pennsylvania."[1]

"Oh, yes, it was West; now I remember all about it—it was husband told me—his parents were wretchedly poor; wer'nt they, Gertrude, dear?"

"Too poor, I believe, to educate him."

"Oh, yes; that is just what husband told me—and being too poor, and being born, as it were, a painter, he invented colors—or brushes—which was it, Gertrude, dear?"

"Neither, I believe," replied Gertrude, suppressing a smile, and glad of an opportunity to shelter Mrs. Upton's ignorance,

---

1 Benjamin West (see p. 144, note 1). The conversation that follows suggests Mr. Stuart's ignorance of West's American roots.

and save her friends from her farther garrulity, she proceeded to relate the well known story of West having made his first brush from the hairs of a cat's tail, and of his having, instructed by the Indians, compounded his first colors from the vegetable productions of the wilds around him. Mr. Stuart took out his tablets. apparently to note down the particulars Miss Clarence had related. "I beg your pardon," he said, "have the goodness again, Miss Clarence, to tell me the name of the painter of whom you spoke."

"West."

"West! ah, the same with our celebrated artist."

"Is there an English artist of that name?" asked Mrs. Layton, with seeming good faith.

"Indeed is there, madam, an exceeding clever person too, Sir Benjamin West; his name is known throughout Europe, though it may not have reached America yet, owing probably to the ignorance of the fine arts here. My eldest brother received with the estate two of his finest productions. One of the happy effects of our law of entail, is that it fosters genius by preserving in families the chef d'œuvres[1] of the arts. It is much to be regretted," he continued turning to Mr. Clarence, "that your legislators have deemed this law of primogeniture incompatible with your republican institutions. It is an unfortunate mistake, which will for ever retard your advance in the sciences, arts, and manners."[2]

"Do manners go with the estate? How can that be?" asked Mrs. Upton in all simplicity. Whatever replies to this question might have been suggested by the presence of the *unportioned* younger son, they were suppressed by the common instincts of good breeding, and dinner fortunately being announced, the party repaired to the dining-room, where we shall leave them to the levelling process of satisfying appetites whetted to their keenest edge by an hour's delay of a country dinner. Perhaps, in confirmation of the assertion already made of Miss Clarence's housewifery, it should be stated, that there was not a dish on table of which Mrs. Upton did not taste, and ask a receipt.[3]

---

1 Masterpieces.

2 Sedgwick's note in the 1830 edition: There may appear to be a striking coincidence between the opinions of our traveller and those announced in Captain Basil Hall's travels; but no allusion was intended to those volumes. This chapter was written a year before their appearance.

3 Recipe.

The dinner being over, Mrs. Layton, evidently anxious for some private conversation with her daughter, proposed a stroll in the wood.

She arranged the party according to her own wishes. "Mr. Clarence," she said, "you are, I believe, condemned to some business discussions with the judge. Mrs. Upton, Miss Clarence, I am sure, will give you a quiet seat in the library, and her receipt book. Miss Clarence, you will do Mr. Stuart the honor to point out to him the beauties of an American forest; and Emilie shall be my Ariadne.[1] I wish," she added in a voice spoken alone to Miss Layton's ear, "that like her you were dreaming of love."

"Pshaw! mother," replied Emilie. There was nothing in her words, but there was something in her manner and looks that abated her mother's hopes. She had, however, too much at stake to leave any art untried to achieve her object; and when, after an hour's walk, Miss Clarence again met the mother and daughter, Emilie's cheek was flushed, and her eyes red with weeping. Her practised mother veiled her own feelings, and inquired of Mr. Stuart, with as much carelessness as if she had thought of nothing else since they parted, "how he liked an American forest?"

"With such a companion," he replied, courteously bowing to Miss Clarence, "quite agreeable, but in itself monotonous."

"A quality, I presume," answered Mrs. Layton, "peculiar to American forests. But, my dear girls, where are you going?—spare me a little longer from the din of Mrs. Upton's tongue. I had as lief be doomed to turn the crank of a hand-organ.[2] My dear Miss Clarence, you must not be all Emilie's friend. Sit down on this rustic bench with me, and let Emilie show Mr. Stuart the pretty points of view about the place. He has come forty miles to see the lake, or the fair lady of the lake," she whispered, as the gentleman withdrew with Miss Layton. "I see everywhere about your place, Miss Clarence," continued Mrs. Layton, plucking a honeysuckle from a luxuriant vine that embowered the seat where she had placed herself, "indications of the refinement of your taste. Flowers have always seemed to me the natural allies and organs of a delicate and sensitive spirit. I admire the oriental custom of eliciting from them a sort of hieroglyphic language, to express the inspirations of love—love, 'the perfume and suppliance of a

---

1 In Greek mythology, Ariadne, the daughter of Minos and Pasiphae, experiences great suffering and sorrow in love (in various versions, with Theseus or Dionysus).

2 In the 1849 edition, Sedgwick replaces this sentence with: I had as lief be doomed to a swarm of musquitos—she stings as well as hums.

moment,'[1] so beautifully shadowed forth in their sweet and fleeting life. I see you do not agree with me."

"Not entirely. Flowers have always seemed to me to be the vehicle of another language: to express their Creator's love, and, if I may say so, his gracious and minute attention to our pleasures. Their beauty, their variety, their fragrance, are gratuities, for no other purpose, as far as we can see, but to gratify our senses, and through those avenues to reach the mind, that by their ministry may communicate with the Giver. To me the sight of a flower is like the voice of a friend. You smile, but I have great authority on my side. Why was it that the French heroine and martyr could exclaim, 'J'oublie l'injustice des hommes, leurs sottises, et mes maux avec des livres et des fleurs,'[2] but because they conveyed to her the expression of a love that made all mortal evils appear in their actual insignificance."

"Bless me, my dear Miss Clarence! how seclusion in a romantic country does lead one to refine and spin out pretty little cobweb systems of one's own. Now my inference would have been that Madame Roland's books and flowers helped her to forget cabals and guillotines, and perhaps I should have come as near the truth as you. You are a very Swedenborgian[3] in your exposition of nature. However, you have no mawkish, parade sentiment, and your hidden and spiritual meanings certainly exalt flowers above mere ministers to the senses. But how did we fall into this flourishing talk? I detained you here to make a confession to you."

"A confession to me!"

"Yes; you know I told you you must be my friend as well as Emilie's." 'Ah,' thought Gertrude, 'she is going to confide to me poor Emilie's affair. I will have the boldness to give her my real opinion.' Mrs. Layton proceeded, "I must be frank with you, Miss Clarence—frankness is my nature. I have wronged you."

"Wronged *me*, Mrs. Layton?"

"Yes, my dear Miss Clarence, in the tenderest point in which a woman can be injured; but do not be alarmed, the injury is not irreparable. You recollect the day you called on me at Mrs. Upton's with that woe-begone, love-stricken devotee of yours?"

---

1 Shakespeare's *Hamlet* I.iii.9.

2 "I forget the injustice of men, their follies, and my pain with books and flowers." From Madame Roland's *Mémoires*, 1795.

3 Reference to the doctrine of correspondences between the natural world or material plane and the spiritual, advanced by followers of Emmanuel Swedenborg (Swedish, 1688-1772) and later adopted by the American Transcendentalists.

"Mr. Seton?"

"Yes, Mr. Seton. Now spare me that sentimental, rebuking look. I will not be irreverent to the youth, though I know better than to give credit to the gossip of Goody Upton, and her cummers[1] about you. His love-passages, poor fellow, will never lead to your hymeneal altar. But to my confession. You must know that on the aforesaid day I had a fit of the blues, and I saw every thing, even you, through a murky cloud. To speak literally, (ergo disagreeably,) I did not perceive one of your charms."

"Oh, is that all, Mrs. Layton?—woman as I am, I can pardon that."

"All! no, if it were, I would not have mentioned it, for one *woman's* opinion of another is a mere bagatelle. Idleness, you know, is the parent of all sin. I had nothing to do, and moved and incited thereto by the demon of ennui, I sat down and described you to one of my correspondents as you had appeared to my distempered vision."

"And is *that* all?"

"Yes, that is all; but that you may know the whole head and front of my offending I must show you my correspondent's reply."

"Do so—that may make a merit of my pardon."

Mrs. Layton took a letter from her reticule, but before she opened it she said, "I must premise in my own justification, not to conciliate you, that when I met you to-day you seemed perfectly transformed from the little demure lady you appeared at first. I feel now as if I had known you a year and could interpret every look of your expressive face. Something had happened this morning—I am sure of it—to give a certain elevation to your feelings. I 'would not flatter Neptune for his trident, nor Jove for his power to thunder.'[2] I could not flatter *you*, Miss Clarence, and it is no flattery to say your beauty is of that character which Montesquieu pronounces the most effective.[3] It results from certain changes and flashes of expression—it produces the emotion of surprise. When you speak and show those brilliant teeth of yours, your face is worth all the rose and lily beauties in Christendom. You remind me of Gibbon's description of Zenobia[4]—do you remember it?"

---

1 A female companion or gossip.

2 Shakespeare's *Coriolanus* III.i.255-56.

3 Charles-Louis de Secondat, Baron de Montesquieu (French, 1689-1755), writer.

4 Edward Gibbon, *The History of the Decline and Fall of the Roman Empire* (1776, 1781, 1788). Mrs. Layton perhaps refers to this passage: "Zenobia was esteemed the most lovely as well as the most heroic of her sex. She

"No; I seldom remember a description of personal beauty."

"I never forget it. You have not been enough in the world to learn that beauty is the *sine qua non*[1] to a woman—a young woman—unless, indeed, she has fortune."

"We are graduated by a flattering scale, truly!"

"Yes, my dear girl, but you may as well know it; there is no use in going hoodwinked into society! But now for our document." Mrs. Layton unfolded Gerald Roscoe's letter, which our readers have already perused, and read aloud from the passage beginning, 'Is it natural depravity,' and ending with the anecdote of Miss Eunice Peabody. When she had finished reading, 'a comely little body, amiable and rather clever,' "is a quotation from my letter," she said, "and was my libellous description of you, Miss Clarence."

"Libellous! Mrs. Layton. I declare to you after your frightful note of preparation it sounds to me quite complimentary; but who is the gentleman to whom I have this picturesque introduction?"

"Ah! there's the rub. He is undoubtedly the most attractive young man in New York—the prince of clever fellows; and, honored am I in the fact—my selected, and favorite, and most intimate friend."

'Oh!' thought Gertrude, 'Emilie said Roscoe was her mother's most intimate friend,' and the pang that shot through her heart at this recollection was evident in her face, for Mrs. Layton paused a moment before she added—"Gerald Roscoe." At this confirmation of her mental conjecture, Gertrude involuntarily covered her face with her hands, and then, disconcerted to the last degree at having betrayed her sensations, she said, half articulately, something of her being taken by surprise at the mention of Gerald Roscoe's name, that he was her father's friend, but she concluded with hoping Mrs. Layton would not think she cared at all about it. But Mrs. Layton was quite too keen and sagacious an observer to be imposed on for a moment by such awkward hypocrisy as

---

was of a dark complexion (for in speaking of a lady these trifles become important). Her teeth were of a pearly whiteness, and her large black eyes sparkled with uncommon fire, tempered by the most attractive sweetness. Her voice was strong and harmonious. Her manly understanding was strengthened and adorned by study. She was not ignorant of the Latin tongue, but possessed in equal perfection the Greek, the Syriac, and the Egyptian languages" (Chapter XI, "Character of Zenobia—Her Beauty and Learning"). In the third century CE, Zenobia ruled as a queen in Palmyra (present-day Syria) and was renowned as a woman warrior.

1 Indispensable (Latin).

Gertrude's.[1] She saw she did care a great deal about it, and giving a feminine interpretation to her emotion, and anxious to efface every unpleasant impression from her mind, she said in her sweetest manner, "I enjoy in anticipation Roscoe's surprise when he shall see you. It will be quite a *coup de théâtre*.[2] On the whole, Gertrude—I must call you Gertrude—*dear* Gertrude—I think I may claim to have done you a favor. I have prepared Roscoe's mind for an agreeable surprise, and for the still more agreeable feeling that his taste is far superior to mine—that to him belongs the merit of a discoverer, and as he is after all but a man, he will enjoy this, and I shall enjoy particularly your triumph over his first impressions."

'Ah,' thought Gertrude, 'those impressions will never be removed, I shall be paralyzed, a very Eunice Peabody, if ever I meet him.' But she smiled at Mrs. Layton's castle-building, and though she assured that lady that nothing was more improbable than that she should ever encounter Gerald Roscoe, as he never left town, and she never went there, yet she did find something very agreeable in Mrs. Layton's perspective; and being human and youthful, she was not insensible to the flatteries addressed to her by the most fascinating woman she had ever seen.

Mrs. Layton's expressions of admiration were not all flattery. There was something in Gertrude that really excited her imagination. She saw she was of a very different order from the ordinary run of well-bred, well-informed, decorous, pleasing young ladies—a class particularly repulsive and tiresome to Mrs. Layton. She foresaw that Miss Clarence, far removed as she was from being a beauty would, set off by the *éclat* of fortune, become a *distingué*[3] whenever she appeared in society, and she took such measures to ingratiate herself as she had found most generally successful. She had shown Roscoe's letter to manifest and enhance the value of her changed opinion. She spared no pains to efface the impression the letter evidently left on Gertrude's mind. She taxed all her arts of pleasing—talked of herself, alluded to her faults, so eloquently, that the manner was a beautiful drapery that covered up and concealed the matter. She spoke with generous confidence of the adverse circumstances of her matrimonial destiny, and Gertrude, in her simplicity, not doubting that she was

---

1 In the 1849 edition, Sedgwick replaces "such awkward hypocrisy as Gertrude's" with "by Gertrude's disclaimer."
2 Dramatic turn of events.
3 Distinguished person.

the sole depository of this revelation, felt a secret self-gratulation in the qualities that had elicited so singular a trust, and the tenderest sympathy with the sufferer of unprovoked wrongs. Then Mrs. Layton again reverted to Roscoe, the person of all others of whom Gertrude was most curious to hear. She had a kind of dot and line art in sketching characters, and with a few masterly touches presented a vivid image. She spoke of society; and its vanities, excitements and follies, like bubbles catching the sun's rays, kindled in the light of her imagination.

Gertrude listened and felt that her secluded life was a paralyzed, barren existence. Her attention was rivetted and delighted till they were both aroused by the footsteps of a servant, who came to say that Judge Upton's carriage was at the door. Half way to the piazza they were met by Mrs. Upton. "Gertrude, dear," she said, "I hope you *will* excuse our going rather early. You know I am an anxious mother, and the Judge is so important at home—but we have had a charming day! I am sure Mr. Stuart has been delighted. I asked him if he had ever seen any thing superior to Clarenceville as a whole, and I assure you he did not say yes. Indeed, sub rosa,[1] (you understand, between you and I,) I do think you have made a conquest."

"Do not, I entreat you, Mrs. Upton, ask the gentleman whether I have or not."

"Oh no, my dear soul; *do* you think I would do any thing so out of the way? I understand a thing or two; but I do long to know which will carry the day, you or Emilie—fortune versus—as husband says—versus beauty. One thing I am certain of, we shall all be in the book."

"Not all," said Mrs. Layton, and added in a whisper to Gertrude, "who but Shakspeare could have delineated Slender?"[2]

Gertrude was surprised and disappointed at finding Emilie on the piazza, prepared to return with her mother; but there was no opportunity for expostulation. Judge Upton stood at the open carriage door, as impatient as if a council of war were awaiting his arrival at home, and the ladies were compelled to abridge their adieus.

When Mr. Clarence had made his last bow to his departing guests, he seated himself on the piazza. "There goes our English visiter, Gertrude," said he, "enriched no doubt with precious morceaus[3] for his diary. Judge Upton will represent the class of

---

1 Secretly (Latin).
2 A dim-witted character in Shakespeare's *The Merry Wives of Windsor*.
3 Bits, or pieces.

American country-gentlemen, and his miscellaneous help-meet will sit for an American *lady*. I heard him ask Mrs. Upton, who has, it must be confessed, an anomalous mode of assorting her viands," (Mr. Clarence spoke with the disgust of a dyspeptic rather than a Chesterfieldian,) "whether it were common for the Americans to eat salad with fish? Notwithstanding her everlasting good nature, she was a little touched at his surveillance, and for once replied without her prefix 'husband says,' that she supposed we had a *right* to eat such things together as pleased us best."

"It is unfortunate," said Gertrude, "that travellers should fall into such hands."

"No, no, Gertrude; it makes no difference with such travellers. They come predetermined to find fault—to measure every thing they see by the English standard they carry in their minds, and which they conceive to be as perfect as those eternal patterns after which some ancient philosophers supposed the Creator to have fashioned the universe. I had a good deal of conversation with this young man, and I think he is about as well qualified to describe our country, and judge of its real condition, as the fish are to pass their opinion on the capacities and habitudes of the birds. I do not mean that ours is the superior condition, but that we are of different elements. It does annoy me, I confess, excessively, that such fellows should influence the minds of men. I do not care so much about the impression they make in their own country, as the effect they have in ours, in keeping alive jealousies, distrusts, and malignant resentments, and stirring up in young minds a keen sense of injustice, and a feeling of dislike bordering on hatred to England—England, our noble mother country. I would have our children taught to regard her with filial veneration—to remember that their fathers participated in her high historic deeds—that they trod the same ground and breathed the same air with Shakspeare, and Milton, and Locke, and Bacon.[1] I would have them esteem England as first in science, in literature, in the arts, in inventions, in philanthropy, in whatever elevates and refines humanity. I would have them love and cherish her name, and remember that she is still the mother and sovereign of their minds."

"But my dear, dear father, you are giving England the supremacy and preference over our own country."

"Our country! she speaks for herself, my child; if there were not a voice lifted throughout all this wide spread land of peace

---

1 English writers Shakespeare, John Milton (1608-74), John Locke (1632-1704) and Francis Bacon (1561-1626).

and plenty, yet how 'loud would be the praise!' I do not wish to hear her flattered by foreigners, or boasted or lauded by our own people. Nor do I fear, on her account, any thing that can be said by these petty tourists, who, like noisome insects, defile the fabric they cannot comprehend."

CHAPTER XIII.

"Is there in human form that bears a heart—
A wretch! a villain! lost to love and truth!
That can with studied, sly, ensnaring art,
Betray sweet Jenny's unsuspecting youth?"[1]
BURNS.

"Gerald Roscoe to Mrs. Layton.

"ON looking over your letter a second time, my dear Mrs. Layton, I find there is enough of it unanswered to give me a pretence for addressing you again; and as I know no more agreeable employment of one of my many leisure hours than communicating with you, I will contrast your picture of the miseries of rustic hospitality and rustic habits, with the trials of a poor devil, condemned to the vulgarity and necessity of dragging through the summer months in town. We all look at our present, petty vexations, through the magnifying end of the glass, and then turning our instrument, give to the condition of others, the softness and enchantment of distance.

"But to my picture. Behold me then, after having waited through the day in my *clientless* office, retired to my humble lodging, No.— Walker-street, in a garret apartment, (by courtesy styled the attic,) as hot, even after the sun is down, as a well-heated oven when the fire is withdrawn, or as hot as you might imagine 'accommodations for a single gentleman' in tophet.[2] The room is fifteen feet square, or rather the floor, as the ceiling descends at an angle of forty-five degrees, so that whenever I pass the centre of my apartment I am compelled to a perpetual salam, or to having my head *organized* in a manner that would confound the metaphysical materialism of a German.

"My dear mother, nobly as she has conformed herself to our fallen fortunes, has not yet been able to dispense with certain

---

1 From "The Cotter's Saturday Night" (1785) by Robert Burns.
2 Hell.

personal refinements for herself, or for her unworthy son. I believe in my soul, she has never wafted a sigh from our land-lady's sordid little parlor to the almost forgotten splendors of our drawing-room; but there is something intolerably offensive to her habits and tastes in the arrangements of a plebeian bedroom. Accordingly she has fitted up my apartment with what she considers necessaries; but that first necessity—that chiefest of all luxuries—space, she cannot command; nor can all her ingenuity overcome the principle of resistance in matter, so that my 'indispensable' furniture limits my locomotive faculties to six feet by four. The knocks I get in any one day against my bureaus, writing-table, book-case, &c., would convert a Berkleian philosopher.[1]

"I have but one window, an offset from the roof, to which my dormant ceiling forms a covert way. My horizon is bounded by tiled roofs and square chimneys. No graceful outlines of foliage; no broad lake to sparkle and dimple on the verge of the starry canopy; no 'heaven-kissing hill;'[2] but chimneys and roofs, and roofs and chimneys, for one who counts it high pleasure to behold

'The lofty woods—the forest wide and long,
Adorn'd with leaves and branches fresh and green,
In whose cool bowers the birds, with many a song,
Do welcome with their quire the summer's queen:
The meadows fair, where Flora's gifts among
Are intermix'd with verdant grass between;
The silver scaled fish that softly swim
Within the sweet brook's crystal, watry stream.'[3]

"These are the sorrows of my exile from nature in this her glorious ascendant. I say nothing, my dear Mrs. L., of being chained to the city, when the sweet spirits that gave it life are fled. In short, I will say nothing more of my miseries and privations. I will even confess that my little cell has its pleasures; humble though they be, still they are pleasures. I do not mean the dreams and visions that sport about the brain of a young man who has his own fortunes to carve in the world, and who of course indemnifies himself for

---

1 Adherent of the philosophy of George Berkeley (Irish, 1685-1753), an idealist and immaterialist.

2 Shakespeare's *Hamlet* III.iv.60.

3 From *The Compleat Angler* (1653) by Izaak Walton (English, 1593-1683).

the absolute negation of his present condition by the brilliant apparition of the future. It is well for us that our modesty is not gauged by our anticipations! My humble attic pleasure consists in looking down, like Don Cleofas,[1] on my neighbors—in guessing at their spirit and history from their outward world. You, my dear madam, who live in the courtly luxury of —— street, if your eye ever glanced through your curtained window at the yards of your neighbors, would only see the servile labors of their domestics. You can therefore have no imagination of the revelations of life to my eye. A curious contrast there is between the front and rear of these establishments of our humble citizens—the formal aspect of the ambitious front parlor, and the *laisser aller*[2] style of the back apartments. Suffer me, in this dearth of parties, operas, and whatever makes an accredited drawing-room topic, to introduce you to one of my neighbors and his '*petit paradis*,'[3] for so Abéille[4] calls and considers his yard, a territory of about thirty feet by fourteen. Poor Abéille!—poor—what can make a Frenchman poor? They ride through life on the 'virtuoso's saddle, which will be sure to amble when the world is at the hardest trot.'[5] They have heaven's charter for happiness.

"Abéille was a seigneur of St. Domingo, and possessed one of the richest estates of that Hesperian island.[6] Did you never observe that a Frenchman's temperament is the reverse of the ungracious state that 'never is, but always to be blessed.'[7] Let his present condition be abject as it will, he *has been* blest. Abéille revels now in the retrospective glories of his seigniory, from which the poor

---

1   Character in *Le Diable Boiteux* (1707), *The Limping Devil*, by Alain-René Lesage (French, 1668-1747), novelist and playwright, as well as in *The Devil Upon Two Sticks in England, Being a Continuation of Le Diable Boiteux* (1790) by William Combe (English, 1741-1823).
2   Whatever goes.
3   Little paradise.
4   Abéille is a surname, but it is also the French word for "bee."
5   From the Dedication of *Pastorals of Virgil* by Dryden.
6   A seigneur is a lord, a person of high rank. St. Domingue, a French sugar colony in the Caribbean, was renamed Haiti after a successful slave-led revolution (1791-1804) overthrew French authority, creating the world's first black republic. Post-revolution, Americans continued to refer to the nation by variations of its colonial name, including St. Domingo. Hesperian refers to a western location, as in the designation of the West Indies.
7   From Pope's *Essay on Man, Epistle 1, Of the Nature and State of Man, with Respect to the Universe* (1733-34).

fellow was happy to escape, during the troubles,[1] with his life, his family, and a few jewels, with the avails of which he has since purchased this little property, and a scene of perfect *French* happiness it is. Abéille has two lodgers, an old bachelor, bitten with the mania of learning French, and a clerk qualifying himself for a supercargo. He teaches young ladies to paint flowers. His pretty daughters, Felicité and Angélique, embroider muslin and weave lace, and by these means, and the infinite ingenuity of a French *ménage* they contrive to live in independence, and so far from any vain misery about their past magnificence, it seems merely to cast a vivid hue—a sort of sunset glory over their present mediocrity.

"Abéille's little parterre[2] gives him far more pleasure, he confesses, than he ever received from his West-India plantation. This parterre is the triumph of taste over expense. He has covered with a trellis a vile one story back-building, that protrudes its hideous form the whole length of the yard, and conducted over it a grape-vine, that yields fruit as delicious and plentiful as if it grew in sunny France. The high board-fence, over which once flaunted a vulgar creeper, is now embossed with a multi-flora. In the angle of the yard next the house, and concealing with exquisite art an ugly indentation of the wall, is a moss-rose, Abéille's *chef d'œuvre*. This he has fed, watered, pruned, and in every way cherished, till it has surmounted the fence; and to-day I saw him gazing at a cluster of buds on the very summit, as a victor would have looked on his laurel-crown. At the extremity of the yard is a series of shelves arranged like the benches of an ampitheatre, (mark the economy of space and sunshine!) filled with pots containing the finest flowers of all seasons. The back windows are festooned, not screened—a Frenchman never blinds his windows—with honeysuckles, coquetting their way to two bird cages, where, embowered and perfumed, are perched canaries and mocking-birds, who enjoy here every sweet in nature but liberty, and the little servile rogues sing as if they had forgotten that; and to finish all, the few unoccupied feet of the '*petit paradis*,' just leaving space for Abéille

---

1 In the 1849 edition, Sedgwick clarifies this statement, replacing "the troubles" with "during the disastrous period of '92," the time following the April 1792 decree granting French citizenship to all property-owning free men of color, an act intended to gain the support of this population in suppressing the slave revolt, but which had the unintended consequence of further inflaming tensions between whites and people of color and leading to armed conflict between the groups and the departure of many white colonists and their families.

2 Flower bed.

to meander among the flowers, are set with medallions of carnations, tulips, hyacinths, and mignonette. I must not omit the tame crow, Abéille's esquire, who follows him like his shadow, and madame's pets and darlings, an enormous parrot, the most accomplished of his tribe—a Mathews among parrots[1]—and the largest and ugliest shock that ever lay in a Frenchwoman's lap. There sits madame, at this moment, coquetting with the parrot, scolding Belle, and taking snuff, her only occupations in life. 'Pauvre femme,' Abéille says, 'elle ne sait pas travailler—toutes les femmes de St. Domingue sont ainsi paresseuses, mais, elle est si bonne, si œconome, et si fidelle!'[2] 'Pauvre femme' indeed! Abéille looks at her through the vista of long past time, or he would not account the latter quality such a virtue. But if madame does not, her pretty daughters do know how to work. Felicité wrought herself into the heart of a youth, who in spite of her poverty, and in spite of the Yankee prejudice of all his kindred against a *French* girl, married her, and toiled hard to support her, when last week, like the gifts of a fairy tale, came a rich legacy to Felicité from Port-au-Prince, the bequest of a ci-devant[3] slave. Never were people happier. I see them now prettily grouped at their chamber-window, Felicité leaning on her husband's shoulder, and playing bopeep with her child, the child in the arms of her old maiden aunt 'Eli, who has forgotten to put on her false curls, even forgotten her matin mass[4] ever since this bantling came into the world. So easy is it, my dear Mrs. Layton, for the affections of your sex to revert to their natural and happiest channel.

"But the prettiest flower of my neighbor's garden, the genius loci of his *petit paradis*, is Angélique. She is much younger than her sister. From my observations from winter to summer for the last three years, I take it she is about the poetic age of seventeen.

"With all the facilities of my observatory, and the advantage of occasional explanatory notes from Abéille, I am extremely puzzled by Angélique. During the past winter, I used every evening to see her, the very soul of gaiety, at the little *réunions*[5] at her father's. Her sylph-like figure was always flitting over the floor. She danced with

---

1 Charles Mathews (English, 1776-1835), comic actor and theater manager, known for his mimicry and ventriloquism; he performed in the United States in 1822 and 1823.
2 'Poor woman' ... 'She doesn't know how to work—all the women from St. Domingue are thus lazy, but she is so good, so frugal, so faithful.'
3 Former.
4 Catholic morning mass.
5 Gatherings.

her father's old French friends, and frolicked with the children, the veriest romp and trickster among them. She would sew the skirts of pére[1] Baillé's coat to old 'Eli's gown; drop icicles under the boys' collars, and play off on all, young and old, her feats of fearless frolic. As the spring opened, I heard her sweet voice outsinging the birds, her light heart seemed instinctively to echo their joyous notes; and many a time have I thrown down my book, and involuntarily responded to her merry peals of laughter. Soon after this there was a sudden transition from the gay temper of the girl to the elaborate arts of the young lady. She dressed ambitiously, always with exquisite taste, as if she had studied her father's flowers for the harmony of colors, but with a restless vanity and expense that seemed the outbreaking of her West-India nature. A few weeks since she had the fever of sentiment upon her—would sit whole evenings by her window alone, and sang more plaintive ditties than I supposed there were in the French language. Now she sings nothing, gay or sad, but sits all day over her lace without raising her eyes. Her face is so pale and pensive that I fancy, even at this distance, I see the tears dropping on her work.

"Her father called me to the fence to-day to give me a carnation. I remarked to him, that mademoiselle was too constantly at her work. 'Yes,' he said, 'but she will work and she is so triste,[2] Monsieur Roscoe. Sacristie![3] we are all triste, when Angélique will not smile.' 'Ah! monsieur, mon cœur pleure.'[4] I felt a sort of shivering as if a storm were gathering over this sunny spot. Heaven grant that this little humble *paradis* may not be infested by evil spirits. Do not, my dear Mrs. Layton, give the reins to your feminine fancy. My interest in Angélique is all '*en philosophe,*' or if you please, '*en philanthropiste;*'[5] a little softer and deeper it may be, than 'Eli or even Felicité, or any less beautiful than Angélique could excite.

"I left my letter last evening and strolled down to the Battery. It should have been a moon-light night but the clouds had interposed, and the few loiterers that remained there chose the broad walk at the water's-side. I saw an acquaintance whom I was in no humor to join, and I retired to a more secluded walk, where I encountered a pair who had evidently gone there to avoid observers, for on seeing

---

1 Father, a title of respect for a Catholic priest.
2 Sad.
3 God forbid!
4 'Sir, my heart weeps.'
5 Purely philosophical; purely philanthropic.

me approach they turned abruptly and departed. Soon after, in going up Broadway, I met the same couple. They were just separating; the lady came towards me; she was shawled and veiled, but as I was passing her, her veil caught in the railing of an area and her face was exposed. It was, as I had conjectured, Angélique. I walked on without seeming to notice her, and I perceived that her attendant had turned and was hastily retracing his steps after her. I cast a scrutinizing glance at him, and though his hat was drawn close over his eyes, and he held his handkerchief to his face, I believed then, and still believe, he was *Pedrillo!* He has a certain gait and air that cannot be mistaken, and though he had not on the famous Spanish identifying cloak that you used to say was managed more gracefully than any other in Broadway, yet I am sure I am right in my conjecture. If I am, 'curse on his perjured arts!'"[1]

––––––––––––

"My dear Mrs. Layton:—My letter had swollen to such an unreasonable bulk that I threw it aside as not worth the postage. But some facts having come to my ear which have made me give unwilling credence to the possibility that you may be induced to favor Pedrillo's suit to Emilie, I have determined to communicate certain particulars to you, that I think will influence your opinion of this gentleman.

"The evening after the encounter with Pedrillo I have already mentioned, I was returning late to my lodgings—there should have been a waning moon to light the city, but the heavens were overcast, one of the possible vicisitudes of weather, which, (if we may judge from the economy of lamp oil,) is not anticipated by our corporation. The night was dark and drizzling. It was past one o'clock. I was musing on the profound stillness—what stillness is so eloquent as that of a populous city?—and in part confused by the darkness, I turned down White instead of Walker street. I did not perceive my mistake till I had made some progress, and then my attention was attracted by a carriage drawn up close to the flagging; the steps were down, the door open, and the coachman on his box. There was no light from the adjoining houses; no sound, no indication of any kind that a creature was awake there. I thought the poor devil of a coachman overwearied had fallen asleep on his box, and I stopped with the intention of waking him, when I heard three low notes whistled by some person a

––––––––––––

1   From Burns's "The Cotter's Saturday Night" (1785).

few doors in advance of me, and directly half the blind of a parlor window was opened, and by the faint light that penetrated the misty atmosphere, I perceived a man's figure before the window of *Abéille's* house. Imperfect and varying as the light was, I saw the person was addressing imploring and impatient gestures to some one within. My first impulse was that natural to a mind of common manliness and delicacy, to avoid any interference with the secret purposes of another, and I crossed the street, designing to pass immediately down on the other side. But as the purpose of this untimely visit flashed upon my mind, I felt that there was something cowardly in my retreat. It might be possible, even at this late moment to save the infirm Angélique (for I had truly divined the actors in the scene) from the power of the villain Pedrillo. I was fortified in my hope when I saw Angélique, in the act of putting her hat on her head, throw it from her, and cautiously raise the window-sash. She spoke to Pedrillo, but in so low a voice that I only caught a few words. Something she said of her mother being sick. That she faltered in her purpose of quitting the paternal roof was plain from Pedrillo's vehement gestures, and from the agony of indecision with which she paced the room, wringing her hands, and balancing, no doubt, the pleadings of honor and filial duty, against the passionate persuasions of her lover.

"I too thought of poor Abéille—the fond old father—of his '*petit paradis*,' and his cheerful and grateful enjoyment of the wreck of his splendid fortune, and of this his loveliest flower trampled in the dust. Images of the ruin and desolation that awaited the amiable Frenchman nerved my resolution, and the possibility that I might avert the instant danger, made my heart throb as if my own dearest treasure were in jeopardy. What, thought I, ought I to do? What can I do, to counteract one who has so far succeeded in his purposes?

"I may alarm the neighbors by my outcries, and rouse Abéille, but the wretch will escape with his prey, before he can be intercepted: or, at best, Angélique will be disgraced by the exposure of her intentions. Thus puzzled, I ceased to measure obstacles, dismissed all calculations, and just followed the impulse and guidance of my feelings. I advanced with cautious foot-steps towards Abéille's door-step. Pedrillo was already on it, and as yet unaware of my proximity.

"The light moved from the parlor, and flashed through the fanlight above the street-door. Angélique had then decided her fate. There was another pause in her movement. I was now so near to Pedrillo that I heard him breathe through his shut teeth, 'Ye furies! why does not she open the door?' and as if answering to his words, Angélique gave audible tokens of her decision. The bolts were slowly withdrawn, the door opened, and Pedrillo sprang forward to receive his prize, when with one arm I hurled him back. I know not how far he fell, nor where, I had no time to give him one glance; with my other arm I had grasped Angélique, and dragging her within the door, I instantly reclosed and rebolted it.

"I never shall forget, and I am sure I can never describe, Angélique's first look of terror, astonishment, and inquiry, and the overwhelming shame with which she dropped her head on her bosom, when she recognised me. Fortunately she did not speak. I listened intently for some indication of our baffled knight's intentions, at this unexpected turn in his affairs. I heard nothing till the sound of the retiring carriage-wheels proved that he had retreated. I then graced myself with an apology to Angélique. I am not sure that she was not, when her first surprise was over, a little vexed with my interference, but I was so fortunate as to give a better direction to her feelings, and without preaching about her duties, or dictating them, I set before her such a picture of her fond old father, that her tender heart returned to its loyalty to him, to duty, and to happiness, and shuddering at the precipice from which she had escaped, she most solemnly vowed for ever to renounce, and shun Pedrillo.

"That it is better to save than to destroy, no one will dispute. I believe it is easier—far easier to persuade the infirm to virtue than to vice. There is an unbroken chord in every human heart, that vibrates to the voice of truth. There is there an undying spark from the altar of God, that may be kindled to a flame by the breath of virtue. If we felt this truth more deeply, we should not be so reckless of the happiness of our fellow-beings, and so negligent of any means we may possess of cherishing and stimulating their virtue.

"I did not embarrass Angélique with my presence one moment after I was assured that her right resolution was fixed; but I hesitated whether to retire through Abéille's yard to my lodgings, or to go into the street, where Pedrillo might possibly still be lurking. I wished that, if possible, he should think Angélique had been rescued by some one who had a natural right to interpose in her behalf. But as I thought there was little chance of encountering him, and as I had knocked off my hat in entering the house, I withdrew that way in the hope of finding it. I did not; and I have since suspected that Pedrillo ascertained my name from it, for I have met him once since, and I thought his face flushed and his brow lowered as he passed me.

"Now, my dear Mrs. Layton, have I not by giving you a true account of the sober part I played in this little drama, proved to you my disbelief in the slander that claims the paramount favor of your sex for men *à bonnes fortunes?*[1] However, to confess the truth, my motive in the communication was quite foreign to myself; but I must indulge my egotism by relating my own part in the characteristic finishing of the tale. Old Abéille came to my room this morning with a note from Angélique. She informed me that her poor mother had just died; that she had bestowed 'such praise' on her when she gave her her last blessing. 'The praise,' she said, 'she had not deserved by her virtue, she would by her penitence, and she had fallen on her knees and confessed all to her mother; and her mother had then blessed her more fervently than ever, and blessed Monsieur Roscoe, both in one breath. And if the prayer of the dying was heard,' adds Angélique, 'no trouble nor sin will ever come nigh to Monsieur Roscoe, nor to any thing Monsieur loves.' Her note concludes with the information that she is going to the convent at Baltimore 'to pray to God and make penitence *for a little while.*' It was evident the old man had a burden on his heart that could only be relieved by words; but there are feelings of a nature and force to check the fluency even of a Frenchman; and Abéille was mute, save in the eloquence of tears. He took out his snuff-box, which serves him on all occasions as a link to mend the broken chain of his ideas; but now it would not do. I had not yet read Angélique's note, and I naturally referred his emotion to the death of his wife, to which I adverted in a tone of condolence. 'Ah, 'tis not that, Monsieur Roscoe,' he said, 'il faut mourir[2]—and my wife—pauvre femme!—was good to die. Certainement c'est un grand malheur;[3] but every body can speak of his wife's death—but, sacristié! when I think of *that*, my tongue will not move, though my heart is full of gratitude to you, Monsieur Roscoe. Ah, you have saved us all, et de quelle horreur!'[4] Here Abéille burst into a fresh flood of tears, and again had recourse to his snuff-box. I could no longer appear ignorant of his meaning. 'My good friend,' said I, 'I understand you perfectly; but this is not a subject to talk about. Let me only say to you, that Angélique was even more ready to spring from the toils than I

---

1 An *homme à bonne fortune* (a lucky or fortunate man) is one who is fortunate in obtaining the favors of women.

2 'One has to die.'

3 'Certainly, it's a great sadness.'

4 'And from such a horror!'

Ugh (at the situation where a girl's virginity is enough to ruin a family or be considered a horror worse than death)

was to extricate her.' 'Ah, Dieu soit béni—veritablement—elle est un ange.[1] Ah, Monsieur Roscoe, you have said that good word of ma petite pour m'encourager. Vous savez,' he continued, for now he had recovered all his volubility, 'vous savez quelle est belle—la reine de toutes mes fleurs—ah! n'est-ce pas, Monsieur—and she is always so douce et gaie—si gaie—toujours—toujours[2]—and now, Monsieur Roscoe, we must speak English; *that* always have a very plain meaning. My claim on my country is partly allowed, and I have received fifty thousand francs.[3] Now I do not want this money; I am very happy, and my poor girl shall have it all— ten thousand dollars—and when she has made her penitence you shall have her hand, Monsieur Roscoe, and all the money in it. Ah, do not speak—vous le méritez.'[4]

"I certainly was not prepared to reply to so unexpected an expression of Abéille's gratitude. However, I had frankness enough to say that marriage must be an affair of the heart entirely. 'You,' I said, 'my friend Abéille, cannot answer for Angélique at the end of a twelvemonth, nor can I foresee in what disposition I shall then find myself.' 'Ah but,' interrupted Abéille, 'we will shorten Angélique's retirement to a few weeks—elle est si jeune,—il ne faut pas penser et prier Dieu[5] too long.' I was driven to an evasion; for I have too much chivalry interwoven in the very web of my nature to reject a 'fair ladye' in plain terms, and I said, scarcely controlling a smile at the resemblance of my reply to the formula of a docile miss, at her first offer; I said that my mother felt on these subjects quite '*en Américaine*,'[6]—that she had her prejudices, and I feared it would break her heart if I married any other than one of my own countrywomen, and therefore I must not admit the thought of aspiring to the hand of Mademoiselle Angélique.

---

1 'Ah, God be blessed—truly—she is an angel.'
2 'Ah, Mr. Roscoe, you have said that good word of my little girl to encourage me. You know,' ... 'you know that she is beautiful—the queen of all my flowers—ah! isn't it true, Sir—and she is always so sweet and gay—so gay—always—always.'
3 On 17 April 1825, King Charles X of France issued an Ordinance recognizing Haitian independence in return for Haiti's payment to France of monies to be distributed to planters who lost property in the slave rebellion and revolution. Abéille, a former plantation owner, has filed a claim with French authorities for reparations and received partial payment on the claim.
4 'You deserve it.'
5 'She is so young—one must not think and to pray to God too long.'
6 As an American.

"'Est-il possible,' cried Abéille, 'q'une femme raisonnable, peut être capable de telles sottises, pauvre garçon!'[1] This was spoken in a tone of deep commiseration. 'I pray the *bon Dieu* will reward your filial piety; but where will madame find une Américaine comparable à mon Angélique? Toujours, toujours you shall be mon fils, if you cannot be the mari of my belle Angélique. Eh bien!—chacun à son goût—mais, une Américaine préférable à mon Angélique!'[2] The old man took a double pinch of snuff. 'Adieu, Monsieur Roscoe; you will come to the cathédrale to hear the miserére[3] chanted for poor Madame Abéille.' I assured him I would do so, and thereupon we parted.

"My dear Mrs. Layton, allow me the happiness of soon hearing from your own lips, or your own pen, that Señor Pedrillo's suit has met its merited fate.

"And in the meantime, believe me, as ever,

"Your devoted friend and servant,

"GERALD ROSCOE."

Roscoe was right in his conjecture that Pedrillo had ascertained who had intercepted his success. When he rose from the prostrate position in the middle of the street where Roscoe had thrown him, he stumbled over a hat. He perceived that the noise at Abéille's door had attracted the observation of one of the guardians of the night, and he thought proper to retreat. He took the hat with him, and when he exposed it to the light, he found within it the name that of all others was most likely to give a keen edge to his resentment. He had met Roscoe often at Mrs. Layton's, and had had some corroding suspicions that Emilie's indifference to his addresses proceeded from preference to Roscoe. He tore off the name, and threw the hat into the street, saying as he did so, "I have found out the *object*, and I will make the *opportunity* of revenge."

It must be confessed there is a charm to our republican society, in a foreign name and aristocratic pretensions, like the fascinations of a fairy tale to children. Our tastes are yet governed by ancient *préstiges*—cast in the old mould. We profess the generous principle that each individual has a right to his own eminence,

---

1 'Is it possible ... that a reasonable woman could be capable of such nonsense, poor boy!'

2 'but where will madame find an American girl comparable to my Angélique? Always, always you shall be my son if you cannot be the husband of my beautiful Angélique. And so—to each his own—but an American girl preferred over my Angélique!'

3 Part of the Office of the Dead (Catholic), the funeral rites.

whether his sires commanded the heights, or drudged obscurely in the humblest vale of life; but artificial distinctions still influence our imaginations, and the spell has not been dissolved by the repeated detection of the pretensions of impostors with foreign manners, and high-sounding titles who have obtained the entrée[1] of our fashionable circles.[2]

Henriques Pedrillo had far more plausible claims to favor than certain other vagrant foreigners who have played among us too absurd and notorious a part to be yet forgotten. He had in the first place 'nature's aristocracy,' a person and face of uncommon symmetry and elegance, and these advantages he cherished and set off with consummate art, steering a middle course between coxcombry and negligence, the Scylla and Charybdis[3] of the gentleman's toilette. His conversation did not indicate any more erudition than he might have imbibed at the playhouse, and by a moderate intercourse with cultivated society. He spoke English, French, and Spanish equally well; and so well as to leave his hearer in doubt which was his vernacular; and he had the insinuating address—the devotion of look and manner, in his intercourse with ladies, that marks the exotic in America. In common with most Spaniards who come among us, he cast his nativity in old Castile, though he confessed he had been driven to the new world to repair the abated fortunes of his ancient family. He was not precise in communicating the particulars of his career; but the grand circumstance of success, if it did not extinguish curiosity, at least repressed its expression. He had been recently known to some of our first merchants, as the principal in a rich house in the Havana. This was enough to satisfy the slight scrupulosity Jasper Layton

---

1 Admittance.
2 Sedgwick's note added in the 1849 edition: Among the more serious changes that nineteen years have made in our society, certain follies of fashionable life have been undergoing the process of evaporation. In the drawing-rooms of '49, we find a far more rational estimate of the relative claims of our own citizens, and foreign pretenders, than existed in 1830. We believe it would be difficult now for a soi-disant [so-called] noble to play off the impostures upon the credulity of our fashionable world that were not uncommon a quarter of a century since. The revolutions of Europe have let in much light, and the most ignorant and benighted are beginning to comprehend the dignity and happiness of the citizenship of our republic.
3 Respectively, the rock and whirlpool off the Italian coast, used figuratively to indicate serious danger (such as shipwreck) even as one is trying to avoid it.

might have felt in introducing him to his wife and daughter. Mrs. Layton at first courted Pedrillo merely as a brilliant acquisition to her *coterie*.[1] She confessed she had no affinities for American character—tame, unexcitable, and unadorned as she deemed it. She spoke French and Spanish remarkably well, and the desire to demonstrate these accomplishments did not betray a very culpable vanity. She first sedulously cultivated Pedrillo's acquaintance; 'Eve did first eat;' but Mrs. Layton, no more than our first mother, foresaw the fatal consequences of what appeared a trivial act. Their relations soon became interesting and complicated. Pedrillo was captivated by Emilie's pre-eminent beauty. Her innocence and sweetness touched all that remained of unextinguished goodness in his nature. The evil spirits look back with lingering affection to the heaven they have forfeited.

Layton, a man of lavish expense, found Pedrillo a most convenient friend. Pedrillo was profuse, but not careless. He had the acute habits of a man of business, and even in his pleasures he nicely balanced the amount he gave against the consideration he expected to receive. When, therefore, he from time to time, lent Jasper Layton large sums of money, he gloried in the secret consciousness of the power he was accumulating. Their intimacy grew till Layton gave him the last proof of his confidence and good fellowship, by introducing him to a club of gentlemen who met privately every night at a gambling-house, and indulged there to great excess this keen and destructive passion.

Pedrillo had acquired in scenes of stirring excitement and imminent peril, such command over his turbulent passions, that to the eye of an observer the fire that was merely covered, seemed extinguished. So at least it appeared to Layton, when after a night of various fortune and feverish excitement, they emerged from their club-room, just as the city lamps were dimmed by the approaching day. "Pedrillo, my dear fellow," said Layton, "you are a philosopher: you win and lose with equal nonchalance—I—I confess it—I am giddy with my unexpected luck."

"*Unexpected?*" replied Pedrillo.

"Yes, unhoped for; Pedrillo, I will tell you a secret. When I entered that room to-night I was utterly ruined."

"A secret!—ha! ha!"

"A secret—yes, *you* might have guessed it, for God knows you were deeply concerned in it—but all scores are wiped out now, hey, Pedrillo? That last bragger cleared off the last five

---

1 Inner circle of intimates.

thousand—and my loss to that devilish fellow Martin, that is balanced too; thank Heaven I am my own man again; a timely whirl of the wheel it was. Fortune, blind goddess as thou art, I still will worship thee!"

"Do we visit her temple to-morrow night?"

"Certainly."

"*Au revoir*, then." They parted; Layton went one way, intoxicated with success, humming glees and catches, now twisting his cane around his fingers, now striking it on the pavement, and even attracting the eye of the drowsy watchmen by his irregular movements. His spirits would have fled if he had penetrated Pedrillo's bosom, and seen the keen, vigilant suspicion he had awakened there.

The next night they met again at the gaming-table. Fortune maintained her perch on Layton's cards; Pedrillo lost large sums. Again they left the house together. Pedrillo appeared even more unmoved than he had on the preceding night. He congratulated Layton with as much seeming unconcern as if the subject in question were a mercantile speculation in which he had no personal concern. Layton was in ecstacies—"You may defy the world, Pedrillo!" he said in a tone of the highest good humor, "and all its turns, tricks, and shufflings. Those poor devils we have left behind us are ready to cut their own throats, or mine. Zounds! my dear fellow, you are high-souled and whole-souled—"

"Have you heard from Miss Emilie, to-day?" asked Pedrillo, rather abruptly interrupting his companion's strain of lavish compliment.

"Yes."

"Does she permit me to follow her?"

Layton's elated tone was changed to one more conciliatory, as he replied, "Why, to tell you the truth, Pedrillo, she seems disinclined; and on the whole we may as well consider the affair as ended."

"*When* did you come to that conclusion, sir?"

"When? what difference does that make, if it be a wise conclusion?"

"Do we meet to-morrow night?"

"As you please; after my run of luck it does not become me to propose it."

"We meet then; and *after* we will speak of Miss Emilie."

"*Eh bien*; but of course Pedrillo, you understand that I shall never consent to put any force on her inclinations."

"You shall do as you choose"—and he added mentally, "you shall *choose* it, Jasper Layton, as surely as a man chooses life rather than death."

The next evening found them at their accustomed haunt. After Pedrillo and Layton had played one game, Pedrillo threw up the cards, alleging a pain and dizziness in his head. Another took his place. He continued to stride up and down the room, sometimes pausing beside Layton, and always keeping his eye fixed on him. Layton had a dim consciousness, as some sensitive persons have in their sleep, of a steady gaze, and once or twice he looked up, startled and inquiring, but instantly his attention reverted to the portentous interests of the game. From time to time angry and half-smothered exclamations broke from his companions, at his obstinate luck; still they continued with fatal desperation to wager and lose, and when the play was finished, they had lost, and Layton had won all. Accustomed as they were to sudden and violent fluctuations of fortune, their continued losses on the present occasion had exhausted their patience, and deprived them of the power of quelling the expression of their excited passions. Despair, madness, and worse than all, suspicion, burst forth in loud imprecations, or in half audible murmurs. Layton's cheek burnt, and his hand trembled, with triumph, or resentment, or consciousness, but he uttered not one word; and when, as they left the apartment, he, as usual, thrust his arm into Pedrillo's, Pedrillo withdrew from him, and fixed on him a cold penetrating glance that thrilled through his soul. He involuntarily shivered—they emerged from the long dark passage, that led from their secret haunt to the street, into a damp, hot, steaming atmosphere. "A singular morning for agues!" said Pedrillo, looking contemptuously at Layton, while he took off his own hat and fanned himself, as if to stir some living principle in the suffocating air. Layton turned his eye timidly to Pedrillo; their glances met—a keen intelligence, a malignant triumph, and pitiless contempt, spoke in Pedrillo's; the shame, and fear, and misery of detected villany, in Layton's. They walked on in silence to the head of the street, where, instead of parting as usual, Pedrillo drew nearer to Layton, took his arm, and went on with him. "A word to the wise," he said, in a low thrilling voice, "a word to the wise, for wise I think you will be after this folly—the ass should not attempt a cheat in the presence of the fox, Layton. I suspected your trick the first night—the second my suspicions were confirmed—to-night I have detected you. Let this pass. You have been rash—imprudent in your practice, my good friend; you should have calculated more nicely the chances of detection. Other suspicions than mine are awakened, but there is an immeasurable distance between suspicion and certainty, and we may continue to widen that distance; that is, if," and as he finished his sentence, every word seemed measured and weighed, and sunk like lead into Layton's heart,—"if in future we are friends?"

The tone was interrogative, and Layton replied gaspingly, "certainly, certainly."

"Well, very well; we understand each other, do we not?"

"Yes, yes, perfectly."

"Then let that pass—'Il ne faut pas être plus sage qu'il ne faut'[1]—details are disagreeable and you are sure, quite sure there is a clear mutual comprehension?"

Layton felt at every word as if a new manacle were rivetted on him. Still, safety on any terms, were better than destruction, and while he writhed under the power, he dared not resist; "Proceed," he cried, "for God's sake—you know I understand you."

"Then, Layton," he resumed in a familiar, everyday tone of voice, "my lips are sealed—as to the few thousands you have won from me, retain them, as a consideration in part for the treasure you ensure me—*ensure* me, mark my words; and, Layton, if in future you get becalmed, do not attempt to raise the wind by such desperate expedients. There are a few situations in life where honesty *is* the best policy, and the gaming table is one of them. But before we part, let us settle our plan of action. Suspicion is awake, go again to-morrow night, and lose your winnings liberally! this will baffle their sagacity, and what is more, appease their resentment. Do you like my counsel?"

"I will take it."

"Good night then, or rather good morning, for I think the sun is glimmering through the scalding fog." They parted, and Layton sprang on his own door-step, as a newly captured slave would dart from the presence of his master. "One word," said Pedrillo, turning back, "you write to Miss Emilie to-morrow?"

"Yes, yes, I will communicate my determination to her."

"Oh! 'of course,'" replied Pedrillo, with a 'laughing devil in his eye,' and quoting Layton's last words of the preceding evening, "'of course you will put no force on her inclinations.'" An oath

---

1 One must not be wiser than necessary. Adapted from "Ce n'est pas être sage qu'être plus sage qu'il ne faut." / "It is not wise to be wiser than one has to be." Philippe Quinault (French, 1635-88), dramatist and librettist. "It is not wise to be wiser than one has to be."

rose to Layton's lips, but he suppressed all expression till secure from observation in his own room, he gave vent to a burst of passion; but resentment, remorse, and parental tenderness, were now alike unavailing. He was inextricably involved with Pedrillo, and his own safety could only be secured by the sacrifice of his beautiful child. Jasper Layton was the only son of a man of talent, virtue, and fortune, and he never quite lost the sense of the responsibility such an inheritance involved; and to the last, the fear of publicly disgracing his honorable name, was a source of the keenest suffering to him. Unfortunately he came into possession, by his father's death, of a large fortune, before he had sufficient strength of principle, or habit, to encounter its temptations. He was not destitute of kind, or even tender affections; but what good thing thrives without culture? and frivolous pursuits and selfish indulgences had rendered his callous. Still, they had not perished, and it was after many heart-writhings, and after a long interview with Pedrillo on the subsequent morning, that he wrote the following letter to his wife—to a wife who, if she had rightly employed her superior powers, might have saved him from the wreck of virtue and happiness.

"Madam—I enclose you a remittance, according to the *conjugal* request you did me the honor to transmit through Gerald Roscoe, Esq.; and at the same time, I take the liberty to forewarn you, that unless you second—energetically second, my views and wishes in the ———— affair, I shall lose the ability, as I have long ago lost the inclination, to answer the demands arising from your habits of reckless expense. I expect you to be at Trenton by the first of next month. Pedrillo will follow you there; and there, or at Utica (he leaves all minor points to her decision) he expects to receive Emilie's hand. He loves Emilie—upon my soul I believe he does—devotedly.

"God knows I have taken every care of her happiness in my arrangements with P————. He has made a magnificent settlement on her, and promises never, but with her consent, to take her to Cuba. Do not moralize (it is not your forte) about P.'s foibles. I know the world; we must take our choice between unmasked frailty, and hypocrisy. I, for one, prefer the former. P.'s liberality covers a multitude of sins. Women *must* be married. Emilie, poor girl, will not it is true, marry for love; but *we* married for love! and what has come of it? ha! ha! It is well enough for boys and girls to dream about, and novelists to string their stories on; but you and I know it is all cursed dupery. All that can be *secured* in matrimonial life is pecuniary independence. To this I have attended with parental fidelity.

"You must do your part; your influence over E. is unbounded; and if you choose to exercise it, you can *incline* her (force is of course out of the question) to do that, on which, let me tell you, madam, your as well as my happiness—happiness! existence depends. We are ruined, *dishonored*, if this affair is not brought to a fortunate conclusion. I tell you this because it is necessary you should know the worst, to second me as you should; but make no unessential communications to poor E. God preserve that cheek from shame that has never been dyed but with the pure blush of innocence.

"Do your part, I beseech you, and do it well, and effectually; you *can* act like a woman of sense. But I am urging where I should command. Remember you have other children, and will have future wants. Can you look poverty and disgrace in the face? If not, you know the alternative.

"Yours, &c.

"JASPER LAYTON."

While the episode in Pedrillo's life related in Roscoe's letter, and the transactions of the gaming-house were passing in New York, Gertrude Clarence was enjoying an almost daily interchange of visits with her new friends, and an acquaintance that promised nothing but happiness was ripening into intimacy. Mrs. Layton found herself compelled by the receipt of her husband's letter, suddenly to suspend this intercourse, and she despatched the following note to Gertrude, in which, as will be seen, she did not hint at the place of her destination after she left Upton's-purchase. She had her reasons for this reserve. She feared that Mrs. Upton would propose to accompany her, as a ride to Trenton from her residence was a convenient and tempting jaunt of pleasure; and she meant that her going there should appear to have been the consequence of a subsequent arrangement.

"It is with inexpressible sorrow, my sweetest friend, that I am compelled to bid you adieu without again seeing you. We take our departure early in the morning. Poor Em' is quite heartbroken about it. We are both under the tyranny of destiny. I resign all to the despot, save my affections; and of those, you, dearest, have taken complete possession. It is not because you are a heroine of the nineteenth century; that is, practical, rational, dutiful, and all the tedious *et ceteras* that I admire you. No, these are qualities that, natural hierarchy

Common as working
class / common as
not average

like bread and water, are the gross elements of every day life, but
they have nothing to do with that fine accord of finely touched
spirits that common minds can no more attain than common
senses can take in the music of the spheres.[1] There is no describing it, but we understand it; do we not? Dear Gertrude, you must
be my friend, you must love me; you will have much to forgive
in me. I am a wayward creature. Oh, heavens! how inferior to
you! but there have been crosses in my destiny. Had I known you
sooner, your bland influence would have given a different color
to my life. You understand me. I disdain the Procrustes standard
of pattern ladies who admit none to the heaven of their favor, but
those who can walk on a mathematical line, like that along which
a Mahometan passes to his paradise.[2]

"My best regards to your father. I wish he could have looked
into my heart and seen how I was charmed with his manners to
you; the chivalric tenderness of the lover mingling with the calm
sentiment of the father. Would that poor Em' had ——— but on
certain subjects unhappy woman is forbidden to speak. To you,
my loveliest friend, a husband would be a superfluity—at present.
But to poor Em' how necessary. You *must* come to us this winter.
I shall make a formal attack on your father to that effect. I shall
bring out all the arts of diplomacy; but I shall need no arts. I have
good sense on my side, and 'good sense' is the oracle of every
man past forty. Clarenceville is, I allow, in the summer, a most
delicious residence, the favored haunt, the home of the genius
of mountain and lake; but in winter, when the grass withers, the
leaves fall, the running stream runs no longer, and the winds are
howling through these sublime forests, (a nervous sound of a dark
day or cloudy night,) then come to the luxuries of civilization in
town. Man was not made to contend alone with nature; and, with
honest Touchstone, I confess that the country in respect 'it is in
the green fields, is pleasant; but (at all seasons) in respect it's far
from court, it is tedious.'[3] But pardon me, I had forgotten this

---

1 Attributed to Pythagoras, the theory of the "music of the spheres" is the
 perfect harmonic interval or ratio, also an expression of the harmony
 or correspondences among music, the physical world, and the spiritual
 world.

2 A Procrustes standard is arbitrary, serving only to create conformity. In
 Greek mythology, Procrustes, a son of Poseidon, tortured his victims by
 stretching them, or cutting off their limbs, so that they would fit into his
 iron bed. A Mahometan is a Muslim, a follower of Mohammed.

3 Touchstone, a professional court clown and skeptic of the virtues of
 country life in Shakespeare's *As You Like It* says of the shepherd's life:

was a note. One is so beguiled into forgetfulness of every thing else when communing with you, dearest! Emilie begs me to say farewell for her."

Here followed half a dozen lines so carefully effaced, that the keenest curiosity could not discover a word. The note proceeded:

"These crossed lines prove how involuntarily my heart flows out to you—how unwillingly it bears the cold restraint of prudence; but, after a few days, such restrictions will be unnecessary. Till then, believe me, dear Gertrude,

"Yours, most truly,

"GRACE LAYTON.

"N. B. My mind was so engaged with matters of deeper interest that I forgot to mention the total wreck of poor Upton's expectations of making a family piece in an English book. She has exhausted her hospitalities on this son of an English baronet, in the hope of seeing herself, and the Judge, and all the little Uptons in print, when lo! she has found this morning, in the course of one of her housewife explorations, a leaf from the traveller's note-book. I can stop to give you but a few specimens from the memorandum. I am vexed at the fellow's impertinence towards you; but you are a *femme raisonnable*,[1] and know that fortune must be thus taxed. 'Mem. Upton's-purchase, residence of a country justice—convenient vicinity to some celebrated lake-scenery—staid here on that account. American scenery quite savage—Justice U. an abyss of ignorance—wife, a mighty vulgar little person—children, pests—no *servants*—two *helps*. Dined at Clarenceville. The C.s great people in America—giants in Lilliput!—Amer'n table barbarisms—porter and salad with meats! peas with currie!—no poultry—no butcher's meat. Query, do the inferior animals as well as man uniformly degenerate, and become scarce in America? Miss C. an only daughter—a prodigious fortune—pretty good air too—do very well *caught young*—but can't go again. Devilish pretty girl here—mother a knowing one.' You see, dear Gertrude, we have all a part in these precious notes. Poor little Upton half cried as she read them. We are philosophers and may laugh. Again, and at each moment more tenderly,

"Yours, G. L.

"Now, in respect it is in the fields, it pleaseth me well; but in respect it is not in the court, it is tedious" (III.ii.17-18).

1 Reasonable or sensible woman.

"One more nota bene and I have done. I have just received a folio[1] from Gerald Roscoe—Oh! what a lover he will be! how I could have loved such a man! Who is it that says (too truly!) that 'la puissance d'aimer est trop grande, elle l'est trop dans les ames ardentes!'[2]

"Farewell, dearest,

"G. L."

Gertrude wondered that Mrs. Layton should be so reserved about Emilie's affairs, when she manifested such singular confidence, and unbounded tenderness; for measuring her new friend by her own purity and truth, she gave full credit to all her expressions. Contrasted with the simple regard and unexaggerated language of Gertrude's common acquaintance, they were like the luscious fruits of the tropics, compared with our cold northern productions.

But she had now no time to analyze her fascinating friend. The jaunt to Trenton, to which her father had at once consented, on Seton's account had been delayed from day to day, for two weeks, from the daily occurrence of the rural affairs of midsummer, that seem to country gentlemen, of the first importance. In the mean while, Seton was becoming worse. The family physician, announced the approach of a nervous fever, that could only be averted by change of air; and Mr. Clarence put aside every other concern; and, on the very day of Mrs. Layton's departure, he set off with Gertrude and Seton, and servants competent to the care of the invalid, in case he failed to derive the benefit they hoped, from the journey. Mr. Clarence was usually particularly annoyed by the discomforts of travelling; his philosophy completely subdued by bad roads, bad coffee, bad bread, and worst and chiefest of all plagues, by the piratical 'red rovers' that 'murder sleep;'[3] but his benevolence now got the better of the habits generated by ill health and indulgence—he thought, and cared only for Seton.

If the unhappy patient's malady had been within the reach of art, it must have been subdued by Gertrude's ministrations; for with that exquisite sensibility, which vibrates to every motion of

---

1 Collection of papers, letters.
2 'The power to love is too great, and it is all too common in passionate souls.' De Staël, *Corrine*.
3 Reference to *The Red Rover* (1827), a romance that also incorporates piracy and mistaken/disguised identities, by Sedgwick's contemporary, James Fenimore Cooper (American, 1789-1851).

another's spirit, she watched all the variations of his mind, and imparted or withheld the sunshine of her own, as best suited his humor; but, in spite of skill and patience, and sisterly vigilance, the nervous fever predicted by the physician made hourly encroachments; and the necessity of a few hours' delay at one of the noisiest inns of that noisiest of all *growing* towns, thronged busy Utica, exasperated the disease to an alarming degree.

As may be supposed, Mr. Clarence had not come to the most public hotel of a town, abounding in every species and grade of receptacle for travellers, till he had unsuccessfully applied for admittance to the other more private, but now overflowing houses.

The travellers, on alighting, were shown into the common receiving parlor, a large apartment opening into the public hall, and near the general entrance door. Mr. Clarence, after vainly attempting to obtain audience of the official departments of the house, and after a fruitless quest for some private and unoccupied apartment, was compelled to content himself with securing the exclusive possession of a settee, which had the advantage of a position removed as far as the dimensions of the apartment admitted, from either of the general passage doors, through which the full tide of human existence ebbed and flowed. Here, he, Gertrude, and Seton, seated themselves; and here they might for a little time, but for poor Seton, have been well enough amused with the contrast to the seclusion, quiet, and elegance of their home.

The front windows of the apartment looked into the most public, and *par excellence* the busiest street of the town, the avenue to the great northern turn-pike. Stage-coaches were waiting, arriving, departing, driving to and fro, as if all the world were a stage-coach, and all the men and women merely travellers.[1]

The 'window privilege' (as our New-England friends would say) at the side of the room, was no way inferior to that in front. This afforded a view of the canal, and of the general debouching place of its packet-boats—all elements are here tributary to the *forwarding* system.

There were servants and porters hustling baggage off and on the boats—stage-coach proprietors persecuting the jaded passengers with rival claims to patronage—agents clothed in official importance—idlers, for even here are idlers, and all 'as their tempers

---

1 Adaptation of lines from Shakespeare's *As You Like It* II.vii.138-39 ("All the world's a stage, / And all the men and women merely players."), suggesting the theatricality of the scene and the various roles assumed by the travelers.

were,' muttering, sneering, scolding, joking, laughing, or silently submitting to their fate. The way-worn, weary travellers, as they poured into the hotel, seemed the victims, instead of the authors, of this hurly-burly.

A female, with a highly decorated pongee riding-dress, gaudy ear-rings, a watch at her side, with half a dozen seals, and a gold safety chain, as big as a cable around her neck—in short, with the aspect of a half gentlewoman, seated herself beside Miss Clarence, and very unceremoniously began a conversation with her. "Are you going on in the pioneer line, Ma'am?" "No." "Oh, in the telegraph—so are we, it is much more select; but I tell my husband, that all the stages are too levelling to suit me"—a pause ensued, and soon after the lady beckoned to her husband. "My dear, who is that foreign looking gentleman, that says he is going on in the pioneer-line?" "The Duke of Monte-Bello!"[1] The lady looked all aghast at the untimely discovery, that levels might be raised as well as lowered in a stage-coach.

The only apparently perfectly cool member of this bustling community, was a ruddy-faced, tight-built, active, little man, not far declined from his meridian, who was walking in and out, and up and down the room, addressing the individuals of this motley crowd, with the easy air of a citizen of the world. He approached Mr. Clarence, and by way of an introductory salutation observed, that it was a 'warmish day.' The mercury stood at ninety, and Mr. Clarence's blood at fever heat.

"Intensely hot," he replied, without turning his head or moving his eye from the ark-like boats, which were gliding under the bridge that crossed the canal.

"A pretty sight that!" continued the good-natured man, "especially, to one, who, like myself, has travelled through this town many and many a day, in fair weather and foul, with the mail on my back."

"You, my friend, you do not look older than myself!"

"I think I have some dozen years the advantage of you, sir; but I have led a stirring kind of a life, and kept my blood warm, and courage up. Yes, sir, just where the grand *canaul* goes, I used to whistle along a foot-path; and here, where the folks are now as thick as blades of grass in June, stood my log-house; and my wife, and four flax-headed little boys, were all the inhabitants. I love to

---

1   The Pioneer Line and the Telegraph Line were stagecoaches. The Duke of Montebello is Jean Lannes (French, 1769-1809), a general in Napoleon's army.

look back upon those times, though I have now seventy drivers in my employ; but we grow with the country, and get to be gentlemen before we know it; excuse me, sir, my coaches are getting under way."

A fresh bustle now broke out; Babel was nothing to it; for no post-coaches stood at its devoted doors. "Hurra for the western passengers!" "Gentlemen and ladies for Sacket's harbor—all ready!" "Hurra for Trenton!" "Pioneer line—ready!" "Gentlemen and ladies for the Telegraph!" "The bell is ringing for the Adams boat—going out!" "Horn blowing for the Jackson[1]—coming in."

Where was poor Seton, and his nerves, in this *mélée*.[2] "It will certainly kill him," thought Gertrude, and calling to a black fellow, who was hurrying hither and thither, as if he were the ruling spirit of the scene; "my good friend," she said, imploringly, "cannot you get a private room, for that sick gentleman?"

Blackey[3] grinned from ear to ear; "Missess can't suspect a private room in a public-house."

Happily, his reply, half impudent, and half simple, caught the ear of our friend, the some-time mail-bearer; who ordered the servant, instantly, to find private apartments, and accompanied his command with such demonstrations of his having 'come to be a gentleman,' as none may give, in our country, but those who have *worked* their passage to that elevation; and none will receive, but those, whose color stamps their subordination. When blackey had recovered from the impetus, that had hurled him from one extremity of the room to the other, his chastiser ordered him to show the lady to the square-room; and said, he would himself conduct the gentlemen to the best apartments the house afforded. Most gratefully did they all follow, blessing the timely interposition of the bustling little man in authority.

Miss Clarence took possession of her apartment, opened the sashes, closed the blinds, and was just throwing herself upon the bed, when, a horribly scrawled half-sheet of paper, caught her eye. She picked it up, and taking it for granted, that it was some discarded scrawl, and without once doubting, whether it were proper to read it, and having nothing else to do, she began it; and once begun, it was read, and re-read. There was no address, no signature; it was not folded, or finished. It ran thus:

---

1 US Presidents John Quincy Adams and Andrew Jackson.

2 Crowd.

3 In the 1849 edition, Sedgwick replaces "Blackey" with "The servant" and, in the next paragraph, with "the man." *thank god*

"You will be surprised at this addenda to the folio I have just despatched; if, indeed, you can decipher it, written, as it must be, with a bar-room pen, and diluted ink. Since I put that in the P. Office, I have had positive information—there is no longer any doubt remaining. The poor girl is passive, and P. is to follow them to Trenton. What horrible infatuation! You may think me as infatuated to hope to prevent it; but I cannot look on, and see a creature so young, so innocent, and so lovely, on the brink of a precipice, and not stretch out my arm to rescue her from destruction. I will communicate the terrible suspicions that are abroad; if my efforts are abortive, why, I shall have made them, and that will be some consolation. I think if I see ——, I can dissipate her delusion; if, indeed, it be delusion; but if, as I rather think, it is a timid submission to tyranny, I shall try to rouse her courage to rebellion. This crusade, of course, prevents my paying my respects at Clarenceville; I understand there are troops of pilgrims to that shrine. Let them bow before the golden idol—I reserve my worship, for the image to be set up in my heart. Report says that Miss C——"

Here the letter had been interrupted, and as Gertrude hoped, unintentionally left, for she could not believe that a person who could indite a decent epistle would expose such allusions to public inspection. 'Who could have written it?' She ran over the whole catalogue of her own, and her father's acquaintance. Not one appeared as the probable writer. She thought of Gerald Roscoe, but she was familiar with his autograph, and, 'thank Heaven, it was not he,' she ejaculated audibly, and smiled involuntarily at the sensation of escape she derived from this assurance. 'Why was it she had rather it had been any other man living than Gerald Roscoe?' Before she had given this self-interogation fair hearing, and while she was folding the manuscript with the intention of showing it to her father, she heard a tap at the door, and the voice of the negroservant, saying, 'Won't missess please to hand me a written letter, lying on the table under a handkerchief, and won't missess please to keep the handkerchief tight over it, *case* the gentleman's very *pa'tic'lar* not to have me, nor nobody read it."

She looked around the room, saw a cambric handkerchief, not far from the place where she had found the letter, and scrupulously covered it; but she did not transfer it to the servant till (as every woman will believe) she had vainly investigated every corner for a mark. She was gratified with this indirect assurance that the exposure of the letter had been accidental and limited to herself, and probably owing to the draft of wind occasioned by her throwing open the window when she entered the apartment.

But what could console the high-minded Gertrude Clarence for the conviction that continually pressed on her from every quarter, and in every form, that the accident of fortune, a distinction that she had never sought, and never valued, exposed her to slights and ridicule; to be dreaded and avoided by one class, courted and flattered by another. She thought of Seton, and it cannot be questioned that she felt a glow of satisfaction that she had excited one pure, disinterested sentiment; and a secret regret that affection was in its nature so independent and inflexible, that, though she would, she could not love him who so well deserved her love. Then came the bitterest reflection of all; her fortune had envenomed the shaft that wounded Seton's peace.

What would become of envy and covetousness, and all their train of discontent, evil, and sin, if the external veil were lifted, and the eye could penetrate the secrets of the heart?

Miss Clarence was roused from a long reverie to which we have merely given the clue, by a notice that Mr. Seton was so much refreshed as to be able to proceed on his journey.

Nothing can be more beautiful, more soothing and refreshing, than the coming on of evening after the fierce heat of one of our midsummer days. It is a compensation for the languor and exhaustion of mid-day—or rather it is the best preparation for the full and exquisite enjoyment of the delicious coolness, the deepening shadows, and the fragrance that exhales from woods, flowers, and fields. A summer's evening in the country is a paradise regained; but, alas! evil spirits could leap the bounds of paradise; and melancholy interposed her black pall between poor Seton and the outward world. In vain did Gertrude point out the rich hills and valleys of Oneida—the almost boundless view of a country so recently redeemed from savages and savage wildness, and now rich, populous, and cultivated. He scarcely raised his heavy eyelids; and his faint and irrelevant replies indicated that his brain was already touched by his disease.

All other interest was now lost in anxiety to reach Trenton; and after as rapid a drive, as roads, at their best indifferent, would permit, they arrived at the 'rural resort,' the neat inn in the vicinity of the falls.[1] Fortunately there were no visiters there at the moment

---

1   The Rural Resort in Trenton Falls was established in 1822 by John
    Sherman, a Unitarian minister who began residing in the area in 1806.
    Overnight guests were first accommodated in 1825.

of our travellers' arrival, and they had an opportunity of selecting their apartments, and for Seton, the most retired and commodious one the house afforded, to which he was borne in the arms of his attendants.

The consciousness of sacrificing one's private inclinations and comforts for the good of another is always pleasant to a benevolent mind; and Mr. Clarence, whom nothing but an errand of kindness would have tempted from his home to a gathering-place, was in unexpected good spirits. He already 'felt quite renewed by his journey.' 'Gertrude looked better than he had seen her for six months.' 'He was sure Louis wanted nothing but a little rest.' He was delighted with the deep retirement and *ruralities* of the situation, and 'charmed with the neatness, civility, and quiet of the house.' The last quality was not of long duration. One or two stage-coaches arrived, and the consequent and inevitable bustle ensued. The guests were judiciously disposed in a part of the house as remote as possible from that occupied by Mr. Clarence; and Gertrude passed the evening in her father's apartment, reading aloud to him, according to her usual custom. The lecture was of course interrupted by Mr. Clarence's frequent visits to Seton's room. His mind was still wandering, and his fever increasing; but after a while, a powerful opiate took effect, and he sunk into an unquiet, artificial sleep. His attendant, however, reported that he was doing well, and Gertrude, after giving her last minute directions, bade her father 'good night.'

As she shut the door of his apartment, her book in one hand, and lamp in the other, her foot was entangled in the cloak of a gentleman who was standing muffled in the little gallery. In extricating herself from the awkward embarrassment, her lamp fell. The gentleman recovered it, and gracefully apologizing for the accident, he relighted the lamp by the lantern suspended in the gallery. This was an operose business. The cloak encumbered him, he threw it aside, and Gertrude could not but notice, with a curiosity stimulated by the concealment for which the cloak had obviously been worn—for nothing could be more agreeably tempered than the atmosphere—the fine figure and classic head thus accidentally and unintentionally disclosed. Every one knows how slow and almost impossible the process of ignition appears when waited for. The gentleman made some commonplace, but, as Gertrude thought, pleasant remark about it, which was suddenly cut off by a servant, who came up the stairs and whispered to him. He returned the lamp to Miss Clarence, bowed, and hurried away. She turned to inquire the stranger's name of the servant, but half ashamed of her curiosity, she hesitated, and while she hesitated, he disappeared.

Gertrude then went to her own apartment. After remaining there a while, she missed her keys, and recollecting she had left the bag that contained them in the parlor, she went down stairs in quest of them. As she approached the parlor-door which stood a-jar, she heard voices in low and earnest conversation. She listened; one was Mrs. Layton, her heart beat, and she sprang forward, and again stopped, for she perceived that her friend was deeply absorbed in a *tête à tête*,[1] evidently private, with the stranger whom she had met in the gallery. They had been quite too much interested in their own affairs to hear Miss Clarence's light tread, and there being no light in the passage, she stood for a moment without the fear of observation. Mrs. Layton leant against the window, her handkerchief at her eyes, and her back to the light, which fell strongly on the stranger's face. His fine features were kindled with a glow of earnest feeling, he spoke in a tone of mingled supplication and remonstrance. 'Such a man could scarcely speak in vain,' thought Gertrude, as she turned away, and stole back to her own apartment. There she revolved in her own mind the probable meaning of Mrs. Layton's unexpected appearance at Trenton— the obscure intimations in relation to Emilie in her farewell note— this private interview with the elegant stranger—the Utica scrawl; and she would probably have arrived at the right exposition, if that had not involved Mrs. Layton in deep reproach. Of course, that was rejected; and after going round, in the same circle, she gave up the subject as inexplicable, and resigned her mind to the sweet fancies awakened by a dewy moonlight evening.

Gertrude Clarence, in daylight, and amidst the real affairs of life, was truly what Mrs. Layton had called her, a fit heroine for the nineteenth century; practical, efficient, direct, and decided— a rational woman—that beau-ideal of all devotees to the ruling spirit of the age—utility. But it must be confessed she had certain infirmities of olden and romantic times clinging to her; that she loved in moonlight and retirement, to abandon herself to the visions of her imagination; that she sought and loved the beauty and mystery of nature; that she gave her faith to the poetry of life—the sublime virtue that is sometimes manifested in actual human existence,—and that always visits the dreams of the enthusiast, as the fair forms of their divinities were presented to the inspired vision of the Grecian sculptors.

---

1 Private, one-on-one conversation.

CHAPTER XIV.

"Is't possible that on so little acquaintance you should like
her?—that but seeing you should love her?"
AS YOU LIKE IT.[1]

WE have violated the consecrated privacy in which Miss Clarence
sheltered her romantic taste, to prepare our readers for a sally that
might otherwise appear extravagant. It was a night to call forth all
the secret correspondencies between the spirit and the outward
world; a night when the soul responds harmonious to the voice of
nature; when the intellectual life, that like the electric principle,
pervades the material world, becomes visible and audible, is seen
in the starry depths of heaven, and speaks in the 'viewless air.'[2] It
was a night—just such as every body has seen, though perchance
not thus marked—in midsummer, sweet, bright, and soft. There
had been a slight shower, and the atmosphere was charged with
the perfume of all the wild flowers that abound in the forest in
June—the month of flowers. The clouds had broken away and dispersed, save here and there a few light silvery forms, that as they
melted away in the moon-light, seemed the very coinage of the
brain, shaped in fancy's changing mould; now winged spirits, now
graces wreathing themselves in flowers; now fairies at their elfin
gambols, and now—nothing. On such a night it is treason against
nature to steep the senses in sleep; voluntarily to close the natural
entrances to all this glory; at least, so thought Gertrude, and obeying a sudden impulse, she threw on her shawl, and creeping softly
down stairs, she entered the apartment where the only member of
the family who was out of bed, was drowsily adjusting his ledger.
"I am going down to the falls," she said.

"Miss! you'll see them far plainer by daylight."

Gertrude did not think it worth while to explain the advantage of the *claire obscure*,[3] and simply requested a lamp might
be left standing in the entry for her. The man assented without
expressing any inconvenient curiosity or surprise. The head of
the financial department of the 'rural resort' was a little ancient

---

1 Shakespeare's *As You Like It* V.ii.1-2.
2 Perhaps from "The Spirit of the Air" (1823) by James Gates Percival
(American, 1795-1856): "I am the spirit of the viewless air"; or from "To
a Departed Spirit" (in *The Literary Souvenir*, 1828/1829, and in *Songs of
the Affections, with Other Poems*, 1830) by Felicia Hemans (English, 1793-
1835): "From the bright stars, or from the viewless air."
3 Chiaroscuro (Italian), the interplay of light and shadow.

gentleman, (gentleman by courtesy—illimitable republican courtesy!) who trudged on in his narrow walk of life without looking to the right or left to scan the motives, or even observe the conduct of his fellow-travellers. That a lady should desire to see the falls by moonlight, appeared to him no more strange than that she should wish to view them by daylight.[1] If he valued falls, it was as 'water privileges;' and the only 'view' he took of picturesque objects was of their effect on the bright side of the landlord's ledger. Gertrude, therefore, happily escaped a remonstrance, and soon found herself in the little path traversing the deep wood which borders the precipitous bank of the West Canada creek—a narrow, deeply embedded stream, that after winding, leaping, and foaming in its unnoticed solitude for centuries, has, within the last few years, become one of the staple curiosities of the country.

Miss Clarence had passed a few weeks of the preceding summer at Trenton, and was secure in her familiarity with the forest-paths. It seemed as if all nature were hushed in silence to listen to the music of the dashing waters. Not a breath of air was stirring. The leaves reposed in the still atmosphere. The moon looked as if she were immoveably set in the far, cloudless depths of the heavens, and where her rays stole in through the lofty branches, and slept on the moss-grown trunks, or dewy herbage, not the slightest quivering of the leaves broke or varied the clear defined outline of the bright spaces. There is something vast and oppressive in such immobility and stillness, and Gertrude felt, in approaching the brawling, noisy, little stream, as if it were a living soul—a being endowed with feeling and sympathy, and voice to speak them. She rapidly descended the several flights of steps, that afford but a slippery and inconvenient passage down a precipitous rock of a hundred feet in height—so grudgingly does art seem to have lent her aid to her mistress nature—but here nature may well scoff at her handmaid's negligence, for here she reigns a queen of beauty; every heart does her homage; every heart! the very trees, as they bend from the walled banks and almost embower the sportive stream, seem in the act of reverence.

Gertrude pursued the usual walk along the margin of the stream, now passing with security over the broad, flat rocks, and now cautiously creeping around the jutting buttresses, whose bases are fretted by the foaming torrent, and whose sides afford

---

1 In the 1849 edition, Sedgwick inserts this sentence: The mere pleasure of looking at falls by daylight or moon-light, was like the child's joy in blowing up soap-bubbles; something there was above and beyond.

a perilous passage along a shelving ledge, scarcely wide enough for a heron's foot. Fortunately, Gertrude had none of the physical sensitiveness that renders some persons incapable of approaching a rapid stream without dizziness. Self-possessed, and sure-footed, she passed the most difficult passages without fear and without danger. She ascended to the summit of the first fall by the natural and rough stair-way, and pursuing her walk, canopied by the over-arching rocks, and creeping along the shelving shore, she attained the side of the foaming, deep abyss, into which the stream rushes at two bold leaps. She stood for some moments gazing on the torrent, and almost deafened by its roar, when she was startled by a footstep close to her. She turned, and saw the stranger who seemed, that evening, destined to cross her path at every turn. He bowed respectfully, and said he had not expected the pleasure of meeting any one at that extraordinary hour—but he added, 'no hour could be more fit for a devotee to nature to visit her sanctuary.'

Gertrude thought there was something like a sarcastic smile playing about his lip, as if his reading of 'a devotee to nature,' was 'a mighty romantic young lady,' a construction she felt was warranted, but a light in which she did not quite like to appear.

"Neither did I," she said, returning the stranger's smile, "think of the possibility of meeting any one this evening. I came simply for the pleasure of seeing the falls by moon-light—by all other lights I am familiar with them."

"But no other light can," replied the stranger, "be so well adapted to them. Broad day light, and a party of exclaiming, professed admirers of scenery, convert the most poetic passages into dull prose."

"Yes," said Gertrude, pleased with a feeling so exactly corresponding with her own. "Solitude and moon-light are certainly the best accompaniments to fine scenery. They are like the vehicle of music to the inspirations of the poet."

"And this is fine scenery," said the stranger; "I have been scrambling along the bank for two miles above this place, and never have I seen such various and startling beauty. The river has so many abrupt turns, and graceful sweeps—at every step there is a new picture, as if you had turned another leaf in the book of nature. I have seen three falls, above this, of less magnitude, and I have been told they occur, at intervals, for several miles. But the falls are only one feature. The sides of the stream are varied and every where beautiful. In some places richly wooded; in others, stern, bare, perpendicular rocks—now sending over their beetling summits a little cascade, that falls at your feet in diamond drops, and then crested with a hanging cedar that waves like a warrior's plume—now receding and sloping, and mantled with moss and fern, or sending out from their clefts, sturdy trees—sylvan sentinels on nature's battlements. In one place the rocks recede and are concave, and the river appears like an imprisoned lake, or a magician's well,—there, I confess, I listened for an 'open sessime,'[1] and thought it possible I might see an enchanted damsel, walk forth, with her golden pitcher."

"But you saw none," said Gertrude. "Ours is not the country of enchantments—nature is *merely* nature here. Neither enriched nor embellished, nor rendered sublime by traditionary tales, nor supernatural graces, or terrors."

"No, thank heaven, no terrors. I was never better pleased than now, with living in a country where a lady may walk forth, at midnight, without fear or danger."

Gertrude felt the awkwardness of her position, the moment it was alluded to, and she rather abruptly asked the stranger, 'if he had ever seen Niagara?'

'He was ashamed to confess he had not. It was the fashion,' he said, 'to compare Trenton to Niagara, but he thought Trenton must be about as much like Niagara, as a frolicsome child was like to Hercules, or the finite to the infinite.'

"And yet," said Gertrude, "I hear the comparison often made, and Trenton often preferred. She is a younger favorite and has the advantage of youth and novelty over the sublime torrent. She has not been heard of by every body in the four quarters of the globe; nor seen and talked of by half the world. We feel something of the pride of discoverers in vaunting her beauty. She has too, her caprices and changes, and does not show the same face to all. This is one of her peculiar charms. There is such a pleasure in saying, 'Oh what a pity you did not see the falls as we did!' and 'ah,' with a shrug, '*we* but just escaped with our lives. There had immense rains fallen, and the passes were all but impassable.' There are no such lucky chances of superiority at Niagara. Like a monarch, Niagara always appears in the same state and magnificence. It pays no visible tribute to the elements; it is neither materially abated nor augmented by them. Niagara is like the ocean, alone and incomparable in its grandeur." It was apparent that Gertrude had seen Niagara, and the stranger naturally asked her many questions

---

1 "Open sesame," password from "Ali Baba and the Forty Thieves." Sedgwick uses an alternate spelling.

in relation to it. From Niagara he adverted to kindred topics. Not a water-fall, natural bridge, or mountain-resort, was passed by, till the meeting was protracted to the last limit of propriety. There is a peculiar pleasure in meeting with a stranger who discovers at once kindred tastes and feelings with our own. If it be a single sentiment, it is sometimes like a word in the 'correspondencies,' of a certain mystical sect, which may be a key to a whole volume. Acquaintance makes rapid strides in such circumstances; and it was not singular that the stranger, whose imagination was no doubt stimulated by the time and place of their encounter, should linger in Gertrude's presence. He felt there was no propriety in detaining her any longer, if she intended to prosecute her walk; nor, much as he desired to do it, could he, after her declaration, that she had come out for a solitary stroll, offer to attend her; and inwardly praying she might say no, he asked if she meant to proceed farther. She answered—for she was not in the palace of truth, nor dared she follow her inclinations—'yes,' and the stranger, with evident reluctance, bade her good night, and soon disappeared.[1]

Gertrude now proceeded very slowly up the next acclivity. The walk had lost its charms. Her mind was entirely occupied with the stranger, and with conjectures who he could be. 'He did not seem,' she thought, 'to remember our first meeting this evening; his mind must have been intent on his approaching interview with Mrs. Layton. If I had had but one glance at him, I should never have forgotten him.' She pondered over his interview with Mrs. Layton. 'Could he be her husband? No, he was far too young. Could he be Emilie's lover? No, such a lover could never need the interposition of parental authority.' Suddenly, and at the thought she stopped stock still, it occurred to her that he wonderfully resembled the image of Gerald Roscoe, impressed on her mind by her father's often repeated descriptions. She passed the stranger's features in review: his dark complexion, bold expanded forehead, singularly black hair, a stature and form cast in the heroic mould;

---

1 In the 1849 edition, Sedgwick inserts the following passage at the beginning of the next paragraph, likely in response to criticism leveled against Gertrude's free behavior by readers of the 1830 edition: Gertrude's first sensation at his departure was relief. She was happily exempt from those minor fears that vex most women's lives, and companionless as she was at her home, she must have lost the immense enjoyment of rural life, moonlight walks, or submitted to the annoyance of a servant's attendance. She was so much accustomed to roaming alone about Clarenceville at all hours, that the impropriety of such a ramble at Trenton had not occurred to her.

the prevailing darkness of his face, relieved by a smile that disclosed a set of as white and beautiful teeth as ever decorated a mouth. 'How often has my father said,' thought Gertrude, 'that Gerald's smile was electrifying;' that it was 'like the sun bursting through a cloud—a smile of intelligence, arch, sportive, and good-humored.' 'Could this stranger be described more accurately?'

Gertrude was startled and roused from her reverie by what she fancied to be a strain of music. It seemed wafted over the torrent, and not mingling with its din, as if the breathing of some spirit above her. There was no visible agent. 'Am I deceived by the solitude, the scene, the hour, or is it an unearthly sound?' thought she. She looked timidly around, and as she listened, the strain sounded familiar. "It cannot be!" she exclaimed, and yet impelled by an irresistible impulse, she sprang forward in the direction whence the sound came. "Should it be he!" she cried fearfully, and hurrying through a tangled path, she came out on a broad projecting rock, that although a few feet below the summit of the lower fall, commanded a full view of it. On that summit stood a figure enveloped in a white dress, and so shaded by branches, that hung like banners over the glittering waters, that it was impossible to say whether the figure were man or woman; whether it were human, or some strange visitant from another world. While Gertrude gazed fearfully, the person advanced to the brink of the water, threw the flute into the torrent, bent over it, and clasped his hands as if in prayer. "Louis!—Louis Seton! oh, God of mercy, save him!" shrieked Gertrude. The scream of agony reached his ear, and arrested him; he looked wildly around. She reiterated her cries and waved her handkerchief. He saw her and descended the cliff towards her so swiftly and recklessly that she covered her eyes in terror, lest she should see him plunge into the abyss.

As he drew near, she ventured again to look at him. His cheeks were crimsoned with fever, his eyes had a supernatural brightness, his fair brow was as pale as marble, and his long flaxen hair, which had at all times a sentimental and student-like air, was in the wildest disorder. He had carelessly thrown over his under garments a white dressing-gown, and his whole appearance confirmed Gertrude in her first impression, that he was delirious. But when he said, in his usual low-toned gentle voice, "You called me—did you not, Gertrude?" She replied, half reassured, and still half doubtful, "Yes; I feared you were venturing too near the fall, and," she added, with a smile of admirable self-possession, "I thought myself fortunate to meet you just at the very moment I was returning home-ward, and dreading to retrace the way alone."

"Oh, do not go yet! Why go away from this beautiful scene? It is a glimpse of heaven; I will never leave it but for a brighter," he added, in a tone of unwonted decision and confidence; "Sit down on this rock, Gertrude—I did not expect this—this is the first blissful hour of my life. Do not look so terrified—this is the gate of heaven—you shall see how I will throw off the load of life, and leap through it; Oh, it was very good of you, to come out to see this—come, sit down!"

There was something irresistibly appealing, and affecting in his manner, and Gertrude smothered her fears and sat down; "I dreamed," he continued, "an angel would show me the way—it's very strange—I cannot account for it;" he passed his hand over his brow, like one who would disentangle his recollections, "I do not think, Gertrude, it ever occurred to me, that you were to be that angel."

"But I am," said Gertrude, rising, and hoping to govern him, by humoring his wild fancies, "I am, and you are bound to follow whither I lead. Come, we must hasten home, Louis—follow me, I intreat you." He rose and followed, half-singing, and half-screaming.

'This will not do, I am exciting his delirium,' thought Gertrude; and stopping suddenly, she said, with all the composure she could command, "I ought, indeed, to be an angel to flit over these rocks at this unearthly rate. We had best return to our every-day characters, Louis; it is childish to risk our lives, in this foolish way."

Her natural tone and manner, for a moment, restored Seton to himself, and his thoughts reverted to their accustomed channel. "It is then a delusion," he said "yes—yes, life is a delusion—hope a delusion—and yet, who can live without hope? I cannot, and why should I, passively, remain here to suffer? Gertrude, did you see my flute, as it silently floated away? but a moment before, the woods rung with the music, my troubled heart poured into it. Think you, Gertrude, it would be as easy to still that heart, as the poor instrument?"

"But the heart is not yours, Louis," said Gertrude, assuming a playfulness, difficult to affect, while she was in a panic; "you gave me your heart, you know, and you have no right to resume it."

"Yes, I gave it to you, Gertrude, and it was a good gift—a true loving heart—but you would not take it—you could not—you know you said so—but, one thing I tell you, Miss Clarence, you will go forth into the world, you will be sought, and flattered, and you will learn, from bitter experience, the value of a true, faithful heart—no wealth can buy it—wealth! wealth! that was a cruel letter; it was the last drop in the cup. Gertrude, I felt as if I were going mad, yesterday—but I am well, quite well, now."

Gertrude became more alarmed, at every new incoherency; and felt her total helplessness, should he again attempt the violence on himself, he had purposed. It struck her, that she might, possibly, lure him onward, by addressing his love of his art, next to his love for her, his strongest passion; without replying, or adverting, to any thing he had said. "Come, Louis!" she exclaimed, "we are wasting time—you promised me, some moon-light sketches of the falls; and, farther on, there is a beautiful view—if we do not hasten, we shall lose the best light for it." She walked at as quick a pace as she dared; and Seton, obedient as a bird to his lady's whistle, followed her. They proceeded on their return, beyond the first fall; and Gertrude meant to lead him on, without alluding again to the view, but his painter's eye, as it rolled from shore to shore, caught the point of sight. "Ah! here it is," he said, "beautiful as a painter's dream—but I have no port-folio, no paper—never mind, I can draw on the impalpable air. I will put you in the fore-ground—you were in the fore-ground of all my pictures—my air-drawn pictures," he added, with a faint smile.

"But I must have a picture, that I can see—here, take my handkerchief—you can make a perpendicular and a horizontal line, and write light and shadow, that is enough, you know, for an artist's sketch."

He kissed the handkerchief devoutly, spread it on his knee, took a pencil from his pocket, and contemplated the scene intently; the preparation for an habitual occupation, restored for a time, the equilibrium of his mind; his thoughts returned to their natural channel. "Such scenes as these," he said, "are the despair of the painter."

"Why the despair? you never fail in your water views. Mrs. Layton said she was afraid to let Argus see your picture of the lake, lest he should try to lap the water."

"Ah, that was sleeping water; but who can paint this beautiful motion—this sound, the voice of the waterfall—the spray, the most etherial of all material things—the light mist rising, and floating around those over-hanging woods, like the drapery of spirits, made visible to mortal sense?"

"But you can imitate the most exquisite tints of flowers; and surely, you can paint these wild geraniums, and blue-bells."

"Yes, I can imitate them; but in the still picture, will they speak to us as they do now, looking out in wild and tender beauty, from the crevices of these stupendous rocks? I can paint the vines that richly fringe those beetling crags, I might attempt their expression of security; but can I give their light fantastic grace, their brightening and deepening hues, as they wave in the gentlest breath of heaven?"

"Oh, no, certainly not! you cannot make all the elements of nature tributary to your art; you cannot work miracles; you can but repeat in the picture, one aspect of the scene. You can give the deep amber tint of the water, but not every varying shade it takes from the passing clouds. You can imitate these wild, broken shores, but not the musical trickling of the drops, as they swell, and fall from ledge to ledge. A picture is, of course, dumb nature; it addresses but one sense; it is what you *can* do, that constitutes the glory of your art; and it is a weakness, Louis, to dwell on what you cannot do."

Gertrude had unwarily touched the wrong key. Seton sprang to his feet—"a weakness, is it Gertrude? do *you* reproach me with my weakness?—Yes, it is the extreme of weakness; but I have struggled against it—far, far worse, I have quietly endured it: I will not longer—why should I? The world cares not for me; nor I for the world. I have floated on its dark, troubled surface, like those bubbles on the stream—they dissolve and are forgotten. So shall I be."

He spoke with the resolute tone of despair. Gertrude's heart sunk within her; but calling forth all her courage, she said, "I agree with you, Louis; the world has dark, tiresome passages enough; but even the worst of them, like our rugged path here, may be cheered by a light from above. The light always shines. Cannot you open your bosom to it?"

"Gertrude!" he replied, with a bitter smile; "do not mock me: tell those fretted waters to give back the image of the heavens, serene and unbroken: bid the stream glide quietly over these sharp rocks: ask that solitary pine to go and bend among its fellows. It is far easier to contend with nature, than with the elements of the soul. I am wearied with the conflict. I have struggled, and I am subdued. I have had such horrid dreams. My cruel brother grinning at me—the world's laugh and scorn ringing in my ears—your voice, louder than all the rest."[1]

"Do not think of it—it was a dream—nothing but a dream, Louis."

---

1 In the 1849 edition, Sedgwick omits the adjective 'cruel' from the description of Seton's brother and revises the end of the sentence:—your voice, Gertrude, low—low, but yet audible, chiming in with the rest.

"Yes it was a dream: and now you speak to me in your own kind voice—this is reality." He took her hand and pressed it to his scorching lips: "I have heard the parting spirit had always some intimation of the future—of good, or evil: this is good—this is light to my heart: I have no more fear. Farewell—farewell!" Again and again he kissed her hand: "it is over now, Gertrude," and he sprang towards the rushing stream.

Gertrude grasped his arm, and, shivering with terror, detained him forcibly. "Have you no pity on me, Louis? do not leave me here alone; attend me round these dreadful rocks; I shall never get back to my father without your help; you can return directly. Come, do not—do not," she continued, imploringly, "refuse me this last kindness; come, quickly." She moved forward, and perceiving that he followed, she ran along the broken shore, sprang from the rolling stones, and leaped from crag to crag, forgetful of all dangers but one, till she came to the last projecting rock, where the foot-hold is extremely narrow, and rendered most perilous by the agitation of the water, which at times lashes the side of the rock, but five or six feet below the narrow margin, on which the passenger treads, in a position not quite upright, but rather inclining over the stream. The hazard of this passage was extreme. Seton still followed and was close to her, but the spell that had controlled him so far, might break at any moment. The incoherent sounds he uttered at every step, now escaping in indistinct murmurs, and then swelling to shrieks, indicated, too truly, the rapid access of his delirium. Gertrude's courage failed—a nervous sickness came over her—her head turned, her feet faltered, and she retreated a few steps, and sunk to the ground.

It was but a momentary weakness; she ejaculated a prayer for resolution and strength, and sprang to her feet again. "I am rested now, Louis," she said; "once round this rock, we are almost home; follow me, dear Louis." She advanced to the perilous path, and proceeded around the projecting cliff, without again faltering.

Seton followed to the front of the rock and there stopped, and stood fixed and immoveable, as if he were part of it. His face was towards Gertrude, but his eye was glazed and turned upwards: it appeared that his senses were paralyzed, and that he neither saw, heard, nor felt; for though Gertrude urged, supplicated, and wrung her hands in agony, he maintained the same, statue-like stillness, looking like an image carved in the rock, before which a terror-struck suppliant was standing. Gertrude dared not advance towards him—his position did not admit assistance—and the slightest movement, even though involuntary, might prove fatal.

She cried to Heaven for aid, but while the unavailing prayer was on her lips, Seton slipped gently from the rock into the current below. In another breath his body swept past her. A little lower down, the current was less impetuous; a few yards lower still it was broken by the rocks and tossed in rapids. He evidently struggled against the current. "Oh! he tries to save himself," cried Gertrude. An eddy seemed to favor his efforts, and impel him towards the shore. "Merciful God, help him!" she screamed, and sprang forward, in the hope that she might herself extend some aid; but, instantly, a counter-current swept him off towards the rapids, and his destruction seemed near and inevitable. Gertrude gazed after him, speechless, motionless—as if awaiting the doom of fate. Suddenly there was a plash in the water, and a person appeared approaching the descending body. "Should he resist—" cried Gertrude. But he did not resist. It was at the calmest and most favorable point in the whole stream for such an interposition, and perilous as it was, it succeeded; and Seton, who had not yet quite lost his consciousness, was drawn in safety to the rocks. Gertrude flew to him. She knelt beside him, and dried the water from his face and neck with her shawl. His preserver was active and efficient. He supported Seton's head on his breast, and chafed his hands and arms.

Seton was for a few moments incapable of motion or articulation, but he looked intelligently at Gertrude, and as if he felt to the heart's core, the joy and gratitude that lit up her face with an almost supernatural brightness. When her first emotion gave place to a more natural tone of feeling, she would have fainted—but she never fainted: she would have wept, but there was still something to be done. She attempted to rise, but her limbs trembled to such a degree as to be useless. "I pray you to make no effort." Gertrude started at the voice, and, for the first time, looking at Seton's preserver, she perceived he was the stranger. He smiled at the sudden recognition apparent on her countenance. "I have been lingering at the steps here," he said, as if in reply to her looks, "detained by my good fortune for your service. You are suffering even more than your friend from this accident." And so she appeared, for Seton was stimulated by fever. "You both need more assistance than I alone can give you. I will go for aid, and return instantly."

"Oh, not for the world," replied Gertrude, for she felt the importance to Seton of keeping the adventure a secret, "not for the world," she reiterated. She perceived the stranger smiled archly at her earnestness, and she guessed at his interpretation. 'He thinks this, no doubt, an appointed meeting of lovers, and Louis's fall accidental; that at least is a happy mistake.' In one particular she was determined to rectify his misconception. "I came here," she continued, "without the slightest expectation of meeting any one. I therefore can have neither reluctance nor fear to be left alone. This foolish trembling will be over in a few moments, and I will then follow you if you will have the goodness to give your arm to my friend—it has already done us a service for which we have no words to thank you."

Seton now for the first time broke silence and attempted, though confused and embarrassed, to express his gratitude. "I beg you not to waste your strength in this way," said the stranger, "I will take it for granted, that you are infinitely obliged to me, for a service that cost me nothing but a little wetting, a circumstance not altogether disagreeable on a hot evening. I really have not encountered the slightest danger; but if I may make a merit of this accidental service," he continued, bowing courteously to Miss Clarence, "I claim the right to return and escort you, after I have attended your friend."

"We are so deeply your debtors, that you may impose your own conditions. I will await you if necessary—or meet you."

"If necessary! pardon me then, if I put some constraint on your courtesy. The evening is becoming cool, allow me to wrap my cloak about you; it shall be fetters and warder till my return." As he spoke, he took his cloak from the ground where he had hastily thrown it, and adjusted it around Miss Clarence. At another time Gertrude might have felt a girlish and natural diffidence at receiving such attentions from a stranger; but serious emotions give to these little punctilios their due insignificance and she received his kindness as quietly as if it were warranted by old acquaintance. Seton's unnatural strength was the only indication of the continuance of his fever. He was tranquil and it appeared probable from the exertions he had made for self-preservation that his first immersion in the water had stimulated his reason. Gertrude watched him anxiously till he disappeared from her in ascending the steps, and then she gave utterance to her devout gratitude for his preservation from death, by an interposition that appeared to her to have been miraculously provided. Accustomed to think and decide independently, she determined to keep poor Seton's sad affair, so far as depended on herself, a profound secret. 'Even my father, kind and indulgent as he is,' she thought, 'would not deem it quite prudent to retain Louis after this; but have I not solemnly promised to be a sister to him? and when he most needs a sister's love and care, I will not abandon him.' From Seton her thoughts naturally turned to the stranger. 'How very strange our repeated

meetings,' she thought, 'how heroic his rescue of Louis! and yet
(she was constrained to confess it) a common man would have
done the same, but not in the same manner. There was a careless
grace about him, as if great actions were at least familiar to his
imagination.' All her reflections ended in the natural query, 'who
can he be?' Suddenly it occurred to her that his cloak might be
labelled, and instantly throwing it from her shoulders, she sought
and found, neatly wrought in large black letters, *Gerald Roscoe*.

Is it fair farther to expound Gertrude's thoughts? It must be
told, that stimulated by an entire new set of emotions, she rose,
threw the cloak from her, adjusted her hair, which she was mortified to find had fallen down, and which, as dame nature had given
it neither the canonical heroine wave, or curl, could not but be
ungraceful in disorder.

It certainly appeared to her that destiny had maliciously arranged the circumstances of her introduction to the hero of her
imagination. How often in those reveries in which young ladies
will indulge when they weave the plot of a little personal romance—how often had she contrived the particulars of their first
meeting—like a skilful painter, and with pardonable vanity, arranged the lights and shadows to give the best effect to the picture.
And now to be first seen by him rambling over perilous rocks, at
the witching time of night, and suspected, as she knew she must
be, of an appointment with a young man of Seton's appearance,
and in such a fantastical dress, and she such a figure! She remembered the smile she had detected on Roscoe's lips, and the thought
that she had at least appeared ridiculous to him, was intolerable.
Then she recollected the Utica scrawl, and was compelled to admit the conviction that Roscoe had written it. This wounded her;
it touched her feelings where they were most vulnerable; and, indignant and resentful, she determined to hasten up the steps and
avoid, if possible, speaking with him again. The cloak she left on
the rock. She could no more have touched it than if it had been
Hercules's fatal tunic.[1] She forgot that a few moments before she
could scarcely support her own weight, ascended the several flights
of steps without halting, and had reached the very last, when she
met Roscoe returning. She was embarrassed and breathless, and
without stopping—without the slightest acknowledgement of his
courtesy, or apology for the trouble she gave him, "You will find
your cloak," she said, "on the rocks—good night, sir." But Roscoe

1 The garment soaked with poisonous centaur's blood, sent to Hercules by
his wife Deianira when she suspected his infidelity.

did not appear to notice her abruptness. "I expected," he said, turning and offering his arm, which she declined—he mended his phrase, "I hoped to have had the pleasure of finding you there too—I beg you will not walk so rapidly—you have no occasion for anxiety about your friend; he reached the house without difficulty—and his own room,"—he added, with as Gertrude thought, a very significant emphasis—"his own room *without observation.* I am quite sure of it, for I remained in the entry till I heard his door close." Miss Clarence made no reply, and they walked on a few paces in silence. Roscoe then said, "I am curious to learn how the accident happened. I asked your friend, but he evaded my inquiry—he perhaps felt that his foot ought not to have faltered, where yours trod safely."

Gertrude, in her confusion, and desire to shelter Seton, said, "he was weak from recent illness."

"An imprudent exposure for an invalid!" returned Roscoe, with another of his provoking smiles, "but I honor his self-forgetfulness in so romantic a cause, and only wonder that a prosaic personage like myself has been allowed to appear in the drama, though it be only to turn the wheel of fortune for others, and be dismissed and forgotten, when I have enacted my inglorious part." They had now reached the door-steps, and he added in a lower voice, "I am compelled to return immediately to the village, and proceed thence in the stage-coach—may I presume to ask the names of my new acquaintance?"

"Oh, no—do not ask them—do not, I entreat you, inquire them—do not ever speak of what has happened to-night. The life," she continued, for she had now quite recovered the power of thought and speech, "the life you have preserved would be worthless if there were any exposure."

"Shall I make a vow of secresy?" he asked, bending his knee gracefully to the step, gallantly taking her hand, and speaking in a tone of raillery that Gertrude felt made her pathetic appeal almost ridiculous, "I do make it," he added with mock solemnity, "craving only an exception in favor of one friend, a safe confidante—my mother. I call on the bright moon to witness my vow," and in token of sealing it, his lips approached her hand, but without presuming to touch it. "Now I have pledged the honor of a true knight—do I not deserve a dispensation in my favor?"

While Gertrude hesitated, resolved not to give her name, and feeling that it was almost childish to withhold it, a window-sash above their heads was gently raised, and murmuring a heart-felt 'God bless you,' she escaped into the entry. There she lingered long enough to ascertain that Mrs. Layton was speaking to Roscoe; and then, after listening at Seton's door, and finding all quiet there, she retired to her room to revolve over and over again, and to place in various lights and shadows, the events of the evening.

She had seen Roscoe at last! and in spite of her personal mortification and vexation, she liked him—she could not help it—she rejoiced in her inmost soul, that she was still unknown to him as the dreaded *rich* Miss Clarence, and she finally fell asleep with the secret, sweet consciousness, that she had not impressed him as altogether the counter part of '*Miss Eunice Peabody!*'

CHAPTER XV.

"Surtout lorsqu'on a l'air de plaisanter avec le sort, et de compter sur le bonheur, il se passe quelque chose de redoubtable dans le tissu de notre histoire, et les fatales sœurs viennent y mêler leur fils noir, et brouiller l'œuvre de nos mains."[1]
CORINNE.

MISS Clarence was up at gray dawn, awaiting intelligence from Seton. She had directed his nurse, to inform her how he passed the night; and, though conscious she was better informed than any one else, she was anxious to learn the effect of his wild sally. John soon appeared. "Mr. Seton," he said, "lay in a dead sleep, but was nothing worse. I have not closed my eyes" continued John, "the whole blessed night, but one bare minute, and then while I dosed, as it were, Mr. Louis took the advantage to slip down stairs, and pump some water on his head, that was fiery hot, and the poor young gentleman came back, as wet as a drowned kitten; I was scared half out of my wits; but I put on him dry clothes, and got him quite comfortable, and I hope Miss Gertrude, nor Mr. Clarence, won't take it amiss that I was overcome with that wink of sleep."

But Miss Gertrude, though the gentlest of kind mistresses, did take it very much amiss; and reproved John, with the utmost severity, that the offence, according to his statement of it, (which she was compelled to receive,) admitted. Those are to be deeply

---

1 "Especially when one pretends to toy with destiny and counts on happiness, something formidable changes the tissue of our history and the fatal sisters [the three Fates] come to mix their black threads in it, and ruin the work of our hands." From *Corinne* by de Staël.

compassionated, who are obliged to trust to menials and strangers, for offices, in which affection alone can overcome the weariness of mind and body! Gertrude felt too late that she had rashly undertaken a task she could not execute. 'Oh, were I his sister indeed!' she thought 'I would never leave him!' She blamed herself for urging his coming to Trenton, and wished nothing more than to get back to Clarenceville, where secluded from observation, she might share the personal care of him with her women; but the physician, at his morning visit, declared a return impossible—he would not even sanction a removal to a private house, but ordered the patient's room to be made perfectly dark, and prescribed the usual remedies for a brain fever.

Miss Clarence was not exempt from the reserve, fastidiousness it may be, so sedulously cherished in the education of our country-women. But every thing was well proportioned, and well balanced in her mind; she never sacrificed the greater to the less. The moment she ascertained that Seton's reason was so far alienated, that he would probably be quite unconscious of her presence—and that it could certainly be of no disservice to him, she went to his room, sat at his bed-side, and watched him, as if he were in truth her brother. He was alternately torpid and silent, or violent and raving. The only indication that a spark of reason remained, was in the passiveness with which he received from Gertrude, what he rejected from every other hand.

In the evening there was a slight remission of his fever, and Gertrude went to her own apartment, where Emilie Layton, who had sent her repeated messages during the day, was awaiting her. The affectionate girl threw herself into Gertrude's arms—expressed her delight at meeting her in the unqualified terms of youthful ecstasy, and her extreme pity for 'poor Mr. Seton.' After informing her that her mother was longing to see her, but that she had been in bed all day, with a violent head-ache, she was silent, evidently embarrassed, and perplexed. She unclasped and clasped her bracelet twenty times, twisted every feather of her fan awry, and at last, throwing her handkerchief over her face, she said, "dear Gertrude, I am engaged to be married to Mr. Pedrillo."

"Emilie!" exclaimed Gertrude.

Nothing could be more simple and bare, than the exclamation; but it was a key-note to Emilie's ear. "I knew you would think so, Gertrude," she said, as if replying to a long remonstrance—"I told mama you would—but it is not so very—*very* bad;" and she laid her head on Gertrude's shoulder, and sobbed aloud.

"But my dear, sweet Emilie, if it be bad at all?"

"Well, I don't know that I can say it is bad at all—at least, it would not be, if——"

"If what? speak out, Emilie."

"Oh! I had rather speak out to you, than not; I am sure my heart will feel the lighter for it. You are so reasonable, and so judicious, and all that, Gertrude, that I suppose you have not felt so; but I expected to be in love when I married. Ever since I first thought of it at all, though I can't remember when that was, I have expected to love, and adore my husband—I have always said, I would never marry any man, that I was not willing to die for."

"And 'judicious and reasonable' as you think me, neither would I, Emilie."

"Would not you, Gertrude? would not *you?*—then, it is right—I am sure it is right;" and her beautiful face brightened all over; but, instantly, a shadow crossed it—as much of a shadow, as can appear on a freshly blown rose, and sighing heavily, she added, "but it is no use now—it is all settled."

"Irrevocably?"

"Irrevocably; mother says, to recede would be ruinous to us all; she has not explained to me how, because she cannot bear to make me as miserable as she is. If I can make them all happy, I ought—ought I not, Gertrude?"

"If you can, without too great a sacrifice, Emilie."

"It seems to me a great sacrifice; I do not, and never can love Mr. Pedrillo, and you know, I must never love any body else; so it is a total sacrifice of my affections; but that is all. I like Mr. Pedrillo—at least, I should, if he did not want me to love him. Mother says, she is certain, that after I have been married a year, I shall like him better than nine women out of ten like their husbands. He is very kind, and generous to me; he gave me these splendid bracelets; but Gertrude, when I put them on I could not help thinking of the natives of Cuba, you know, who thought, poor simpletons, that the Spaniards were only decorating them with beautiful ornaments, when they were fastening manacles on their wrists. I always hated Spaniards—I am sorry Mr. Pedrillo is a Spaniard—I cannot forget it, though he does not look at all Spanish. Mama says, he is probably descended from one of the Irish Catholic families that emigrated to Spain. He is called very handsome, Gertrude," she continued in as plaintive a voice as if she were counting her griefs; "he is very gay when he is pleased; he has seen a great deal of the world though he is not very old—not more than forty."

"Forty! Emilie; and you seventeen!"

"So it seemed to me, Gertrude. I told mama forty seemed to me as old as the hills, but she quite laughed at me and quoted something from Molière, about his being the better fitted to guide my youth."

"I presume he is a man of fortune, Emilie?"

"Oh yes, indeed; that is the worst of it; if it were not for that, I could do as I please."

Gertrude's heart was full of sympathy, tenderness, and compassion for the unresisting victim, but she hesitated to express her feelings. 'Why should she increase the reluctance that must be unavailing? Were it not better to employ her influence over Emilie to reconcile her to the now inevitable event.' She tried to look at the affair in the most favorable point of view, and as there are few substances so black that they will not reflect some light, so there are few circumstances in life but that have, as the prosers say, 'their advantages as well as disadvantages.' "I should certainly have carved out for you a different fate, dear Emilie," she said— "to love, as well as to be beloved, is always our young dream."

"Yes, indeed! and is it not hard to awake so very soon from it?"

"Yes; but it might prove an illusion, and you awake to some blessed realities. You might cease to love, but you can never lose the happiness that springs from a difficult sacrifice to filial sentiment."

"That is true, Gertrude, and I will make the most of it. Mama would have been so wretched—she has so much feeling."

Gertrude recollected the Utica scrawl, and the impassioned interview that she had witnessed between Mrs. Layton and Roscoe, and some painful distrusts of that lady crossed her mind. The *feeling* that required all the sacrifice to come from others, appeared to her very questionable. "Do not look so troubled about me, dear Gertrude," continued Emilie, rightly interpreting Gertrude's expression. "I never take any thing very hard. Aunt Mary used to say I was born under a mid-day sun—there were no shadows in my path. If she had but lived!—but there is no use in wishing." Emilie was interrupted by a summons to Gertrude from Seton's physician.

"Stop one moment," said Emilie; "I have not yet told you that Mr. Pedrillo is to be here in a few days, and that mama hopes to be able to see you to-morrow; but she begs you will not speak of this affair to her; 'her nerves,' she says, 'are so torn to pieces,' and—oh! I forgot to mention that I want you to come down stairs to-morrow, there is a Miss Marion here who wishes excessively to see you; and her brother—and indeed, Gertrude, you should come down, for in spite of all I say, every body believes that you must be engaged to Mr. Seton." Gertrude was solicitous to avoid such an interpretation of her devotion to Seton, and she promised Emilie she would make her appearance on the following day. But the following day found her occupied, weary, and heart-sick, and she declined joining the society below stairs.

Day after day passed, and there was no abatement of Seton's malady. The scene was sad and monotonous to Gertrude, but there were various incidents occurring that were destined to affect the fortunes of those in whom she was interested.

Nothing is more characteristic of our country than the business-like way in which pleasure is pursued. The very few genuine idlers have not yet learned grace or ease in their '*idlesse*.'[1] A genuine idler—a man of entire leisure, is a *rara avis*.[2] The Duke of Saxe-Weimar was asked by an honest Yankee, 'what business he followed for a living?'[3] The host of travellers who run away from their offices, counters, and farms, for a few hot weeks in mid-summer, hurry from post to post, as if they were in truth 'following the business of travelling for a living.' Trenton is one of the picturesque stations that must be visited, but being situated between Niagara and Saratoga, the chief points of attraction, Trenton is the game shot on the wing. Most travellers leave Utica in the morning coach—arrive at Trenton at mid-day—hurry to 'the steps,' and the brink of the 'great fall'—eat their dinner, and proceed on their route, in the full complacency of having seen Trenton! Two or three parties remaining there for several days, was a rare phenomenon. The Marions alluded to by Emilie, were Virginians. The mother, son, and daughter, comprised all that remained of their family—a family that, from its earliest existence, had been among the most distinguished of the 'ancient dominion.' The blood of English nobles ran in their veins, and was not, in their estimation, less honorable for having, in its transmission to them, warmed the hearts of pure republican patriots. They were the very reverse of the character which (we are ashamed to confess) is often ascribed by northern prejudice and bigotry to our southern brethren.[4] Active in body and mind, spirited, gifted, cultivated, kind-hearted,

---

1 Idleness.

2 Rare bird (Latin); an oddity.

3 Karl Bernhard (German, 1792-1862), Duke of Saxe-Weimer Eisenach, author of *Travels Through North America, during the years 1825 and 1826* (1828), that includes a report of his own visit to Trenton Falls, New York.

4 In the 1849 edition, Sedgwick replaces this sentence with: They were the very reverse of the character which is ascribed sometimes most unjustly to our southern brethren.

and indulgent to all human kind—even to their slaves—to such a degree, that never was a family better loved or better served by its dependents; and so far from possessing riches, (which some among us fancy lose their wings when they perch on a southern plantation,) they had an hereditary carelessness of pecuniary matters, which, combining with the general deterioration of southern property, menaced them with alarming embarrassments.

Augusta Marion had endured severe afflictions, but she did not increase their force by resistance. She had not the usual sweetness and gentleness of deportment that characterizes the manners of the ladies of the south. On the contrary, she had a startling abruptness; but as it was the natural expression of an impulsive character, of a quick succession and rapid combination of ideas, and as she had a tender heart and good temper, (in spite of now and then a momentary heat and flash,) her manner became rather agreeable, as suited to the individual, and characteristic of her. She was sagacious, and her enemies said sarcastic; but if so, her arrows were never poisoned, and never aimed at a reptile that was not noxious.

Randolph Marion, the brother, was the hope, pride, and delight of mother and sister—a man that every body might love and admire, and own they did so without being asked for a reason, for the reason was apparent. He had nothing in excess, but all gentlemanly points and qualities in full measure. He was not a genius, but talented—not learned, but well informed—not 'too handsome for any thing,' but well-looking enough for any body. He was not a wit, nor the mirror of fashion, nor pink of courtesy; but good-humored and well-bred. In short, he had just that standard of character that attracts the regard of others, without alarming their self-love.

The Marions, or rather we should say Augusta Marion, was Emilie's constant theme during her interviews with Gertrude. 'She was certainly,' she said, 'except her dear Gertrude, the most charming woman in the world, so agreeable and so witty!' Once or twice the name of Randolph Marion escaped her, but without note or comment. 'She had known them both two years before in Philadelphia, and she had always thought Miss Marion most entirely captivating, and so did her aunt Mary.'

Gertrude was delighted to see that Emilie could crop the flowers in her path. Neither of them perceived they grew on the brink of a precipice. Emilie seldom adverted to her engagement. Like death, it was future and inevitable, but its period was not fixed, to her knowledge, and she felt in regard to it, all the relief of uncertainty. Little did she suspect that her mother had promised that the marriage should take place as soon after Pedrillo's appearance at Trenton as he should request.

Mrs. Layton was still secluded in her own apartment, and beguiled Gertrude and Emilie—and herself too—with exaggerated expressions of sensibility and suffering! 'She could not see Gertrude,' so said the little twisted pencil-scrawled notes which she sent her twice and thrice a day, 'an indifferent person she could meet without emotion; but her nerves and affections were so interwoven that one could not be touched without the other vibrating. She was sustained by the consciousness of performing a necessary duty, but she had nothing of the martyr in her composition, and she shrunk from the fagot and the pile. She thanked Heaven, poor Em' had not the sad inheritance of her sensibility. In a few days she hoped to see Gertrude—but now her nerves required solitude and a dark room.'

Of all the mysteries and obliquities of the human mind, the arts of self-delusion are the most curious. No doubt Mrs. Layton's imagination figured the fagot and the pile, but was it the martyr or the culprit that suffered?

"Dear Gertrude," said Emilie, bursting into her apartment, and looking as bright and fresh as a sunny morning in June, "we are all going to the falls this afternoon—do promise you will go with us." Mr. Clarence, who chanced to enter the room at the same moment, enforced Emilie's entreaties, and Gertrude promised to join her in the parlor in the course of half an hour. Accordingly she went to the parlor at the appointed time; but finding no one there, she passed into a small adjoining apartment, and while she was awaiting Emilie she examined a collection of minerals belonging to mine host of the 'rural resort,' a versatile genius, who is well known to have diversified the labors of his calling with occasional lectures on the popular sciences.[1] Directly, two other persons entered the parlor, but as their voices were unknown to her, she remained where she was, secluded from observation.

After some common-place remarks about the weather, the lady said abruptly, "Have you made up your mind, Randolph?"

"About what, Augusta?"

"Pshaw! don't blush so—upon my honor, I did not allude to Emilie Layton."

"I did not imagine you did, Augusta."

---

1 John Sherman's *A Description of Trenton Falls* (1827) includes extensive description of the geology of the falls and fossil evidence at the site and in his collection.

"Oh, not at all; and you were not thinking of her—were you?"

"And if I were?"

"*If*, indeed! No, no, Randolph, you must not enact the lover there—a beautiful gem she is—but not for your cabinet. Did you ever see such rich hazle eyes, and dark eye-lashes, with such fair hair, and exquisite skin?—did you ever, Randolph?"

"Why do you ask me, Augusta?—you know I never did."

"And such dimples and lips—and her fairy Fanella figure—and her exquisite little feet. I do not believe Pauline Borghese's were as pretty, though it was her custom to denude them to the admiring eyes of her visiters—do you, Randolph?[1] Well may you look grave. It was a cross accident that cast her in your way just now, when such an opportunity of falling eligibly in love is at hand—when, for once, love and reason might meet together in good fellowship."

"As they never did meet, Augusta."

"Ah, that is the cant of one and twenty. But matters are differently arranged with such veterans as mama and I. You should hear some of our colloquies. Dear mama! nothing is more amusing than the struggles of her natural tastes against the vulgar necessities of this 'bank-note world.' In your selection of a wife—and mama has no doubt you can select from the whole sex—she would not allow the lady's fortune to be even a make-weight in the scale of your favor; but the trifling accessory—the little accident of fortune 'removes the only objection to Randolph's marriage,' so says mama. 'Removes the objection!' was ever a pecuniary motive more ingeniously stated, and in singleness of heart too. And truly, Randolph, if this Miss Clarence is the paragon of excellence that Emilie represents her, the one objection is removed."

"But, Augusta, what if there be in my heart a thousand and one objections?"

"To Miss Clarence?"

"Pshaw! no. What am I to Hecuba, or what is Hecuba to me?"[2]

"I understand you—the objections are to marrying any woman, save one?"

Marion shut the outer door, and then replied, "Yes, Augusta, save one. From you, my dear sister, I have no concealments."

---

1   Pauline Bonaparte Borghese (1780-1825), sister to Napoleon Bonaparte, was well known for her beauty and love affairs.

2   Reference to Hamlet's line, "What's Hecuba to him, or he to Hecuba, / That he should weep for her?" in Shakespeare's *Hamlet* II.ii.559. Hecuba, wife of Priam (ruler of Troy); Hamlet and the players repeat the story of Priam's slaughter, witnessed by Hecuba.

Miss Marion made no reply for some moments—when she did, her voice was changed from raillery to tender seriousness, "I am sorry, Randolph—heartily sorry—but cannot blame you. All the loves and graces have combined in that pretty creature against your prudence; and then her beauty is so true an index of her sweet, innocent spirit. Well, it can't be helped, and so there's an end of it. No, I do not blame you. On the very verge of the frigid zone of old maidism as I am, there is nothing I so truly sympathize with as a youthful, reckless, true love—a love that hopes, expects, and believes all things—and fears nothing. Randolph, from the time we knew Emilie in Philadelphia, and you used to carry her music-book to school for her, I have had a presentiment of this, and when we met here, I was sure you had turned the critical page in the book of fate."

"And you permitted me to read it without advice or warning. God bless you, my dear Augusta."

Nothing makes a young heart overflow with gratitude like meeting (especially if unexpected) with hearty sympathy in a love affair. Randolph Marion was a pattern of fraternal affection, but never had he felt more tenderly towards his sister than at this moment; and when she proceeded to give him more unequivocal proofs of her sympathy, his feelings were raised to a higher pitch than tenderness.

"Randolph," she said, "I am frank and direct, and must to the point. I like to remove all moveable obstacles. I do not mean to be pathetic; but you know 'there are but two of us,' and between us two but one heart. I have some fortune, thanks to aunt Molly—there are sad rents in our patrimonial estate—take what I have and repair them, and in return, my dear brother, give me in fee simple a rocking-chair at your fire-side, and that, with a life estate in your heart, is all I ask."[1]

Marion threw his arms around his sister's neck, and expressed in a few broken sentences his admiration of her generosity, and his determination not to accept it.

"It is no sudden impulse of generosity, Randolph, but that which I have long expected and determined to do. Since the event that fatally and for ever extinguished my hopes, nothing remains for me but to make others happy; and that, I suspect, after all, is the surest way of making myself so." At this moment the door opened, and Emilie appeared. She perceived the brother and sister

---

1   In fee simple: absolute, complete ownership. Life estate: ownership or possession for the term of the possessor's natural life.

were deeply engaged, and was retreating, but they both begged her to come in, and she then asked 'if Miss Clarence were not there?'

"Heaven forefend!" exclaimed Miss Marion, resuming her natural tone of gaiety.

"She must have come in here," continued Emilie, "her father told me she was here, and the servant says he saw her come in here."

Poor Gertrude had been on the rack for the last ten minutes. There had been no point in the conversation from its start, when she could, without extreme embarrassment, make her appearance. As it had proceeded, she had become as anxious to avoid observation, as ever a hidden criminal was to escape detection. She would have jumped out of the window if there had been an open window; but there was none—no possible escape—and she had stood, like a statue, hoping that some kind chance would call the parties away before she was compelled to make her egress. Emilie approached the door of the inner room, and nothing could in any degree relieve her but an adroit movement. She advanced from her seclusion.

"Gertrude," exclaimed Emilie, "you are here after all!"

The Marions looked thunderstruck. There was tinge enough on Gertrude's cheek to manifest her full consciousness of the awkward position in which she stood. Emilie began the usual form of an introduction.

Gertrude interrupted her, then recovering her self-possession, she said, "An introduction is superfluous, Emilie, you would hand me across the vestibule—I am already in the inner temple—and your friends must believe," she continued, turning to them, her fine countenance animated with the feelings they had inspired, "your friends must believe that I feel its beauty too much, ever to violate its sanctity."

Miss Marion obeyed the impulse of her warm heart and took Gertrude's hand. "We are friends for ever," she said, "and Randolph is in love, literally at first sight." He certainly looked all admiration. "Do not, my dear Emilie," she continued, "stare as if we had all of a sudden fallen to talking Greek—don't ask, even with your eyes, for an explanation. Here is Mr. Clarence looking as if it were time for us to proceed on our walk." They did so—and when they came to the steps, Mr. Clarence turned off, saying that he had arrived at an age when a man must be excused for preferring to look down upon a water-fall to the inconvenience of descending to look up. The ladies accepted his excuse and promised to join him at the shantee on the brink of the great fall. Emilie took

Marion's offered arm, without dreaming of the projects that were agitating his bosom, or the hopes that were hovering on his lips for expression. She was at the happy age when the feelings are enjoyed, without being analyzed. She lived in the present bright hour, careless of the future, for whatever was future seemed to her, as to a child, distant. When they reached the flat rocks at the bottom of the steps, Gertrude was affected by the recollection of the scene she had witnessed when last there. Miss Marion observed her unnatural paleness, and imputing it to the debility consequent on her fatigue and anxiety, she insisted on sitting down with her, and permitting Randolph and Emilie to precede them. Randolph was nothing loath to this arrangement, and he soon disappeared with his fair companion. The circumstances of Gertrude's introduction to Miss Marion, enabled them to dispense with the usual preliminaries to acquaintance. They understood one another, and feeling that they did so, they interchanged thoughts on various subjects with the familiarity of friends. Miss Marion did not speak of Emilie, and Gertrude dared not intimate that her destiny was already fixed. They talked of Mrs. Layton, about whom Miss Marion was quite curious. She had never seen her, and had no very favorable impression of her. "I would fain believe, Miss Clarence," she said, "that she deserves the admiration you express of her, but I am certain I should not like her. The happy age of delusion—the luxury of believing all things are what they seem, is past to me. Experience has been to me like the magical unguent with which poor Lelia anointed her eyes, that enabled her mortal vision to penetrate through all disguises into the sins and miseries of fairy land. Mrs. Layton is a woman of fashion—a belle at forty! No, I am sure I shall not like her. Thank Heaven, Emilie has not been long enough in her atmosphere—a malaria it is—to be infected by her." Gertrude interrupted Miss Marion to ask if she knew the gentleman who had just descended the steps, and who after a keen glance at them, eagerly surveyed the only traversable path. "I think I have seen him before," she said, after a moment's consideration. "Oh, yes, that dog I recollect perfectly." She pointed to a beautiful liver-colored little spaniel, with white tips to his feet and ears, and his sides fleckered with spots so white and distinct, that they appeared like wreaths of snow just lightly thrown there. "I remember now, it was on board the steam-boat I met them—the dog is a perfect beauty." The dog, as if conscious of the admiring gaze of the ladies, and like a flattered belle, anxious to show off his commended graces, plunged into the water. The current was stronger than he anticipated, and he seemed in imminent danger of being swept away; but he courageously buffetted the waves, whimpering and keeping his eye fixed on his master, who sprang to the brink of the water, crying, "Bravo! bravo! Triton, my good fellow! bravo!—courage mon petit!"[1] He looked as if he would plunge in for his favorite, if it were necessary. But it was not—Triton came safe to land, and while he was shaking a shower from his pretty sides, and receiving his master's caresses, Gertrude anxiously demanded of Miss Marion if she knew the gentleman's name. "I do not—I meant to have inquired—it is such a burden off your mind when you find out a stranger's name—he is evidently a foreigner."

"A foreigner!" echoed Miss Clarence.

"You start, as if a foreigner were of course a pirate, or a great bandit."

The only foreigner Gertrude thought of, at that moment, certainly seemed to her to belong to the class of spoilers. Though Emilie had told her, Pedrillo did not look like a Spaniard, yet Gertrude's imagination had pictured him with dark eyes; with a face of more shade than light, and in every shadow lurking some deep mystery or bad design. The gentleman had large and very light blue eyes, and a fair, clear complexion, though rather deepening to the hue of the *bon vivant*,[2] and Gertrude thought at first sight, (for we would put in a saving clause for her sagacity,) had rather an open, agreeable expression.

"What does your practised eye," she asked Miss Marion, "see of the foreigner in that gentleman?"

"What! why, in the first place, observe his air—the *tout-en-semble*[3]—he has nothing of the don't care, negligent demeanour of our countrymen who, from living always among their equals, from having no superiors to obey, nor inferiors to command, get this easy, indifferent, and careless manner. Our quiet, plodding, uneventful, comfortable lives, are stamped on our faces. They are as different from the Europeans, as the appearance of a tame animal, from a wild one. After the smooth surface of youth is broken up, the face bears the record of individual experience. I was struck with this, in looking at David's picture of the coronation.[4] The remarkable men there clustered around their master, the miracle of the age, looked as if they had lived in an atmosphere of pure

---

1 My little one.
2 One who lives well, indulging in sensuous enjoyments.
3 All together, complete.
4 "The Coronation of Napoleon I" (1808) by painter Jacques-Louis David (French, 1784-1825).

oxygen. I remember turning my eyes from the picture to the sober citizens who were gazing at it, and thinking that their faces were as spiritless as shaking Quakers."

"But these are indications to the gifted eye," said Gertrude.

"There are others then, more obvious. Just cast your eye on this gentleman, now his hat is off; you may, for he does not seem conscious of our existence—that profusion of hair, would be a curiosity on an American head, over five and twenty; and this gentleman has some dozen years more than that—and observe, as he passes his hand over his face, those large, richly set rings. I never saw an American (I mean, of course a man past boyishness and dandyism) with more than one, and that, some simple token or memorial; and finally, see the string of little silver bells on his dog's collar—an American would not venture an appendage so pretty and fantastical. But see, he is coming towards us, and means to speak—of course he is not an Englishman."

The stranger bowed courteously, and made some commonplace remarks on the scenery. Whether his accent were foreign, or merely peculiar to the individual, it was difficult to determine. He compared the falls to those on the Caatskill—the Cohoes, the falls of the Genesee, Niagara, la Chaudiére, and Montmorenci. This was all American, and Gertrude began to think her companion's sagacity was at fault; but in the next breath, he spoke of the falls of the Clyde, of Tivoli, and Schuffhausen, as if equally familiar with them.[1] He affected nothing of the amateur of nature, but appeared the citizen of the world, who, habitually adapts himself to the taste of the company in which he happens to fall. The ladies rose to pursue their walk, and he bowed, and preceded them at so quick a pace that he was soon out of sight. Brief as their interview had been, Gertrude was satisfied that Miss Marion was right in her conjectures, and instinctively as she shrunk from it, she believed that she ought to rejoice in Pedrillo's arrival. The sooner poor Marion was awakened from his dream, the better; and certainly too, the sooner Emilie was recalled from the labyrinth, into which she was blindly plunging. But even her deep interest in her friend was driven from Gertrude's mind, at repassing the rocks on which she had suffered with Seton the agonies of deadly fear and despair—some gentler remembrances beamed athwart her mind.

---

1 Waterfalls in New York (the Catskills, Cohoes, Genesee, Niagara), Quebec, Canada (la Chaudière, Montmorenci), Scotland (the Clyde), Italy (Tivoli), and Switzerland (Schuffhausen).

An abrupt turn in their walk, now again brought the ladies in view of, and near to the stranger. He stood partly concealed by a cluster of dwarf-beeches, his face half averted from them, but still they could see that his brow was contracted, his lips compressed, and his eye eagerly fixed on some object; and instantly Gertrude perceived that object was Emilie, and she felt assured the stranger was Pedrillo. Emilie stood beyond, and far above them, on the flat surface of a projecting rock. Her Leghorn cottage-hat, tied with pink ribbons, had fallen back, and Randolph was interweaving her beautiful tresses with wild flowers. She appeared as lovely, and both were as happy as spirits of paradise; and Pedrillo seemed to regard them with that oblique and evil eye, that Satan bent on our first parents in their blest abode—that eye of mingled and contending passions, that expresses the ruined soul. Both the ladies stopped, and stood motionless.

All parties were near the great fall. Mr. Clarence was in the porch of the little shantee that overlooks the cascade. Randolph and Emilie had ascended some distance above the basin of the torrent, by the foot-path, that winding around the perpendicular rocks, and mounting the bare sides of those that are less precipitous, affords a safe, and not very difficult ascent to the cautious and agile passenger. As we have said, Emilie and Marion were standing on the platform of a projecting rock, when Pedrillo first discerned them—there they stood, the world forgetting. It was one of those few blissful moments of life, that borrows nothing from memory, and asks nothing from hope. Such moments are too often a prelude to weary hours of sorrow; they were fleeting to Emilie, for recalled to actual existence by a strong and unequivocal expression of Randolph's tenderness, her engagement darted into her mind; she started as if a dagger had pierced her heart, and turned from her lover. As she did so, she saw Pedrillo; she encountered his glance, and she felt to her inmost soul all it conveyed. She uttered a faint exclamation and turned from the rock to ascend the cliff. She left his side, or rather sprang from him so abruptly, that Marion was not aware of her intention till she was some feet in advance of him. "Be careful, Emilie!" he cried, "Stop! for Heaven's sake, stop—let me precede you. Emilie! Emilie! stop!" he continued, as she, without hearing or heeding him, pressed on. "Just ahead of you, is a most perilous place—for God's sake, stop! Emilie! Emilie! you are below the path!"

Still she heeded not, but pressed on with that fearlessness that sometimes secures from accident. But here there was but one security—but one safe path, and from that she had unconsciously deviated. Mr. Clarence saw from above her imminent peril, and screamed to her to stop. Gertrude and Miss Marion perceived, that one more step, and her fate was inevitable; and in the same breath, they uttered a shriek of terror. Pedrillo, too, in a voice that resounded from shore to shore, shouted 'Beware!' Randolph, only, was silent; almost petrified by the immediate presence of the danger of which he saw the full extent without a hope to rescue her. The panic was now fully communicated to Emilie. The shouts above and below confounded her, without conveying any distinct intimation to her mind. Already her foot was on some loose stones that projected over the edge of the precipice, and only half sustained by the earth in which they were embedded, must be dislodged by the slightest force. She felt them sliding from beneath her feet, and made one more leap forward, but there the support was still more treacherous—the stones gave way at the first touch of her foot, and she felt herself sinking with them. Instinctively she stretched out her arms, and grasped a bough of hanging cedar that depended over the cliff. Her hold was too weak to sustain the weight of her body, and yet tenacious enough to check her descent. Many feet, sheer down the precipice she went, her hands slipping near to the extremity of the limb where though scarcely as thick as a common sized rope, it yet supported her.

So powerful is the instinct of self-preservation, that the most weak, and timid, and inexperienced, left alone, without any possibility of help but in the energy of their own efforts, have manifested an amazing power in perceiving and grasping at any means of salvation from destruction. Her friends were gazing in despair. They saw the limb swing back from her released grasp, and believed that all was over. Not Randolph, for he had already descended the precipice with desperate velocity, and from below he saw Emilie, with the Heaven inspired instinct that would have guided a kid over a mountain crag, gently release one hand from the bough and grasp some fibrous twigs, that shot out from a fissure in the rock—and just where she needed the support, and where alone it would avail her, there was a cleft in which she placed her feet. One giddy glance she gave to the precipice below, and the foaming abyss that lashed its side, then turned her face, pressed her brow to the rock, and resolutely closed her eyes to shut out the appalling scene. Pedrillo and Marion now explored the precipice with intense and almost equal anxiety, to find some mode of rescuing her from the frightful position, that it was evident she could not long maintain. At the same moment they perceived a fissure in, or rather a ledge, of the rock, just wide enough for a possible, though most perilous passage, from the platform from which Emilie had started to a place a few feet below, and parallel to that where she now was. Both at the same instant sprang towards the platform. Pedrillo was nearest and first attained it, and thus secured himself the precedence on the narrow ledge. Marion's satisfaction at seeing him rapidly approach Emilie to give her the aid, which, if it came not soon would come too late, was strangely mingled with disappointment at thus being rendered, by the interposition of a stranger, useless to her for whose safety he would freely have given his life. But he soon lost every other feeling in the apprehension that some misstep—some miscalculated aid, might farther endanger the life, that was now suspended by a single thread. Once or twice Emilie half turned her face towards him. It was as pale as marble; and even at that distance, it was evident from a certain relaxation of attitude, that her strength and courage were sinking away. What, then, was his astonishment at seeing Pedrillo, after reaching the extremity of the ledge—the point where, if at all assistance was to be given, stand for a moment, survey the abyss, and then return towards the platform. In an instant he reached it. "Some other mode must be tried," he said, "the ledge at its extremity is inconceivably narrow—there is not breadth enough for a bird's claw—my head became giddy—at the least attempt to aid Miss Layton I must have lost my balance, and we should have been precipitated into the abyss. Follow me, sir," he continued, with the air of one who has a right to command; "there are persons at the shantee who can help us—ropes must be let down—there is no time to be lost."

"Not an instant," said Marion, "and but one way to save her;" and he passed on to the ledge, with the evident determination 'to do, or die.'

"Oh stop!—my brother—Randolph, stop!" cried Augusta Marion, who, with Gertrude, had attained the platform, and was standing there, both most agitated witnesses of the whole scene.

But Randolph would not heed her; and Gertrude, with a firmness that was a guardian angel in all exigencies, followed Marion saying, "I am sure I can give your brother assistance—I am used to these rocks—be calm, Miss Marion, and do not look at us."

"Noble creature! God help them!" ejaculated the terrified sister, and clasping her hands she sunk on her knees; but her lips did not move—her heart scarcely beat—her whole soul was fixed in one intent breathless interest.

But what was her suffering to that of the father, who stood on the verge of the cliff and saw Gertrude, she in whom all his affections and every hope were concentrated, voluntarily place her life in peril; and that peril, to his view, aggravated by the distance and depth below him!

In the mean time, Pedrillo mounted the rocks, intent on his own project of rescuing Emilie. He had not proceeded far, when his little dog, Triton, who seemed to have become aware that danger pervaded the place, sprang yelping after him and before him, as if to arrest his progress. Pedrillo, in his eagerness, stumbled over him and fell; and in his fall he sprained his ankle so as to be utterly disabled, and was obliged to crawl back to the platform, and there endure an irritation of mind that far surpassed the anguish inflicted by his hurt, though that was by no means trifling. His love for Emilie was the strongest and tenderest sentiment of which he was capable, and he was now condemned to remain in utter inaction, and see her beautiful form mutilated, crushed, destroyed; or, an idea scarcely more tolerable, see her saved from this perdition by the superior devotion and skill of this young stranger rival. Has Dante described a penal suffering more acute than Pedrillo's?[1]

Marion, closely followed by Gertrude, soon reached the extremity of the ledge. He seemed not even to perceive the danger from which Pedrillo had retreated. Emilie was not conscious of his approach till he pronounced her name. She then looked towards him with speechless agony. Her deathly paleness, the nervous convulsion of her features, and the tremulous motion of her whole body struck a panic to his heart. His eye turned to Gertrude. "Oh God!" he murmured. His voice and look expressed his utter despair.

"Be calm," she replied, "we can save her—I am sure of it—only be firm. Emilie—Emilie," she added, in an almost cheerful voice, "be resolute for one minute more, and you will be safe." Again Emilie turned her head, and still she looked like a dying victim on the rack. Gertrude did not venture to raise her eye to her. With the inspiration of heroic courage and devotion, she bent her whole mind to the action. Not a thought was spared to fear or danger. "You see," she said to Marion, taking her hands from the rock and standing upright with a careless freedom of attitude, "you see I have ample space for my feet. I stand with as perfect security here, as on a parlor-floor. Here too, are some twigs above me, by which I can hold. My position is firm and safe." "You"—she

---

1 Dante Alighieri (Italian, c. 1265-1321), in *The Inferno*, the first volume of *The Divine Comedy*, depicts travels through the nine circles of Hell.

continued, depressing her voice to the lowest audible tone—"you have a narrow, precarious foot-hold; but by grasping my hand you may secure your balance. Now consider how you can get Emilie where we are."

Gertrude's self-possession and intrepidity inspirited Marion. "We can save her," he exclaimed, "if she will let us. Do you speak to her—I cannot."

"My dear Emilie," she said, "the danger is already past, if you will think so. Fix your eye on us, and mind Mr. Marion's directions." The poor girl felt already the inspiration of hope. She did as she was directed, and as she turned her face towards them, they perceived she was much less frightfully pale and agitated. Marion gave one hand to Gertrude, and extending the other, "place your feet," he said, "Emilie in my hand. It is as firm as if it were braced with irons—keep your hands upon the rocks—they will support and balance you. One single yard from this spot, and you will be in perfect safety." Once Emilie advanced her foot, and withdrew it. "Do not draw back, Emilie," cried Gertrude and Marion in one breath—"do not draw back—fear nothing—keep hold of the twigs till your feet are firmly placed." She did so—they retreated one step. Marion's hand was firm and unbending as adamant—another step—and another, and Marion slowly depressed his hand, and Emilie's feet were on the rock, on the same level with his. Not one word was spoken. He placed his arm around her, and thus sustained her, trembling like an aspen leaf, to the platform, and there she sank on his bosom, and both lost all thought and feeling, save an obscure but most delicious consciousness of safety and love. How long they remained thus they knew not. What mortal art can measure or define such moments? They seem to partake of the immortal essence of the high feeling infused into them—to belong to eternity.

Gertrude had passed the platform, and gone to meet her father, whom she saw approaching. In his arms she was now folded, receiving all the expression he could give to his joy, and pride, and gratitude, and love.

Pedrillo had withdrawn a little from the platform, and though he still stood near Emilie and Marion, they were unconscious of his proximity. With a feeling that she was now all his own, Marion imprinted a kiss on her brow. Pedrillo started forward, "Miss Layton," he exclaimed, in a voice of passion, "have you forgotten?"— He paused. If the rocks had yawned to engulf her, Emilie would not have been more shocked. She became as agitated as when she hung over the abyss. A more dreadful abyss, was present to her imagination. She shrunk away from Marion, and covered her face with her hands.

"What is the meaning of this impertinent intrusion?" demanded Marion.

"Impertinent!" retorted Pedrillo, "and what name do you give, sir, to the advantage you have taken of the accidental service rendered to my affianced wife?"

There was an assurance in Pedrillo's voice and manner that left little to be hoped. Marion turned a look on Emilie that said every thing—he spoke but one word, "Emilie?"

"It is all true," she replied.

geet —) "Would to God then we had perished together!"

A check was now put upon the expression of the excited feeling of all parties. Mr. Clarence approached. Emilie's face was covered and leaning on Miss Marion's shoulder, who, half comprehending, and fully pitying her, sustained her in her arms. "My poor little Emilie," said Mr. Clarence, tenderly embracing her, "I do not wonder you cannot get over this dreadful fright. We must get you home to your mother. Where's Marion? Ah, there he goes, running away from our compliments. It was a knightly feat, but he should not withdraw till the 'fair ladye' is in her bower again."

And how to get the ladies to their bower again was the next consideration; but as this was achieved by ordinary means, we shall not detain our readers with the details.

The ladies were all, of course, compelled by Mr. Clarence's tender watchfulness over their health to retire for repose. Gertrude was relieved from a vain attempt to compose her spirits, by an urgent request from Mrs. Layton that she would come to her room. She received her with extravagant demonstrations of joy and tenderness. Flattering as they were, they awakened a passing query in Gertrude's mind why the pleasure that was so fervent had been so long deferred. "My precious Gertrude," began Mrs. Layton, after the first greetings were over, "you may have some faint idea how much I have suffered for the last ten days, from the fact of my not being able to see you. It is hard for one who has Heaven's chartered freedom of mind, to be bound by the stern fatalism of circumstances. I can only allude to certain affairs. If I were at liberty I should open my heart to you, Gertrude, of all persons in the world; but you already know enough from my poor Em' to imagine my relief from having the evil day put off."

"Thank Heaven," exclaimed Gertrude, "it is then put off."

"Of course—Pedrillo is unable to move—what a frightful predicament poor Em' was in, on those rocks; and she tells me, you behaved so sweetly, Gertrude. By the way, dearest, do tell me something of this young Marion who enacted the hero to-day—rather officiously, I think—I am provoked that he should thrust himself forward, and deprive Pedrillo of such an opportunity of rendering Emilie a romantic service." Gertrude inferred from the light tone, in which Mrs. Layton spoke of the affair, that she was not at all aware of Emilie's hair-breadth escape, and she described the frightfulness of her danger, Pedrillo's attention to his own safety, and Marion's devotion to the single object of Emilie's preservation. Mrs. Layton listened with great apparent interest, expressed her surprise that Emilie had been so incommunicative, and concluded by saying, she supposed "the poor child had been scared out of her wits. She scarcely spoke to me after her return; and said, she should lie down in her own room, and begged not to be disturbed—she is taking an honest nap I have no doubt—she is just like her father—I should not have slept for a month, after such an affair. Well, it is fortunate for her, that she has so little imagination. It will make small difference to her, who enacts the hero—she is not like you and me, Gertrude; she never will suffer the sad, sad experience of a heart of sensibility, its cravings, its yearnings, its unbounded desires, its vain regrets—No, no, Emilie's life will flow on, as the scripture has it, like still waters in green pastures."[1]

"Oh, Mrs. Layton, I am afraid your expectations are too sanguine. Her childhood has been serene, but to pursue your figure, the stream that is destined to frightful precipices, may hold its infant course through flowery and still pastures."

"It may; but we are misled, by talking figuratively. The fact is, I see, (for I am not blinded by maternal affection,) I see that Emilie is a *mediocre* character; if she were not, would not her own beauty excite her more? She will just live *even on*, content with what would be to you and me, perfect stagnation, ordinary connubial life—it is a safe, but certainly, not a very alluring destiny. Believe me, dearest, married life rarely affords much excitement to the sensibilities, or scope to the imagination."

Gertrude shrunk from expressing her maiden meditations, on this subject. They were high and romantic, or, might be called so, by those who are fond of affixing that doubtful epithet, to the aspirations of those, who modify their hopes by the capabilities of our race, rather than graduate them by its history. Mrs. Layton guessed her thoughts; "My sweet friend," she said, "I see your

---

1 Refers to Psalm 23.

mental revoltings from my views of life. Mine are the result of my peculiar position; I am not a philosopher, and my opinions are deduced from individual experience; so, do not let me cast the shadows of my past, over the bright field of your future. We will not talk of shadows; I feel particularly light-hearted. As I said before, the evil day, which God knows I have done all I could to avert, is at any rate deferred. Pedrillo has too much respect for the graces, to go hobbling to the hymeneal altar. I shall have time to recruit my spirits; and poor Em', to cultivate a more tender sentiment for her suitor. Indeed, I think he ought to excite it; he is uncommonly elegant, and a foreigner; and that is, after all, an advantage *dans les petites affaires du cœur.*[1] The men of our country, particularly our northern country, are so deficient in all the embellishments—the mysterious, indescribable little arts, that excite the imagination; they are upright and downright—and have such a smack of home about them. If they reach the heart, it is by the turnpike-road of common sense, not by the obscure, devious, mysterious, but delicious avenue of the imagination. You agree with me, at least you feel with me, Gertrude?"

"I am listening to you, but I really have no opinion on the subject; I have seen so little of society, that I have made few comparisons. My predilection, I confess, is in favor of my own countrymen; they may have a less polished exterior, but they seem to me, to have more independence of manner, more naturalness, and simplicity."

"Certainly, they have—but less of these prime qualities than savages—you smile, but you will think with me, when you have passed a winter in town—the thing I have set my heart on. By the way, poor Louis Seton! Gertrude, a *sentiment* is so necessary to us; so much is it, as has been said, the 'history of a woman's life,' that, shut up, as you have been, at Clarenceville, with this 'man of feeling,' I am amazed you have escaped something more serious than a passing *tendresse.*[2] Now, no protestations—susceptibility is absolutely essential to an attractive woman. But come, dearest, one of my reasons, though the least urgent, for sending for you, was, to beg you to present me to these Marions. It is incumbent on me, to make my acknowledgments to our knight of the rocks."

The ladies proceeded together to the parlor, and there learned, to Gertrude's mortification, and Mrs. Layton's well concealed

---

1 In the little affairs of the heart.
2 Fondness.

satisfaction, that the Marions had taken their final departure from the 'rural resort,' half an hour before. A servant gave Miss Clarence a note from Miss Marion; it ran as follows:

"My dear Miss Clarence—I have forborne to disturb your repose after your perilous adventure, to announce our abrupt departure. Accident introduced you into our family cabinet, and as you are apprised of its secrets, you will not wonder at poor Randolph's feelings, in consequence of the disclosures of to-day. My heart pleads for Emilie, but my reason tells me, that it is wisest, discretest, best, to shun any farther intercourse with so beautiful a creature, who is so careless of obligations and consequences. Depend on it, Miss Clarence, I am right in my opinion of the mother; and though I grieve to say it, poor Emilie has bad blood in her veins. I am sustaining the part of a rigid moralist with Randolph, while my womanish heart is melting within me. I cannot regard the sweet girl in any other light, than as a victim—the faults of seventeen are not deliberate—but I talk as sternly to Randolph, as if I were Junius Brutus.[1] In compliance with a kind invitation from your father, we have promised to visit Clarenceville, on our return from Niagara.

"'Till then, adieu, my dear Miss Clarence,
"and allow me to be
"your friend and admirer,
"A. MARION."

Pedrillo was on a sofa in the parlor, when the ladies entered; and while Gertrude was reading her note, he and Mrs. Layton were carrying on a subdued, but impassioned conference; the result of which was a request from Mrs. Layton, that Miss Clarence would do her the favor to request Emilie, provided she found her awake and sufficiently recovered, to make her appearance in the parlor.

Gertrude found her friend, neither sleeping, nor recovered; but sitting in a most disconsolate attitude, bending over an open letter, which she had drenched with her tears. "Oh, Gertrude!" she said, "look at this—is it not cruel?" It was from Marion, and began with the text of all disappointed lovers.

---

1 Lucius Junius Brutus, founder of the Republic of Rome in 509 BCE.

"Frailty, thy name is woman![1] Must I apply this condemnation to Emilie Layton? Why have I lived to find that she, whom my devoted love invested with perfection, is capable of deliberate coquetry. Am I in my senses? Could Emilie Layton, she, who appeared full of all kind and gentle thoughts, could she, on the eve of marriage with another, trifle with a heart she knew was all her own? She has done so—your own lips Emilie, have confessed the truth—your vows *are* plighted to another—it is not slander—it is not a dream—again and again I repeat the first prayer of my pierced soul, 'would that we had perished together.' But, my sister waits for me: she talks of recovered tranquillity—but what tranquillity can be in reversion for him, who bears in his bosom, a poisoned shaft? the bitter remembrance of her unworthiness, to whom he would have devoted his existence; for whom he would have encountered death itself, without a pang.

"Farewell, Emilie—farewell for ever,

"R. MARION."

Gertrude quite forgot the errand on which she had come to Emilie, in her efforts to console her. "I should care for nothing else in the wide world," said the poor girl, "if Randolph only knew how innocent I have been."

"That he may know in future, Emilie, but at present—"

"Oh I know I must not vindicate myself—I must suffer, and suffer in silence, and if my heart breaks I must not tell him that I loved him—loved him with far truer love than his; for I never would have believed any evil of him. I did not know till now—indeed, Gertrude, I did not, that I loved Randolph. I knew that I was always thinking of him, but I did not know *that* was love. I knew that I felt restless away from him, even with you, and happy if I were but near him without speaking, and without hearing his voice; but I did not know *that* was love. Even on that dreadful rock, Gertrude, I felt that I had rather be swallowed up in the abyss than be saved by Pedrillo, when Randolph was so near to me, and yet I did not know *that* was love. But when Mr. Pedrillo claimed me, and Randolph pronounced my name, then the whole truth flashed on me; and yet I had better die than speak the one true word to Randolph. And with this on my heart I must go to the altar with Mr. Pedrillo—and very soon too—mama hinted that to-day."

---

1 Shakespeare's *Hamlet* I.ii.146.

"Not soon, Emilie—perhaps never. Mr. Pedrillo was maimed on the rocks, and he has himself deferred the marriage."

"Thank Heaven! but what reason is there, Gertrude, to hope this detested marriage may never take place?"

"Every thing future, Emilie, is uncertain—every thing—but that if you disclose to your mother the actual state of your feelings, she will herself break off this engagement."

"Never—never, Gertrude. Mama has reasons that she does not tell me. She never would have made me write that solemn promise to papa, if it were not *necessary* to perform it. I do not know how I could do it, only that I always have to do every thing mama wishes. Mama was so sure I should like Mr. Pedrillo, and I thought she knew best. I did not hate him then—but now the very thought of him makes me shiver."

Gertrude was well aware that Mrs. Layton would not wish Emilie to show herself to Pedrillo in her present state of mind, and after ministering all possible consolations to her, she undertook to make her apology to her mother. She received it with the best grace possible. Not so Pedrillo. His cup of irritations was full, and one added drop made it overflow. He wrought himself first into a passion, and then into a fever, which produced so violent an inflammation in his wounded limb, that on the following morning the physician gave his professional opinion that the gentleman might be detained at Trenton several weeks. In this state of affairs Mrs. Layton felt her position to be rather awkward, and she and Emilie, after a tender parting with Gertrude, took their departure for New York.

Mr. Clarence and Gertrude were still detained at Trenton for some weeks. Seton's convalescence was slow and imperfect, and his melancholy continued, like an incubus, in spite of all their efforts to alleviate it. When his health was sufficiently restored to bear a removal, Mr. Clarence proposed, that instead of returning to Clarenceville, he should proceed to New York, and there embark for Italy, where in a genial climate, and in the pursuit of his art, he might regain his health and happiness. Mr. Clarence, who seemed always to regard his fortune as a trust for others, assured him that he should place at his disposal a sum that would render his residence abroad, easy and respectable. Seton heard him without reply, but with evident emotion.

On the following morning they were to leave Trenton. Seton did not appear at breakfast. Mr. Clarence went to his room, and found that he had gone, and had left a note addressed to him. It was full of expressions of gratitude and tenderness to Mr. Clarence and

Gertrude; but it was most afflicting to see that those sentiments, whose essence seems to be happiness, were so transmuted in his distempered mind, that sweet fountains distilled bitter waters.

"Why," he said, "seek to prolong a burdensome existence? He was a weed driven on the tempestuous waves—the idle sand blown over the desert of life. He cast a blight on every thing about him." The note was written in the deepest despondency, and concluded with a request that no inquiry might be made after him, and a most affecting and eternal farewell.

This request was so far from being complied with, that Mr. Clarence instituted the most assiduous inquiries. He traced him to Utica, but no farther. His family connections knew nothing of him, and Mr. Clarence and Gertrude were driven to the horrible conclusion that he had committed the last act of despair.

END OF VOL. I.

CLARENCE;
OR,
A TALE OF OUR OWN TIMES.

BY THE
AUTHOR OF "HOPE LESLIE," &c. &c.

"Return, return, and in thy heart engraven keep my lore,
The lesser wealth, the lighter load—small blame betides the
poor."

BISHOP HEBER

IN TWO VOLUMES.

VOL. II.

PHILADELPHIA.
CAREY & LEA .—CHESTNUT STREET.
1830.

CLARENCE;
OR,
A TALE OF OUR OWN TIMES.

CHAPTER I.

"I'll no say men are villains a',
The real harden'd wicked,
Wha hae nae check but human law,
Are to a few restricked."[1]
BURNS.

PEDRILLO's detention at Trenton was protracted day after day, and week after week. His inflammatory constitution, and impatient temper, acted reciprocally upon each other; and a wound, that with a tranquil temperament would, by the process of nature, have been cured in a week, produced a suffering and languishing sickness. So surely and dreadfully are physical evils aggravated by moral causes, that those who would enjoy a sound body, should cherish a sound mind.

He passed the weary hours in alternately execrating poor little Triton, as the cause of his accident, and then caressing him as the only solace of his solitude; in cursing his own ill-luck, waterfalls, country-doctors—in short, every thing that had the most innocent relation to his misfortune. Time at last, did its beneficent work, and late in the autumn, Pedrillo returned to New York, without a blemish on his fine person.

A few weeks had wrought a sad change in Emilie. The careless, irrepressible joy of youth was gone; her manners had the indifference and languor of those, whose interests in life are paralyzed by use and time; the bloom had faded from her cheek, and was only replaced by the exquisite, but transient hue of feeling. Her eyes were habitually cast down, as if to shelter from observation, the secret sorrow that was betrayed in their tender melancholy. She submitted to the fate that awaited her, without any other remonstrance, or repining, than the mute signs we have described, which should indeed have spoken daggers to her parents. She began to fancy herself callous to the future. 'Why should she care what became of her?' thus she reasoned—'if Randolph Marion no longer cared for her, and she was sure that he did not, nor in any circumstances ever would.'

---

1 From "Epistle to a Young Friend" (1786).

She had seen him once since his unkind parting at Trenton. He, and his sister, passed through New York, on their way to Virginia, and she accidentally encountered them in a shop. Randolph bowed coldly; Miss Marion, always kind, in and out of rule, addressed her with cordiality; but a cordiality so flurried, that it betrayed its meaning. She said that they were hurrying through town, and made some apology for not calling to see her, which like most such apologies, only augmented the embarrassment it was meant to allay. Emilie did not distinctly comprehend a word Miss Marion said—she did not know whether she replied or not. She was only conscious that Randolph was standing near her; and was, as she thought, in the coolest manner possible, discussing with the shop-keeper, the quality of some French cravats.[1] Once she looked towards him, she could not help it, but his eye was averted, and she hastened away, to bewail in secret the injustice and inconstancy of man, and the hard fate of woman, destined to love on without requital, and to suffer without sympathy.

In the mean time, Mrs. Layton flowed down the current of life, with her usual habits of self-indulgence and expense. She maintained her intimacy with Gerald Roscoe, an intimacy, that might have degenerated into a *liaison*[2] of a more doubtful nature, in circumstances where moral restraints are less salutary, and severe, and pervading; and the eye of the public less vigilant, than in our fortunate country. We would not insinuate that Mrs. Layton had any more vicious propensity, than a love for admiration; but what is more corrupting, than an insatiable passion for admiration? an unextinguishable love of coquetry? They can only be gratified by influencing the imagination, through the medium of the passions; and a woman, a wife, a mother, who maintains this most unholy despotism, has already sacrificed the fine spirit of virtue. We would be the last to impeach the virtue of our hero, but it was human, and therefore, needed to be fortified against temptation. There is something very flattering to the vanity of a young man in the preference of a woman of experience; if that experience is set off and enriched, by talent and beauty; if manners lend the aid of their almost omnipotent charm, and a brilliant and piquant conversation nourishes a distaste to common society.

Roscoe's mother had watched the progress of his acquaintance with Mrs. Layton, with great solicitude. She never attempted to govern his conduct by maternal authority, but wisely contented

---

1 Neckbands.
2 Love affair.

herself with the sure and silent influence of her affections, and sentiments. She believed that no virtue could have much vigor or merit, that was not free and independent in its operation; and though her solicitude never slept, she suffered her son (we use the expression without irreverence) 'to work out his own salvation.'

She never exacted sacrifices to her opinion, and he was never reserved in his confidence; so that, to the tie of nature, was added the charm of voluntary friendship.

Mrs. Roscoe perceived that Gerald's romantic encounter with the stranger of Trenton-falls had left a deep impression on his imagination. We cannot say on his heart, though his mother thought, that it was like ground broken up, and richly seeded, and only awaiting a farther, genial, external influence. She sympathized with all the mystery and excitement of the adventure, for she was a true woman; and so far it was a matter of feeling; but in her willing recurrence to the theme of that adventure, she had some reference to the art of the physician, who exterminates one disease, by infusing another. Gerald was at the age of sentiment, and she believed that weeds would best be extirpated by the growth of a preference, congenial to the pure and ardent mind of her son. This might prove an air-built castle at last, but it was raised by hope and love, on a base of truth.

It was not long after Pedrillo's return to town, that a singular coincidence, happened in the Layton family.

The husband and wife were both at home on the same evening, and in the parlor *tête-à-tête*. Layton was stretched on the sofa, and his wife at her piano, singing a popular Italian song. "You should never attempt Italian music, Mrs. L.," said the husband. She sang on. "It requires some assurance to sing that air, after hearing the Signorina Garcia."[1] Still her voice was unfaltering. "My dear Mrs. L., you deserve a place in Matthews' nightingale club,"[2]—"Good Lord! Mrs. L., do stop—I shall have neither ears nor nerves left." Mrs. Layton was still deaf. If 'a soft answer turneth away wrath,'[3] there is nothing kindles it like no answer at all. Layton felt himself insulted by his wife's impassiveness. He thrust the poker into the grate, threw over the shovel, and succeeded in forcing his wife from the piano with his terrible discords. She retreated, however,

ASSHOLE - Abusive

asshole, to be prure

---

1 Signorina Garcia performed in the Italian operas given at the Park Theater in New York City in the 1825-26 season.
2 "The Nightingale Club" is a song from *The Mail Coach Adventures* (1817), one of Charles Mathews's productions.
3 Proverbs 15.1.

without the slightest discomposure, and when her husband had resumed his position, on the sofa, and she had seated herself opposite to him, she asked him, with as much *nonchalance* as she would have referred to any historical truth, "Do you remember, Layton—I think it was the very day after we were engaged—do you remember your shedding tears, at my singing a little Scotch air; do you remember?" He made no reply. "Orpheus' miracle was nothing to mine, he only made the *stones move*."[1]

"But your age of miracles is past, Mrs. L." Mrs. Layton could bear any thing with more philosophy than an allusion to her age, but even that, *from her husband*, could not ruffle her temper, or rather disturb her command of it. "Do you remember," she continued, "my poor father saying, 'this is nothing, Grace, but try ten years hence if you can draw tears from your husband's eyes.'"

"God knows," muttered Layton, "you have done that often enough, but not by *music*."

"And yet there are those that tell me, even now when I sing,

'That Ixion seems no more his pain to feel,
But leans attentive on the standing wheel.'"[2]

"Yes—but your Ixion is not in the infernus of matrimony. It was Gerald Roscoe, I fancy, who made this famous speech to you?" The lady did not reply. Layton whistled, but it was any thing but the Lillabullero from the gentle soul of my uncle Toby.[3] Both parties were silent for the space of half an hour.

"A devilish agreeable time we are having," said Layton.

"I will give you something to make it more—or less agreeable," replied his wife. She rang the bell—ordered the servant to bring down her writing-desk—took from it a roll of papers and threw them to her husband. He opened them, looked at one after another, and between each uttered certain exclamations that express surprise and anger in the most laconic form—threw them all aside, and strode up and down the room.

---

1 In Greek mythology, musician and poet Orpheus, son of Apollo and the Muse Calliope, created music so beautiful that even the stones were moved.

2 From Dryden's "Georgics, Book IV" (1697). In Greek mythology, Ixion, having violated Zeus's pardon by attempting to seduce Zeus's wife, was punished by being bound to an ever-turning fiery wheel.

3 In Sterne's *Tristam Shandy*, Uncle Toby whistles Lillabullero (most commonly spelled Lilliburlero), a traditional Irish melody, rather than respond verbally to statements he finds shocking or absurd.

"There are besides," said Mrs. Layton, "some unwritten accounts, which, while your hand is in, you may as well settle. The children's school-bills—music, dancing, &c., for the last two quarters—Justine's wages since May, and," yawning, "really I do not recollect, but my impression is, there are a mass of them."

"A mass of them—and where am I to get money to pay them?"

"Indeed, I do not know, 'ce n'est pas mon affaire'."[1]

"And what under heaven is your affair, but to involve me in debt after debt, without care, and without remorse?"

"If I have no remorse for contracting debts, I think I should feel some if I were to adopt certain modes of paying them."

"What do you mean by that insinuation?" demanded Layton, turning fiercely round upon his wife.

"Oh, nothing—nothing—but that I should scarcely have the heart to pay my debts by marrying my child to"—

"To whom?—to what? speak out."

"Well then, if I must speak out—to a villain."

"A villain! have a care, madam—what right have you to call Pedrillo a villain?"

"I believe him to be so."

"On what authority?"

"The best authority."

Nothing was farther from Mrs. Layton's intentions when she first retorted her husband's reproaches, than to involve herself in the necessity of imparting the communication she had received from Gerald Roscoe at Trenton. This she knew to be dishonorable in relation to Roscoe, and besides, she meant to maintain the advantage of apparent ignorance of the worse than doubtful character of Emilie's lover. But the pleasure of recrimination overcame her prudence, and she had committed herself so far that she was obliged to proceed, and confess that Roscoe had confided to her the story of the little French girl, and had moreover told her, that there were suspicions abroad that Pedrillo had been connected with a desperate band of men on the South American coast.

Layton flew into the most unbridled passion, cursed her informer as an intermeddler, and the inventor of a tale which he professed utterly to disbelieve—threw out intimations of real or affected jealousy of Roscoe, and concluded by saying, that whatever was the reputation—whatever was the real character of Pedrillo, they were too deeply involved with him to retract. This Mrs. Layton believed, and felt that she had unwittingly given her husband

too involved to severties w/ a 'good guy'

1 'It is not my affair.'

the vantage ground. He had made the contract of Emilie's marriage, as he professed, with faith, in Pedrillo's integrity. She had acquiesced in it believing in his depravity. He reproached her with this. She alleged in defence his command, and the reasons he had assigned for that command. He retorted unqualified reproaches. She received them in apathetic silence, evincing that if she were not invulnerable, he at least could not wound her. This conjugal scene was broken up by a signal that lays many a foul domestic fiend—the ringing of the door-bell. Mrs. Layton retired to her own apartment, and Pedrillo was introduced.

He had come on business, and fortunately, as he said, had for once found Mr. Layton, and found him alone. After very concise preliminaries, he said, with the air of one who has a right to command, that he had decided his marriage should take place in January. The dictatorial manner in which he announced his determination, would, at any time, have been offensive to Layton's pride, but it was more than he could bear in his present irritated state. He replied that no one had a right to dictate his domestic arrangements—that it still depended on his will whether the marriage took place, or not.

"Does it so?" asked Pedrillo tauntingly. "What has so suddenly changed the aspect of our relations?"

"The rein and the whip," replied Layton, "may change hands."

Pedrillo demanded an explanation, and Layton gave it, without alleviating with a doubt the dark tale he unfolded. When he had professed to disbelieve it, he shared the responsibility of the imputed guilt with Pedrillo. He now devolved the whole weight on the shoulders of his principal, and he had no longer a motive to lighten it. Pedrillo admitted in full the affair at Abéille's, and treated it as a mere bagatelle—a matter of course in the life of a man of the world. The more serious charge, he asserted was an entire fabrication—invented by Roscoe in revenge of his superior success with the French girl—the revenge of a jealous and discomfited rival; or if not invented by him, it was an idle rumor to which any stranger was liable, and to which Roscoe had malignantly attempted to give force, and credibility. He was perfectly cool, and self-possessed; and poor Layton, like the insect that struggles for a moment to extricate himself from the meshes of his enemy, became more passive and helpless than ever. Pedrillo was not of a temper to remain satisfied with simply eluding a blow. He returned it with a poisoned shaft. His defeat at Abéille's had been rankling in his bosom ever since, but he could not resent it without bringing the affair to light, and risking an inauspicious influence on his suit to Emilie. He dared not pick a quarrel with Roscoe, lest it should lead to investigations that might prove inconvenient. A channel for his resentment was now opened. With the nice art of a superior mind, he adapted himself precisely to the dimensions and force of the instrument with which he was to operate. He made Layton feel, and feel to his heart's core, that their interests were identified—that they must sink or swim together; and therefore that it was quite as important to his interest as it could be to his (Pedrillo's) to repel Roscoe's charges. Roscoe was next made to appear in the light of an officious, impertinent intermeddler in Layton's domestic affairs. He insinuated that Roscoe had good reasons for cherishing that contempt for her husband which Mrs. Layton did not scruple on any occasion to manifest. From insinuations he proceeded to accusations. He said Roscoe's visit to Trenton was only a part of a system of devotion, to which Layton alone was blind. He magnified Roscoe's little gallantries—recalled his forgotten attentions, and gave to them meaning and importance, and finally filled Layton's confused and darkened mind with images of wrong and insult.

Love is not so often as self-love, the parent of jealousy. Layton's pride was wounded; not his affections, and that combined with his consciousness of guilt, and his secret rankling hatred of Pedrillo, to work him up to a welding heat, and Pedrillo perceived that he might give what form he pleased to the expression of the unhappy man's passions, when their conference was interrupted by the entrance of a visiter.

Mr. Layton was in no humor to be broken in upon. "Did not I tell you, Andrew," he said to the servant, "that I was not at home?"

"Oh, don't scold at Andrew!" said the visiter, Mr. Flint, a man of peace and invincible good nature, "he told me you were not at home, but I came in with a little errand from Mr. Roscoe to Mrs. Layton."

"You did, did you? You are a particular friend of Mr. Roscoe's—are you not?"

Mr. Flint had a decided partiality for intimacies with those, who were graduated a little above him, on the scale of gentility, and he answered unhesitatingly, and with a smile not in the least checked by Layton's rude and hurried manner, "that he was a *very* intimate friend of Mr. Roscoe."

"Then, sir, you will be kind enough to take back an errand to Mr. Roscoe; and tell him, from me, that he is a scoundrel."

"Why, Mr. Layton! I declare I—I don't understand you, sir."

"Tell him then, that he is a d——d, impertinent, lying scoundrel. If *he* does not understand me, he may send you back for an explanation."

"That's no message for one gentleman to carry to another, Mr. Layton; and I must be excused, sir." Flint began to suspect that Layton was heated with wine, and he added, "if you have any real offence with Mr. Roscoe, wait till to-morrow; a reasonable resentment won't work off in a night, and an unreasonable one will disappear with your dreams."

"Reserve your advice, sir, for your friend; he will probably need it. Will you be the bearer of my message?"

"No, sir, excuse me—I have no fancy for carrying about firebrands, especially, to throw in my friend's bosom. Good night, sir. I really advise you to be considerate—good night." He went out, but instantly returned. "Ah! Mr. Pedrillo, I forgot—I put that little wax-head of my father into my pocket, to show to you—here it is."

Pedrillo took it, bit his lips, and turned around to hold the image to the light; and as he did so, he let it fall on the hearth-stone, and broke it to fragments. "God bless me! Mr. Flint, I beg your pardon."

"You are very excusable, sir, but—but I had as lief you had broken my head."

On the same night, after his return to his lodgings, Pedrillo wrote a letter to a friend in the West Indies, from which the following passages are extracted.

"After all I may have made a false play; finessed to my own loss; however, I am sure R. has no proof to substantiate his story; and as we sons of fortune well know, there is a great gulf between suspicion and proof. Still, I may have made a false step; for though I would like to pay off all scores to that driveller, by Layton's hand, a duel is an uncertain mode of revenge, and if L. gets the worst of it, which he may, though a famous shot, I am dished. My adorable submits in holy obedience to the fiat of her father. If this is withdrawn, (thanks to my stars! death alone can withdraw it,) I shall lose her. By Heaven! Felix, the very thought of it, makes every drop of blood in my body rush to my brain.

"But I will not lose her! Did I ever relinquish any thing, on which I had fixed my grasp?

"I once knew a boy—he had lived scarce thirteen years in this wicked world, when a drover, returning from market with a full purse, stopped at his father's house, an inn, no matter where. In the dead of night, the boy stole to the drover's room with a butcher's knife, recently whetted, in one hand. He slept so soundly, though the broad moon shone in his face, that the boy secured the purse, without using the knife. But it proved not useless. The boy's father had suspected, and followed him; and while he was retreating backwards, his eye still fixed on the drover, his father grasped the purse; the boy was no match for him in strength; in daring, he was a match for the devil; he could not extricate the purse by force; he raised the other hand, and gave a single effective stroke with the knife. The bloody fingers (his father's!) relaxed their hold; the boy retained the purse, mounted a prepared horse, and made his escape. Think you that a spirit kindred to that boy's, and fortified with the sinews and muscle of a man, will relinquish an object on which his soul is fixed?

"I shall achieve a victory over this fellow, Roscoe, whether he fight or not. But he will fight; there is nothing in life a young man fears so much, as the scorn and ridicule of his companions; and though Roscoe takes a high tone, and has the reputation of spirit, (which, by the way, any man of his inches, muscle, erect-bearing, and flashing eye, may get,) yet he will not dare encounter the suspicion of sneaking. And yet he will, and he knows it, lose character by fighting. A duel is a ticklish affair, in this part of the world; discreditable with all, but the independent corps who have broken the shackles of society, and the very young men who rant about the 'code of honor,' their 'fine sensibilities,' and such trash. Still, I think he will not dare refuse the challenge. I shall hang him on this horn of the dilemma.

"I meet —— constantly. He has not the slightest suspicion; how should he have, he is scarce five and twenty; yet I dread and hate the sight of him. This evening he showed me a resemblance of *his* father, moulded in wax—it *was* like me. I crushed that likeness, and all form of humanity out of it.

"I am impatient to get away from this country; they have a way of their own, of inquiring out every thing. Those only who can afford to bear the scrutiny, should live among them. I meant to have returned to Cuba, as soon as I had secured the funds in the hands of ——, but the thread of destiny has been strangely spun about me; and I sometimes think that my cradle and my grave—Pshaw, this is drivelling."

CHAPTER II.

"But where you feel your *honor* grip,
Let that aye be your border,
Its slightest touches, instant pause—
Debar a' side pretences;
And resolutely keep its laws,
Uncaring consequences."[1]
BURNS.

"MOTHER," said Gerald Roscoe, on the following morning, as he was going out to his office, "I expect a note from Mrs. Layton, about attending her to the Theatre; be kind enough to open it, and if it requires an answer, send it to me." In the course of the morning, the note came. Mrs. Roscoe opened it. Instead of the expected contents, it ran as follows.

"To Gerald Roscoe, Esq. Sir; your interference in my family affairs, deserves some notice on my part. Your devotion to the *mother*, is not of a nature to require that you should interest yourself in the *morals* of the lover of the daughter. I requested your intimate friend D. Flint, last night, to tell you, from me, that you were an impertinent, meddling, lying scoundrel. I now repeat it—and am ready to give you the satisfaction of a gentleman, or to publish the above character to the world, with the addition of coward. Choose your alternative.

"Jasper Layton."

Mrs. Roscoe read, and read again the note, and felt as a mother must feel who sees the life and reputation of her son menaced. Her first impulse, as soon as her agitation had so far subsided as to enable her to form a purpose, was to go immediately to Layton; to convince him that he was under some fatal mistake (for this she never for a moment doubted); and to intreat him, for her sake, to revoke his note. But, on second thoughts, her good sense, her pride, and just confidence in her son, revolted from this feminine procedure. 'Gerald shall not,' she thought, 'be saved by the cowardly shield of his mother!' She then sat down and wrote him a note, saying, that 'the time had come to test the firmness of his principles;' that in all their conversations on the dreadful crime of duelling, he had admitted that it was contrary to the

---

1   From "Epistle to a Young Friend" (1786).

plainest dictates of reason, and a violation of the law of God. It was enough to remind him of this, she would not urge any inferior considerations. If he were not governed by his duty to Heaven, she would not ask him to be influenced by his love to her—by her dependence on him.

She abstained from expressing an emotion of tenderness, or of fear. 'I will not shackle him,' she said—'but have I not already? Will not the fact of my being privy to the note embarrass him? My noble-minded son, I will trust you.' And, without allowing herself time to shrink from her resolve, she threw her own note into the fire, resealed Layton's so carefully that Gerald could not suspect its having been opened, and sent it to his office. Perhaps this was rash confidence—it certainly would have been, if she had any reason to doubt the strength of his principles, or the firmness of his character; but she trusted to something stronger than her own influence, to something more unerring in its guidance and decision than her opinion—the enlightened conscience of her son.

She knew that men, all men, are jealous, and rightly so, of the interference of women in matters that do not properly come under their cognizance. She knew that they do not allow, even their just weight, to feminine scruples and doubts, because they believe them to have their source in constitutional timidity. Did she not then act with prudence, as well as true delicacy, in leaving the whole affair where it exclusively belonged, in the hands of her son?

But, though she had wrought her mind up to this pitch of resolution and forbearance, she was a prey to the anxieties and tormenting imaginations, so natural to her sex. 'Gerald may be influenced by some hot-headed adviser—the principle that seems strong in the hour of reason, calm discussion, and meditation, is insufficient in the hour of passion—when pride is stung by provocation—when the voice of the world is in the ear, and the fear of God quails before that of man's ridicule. Oh, my son, if you should disappoint me!—if you should fall!—or survive, the destroyer of another!'—These thoughts, and a thousand other disjointed and thick-coming fancies, agitated her, and produced a state of high nervous excitement. She heard the street-door open. It was Gerald's step—some person was with him. She awaited with breathless apprehension the first glance at him—'his face will tell me all,' she thought; but, instead of entering her parlor, he passed hastily up stairs. She rang the bell. Miss Emma, the daughter of her hostess, appeared.

"Do you know who came in with Mr. Roscoe?"

"Mr. Flint. Mr. Roscoe said he had some particular business with him, and he wished not to be disturbed.—But, bless me, ma'am! are you ill?—you are very pale."

"I am not well."

"Shall I sit here for a little while? you look faint, I am afraid to leave you."

"I am not faint, but you may sit down here, Emma, if you will."

There was something sedative in the quiet girl's presence, and for a few moments Mrs. Roscoe was tranquilized; but, like other inadequate sedatives, it soon increased the irritation it should have allayed, and Mrs. Roscoe dismissed her kind attendant, saying, "My nerves are in a sad state to-day, Miss Emma, even the pricking of your needle disturbs me."

Emma did not know that Mrs. Roscoe had nerves, and she went away to relieve her wonder at seeing her in this extraordinary condition, in the natural way—by imparting it.

From that time till dinner, how heavily the hours—the minutes dragged! One might believe that duration, as philosophers have deemed of matter, was ideal, from the length or brevity imparted to it by the mind. Dinner came at its accustomed hour, and Roscoe appeared as usual to all eyes but his mother's. She observed an unusual seriousness and abstraction, evinced by his not noticing her altered appearance, though it was repeatedly remarked by other members of the family; but when she spoke, though merely to decline a common courtesy of the table, the thrilling tone of her voice startled him.

"Are you not well?" he asked, and for an instant he looked earnestly at her; but his thoughts instantly reverted to a secret anxiety, and not waiting her reply, or scarcely noticing whether she replied, he abruptly withdrew from the table, and left the house. Mrs. Roscoe retired to her own room. When summoned to tea, she was found reclining on her sofa, in a high fever. She inquired for her son. He was writing in his own room—'would she have him called?' "No," she said firmly, and 'no,' she repeated to herself, 'he has not offered me his confidence. Oh Heaven! if I have erred—it may be too late, even now, to repair my error!'

Those alone can enter perfectly into Mrs. Roscoe's feelings, who have garnered up their hearts in the virtue of the individual most precious to them. This was the treasure dearer than reputation, than safety, than existence. She was no Spartan mother, and she had the common shrinking from a mortal combat; but, to do full justice to her noble and elevated spirit, it was not the personal risk she most dreaded, it was the crime of murder, in the eye of the immutable law of God—for such she deemed duelling, stripped of all the illusion that custom, false reasoning, and brilliant names, have thrown around it. Her principles, her feeling, her pride, were shocked; she had believed Gerald superior to the influences that sway common minds, and now, in the very first temptation, had he sinned against the clearest convictions of his intellect, and the strongest resolutions of his virtue—had he degraded himself to the level of a worldly and almost obsolete code of honor? But, if he had been infirm of purpose, might she not yet save him? If he had proved her confidence rash and weak, ought she not now to interpose? It was a false delicacy to surrender the sacred right of a mother! Mrs. Roscoe did not longer balance these thoughts, but obeyed their impulse, and hastened to Gerald's apartment. He was not there. A note, directed to her, was lying on the table. It contained but a line, saying, that as he understood she was indisposed, he had not seen her, but left the note to inform her that he was obliged to go out of town on business of some importance, and might not return till the next evening.

It was then too late! and Mrs. Roscoe returned to her own room to pass the agonizing watches of a sleepless night, in vain regrets and torturing apprehension. The morning came, but it brought no relief—hour passed after hour, each sadder than the last. Every sound rang an alarm-bell to her ear. Every approaching footstep menaced her with misery. She wondered, as those do whose minds are concentrated on one harrowing thought, to see the passersby bowing and smiling, and coolly pursuing their customary occupations, and the inmates of the house setting about their usual employments, and making preparations for dinner as if it were worth caring about. But the dinner—that diurnal circumstance that maintains its dignity through all the seven stages of man's life—that neither joy nor sorrow, birth nor death, prevents—the dinner came, and by all but Mrs. Roscoe was as usual eaten and enjoyed. She remained in her apartment alone, meditating on the images her imagination had conjured up, when a carriage stopped at the door. Gerald was in it, pale as death, and supported on the arm of a stranger, he was conducted into the house. Mrs. Roscoe threw open the door. "Do not be alarmed, my dear mother," said he, "I have received a trifling wound—I assure you it's nothing more;" and then courteously thanking the stranger for the aid he had rendered him, he lay down on the sofa, and the gentleman withdrew.

Gerald threw back his cloak, and discovered his arm, from which his coat sleeve had been cut. His linen was drenched in blood. "It is a mere flesh wound," he said, "and has been already well-dressed by a surgeon. There is indeed no occasion for your fright, my dear mother," for so he interpreted her gaze and colorless cheek. "You have no sickly feeling at the sight of blood—come, sit by me, and I will tell you all about it. Let me put my arm around you. I shall not, like the gallant Nelson, give you my wounded arm.[1] Do speak to me—kiss me, mother."

All the mother had rushed to her heart at the sight of her son, alive, and safe. Joy that he was so, was the first fervent emotion of her soul. His tenderness overcame her. She sunk on her knees beside him, and clasping her hands, exclaimed, "Oh God, forgive him!" and then dropping her face on his breast and bursting into tears, she added, "Gerald, how could you disappoint me so cruelly?" An explanation followed.

As Roscoe's relation to his mother was brief, and imperfect, and as the merit of a modest man is never placed in full relief in an auto-biography, we shall resume our narrative at our hero's receipt of Layton's note. Roscoe was at a loss to conjecture what could have stimulated him to such an expression of resentment for an offence given some months before. The intimation against Mrs. Layton, he would not for a moment admit as a solution of the mystery. 'It is possible,' he thought, 'that Flint may explain it, and as he is alluded to, though he is not my 'intimate friend,' and not precisely the man I should have selected for my confidence, yet he is an honest fellow, and may be useful in affording me some clue.' Flint, by his request, met him at his lodgings, and as soon as they were closeted in his room, Roscoe showed him the note. Flint related what had passed the preceding evening; but this threw no light on the affair, and Roscoe, after a little farther consideration, arrived at the just conclusion that Mrs. Layton, in a moment of conjugal pique, had betrayed his interview with her at Trenton, and that Layton had been stimulated by Pedrillo to this expression of his resentment and jealousy. When Roscoe had arrived at, and communicated his conclusions to Flint, that gentleman had a hard struggle between his good nature, his real regard for Gerald Roscoe, his desire to participate in a stirring affair, and his sense of right. The latter, as it should, triumphed.

"Well," he said, "I really am sorry for you, Roscoe. I have no fear to fight myself, or back a friend, in a good cause; but one must have that, to go at it with real pluck. One must be willing to take

---

1 Viscount Horatio Nelson (English, 1758-1805), naval commander and hero. His arm was amputated due to injuries sustained in the Battle of Santa Cruz de Tenerife in 1797.

his principal's place in all respects—that is, Roscoe—for I will be frank with you—one is supposed to approve, as well as espouse his friend's quarrel, and so I really must wash my hands of the whole affair."

"Really, my good friend, I am not aware that I have asked your participation in any *affair*—but I should like to know how I have alarmed your conscience?"

"Why I don't like to hurt your feelings, Roscoe—but I do think it is a condemned rascally business to be too attentive to another man's wife."

"If by 'too attentive' you mean, Flint, to express gallantries which afford a foundation for Layton's jealousy, I assure you, on my honor, that he has done foul injustice to his wife and to myself."

"Thank the Lord," cried Flint, rubbing his hands and pluming the wings of his active spirit for adventure, "then I'm your man, Roscoe—we'll give 'em as good as they send. 'Impertinent lying scoundrel' indeed! The words have been ringing in my ears ever since last night. I am right glad you don't deserve a shadow of them. You must overlook my misgivings. Mrs. Layton is a very sensible lady, but then you know she is not a person that one feels quite sure of—and I have thought myself sometimes that she was so partial to you it might turn your head."

"Thank you for your solicitude. A head of weightier material than mine might be made giddy by the preference of such a woman as Mrs. Layton, and that mine is not, is a proof, not of my virtue, but that she has not essayed her powers against it."

"Ah, that is very well—give the d—l his due, and a woman more than her due, is a good rule."

"For the *cour d'amour*[1] it may be—but I speak, Flint, according to the forms of a court with which you and I are more familiar—the truth—the whole truth—and nothing but the truth."

"Well, I am glad of it. I am entirely satisfied, I warrant you. Now let us proceed to assure the gentleman he shall have the satisfaction he demands."

Roscoe was amused with the half kind-hearted, half officious, and truly characteristic eagerness with which Flint had made himself part and parcel of the whole affair; but accident had admitted him to his confidence, and he felt that there would be rather more pride than delicacy in now excluding him. "I have no intention of ever giving that satisfaction," he replied.

---

1   Court of love.

"What!" exclaimed Flint, and never was more surprise and amazement expressed in one word.

Roscoe calmly repeated.

"Why, Roscoe!" and he added in a tone in which he never spoke before or since—lowered and faltering, "you ar'n't *afraid*—are you?"

Roscoe smiled. "Did ever man plead guilty to such an interrogatory, Flint? I honestly believe most duelists might, and that they go out because they fear the laugh of the world, and the suspicion of cowardice, more than they fear death, or the judgment after death. The greater fear masters the less. Moreau said he could make any coward fight well, by making him more afraid to retreat than to advance.[1] It is a fear paramount to my fear of the world's laugh that would compel me, in all circumstances, to refuse to fight—or rather, to express myself in terms more soothing to my self-love—that would inspire me with courage not to fight."

"Oh, I understand you now—you are afraid of killing a man."

"That would be disagreeable, Flint; but I might avoid that, you know, and I should be quite as much afraid of being killed. As to both these fears, I plead not guilty."

"Well then, for mercy's sake, what is your fear?"

"The fear of God—the fear of violating his law."

"Oh!" exclaimed Flint, with the satisfaction of one who has been scrambling through a tangled path, and suddenly emerges into the high-way, "Oh, Roscoe, I did not know you was a professor!"

Professor, with the largest part of Christians in New England, of which part of our country Mr. Flint had the honor to be a native, is the technical term for an individual who is enrolled as a member of a particular church, and has partaken its sacraments. "To be sure," he added, "you are pledged if you are a professor, and you have a perfect excuse for getting off, if you choose."

"But I shall not allege that ground of excuse, which has always seemed to me like the pretext of a boy when caught, 'I said no play.' And indeed I am not a *professor*, nor pledged any more than every man is who confesses himself responsible to the Supreme Being. Does not that single and almost universally admitted article of belief require us to cherish the gift of life, and to apply it to the purposes for which it was bestowed? I honor the sentiment in

---

1   Jean-Victor Marie Moreau (French, 1763-1813), military commander
     under Napoleon Bonaparte, later exiled (during which time he resided in
     the US), ultimately returned to Europe as military adviser to European
     leaders seeking Napoleon's defeat.

which duelling originated. It is a modification of the same principle that made the martyr. The principle that truth and honor are better than life. But their application is widely different. The martyr offers his life to support what he believes to be divine truth, and in obedience to the divine law, which demands fidelity to that truth. The duellist surrenders his life to the false and fantastical laws of the court of honor, and in direct violation of the law of Heaven."

"Well, I declare, Roscoe, I never thought of all that."

"No, my good friend, but 'all that' and a great deal more you, and every man of sense and just feeling, would think of, if you applied your minds to the subject before the exigency for action occurs."

"How comes it then," asked Flint, who could not at once elevate himself above the atmosphere of human authority, "how comes it then that so many great and good men have fought duels?"

"I deny that many good and great men have fought duels. Would to Heaven there had not been, most conspicuous among them, the noble name of that man, whose fine intellect, and generous affections were lavished on his country, but who threw a dreadful weight into the balance against all the good he had done her, when he gave the authority of his name to this barbarous practice."[1]

"But I guess, Roscoe, that last act of his life was blotted out by the tears of the recording angel, as they say."

"I hope so; but I would rather trust to its being effaced by his reluctance to yield himself to the slavery of usage, and by his deep subsequent penitence, than to the tears of the recording angel, who, since he let fall the drop on the Corporal's oath,[2] has been made to shed such oceans over human infirmity, that the fountain must be pretty nearly exhausted."

---

1 Gerald Roscoe implicitly refers to Alexander Hamilton (1755?-1804). Born in the West Indies to English parents, he was first US Secretary of the Treasury and a friend and close political ally of Sedgwick's father Theodore. On 11 July 1804, Hamilton and Aaron Burr (1756-1836), then US Vice-President, dueled at Weehawken, New Jersey. Hamilton's wounds were fatal, while Burr retained his political office.

2 Reference to a well-known episode in Sterne's *Tristam Shandy*, involving Uncle Toby and his faithful servant, Corporal Trim, in which an exclaimed oath is expunged by the tears of the recording angel. Roscoe's point is that it would have been better to have not participated in the duel.

"Well," said Flint, after a little meditation, "I believe you are right; but let me ask you one candid question, Roscoe. Don't you expect to lose reputation by refusing to fight?"

"You set me a noble example of candor in your home questions, Flint," replied Roscoe, smiling, "and I will answer you candidly, that with a certain class I do. But they happen to be those whose opinions I do not particularly value; and even if I lost reputation with the most dignified portion of society, with all society, it would not alter the merits of the question. Reputation must be graduated according to the opinions of the community we live in—they are a party to it. My character is my own; no man can give it, and, thank God no man can take it away—it is a sacred trust confided to me alone."

"Then it would not alter your views, if you lived in Kentucky, or Georgia?"

"Certainly not my views, for the rule that governs me is of universal authority. But I dare not assume that I should have the courage there to abide by my principles. Few men's morals are superior to the standard that obtains in the community in which they reside; and even if their theory is better, it requires more moral heroism than most men possess to put in practice. Therefore the latitude in which a man lives should affect our estimation of the turpitude of the crime. In New York we have no such extenuation; the opinion of the enlightened is against duelling, as a most unreasonable as well as criminal practice. The good sense of the community is against it, and a man really gets no honor for an *affair*, but with a few scores of half-fledged boys, and men of doubtful principles, whose opinions or conduct would never be quoted on any point of morals. In New England it is even better than here. There the universal sense is against it, and there a man is disgraced by fighting a duel; and you, I think, Flint, would be the last man to pronounce your countrymen wanting in courage, or a nice sense of honor."

"That I should; and if any man accused them of it, I would"— he paused; his mind was in a new region, and he was not sure how far his friend went in rejecting all militant demonstrations.

Roscoe supplied the hiatus, "fight them, hey, Flint?"

"No, Roscoe, I would get you to *convince* them."

"Spoken *en avocat*,[1] my good fellow, and be assured you may command my pacific efforts at any time, in return for your offer of a hazardous service, for which I am really obliged to you."

---

1 As an attorney or lawyer (*avocat*).

Roscoe opened his writing desk, and Flint reluctantly took his leave to withdraw.

"I declare," he said, and with evident sincerity, "I should like to do something about it—sha'nt I carry your note, Roscoe?"

"No, I thank you; I believe such servile offices are dignified only when done in the service of Mars."

"What do you mean to write?"

"What I should in any other case—the simple truth."

"Supposing he posts you?"

"That I can't help."

"Supposing he offers to cane you?"

"That, please Heaven, I shall help."

"And return, won't you?"

"To the very best of my ability, Flint."

"I am glad of that—I am glad of that. I was afraid you believed in non-resistance. I hope you will have a chance—good morning;" and quite satisfied, and in high good humor, he departed. He had gone quite down the stairs, when he returned, ran up to Roscoe's room, and stood with the door in his hand, saying,

"I meant to have told you that I always thought there was no reason in it; for instance, if you had wronged Layton as much as he thinks for, what good could it do him to lose his life or take yours? I knew they didn't fight duels in New England, but I wonder I did not think of it. They are always beforehand with every improvement in New England."

"Yes," said Roscoe, bowing in token of his acquiescence in his friend's complacent nationality; "yes, Flint, the sun always rises in the east—but good morning; at this rate it will set with us before I have finished my note"—and thus definitely dismissed, Flint took his final departure.

"Gerald Roscoe's Note to Jasper Layton.

"Sir,—As duelling is, in my estimation, a violation of the immutable law of God, and can never be a reparation, or an atonement for an injury, I should in every supposable case avoid giving, and decline receiving, the 'satisfaction of a gentleman,' in the technical acceptation of that phrase. Any other mode of satisfaction which a just and honorable man may give or require, for real or fancied injuries, I am ready to afford you, and shall demand from you.

"From the words which you have made emphatic in your note, I must infer that you have lent your ear to base insinuations touching the honor of your wife. Be assured, sir, that I have never presumed to address a gallantry to Mrs. Layton, which might not have been offered in the presence of her husband and children.

"Your assertion that I have meddled with your family affairs is not without foundation. I did *meddle* with them so far as to apprise Mrs. Layton of the real character of her daughter's suitor. How far a disinterested effort to prevent the alliance of your child with a man who to my certain knowledge, has been guilty of base conduct, and who lies under the suspicion of foul crimes—how far such an effort deserves the father's resentment, I must beg you deliberately to estimate.

"You have bestowed on me epithets, which you will do well for your own sake, to recall. Thank God, I do not deserve them, and therefore cannot, on my own account, invest them with the slightest importance.

"Your ob't[1] servant,

"G. ROSCOE."

Roscoe despatched his note, and, as has been seen, joined his mother at dinner. Not suspecting she was acquainted with the affair, he did not guard against his apparent absence of mind, but suffered his thoughts to run in their natural channel. Though perfectly assured in the course he had adopted he felt, as may be imagined, a deep interest in the effect of his note on Layton, and the final issue of the business; and he did not, it must be confessed, feel quite so composed and apathetic under the burden of the stinging epithets bestowed by Layton, as he assumed to be, or as he honestly thought he ought to be. Most men would rather die a thousand deaths, than in the eye of the world deserve such words; and though idle breath they be, and from a despised source, yet with a man of high honor and susceptible feeling, they wound more painfully than the keenest weapon.

After dinner, Roscoe as usual went to his office. He heard nothing farther from Layton. In the afternoon, he was obliged, as he had alleged to his mother, to leave town on professional business. He did not return till the following afternoon. He was then hastily walking up town. There was, as usual at that hour of the day, a press in Broadway, and he was turning into Park-place to avoid it; when he saw Layton and Pedrillo coming toward him. He could not then proceed up the street, or stop, without evidently doing it in relation to them; and he pursued, but very slowly, the way he had intended. He heard hurried footsteps behind him. He

1 Obedient.

slackened his pace, and he heard Layton say in a loud voice, "the cowardly rascal hopes to escape us."

Roscoe turned short round. "Do you mean that for me, sir?" he demanded.

"Yes," replied Layton, "and I mean this for you;" and as he spoke, he elevated a heavy cane, and aimed a blow at Roscoe, but the weapon did not touch him, he parried it, and grappled with Layton—a desperate struggle ensued. Roscoe unfortunately was embarrassed by a cloak, his foot was entangled, and he staggered backwards; Layton perceived his advantage and pressed on him with redoubled vigor; Roscoe had nearly fallen to the ground, when the fastening of the cloak gave way; it fell off, and disencumbered, he sprang forward, and by superior strength, or skill, or coolness, succeeded in wresting the cane from Layton's hand. When the resistance of his struggle ceased, Layton recoiled several feet. Roscoe maintained his ground. Pedrillo sprang towards Layton, and gave him his cane. "Do your business quickly," he said, and added in a voice, audible only to Layton, "you are no match for him in strength—touch the spring."

Roscoe threw down the weapon which he had wrested from his adversary, as if he disdained any other aid than the stout arm, that had already achieved one victory, and met Layton more than half way, as he advanced towards him. The passengers in the street had now taken the alarm, and were rushing towards the scene of contest. Some natural lovers of 'the fancy,'[1] shouted 'fair play,' 'fair play,' 'take away the cane!' The possession of this weapon, however, gave Layton, perhaps no more than an equality with his superior antagonist. Roscoe eluded his blow, and they again grappled. The street now rung with the pacific cries of 'separate them!—part them!'—but before a hand could be interposed, Layton fell in the fierce encounter, and stung with the consciousness of being a second time overcome, and maddened with passion, he obeyed Pedrillo's injunction, and touched a spring that gave an impulse to a dirk concealed in the cane. If he had willed it so, it was not possible in his hampered position to direct the weapon; fortunately the random stroke touched no vital point, but merely penetrated a fleshy part of the arm. Layton had no nerves for a bloody business; and Roscoe easily extricated the cane from his relaxing grasp, withdrew the blade from his arm, and before it was observed, or even suspected by the spectators, that he had received a wound, he released Layton, adroitly returned the blade

---

1 Professional boxing.

to its case, and the cane to his antagonist, saying in a low voice, "guard against such accidents in future." His cloak was lying on the ground; he hastily wrapped it around him, to conceal the blood that he felt to be penetrating his garments. One of the spectators, of quicker and cooler observation than the rest, had from the motions of the parties, suspected foul play. He saw that Roscoe, though perfectly cool and undaunted, had the mortal paleness, that is incident to a sudden loss of blood; and looking narrowly at him, he perceived the blood trickling from beneath his cloak. "The gentleman is wounded!" he cried. The mob, ever greedy of excitement, caught the words, and 'foul play!' 'foul play!' 'seize the fellow!' rung from one to another. Layton had joined Pedrillo, and arm in arm with him, was walking away at a hurried pace, when half a dozen hands arrested him at once. "I beseech you, my friends," said Roscoe, who was now obliged to lean against an iron railing for support, "I beseech you to release that gentleman. I am sure my wound was accidental."

"Those that carry edged tools must answer for them!" shouted one.

"Yes, yes," cried another, elevating the cane he had snatched from Layton, "see here, this dirk requires a nice hand and strong pressure—off to the police office with him."

"My friends," repeated Roscoe, "I entreat you to hear me. You are doing injustice. The gentleman attacked me with a common cane; such as half a dozen among you have in your hands at this moment." He then proceeded so earnestly and skilfully, to place the suspicious circumstance in the most favorable light for Layton, that if he did not remove all doubt, he prevented its expression, and Layton, who had suffered the severest punishment in listening to his own unmerited vindication from Roscoe's lips, was at length permitted to proceed without further molestation, and with the mortifying conviction, that he had been involved in a foolish quarrel, and set on to a cowardly revenge by Pedrillo. In the wreck of his character, there was still left enough of manly feeling, to be touched by Roscoe's magnanimity; but the faint spark that might have been cherished into life and action, was deadened by the presence of his evil genius.

Roscoe was put into a carriage, and conveyed to a surgeon's; and thence, as has been seen, to his mother's. His conduct was the general theme of the hour's applause. His physical superiority, (the want of which a mob never pardons,) gave a value and grace to his generosity. It was equally manifest that there is in the bosoms of men, the rudest, most ignorant, and vulgar, a chord that responds to every unequivocal manifestation of moral superiority.

CHAPTER III.

"Il faut briguer la faveur de ceux à qui l'on veut du bien, plûtot que de ceux de qui l'on espère du bien."[1]
LA BRUYERE.

ON the morning following their rencontre,[2] Layton sent a half apologetic letter to Roscoe. The conflict was apparent between his sense of justice and gentlemanly feeling on the one side, and his pride and humiliation on the other. Roscoe was satisfied, and heartily pitied him, but of course there could be no renewal of their intercourse. Mrs. Layton deplored the privation of Roscoe's exciting society, and after deeply considering how she could best solace herself for the loss, she addressed a letter to Gertrude Clarence, to which the following is a reply:

"Miss Clarence to Mrs. Layton.
"*Clarenceville, 1st Nov.* 18—.
"My dear friend—It is almost cruel of you to enforce your kind invitation with such glowing pictures of the variety and excitement of a winter in New York, and quite barbarous to ask me if I do not begin to feel the ennui of country life, when I am obliged to confess that I do. Since my return from Trenton, I have felt a craving that 'country-contentments' do not satisfy. I used to go round and round in the same circle, and experience neither satiety nor deficiency. I read and study as usual with my father, but the spirit is gone. I used to find amusement in the occasional visits of our simple village friends, and could, without effort, manifest the expected interest in the success of an application for a new bank, or turnpike-road, or the formation of a new 'society.' I could listen with becoming attention to Col. Norton's stories of the revolution,[3] though I knew them all by heart—to good old Mrs. Wyman's graphic details of her anomalous diseases, and even to your friend Mrs. Upton's domestic chronicles. I have ridden half a dozen miles to find out whether our pretty little busy bee,

---

1   "One should court the favor of those to whom one wishes well, rather than from those from whom one hopes to obtain some good." From *Les Caractères de Théophraste, traduits du Grec, avec les caractères et les moeurs de ce siècle* (*The Characters of Theophrastus, Translated from the Greek, with the Characters or Manners of This Century*), 1688, by Jean de La Bruyère (French, 1645-96), essayist.
2   Encounter.
3   The American Revolutionary War of 1775-83.

Sally Ellis, or her bouncing notable rival obtained the premium for the best flannel at the fair, and—dare I confess it to *you*, Mrs. Layton?—I have been as eager to know which of our rustic friends received the premiums of the Agricultural Society—premiums for *rich crops* and *fat bullocks*—as if they were the crowns decreed in Olympian games. But, alas! it is all over now—these things move me no longer. I have not opened my piano since the Marions left us, and my drawing, my former delight, I have abandoned. It is too indissolubly associated with the sad memory of Louis Seton. If you love me, my dear Mrs. Layton, spare me any farther raillery on this subject—I cannot bear it. I have known nothing in my short life, so painful as being the accidental cause of suffering to a mind, pure, elevated, and susceptible as Louis Seton's, and certainly nothing so perplexing to my faith, as that such a mind should be doomed to misery! My father, who is my oracle in all dark matters, says these are mysteries of which we must quietly await the solution—that we are here as travellers in a strange and misty country, where objects are seen obscurely, and their relations and dependencies are quite hidden. But we are safe while we fix the eye of faith on the goodness of Providence—His perfect, illimitable, and immutable goodness. This is the beacon-light— the central truth of the moral universe. I am announcing high speculations in a very metaphysical sort of a way; but I am as the humble cottager who receives through her narrow window a few rays of light—few, but sufficient to brighten her small sphere of duty, and to preserve her from either faltering or fear.

"Why do I not hear from my dear Emilie? Why are you silent in relation to her? Must I give the natural interpretation to this silence?

"Marion staid with us a month, and though we made every effort to animate him, his melancholy did not relax in the least. I wish, if you have an apt occasion, you would assure Mr. Gerald Roscoe that he has been misinformed—that Randolph Marion has not been 'paying his court to the great heiress.' I believe I quote Mr. Roscoe's flattering words. Poor Randolph! his destiny is a far more enviable one, suffering as it may be, than a heartless devotion to an heiress.

"I was interrupted by a summons from my father. He has made it his request that I should accept your invitation. You know I could only go by his request. 'He cannot,' he says, 'stay at Clarenceville without me, and a tour through the southern states may benefit his health.' Thus it is all delightfully arranged, and I shall be with you in the course of ten days.

"My father's *southern* tour may confirm your suspicions in relation to Miss Marion. You certainly condole with me, most gracefully, on the prospect of a step-mother, and the possible contingency of a divided, and subdivided inheritance. Honestly, my dear Mrs. Layton, such probabilities would, in my opinion, make me a subject rather of congratulation, than condolence. Miss Marion's visit to us has confirmed all my predilections in her favor. She is intelligent, active, and gay. Her gaiety is the sparkling of a clear and pure fountain—and, my father says, the result of a happy physical constitution; for you know, he thinks with the Frenchwoman, '*que tout cela dépend de la maniére que le sang circule.*'[1] You may think this view of my friend precludes sentiment—or that my father is past the period of romantic attachment; but I doubt if age, or accident, or any thing but voluntary abuse, can deprive the affections of their finest essence. There is, I assure you, in neither party a want of sentiment, nor an excess of it—no obstacle what ever to the event you predict, but such as the world never takes account of when it sends forth its rumors. The parties themselves have never thought of it, and have both an entire indisposition to matrimony. These, you know, may be as effective obstacles as that *only* one which poor Sir Hugh's benevolent efforts could not overcome in the case of Dr. Orkborne and Miss Margland[2]—their 'mortal mutual aversion.'

"But I am spinning out my letter when my thoughts are busy with the delight of seeing you. Adieu then till we meet. My tenderest love to Emilie.

"Most affectionately yours,
"GERTRUDE CLARENCE."

Miss Clarence, after mending her pen, laying it down and resuming it half a dozen times, added the following postscript. Every body knows a lady's P. S. contains that which is nearest her heart.

---

1 That all of that depends on how the blood circulates. Johnson's *Rasselas* (1759): "I always remember a remark made to me by a Turkish lady, educated in France: 'Ma foi, Monsieur, notre bonheur dépend de la façon que notre sang circule.'"
2 Characters in the novel *Camilla, or A Picture of Youth* (1796) by Fanny Burney (English, 1752-1840).

"P. S. I am exceedingly obliged to you, my dear Mrs. L., for your assurance that you have been mindful of my request that you would not mention to your friend, *G. R.*, the fact of my having been at Trenton with you. You ridicule what you call a 'true *femality*,' and define that to be something without rhyme or reason. But you say you love me the better for it, and I am content with whatever produces this result.

"G. C."

At the appointed time Miss Clarence arrived in New York, and was welcomed by Mrs. Layton and Emilie with unequivocal demonstrations of joy. Mr. Layton, too, received her with the courtesy of a man of the world. Scarcely aware of the strength of her prejudices against him, she was surprised at his agreeable exterior, and bland manners. He had originally been very handsome, and though his heavy drooping eye-lids, and mottled cheek, indicated a man of irregular habits, his features still retained the beauty of symmetry, and his figure the ease and grace of a man of fashion.

There was an air of luxury and refinement in Mrs. Layton's establishment, beyond that usually produced by the union of fortune and fashion. Her taste and imagination, and that love of the *recherchée*,[1] that is perhaps a subtle form of vanity, had led her to avoid whatever was common-place. Even the names of her children indicated her artificial taste. She relieved the simplicity of Emily, a name adopted in compliment to her grandmother, by giving it a French termination; and subsequently gratified her fancy by selecting for her younger children the rare names of Gabrielle, Victorine, Julian, and Eugene. In the arrangement of her house, she avoided the usual modes of vulgar wealth. She tolerated no servile imitation of French ornament; no vases of flaunting artificial flowers, in full eternal bloom; no pier tables covered with French china, kept for show, *not* 'wisely,' and looking much like a porcelain dealer's specimens, or a little girl's baby-house; no gaudy time-piece, confounding all mythology, or, like the Roman Pantheon, embracing all; in short, there was nothing common-place, nothing that indicated the uninspired, undirected art of the fabricator. The very curtains and carpets betrayed, in their web, the fancy of the fair mistress of the mansion. There were few ornaments in the apartments, but they were of the most exquisite and costly kinds. Lamps of the purest classic form—the prettiest alumette[2] cases and fire-skreens that ever came from the hand of

---

1   Uncommon, exquisite; also what is sought after or in demand.
2   Match, thus match-cases.

a gifted Parisienne—flowers compounded of shells, and wrought into card-racks, that might have served the pretty Naiads themselves, if perchance visiting cards are the tokens of sub-marine courtesies, and a Cupid, of Italian sculpture, bearing on his wing a time-piece, and looking askance, with a mischievous smile, at this emblem of the sternest of tyrants.

On a pedestal in one corner of one of the drawing-rooms, stood a bust of the Princess Borghese, said to bear a striking resemblance to Mrs. Layton, and on that account presented to her by a young Italian, who had given her lessons, en amateur,[1] in his native language. Opposite to it was a Cupid and Psyche.[2]

Connected with the drawing-rooms there was a library, filled with the flowers of foreign literature, and the popular productions of the day, and embellished with a veiled copy of Vanderlyn's Ariadne,[3] and a beautiful portrait of Mrs. Layton, in the character of Armida.[4] We do not furnish inventories, but merely data, to indicate the character of that establishment in which our heroine was now to be introduced to the society of New York. So much of it as was comprised within the large and fashionable circle of Mrs. Layton's acquaintance, poured in upon her on the first notice of her arrival, to offer courtesies in every accredited form.

Mr. Clarence was detained for a few days in Albany. When he rejoined his daughter in New York, and as soon as the first greetings were over, he said, "Of course, my child, you have explained to Gerald Roscoe the Trenton affair?"

We ought to state, that Gertrude after the disappearance of Seton, communicated to her father the story of the eventful night at Trenton. We will not say that she was quite as confidential to him as we have been to our readers, but she was as much so as could reasonably be expected; that is, she communicated the leading facts, which bore about the same proportion to the emotions

---

1 As an amateur, not as a professional.

2 Perhaps a sculpture of these figures, or a reproduction of the painting
   Cupid and Psyche (1798) by painter Baron François Gérard (French,
   1770-1837). Cupid: Roman god of love, known as Eros in Greek mythology; Psyche, a beautiful Greek princess with whom Cupid falls in love
   and whom Zeus makes immortal.

3 John Vanderlyn (American, 1775-1852). His painting Ariadne Asleep on
   the Island of Naxos (1809-14) was likely veiled to conceal a nude, provocatively posed Ariadne.

4 The witch or sorceress in the Italian poet Torquato Tasso's epic poem
   Jerusalem Delivered (1581) as well as Franz Joseph Haydn's opera Armida
   (1784).

they had elicited, as a little fire does to the volume of smoke that evolves from it. Gertrude replied to her father's interrogatory, "I have not seen Mr. Roscoe."

"Not seen him! that's most extraordinary. He certainly knows you are in town, for he has replied to the letter I sent by you. My child! you are ruining the lock of that work-box."

She was zealously turning and re-turning the key. "Mr. Roscoe does not, I believe, visit here now," she replied; "Mrs. Layton says he has some coolness with her husband."

"That's no reason why he should not pay his respects to you. Of course Mrs. Roscoe has called?"

"No, papa—she does not visit Mrs. Layton."

"Nonsense! my oldest and dearest friends to stand on such punctilios as these; I do not understand it—it is not like them. I shall go immediately and find out the meaning of it."

"Oh, papa!" Gertrude checked the remonstrance that rose to her lips, and merely said, "At least, I beg you will say nothing to Gerald Roscoe of my having been the person whom he met at Trenton."

"Certainly not—if you choose to have the pleasure of surprising him when you meet—well, there's no harm in that;" and away went Mr. Clarence on a quest that was destined to prove rather unsatisfactory.

Gertrude mistook in supposing that Mrs. Roscoe had not called on her. Eager to see and to pay every respect to the daughter of her friend, she went to Mrs. Layton's on the very first day of Gertrude's arrival. Miss Clarence was at home, but it did not quite suit the convenience of the servant, whose affairs were in arrears, that she should be so, and he refused her, received Mrs. Roscoe's card, and suppressed it. On the following day Mrs. Roscoe wrote a note to Miss Clarence, saying, that she was unfortunately prevented by indisposition from repeating her call on that day, expressing her earnest desire to see her, &c. &c. The note was sent, but mislaid at Mrs. Layton's, and never reached Gertrude. Two days after she again called, was told Miss Clarence was at home, and was shown into the parlor, and announced to Miss Layton, who was receiving morning company. Mrs. Layton was not present. Miss Layton did not know Mrs. Roscoe, and did not hear the name distinctly; and the coldness and seeming indifference which the poor girl now manifested alike to all, Mrs. Roscoe fancied was marked to her. Visiter after visiter appeared. It chanced that there were one or two among them, who had formerly courted even a look from Mrs. Roscoe, and who now recognised her with a supercilious bow, or what is far more annoying, a greeting evidently meant to be condescending. Mrs. Roscoe was entirely superior to their slights or favors, but not to being disturbed by their ignorance that she was so. Her own delicacy forbade her enlightening them and, with her impatience aggravated by these little irritations, she sat for a full half hour watching every opening of the door. No one can possibly estimate, or it may be, excuse her vexation, who has not waited for half an hour, and at the end of it been told, as she was, by the heedless servant, "Oh, ma'am, I thought you inquired for the ladies—Miss Clarence is not at home." Miss Layton now perceived that the lady had suffered some negligence, and she advanced with an apology. Mrs. Roscoe left her compliments for Miss Clarence, and withdrew. Pedrillo entered as Mrs. Roscoe retired, and so suddenly and completely displaced her image, that Emilie never thought of her again. These little mistakes and neglects left both parties with the impression that each was aggrieved. Gertrude, of course, never returned the visits, and Mrs. Roscoe did not repeat them.

Mr. Clarence went to Mrs. Roscoe's lodgings, in the full confidence of a satisfactory *éclaircissement*.[1] He was sincerely and deeply attached to the Roscoes; and certainly, the strongest wish of his heart, was, that his daughter should be favorably known to them; but he was far too proud of her, and too delicate, to solicit even Gerald Roscoe's attentions.

He was told that Mrs. Roscoe was at home, but 'engaged.' He sent up his card, with a request to see her. She was really indispensably engaged, but she did not think it worth while to detain him with an explanation of particulars; and she returned word that she was extremely sorry, but she could not then see Mr. Clarence. He left a request that Mr. Roscoe would call at his lodgings, in the course of the day, and went away more annoyed than he was willing to admit, even to himself.

Roscoe was out of town, and did not return till late at night. In the morning, before breakfast, he called on Mr. Clarence. *Before breakfast*, as our readers well know, was the dark hour to Mr. Clarence. Instead of meeting Roscoe with the cordial greeting he anticipated, he received him coldly, and pettishly, and proceeded immediately to talk of some business concerns, that required Roscoe's immediate attention, as Mr. Clarence was to leave town in the twelve o'clock boat.

---

1 Explanation.

Roscoe was hurt and disappointed by Mr. Clarence's reception. He had cherished a filial affection for him; and shocked by his apparent indifference, he forgot to account for his not having called the day before. He thought Mr. Clarence betrayed an undue interest about his pecuniary concerns—'this detestable money!' he said to himself, 'it spoils every body!' He left Mr. Clarence to execute his business, and engaged to meet him again at the boat. He encountered some unexpected delays, and just got to the wharf in time to exchange one word with Mr. Clarence, as the boat, like a hound springing from his leash, darted away.

'Adieu,' thought Mr. Clarence, as he returned Roscoe's farewell bow, 'to my long cherished hopes. What folly ever to stake our happiness on that which depends on the mind of another. Well, certainly the Roscoes were the last persons, whose coldness and negligence, I should have expected.'

The circumstances here detailed, may seem very trifling; but has not many a friendship been wrecked by mistakes and misconceptions as trifling; and should not those who know the value of this treasure, carefully guard it, and maintain it, on an elevation which these earthly vapors cannot reach.

CHAPTER IV.

"I know not whether the vicious or the ignorant man be most cursed by the possession of riches."
ANON.

"GOOD morning, my dear girls," said Mrs. Layton, entering Miss Clarence's apartment, "you see, Gertrude, I do not consider you in the light of a stranger. I never go down to breakfast. There is no *couleur de rose*[1] in the morning tints of a domestic horizon. I hope *mio caro sposo*[2] is civil to you."

"No one could be kinder."

"Oh, he is the pink of courtesy—to strangers—Pshaw! I forgot Emilie was in the room. You really look like the pattern-girls of a boarding-school; do you mean to immure yourselves all day with your books?"

"I assure you I have no such juvenile intentions," replied Gertrude, "I have business out this morning."

---

1 Rose color.
2 My dear husband (Italian).

"Business! shopping of course?—a young lady can have no other business; commissions for the barbarians of Clarenceville? or a *bargain* for Harriet Upton?"

"No, no, Mrs. Upton would not trust me."

"Oh, then for yourself, of course?"

"No, Mrs. Layton, shopping is not my errand."

"I am glad of it. There is nothing so rustic and *countrified*, as the *empressement*,[1] with which country ladies rush forth to new hat, new shoe, and new dress themselves. You would lose your beautiful individuality, if you were to identify yourself with these people, in any particular—and besides, I had rather direct your sacrifices to the graces."

"My dear Mrs. Layton! did not you commend my taste, in my new hat and pelisse?"

"Certainly I did. There is genius in dress, as in every thing else; and though not a particle of science, you have some inspiration on the subject. Your dress harmonizes with a certain air of refinement and elegance, that seems to be native to you. You do not, however, comprehend all the power of dress—I do—I have studied it as a science, and to a woman, 'it is fairly worth the seven.'[2] But your business, Gertrude, what is it?"

"I am afraid you will think it quite as rustic, as shopping for country acquaintance. I am going to look up some of the friends of my childhood; our former humble neighbors of Barclay-street."

"Lord! have not you forgotten them?"

"My father has left me a list to assist my recollections."

"*Eh bien!* These sweet charities of life should not be neglected. But, dear Gertrude, you must not expect to find these people where you left them seven years ago; half the inhabitants of our city, move every May-day."[3]

"I foresaw that embarrassment, and sent Nancy to purchase me a Directory."

Mrs. Layton laughed. "There is certainly something novel in this enterprise of yours, Gertrude. A young lady of fashion and fortune setting off with a Directory, to seek out acquaintance of seven years since—and when time has so gently dropped the curtain of oblivion over them. But it *is* very amiable. You go first to the Roscoes, I presume?"

---

1   Eagerness, alacrity.

2   From Epistle IV. Of the Use of Riches, in *Moral Essays* (1731-35) by Alexander Pope.

3   In nineteenth-century New York City, rental leases typically expired on 1 May, thus creating a 'May-day' rush of moving to new lodgings.

"No, I do not go there at all."

"You are right. They have behaved shabbily. Where, then, do you go?" Gertrude gave Mrs. Layton her list. Mrs. Layton smiled as she returned it, "Go, my dearest, and get over it as soon as possible—and be careful and not commit yourself. These are the sort of people who will invite you to 'run in at any time'—'to be sociable'—'to come and pass an evening'—they 'are never engaged.' If they name any specific time, say you are engaged, and leave the rest to Heaven and me."

Thus instructed, Gertrude left Mrs. Layton, and was in the parlor, awaiting the carriage, when a short, snug looking little gentleman, with an erect attitude, and that lofty bearing of the head by which short men endeavour to indemnify themselves for the stinted kindness of nature, entered the apartment. The stranger had a round sleek face, shiny hair, prominent, bright blue, and rather handsome though inexpressive eyes, and a mouth filled and crowded with short, regular, and white teeth. He smiled—and never did smile more truly indicate imperturbable good-temper, and perpetual good-humor—he smiled as he announced himself as 'Mr. D. Flint,' and apologized for the early hour at which he had called. He 'had been disappointed so often in his efforts to see Miss Clarence, that he was determined to make sure of the pleasure now.' A servant announced the carriage. Mr. Flint handed Miss Clarence into it, and when there, and before Gertrude could frame a polite negative to his request that he might have the honor of attending her, he seated himself beside her, and asked where he should order the coachman to drive. "To Fountain's," she replied, resolving she would drop her companion there. As if knowing he had short space, Mr. Flint improved it to the utmost. He described all the fashionable amusements—all the stars of the ascendant, and all as his familiars—promised to introduce this and that gentleman to her, persons of whom she had often heard, though never of Mr. D. Flint—discussed the last play—volunteered to send her the last new novel—offered to go to this place with her, and that place for her, and, in short, before they reached Fountain's, he had fairly woven himself into the woof and warp of her futurity. As the carriage turned towards the shop-door, it was intercepted by another vehicle, and obliged to pause for a moment. At that critical moment, Gertrude's eye fell on Roscoe. He walked past, all unconscious that the individual whom of all others in the world, he most desired to meet, was within his field of vision. "Did you know the gentleman you were looking at?" asked Mr. Flint. Miss Clarence blushed as if she were betraying a secret, and replied, 'she was not sure she knew to what gentleman he alluded.'

"Oh, then I was wrong. I thought you bowed to Mr. Roscoe—a particular friend of mine." Miss Clarence was more than half vexed at this interpretation of her eager glance, and as Mr. Flint handed her from the carriage, she bade him a hasty and most decided 'good morning.' Mr. D. Flint, not at all discomfited at his abrupt dissmission, felt much like one of the enterprising race of *squatters*, who having planted himself on the territory of some great proprietor, makes his *improvements* with the happy confidence that possession will gradually mature into right.

Miss Clarence directed the coachman to drive to Mr. Stephen Brown's, 3**, Broadway. 'My friends have risen in the world,' thought she, as the carriage stopped against a very elegant four-story house.

Stephen Brown had begun life in the humble calling of a journeyman tailor. His own industry aided by a thrifty help-meet rapidly advanced his fortunes. He abjured the goose, (even a goose should have taught him better,) and followed his ascending star to a retail-shop in Chatham-street. A profitable little concern it proved, and Brown was translated to the higher commercial sphere of Maiden-lane. Here he acquired property rapidly—the appetite, as usual, grew by what it fed on. From buying goods, Brown proceeded to buying lots. He was one of the few fortunate speculators, and the prudent age of fifty found him living in his own luxuriously furnished house in Broadway, with an income of $20,000.

Miss Clarence had known these people when, at a humble stage in their progress, they lived near her father. They had but one child—a good-natured, lawless urchin, whom she remembered as her brother Frank's favorite comrade in his boldest sports. The Browns sedulously cultivated this intimacy. They were ambitious to bring up 'little Stevy,' as they fondly called him, to be a gentleman, and they perceived that Frank Carroll had certain instincts of that race which were not native to their son. They sent 'Stevy' to the same schools with Frank, and won Frank's heart by those little personal favors and indulgencies agreeable to men and boys. Miss Clarence had a very distinct recollection of the gifts and the rides Frank received from the Browns. She had a kindly remembrance of 'little Stevy' too. She cherished every association with her brother, and it was the impulse of sisterly tenderness that now prompted her to seek out the Browns.

Mrs. Brown was at home, and Miss Clarence was ushered into an immense parlor, overloaded with costly, ill-assorted, and cumbrous furniture, where the very walls, all shining and staring with gilt frames, and fresh glaring pictures, seemed to say, 'we can afford to pay for it.' A chandelier of sufficient magnitude to light a theatre, hung in the apartment. An immense mantel-glass, half frame, reflected the gaudy and crowded decorations of the mantel-piece. Sofas, side-boards, (there were two of them, respectable pieces of architecture,) piano, book-cases, the furniture of drawing-room, dining-room, and library, arranged side by side, indicated that the proprietors of the mansion had received their ideas from the ware-house, and had made no progress beyond cost and possession. Our heroine was making her own inferences in regard to their character, from the physiognomy of the apartment, when the servant returned with the message that Mrs. Brown said, 'If the lady wa'n't no company, she might walk down in the basement.' Miss Clarence went, and was introduced to an apartment and a scene, which we shall exactly describe. The room was furnished with the well preserved luxuries of the Browns' best parlor in Chatham-street—the only luxuries they ever had enjoyed. There were the gaudily painted Windsor chairs—the little, round, shining, mahogany candle-stand—the motherly rocking-chair, with its patch-work cushion—the tall brass andirons—the chimney ornaments, wax fruit, plated candlesticks, and China figures—and edifying scripture prints, in neat black frames, adorning the walls.

Stephen Brown, the proprietor of this magnificent mansion, and of blocks of unmortgaged, unencumbered[1] houses, was seated on a *table*, cross-legged, his shears beside him, and his goose[2] at the fire, putting new cuffs on an old coat—his help-meet the while assorting shreds and patches for a rag carpet! What signified it that the one could have purchased the wardrobe of a prince, and the floors of the other were overlaid with the richest Brussels? This scene, and these occupations awakened a train of agreeable associations, touched the chords that once vibrated to the highest happiness of which they were susceptible—the consciousness of successful diligence. Neither of the honest pair recognized, in the elegant young lady who entered, the little girl they had formerly known. Mrs. Brown untied her apron and huddled it, with her work, into a covered basket, pushed up the bows of her cap, smoothed down her shawl, and threw a reproving but unavailing glance at her husband, who, after peering over his spectacles at the stranger, pursued his work.

---

1   Free of debt, lien, or other legal or financial claim.
2   Heavy iron used by tailors to smooth fabric.

"You do not remember Gertrude Clarence"—said our heroine, kindly offering her hand to Mrs. Brown, "you have not forgotten the Carrolls of Barclay-street?" The name with which Mrs. Brown was most familiar, revived her memory—she welcomed Gertrude heartily; and Brown suspended his stitches to say he was glad to see her, and to inquire after her father. "I should not have thought," said the old woman, apologetically, "of sending for you down to the basement, if I had surmised who it was, but I thought it was one of them society ladies, what brings round the subscription papers. It is a wonder I did not know you. You have got that same good look, though you are taller and handsomer; but, la! we all alter, some go on from spring to summer, and some from summer to winter," she shook her head, and sighed.

"But I do not perceive any change in you, Mrs. Brown, you are looking just as you did when you gave my dear brother that pretty little terrier-dog."

"Lord bless us! how well I remember it! Them were happy days. It was the time he saved Stevy's life, as it were, when they were skating together."

"Better lost than saved," muttered Brown, in so low a voice, that Gertrude did not distinctly hear him. She inferred, however, that something had befallen 'the only child.' "Your son is living, I trust?" she said.

"Yes—a living trouble," replied the old man, harshly. The mother sighed, and Gertrude essayed to turn the conversation into a more agreeable channel. "You have a very fine house here, Mrs. Brown," she said.

"Our neighbors have not got no better, I guess—you took notice of the parlors, Miss Clarence—you see we have not spared nothing—but, mercy's sake!" she added, lowering her voice, "what good does it do us, so long as Stevy is as he is?"

Our heroine ventured to explore the maternal sorrow a little farther, and ascertained that Stephen had forfeited his father's favor by his idle and expensive life, and was just now exiled from his home, and under his father's ban. After listening to Mrs. Brown's details, Gertrude, anxious to pour oil into the mother's wounds, replied in her kindest voice, "Oh, Mrs. Brown, most young men, with Stephen's expectations, are wild and idle—prodigal sons for a little while; but they come home to their father's house at last— and no doubt poor Stephen will."

"Bless you! that's so considerate. I tell *him* so," and she glanced her eye towards her husband, and taking advantage of his being slightly deaf, and her back towards him, she proceeded to pour her griefs into Gertrude's ear. "It's having a rich father that's ruined poor Steve—never was a better heart—never—but the poor boy has fallen into bad company, and thinking he must get the old man's money at last, he's gone all lengths. If it had not been for lawyer Roscoe—God Almighty bless him! if it had not been for him, Stevy would have gone to the penitentiary; not that he was guilty to that degree, but he was snarled in with them that was. Mr. Gerald Roscoe saw right through it, and he took it up, and argufyed it in court—and la! who could help believing him; and he cleared him, he did. And then he came here himself to tell us of it with such a beautiful smile—oh, a kingdom could not buy that smile! but *him* never so much as thanked Mr. Roscoe, and only just said, 'you may take your labor for your pains—not a shilling of my money shall go for the fellow, even if it were to save him from a halter.' Do you think Mr. Roscoe took offence? not a bit—he never minded the old man's words any more than he would his stitches; but when *him* was through speaking, he said, "You mistake me, friend Brown, I neither expected nor desire your money. I undertook your son's cause on account of his having been honored with the friendship of a little favorite of mine, Frank Carroll."

"My brother!" exclaimed Gertrude, "did he say that?"

"To be sure he did, and that after looking into the business, and finding poor Steve was innocent, he had for his own sake, done all in his power for him. And then he spoke so pretty for the poor boy, and begged us to take him home once more, and make his father's house the pleasant place to him, and let him have his friends here like other gentlemen, and get him married to some pretty, nice, discreet girl, and so on; and then he said, our money would be worth something to us. But, la! I can't give you no idea of it—I never heard any body talk so—my heart melted and was hot like within me—dear! a man's heart is harder—*him* never shed a tear nor spoke a word—nor he has never mentioned Stevy since, till just what he said to you."

"He has not forgotten him, though," replied Gertrude, in the same discreetly low voice which the mother used; "do you keep up a secret intercourse with your son?" Mrs. Brown eagerly bowed an assent. "Then use all your influence to persuade him to persevere in good conduct, and he will certainly win his way back to his father's heart and house." Gertrude rose to take leave. In answer to Mrs. Brown's inquiry of 'where she put up?' she mentioned 'Mrs. Layton's'. The name struck Brown—he dropped his shears, "Layton—Jasper Layton," he demanded, "in ——— street?"

"Yes."

"Then, Miss, I advise you to have all your eyes about you—you'll want 'em. That man is on the high road to ruin—in straits for money, and he won't scruple borrowing from a lady—he stopped here in his gig and tandem yesterday—as if I'd lend a penny to a blade that drives a tandem; and then he came turning and twisting to his business. 'A very superb house you have here, Mr. Brown, an elegant room this—rich furniture—you must be a happy man, Mr. Brown.'" "Happy! happy!" repeated Brown, as if the words brought out all the discords of his nature, "happy I've never been since I've earned more than I've spent; to be sure, sometimes when I sit down in this room with just my old furniture about me, with the old shears and goose, and put in a new patch, or set a new cuff, it does *feel good*—it brings back old times, when I sat over my needle, cracking my jokes from morning till night; and my old woman, not groaning and sighing as she does now-a-days, but singing like a lark over her wash-tub, with one foot on"—Brown's words seemed to choke him, and a child-like flood of tears gushed from his eyes—"on *Stevy's cradle*."

Gertrude, obeying the impulse of that sweet and generous nature, that made her estimate the affections of every human creature, however sordid and mean, as too precious to be contemned, advanced to the table on which Brown was still seated, and resting her hands on it, she looked at him with an animated expression of appeal and intercession, that seemed to confound and overpower his senses; for he covered his face with his hands; "Oh, bring your son home again, Mr. Brown—try him once more—forgive the past."

"There's too much to be forgiven," interrupted Brown.

"But, my good friend, those that are forgiven much, you know, love much. Stephen will feel your kindness—he always had a good heart—a very good, kind heart."

"Did *he* ask you to speak to me?" said Brown, letting fall his hands, and looking piercingly at Gertrude.

"No."

"Did the old woman?"

Gertrude could hardly forbear a smile at Brown's suspicion of sinister influence. "No, indeed," she said, "it was yourself Mr. Brown, that induced me to speak for your son—I perceived your heart was turning towards him."

"That's true! that's true!" exclaimed Brown, leaping from the table, "my feelings have been working like barm, ever since Mr. Roscoe spoke to me;—if I thought—if I thought he would not go astray again—"

"Oh, try him—how often we all go astray, and yet does that prevent our expecting the forgiveness of our Father in heaven, when at each offence we ask it?"

"That's true again—and I've thought to myself, that I did not know how the Lord could forgive me, who am but his creature, and I be so hard to my own flesh and blood."

Gertrude saw the point was gained. "I shall come again, my friends," she said, "to see you—and to see Stephen, my dear brother's old friend; and I am sure that I shall find it *feels good* to you all again." The old woman who had been overpowered with emotions of surprise, and joy, and gratitude, now felt them all merged in admiration of Gertrude, which she expressed in a mode peculiarly feminine. "Oh Miss Clarence! you and Mr. Gerald Roscoe, have been such angels to us! you are just alike—you need not shake your head—I thought of it the moment you began to speak about Stevy—I am sure, if ever there was a match made in heaven—"

"My good friend! Mr. Roscoe and I are strangers to each other."

"La! that's nothing. I can make you acquainted; come here and drink tea with me to-morrow evening, I will invite him, and then if—"

"If Stephen is here," said Brown, finishing her halting sentence, "there are no *ifs* in the case—Stephen shall be here."

Dame Brown's auspices, were not precisely those under which Miss Clarence preferred to be introduced to Gerald Roscoe; and availing herself of Mrs. Layton's hint, she pleaded an engagement, and terminated a visit that seemed to the Browns, Heaven-directed. Mingled with the pleasure of having been the instrument of good to others, there was, in Gertrude's bosom, a sweet, and cherished sentiment of sympathy with Roscoe, arising from that best and truest of all magnetism, correspondent virtue.

We say she cherished this feeling—she did so, in spite of a very vigorous resolution to expel it; for she knew that as Miss Clarence she was as yet, to him an object of indifference, bordering on dislike; and she dreaded lest any favorable impressions he might have received at Trenton-falls, should be effaced as soon as he identified the stranger he met there, with the heiress of Clarenceville. 'I cannot but wish,' she thought, 'that he who has been so beloved of my father, and who manifests such fond recollections of Frank, should be my friend'—and revolving this, and kindred thoughts in her mind, she proceeded from the Browns' to Mrs. Stanley's. Here she was again surprised to find a lady, whom she remembered as a bustling notable woman, on the shady side of fortune, emerged into its luxuries and sunshine. Mrs. Stanley had been thrown out of her natural orbit; and as an itinerant lecturer remarked of the unlucky asteroides, she was of no 'farther use to society.' She would have made a most meritorious shop-keeper, or a surpassing milliner. There are few persons fit to be trusted with the selection of a mode of life, or who suspect how much they owe to Providence, for assigning to them an inevitable occupation. In our country, the idlers of fortune, are to be compassionated. We have as yet no provisions for such a class; they are not numerous enough to form a class, and each individual is left to his own resources.

A rich, motherless, uneducated, unintellectual woman, is one of the most pitiable of these sufferers. If she has no taste for the management of public charities, and no nerves to keep her at home; if she is healthy and active, she takes to morning visiting, shopping, frequenting auctions, and to that most vapid of all modes of human congregating—tea-parties. —also, shitting on extraverts again

Mrs. Stanley was issuing from her door, as Gertrude entered it. She expressed a sincere pleasure at seeing her, but her politeness soon became constrained, and her relief was manifest, when Gertrude rose to take leave, and inquired for a direction to Mrs. Booth's. "My dear, how fortunate!" exclaimed the good lady, "I am just going to an auction in our neighborhood. Mrs. Booth will certainly be there; she is at all the auctions; though, poor soul, she lives at the world's end—how lucky you mentioned her! You will have a fine chance, if you wish to buy any thing, Miss Clarence— the auction is out of season, and I expect the things will go off a bargain." Miss Clarence assured the lady that 'she should make no purchases, but should be glad to avail herself of so good an opportunity, to pay her respects to an old friend'; and accordingly, she suffered herself to be conducted to the durance of an auction. Mrs. Stanley was evidently on the *qui vive*, as much interested and fluttered, as if she were about to purchase the cargo of an India-man.[1]

Our heroine had no very definite idea of an auction. She knew it was an occasion on which commodities were bought and sold; but she was quite unprepared for such a scene as is exhibited at a sale of fashionable furniture in a private house, and astounded by the crowd, the pushing and jostling, the smiling impertinence of some, and nonchalance and hardihood of others, she dropped her veil and followed her companion timidly. Mrs. Stanley, with the intrepidity of the leader of a forlorn hope, pressed through the

---

1   Merchant ship engaged in trade with India.

crevices that were civilly made for her by the men who occupied the entry, the flank of the battleground, and entered one of the two spacious apartments, filled with fine furniture, and a motley crowd of all ranks, from the buyers of the costly articles of the drawing-room, to the humble purchasers of the meanest wares of the kitchen.

The sale had begun, and the ladies, (precedence in our country is always, even on the levelling arena of an auction-room, ceded to the females,) the ladies were hovering—brooding better expresses the intentness of their attention—brooding over a table filled with light articles. There stood the hardy pawnbroker mentally appraising every article, as was evident from her keen glances and compressed lips, according to the standard of her own price current. Next were old housekeepers, familiar spirits there, their unconcern and tranquil assurance contrasting well with the eager, agitated expression of the novices, who had come with the honest intention to buy as well as bid, and whose eyes were rivetted to the elected article with that earnest look of appropriation that marks the unpractised purchaser—then there were young ladies leaning on their fathers' arms, their wishes curbed by the parental presence, and old ladies made prudent by experience—troops of young married women, possible buyers; and troops of idlers, who loved better to see this slight agitation of hope and fear, than to stagnate at home.

There were but few persons of fashion present, and they seemed to disdain the element in which they moved, though they condescended to compromise between their pride and their desire to obtain possession of a costly article at an under price. The pervading spirit of trade and speculation spares neither age nor condition in our commercial city.

Our heroine, unknown and unnoticed, was sufficiently amused observing others, when Mrs. Stanley touched her arm, "My dear Miss Clarence! just hear what a bargain that dinner-set is going— let me bid on it for you."

"Excuse me, ma'am—my father has an abundance of china."

"Oh, but it is *such* a bargain!"

"I cannot abstract the bargain from the article, and that I do not happen to want."

"But, my dear, china never comes amiss, a store is no sore— fifty dollars only is bid for it—if I but had a place to put it in! I know," she added, in a confidential tone, "the whole history of that china. Mr. ——, you know who I mean—the ambassador, brought it out with him. He died soon after, and it went off at his auction at twice the first cost. Mrs. Pratt bought it; her husband—a peculiar man, Mr. Pratt—sent it right off to Boyd's auction-room. Hilson—Hilson, Knapp & Co., you know, bought it there; he failed the next week, and I bid upon it at his auction—Mrs. Hall overbid me; she died, poor thing, without using it, and Mr. Hall has determined to break up housekeeping—he is so afflicted. Oh, gone, at sixty dollars! what a sacrifice!"

"Is that gentleman, Mr. Hall?" asked Gertrude, glancing her eye at a person who stood opposite to her, with a long weed depending from his hat, and dangling on his shoulder, to which he seemed to have committed the task of mourning, while he was absorbed in magnifying the value of the article under the hammer, by certain flourishing notes and comments, "A capital time-piece, ma'am—given to poor Mrs. Hall by her late father. He selected it himself in Paris."

"You may confide in the sofa, ma'am—it is Phyfe's make—poor Mrs. Hall never bought any furniture but Phyfe's."[1]

"Yes, madam, the carpets have been in wear one year, but poor Mrs. Hall has been shut up in her room, and seen no company in that time."

Gertrude, who well knew that the prefix of 'poor' is, in common parlance, equivalent to deceased, was smiling at the 'afflicted' husband's tender allusions to his departed consort, when Mrs. Stanley again touched her arm. "Do you know the gentleman in the next room, who is leaning against the corner of the mantel-piece? there, he is looking at you."

"Yes—no—yes," answered Gertrude, betraying in her contra-dictory replies, as well as in the instant flushing of her cheek, the emotions excited by thus accidentally encountering Gerald Ros-coe's eye. He instantly bowed, and was taking off his hat, when his elbow hit a lamp on the corner of the mantelpiece. "Goodness me! he has broken that lamp!" exclaimed Mrs. Stanley—"no, no, he has caught it—that was handsomely done! who is he?" Gertrude made no reply. "How strange you don't remember his name, Miss Clarence, he is a very genteel looking man—twenty dollars only for that castor—my! what a bargain."

Gertrude, conscious of her burning cheek, and afraid her companion might observe it, was relieved by the reverting of her attention to the sales. She ventured one more timid and but half

---

1 Duncan Phyfe (1768-1854), an emigrant from Scotland, was a New York City cabinetmaker known for making furniture of high quality and graceful style.

permitted glance towards Roscoe. He had left the place where he stood, and as Gertrude thought, might possibly be making his way to her, 'I can never encounter a meeting and explanation in this odious auction-room,' she thought, and, determining to avoid it by a sudden retreat, she was making a hurried apology and adieu to Mrs. Stanley, when that lady recollecting herself, exclaimed, "My dear! you forget you came here to see Mrs. Booth; there the old lady sits right behind us—twenty-five—twenty-five for that glass dish—no great catch—I'll just mention your name, dear, to old Mrs. Booth—poor soul, she is so deaf!"

"Oh, then," said Gertrude, appalled by the idea of hearing her name screamed where she most particularly wished it should not be spoken at all, "Oh, then, some other time—I entreat, Mrs. Stanley." But before the protest reached the lady's mind, she had forced her way to Mrs. Booth, taken Gertrude's arm, pronounced her name, and returned to the table. Mrs. Booth, with the eagerness not to be at fault, common to deaf persons, caught the name, and uttered in a high key, "Mrs. Lawrence! how *do* you do, my dear?" At this moment Roscoe had penetrated through the crowd, and, unperceived by Gertrude, stood a little behind her, but near enough to hear whatever might pass between her and Mrs. Booth. "I am right glad to see you, my dear!—such a surprise! how are papa and mama, and husband?" Gertrude could not explain that she had no right to answer for more than one of the parties named, and she merely bowed and smiled as complacently as she could. "Any children yet, dear?" continued the kind-hearted querist. Gertrude most definitively shook her head. "Never mind, dear—uncertain comforts. You like living in the western country, don't you? And Mr. Lawrence is a great farmer, I hear. You are looking amazing well—not a day older than when you were married. Did your husband come to town with you, dear? La! if here is not Mr. Gerald Roscoe—waiting as patient as Job, to speak to me—Mrs. Lawrence, Mr. Roscoe."

Roscoe looked like a man suddenly awakened, from whom a delightful dream is fleeting. He however had the self-possession to bow and express his pleasure at meeting *Mrs. Lawrence*. "Such a surprise," he said, significantly quoting Mrs. Booth's words—and added, "I forced my way through the crowd to pay my respects to you," he depressed his voice, "and to pray you to release me from the promise I made you. My good deaf friend's introduction has rendered my request unnecessary. I am obliged to her for a favor that I confess I would rather have received from *Mrs. Lawrence* herself." Gertrude deliberated for a moment whether she should rectify his mistake, or whether she should prolong, while accident befriended her, the mystery in which accident had enveloped her. She did not quite like to appear the humdrum personage—the Mrs. Lawrence of several years standing, whom she personated in the old lady's presentation; and she therefore said, with a mischievous pleasure in the perplexity she was inflicting, "Mrs. Booth has mistaken me for a married friend of hers, and Mr. Roscoe will perceive the propriety of not inquiring into a mystery which is so evidently protected by destiny."

Roscoe bowed. "I submit," he said, "and I confess I prefer the continuance of the mystery to the solution the old lady forced on me. I began to think the atmosphere of an auction-room as fatal to romance, as day-light to a ghost."

"It is certainly a place of disenchantment," said Gertrude; and anxious to give the conversation a new direction, she continued, "I came here with a lady whom I had invested with the charms that memory gives to those who are associated with our earliest pleasures. She took me, for the first time, with the companion of my childhood"—a shade passed over Gertrude's expressive face at this allusion to her brother, and suggested to Roscoe the identity of this tenderly remembered companion with the hero of the Trenton adventure. There was an involuntary exchange of glances, and Miss Clarence began again: "She took us to the theatre, the circus, and the museum, and she was identified in my imagination with the excitement of those scenes. But the spell is completely broken here. Nothing in life seems to interest her so much as an auction bargain."

"There is her kindred spirit," said Roscoe, pointing to the very lady in question, "I am told she attends all these places as punctually as the auctioneer himself—that her house is a perfect warehouse of 'uncommon bargains.' My poor old friend, Mrs. Booth, is a more rational woman. She frequents the auctions, as a certain philosopher went to a hanging, '*en amateur*.' She is perfectly deaf, and can take no part in individual hopes, success, and disappointment, but she feels the *ground-swell*, and enjoys a sympathetic agitation from the general movement on the surface of human affairs."

"Human affairs!" exclaimed Gertrude, "we can hardly wonder at those philosophers who have treated our race as a subject for contempt and ridicule, rather than of admiration and hope. The most sanguine believer in perfectability is in danger of forgetting the capacities of man, and giving up his creed altogether when he looks upon the actual interests and pursuits that occupy him. But I perceive," she continued, misinterpreting Roscoe's smile, "that

I am making myself very ridiculous—a prosing, reflecting recluse is quite out of place in this assembly. What picture is that the auctioneer is puffing at such a rate?"

Roscoe could not answer the question; the crowd prevented his seeing it. The man of the hammer proceeded with professional eloquence and pathos, "Five dollars—five dollars only is offered—this is too bad, ladies—a first rate picture in my humble opinion."

"Who is the painter?" inquired a professed connoisseur. "The painter, sir?—I really don't know precisely—doubtless some great young artist."

"Doughty, perhaps," suggested a kind friend, while a humble disciple of the fine arts pronounced 'it beyond all dispute a production of Cole's.[1] It had his clear outline—his rich coloring.'

"A landscape by Cole," cried the auctioneer, nodding gratefully to the sponsor, "a landscape by Cole—a very celebrated painter, Mr. Cole—six dollars—six dollars only offered for a picture by Cole."[2]

"It is not very large," said a cheapening voice.

"If it were in a handsome frame," said our friend, Mrs. Stanley, "I would buy it myself. Six dollars *is* a bargain for one of Cole's landscapes."

"If one could only tell the design," cried a caviller.

"The design," replied the ready auctioneer, "why it's evident the design is something of the water-fall kind, and that fine figure of the lady kneeling, is put in for the beauty of it."

"Mama," whispered a young lady who had made the grand summer tour, "it looks just like those sweet Trenton-falls—do bid for it."

---

1 Thomas Doughty (American, 1793-1856), painter of the Hudson River School, known for his landscapes; Thomas Cole (1801-48), emigrant from England, considered the founder of the Hudson River School. *The Art of Trenton Falls* (Museum of Art/Muson-Williams-Proctor Institute, Syracuse UP, 1989) reports that Cole was commissioned to paint Trenton Falls' scenes, but the paintings, if completed, are not now known (16).

2 Sedgwick's note in the 1849 edition: Since this sentence was penned Cole has painted his most admired picture—has extended his reputation, and has closed a life that infused its moral essence into his pictures. We know no pictures where the characteristics of the man are more strikingly and unmistakeably impressed. He distilled from nature, poetry, and that which should accompany it—truth, purity, and religious aspiration. His Landscapes are in the highest sense pantheistic. The divinity is every where present in them. We look with almost superstitious reverence upon his last unfinished picture, and feel as if he must have closed his eyes here to open them on scenes which would enable him to perfect it.

"Seven dollars!" called out the compliant mama.

"Seven dollars—thank you, madam—going at seven dollars—bless me, ladies! one of those eyes is worth more than seven dollars—upon my word they are speaking."

At this moment Miss Clarence observed a woman who stood near the auctioneer look curiously alternately at her and at the picture, then whisper something to the person next her, who after doing the same thing, nodded affirmatively to her companion, and said so emphatically that Gertrude comprehended the motion of her lips, 'striking indeed!'

"Come ladies," cried the auctioneer, "favor me with one bid more—it is really too good to be sacrificed—something out of Scott or Byron, 'though I can't give chapter and verse,' or perhaps," he added, making a timely application of some classical scraps, picked up in his professional career, "perhaps it is Hero, or Sappho, they are always painted near rocks and water."[1] Roscoe and Miss Clarence both laughed at the ingenious conjecture of the man of business; and Roscoe suggested that the picture should be elevated, as it could not be seen where he stood. The picture was instantly raised, and presented to them both, a scene too deeply impressed on their imagination, ever to be mistaken or forgotten. It was indeed Trenton-falls; precisely as they appeared, on the night of their adventure, with Seton. The moon just risen above the eastern cliffs, tipped the crests of the trees with its silvery light, played on the torrent that foamed and wreathed in its smiles, and concentrated its rays on the figure of Gertrude, who appeared kneeling on the rocks, just without the dark line of shadow, that veiled the western shore.

There were no other figures in the picture, but imagination instantly supplied them; and it seemed to Roscoe, that he again stood on those rocks—again saw Seton unclose his eyes, and Gertrude raise hers to Heaven, with the fervent expression of a beatified spirit.

"Oh Louis!" exclaimed Gertrude, involuntarily, then laid her hand imploringly on Roscoe's arm, then conscious every eye was turned towards her, she shrunk from his side, and disappeared. Roscoe's eye was rivetted to her retreating figure, but instantly recovering his self-possession, he assumed the air of an ordinary bidder, and called out to the auctioneer, "fifty dollars."

---

1   In Greek mythology, Hero, priestess of Aphrodite, was Leander's lover.
Sappho (c. 615-c. 550 BCE) was the Greek poetess of the isle of Lesbos.

No competitor spoke. The picture was knocked down to Roscoe. The amateurs, the pawn-brokers, the bargain-buyers, the whole host of veteran auction *tenders*, exchanged nods and smiles of derision and pity, for there were kind-hearted creatures among them, at the *gullibility* of the novice. Even the auctioneer himself, could not suppress a complacent smile, when he transferred the picture to Roscoe, who deviating from the ordinary mode of business, gave a check for the amount, and requested immediate possession. Curiosity spread through the rooms. The picture was at once invested with a mysterious charm, and a factitious value. Half a dozen voices in a breath, begged another view. Roscoe, very politely regretted that it was not in his power to oblige the ladies, said he paid an extraordinary price for the exclusive right to look at the picture—coolly rolled up the canvass and withdrew; envied at last, as the possessor of a secret, and a *bargain*.

CHAPTER V.

"Who'er thou art, were mine the spell,
To call Fate's joys, or blunt his dart,
There should not be one hand or heart,
But served or wished thee well."[1]
HALLECK.

MISS CLARENCE left the auction room, overpowered by confused and painful feelings. The mortification of seeing her own portrait, however disguised by the romantic position in which she was placed, exposed at a public sale, and bid upon by Roscoe, at first blunted every other sensation. But considerations of deeper, and more painful, as well as of more generous interest, soon arose in her mind, and entirely possessed it. Seton was living—was enduring the extremity of misery, for nothing short of that, could have induced him to part with a picture, which proved with what tenacity, with what fond partiality, he had retained her image. Estimating her personal charms, more humbly than any one else would have done, Gertrude esteemed the portrait, a lover's apotheosis of his mistress.

---

1 From "Woman (Written in the Album of an Unknown Lady)," 1824, by
Fitz-Greene Halleck (American, 1790-1867), a member of Sedgwick's
social circle.

She had penetrated the crowded passage, and reached the outer door, when it occurred to her, that she might possibly obtain some clue to Seton, by ascertaining from the auctioneer how the picture came into his hands; and she turned to retrace her way to the parlor, but she was daunted by perceiving that her undecided movements were observed by those who had noticed her flushed and agitated countenance, as she had hurried through the entry; and naturally interpreting others by her own consciousness, she believed the resemblance of the picture had been generally detected; and she felt herself at the mercy of whatever conjectures and inferences the vulgar and curious might make. More than ever embarrassed, she turned again towards the door, got into the carriage, and obeying a sudden impulse, ordered the coachman to drive to No.— Walker-street—Mrs. Roscoe's address. At first occupied with the single desire to obtain Roscoe's co-operation in finding Seton, she determined to dissipate the little mystery in which she was involved. 'But why was this necessary to effect her purpose? at least,' she thought, listening to those long cherished feelings that were resuming their force, 'at least, why not retain my innocent incognita, till there is some object to be effected by resigning it. It certainly would not stimulate Gerald Roscoe's zeal, to know he was serving Miss *Clarence*.'

How much Gertrude's desire to see Roscoe's mother—the woman of all her sex, she most desired to know, influenced her in selecting the mode of searching out Seton, we leave to those to determine, who are skillful in unravelling the intricate web of human motives. Certain it is that when Mrs. Roscoe's door was opened to her, and she was told that lady was at home, she would have exchanged her location for any other on the habitable globe. She was however, somewhat reassured by finding the parlor vacant. The landlady who admitted her, went to summon Mrs. Roscoe, and Gertrude was left to her own meditations. 'This then' she thought, 'is the abode of the Roscoes—what a change, from the sumptuous style in which they once lived! And yet it does not differ much from the picture my imagination has drawn, for here are the indications of taste, and refinement, and intellectual occupation.' Her eye ran rapidly over the apartment. Nothing could be more simple than the furniture, but there was that grace and propriety in its arrangement, that marks the habits and taste of a lady. A piano, a guitar, and a flute, with music books, a few volumes of the best French and Italian authors, some choice English books, the best foreign and domestic reviews, a port-folio of drawings, a freshly painted bunch of flowers, copied from some natural ones still blooming in a tumbler, indicated the luxuries in which the Roscoes still indulged.

While Gertrude was eagerly gathering a little history from these particulars, the mistress of the house returned. She evidently thought some apology necessary for the delay of Mrs. Roscoe's appearance, and while she mended the fire, "I am sure," she said, "Mrs. Roscoe will be down directly; it is quite contrary to her habits to keep any one waiting. She has broken my Emma of ever fixing after company comes. She says we have no right to sacrifice others' time to our vanity, and Emma looks upon every thing she says just like the proverbs."

Gertrude wondered that a lady whose punctuality was so exact, should be so dilatory on this occasion. Her impatience arose from the fear that Roscoe might return before she should get away. "Perhaps," she said, rising with the intention of going, "perhaps Mrs. Roscoe is particularly engaged."

"Oh, no, Miss, nothing that will keep her more than a minute. Mr. Gerald came in just the minute before you did, with some great news, I suppose, for he was all out of breath, and he's telling it to his mother. It's nothing disagreeable," she continued, observing Gertrude's countenance change, "I never saw two persons look happier. I should think Mr. Gerald had drawn a prize in the lottery."

"I will not disturb them, then," said Gertrude, moving towards the door.

"You'll not disturb them in the least, ma'am—there they are coming now." Gertrude heard their footsteps descending the stairs: to retreat without being seen was impossible—to remain calmly where she was seemed to Gertrude quite as much so. They paused at the foot of the stairs, and were in earnest conversation. Gertrude, unconscious what she did, took up a book.

"My John's Spanish grammar," said the landlady, anxious to fill up the awkward chasm, and having the liberal communicativeness natural to persons of her order, who have rather a sympathetic turn of mind, she proceeded, "Mrs. Roscoe is giving my son lessons in Spanish. He is going out supercargo to south America, and she is as much engaged in it as if it was her own interest."

"Does Mrs. Roscoe understand Spanish?" asked Miss Clarence, hardly knowing what she said.

"La! yes, Miss, and every thing else I believe. She has taught the world and all, to my Emma, so she gets a genteel living as governess."

"I thought Mrs. Roscoe was an invalid."

"She is of the delicate kind, but she keeps off the thoughts of it by being always busy doing good to somebody, instead of pining and going to bed as some ladies do. I never knew her give up but once."

"When was that?" asked Gertrude, who was sustaining her part in the conversation with about as much interest as a person does while sitting in a dentist's chair, awaiting the coming of that dreaded executioner.

"Why that, Miss," replied the landlady, "was when that dreadful business of Mr. Gerald Roscoe's and the Laytons was going on."

'What do you mean?' Gertrude would have inquired, for her curiosity was now thoroughly awakened. But again she heard approaching footsteps. The loudest, firmest step was, however, evidently retreating, and she breathed more freely—the door was half opened, and she heard Roscoe, who was leaving the house, turn back and say, "Oh, I forgot to ask you if you went to see Miss Clarence this morning?"

"Yes, I went; but there were half a dozen carriages at the door, and I did not go in—and on the whole I believe I shall not go at all."

"You are right. It can be of no consequence to her." The outer door closed, and Mrs. Roscoe entered. The blush of alarmed and conflicting feelings was still on Gertrude's cheek. She was in the presence of the woman who of all others she most wished to please, and she was nearly deprived of the faculties of speech and motion. Mrs. Roscoe apologized for having kept her waiting. There was a gentle courtesy and softness in her manners that seemed rather to appeal for the indulgence of others, than to indicate they needed it. Gertrude was somewhat re-assured, made a bold effort, and remarked that 'it was unusually cold.' Mrs. Roscoe thought on the contrary 'it was the warmest weather ever known at that season.'

Gertrude abandoned that ground, and observed that our climate, was inconstant. Nobody could controvert this position, and there was a full stop. Mrs. Roscoe rung for more coal, begged Gertrude to draw nearer to the fire, and exhausted all the little resources of politeness. Fortunately Gertrude in removing her chair, knocked down the Spanish grammar, and now recovering in some degree the possession of her mind, she made a graceful allusion to what the landlady had said of Mrs. Roscoe's occupations.

"Ah, poor Mrs. Smith! no Pharisee[1] ever had a more faithful trumpeter than she is to me."

---

1 Sub-group within Judaism known for strict interpretation and adherence to Mosaic law in the pre-Christian period; more generally, a formalistic or self-righteous person.

"The voice of the trumpeter could hardly be mistaken for the genuine expression of gratitude."

"But I am really the debtor to my good landlady; those know not how much they bestow, who give us objects of interest, and means of agreeable occupation." The ice was now broken, and never did a little boat set free more gladly bound over the waves, than Gertrude skimmed over the light topics that followed, till she was checked by the very natural thought, that there was no propriety in deferring to announce her business. Mrs. Roscoe interpreted the embarrassed pause in the conversation; she saw that Gertrude's was the diffidence of excited sensibility, not of *gaucherie*,[1] and skilfully extending the aid of a leading question, she said, "There is perhaps a misunderstanding. Mrs. Smith is a blunderer—you did not say you had business with me?"

"Yes, indeed I did," said Gertrude, recovering herself, "but Mrs. Roscoe must blame herself if the pleasure of seeing her has put every thing else out of my head; I ought not to have forgotten that I had no pretence for my intrusion but business. I met Mr. Gerald Roscoe"—there may be those who having felt similar emotions at pronouncing simply a name, will pardon Gertrude for faltering at "Roscoe," for the deep mortifying crimson that overspread her face, and for the tremulous tone in which she blundered through the simplest sentence possible—"I met Mr. Gerald Roscoe at an auction this morning"—she would have proceeded to speak of the picture, but the words and the blush were enough—Mrs. Roscoe interrupted her, took her hand, and said, her eyes beaming with animation, "I understand all—I have the pleasure of seeing the lady of Trenton-falls. My son has already told me of his fortunate meeting with you this morning, and of his,"—

"His bidding on a picture for me," said Gertrude, eagerly putting this interpretation on a wish she had implied by laying her hand on Roscoe's arm.

"No," replied Mrs. Roscoe, with a smile, "that was not precisely Mr. Roscoe's understanding—he flattered himself that the fortunate purchase was his own—but the fates are against him; on coming out of the auction room he met the painter of the picture"—

"Good Heaven!" exclaimed Gertrude, her cheek suddenly losing its heightened color, and becoming as pale as marble, "did he see him?"

"Yes—and he claimed the picture with such fervent feeling, that my son, reluctant as he was to part with it, resigned it to him. He took it, intreated not to be followed, and disappeared."

---

1 Awkwardness, or clumsiness.

"Then all clue to him is again lost!"

"Will you give my son authority to search for him?"

"Certainly—he will oblige me infinitely."

Gertrude rose to take leave; Mrs. Roscoe laid her hand on Gertrude's arm, "My young friend," she said, "we must not part strangers—strangers we are not; but I have as yet thought of you as a vision with which my imagination only could be familiar. I am delighted to have the assurance of my senses of your actual substantial existence—you must not leave me now. It is quite time for my son to return; let him have the pleasure of receiving your commission from your own lips."

"Oh, no, I cannot, indeed," Gertrude replied, in a manner so flurried that it was evident Mrs. Roscoe had suggested the strongest motive for her instant departure. "Then," said Mrs. Roscoe, detaining the hand Gertrude had extended to her, "at least give me your name; we should know a lady who moves in daylight, and carries a card-case, by a less romantic designation than 'the lady of Trenton-falls.'"

This rational request placed Gertrude's incognita in a very ridiculous light, and feeling that it did so, she opened her card-case; but recollecting that the step she had taken, though quite proper for a stranger, was awkward for Miss Clarence, and recollecting too that she had been neglected, shunned, and, as she believed, contemned by both mother and son, she reverted to her first decision, and closing the card-case, said, "Pardon me, Mrs. Roscoe, my name, unhappily, would dispel the little interest which it has been my good fortune to excite, and for which, mortifying as the confession is, I know I am indebted to the accident of a trifling mystery. It will be enough for Mr. Roscoe to know that his inquiries may relieve the most painful solicitude of one whom he has twice materially served."

"My son wants nothing to stimulate his zeal, though he may not be too modest to ask for your name to reward it; but pardon me, I perceive the subject is painful to you. My son has it already in his power to communicate some circumstances in relation to your friend, of which you are ignorant. He knows that the young man passes by an assumed name, and at present sedulously conceals his place of abode; something more he may have to tell, if you allow him the opportunity."

"Certainly; I will send my servant here to-morrow for any information he may be able to give me, and I beg that you, Mrs. Roscoe, will express to him my sense of his kindness." She then departed, leaving Mrs. Roscoe in a half pleasing, half painful state of uncertainty, but with a positive unqualified interest in Gertrude, and sympathy with Gerald.

"I have measured and weighed every circumstance," she said, after having related the particulars of Gertrude's visit to her son, "and I can hit on no solution more rational than the first that occurred to me. Your heroine, Gerald, has undoubtedly a clandestine attachment to this poor youth—she is evidently a woman of education, of thorough good-breeding, of sentiment, and uncommon refinement; this painter is some 'young Edwin'[1] of lowly fortune, frowned upon by her parents or guardians, and she is naturally anxious to maintain secrecy, while she still perseveres in her interest in the young man—poor girl, I shall pity her when she comes to know the history of his sufferings."

Roscoe shook his head. "For Heaven's sake, my dear mother," he said, "do hit upon some other solution—this is purely feminine, and savors of old-fashioned ballad sentimentality."

"Really, Gerald, it does not become a youth, who falls in love at first sight with a nameless, mysterious fair one, to rebuke his mother's sentimentality—what other solution do you prefer? Would you be resigned to the truth that her name was a dishonored one? disgraced by either parent?"

"I would prefer any reason for her mystery, independent of herself."

"Any explanation that left her affections free, and attainable, Gerald?"

"Pretty well probed, mother. Yes, I would."

"Amen, my son; I have no fears that you will suffer from a predilection which as yet is a mere fancy; to tell the truth, I am half in love with the sweet girl myself. Abandon yourself to destiny, Gerald; if her affections are pledged, or if she is not worthy of yours, you will find it out in time; diseases have their day, and incurable love is not the malady of ours."

"Love! Heaven preserve us! mother, you do not fancy I am seriously in love?"

Mrs. Roscoe laughed—Gerald laughed, and blushed, and looked—we blush too, to apply the degrading epithet to the fine face of our hero, but it is the only one that accurately describes a certain expression that 'happeneth to all men'—Gerald Roscoe looked *sheepish*, and thus, for the time, the discussion ended.

---

1   Refers to the nineteenth-century English folksong "Young Edwin in the Lowlands Low," popular also in the US.

Meanwhile Gertrude, whose perseverance in her mystery, we by no means approve, nor would hold forth as a possible precedent for any of our young friends, was congratulating herself on her success, little dreaming of the suspicions to which she had made herself liable. The visit had been as interesting to her as a voyage of discovery. Every thing she had seen and heard at Mrs. Roscoe's had tended to confirm her favorable impressions of that lady. She contrasted her elevated and happy mode of life, with Mrs. Layton's indolence, indulgence, and sacrifices to fashion; with the ignorance and vulgar expense of the Browns and the Stanleys; and she learned more of true philosophy and political economy from the morning's observation, than she would have gathered from volumes of dull treatises—more of the just use of property, and the true art of happiness.

The following morning she sent a servant with a note to Mr. Roscoe, containing a simple request, that he would send her whatever information he had obtained of her friend. The servant returned with a note. Gertrude inquired of her messenger if any questions had been put to him. "No; the gentleman had given him the note without speaking one word;" and Gertrude, ashamed that she had for a moment suspected Roscoe's interest or curiosity might overcome his delicacy, retired to her room, locked her door, and closed her blinds, before she read the note. Strange are the outward signs of hidden feelings!

The note ran as follows:

"I am mortified that I cannot relieve a 'solicitude,' (worth the sufferings of its object to have excited,) by any satisfactory information of your friend. I have ascertained merely, that the picture, in the absence of its owner and painter, (for who but a witness of that scene could have made such a presentment of it?) was sent by his landlady to auction. He returned, and found it gone—and alarmed at his loss and still more at the desecration of the picture by an exposure to a public sale, he repaired to the auction. I met him, as my mother has already informed you, and perceiving to what a degree his sensibility was excited, I taxed my wits and my magnanimity, and, without any absolute sacrifice of veracity, made it appear that the picture had not been seen by any eye but mine, and that I had assumed it as a trust for him. He took it, and thanked me, as if he had received something very like a gift of life; and then intreating that I would not inquire for him, and assuring me that I should hear from him at some future time, he left me. At your bidding, I have violated his wishes, and made a most thorough search for him. All I can ascertain is, that he is constantly occupied with his art, and is solicitous to remain concealed. He has changed his lodgings, after having told his landlady that inquiry after him would be fruitless. My mother imprudently told you I had something to communicate of this person; but, unhappily, it is nothing that can enlighten you as to his present condition, or relieve any anxiety you may feel as to what may have been his past sufferings. He has suffered long and severely from a malady of the mind, which was finally relieved by judicious care and medical art. For many weeks past, I have reason to believe, his external condition has been tolerable. Whatever sorrows of the heart he may still endure, are, perhaps, quite as much to be envied as pitied.

"My mother bids me ask if there is not one drop of pity in your woman's heart for the pains and penalties of curiosity? For myself, I am at last resigned to the penance you have inflicted. I am grateful to fortune for past favors, and take them to be an earnest of her future smiles. The vision of a moonlight night, in the bewildering scenes of Trenton, might be the coinage of the o'er-wrought fancy; but daylight, a city, and an auction-room, are not visited by spirits, and a form that moves on our *pavé*[1] and in our hackney-coaches, cannot escape the eye, always in quest of it—so says my awakened hope. I have made a covenant with my lips, and shall ask no questions, but humbly await the hour when you, or kind chance, shall reward my forbearance. I shall not wait long, if you are but half as much impressed as I am with my own greatness in this matter. If I can be of any farther use to you, I pray you to command the services of

"Your very humble servant,
"Gerald Roscoe."

Gertrude's solicitude for Seton was rather augmented than abated by this communication. It was evident that Roscoe knew more particulars of Seton's suffering than he imparted, and she was left to conjecture, but not to exceed in her most distressful imaginings, the real truth.

The main subject of Roscoe's letter did not so utterly engross her but that she scanned every word. 'There is nothing in it,' thought she, after having thoroughly weighed it—'nothing more than bare curiosity—and why should I expect to find any thing else? Poor Louis—how can my thoughts wander from you!' Gertrude

---

1 Cobblestone streets.

was yet to learn that expectations arise unbidden and unauthorized—that duty cannot control or guide our subtle thoughts. Hers reverted to Roscoe. 'Perhaps I have done wrong—this assumption of mystery—my gratuitous visit, are certainly contrary to my father's maxim—that a young woman should never depart from the established and salutary rules of society—that she should live within the barriers. But is not this fastidiousness? Life would be dull enough if we must for ever walk in the trodden path—never follow the inspiration of feeling. Still, my going there, betrayed my feelings—what feelings! How unlike Roscoe's letter is, to Louis' distant, delicate, fearful devotion; but why should there be any resemblance? What could that talking woman mean by his affair with the Laytons.'

"Shall I take out your pink, or fawn colored dress for this evening?" asked Gertrude's maid, who entered, and interrupted and put to flight her sweet meditations. The important decision between the rival colors was soon made, and Gertrude joined a brilliant musical party in the drawing-room.

CHAPTER VI.

"These are not the romantic times,
So beautiful in Spencer's rhymes,
So dazzling to the dreaming boy;
Ours are the days of fact, not fable,
Of Knights, but not of the Round table."[1]
HALLECK.

MISS CLARENCE had now been long enough in town, to get fairly started in the career of fashionable life. She had been visited by the *haut ton*[2] of the city; and was already besieged by half a score of aspirants for her matrimonial favor. There were among them genteel young men, who made their approaches and their retreats, in the delicate mode, prescribed by the received usages of society. Such persons fill a respectable niche in life, but are not destined to 'adorn a tale;' we shall therefore, omit them in our *dramatis personæ*.

By far the most important personage among our heroine's lovers, was the *ci-devant* friend of the Roscoes, Stephen Morley, Esq.

---

1 From "Alnwick Castle," Part 19 (1827) by Halleck.
2 The best of society (literally, "high class").

No longer the cringing, sycophantic, all-calculating Mr. Morley, for these qualities had achieved their end, and obtained their reward. He had risen to be a dispenser, instead of a seeker of political favors; he stood high in office, and higher in hope—so elevated that many believed that the most exalted post in our country, was within his possible grasp—it certainly was in the eye of his ambition.

Mr. Morley, it was true, was some twenty or thirty years older than Miss Clarence, but he reasoned (and it must be confessed *sub modo*[1]) 'that Miss Clarence, though young, was not beautiful'—he had half a dozen well-grown children; but 'she was neither gay nor girlish, and after all, what were these trifles weighed against the name of Morley, with the cabalistic prefix of Judge, Governor, Secretary, or President?—Thane of Glamis—Cawdor—King!'[2]

Next in importance, was Major Daisy. Let not the reader mistake, the major was no *champ de mars*[3] hero, but a gentle carpet knight. It might almost be said, that he was born to his title, for he received it as commander-in-chief of a nursery regiment, and had probably retained it on the principle of attraction in opposites. It was true of the Major, as of many nobler victims, that 'Fortune smiled deceitful on his birth;'[4] he was lapped in luxury, but when it was time for him to have walked alone, viz. when he had advanced some thirty years on the journey of life, the rich house of his father, Daisy & Co., did what most others, rich and poor, do in our city, failed; and the major, not being of a temper to turn the tide of fortune, played the philosopher, and took the easy part of submitting to evils, he had not energy to resist. The world used him kindly. It fared with him, as with few who do not hold the golden key; the *passe-partout*[5] in a society of moneyed aristocracy—he retained his place in the *beau-monde*.[6] For this he was indebted to old and confirmed associations. But what made Major Daisy an Areopagite[7] in the female fashionable world, must be incomprehensible to those who do not know how important it is in that dominion of debateable land, of uncertain boundaries,

---

1 Subject to a modification or qualification (Latin).
2 References to Shakespeare's Macbeth, Thane of Glamis, who becomes Thane of Cawdor.
3 Battlefield (literally, "field of Mars," Roman god of warfare).
4 From "Autumn" (1730) by James Thomson (English, 1700-48).
5 Skeleton key (literally, "go anywhere").
6 Upper-class society (literally, "beautiful people").
7 Member of the Areopagus, the highest judicial and legislative council in ancient Athens.

and of ever falling barriers, that some infallible hand should hold a scale by which to graduate the pretensions to gentility. Instead of the tiresome investigation at the ascension of a new family in the firmament of fashion, of 'who are they?' 'whom do they visit?' or 'who visits them'—the simple appeal to the Major, 'are they *genteel*?' laid all doubt and discussion at rest.

Then the Major had acquired a great reputation, (as some other tribunals do, simply by giving judgment,) in the questions of fashion and *belleism*.[1] If the mothers relied on him in matters of more vital importance, the daughters listened, as devotees to an oracle, to his opinion, of 'who was the best dressed lady at the fancy-ball,' and the Major's decision that, such a fair-one was '*the* decided belle,' was the fiat of fate. He knew at a *coup-d'oeil*[2] whether a hat were *really* Parisian, or of home manufacture—could tell a *real* blond, or camel's hair, at a bird's-eye view—was a connoisseur in pretty feet, and an exquisite judge of perfumes. To conclude all, the Major, like most *poor gentlemen*, dressed with elaborate neatness and taste—and, (to the utter perplexity of that large class of persons, who tax their wits to solve the problem of their neighbor's expenditures,) with very genteel expense.

Major Daisy had rather an undue portion of the better part of valor in his composition. He had been all his life afraid of committing himself in a connubial pursuit. There was nothing but death which he dreaded so much as a refusal; but of late, there had come a small voice from his inmost soul, saying, if ever he meant to marry, it was time to think of it. By a singular coincidence, it happened that this oracle gave out its intimations about the time Miss Clarence became an inmate in the family of Mrs. Layton, with whom the Major was on the footing of an old and intimate friend, and contemporary.

The rival whom the Major most feared, and with least reason, was a young scion of the old and universal family of *Smiths*. Mr. John Smith, Jr. the only son of a rich broker—a vulgar, half-bred youth, recently moulded into a dandy; and as that implies the negation of every thing manly, and worth describing, we shall pass him over, only saying, that he presumed to our heroine's hand, incited thereto, by certain refined suggestions from his father, such as, 'John, my boy, there's a chance for you!—a nice girl they say—her father is heavy, I know all about that—like to like, birds

---

1 Hyphenated as belle-ism in the 1849 edition, suggesting not a study of beauty (the literal meaning), but the study of young women of fashion.
2 Glance.

of a feather—fortune to fortune—that's the way to roll up the ball, my boy—set about it, John.' And the exemplary son, with infinite self-complacency, obeyed the paternal mandate.

Mr. D. Flint, who has already been repeatedly presented to our readers, must make of the lovers a *partie quatré*.[1] Flint was of the emigrating race of New England, and from the heart of it; and a fair specimen of a class not rare in that enterprising land. He was a lawyer, but even the arts of that profession, which is supposed to sharpen all the wits, could not improve his natural faculty of 'getting along,' and pushing along. He came to the city without acquaintance, friends, or patronage of any sort; but by dint of indefatigable industry, vigilant activity, and irrepressible forwardness, he penetrated to the foremost ranks of business, and obtained an uncontested circulation in the fashionable circles. This latter was accomplished much in the same way as the cat's celebrated ascent of the well, 'three steps up, and two steps down;' but though the rebuffs he received, were innumerable, he was never disheartened by them. If utterly destitute of that *tact* which is the best guide in the art of pleasing, he was entirely free from the sensitiveness that is curiously compounded of sensibility, pride, self-love, and selfishness. He never took offence—the delicate intimations of the refined, the coarse joke, the rough reproach, disdain, contempt, neglect, all glanced from his armor proof of triple steel—good nature, self-complacency, and insensibility. He was perfectly free from affectation, save in the single point of concealing his Christian name; of this he had unwarily made a mystery, when he first came to town; and his reluctance to disclose it had been confirmed by some of his mischievous acquaintance, who had appended to the initial *D.* every ridiculous prefix in the language. He was not only free in all other respects from affectation, but he had not aimed at polish, or even quite freed himself from a rusticity of dialect, that betrayed his early associations. If told any thing that excited his wonder—this was rare, for true to the character of his all-knowing countrymen, he had

——— "a natural talent for foreseeing
And knowing all things;" ———[2]

but if perchance, taken by surprise, he would exclaim 'do tell!' or 'you don't!' instead of those expletives of custom, '*Mon*

---

1 A fourth party.
2 From "Connecticut" (1826) by Halleck.

Dieu!'[1]—'God bless me!'—and notwithstanding the proverbial vulgarity of these provincialisms, he *guessed, concluded,* or *calculated,* in every sentence.

We hope to be forgiven for calling this portrait a national sketch: 'Who may we take liberties with if not with our relations?' and we must not be suspected of disloyalty to our race, though the man is not always painted triumphing over the lion—the New Englandman superior to every other. Besides, we sincerely like Mr. D. Flint, and the class of character to which he belongs. If deficient in the niceties of feeling, he abounded in active useful kindness. If unpolished, he was honest; and if unrefined, he afforded a sort of safety valve for the over refinement and irascibility of others.

These were the satellites that revolved around the envied heiress! and these were assembled about her one evening when Mr. Flint, always the first to move, proposed they should go to the Athenæum lecture. Miss Clarence assented, glad of any opportunity of escaping from the siege of her suitors. Mr. Morley was quite too much a man of affairs to waste an hour at a lecture of any kind, and he withdrew. Mr. Smith "would go if Miss Clarence wished, for," he gently murmured, "I am like him *which* divided the world into *one* part—that where she is."

"Oh, my poor friend, Rousseau!"[2] exclaimed Mrs. Layton, at this version of one of the most felicitous passages of her favorite author, "it is too hard that you should fall on evil tongues, as well as evil times. But come, Pedrillo, the world is *divided* into *one* hemisphere to you too, I believe, what say you to killing an hour, or rather permitting it to die a natural death at the Athenæum."

Pedrillo replied, to Mrs. Layton's ear alone, 'that the Athenæum was a bore, and he preferred remaining at home, provided Miss Emilie did the honors of the house in her mother's absence.' Emilie was appealed to, but on every occasion—with and without reason—she shrunk from Pedrillo, and she expressed an earnest wish to accompany her friend to the Athenæum; whereupon Pedrillo bowed, and declared he should be most happy to attend her. Mr. Flint murmured at these preliminaries. He was for making the most of every thing. 'The lecture was on astronomy—there

---

1 My God!

2 Jean-Jacques Rousseau (French, 1712-78), philosopher. The line is from Letter IV of *Julie, ou La Nouvelle Héloïse / Julie, or the New Heloise* (1761): "Le monde n'est jamais divisé pour moi qu'en deux régions; celle où elle est, et celle où elle n'est pas." / "For me, the world is never divided into more than two regions: the one where she is, and the one where she is not."

were to be fine transparencies exhibited, and the ladies would lose their chance of good seats by this delay.'

"Pshaw, Mr. Flint," said Mrs. Layton, "are you under the delusion of imagining we go to the Athenæum to see, or to hear?"

"What do you go for, then?" honestly asked Flint.

"To be seen, my good friend—to fulfil our destiny, and be the observed of all observers. Blues, pedants, and school-boys may go to stare, and listen; but we of the privileged class have, thank Heaven, a dispensation."

"Privileged class! what a happy expression!" exclaimed Mr. George Smith, eying himself obliquely in the mantel-glass.

"Pardon me, madam, I do not agree with you," said Major Daisy. "The Athenæum lectures afford a remarkably genteel way of getting information, and are as little tiresome as astronomy, and philosophy, and all that sort of thing, can be made. You know —— is of my opinion—he remarked in last evening's paper that the tone of society had improved since their institution."

"They are certainly useful," said Mr. Flint.

"*Oh l'utile—t'utile—Je te deteste*,"[1] exclaimed Mrs. Layton. "How do you like my hat, Daisy?" The ladies were adjusting their cloaks and hats.

"*Admirable, Madame!*—from the *Rue Italienne*—is it not?"

"You have the best eye in the city—yes—Miss Thompson imported it for me. You see it is a *demi-saison*[2]—the flowers half hidden by the feathers—the reign of summer yielding to winter. And then observe how happily it is adapted to the *demi-saison* of life—alas the while!"

"I declare it is a very pretty-looking hat," said Mr. Flint. "What was the price of it, Mrs. Layton?"

"Pardon me, Mr. Flint, that is the only particular I never inquire about." Mrs. Layton was right; such vulgar queries are for those who mean to pay, or at least *not* to postpone payment indefinitely.

The party was now equipped and proceeded to their destination. "I told you so—we are too late," said Mr. Flint, on opening the door, and finding the room full to overflowing.

"A room is never too full," replied the gallant major, "for certain persons to find a place."

"A very good rule, Major, and another is, Miss Clarence, to be quite unconscious that the seat you happen to prefer is occupied—now follow me." Suiting the action to the word, Mrs.

---

1 "Oh, usefulness—usefulness—I detest you."

2 Half-season.

Layton pushed her way to the upper end of the room, declining gracefully, as she proceeded, numerous offers of seats, till she obtained the conspicuous position at which she aimed. Gertrude was amazed at what would have startled a novice only, the ease with which a lady of fashionable notoriety can doff the prescriptive delicacy of her sex, and force her way to a commanding station, with a boldness that would better become a military chieftain. The lecturer paused at the bustle occasioned by the entrance of the brilliant party. Mrs. Layton always commanded notice. Her daughter, a newly risen star in the fashionable hemisphere, had not yet sated curiosity, and our heroine was known—we grieve so often to repeat the unprized distinction—as 'Miss Clarence—the great fortune.'

In our commercial city every thing is inspired or infected by the bustling genius of the place. Even scientific associations, and literary institutions, are modified by the habits of business. The merchant, who has a hundred argosies at sea, can give but brief attention to any thing but the chances and losses of trade; and thus it happens that at the Athenæum, the most fashionable of our literary resorts, *four* lectures only are allowed to the discussion of the most useful arts—to the most abstruse science—to the inexhaustible topic of metaphysics—to the fascinating themes of German and English literature. If poetry is the subject, the lecturer must discuss its origin, its nature, its uses and abuses—he must sail down the stream of time from Hesiod to the last stanza by Moore, or Halleck, or Bryant.[1] He must prove that if our soil has as yet produced few flowers of poesy, we have a greater capacity to develope than any other people, (for our patriotic audiences are not quite satisfied without this sacrifice to the local divinities,) and he must do all this in four lectures of one hour each, 'counted by the stopwatch, my lord.' In this brief space the geologist scales the Andes, dives to the primitive rocks, and imparts his revelations of antediluvian worlds. The astronomer comprises the brilliant discoveries of his science within this Procrustes measure. Doubtless there are fortunate and dexterous individuals, who in this match of knowledge against time may, like persons running through the Hesperian gardens, catch some of the golden fruit as it falls.[2] But miracles are past, and for the most part we must say, 'Alas, for this multitude, for they go empty away!'

---

1 Hesiod, Greek poet of the eighth century BCE; Thomas Moore (Irish, 1779-1852); Fitz-Greene Halleck; William Cullen Bryant.
2 Garden in Greek mythology in which golden apples grew.

A limited time is not the only difficulty with which the lecturer has to contend. He must possess a rare art who commands the attention of a popular assembly constituted of young ladies just escaped from the thraldom of school—their *beaux* just launched on the tide of fashion—married pairs, seeking a refuge from conjugal ennui—a few complaisant literati, who go '*pour encourager les autres*,'[1] and a very few honest devotees in every temple of knowledge. But even in such an auditory 'the air, a chartered libertine is still',[2] while —— defines and magnifies the art his genius illustrates; and while —— kindles up the dim speculations of metaphysics with the light of his genius, and imparts to their abstractions the vivifying essence of his wit.

The particular attraction of the evening we have selected, was some fine transparencies. Gertrude had taken an unambitious seat behind Mrs. Layton. "I am afraid," she said, "my *rue Italienne* is in your way, my darling,—my feathers *de trop*,[3] are they not?—You cannot see any body?"

"I cannot see the lecturer, and as I must honestly confess, I am smitten with the rustic desire to see the transparencies, I will trouble Mr. Pedrillo to conduct me to an unoccupied place just below us."

"Rather an eccentric movement for a fashionable young lady, but '*chacun à son gout!*'[4] go, we will not lose sight of you."

Pedrillo saw her ensconced in a position that promised to be a favorable point of sight; but here too a phalanx of plumes waved and nodded before her, and the fair wearers were reconnoitering the company through their eye-glasses, and interchanging their remarks on new dresses and new faces. Pedrillo left her, saying, he could not presume to divide her attention with the lecturer, and resumed his station at Emilie's side. The lights were soon after all extinguished to give full effect to the transparencies, and directly two gentlemen took an unoccupied place before Gertrude. The one, she recognised by his voice to be Flint, who had left his party to speak, as he said, 'to a member of Congress—a particular friend,' and the other was Gerald Roscoe. The gentlemen were as sincere as she had been in their wish to give their attention to the lecturer, but it was impossible; the fairer part of the audience had taken advantage of the entertainment being chiefly addressed to

---

1 To encourage the others.

2 Shakespeare's *Henry V* I.i.48.

3 Too much.

4 Each to his own taste.

the eye, and were indulging in whispered *tête-à-têtes*. The gentlemen followed their example, holding their hats before their faces to secure their communications from general circulation, and thus giving them more distinctly to their back auditor.

"Have you met Miss Clarence yet?" asked Flint.

"No—never."

"I will introduce you to her after the lecture; I am quite intimate with her."

"Thank you—I have already been offered that honor once to-day by the mother of our client, Stevy Brown; the poor dog is at home again, in high favor with the old tailor; and his wife, who is very much my friend, and overflowing with gratitude to Miss C. for some part she had in the reconciliation, predicts a match between us, and actually sent for me to-day, to propose we should help on our destiny by meeting at a sociable tea-drinking at her house!"

"Well—what did you do about it?"

"Heavens, Flint! I should think even your business spirit would shrink from such an encounter."

"I don't know that—it is not best to be too romantic; but I am glad at any rate that you declined the meeting. You are such a favorite with the girls, Roscoe, that I had rather not have you for a rival."

"The danger of my rivalship, Flint, would depend on the eagerness of the competition, and that on the value of the prize to be striven for."

"Oh, certainly—and the prize in this case *is* worth striving for. I should despise marrying for fortune alone as much as any man, but I presume fortune don't disqualify—I can tell you, Roscoe, Miss Clarence is a very sensible young lady."

"Heaven defend us from your very sensible young ladies!"

"Oh, well, she is very fashionable, if you prefer that, and very much admired."

"So I am told by Morley, Daisy, & Co.—a goodly company, truly—all, all honorable men. The value of their admiration can be pretty accurately calculated—what is the amount of the stock, Flint—the consideration for which these gentlemen will give their matrimonial bonds?"[1]

"Now you are too severe, Roscoe. There are several ladies in the city as much of an object as Miss Clarence; but then, I must

---

1   In the 1849 edition, Sedgwick amends this phrase to "matrimonial bond and mortgage."

own, there is an advantage in having an elegant sufficiency, secured from all contingencies."

"I am ignorant of the terms of the trade, Flint; what do you mean by an elegant sufficiency?"

"A hundred thousand dollars. I know, on the best authority, that the old man has secured her that, so that if he marries again, and some folks think he will, or if he lives for ever—dyspepsia never kills any body, you know—still there is enough for any reasonable man. I tell you again, Roscoe, Miss Clarence would not be a bad bargain without her money. Upon my honor, I would as soon sell my soul as marry for money alone—but she comes up to my rule, viz. never to marry a woman with a fortune that I would not marry if I had the fortune, and she were without it—that's about fair, is it not?"

Roscoe was struck with this *naïve exposé*[1] of sordid calculation, just notions, and honest feeling, and he was on the point of wasting a little sentiment on Flint, in a remonstrance against this admixture of the pure and base, but he remembered in time that there is nothing more quixotic than to attempt to change the current of a man's mind by a single impulse, and he contented himself with saying, "I am no casuist in these matters; I conceived an early prejudice, a sort of natural antipathy against a *fortune*—that I believe is the technical term for a prize-lady."

"You don't say so—that's very odd."

"It may be so, but as a natural antipathy is a feeling of which we do not know the origin, and which we never hope or try to overcome, you may venture to introduce me to Miss C. without any fear of competition."

Flint had a profound respect for Roscoe's opinion, and after a short interval of silence, he said, "Do tell me why you so much object to marrying a fortune?"

Roscoe replied, in the words of an old ballad,

"Her oxen may die i' the house, Billie,
And her kye into the byre,
And I shall hae nothing to mysel,
But a fat fadge by the fyre."[2]

Gertrude smiled, she could not help it, at the ridiculous light in which Roscoe had placed her; but a captive at the stake would

---

1 Naïve statement.
2 From "Lord Thomas and Fair Annet," a traditional English ballad.

have had no reason to envy her, delicate as she was almost to fastidiousness, while she heard her market value so coarsely set forth by Flint, and her father, who was embalmed in her heart in the sanctity of filial love, spoken of as the 'old man,' whose projects, health, and life were of value only as enhancing, or diminishing her chances of wealth—and this to Roscoe too. Gertrude felt for the first time the full force of a sentiment that she had almost unconsciously cherished. If a woman would make discoveries in that intricate region, her heart, let her analyze the solicitude she feels about the light in which she is presented even to the imagination of him whom she prefers. The estimation of the most indifferent or despised becomes of consequence, when it may color with one shade the opinion of that individual. 'Is it not possible,' thought Gertrude, 'to escape this introduction,—I cannot—I will not become at once in his eyes this detested 'prize-lady'—what an odious term! this object of the pursuit of 'Morley, Daisy, & Co.'—this 'fat fadge' of his perspective;' and dreading any thing less than the threatened presentation and consequent éclaircissement, she determined to make her way to Mrs. Layton, and on some pretext retire from the lecture-room, before she again encountered Flint. She had half-risen, when she was arrested by some disorder in that part of the room where she had left her party, and directly the cause was explained by several voices exclaiming, 'there's a lady fainting!'—'open a window'—'make room there!' The lecturer stopped. A candle was lighted at his lamp, and Gertrude saw Emilie supported, almost carried in Randolph Marion's arms, and followed by Pedrillo and her mother. Marion's face was pale and agitated. Flint sprang forward with his usual alacrity to offer assistance; Gertrude lost every other consideration in her interest for her friend, and would have followed, but she heard Mrs. Layton say, "It is merely the heat of the room—come with us, Mr. Flint—Major Daisy stays for Miss Clarence—run forward, Mr. Flint, and see if there is a carriage at the door—if not, get one." Never was there a more useful man for an exigency than Flint. Roscoe had stepped forward to assist the retiring party, but after exchanging a word with Mrs. Layton, he resumed his place. Miss Clarence was before him, and the candle still near enough to reveal her features. Their eyes encountered. She bowed, but with the coldest reserve, for at that moment she felt her identity with the 'prize-lady' only. Roscoe's surprise and pleasure at meeting her prevented his observing her coldness. "Is it possible," he exclaimed, with the utmost animation, "that I have been unconsciously near you; I shall never again believe in those delicate spiritual intimations that are supposed to be conveyed without the intervention of the senses." Gertrude secretly wished that the senses too had suspended their ministry, that her ear had been deaf to those sounds that seemed now to paralyze the organs of speech.

Roscoe looked curiously round in quest of some person, or persons, who should appear to be of Miss Clarence's party. She saw his curious survey, enjoyed his perplexity, and kept her attention apparently fixed on the lecturer. "It is a pity my friend, Mr. ——, does not speak loud enough to be heard," said Roscoe, "since he is so fortunate as to engross your attention."

"It aids one materially in hearing, to listen," replied Gertrude.

"A good hit," said an elderly gentleman, who sat next Miss Clarence; "a word, young man," he continued, drawing Roscoe towards him, "I advise you not to interrupt that young woman any longer; she comes here for some profitable purpose—she is a teacher in the High-school, I surmise."

'She certainly listens most dutifully,' thought Roscoe, 'but this good gentleman's surmise is not mine.' "If the lady is a teacher, sir," he replied, with the utmost good humor, "I am a learner, and you must allow me to use my golden opportunity. 'The gods send opportunities—the wise man profits by them,' you know"—he quoted the Latin saying in its original. His admonisher was so propitiated by the implied compliment to his learning, that, though he did not understand a word of it, Roscoe might have talked through the lecture without any further reproof from him.

The lecture was evidently drawing to a close, and Gertrude heartily wished that, like Cinderella, she had some good fairy at hand to assist her departure; and Roscoe secretly exulted that now at least she could not disappear without affording him some clue by which to ascertain her name—all that seemed to him unknown. So satisfactory is that internal conviction that is wrought by the character and manners. Roscoe availed himself of a pause, while the lecturer was adjusting a transparency. "I shall hope again to meet you here; pardon this uncourteous *you*—our barbarous language has no more gentle substitute for the name. Do not," he added, in a lowered and earnest tone, "do not leave it to destiny any farther to weave the web of our acquaintance; allow me to seek you elsewhere, or, at least, to expect to meet you again here?"

"Have you forgotten," asked Gertrude, referring to an expression in Roscoe's note, "have you forgotten your voluntary 'covenant with your lips?'"

"Pardon me—that covenant only extended to impertinent questions of others, and indirect inquiries."

"But those were not the terms of the compact, and you have given me new reasons this evening for enforcing it."

"Impossible! what can I have said or done to deserve such a mark of your displeasure?"

"Not my displeasure—exactly," she said—and 'not my displeasure at all,' spoke the sweet smile that beamed from her lips; but now the candles were re-lighted, and she perceived Major Daisy eagerly making his way through the crowd to her. She abruptly left Roscoe, and met Daisy. She had dropped her veil to prevent all recognitions from her acquaintance. "Do not speak to me," she said, as the major was beginning to describe the anxiety with which he had looked for her, "there is a person here I wish particularly to avoid—let me pass out as if entirely unknown." Daisy, not doubting she wished to cut some vulgar acquaintance, implicitly obeyed her, admiring the facility with which she was acquiring the arts of polite life. She thus succeeded in completely eluding the vigilance of Roscoe. His eye followed her till she was lost in the crowd; but he saw no one join her, and he was not without some uncomfortable reflections on the singularity of a lady violating the common forms of society. Yet there was so marked a propriety and delicacy in Gertrude's deportment, that it seemed ridiculous to doubt her. He racked his brain to conjecture what she could have meant by alleging that he had that very evening given 'her new reason for her mystery.' 'She might,' he thought, 'have overheard my discussion with Flint; but I said nothing dishonorable to her sex—or any individual of the blessed community but poor Miss Clarence. Heaven forgive me, for my antipathy to that girl's name even—Well, I will home to my mother, and see if female ingenuity can help me to unravel this mystery.'

CHAPTER VII.

"Laissez moi faire.—Il ne faut pas se laisser mener comme un oison; et, pourvu que l'honneur n'y soit pas offense on se peut libèrer un peu de la tyrannie d'un père."[1]
MOLIÈRE.

ON the night after the lecture at the Athenæum, Miss Clarence had just laid her head on the pillow, when she heard her door gently opened, and saw Emilie enter. "Oh, Gertrude," she said, "how could you go to bed without coming to see me?"

"My dear Emilie! I was prevented by your mother. She told me you were exhausted by your indisposition at the lecture, and had fallen asleep, and Justine had requested no one would disturb you."

"How can mama!" Emilie checked herself and added, "I have not been asleep—I cannot sleep—but I will not disturb you Gertrude. Only kiss me once, and tell me you love me, and feel for me." She knelt beside Gertrude, and laid her face on her friend's bosom. Nothing could be more exquisite than her figure at this moment, as the moonlight fell on it. Her flowing night-dress set off the symmetry of her nymph-like form; her hair, parted with a careless grace, lay on her brow in massy waving folds; her cheeks were flushed with recent agitation, and her eyes, the ministers of her soul, revealed its sadness. Her attitude seemed to solicit pity, and Gertrude, full of the quick-stirring sympathies of youth and ardent feeling, obeyed their impulse. "Come into my bed, Emilie," she said, "and lie in my arms, and pour out your heart to me as to a second self. Every one of your feelings shall be a sacred trust, and I will think and act for you as I would for myself."

Never did a child, with its little burden of untold grief, spring more eagerly to its mother's bosom, than Emilie to the arms of her friend. She felt there as if she were at home, and at rest, and no evil could approach her! She wept without fear, and without measure. "I never was used," she said, "to shutting up my thoughts and feelings in my own bosom, and it has seemed to me as if my heart would burst. Mama has charged me so often not to say any thing to you on a certain subject—but I never promised her—do you

---

1   "Trust me, one must not let oneself be treated like a gosling, and
     provided that honor is not offended, one may free oneself a little from
     a father's tyranny." From Molière, L'Amour Médecin (The Love Doctor),
     1665.

think it was wrong, to let you Gertrude, who are such a true friend to us all, to let you know what was in my mind?"

"You cannot help it, Emilie, for I already guess and fear all that is not told. Have I not understood your not writing to me?—your reserve since I have been with you? Have I not observed your drooping eye—your timid, shrinking look, whenever Pedrillo appears?"

"Oh, I hate him!" interrupted Emilie—it was the ungentlest word she ever spoke.

"Did I not see you to-night in Randolph Marion's arms?"

"Did you see that, Gertrude?—then you know—no, that you cannot know—"

"Randolph's agitated countenance, Emilie, and your emotions have left you little to disclose—he still loves you?"

"I think—I believe—I *hope* he does. Is it not strange, Gertrude, that I can hope it, when his love must be useless to me, and misery to himself?"

"No, Emilie, the hope of a requital is the first and last demand of affection—the first and last breath of its existence."

"Then it was not a sin in me to feel such a gush of joy when our eyes met, and I perceived in that one brief glance that I was still beloved. Gertrude, I forgot where I was—I thought of nothing but that Randolph still loved me. Mr. Pedrillo must have observed us—he whispered in my ear 'beware!' I felt as if a serpent had stung me. Then the room whirled round, and I knew nothing more till I was standing on the college steps, leaning on Randolph's bosom, and supported by his arms—he resigned me to mama—pressed my hand to his lips—yes, before Pedrillo's eyes, and *mama's*—and then he said 'Emilie, forgive me!' and darted away. He spoke but those three words, but did they not say he had wronged me by that cruel letter at Trenton? did not they indicate that he still loves me?——but if he does"——

"Is it not possible, Emilie, to avoid this horrid marriage?"

"No—no—that man is as relentless as the grave—we are all in his power. *My price is paid*, Gertrude—my mother has told me so." The poor girl averted her face as if she would have hidden her shame at the insupportable thought of the infamous traffic in which she was sacrificed.

Gertrude started up. "Your *price*, Emilie!" she exclaimed, "Is it *money* that is in question?—can money redeem you from this dreadful fate?"

"It is not money alone," replied Emilie, in a tone that proved she had not caught a ray of hope from the animated voice of her friend, "there is some dreadful mystery, Gertrude, mama does not understand it, but ruin—absolute, hopeless ruin, awaits us all if this marriage is not accomplished. Oh, I could have laid down my life—I could have sold myself to slavery, but to marry a man I so detest—and fear—and Randolph still loving me—but you cannot help me, my noble, generous Gertrude—there is no help for me."

"I do not despair, Emilie," replied Gertrude, to whose strong and resolute mind no obstacle seemed insuperable, when her friend's preservation was the object to be obtained; "I do not despair—there is a limit to parental rights—you do not owe and you must not yield a passive and destructive obedience to the authority of your parents. You have a right to know what this ruin is which you are to avert by self-immolation. We will try to the utmost to close this mysterious gulf without burying you within it. Your marriage has been once deferred by the intervention of Heaven—try now what a heaven-inspired resolution can do."

"When I listen to you, Gertrude, it seems possible."

"It is possible. Is Pedrillo urgent as to the time?—Has your father named a day to you?"

"Not the day precisely; but I see there is no escape—he told me this morning, it must not be much longer delayed."

"At any rate," said Gertrude, after a little consideration, "there will be time enough for me to receive a letter from my father. Rest assured, Emilie, that whatever can be done to save you I will do—now compose yourself and go to sleep." Emilie did not comprehend what her friend meant to do, or could do; but she seemed to repose tranquilly on her promise, and like a vine that has drooped till its delicate tendrils caught a support, she clung to Gertrude in secure dependence, and soon fell asleep as quiet as a child in the sanctuary of its mother's arms.

The next morning as Gertrude was indulging the children, and herself no less than the children, in a game of romps in the nursery, she received a summons to Mrs. Layton's apartment. She found that lady reclining on her sofa, her window-curtains so arranged as to admit only a flattering twilight. A new novel, a new poem, bouquets of fresh flowers, and half a dozen notes on perfumed and colored paper, lay on the table before her. She was reading an ode to childhood, and her eyes were suffused with the tears which the poet's imagination had called forth. Before Gertrude had closed the door, the children, disappointed at being so suddenly deprived of their favorite pleasure, came shouting after her. "Shut them out—shut them out," cried Mrs. Layton, "I cannot have my room turned into a *ménagerie*[1]—ah, thank Heaven, now we are quiet again. Come and sit with me, dearest, not 'under the green wood-tree'—that is the luxury of Clarenceville—but on my sofa, where we can better defy 'winter and rough weather.'[2] Here is a harvest for you, the rarest and most costly flowers delicately directed to 'Mrs. L., for herself, *her friend*, and Miss Emilie'—a proposition from the major that we should make up a party for the masquerade—and lastly, a diplomatic letter from Mr. Morley. Listen to it, Gertrude, for though addressed to me, it has been studiously adapted to your ear."

"My dear Madam—I have just received a letter from Mr. Clarence, who was a particular friend of my father."

Ha! ha! Gertrude, love plays strange things with chronology— Morley is full five and forty, which I take to be half a lustre in advance of your father; but allons![3]

"He recommends a friend of his, Mr. Randolph Marion, for the office of ——, and says, what may be true though flattering, that my influence will decide who shall be the successful candidate. Nothing in life would give me greater pleasure than to oblige Mr. Clarence, but I am unfortunately in a degree committed to a very zealous and useful member of our party. If however your fair friend, Miss C. is interested in Marion, (I do not mean *en amante*,[4] for I understand there is no interest of a delicate nature in question,) I shall make every effort and sacrifice to oblige her. Will you assure her of this, after ascertaining her wishes in the most recherchée[5] manner imaginable. Your sex are born diplomatists. Oh that you, my dear Madam, would vouchsafe to be my minister plenipotentiary '*dans les affaires du cœur!*'[6]
  "I remain, Madam,
  "Yours, with infinite respect,
  "and regard, &c. &c. &c.
  "*STEPHEN MORLEY*"

---

1 Place where wild animals are kept, and often exhibited.
2 Lines from Shakespeare's poem "Under the Greenwood Tree."
3 Listen!
4 As a lover.
5 Studied or meticulous, suggesting a hidden or subtle inquiry.
6 In the affairs of the heart.

"*Les affaires du cœur!*" repeated Mrs. Layton, "Oh Love, what hypocrisies are practised in thy name!—but what says my 'fair friend' to Mr. Morley?"

"That he can in no way do me so great a favor as by securing the appointment of Randolph Marion."

"But my 'fair friend' must understand that the exchange of equivalents is a favorite principle, in the political economy of certain politicians; and that Mr. Morley expects that the gift of this office to Marion, shall be a make-weight to turn the matrimonial scale in his favor?"

"I shall not be deterred by any fastidious reference to Mr. Morley's expectations, from getting an advantage in this barter trade, of which I am the unhappy object—particularly as the advantage is one in which I have no personal interest, I will myself write a reply to Mr. Morley, and if—if Marion obtains the office, will it not be possible, Mrs. Layton?"

Nothing could be less explicit than Gertrude's words; nothing more so, than her eager, penetrating look. Mrs. Layton understood her perfectly, and replied emphatically, and with chilling coldness, "not possible."

Gertrude, with abated, not extinguished hope, wrote the note, and despatched it to Morley. That finished, "the next affairs in order," said Mrs. Layton, "are these bouquets from our lack-brain suitors, Daisy and Smith. I gave them some lessons, last evening, in the vocabulary of flowers. Daisy has sent the emblems of all the passions, sentiments, and emotions of humanity, so that if he finds it convenient not to mean one, he can mean another. My friend Daisy understands that part of wisdom, which is wariness, but poor Smith has staked all on a single die. Here is his declaration, in a half bushel of rose-buds!"

"And am I expected to comprehend their symbolical language?"

"Oh, no; give yourself no farther trouble, than to grace the flowers in the wearing, and answer the gentlemen when they speak their accustomed language which, Heaven knows, is far enough from that of these sweet interpreters of 'thoughts that breathe.'[1] Here is a note from Flint; honest, practical, every-day Flint. He asks me to lend him Rousseau's Heloise![2] Mr. *D.* Flint, translated to the sublimated region of sentiment; what a triumph for you, Gertrude! But you have such a superb indifference to

---

1 From "The Progress of Poesy: A Pindaric Ode" (1757) by Thomas Gray (English, 1716-71).

2 Rousseau's *Julie, or the New Heloise* (1761).

all these honors—what are you examining so critically?—the autograph of my friend Gerald Roscoe; a note I have just received from him inquiring after Emilie's health; he was at the lecture last evening; he seems in a sentimental mood; *ah! l'éstrange chose que le sentiment!*[1] But it is as natural to Roscoe, as soaring to the lark; while poor Flint is like a stage-cupid, with paste-board wings. Gertrude, you are welcome to your lovers, while I have Roscoe. Spare your blushes, dearest." Gertrude did blush, but it was at her private interpretation of Roscoe's sentimental mood. Mrs. Layton proceeded, "I mean while I have Roscoe for my *friend*. He would never fall in love with a married woman, at least, never *tell* his love; he is too *American* for that, though *grâce à Dieu*,[2] not precise. But we have not yet decided on our answer to Daisy, will you go to the masquerade? in mask of course, for I never remain a spectator, where I may be an actor. Now you look as if you were going to raise objections, and be afraid of what papa will say."

"No, I have no fear of the kind, I assure you, Mrs. Layton. My father has no wish to be an external conscience to me. He has given me certain principles, but he leaves me at perfect liberty in their application."

Mrs. Layton shook her head: "I always shudder when a girl, minus twenty, begins to talk of principles. Spare me! spare me the virtue, that is weighed in the balance, and squared by the rule. Ma chère,[3] you would be infinitely more fascinating, if you would break through this thraldom."

"A thraldom, Mrs. Layton, of which I am unconscious, cannot be very oppressive. No condition admits greater liberty than mine, a liberty that has no other limit than the bounds set to protect our virtue."

"Heaven preserve us, Gertrude! I had no intention of calling all this forth by a simple proposition to join a masquerading party. You have raised a whirlwind to blow away a feather. In one word, will you go, *en masque*?"[4]

"In one word then, Mrs. Layton, no."

"*Eh bien*—that is settled." Rather an awkward pause ensued, and was broken off, to the relief of both parties, by the entrance of a milliner's girl, whom her mistress, Madame, had sent to Mrs. Layton with some beautiful specimens of newly arrived

---

1 Oh! What a strange thing is feeling!
2 Thank God.
3 My sweet, my dear.
4 In costume, or with a mask.

Parisian finery. "Beautiful! beautiful!" exclaimed Mrs. Layton, as she opened the box; "ah, Gertrude, the advantages of fortune are countless—you can indulge yourself in these luxuries to any extent."

Miss Clarence did not seem disposed to avail herself of the privilege, while Mrs. Layton with the utmost eagerness selected some of the most costly articles for Emilie and laid them aside, and then tried on and decided to retain, a *Gabrielle pélérine*,[1] a *Vallière cap*,[2] and *Henri quatre*[3] ruff. "Now, my good girl," she said, "take the rest back, and tell Madame I am infinitely obliged to her for giving me the first choice."

"Madame," said the girl, modestly, "Madame pinned the price to each article."

"Yes—but she must know the prices?"

"Yes, ma'am—but Madame told me not to leave the articles unless you paid for them."

"Madame is excessively nice," said Mrs. Layton, coloring and throwing back the articles she had selected for herself, but, instantly resuming the Gabrielle, "I must have this," she said, "it is so graceful and piquante,[4] and really I have nothing else fit to wear this evening." She emptied her purse of its contents, five-and-twenty dollars, precisely the amount of the Gabrielle. She gave the money to the girl, who was re-folding and replacing the articles she had first lain aside, "Stop, I keep those," she said, and turning to Gertrude, added, in a half whisper, "they are for Emilie—you know it is indispensable she should be prepared for a certain occasion—what *shall* I do about them?"

Gertrude felt embarrassed; she perceived Mrs. Layton expected she would offer to relieve her from her dilemma, in the obvious way, by advancing the money; but this she was resolved not to do, and she replied coldly, "I really cannot advise you."

Mrs. Layton looked displeased—and saying, in a suppressed voice, "there is one alternative, though not a very pleasant one," she wrote a note, and gave it to the girl—"Take it to the City-Hotel," she said, "inquire for Mr. Pedrillo—give it into his hands—he will give you the money."

---

1 Pélérine: small cape covering the shoulders with ends meeting in a point at the front; Gabrielle-styled suggests that the fabric is sewn in a series of puffs accentuating the pélérine.

2 A cape in the style of Louise de Vallière (French, 1644-1710), mistress to King Louis XIV.

3 Henry IV-style ruff, worn about the neck.

4 Vivid.

"Mrs. Layton!" exclaimed Gertrude, starting up and losing all her assumed coldness, "do not, I beseech you, do that—allow me to pay for the articles."

"As you please," replied Mrs. Layton, in the most frigid manner. Gertrude flew to her apartment, returned with her purse, paid the amount, and the girl withdrew. Gertrude would have withdrawn too, but Mrs. Layton, who had completely recovered her self-possession, said, "you must not leave me, dear Gertrude, till you have forgiven me for my momentary displeasure; I misunderstood you, but there is nothing that so shocks my feelings, as the appearance of selfishness."

There was something almost ludicrous to Gertrude, in the sudden *bouleversement*[1] of her ideas occasioned by this speech. She expected Mrs. Layton would devise some ingenious cover or extenuation for her own culpable selfishness and indulged vanity, but she was quite unprepared for this extravagant self-delusion. Her heart ached too at the sight of the ornaments that were destined to adorn the victim for the altar, and she stood between the tragic and the comic muse, not knowing whether to laugh or cry, when she was opportunely relieved by another visiter.

An old woman entered the apartment and approached Mrs. Layton, courtseying again and again, in that submissive deferential manner that is so foreign, so *anti-American*. Her accent was Swiss, and her costume neat and national. She began with an apology, "She would not have troubled the lady just now, but the old man at home was starving with cold, and another besides, who had the chills of death on him—God help him—and Justine said"—

"You are Justine's mother, then," interrupted Mrs. Layton.

"Yes, indeed, lady—I've been here so often I thought the lady knew me; and Justine—God bless the child—Justine said the five-and-twenty dollars were waiting for me since the morning in the lady's hands."

Mrs. Layton had indeed at the first glance too perfectly recognised the old woman, and anticipated her claims. She had, after a hundred broken promises to Justine, her maid, to whom she owed a much larger sum, told her, not two hours before, that she had twenty-five dollars ready for her; and she now felt all the mortification—not of failing to perform her contract, to such trifles she was accustomed—but of an exposure before Gertrude, and while the Gabriélle lay as a mute witness before her. Mrs. Layton rather prided herself on speaking the truth; it was a matter of taste

---

1 Overturning, disruption, or upheaval.

with her, and she adhered to it unless driven to extremities. She was even frank, so far as frankness consisted in gracefully confessing faults that could not be concealed; but those that are grossly deficient in one virtue, will not be found martyrs to another, and rather than it should appear to Gertrude, that she had given for the Gabriélle the very money due and promised to Justine, she said, though with evident confusion, "Your daughter mistakes, my good woman, I told her I would have the money for her tomorrow morning."

"God help us, then!" replied the old woman, bursting into tears, "it is always so—to-morrow, and to-morrow, and to-morrow—we shall all be dead before your to-morrow comes to us, madam."

"Allow me to lend you the twenty-five dollars, Mrs. Layton," said Gertrude. Mrs. Layton nodded her acceptance, took the bills, and transferred them to the woman, who thus unexpectedly relieved, turned her streaming eyes to the source whence the relief came. She had not before noticed Gertrude. She now courtesied low to her, and, in the excess of her gratitude, kissed her hands; and looking at her again, she seemed struck with some new emotion, and murmured and repeated, "it is—it is—it must be—for the love of Heaven, my young lady, let me speak with you alone!" Gertrude, at an utter loss to conjecture the reason of this sudden and mysterious interest, accompanied the old woman into the entry. As soon as they were alone, "If there is mercy in your heart, young lady," she said, "go along with me—there's not a moment to be lost—Justine will tell you so." She opened the nursery-door, summoned Justine, and whispered to her, and Justine said earnestly, though with less impetuosity than her mother, "Indeed, Miss, you had best go with her—ye need fear nothing. She may mistake, but if she's right, ye'll be sorry one day, tender-hearted as ye are, if ye refuse her—that is, if it is as my mother thinks, ye'll grieve that ye did not go—indeed ye will."

"For the love of God, Justine, stop talking, and bring the young lady's hat for her." The hat and cloak were brought, and Gertrude, feeling much like a person groping in utter darkness, accompanied her conductor to a miserable little dwelling, at the upper extremity of Elm-street.

CHAPTER VIII.

"O Death!——
The great, the wealthy, fear thy blow,
From pomp and pleasure torn;
But oh! a bless'd relief to those,
That weary-laden mourn."[1]
BURNS.

GERTRUDE'S conductor had hurried on in advance of her, partly as it seemed to preserve a respectful distance, and partly to avoid any communication with her. When she was within her humble dwelling, she mounted to the second story, and winding her way through a dark narrow passage to the extremity of a back building, she reached a door, at which she stopped for a moment, then placing her finger on her lips, in token of silence, she signed to Miss Clarence to await her, opened the door, and disappeared. Gertrude heard a low murmur within, but nothing to afford her a clue to the old woman's purpose. 'If I am brought here,' she thought, 'to be moved to charity by an extraordinary spectacle of wretchedness, why this secresy?—why Justine's and her mother's strange allusions?' The door was re-opened, and her name pronounced by a well known voice, in a feeble, tender, and tranquil tone. At the same time, the old woman, in explanation of the part she had acted, held up before Gertrude the picture of Trenton-falls. Gertrude sprang forward, exclaiming "Louis Seton!" She stood beside him, pressed his pale, emaciated hand to her lips, and expressed in her asking eye, what her tongue could not utter. The old woman remained at the door, wringing her hands, and giving vent in her own language, to her interpretation of a scene that appeared in her simple view, to tell the common tale of true love and a broken heart on one side; and of disdain, and late relenting on the other.

Seton was wrapped in a flannel gown, and sustained by pillows in an upright position. His bed was drawn as near as possible to the hearth. A single chair, and a small table, on which lay some implements of his art, and a bible, and some vials, were all the furniture of his room; its neatness and order indicated the kind care of his hostess.

His form was attenuated, his hands bloodless, a consuming color burned in his hollow cheeks, his brow was pale and fixed

---

1 From "Man Was Made to Mourn: A Dirge" (1784).

as marble, his eye bright as if the soul had there concentrated all its fires, and his mouth, that flexible feature that first betrays the mutations of feeling, was serene and rigid, as if the seal of death were already set upon it.

At the first sight of Gertrude, a faint color overspread his brow and temples; his lips trembled, and his bosom heaved, he very soon however recovered his composure, and said, "do not weep, my dear friend, but rather rejoice with me."

"Nay, nay," cried the old woman, advancing, "weep on, child; for the love of Christ, weep on, till his dying lips shall speak the word of peace to you."

"Dying!" echoed Gertrude, for that was the only word that had made a distinct impression on her sense; "dying! oh, it cannot be. He must have a physician, and better lodgings. My good friend, hasten back to Mrs. Layton's, and bring my servant here."

"Bless you, young lady, it's too late; it's a miracle he has lasted to see ye; and ye'd better use the spared minutes to lighten your conscience."

Seton smiled faintly. "She is right, Gertrude, I am dying, but do not let that grieve you; death is to me, the happiest circumstance of my existence;" then turning to the old woman, he added, "Marie, I have nothing to forgive this lady; she has been an angel of mercy to me."

"God forgive me! she looks like it; ah, pity," she exclaimed, as the other natural solution of this sad meeting occurred to her simple mind, "ah pity, pity that ye ever parted! pity that ye have so met!"

Seton manifested no emotion at these vehement exclamations, but calmly told Marie, he had much to communicate to his friend; and she, after mending the fire, and arranging some emollients, provided by a dispensary-physician, left the apartment!

"Oh Louis," said Gertrude, "why have you let us remain in such cruel ignorance of your condition; you have not surely ever for a moment, doubted my father's sincere affection for you—or mine?"

"No, Gertrude, never."

"And you certainly knew, there was nothing I desired so much, as to serve you."

"Yes, I well knew there was nothing too much to expect from you, and your noble-minded father; but I have been sick, and diseased in mind, Gertrude."

"And was that a reason why you should fly from the offices of affection."

"Reason! I have been deprived of reason, and long before my reason was gone, my feelings were diseased and perverted, and my pride unsubdued, I shrunk from an accumulating load of obligation. One generous feeling I had. I could not bear to be to you, Gertrude, like the veiled skeletons at the feasts of the Egyptians, for ever presenting before you gloomy images, and calling up sad thoughts."

"Oh, how wrong you were, Louis! I had so few objects of affection! Next to my father, you were most important to my happiness."

Louis pressed her hand to his lips. "I was wrong," he said; "I underrated the generosity of your affection, and I grossly magnified my own miseries, but it's all past now; you will forgive me, Gertrude?"

"Forgive you! do not speak of forgiveness—I never, never shall forget that you have suffered such extremity; and that it has come to this—"

"My dear friend, do not afflict yourself thus—my troubles have all ended happily." There was a singular contrast and change, in both Gertrude and Seton. He was collected and serene, as if he had already touched the shore of eternal peace. She agitated, as one still tempest-tost on the uncertain waves of life. But after a little while, she regained her usual ascendancy over her emotions, and ashamed that she had for a moment disturbed his holy peace, she sat down beside him, and listened with tolerable composure, to his relation of the particulars of his life, since they parted. During his recital he had frequent turns of fainting, but they were relieved by intervals of rest.

"My life is so far spent," he said, "that I can only glance at the past. There was much, of which you were ignorant, Gertrude, that aggravated my malady before we left Clarenceville for Trenton. The immediate cause of my melancholy was suspected, if not known, and I was subjected to the gossiping scrutiny of our neighbors, and the vulgar intimations of the servants. Coarse minds graduate others by their external condition. You were rich, and I was poor, and therefore in their estimation, on their level. You remember the circumstances that led me to betray my cherished passion. My nerves were laid bare by this exposure, and while I shrunk from the slightest touch, I was told that one said, 'it was a shame for a beggarly drawing-master to take advantage of Mr. Clarence's generosity,' and another said, 'still waters run deep, but who would have thought of Louis Seton playing such a game?' and 'she has served him right—she will carry her fortune to a better market than Louis Seton's.'"

"Oh spare me—spare me, Louis."

"I repeat this to you, Gertrude, because it is my only apology for having yielded to a sickly sensibility, compounded of physical weakness, pride, and humility."

"I want to know no more, Louis; you have suffered, and I have been the cause."

"The cause was innocent, and the suffering is past, Gertrude—therefore listen patiently. We went to Trenton. Delirious as I was, I perfectly remembered our progress over those wild rocks—with what skill and resolution you lured me on and protracted my last act of madness, till I was saved by a wonderful intervention. At the time I believed my preserver to be a supernatural being. I fancied, in the lawless vagaries of my mind, that his face had been revealed to me in a dream; but afterwards I remembered the resemblance was to a head you once painted from memory—the face of a beautiful youth, the friend, as you told me, of your brother. Gertrude, do not avert your face. I know not what that deep blush means, but nothing it *can* mean would disturb me now. How am I changed! Do you remember that, proud of your proficiency in my art, I wished to show the head to your father, and that to end my importunity you threw it in the fire? What hours of tormenting thoughts—what nights of watchfulness did that simple act cost me, so do we selfishly shrink from the appropriation of affections to another, even when unattainable to ourselves." Seton's voice faltered for a moment. "As I retrace my former feelings," he continued, "their shadows cross me. But to return to the night at Trenton. The image of your figure, as I saw you when I first opened my eyes, kneeling, and a celestial expression lighting up your face, remained in my mind in all the freshness of its actual presentment. It abode with me in darkness, in solitude, in misery—in madness, Gertrude.

"After I escaped from your father's beneficent offers at Trenton, I made my way to New-York—I know not how—my recollections of that time are like the confused and imperfect images of a distressful dream. I have since learned that I was found perishing in the street. It was impossible to identify me, and I was taken to the alms-house, and placed with the maniacs, supported by public charity. I cannot now, when all other evils have lost their power to wound me, look back without shuddering, on that period when neglect, injudicious treatment, privation, darkness, a sense of wrong, conscious degradation, misery in every form, exasperated my disease. Oh, Gertrude, is it not strange that men rioting in luxuries, and still more strange that those who are blessed with quiet homes of health and happiness, should permit their brethren suffering under the visitation of the severest of physical evils, to languish in the receptacles of poverty—in the dungeons allotted to crime?"

Gertrude answered this appeal by a solemn resolution, which she afterwards religiously performed, to make a rich offering to an unequivocal and neglected form of charity. Seton proceeded: "Gertrude, the person whose name I have since ascertained to be Roscoe, again appeared to rescue me from a more dreadful fate than that from which he saved me at Trenton. I know not what motive led him to inspect the wards of the alms-house, but there he found me, scratching on the wall the outlines of the scene at Trenton, with a bone which I had taken from my soup, and sharpened for that purpose. He instantly recognised me. I hailed him as God's messenger to me, and besought him to release me. He listened to me—he looked with deep interest at the outline I had traced, and after ascertaining that I was harmless and convalescing, he promised to take me from my imprisonment. The same day he returned, and conveyed me to a farmer's house in a retired spot on Long Island." Seton paused, and Gertrude, released from the intense attention she had given, covered her face and wept without restraint. Her bitter grief for all Seton had endured, was mingled with a feeling very different but scarcely less affecting—a feeling that Heaven had linked her sympathies with Roscoe's, had mysteriously interwoven the chain of their purposes, and feelings. She felt keenly too, the delicacy which Roscoe had manifested in withholding from her the particulars of Seton's sufferings, and of his generous part in ministering to his relief. "Gertrude," resumed Seton, in a voice of the deepest tenderness, "I cannot mistake this emotion—you know Roscoe—it is as it should be—"

She started as if the secrets of her inmost heart had been revealed. She cleared her voice, and made an effort to speak, for she could not permit such an inference from her emotion. Seton laid his hand on hers, "I ask no explanation—no communication, Gertrude." Again he reverted to himself. "Never shall I forget the first days of my emancipation—my keen enjoyment of liberty and nature. It was early in October—the sky was cloudless—the air serene and balmy. Oh, how exquisitely I relished those common and neglected bounties of Heaven! I lived in the open air. The clear soft skies, the transparent atmosphere, all nature seemed to me instinct with the Spirit of God, and it was so, to my awakened mind. The world appeared to me to lie in one dark total eclipse, and myself to be conveyed beyond the reign of shadows—to dwell in light—to be alone in the universe with God.

"These blissful days soon passed, and I was confined to the house by inclement weather. Roscoe sent me some implements for painting—I seized them as a hungry man would have snatched at food. I finished at one sitting the scene at Trenton. I perceived myself the extravagance of the picture, and sat down to the work anew. I painted another, and another, and another. Each was better than the last, and each indicated a correspondent progress in the recovery of reason. The application to an habitual employment restored my thoughts to their natural order of succession, and my feelings to their natural temperature.

"I never communicated my name, or spoke of you to Roscoe. For a long time I retained my first illusion, and believed he was a supernatural being; and it was very long before I could bear to pronounce your name. By degrees these illusions and extravagancies lost their force. I no longer withheld myself from you and your father from pride, or morbid sensibility, but I wished to test my moral strength in solitude, before I encountered new trials; my brothers, I had reason to think, believed me dead—I wished, for a time, to be dead to the world. I wrote to Roscoe, and expressed my gratitude, and acquainted him with my determination.

"It is now eight weeks since I left my place of refuge—a changed man. My mind, like the body refreshed by sleep, awoke to new vigor. The engrossing passion that had absorbed my faculties, was gone—no, not gone, Gertrude, but converted to a peaceful, rational sentiment, that accords with happiness and is immortal in its nature—a sentiment as distinct from the passion that had agitated my being, as the elements are in their natural and gentle ministry from their wildest strife and desolation.[1]

"I was changed too in other respects. The world, 'at best a broken reed, but oft a spear'[2]—the world had lost its power to wound me. The operations of the spirit are so mysterious, the modes of its communication with the Divinity so incomprehensible, that I shrink from attempting to communicate, even to you, Gertrude, the convictions of my own mind. I had new views, new hopes, and

---

1 Sedgwick's note in the 1830 edition: It is remarked by an able medical writer on the diseases of the mind, that persons whose madness has been induced by love rarely retain the passion after the recovery of reason. Such a circumstance is related of one of the princes of Condé.

2 From "Narcissa," The Complaint, Night III, in *Night Thoughts* (1742) by Edward Young (English, 1681-1765).

purposes—whence came they? not from the outward world—they were the inspiration of Heaven.

"I applied myself to painting; the avails of my constant labor were small; and while, from the elated state of my mind, I was unconscious of the presence of disease, consumption was sapping my life—the progress of the malady was accelerated by my rashness. A painter had employed me to finish the draperies of some portraits. I was so exhausted by the labors of the day that I shrunk from walking to my lodgings and I slept on his bare floor. At the end of the week I was carried home; there a new shock awaited me—my picture, my sacred treasure, had been sent to an auction, to raise the pittance due to my landlady. I forgot my sickness and my weakness, and rushed out of the house to recover it. Again I met Roscoe, who seemed always sent to me in my extremity— he had the picture, and restored it to me; and I confess to you I was scarcely less grateful than when he saved my life, or when he restored my liberty. I removed my lodgings to this place. I have painfully earned a subsistence till the last ten days, and since then I have received every kindness from this good old Swiss woman."

"But why, why," asked Gertrude, "have you not written to us?"

"I have twice written, but received no answer; I knew this was accidental. I had relinquished all hope of hearing from you; God be praised that old Marie met you, and was induced by your resemblance to the picture, to ask you to come here."

Gertrude assigned her father's absence from Clarenceville as the cause of Seton's receiving no replies to his letters; and then, but not without an obvious effort, she asked, 'why he had not communicated his wants to Roscoe?'

"I did, yesterday, send a note to the post-office for him, but my hand was tremulous and stiff with cold, and the direction may not be legible. But, truly, Gertrude, I have wanted little; a mortal sickness admits but few alleviations. My attendant has been kind, and what she could not provide for me, I have been satisfied without."

Nature had put forth her mysterious force—Gertrude's presence soothed and stimulated him, and Seton was sustained through his narrative by an energy of feeling that seemed to hold death in abeyance.

He had not spoken continuously, but with frequent and fearful interruptions, and as his voice died away in the conclusion, and his eyes became fixed in an eager, soul-piercing gaze, Gertrude, who had never before seen a human being in extremity, was appalled with the infallible tokens of approaching death. Seton laid her hand on his heart—"it beats feebly," he said, "my life is fast passing away;" and added, with an expression of some concern, "do you fear to stay alone with me, Gertrude?"

"No—no Louis!" she replied, subduing her natural shrinkings, "I have no fear—no wish, but to remain with you."

"I thank God!" said Seton, with a smile of sweet serenity, "my last wish is gratified—your presence, Gertrude, makes my dismissal happier."

Seton's fears of death had long been vanquished by the only force that can subdue its terrors—the force of religious faith. He had studied the Christian revelation faithfully, and he believed it, not with a mere intellectual, cold assent, but with the rapture of the mortal who reads there the charter of his immortality—with the exultation of the prisoner who receives the promise of pardon and release. He found there the solution of his sufferings. What if his life had been a dark and forlorn scene? His brief sorrows had been God's ministers to prepare his spirit for inextinguishable happiness. What if he had wandered in dismal exile through a far and foreign land? His path lay homeward, and could he shrink and tremble when his foot was on the threshold of his Father's house? Oh, no. The decline of life was to him the crumbling of his prison-walls. He had watched with joy, through solitary days and wakeful nights, the decay of the mortal mould that encumbered and imprisoned his longing spirit.

Life had never, in its blithe and morning hour, been bright to him. His childhood had been neglected—his youth sickly—his manhood blasted—his affections, those ordained and sweetest springs of happiness, sources of misery. They were now elevated far above the accidents of life, and ready to expand and rest in the celestial region for which they were created.

Seton's voice was exhausted by the long effort it had sustained. He afterwards spoke little, but no power of language could have added force to his few and brief expressions of faith and tranquillity—to the eloquence of his silence, when his eye was raised in devotion, or beamed with holy revealing from the sanctuary of his soul. Gertrude's spirit rose with his. There was something affecting and elevating in her disregard of the circumstances of death—so appalling to the young and inexperienced—in her tender manifestations of sacred sympathy with the departing spirit. Hour after hour passed away. Marie came in occasionally to render little services. The day was drawing to its close. The old woman beckoned Gertrude to the door. "He is changing fast," she said, and participating to a very old and general superstition, she added, "He will go with the turn of the tide: will you not have some one called?—it is a fearful thing, young lady, to bide alone."

Gertrude, though not without some natural reluctancy, would not permit it to interfere with the wish Seton had expressed, and she again assured Marie that she preferred no person should be summoned—and Marie, sorely against her own judgment, assented; but as she descended the stairs, meditating on the singular boldness of the young lady, she was summoned to the street-door by a loud knocking. She opened it to Gerald Roscoe, and inferring from his eager inquiries, that he was a particular friend of Seton, and rightly judging that there was no time to be lost in the preliminaries of ceremony, she bade him follow her. She opened the door of Seton's apartment, and signed to Roscoe to approach cautiously. He did so, and when he reached the threshold he stood as if he were spellbound. Seton was too far gone, Gertrude too deeply absorbed, to observe him.

The setting sun shone brightly through the only window in the apartment. Seton's eye was turned towards it. As the last ray faded away, he lifted his eye to Gertrude, and said with perfect distinctness, "My last moment is bright too, Gertrude." A slight convulsion passed over his features. He made a sudden effort to raise his head. Gertrude rested it on her bosom. A celestial smile, a quivering light from the soul played over his lips, he half uttered the last prayer of faith, 'Lord Jesus, receive my spirit!' and all was over.——Gertrude remained motionless, bending over the vacant form. The outward world vanished from before her. It seemed to her that the veil was lifted that envelopes the unknown world, and that she touched its blissful shore with the released spirit.

But to return from this high mysterious vision, to the silent chamber, and the lifeless form!—to the penetrating sense of separation and loss!—*this* is the terror of death. Death comes to the body only; it is but the change of that frame that is at one moment the expressive organ of the ever-living spirit, and the next, worthless clay, that mocks our grief with its stillness and immobility. This was the moment of grief and unrepressed tears; afterwards came the grateful considerations that she had been permitted to witness, and in some degree to minister to the peace of Seton's departure—that his conflict with the jarring elements of this world was ended, and that she had seen the demonstrations of the omnipotent power of religion.

Roscoe watched her with intense interest as she bent over Seton, her hands clasped, her face lit with the tenderness of affection, her eye raised in the fervency of devotion. She pressed her lips to Seton's brow. 'She loves him,' thought Roscoe, 'but it is with that excellence with which angels love good men.'

"Ye'd best speak to the young lady," said Marie, who thought that time enough had been allowed to the exclusive indulgence of Miss Clarence's feelings. Gertrude turned at the sound of her voice, and for the first time perceived Gerald Roscoe.

The sight of him excited no selfish emotion. Her feelings were now all in one channel, and he appeared to her only as Seton's friend and benefactor. She advanced, gave him her hand frankly, and expressed her sorrow that he had not come sooner, and her warm unmeasured gratitude for his generous kindness to Seton.

The intercourse of young persons of different sexes is so apt to be embarrassed by the conscious desire to please, and by the artificial modes of polished society, that the genuine motions of the mind are seldom embodied in unpremeditated language. Gertrude had never before met Roscoe without a degree of embarrassment that imparted to her manners a slight shade of constraint; but now, under the influence of deep and strongly excited sensibility, she forgot all that was of peculiar interest in their relation to each other, and talked to him with the freedom of intimate friendship. The occasion gave a tenderness to her manner, and her raised feelings an eloquence to her expressions, that penetrated Roscoe's heart. She did not, as on every former occasion, studiously avoid any allusion to herself, nor measure her phrases as if she were beset with rocks and quicksands. She spoke of her affection for Seton as if he had been her brother, and only veiled a part of the truth when she imputed the disease of his mind, entirely to a morbid sensibility preying on a delicate frame.

Roscoe perceived that Gertrude was off her guard, and seemed utterly to have forgotten the secret she had so sedulously kept. He expected that some accidental word would relieve his curiosity, which though rebuked for a moment, had revived, and put him on the rack of alternate hope, and disappointment. One natural question, one insidious word, might elicit what he so ardently desired to know; but that word would not be generous or honorable, and therefore could not be uttered by him. He was provoked at himself, that this importunate thought should violate the sanctity of such a moment; still it would not down. He turned his eye to Seton's lifeless form. He gazed at Gertrude with a far deeper interest than he had ever before felt; he listened with thrilling interest to all she said, yet that impertinent query, 'who can she be?' disturbed the harmony of his mind, like a creaking hinge. He heard the old woman again mounting the stairs—'now,' he thought, 'her name must be spoken, or something said that will dissolve this spell.' But Marie approached Gertrude, who was silently gazing on Seton, with the last yearnings of affection, and addressed her, according to her usual custom, in the third person—"a carriage was waiting for the lady," she said, "and here was a note from the mistress." Roscoe smiled, in spite of his vexation, at the simple mode in which his hopes were baffled.

The note was from Mrs. Layton, in reply to a line Gertrude had sent, explaining her detention.

"My sweetest Gertrude," said the note, "I send a carriage for you—you must indeed come home—you are exposing yourself to too severe a trial—I should have come immediately to you, but my feelings unfit me for *scenes*. Poor, poor Seton! 'he dies a most rare youth of melancholy.' How affecting such a death, in this heartless world! You probably will prefer that the funeral solemnities should be at Trinity-Church. As soon as we know your wishes, Layton will make all the arrangements.

"Dieu te garde, ma chère.[1]

"G. L."

'Funeral solemnities at Trinity-Church!' repeated Gertrude to herself, 'an ostentatious funeral would be a mockery to him who so shunned the world's eye while living.'

"Mr. Seton," she said, turning to Roscoe, "was as you well know, a total stranger in the city. I am reluctant to leave the last rites to hirelings; and if you, Mr. Roscoe—"

Roscoe interrupted her faltering request, with an assurance that she had only anticipated him—that he should make every necessary arrangement, and should feel himself happy in being permitted to render the last tribute of humanity to her friend.

Gertrude expressed her gratitude for all he had done, and for all he promised to do, with so much warmth and gracefulness that Roscoe felt he had given no equivalent for such thanks from such a source; and yet he thought, 'if she does feel obliged to me, there is a boon withheld, which would requite them a thousandfold.' But this boon was not even hinted at, and Gertrude had actually left the apartment, and was in the carriage on her way home, before the question occurred to her, and then it struck her like an electric flash, whether she had betrayed her name. She reviewed

---

1 God protect you, my dear.

all that had passed; she tried to recall every word, but that she was not able to satisfy herself, is the best proof of the engrossing emotions Seton's death had excited.

The heroines of our times live in a business world, and even funeral rites cannot be a matter of pure sentiment. Miss Clarence had been too long intrusted with the responsibility of pecuniary affairs, to fall into a feminine obliviousness in matters of expense, and as soon as she was in her own apartment, she sent for Justine, and giving her a sum of money, she requested her to place it in her mother's hands, to be appropriated to Mr. Seton's funeral charges. To this, she added a compensation for Marie's services, and a generous reward for her fidelity and kindness.

Justine, accustomed to Mrs. Layton's extravagant expressions of feeling, and her utter neglect of duties, had fallen into the common error of generalizing her individual experience, and honestly believed, that all fine ladies exhibited their sensibilities in nervous affection, and were subject to lapses of memory in money affairs; and she regarded Miss Clarence with a wonder and satisfaction, similar to that of a naturalist, who is analyzing a new species in nature.

"*Mon Dieu!*"[1] she exclaimed, as she stowed away the separate rolls of bills in her pocket-book, "how singular! my sweet young lady you look quite spent, and yet, God bless you—you think of all this as if you had no feelings, and were not a lady, at all."

'Any man may die heroically in company,' said Voltaire.[2] He *lived* in 'company,' and it was his misfortune to find food for his scoffing wit in the perpetual masquerade of artificial society. He fed his own vanity with its natural and abounding nutriment—the follies of his species. But he should have raised his eye from the feet of clay, to the fine gold of the image—he should have penetrated beyond the seats of the money-changers, to the sacred fire that burnt within the holy of holies—to the divine principle in the soul of man. Had he been familiar with the retreats of unaffected and unostentatious virtue—had he witnessed the quiet death of the faithful, unsullied by superstition, exaggeration, or self-delusion, he might have been saved from his unbelief in human virtue, the most dangerous of all skepticism—he might have employed his delightful, unimitated and inimitable talents in developing the noble capacities, and advancing the high destinies of man, instead

---

1 My God!
2 François-Marie Arouet, known as Voltaire (French, 1694-1778), philosopher and writer.

of '*riant comme un démon ou comme un singe des miséres de cette espèce humaine.*'[1]

Let the skeptic enter such a chamber of death, as Louis Seton's, and see the eye of faith kindle with celestial light, as the poor struggler with the evils of life, approaches the moment of release—let him observe the profound peace that earth can no longer trouble; and then let him, *if he can*, employ the mind God has given him, to controvert the immortality of that mind—the truth, that sustains man amid wrong, oppression, disappointment, calamity in every form, and in that fearful visitation which comes alike to all.

CHAPTER IX.

"S'il était reconnu qui'l faut cousidérer la pensée comme une maladie contre laquelle un régime reguliér est nécessaire, on ne saurait rien imaginer de mieux qu'un genre de distraction à la fois s'ètourdissant et insipide."[2]
MAD. DE STAËL.

TEN days subsequent to Seton's death passed away without any incident in the affairs of our dramatis personæ worthy of being recorded. Miss Clarence availed herself of a cold, (an auxiliary always at hand in a New York winter,) as a pretext for remaining in her own apartment. She did not repine at Seton's death, but wisely regarded it as a happy release. She had, however, been too long and too affectionately attached to him not to be deeply affected by the knowledge of his sufferings, and not to yield her mind to the serious emotions, and thoughts that death calls forth.

Nothing could be more opportune than this retirement to Emilie, who under the pretext of devotion to her friend, sheltered herself from the observation of the world, and the ardent attentions of Pedrillo.

Mrs. Layton, conscious that she had fallen in Gertrude's esteem, and ambitious to regain the admiration that had been so flattering to her, exerted with fresh resolution all her powers of fascination. She endured a week's seclusion without apparent ennui.

---

1 Laughing like a devil or a monkey at the miseries of the human race. De Staël, *De L'Allemagne* (1810).

2 "If it were believed that thought was an illness against which regular treatment was necessary, one could imagine nothing better than a kind of distraction at once tiresome and insipid." De Staël, *De L'Allemagne*.

She adapted herself with nice tact to the current of Gertrude's feelings—was serious, sympathetic, and sentimental, but it would not all do. Gertrude had waked from her dream, and imagination could not repeat its illusions. The qualities that had captivated her had vanished in smoke, like the body of the Arabian magician, and Gertrude's incredulity in the reality of that which had once deceived her, was not, like the fisherman's, affected. When an eloquent or enthusiastic strain flowed from Mrs. Layton's lips, 'why,' thought our practical heroine, 'is not that fervid feeling directed to Emilie?'—'why is it not employed to avert her impending fate?' When Mrs. Layton complained of her destiny, and lamented that she had no adequate object to employ her faculties and fill the void in her heart, Gertrude thought of her neglected children. 'If her conjugal happiness is blasted,' she said, 'can a *mother* want objects to elicit her noblest faculties, and her tenderest affections?' As an intimate intercourse brought their minds into close comparison, Gertrude perceived they were not, on any subject, attuned to the same key. They were both well versed in the elegant literature of the day, but their tastes were always in opposition. In poetry, Mrs. Layton preferred that which addressed the passions; Gertrude, that which touched the affections. Mrs. Layton was an idolator of Byron. Her imagination was stimulated by the tragic history of his heroes, whose feelings are all passions, and whose deeds are almost all crimes. She delighted in his descriptions of the outward world—the visible paradise of poetry, which the evil spirit of his mighty genius has sometimes overshadowed with its own image. Gertrude loved all the poets—the glorious company—but she preferred the touching simplicity, the penetrating tenderness of Burns, and the perfect yet poetic fidelity of our own Bryant, the mirror of nature, that like a serene lake, gives back the image of the delicate floweret and the lofty tree, as clearly defined, as soft and beautiful as their originals in the ethereal atmosphere. Mrs. Layton revelled in the Sybilline revelations of Mad. de Staël. Gertrude's soul was thrilled by them, but she preferred Miss Edgeworth[1]—preferred the beneficent genius who has made the actual social world better and happier, to her who by a motion of her wand could create an imaginative world, and disclose a possible,

---

1 Maria Edgeworth (Anglo-Irish, 1768-1849); see Introduction and Appendix A on Sedgwick as the "American Edgeworth." Sedgwick's first work, *A New-England Tale* (1822), was dedicated "to Maria Edgeworth as a slight expression of the writer's sense of her eminent services in the great cause of human virtue and improvement."

but unattainable beauty. Among heroines, Corinne was Mrs. Layton's favorite. Gertrude preferred Rebecca—she who conquered, to her who was the victim of love. Even Jeanie Deans, (pardon her humble taste, gentle reader,) that personification of truth—that unvarnished picture of moral beauty, moved her heart more than the gifted Corinne.[1] It would be an endless task to enumerate the diversity of their tastes in nature, in music, in all the arts. Mrs. Layton's sensibility was the fruit of a highly cultivated imagination; Gertrude's, the instinct of a generous heart. Mrs. Layton required high stimulants, and artificial excitements—the miraculous touch of the prophet to bring it forth. Gertrude's was moved by natural impulses and flowed from an ever-living fountain. Thus opposed in the very texture of their characters, it was impossible for either party to derive much enjoyment from a continued exclusive intercourse, and Mrs. Layton was impatient to plunge again into society, where her ready wit, and graceful facile manners, were available qualities.

"My dear Gertrude," said she, one particularly bright morning, "I cannot consent to your and Emilie's immuring yourselves any longer. Our door-bell will be rung by a dear five hundred friends, at least, to-day; and it is really a farce, when you are so well, and looking so remarkably well, too, to send them away with a mere bulletin of your health—so, unless you choose to permit the real cause of your sentimental seclusion to peep out, I beg you will grace my parlor."

"We are your subjects, and owe you passive obedience," replied Gertrude, who as soon as she perceived her liability to excite curiosity, determined to avoid it.

"You are a dear, reasonable creature, Gertrude, and I wish I had made my request sooner, for really I have been tormented to death with Pedrillo's impatience, (poor fellow! it's no wonder, it will not do for Em' to dilly dally much longer,)—and Layton, too, has been in the worst possible humor—by the way he left a note for you this morning—some one of your honorable suitors has probably chosen him for mediator"—she rung the bell, and ordered the servant to bring Miss Clarence a note from Mr. Layton's dressing-room table. It was brought, and contained no soft intercession, but a nonchalant sort of a request that Miss Clarence would favor him with the loan of five hundred dollars for a few days. Gertrude hesitated for a moment. She habitually regarded

---

1 Corinne of de Staël's *Corinne* (1807), Rebecca of Sir Walter Scott's *Ivan-hoe* (1819), and Jeanie Deans of Scott's *The Heart of Midlothian* (1818).

her fortune, like the other gifts of Providence, as a sacred trust, to be applied to the best uses, and she could not appropriate so considerable a sum without being somewhat disturbed by the belief that it was to be applied to an idle or profligate purpose.

Mrs. Layton who, though she had not chosen to appear so, was really aware of the contents of the note, watched the expression of Gertrude's countenance, and put her own interpretation on it. 'Oh,' thought she, 'how unlike poor me! If I had her wealth, I should not give a second thought to so pitiful a sum! but money does so harden the heart!' Gertrude hesitated but a moment. 'I cannot refuse,' thought she, 'while a guest in his house,' and thus quieting her conscience, she signed a check for the amount, and enclosed it in a note to Layton.

"Ah—is that it?" said Mrs. Layton, looking at her with a smile, and speaking in a tone of surprise. "Poor Layton! alas! alas! Gertrude, we *do* live in a 'bank-note world,' and happy are they who have enough of this mundane trash—But come, my dearest, finish your toilet—thank Heaven, you as well as myself, look the better for its tender mercies—but Emilie—it is too provoking—she has just tucked her wavy locks behind her ears, and she looks like the beau-ideal of painting, or like

"The forms that wove in Fancy's loom,
Float in light visions round the poet's head."[1]

Upon my word, I think she becomes the *penseroso*."[2]

"Oh, mother!" said Emilie. It was but a word—but Gertrude thought a word spoken in such a tone of feeling and remonstrance, should have pierced the mother's heart. Emilie was standing beside her, clasping her bracelet. Gertrude kissed her. "This fair round cheek was made for smiles, not tears, and," she added, glancing her eye at Mrs. Layton, and speaking with an energy not at all agreeable to that lady, "God forbid she should be doomed to them!"

"Amen!" responded Mrs. Layton. And now, young ladies, our orisons[3] being ended, let us descend to mortal affairs"—and smoothing her brow, she led the way down stairs. As they reached

---

1 From "On the Death of a Lady" (1764) by William Mason (English, 1725-97).

2 Reference to "Il Penseroso" (1632) by Milton. Penseroso: melancholy person.

3 Prayers or, less commonly, speech or oration.

the lower entry, the door-bell rang, and Mrs. Layton, glancing her eye through the side-window, exclaimed, "there's Patty Sprague!—I wish she were a thousand miles off." The ladies passed into the parlor and the servant to the door, followed by one of the children who happened to be loitering there. The door was opened, and Miss Patty appeared—"Ah!" said she to the little boy who was springing on the door-step, and pulled back by the servant, "Ah Julian, is mama at home, dear?"

"Yes, Miss Patty," he replied, and like a bird, vexed that the door of his cage was reclosed upon him, he pecked at the first object within his reach. "Yes, Miss Patty, but she said she wished you were a thousand miles off."

"Never tell tales out of school, dearie," rejoined Miss Patty, patting the boy's cheek, and she proceeded to the parlor, without being in the slightest degree checked or irritated. Miss Patty belonged to the single sisterhood; a community, which in the march of civilization, is losing its distinctive characteristics, but is still strikingly marked in the 'lone conspicuity' of some of its members.

Among these few, Miss Patty stood out in such bold relief, that her image would have befitted the banner of the order. She was a belle before the Revolution; had played 'cruel Barbara Allen' to one or two patriots, who unlike poor 'Jemmy Grove,' survived and lived to fight vigorously for their country.[1] She had flirted with British officers, and been actually engaged (she said so!) to a refugee tory, who could not (he did not!) return to keep his vows. Miss Patty, however, bore the sad chances and changes of this mortal life, most kindly. Her vanity, if it had no aliment in the present, and could hope for none in the future, was pampered by memory. She had a good-natured, gossiping, selfish sympathy with the world, but no love, hatred, or malice for any individual of that world. She hoarded her patrimony, and lived by *spending the day* in turn with a large circle of affluent friends; some bound to her by the tie of distant kindred, and others by old acquaintance. If any of her circle fell into adversity, Miss Patty forgot them; and why should such a fly as Miss Patty descend the wheel, when she might as well buzz about those who were on the top? She was generally tolerated, and sometimes welcomed—for she was a walking and talking chronicle—possessed of the last information on the floating topics of the day, and in her humble way, and to

---

1 In the traditional Scottish ballad "Barbara Allen," a dying young man (often called Jemmy Grove) pleads his unrequited love to a cold-hearted Barbara Allen.

our prosing world, she filled the place of a wandering minstrel, or itinerant conteur.[1]

"Glad to see you down stairs, young ladies," she said, as she entered the parlor. "Every body is mourning about your sickness, Miss Clarence—parties put off, and hearts breaking. I have come to spend the day with you, dear"—turning, half confidentially, to Mrs. Layton.

"How unfortunate! Miss Patty—we are engaged out to dine."

"That suits me better yet—I'll sit awhile, and run over and dine with the Porters, and spend tomorrow with you, dear." It was a part of Miss Patty's tactics, to have an engagement one day ahead. She was no philosopher in the abstract; but what is life but a series of philosophical truths? and Miss Patty perceived that her friend consented without much visible reluctance, to an evil twenty-four hours distant; and when it came, it was in the class of inevitables, and of course, submitted to with grace. As soon as Miss Patty had received Mrs. Layton's bow of acquiescence in her arrangement, she turned to the young ladies.

"Dear! how pale and thin Emilie is looking—but it's so with all engaged ladies—I looked just so, before the revolution." Gertrude smiled—she could not help it—at the revolution that must have occurred, since Miss Patty could have resembled the figure of her friend; as pale, certainly, and as beautiful as the most exquisite statue. "You smile, Miss Clarence—you don't remember—oh, no, you can't remember—but, perhaps you never heard about my engagement to Mr. Pinkie?"

"Bless you, Miss Patty!" said Mrs. Layton, eager to avert the history, "indeed she has—who has not heard it?"

"True—true—it was pretty well known. Well, Emmy dear, I hope you will have better luck than I had. I believe you are one of the lucky kind; only think, to come out—be *such* a belle, and engaged to a *real* nabob, before she is seventeen; that's what I call a run of luck!"

"But the game is not finished, and the tables may turn," said Gertrude, with an emphasis that sounded like a celestial prophecy to Emilie; like treason to her mother, and very like envy to Miss Patty.

"That is not hardly fair, Miss Gertrude," she said, "you have brought Emilie's color into her cheeks, with the bare thoughts of it. Never mind, dear, there's no war breaking out now, as in my day, and—but here's the very person in question."

---

1 Storyteller.

Pedrillo entered; and while he, on the score of not having seen Emilie for a week, was raising her reluctant hand to his lips, Miss Patty continued to Gertrude, her handkerchief before her face, and in a depressed tone—"the handsomest man I have seen since the evacuation! nothing boyish, no American slouch—you never saw the British officers, Miss Clarence?"

"I never had that happiness, Miss Patty."

"Then you never saw what I call *men*. Mr. Pedrillo has that same air, so erect, and finished, and *Je ne sais quoi*,[1] as the French say. Poor Mr. Pinkie had it too—but then he was born before the revolution. You know the Americans are very much degenerated."

"No, I was not aware of it," replied Gertrude, with seeming simplicity.

"My dear!—they certainly are. The English travellers and English reviews all say so—they tell me—I don't read such light things—but it is my opinion—and I am sure I ought to be a judge, for as Gerald Roscoe said to me once, 'Miss Patty,' said he, 'you have seen a great deal of life'—you need not smile, Miss Clarence, he did not mean any allusion to my age—he is too much of a gentleman for that. By the way, I met him this morning, and told him I always laid you out for him. 'Oh, bury the thought, Miss Patty,' said he, 'I cannot enter the lists against so many—my superiors and elders'—saucy fellow! I suppose he alluded to Mr. Morley—but, la! what a certain sign it is if you mention a person, he is sure to appear—Good morning, Mr. Morley—I declare, I don't see that you grow old at all."

Mr. Morley, who had entered, bowed rather coolly to the compliment, and then said to Mrs. Layton, though his eye turned most significantly to Gertrude, that he had just received a letter from Washington, announcing Mr. Randolph Marion's appointment.

Gertrude dared not look at Emilie, but she expressed her own pleasure in the most animated terms. Morley was delighted. "My dear Miss Clarence," he said in a low tone, "I am too happy to have obliged you."

"You have obliged me, materially, Mr. Morley, and I am delighted to believe that you will be rewarded for any exertions in my friend's behalf, by the consciousness of having given the public an officer of talent and integrity." This was not precisely the reward—the *quid pro quo*,[2] to which Mr. Morley looked; and this he was

---

1 A certain something (literally, "I don't know what").
2 Something for something (Latin), meaning a return or exchange of a favor.

intimating to Miss Clarence, in oracular phrases, which she fortunately might or might not understand, as suited her, when a troop of fashionable ladies attended by Major Daisy, Flint, and half a dozen other gentlemen, entered. Never did the arrival of a *corps de reserve*[1] prove a more timely relief, than this to poor Emilie; who, in a state of nervous agitation, was giving all her thoughts to Marion's rising fortune; and trying to avert her treacherous cheek from Pedrillo, and close her ear against the ardent language that he was addressing to her, while he appeared to be carelessly playing with a fire-screen.

The usual formula of morning chit-chat was run over; that mystery of mysteries eagerly inquired into, "how *did* you take such a sad cold?"—all the changes rung upon the weather—'it had been very damp'—'it was very fine'—'nothing more capricious than the weather'—'Mrs. L. had a delightful party'—'Mrs. K.'s was very dull'—'none of the L.'s there, on account of the old gentleman's death, *charming* old man he was, pity he had not lived a few days longer.'

A knot of ladies, bold aspirants to the reputation of *fine women*, were announcing their opinion of a new poem, and the last novel. "Is the Corsair a favorite of yours?" "Oh!" replied the sapient young lady, to whom the inquiry was addressed, "Oh, I doat on it—was there ever such a sweet creature as Conrad?"[2]

"No," said another lady, in answer to an innocent query, "I never read *American* novels, there's no high life in them."

The scene was constantly shifting, or rather the actors made their exits, and new ones appeared. The servant stood with the door half open, "Miss Clarence, you feel the draught, shut the door, John," said our attentive friend Flint. John bowed respectfully, but did not move, and the reason of his deferred obedience was presently explained by voices, from the entry, breaking from a whisper into a gentle altercation. "Indeed, Mr. Roscoe, you must come in—it cannot be impossible."

"I would trample on impossibilities at your bidding, Miss Mayo, but—"

The rest of the sentence was intercepted by an exclamation from Flint—"I declare, there's my friend Roscoe; I promised, ten days ago, Miss Clarence, to introduce him to you," and before Gertrude could interpose a word, he darted off to force

---

1 Reserve troops.
2 Conrad, a pirate chief, is the main character in "The Corsair" (1814) by Byron.

his patronage on Roscoe. A more potent voice was now raised, "Come in, Mr. Gerald Roscoe," said Mrs. Layton, "as lady of the manor, and entitled to all waifs and strays, I command you to come in," and Roscoe, preceded by two ladies, who, if they had been a trio, might have been mistaken for the graces in Parisian costume, entered the parlor. Mrs. Layton rose to receive them with something very different in her manner, from the mechanical politeness she addressed to ordinary guests. "For shame, Mr. Roscoe!" she said, "you, unfettered, unbound, and not half so old as the vagrant Greek, to resist the presence, as well as the voice of the syrens; and such syrens,"[1] she added, casting an admiring look at the elegant young ladies before her.

"I did not resist the voice of *the* syren," replied Roscoe, in a tone so depressed, as to be audible only to Mrs. Layton's, and one other ear—strange power of love! Gertrude sat at some distance from Mrs. Layton; her satellites, Morley and Daisy, stood before her. Morley was pouring out diplomatic compliments, fraught with meaning, but they were all lost on her. She was conscious of but one presence. From the first moment Roscoe's voice had reached her, she felt a stifling sensation—her heart beat almost audibly, and her first impulse was to run out of the room, but propriety, dignity, forbade. 'If I betray any emotion,' she thought, 'I shall hate myself—I shall be for ever degraded in his eyes—I cannot support an introduction to him in broad day-light, before all these persons—blockaded too by 'Morley, Daisy, & Co.'—how contemptible he will think my mystery!—why did not I tell him when we last met?—can this horrid suffocating feeling be faintness?—how ridiculous!—how disgraceful!'

"Bless me!" exclaimed Flint, who had returned to Miss Clarence's side, "how excessively pale you look!" Gertrude's alarm was augmented by this exclamation. She made no reply, but kept her eyes riveted to the floor. "She's certainly faint," interrupted Flint, "Ladies, allow me to raise this window." He made a bustling effort to effect this purpose.

"What is the matter?" asked half a dozen voices.

"Miss Clarence is faint," was the reply.

"Indeed I am not," said Gertrude, summoning all her energy to shelter and suppress a momentary weakness, and stimulated by the danger of exposing to Roscoe, an emotion as flattering to him,

---

1 Odysseus, the hero of Homer's epic poem *The Odyssey*, was able to hear and resist the deadly call of the Sirens only by having his crew bind him to the mast of his ship.

as humbling to herself; "indeed I am not in the least faint, I never fainted in my life—pray close that window. You are very good, Mr. Flint, but you made a strange mistake."

"Begging your pardon, Miss Clarence," replied Mr. Flint, with well founded pertinacity, "I don't think I mistook at all. Persons are not always conscious when they are going to faint—you were certainly deathly pale, and I'm pretty sure you breathed short—at any rate, your color came with the first breath of fresh air."

'What odious details,' thought Gertrude, shrinking from the exposure of these particulars; and with a feeling of a doubtful shade, between spirit and temper, she replied, "you must really, Mr. Flint, allow me to judge of my own sensations." She was nerved by the courageous sound of her own voice, and she ventured to cast one rapid glance around the room in quest of Roscoe. He had disappeared. 'Had he seen her?' She did not know, and dared not ask.

"Your alarm, Mr. Flint, was *mal-apropos*,"[1] said Miss Mayo, the eldest of the sisters who had entered with Roscoe. "I was, just at the moment of your frightful exclamations, going to present a friend to Miss Clarence—he disappeared while we were all looking at you, Miss Clarence—Mr. Roscoe, the cleverest young man in New York." Miss Mayo spoke unadvisedly. She did not dream that she could encroach on the self-estimation of any one present; but John Smith and Major Daisy, echoing her last words, 'the cleverest!' in a tone of unfeigned surprise, taught her the indefinite extent of the boundary-lines of vanity.

"Yes," said Miss Patty Sprague, "Miss Mayo is right. I heard the chancellor say, myself, that Gerald Roscoe would be at the head of his profession, in a few years; and I am right glad of it—it is pleasant to see good luck happen to such a genteel family as the Roscoes—I have spent many a pleasant day in his father's house."

"Do you ever spend the day, Miss Patty," asked Mrs. Layton, "with Mrs. Roscoe?"

"No," replied Miss Patty, with a deep sigh, "since she gave up her house, I have somehow lost sight of her."

"Miss Patty's vision, I should imagine, was too imperfect for the dim light of obscured fortunes," said Gertrude in an under voice to Miss Mayo.

"Yes, but just observe with what an eagle-eye she can look at an ascending luminary.—Do you know, Miss Patty, that Mrs. Spencer is going to bring out her pretty daughter, and has sent out invitations for an immense party?"

---

1 Misplaced, inappropriate.

"La! yes, dear, I heard so—a charming, intelligent woman, Mrs. Spencer. I have not been there since Mr. Spencer's failure—I am truly glad they have got up in the world again—I wish, dear, some day when it's convenient, you would give me a cast in your carriage—I should so like to spend a day with them."

"I will certainly *remember* you, Miss Patty," replied Miss Mayo, with an unequivocal smile. "By the way, Mrs. Layton, you have invitations of course to the Spencers; do you go?"

"Really, I threw the notes aside, and have not thought about it. There will be nothing *distingue* there, I fancy.—no especial attraction?"

"No; it will be like other parties: tea-parties are, as Madame de Staël has said, "*une habile invention de la médiocrité pour annuller les facultés de l'esprit*."[1] But as you sometimes submit to the levelling invention, I wish particularly that you would go to Mrs. Spencer's."

"And why?"

"Because, she has a very accomplished daughter, she wishes to bring out."

"Heavens! my dear Miss Mayo, so have fifty other mothers, to whom we should not think of doing such a neighborly office, as helping out their daughters; but Daisy shall decide—he is my oracle. How is it Major Daisy, are those Spencers genteel?"

For once, Major Daisy was at fault. "Really, Mrs. Layton, I cannot say—I am at a loss; but if you, and the ladies will go, I, and some of my friends, will form a phalanx around you; and we can be quite by ourselves, you know."

"Upon my word," said Mr. John Smith, "I think the ladies *does* make a mistake, if they go. My father says, he thinks it's time for *us* to take a stand: He don't think the Spencers *visitable*."

Miss Patty peered over her spectacles at John Smith; and laying her hand on Daisy's arm, she whispered, "Is not that a son of Sam Smith, that drove a hackney coach, when he first came to New York?"

"Yes—it's natural *he* should be on the alert, you know, Miss Patty, about taking a *stand*?"

Miss Patty did not take the pun; and while Daisy was regretting he had wasted it on her, she continued—for her indignation was touched, where alone it was vulnerable; "*Visitable* indeed! The Spencers visitable? I wonder if Mr. Spencer's father did not live in

---

1 "A clever invention of the mediocre to annul the powers of the mind," from *De L'Allemagne*.

Hanover square, and ride in his coach; (and many a time have I rode up to St. Paul's in it. St. Paul's was then quite out of town;) when this young fellow's mother, Judy Brown that was, used to go out dress-making—the *visitable* people to her, were those that paid her day's wages punctually."

"Well," resumed John Smith, unsuspicious of Miss Patty's vituperation; for he had walked to the window, and was reconnoitering the street, through his eye glass; "Well, if the ladies *persists* in going, I shall attend them; though I have written my note, and sealed it with the mushroom seal, and 'where were you yesterday?' I always use that seal for such sort of people—It's very clever to have *appropriated* seals; is not it, Miss Mayo?"

"Extremely, Mr. Smith,—the mushroom is the *élite* of seals for you."

Mr. Smith could not even guess what *élite* meant; but vanity—blessed interpreter! told him it meant something flattering; and he bowed most gratefully to Miss Mayo.

Mr. Flint had been hitherto silent. Unversed in the complicated machinery of gentility, he was too honest, and too good natured, for affectation on the subject; but, impatient for the result, he demanded of Miss Clarence, 'what she meant to do about going; for,' he said, 'if she went he would contrive to get an invitation.'

"Oh!" replied Miss Clarence, who had caught from Miss Mayo, some interest in the success of Mrs. Spencer's party, "I shall certainly go, provided"—

"Provided Mrs. Layton goes," said that lady; anticipating Miss Clarence's conclusion, "assuredly, my dear Gertrude, we shall all say 'ditto to Mr. Burke'[1]—shall we not, gentlemen?" The gentlemen smiled, and bowed their assent. "We are quite safe in going—our distinguished selves out of the question, it is quite enough to say of any party 'the Mayos were there,' their presence is fashion. I perceived you were predetermined to sanction Mrs. Spencer, were you not, Miss Mayo?"

"To accept her invitation, I was, Mrs. Layton; and had made Gerald Roscoe promise to accompany me."

"What a triumph! Roscoe has avoided all parties, this winter."

---

1 A common phrase indicating agreement, drawn from an anecdote of politicians Henry Cruger, Jr. (English and American, 1739-1827) and Edmund Burke (English, 1729-97). When both men were elected to Parliament in 1774, Cruger made this remark after Burke's speech of thanks, indicating that Burke's speech would do for both men. In addition to serving as an MP, Cruger later served his native New York as a state senator (1792-96).

"Yes, Mrs. Layton, and does not every man of special cleverness, after a winter or two?—however, I rallied him unmercifully, upon turning recluse, in New York; and fancying, on the *pavé* of Broadway, that he was walking in the groves of Academus: whereupon, he very graciously said, I reminded him that Plato had placed a statue of Love at the entrance of those groves; and, he added, with his usual gallantry, that he was now perfectly aware, no man could enjoy their seclusion, in peace, till he had rendered homage to the divinity. A pretty compliment to the absolute power of the sex—was it not, Miss Clarence? bless me! you blush as if it were personal; that blush is prophetic! I shall tell my friend Gerald Roscoe—no protestations; good morning—we shall all meet at the Spencers."

"What a pity!" exclaimed John Smith, as the door closed after her, "that Miss Mayo should be *such* a blue."[1]

"Do you remember, Mr. Smith," asked Mrs. Layton, "the reply of Pitt, to the King, when he said General Wolf was mad?"

"No, madam, I can't say I do, in particular."

"'Would to God he would bite some of your majesty's ministers!'[2] It would," continued Mrs. Layton, without regarding the smile of inanity, with which Smith received the witticism, "it would be an infinite relief to the insipidity of fashionable society, if the persons who constitute it, were generally infected with Miss Mayo's zeal for mental accomplishments; but then, one does so shrink from the danger of being called a blue, when one sees, as in Miss Mayo's case, that even youth, beauty, and fashion, cannot save one from the odious appellation."

"As the appellation only suits pretenders," said Miss Clarence, "and is for the most part only bestowed by spiteful ignorance, I cannot imagine that it should require much courage, even in a fashionable young lady, to emulate Miss Mayo's example, and devote her leisure hours to those pursuits that enrich the mind, and extend a woman's civil existence beyond the short reign of youth and beauty."

"Ah, Miss Clarence," said Mr. Morley, "the blues will win the field, if you become their champion."

"Lord!" said John Smith to Major Daisy, in a sort of parenthetical whisper, "is Miss Clarence a blue?—I never heard her talk about books."

---

1   A "bluestocking," or intellectual woman.
2   William Pitt (English, 1708-78), Earl of Chatham and Prime Minister (1766-68); James Wolfe (English, 1727-59), soldier and commander who served notably in the Seven Years' War.

aisy could not reply, for he was listening to find out.

were fit to be a champion, Mr. Morley," replied Miss
nce, modestly, "I would lay the phantom army of blues, that
conjured up to terrify young ladies from their books, and repel
very ignorant and *very* young gentlemen from all cultivated young
women."

"There!" whispered Mr. Smith, with infinite satisfaction, "I
knew she was not a blue!" Daisy was silent, a little doubtful and
fearful. Flint, who had an innate and homebred reverence for
whatever was intellectual and cultivated, rubbed his hands in expressive ecstasy. Mr. Morley thought, in the quiet recesses of his
soul, that it would be a great advantage to have such an intelligent
person as Miss Clarence to conduct the education of his daughters; and all took their leave, satisfied that Miss Clarence had a
right to be, and could afford to be—even a blue, if she pleased.

All had now departed—even Pedrillo, who had lingered through
the whole morning, to enjoy the despotic pleasure of manifesting
his right to monopolize Emilie. Her languid and abstracted manner indicated, and made him feel to his heart's core, that whatever external observance she might render, he could never bind
or touch her affections—their ethereal essence was beyond his, or
even her control.

"Thank Heaven!" exclaimed Mrs. Layton, as the door closed
on the last visiter, "we are released at last. What is so tiresome,
Gertrude, as morning visits?"

"A common-place from your lips, Mrs. Layton!"

"Yes, it is common-place—every body detests them; and yet
what is one to do? We must not undertake to be wiser than our
generation. It is Molière, is it not, who says there is no folly equal
to that of attempting to reform the world?

'C'est une folíe a nulle autre seconde,
De vouloir se mêler de corriger le monde.'"[1]

"Molière is perhaps right, Mrs. Layton; and it may be presumptuous, as well as foolish, to crusade against the follies of others;
but it seems, to me at least, an equal folly in ourselves, to conform
to a custom which you confess to be 'tiresome,' and which is certainly wrong."

"Tiresome, I grant you, but how wrong?"

---

1   "It is madness second to no other / To want to meddle with remedying
the world," from Molière's *Le Misanthrope* (1622).

"Obviously because it consumes the best hours of the day, and coerces, by the tyranny of custom, those who have it in their power to select their own occupations."

"*Miséricorde*,[1] Gertrude! you are sometimes a little *new*. Do you really imagine that these trumpery women who constitute the majority of morning visitors, could be induced to make any rational use of time? Time, my dear child, is like those coins that have no intrinsic worth, but are valued according to the impress put upon them."

Gertrude had too clear a head to be confounded by a simile. "Then certainly," she replied, "it should not pass without any impression. But do not think me so very *new*, Mrs. Layton: I would only ask that you, and those who think like you, would abandon a custom which you confess to be *ennuyant*[2] to those who really like it, and may therefore support it without your glaring inconsistency."

"This is all very sage and very virtuous, Gertrude; but really, my dear friend, when you know a little more of the world as it is, you will relinquish the beau-ideal of a world as it should be. I have quite too humble an opinion of myself, to aspire to turn the current of society from its well-worn channels. I might, as you suggest, institute a sort of hermitage in the midst of the world; but what is an individual separated from the mass—an insignificant drop of water from the great ocean?"

Gertrude smiled at the ridiculous light in which Mrs. Layton had placed her suggestion; and she smiled, and sighed too, as she (assenting to it) mentally repeated Molière's couplet. "My dear Gertrude, is that sigh heaved for your poor friend, or for the wicked world at large? In either case it is not wasted, for we have both enough of sins and sorrows to sigh over. But you are in too melancholy a vein to-day—you are not well. *Apropos*,[3] you were really faint this morning?"

"Slightly so for a moment."

"And so you 'moralized the spectacle'—Ah, well, that is natural. To tell you the honest truth, you and Emilie both look like nuns just from a cloister—your imagination filled with death-heads. Let me send for a carriage. It is but two o'clock—you can ride for a couple of hours, before it is time to dress for dinner."

The young ladies assented, glad of an opportunity of being together, without the fear of interruption.

---

1 Mercy.
2 Boring.
3 By the way (literally, "about that").

CHAPTER X.

"C'est trop d'etre coquette et devote—une femme devrait opter."[1]
LA BRUYERE.

EMILIE'S spirits were stimulated by the recent information of Marion's good fortune; and as soon as the two friends were fairly in the carriage, and away from the door, she said, "Is not this delightful news of Marion? Of course it's nothing to me—it can be nothing; but it would be very strange if I did not feel it."

"*Very* strange, Emilie."

"You smile, Gertrude, and well you may, for it is very odd that any thing can make me happy, even for a moment; but I feel this morning as if, in spite of fate, there were some good in store for me."

Gertrude, far from repressing, cherished, and strengthened the happy presentiments of Emilie's innocent mind. And she had a right to do so, for hers was not the common, easy, and half-selfish sympathy with happiness. She was conscious of a plan, and a determined resolution, if possible, to extricate her friend from her unhappy engagement, and being perhaps unwarrantably sanguine in her hope of success, she felt as if Emilie's elation were a premonition of coming happiness. Alas! how often are wishes mistaken for premonitions! How often the destructive storm is gathering, when the skies are brightest and clearest to mortal vision!

"Emilie," said Gertrude, "is not Marion, now that he has it in his power to secure to you independence, is he not bound as a true knight—a true-love, to ascertain how far you consider your obligations to Pedrillo sacred?"

"He has had no opportunity to do so—perhaps, Gertrude, you do not think Randolph still cares for me?"

"I believe he does—I do not see how any one can help caring for you—loving you tenderly, Emilie; but I want his assurance, in case—"

"In case of what?—do speak, Gertrude."

"Perhaps I have already spoken too much. In case we need his co-operation: Now, Emilie, you must not, positively, ask me any thing further."

"I will not, dear Gertrude—I will obey you in every thing. It *is* very strange that Randolph has not made an effort to see me—that

---

1 "It's too much to be both flirtatious and devoted—a woman should choose." From La Bruyère, *Les Caractères* (1688).

he has not written to me, if he could not see me; yet, I am sure all is right with him. How could he have any hope, when he knows I am to be married, and so soon, to Mr. Pedrillo—how can there possibly," she added, relapsing into her tone of despondency—"how can there possibly be any hope?"

"Oh Emilie, 'if he dare not hope, he does not love;' but here we are coming to the place where I saw the beautiful engraving I promised your mother." She ordered the coachman to stop. The ladies alighted, and entered a fashionable bookstore, to which was attached a show-room for paintings, prints, and other productions of the arts. A gentleman was standing at the counter, tossing over some books; his attention was attracted by their entrance; he turned his face towards them, and instantly it brightened with the pleasure of recognition, and was answered by, at least, an equal animation from Emilie's eyes. It was Marion. He advanced to them. "My dear Miss Clarence," he whispered to Gertrude, "allow me five minutes conversation with Miss Layton."

"There are some new songs, Emilie," said Gertrude, adroitly favoring the request; "you may look them over, while I am selecting the prints;" and passing into the inner room, she endeavored to monopolize the attention of the only clerk in waiting. Her effort was successful—he was too much engrossed with his ready sales to his liberal customer, to listen to the low energetic tones of Marion, or to Emilie's soft tremulous replies. The words escaped Gertrude's ear, but the murmuring sounds were as intelligible as the most expressive notes of a tender song. 'Their loves must not be thwarted,' she thought, as she wiped the gathering tears from her eyes, 'they shall have all my efforts—all my thoughts!' Ah, Gertrude, why that sudden flush? why is that eye so suddenly turned, cast down, and raised again? and where are those thoughts that were to be *all* given to the loves of your friends?

The shop-door had again been opened, and Gertrude, dreading some impertinent interruption, had turned her eye fearfully to Emilie. She encountered Roscoe's sparkling glance. She was abashed and agitated; she longed, yet dreaded to know, whether he had seen her at Mrs. Layton's; she feared to learn from his words, or looks, that he suspected the secret reason of her mystery, and she hoped to pass it off as her sportive concurrence with accident. These, and other thoughts, too rapid and disjointed, to be defined, flashed, like meteors, athwart her mind, and communicated embarrassment to her face and manner, while Roscoe was advancing towards her. Fortunately, all embarrassment is not awkward. There is a charm in the timid eye, the varying cheek, the softness and sensibility of the faltering voice, that the self-possession, the 'loveless wisdom'[1] of maidenly pride, may disdain, but can never equal.

Gertrude had never appeared so interesting to Roscoe, as at this moment. And why? Nothing could seem less affecting, than their present *uncircumstanced* encounter in a print-shop. All their other meetings had occurred when her feelings were strongly excited; but the exciting cause was obviously independent of him. He now perceived—no, not perceived, but hoped—faintly hoped it may be, for he had not a particle of coxcombry, but he did distinctly hope that her too visible emotion, proceeded from a sentiment responding to that which had most insidiously interwoven itself in his affections and anticipations. True love, even when far more assured than Roscoe's, is always unpresuming, and never had he addressed her in so reserved and deferential a manner, as at this moment. 'He certainly knows me'—thought she—'it is just as I expected—what an utter change!' But Roscoe had not seen her at Mrs. Layton's—had not yet identified the lady of his thoughts, with the shunned heiress—the elect of his heart, nameless and unknown, with the daughter of his benefactor and friend. Of this she was assured, by his quickly resuming his customary, frank, and easy tone.

"To whom shall I make out the bill, Miss?" asked the shop-boy, who, since Roscoe had withdrawn his customer's attention, had lost all hope of swelling its amount. Gertrude was at the moment, listening to a criticism of Roscoe, on a fine engraving of Guido's Sybil,[2] and looking him full in the face. He smiled at the interrogatory, and so archly, that in spite of her tremulous fears, she smiled in return. "Poor, simple youth!" said Roscoe in a low voice, "if he gets a satisfactory answer to that question, we will set him to find out the man in the iron mask, or the author of Junius' Letters."[3]

"I did not hear the name, Miss," said the clerk, confounded by the murmur of Roscoe's voice, and uncertain whether the lady had replied.

---

1 From "The Pleasures of Hope" (1799) by Thomas Campbell (Scottish, 1777-1844).

2 *Sibilla* (1635-36) by Guido Reni (Italian, 1575-1642).

3 "The man in the iron mask" (unknown) was imprisoned from 1661 until his death in 1703 (held at the Bastille from 1698 to 1703). Voltaire speculates on his identity in his *The Age of Louis XIV* (1751). Junius is the pseudonym of an author of numerous letters to the London *Public Advertiser* from 1769 to 1772 criticizing the government, revealing corruption, and defending Englishmen's rights.

"You need not trouble yourself to make out a bill," replied Gertrude; "just give me the amount."

"Admirable!" exclaimed Roscoe; "so natural, and easy, and successful a reply!"

"At this stage of our acquaintance," replied Gertrude, in the same tone of raillery in which he had spoken, "I am too much pleased with the success of my riddle, voluntarily to tell it; and I assure you I shall tax my ingenuity to co-operate with kind chance. I confess I am a little surprised that your sagacity has not sooner outwitted both."

"My sagacity! The solution would truly have been the achievement of pure sagacity, since chance is as obedient to your wishes as the 'dainty spirits' of Prospero[1] to his; and you know it is 'in the bond' that I ask no questions."

Gertrude hesitated for a moment in her reply. She began to be herself impatient of the mystery—to feel it to be onerous, and to fear that it was silly. "I withdraw that condition," she said; "if we meet again, I permit you to ask what questions you please— but not now," she added, shrinking from the awkward moment of disclosure.

Roscoe bowed, and expressed his thanks, with a little faltering, and a great deal of animation, and concluded by saying, "if the fortunate moment ever comes, of a satisfactory reply to my *questions*, do not be offended if I am as extravagant in my demonstrations of joy, as Archimedes was when he rushed from the bath, exclaiming, "I've found it—I've found it."[2]

Gertrude received certain intimations from her throbbing heart, that they were dwelling too long on a too interesting topic, and she rather abruptly turned the conversation to some new prints lying on the counter. The attentive clerk was induced, by the expression of her admiration, to display the treasures of his shop. He produced a collection of rare coins and medals, imported for one of the few antiquaries of our country, and a fine set of impressions of Canova's *chef d'oeuvres*.[3] Here were fertile themes of conversation, and Roscoe, for the first time, had an opportunity of eliciting the various knowledge with which Gertrude's mind was enriched. In examining the medals, references to history were unavoidable.

---

1   Prospero is a character in Shakespeare's *The Tempest*. Ariel is his 'tricksy spirit.'
2   Archimedes reportedly exclaimed "Eureka!" (I have found it) upon the discovery of his principle of buoyancy and displacement.
3   Antonio Canova (Venetian, 1757-1822), sculptor.

Without haranguing like a magnificent Corinne, she gracefully recurred to traits of character, and such circumstances illustrative of those traits, as were impressed on her clear and accurate memory. In looking over the prints, her susceptible imagination, alive to all the forms and combinations of beauty, her cultivated taste and nice observation were manifested spontaneously, without effort, and without constraint; and Roscoe enjoyed the rare pleasure that results from congeniality of taste, and similarity of culture. His own mind was enriched with those elegant acquisitions, that are regarded for a professional man in our 'working-day world,' rather embellishments than necessaries. But are they so? And when the 'working-day' is past, and affluence and leisure attained, are there not many who ruefully exclaim; with Sir Andrew Aguecheek, 'Oh that I had followed the arts!'[1]

Never were *tête-à-têtes* less likely to be voluntarily broken off, than those of the parties in the book-seller's shop. Gertrude was however aware of the propriety of withdrawing, and she looked anxiously at Emilie, who was still bending over the music with Marion, as if they were conning a lesson together. Roscoe's eyes followed the direction of Miss Clarence's. "Are those persons known to you?" he asked.

"Yes, the lady is my companion," replied Gertrude, secretly rejoicing that Emilie was so concealed by the large cloak and hood in which she was muffled, that Roscoe had not recognised her; "I must remind her that it is quite time for us to go."

"Oh no—do not; the common instincts of humanity should protect a conversation so interesting as that from interruption; and besides," he added, his ready ingenuity hitting on this device to prolong their interview, "I was just going to have the boldness to ask you to accompany me to the Methodist chapel in John-street. I do not wonder that you smile at the singular proposition—you perhaps have not heard Mr. Summerfield?"[2]

"No, but I have heard much of him as a most eloquent preacher."

---

1 Unable to understand Sir Toby Belch's French ("pourquoi"), Sir Andrew Aguecheek responds with this comic lament; Shakespeare's *Twelfth Night* I.III.92-93.

2 The Reverend John Summerfield (English, 1798-1825) traveled to the United States in 1821 and, admitted to the Methodist Conference, he served New York City as a minister. John Holland's *Memoirs of the Life and Ministry of John Summerfield, A.M.* (1830) records his preaching at John-street in January 1822 and the powerful response of his congregation.

"And wish to hear him, do you not? All ladies follow after eloquent preachers; even my mother, the most regular church-going woman in the bishop's diocess—the most rational of women, has gone with the crowd to-day, and it will not lessen my unbounded respect for one other of the sex, if she too joins the multitude. You can return in a short time, and it may be, strange as it may seem, that your friend will not miss you."

Gertrude was really anxious to hear the celebrated preacher in question, and was probably more influenced than she was herself aware of, by the desire to remain near to Roscoe; and going up to Emilie, she whispered, cautioned her not to prolong her stay imprudently, said she had a little farther to go, and that she would leave the carriage for her, and walk home herself. Emilie readily assented to any arrangement to protract a pleasure that might never be repeated, and Gertrude and Roscoe proceeded to the chapel, which they found filled to overflowing. Pews, aisles, windows, the porch-steps, were crowded; and even the outer persons of this immense concourse were in that hushed and listening attitude, that shows what a potent spell one mind can cast over thousands.

There is a certain deference, of boasted equality, and on the level arena of a church, even in our country, paid to the superiority of personal appearance. One and another gave way a little, a very little, at Roscoe's approach; so that after a few moments of patient perseverance, Gertrude found herself at the entrance of the middle-aisle. The first face she recognised, the first eye she encountered, were those of our *ubiquitous* friend Flint. He nodded familiarly to her. Being himself ensconced at the upper end of a pew, and hemmed in by a file of ladies, he could not offer his seat, he however, contrived to signify to one of the volunteer masters of ceremonies, that there was a vacant seat in a distant pew, to which the lady, to whom he directed his attention, might be conducted. The man offered his services, and Gertrude accepted, simply from the consciousness, that the precise place she occupied, was just at that moment, the most attractive in the world; and Roscoe saw her conducted away from him, with the same sort of vexed disappointment, with which a lover awakes from his dreams, at the moment, when after infinite pains, he has secured proximity to his mistress.

The preacher was young, handsome, and graceful, with a delicious voice, skillfully modulated, and expressive of the tenderness of a seraphic spirit. He presented the most appalling truths to his hearers, and enforced them by an address to their strongest passions—love, and fear. His youth might have seemed to want authority to set forth the terrors of the law, had not his emaciated figure, and hectic cheek indicated that his spirit was on the verge of the unseen world, and fulfilling a celestial commission, and a last duty.

It was not because Gertrude's religious sentiments did not precisely accord with the preacher's, that he failed to interest her. She was not one of those cold and conceited listeners, who criticise when they should feel. Her affections could warm at another's altar, though the fire there was not kindled by the same process that had lighted the sacred flame on her own; and finally, if she was not moved by the popular preacher, it was not from the remotest similarity to the old woman who could only cry in her own parish. If, as Dr. Franklin relates, a poor octogenarian who had been immured for years in her own apartment, employed a confessor to shrive her "vain thoughts," our heroine, just in the uncertain budding time of her sweet hopes, must be forgiven for her truant fancies.[1]

But if she was unmoved, there was a lady at her side almost convulsed by the picture of the final retribution which the preacher presented. She was cloaked, and veiled, and kept her head reclining on the front of the pew. Her tears fell like raindrops into her lap. Gertrude suspected she knew her. 'Can it be!' she thought—she kept her eye steadfastly fixed on her. Her curiosity, and a better feeling than curiosity, was awakened. The lady drew off her glove. If Gertrude had been at a loss to recognise the beautiful hand thus exposed, she could not mistake the rich and rare rings that identified Mrs. Layton's.

Gertrude's first impulse was to press that hand in hers, in token of her sympathy with the gracious feelings awakened; but she was checked by the studious concealment of Mrs. Layton's attitude, and by the fear, that the consciousness of her observation might check the tide of religious thought, which she hoped, like a swollen torrent, would sweep away accumulated rubbish, and leave a fertilized and productive soil. But Gertrude's benevolent hope had a frail foundation.

The agitation of Mrs. Layton's mind, was not the healthful strife of the elements, that leaves a purified atmosphere, but the storm of a tropical region, that marks its track by waste and desolation. Her religion, (if it be not sacrilege, so to apply that

---

1 This anecdote is related in Part I of *The Autobiography of Benjamin Franklin* (1771-90).

sacred name,) was a transient emotion—a passing fervor—a gush of passion, that if it did not lull the cravings of her immortal nature, or still the reproaches of conscience, for a time, at least, overwhelmed them.

Gertrude, in the simplicity of her heart, believed a moral renovation was begun, and already with the sanguine expectation of youth, was counting on its natural fruits, in the mother's zealous co-operation in her daughter's cause, when she was awakened from her reverie, by the close of the service. She eagerly hastened forward to escape Mrs. Layton's notice, and was soon lost in the crowd, from which she disengaged herself and reached home, without again encountering Roscoe, who was lingering and looking for her.

She found Emilie at home, impatiently awaiting her; her cheek was flushed, and her face was radiant. Her air, her step, her voice, her whole being, seemed changed. The inevitable duties of the toilet were to be performed, preparatory to dinner, and the time of grace was short; but short as it was, Emilie found opportunity to communicate the substance of her interview with Marion. He still loved her, truly, devotedly. "And it was from a letter of yours to his sister, Gertrude, which he says, she had not the heart to keep from him, that he learned the true state of the case, that I had never trifled with his feelings, that I was forced into this odious engagement, and that you believed I loved him—you should not have told that, Gertrude; however, it is past, and can't be helped now—and that I should be miserable with Pedrillo—*that*, I'm sure you might say to any body. Randolph came post to New York, and had not been a half hour in the city, when he accidentally heard we were all at the Athenæum, thither he went to meet us. He has since repeatedly called, and never been admitted—he has written to me, and his letters have been enclosed to him, un-opened."

"I have conjectured all this before, Emilie; but what is to come of this interview?"

"Oh! Heaven knows—dear Gertrude; bless you—bless you for writing that letter."

What was to come of it, in Emilie's hope, was plain enough from her benediction. Gertrude shook her head, and said, with a gravity half-real, half-affected, "I was afraid I was at the bottom of this mischief, but I have done what I could to repair it."

"Oh Gertrude!" exclaimed Emilie, mistaking her friend's meaning, "then you told mama?—you advised her to return the letters?"

"Emilie!"

Emilie did not quite comprehend the tone of Gertrude's exclamation. "I am not offended," she said—"I cannot be offended with you. I dare say you thought it was right, or you would not have done it; and as you never was in love, dear Gertrude, you know, you cannot possibly tell what a trial it is."

Gertrude, not thinking an *éclaircissement*[1] at this moment, very important, proceeded to ask Emilie 'if Marion had proposed any thing?'

"Yes, he has, he intreats me—but perhaps, Gertrude, you will think it your duty to tell mama?"

"Nothing you trust me with, Emilie."

"Oh, do not think I doubt you. It is only when I am not quite sure we think exactly alike about what is right, and I judge from my feelings, you know, and therefore, I am very liable to go wrong."

"Never—never Emilie, while they remain so pure and unperverted—but tell me, what did Marion propose?—an elopement, a clandestine marriage?"

"Yes."

"I am glad of it."

Emilie threw her arms around Gertrude's neck, "Are you, Gertrude?—do *you* think it is right?—do *you* think I may consent?"

Gertrude looked in her eager face with a smile, and replied playfully in the words of the Scotch song:

"Come counsel, dear Tittie, don't tarry,
I'll gie you my bonnie black hen,
Gif ye will advise me to marry
The lad I lo'e dearly"—[2]

Dear Emilie, that advice may yet come from my lips, as it springs from my heart at this moment. But a clandestine marriage must be the last resort. We must first see whether your father will not release you from the engagement he has made with Pedrillo."

"He never will—never, Gertrude."

"We will see—and if he will not, why then—but here is Justine, to tell us the carriage is waiting. Keep up your spirits, Emilie, and according to the good old fashioned rule, 'hope for the best, and be prepared for the worst'—the worst shall not come to you, if human effort can avert it."

---

1 Clarification.

2 From "Tam Glen" (1789) by Robert Burns.

Mrs. Layton and Pedrillo were awaiting the young ladies in the parlor. Mrs. Layton showed no traces of the morning's emotions excepting an unusual languor, and a deeper tinge of rouge than usual. Emilie never had appeared more dazzlingly beautiful. Pedrillo siezed her hand with rapture; "God bless me, Miss Emilie," he said, "your ride has wrought miracles. No rose was ever brighter and fresher than the color on your cheek. Miss Layton," he added in a lower tone, "this week is to fulfill my hopes."

"This week!" she echoed, and her boasted color faded to the faintest hue. Nothing farther passed. He handed her to the carriage, and she was compelled to endure, with an aching, and anxious heart, for the remainder of the evening, the stately ceremonies of a formal dinner-party.

CHAPTER XI.

"I had rather be married to a death's head, with a bone in his mouth, than to either of these. God defend me from these." MERCHANT OF VENICE.[1]

THE Penates[2] seldom smile on the breakfast-meal in the happiest families, and where no sacrifices are made to the domestic deities, it is a gloomy gathering enough. On the morning succeeding the dinner-party—dates begin to assume an importance as we draw to the close of our history—Mr. Layton was in his murkiest humor. He did not even, as usual, vent his ill temper on the poor servant in waiting—the common safety-valve of effervescing humors. The cold coffee, the heavy cakes, the missing butter-knife, all were unnoticed. Twice he rose, and it seemed unconsciously, from the breakfast-table—strode up and down the room—paused behind Emilie's chair—patted her head—then turned abruptly away to hide a starting tear—seized the morning paper, sat down by the window, and affected to be reading it. Emilie, whose agitated spirits were ready to take alarm, thought her father's manner portended evil to her; and when he said, "My child, your mother wishes to speak with you as soon as you have finished your breakfast," she turned pale, rose from her untasted coffee, and left the room.

---

1 Spoken by the heiress Portia regarding her suitors in Shakespeare's *The Merchant of Venice* I.ii.49-51.

2 Household gods in Roman mythology.

Gertude would have followed, but Mr. Layton arrested her by a request that she would allow him to speak with her in the library.

Layton's affairs with Pedrillo had come to a fearful crisis. Pedrillo had been excessively irritated by being for ten days denied all access to Emilie; and on the preceding morning, (of which we have given the details,) he had been exasperated by her manifest aversion to him, and by the emotion she had betrayed at the mention of Marion. He was farther outraged by some well meant attempts of Flint to be witty on the precariousness of love affairs; and these little irritations swelled the measure of his impatience, already full, to overflowing. When he met Layton, the passion that had been curbed by the restraints of good-breeding, was expressed without qualification. He insisted on the immediate performance of Layton's contract, and threatened, in case of any further delay, the enforcement of his pecuniary claims, and, what Layton dreaded far more, the disclosure of the fraud he had practised at the gaming-table. Layton was desperate, and promised whatever Pedrillo required.

"Miss Clarence," said Layton, when he had closed the library-door, and after two or three embarrassing hems! "Miss Clarence, I find it excessively awkward to make a request of you, which always comes with a bad grace from a gentleman to a lady, and from me to my guest may appear particularly indelicate. However, I am perfectly aware such fastidiousness is out of place in relation to you, and though I am really oppressed and mortified by the necessity of asking"——

"I beg, Mr. Layton," replied Gertrude, compassionating his embarrassment, "that you will consider my being your guest merely as a circumstance that gives me a facility in serving you."

"You are very good, Miss Clarence, very kind; but it is so difficult to explain to a lady the little pecuniary embarrassments to which gentlemen are liable, that it is humiliating to confess them. However, your goodness overcomes my scruples; and frankly, my dear Miss Clarence, I am in pressing want of a thousand dollars. Can you oblige me by advancing it?"

Gertrude hesitated for a moment; but her plans and resolutions were formed, and not to be lightly shaken. "I am awaiting, Mr. Layton," she replied, "a letter from my father, which will contain some instructions in relation to my pecuniary concerns, and till I hear from him, I cannot dispose of so large a sum."

"But, my dear madam—my dear Miss Clarence, you misunderstand me—dispose! bless me!—I ask only the loan for a very few days."

"So I understand, Mr. Layton."

"And you refuse!—I confess I did not anticipate this; a thousand dollars is a small item of your splendid fortune, Miss Clarence. Would to God I had been endowed with one particle of your admirable prudence!" Though Layton did not quite lose his customary good-breeding, he spoke in a tone of bitter sarcasm that wounded Gertrude to the heart, for she utterly disdained every sordid consideration. She was not however betrayed into any apparent relenting, and he proceeded: "I was perfectly aware that I had no claims, Miss Clarence, but I imagined you might be willing to risk a small sacrifice for the husband and father of friends whom you profess to love."

"I am perfectly aware of all the motives that exist for granting your request, Mr. Layton, and I resist them in very difficult compliance with what I believe to be my duty."

"Duty!—a harsh ungraceful word on a young lady's lips, Miss Clarence. But I am detaining you—I certainly have no intention of appealing to the feelings of a lady who has so stern a sense of *duty*." Layton spoke with unaffected scorn. Nothing could appear more unlovely in his eyes, more unfeminine, and, as he said ungraceful in a lady than consideration in money affairs. He mentally accused Gertrude of parsimony, of miserliness, of utter insensibility to the soft charities of life; but the current of his feelings was changed, when a moment after the door was thrown open, and Emilie rushed in and threw herself at his feet, exclaiming passionately, "Oh, my dear father, pity me!—have mercy on me!"

Her customary manner was so quiet and gentle that there was something frightful in this turbulent emotion. Gertrude sprang towards her—"My dear Emilie," she said, "what does this mean?"

There seemed to be a spell in Gertrude's voice; Emilie was hushed for a moment—she turned her eyes to her friend with the most intense supplication, and then again bursting into heart-piercing cries, she said, "No, no—you cannot help me. Oh, my father, my dear father, if you ever loved me, even when I was a little child—if you once wished to make me happy, do not now abandon me to utter misery! Gertrude—this very week—oh, I shall go wild. My dear father, pity me!—Gertrude, beg for me!"

Gertrude burst into tears. "For God's sake, Mr. Layton," she cried, "save your child from this cruel fate!"

"Do *you* feel!" he exclaimed, gazing at Gertrude, as if he were surprised at her emotion—"do *you* feel? Then even the stones cry out against me"—and giving way to a burst of uncontrollable feeling, he raised Emilie and pressed her to his bosom. "Pity *me*—pity me, my child; I am miserable, condemned, wretched, lost. Speak the word, Emilie—say I shall dissolve this engagement with Pedrillo, and I will—I will go to prison. We will all sink together into this abyss of ruin and misery. Speak, Emilie, and it shall be so."

Emilie was terrified by her father's passionate emotion, and she gathered strength at the first thought of a generous motive for her sacrifice. "Oh, no, no," she replied, "let it be me alone, if there must be a victim—I have expected it—I can bear it." She dropped her head on her father's shoulder.

'Can I,' thought Gertrude, 'look passively on this distressful conflict? why have I not heard from my father?—why should I wait to hear?—he would not be less willing to interpose than I am—I will speak to the wretched man—I will try;' and she was on the point of giving utterance to her purpose, when a servant appeared at the open door with a packet of letters. Her eye ran hastily over the superscriptions. One was from her father. She broke the seal and glanced at its contents, and then turning to Emilie, she threw her arms about her, and said with a look of ineffable joy, "Now, Emilie, I can redeem my promise to you." Emilie looked up bewildered, a faint light dawned on her mind, but it was a light struggling through darkness. There was a strange sickly fluttering about her heart, like that felt by the sufferer who has resigned himself to the executioner when his uncertain sense first catches the cry of pardon.

"I thought you had withdrawn, Miss Clarence," said Mr. Layton, with evident confusion and undisguised displeasure, "I am not aware that your residence under my roof invests you with a right to witness our most private affairs."

Gertrude did not condescend to notice this offensive speech. She replied with a little faltering, for she found it difficult to embody in words her long mediated project, "Mr. Layton, my position in your family has given me a knowledge of your affairs, unsought for and most painful."

"Such assurances are superfluous, madam."

"No, not superfluous," she continued, with unabated gentleness, "for the knowledge that Emilie's happiness was in jeopardy, has inspired me with the hope to serve her."

"By advice and remonstrance, no doubt—the selfish and cold-hearted are ever lavish of such services."

"I waited only for a letter from my father," she proceeded, without seeming to hear him, "it has come, and is what I expected. Mr. Layton, I must be more explicit than you may think becomes me. This is no time to make sacrifices to fastidiousness—Emilie, allow me to speak alone with your father." She kissed Emilie tenderly as she turned to withdraw and whispered, "take heart of grace, my blessed—all must yet be well."

Mr. Layton gazed at Gertrude with an impatient expectation of remonstrance, but she spoke in a voice and with a look like an angel's extending celestial aid to a mortal lost in a labyrinth. "Mr. Layton," she said, "there is no time, and this is no occasion for distrusts on your part, or delays on mine. I have come to the knowledge, no matter how, that you are involved in pecuniary obligations to Mr. Pedrillo. May not the cancelling of these obligations save Emilie from this marriage?"

"What right have you, Miss Clarence, to ask this question; and how, in God's name, am I to cancel any pecuniary obligations?"

"My right," she replied, "is indisputable, for rests on my affection for Emilie, and my hope to save you from an eternal sorrow by satisfying Pedrillo's claims."

"Poor dreaming girl!" exclaimed Layton, half incredulous and half contemptuous, "you talk of satisfying Pedrillo's claims, when your generosity could not stretch to the hazard of one poor thousand dollars."

"No," returned Gertrude, with a smile, "we money-dealers, Mr. Layton, are all calculators—we require an equivalent for our money. Emilie's redemption from this deep misery is worth to me any sacrifice I can make. Her emancipation from this engagement is the equivalent I demand, the only return I wish. No, this is not all; you must promise me not only her freedom, but that she shall be at liberty to give her hand to Randolph Marion, on whom she has already worthily bestowed her heart. If you accede to my terms, you will furnish me with a statement of the amount of Pedrillo's claims."

"Good Heaven!—are you in earnest—have you deliberated?— your father, Miss Clarence?"

"I have already told you that I have only waited for his sanction. Read, if you please, what he says on the subject."

Layton ran his eye hastily over a few paragraphs of the letter, and trembling with new emotions, he exclaimed, "Oh, he has not—you have not dreamt of the hideous amount of my debt to that villain."

"We do not know it, but we should not shrink from any amount within the compass of our fortune. Be more calm, Mr. Layton— take this pencil and give me in writing the sum due."

"Look over me, then," he said, seizing a sheet of paper, "look over me, and arrest my hand when the sum exceeds your intentions. He then recalled and recorded the debts contracted from time to time. He stopped suddenly—"These are thousands, not hundreds, Miss Clarence."

"I understand perfectly"—replied Gertrude, "go on."

He proceeded, till running up the different specifications, he set down the sum total, "Sixty thousand dollars!" he said. "You see now, Miss Clarence, how deep, how hopeless is my ruin."

"Hopeless! do you still doubt that I am in earnest, Mr. Layton?"

"But you cannot design—Miss Clarence, I will not deceive you. I can by no possibility repay any portion of this debt."

"You forget that I have made my own terms, Mr. Layton. Assure me that Emilie is at liberty to indulge the honorable inclinations of her heart, and I will at once convey to you the amount of property you have mentioned."

Layton did not reply—he could not. He was almost frantic with conflicting emotions; a manly shame, that he had underrated and insulted a woman capable of such generosity and forbearance—a thrilling joy at the thought of escaping from thraldom, checked by the stinging consciousness, that he remained Pedrillo's slave, while the secret of his dishonor was in his keeping. He pressed his hands to his throbbing temples—he paced the room, and replied only by incoherent ejaculations, to Gertrude's entreaties, which were urged as if she were suing for her own happiness.

There is a salutary principle in the atmosphere of virtue—a quickening influence in a noble action—an inspiration caught from powerful goodness. 'Will Gertrude Clarence do this for her *friend*,' he thought, 'and shall not I run a risk—sacrifice myself, if it must be, for my *child*? It is but the name of honor that I have to lose!'

But was it not possible to break with Pedrillo, and still preserve that name?—Pedrillo might make the long dreaded disclosure, but he had *no proof*, and would the word of a disappointed man, a revengeful Spaniard, be credited?' Layton felt assured it would not; and without waiting to deliberate further, he poured out his honest thanks to Gertrude, and received the papers that placed at his disposal the price of Emilie's liberty.

Thus authorized to tell Emilie that she was mistress of her own destiny, Gertrude flew to her friend, her face radiant with the happiness she was to communicate. Banished spirits restored to paradise, could not have been more blissful than the two friends; Emilie receiving more than life and liberty, a release from the cruellest enthralment, and at her hands, whose favors had the unction of celestial mercy; and not release only, but the assurance that her affections might now expand in the natural atmosphere of a pure, requited, and acknowledged love.

Delicious as Emilie's sensations were, Gertrude's was even a more elevated joy, for

'If there is a feeling to mortals given,
That has less of earth in it than Heaven,'[1]

it is that quiet inward joy, that springs from the consciousness of benevolent and successful efforts for others; of efforts to which one is not impelled by any authorised claim, which the world does not demand, nor reward, nor can ever know—which can have no motive, nor result in self. A perfectly disinterested action is a demonstration to the spirit of its alliance and communion with the divine nature—an entrance into the joy of its Lord.

Not a shadow dimmed their present sun-shine—not one presaging thought of coming evil—not one transient presentiment of the fatal consequences of that hour's decisions.

As soon as their spirits were sufficiently tranquilized, Emilie sat down to write a note to Marion, and Gertrude to read her letters. Those shorter, and of less consequence than her father's we shall first present; and our readers will confess, they were of a nature to bring down our heroine's feelings to the level of *very* common life.

"To Miss Clarence.

"Respected lady: 'If a man would thrive, he should wive,' therefore, as agent, and acting for my son, (John Smith,) I have the satisfaction of proposing an alliance (matrimonial) between you and him, (that is, my son.) He is a remarkable genteel young man in a drawing-room, (John is)—quite up to any thing, but as that is where you have seen him, (chiefly,) I shall say no more about it, only observing that my son (John) always goes for the first, (he can afford it,) i. e. Wheeler's coats—Whitmarsh's pantaloons—Byrne's boots—&c. &c.—which is, (I take it,) the reason he has made you, valued lady, his choice; you being the first match in the city (at present). John (my son) has been a healthy lad from the egg, and cleanly, (his mother says,) thorough cleanly. A touch of the intermittent, that he is taken down with, (this evening,) makes nothing against it (i.e. against his constitution). As I have found procrastination (in all kinds of business) a bad thing, and to strike while the iron's hot, a safe rule (without exceptions), and as the

---

1   From "The Lady of the Lake" by Scott.

doctor says my son (John) may be down for a week, I concluded (knowing his mind) not to delay, for fear of accidents. As I have not writ a love-letter since I married my wife, I hope you will, ma'am, excuse all mistakes and deficiencies. As soon as I receive a punctual answer, (to the above,) we will arrange all matters of business, (there I'm at home,) to your, and your honored father's wishes. (Errors excepted,) your obedient servant to command, ma'am,

"SAM'L SMITH."

Gertrude read Mr. Smith's letter and threw it into the fire, but before it was consumed, she snatched it out, and preserved it as a happy illustration of the flattering honors, to which an heiress may be doomed. The following brief reply ended this correspondence.

"Miss Clarence presents her compliments to Mr. Samuel Smith. She is very happy to hear that his son—Mr. John Smith—has a good constitution, and laudable habits, but must decline the honor of deriving any advantage from them."

The succeeding epistle was from Mr. *D.* Flint.

"To Miss Clarence.

"Dear girl—I hope you will not deem my address to you at this time premature. I assure you the sentiment that prompts my pen was begun in esteem, and has ripened into love. I declare to you upon my honor, Miss Clarence, that I have never seen a lady, whom my head and heart both so wholly approved as yourself; and I feel very sure that no change of circumstances, or fortune, could ever make any difference in my feelings, but that in all the vicissitudes of this sublunary scene, I should show you every attention which man owes to the weaker sex.

"I wish, on all occasions, to be fair and above-board; and therefore, I deem it my duty to accompany this offer of my hand with a candid account of my family. My father resides in Connecticut. He is an independent farmer, and an honest man—'the noblest work of God,'[1] Miss Clarence. He had not, it is true, the advantages of education, which he gave to me, and which have made my lot so distinguished. My mother is a sensible, and good woman, though rather plain. Her prophetic verse in the last chapter of Proverbs,

---

1 "An honest man's the noblest work of God," from Pope's *An Essay on Man*, Epistle IV (1733-34).

is, as my father often remarks, literally fulfilled, 'her children rise up and call her blessed, her husband also, and he praiseth her.'[1] I promised to be candid, and therefore must state to you, that my eldest brother—the child of a former marriage, and therefore, only my *half*-brother—committed a crime when he was about thirteen, for which, he was obliged to flee the country. It is now more than twenty years since, and as he has never been heard from, and as he was, as I observed above, but my *half*-brother, I hope you will overlook this stain on our name, which has been the greatest of griefs and humiliations to my poor father.

"I am sensible that my parents are not precisely such persons as compose our circle in New York; but as they seldom or never come to town, you will not be mortified by their being brought into comparison with our acquaintance here. It is right, however, to state that, while they live, I shall make them an annual visit, and shall expect of course that Mrs. Flint will wish to accompany me. May my right hand wither, before I fail in any act of duty or kindness to my honored parents!

"And now, my dear girl, I beg you will give a week's consideration to the contents of this letter, and then answer it according to the dictates of your own good sense. May the answer be propitious to the most earnest wish of your devoted friend and lover,

"D. FLINT."

Blunt and *gauche*[2] as our friend Flint was, his coarser qualities were so commingled with simplicity, integrity, and good-heartedness, that our heroine, if she had been compelled to select one from among her professed suitors, would undoubtedly have laid the crown matrimonial on Mr. D. Flint's aspiring brow; but as she was fortunately exempt from so cruel a necessity, she laid the letter aside to be answered as he had requested, at the end of a week, and strictly 'according to the dictates of her good sense.'

The last and most important letter was from Mr. Clarence.

"*Marion Hall, Virginia.*

"My dear child—I have just received your last two letters. I trust no evil will ensue from the delay of the first.

"Poor Seton! His fate has cost me many tears, but I am deeply thankful for his dismissal. I know nothing more distressful than to be condemned to drag through a long life, with broken health,

---

1 Proverbs 31.28.
2 Awkward.

a sensitive temper, and that bitter drug, poverty. His felicity in heaven is, I doubt not, enhanced by his sufferings on earth.

"Roscoe's generous kindness to Louis, is in conformity to my impressions of his character. I was a little captious in relation to the Roscoes when I was in New York, and suffered certain trifling irritations to influence my feelings improperly, and I am afraid, my dear Gertrude, that you have cherished a resentment quite out of proportion to their offences, and inconsistent with your native gentleness. How is it possible, my dear child, that you should have met Roscoe in Louis' room, and not have communicated your name? Suffer me to say, that I think there was rather more pride than dignity in this procedure; or was it rustic girlishness, Gertrude? And have you been making a pretty little romantic mystery of your name? In either case, my child, I entreat that you will put an end to it. I fear that Gerald, when he discovers the truth, will be—no, not disgusted—the word is too harsh—but a little *rebuté*."[1]

Gertrude pondered over the above portion of her letter for at least half an hour, before she proceeded; and then she gave rather a listless and undutiful attention to what followed.

"I thank you, my dear Gertrude, for transmitting to me your impressions, while they are fresh and unmodified by experience, of the society in which you are moving. I am attached to New York from early habit; it was the scene of the happiest portion of my life. It is a noble city—a wide field for every talent—full of excitement, of facilities for the enterprising, stimulants and motives to exertion, and rewards to industry and ability. But that its opulence, its accumulating wealth, its commercial potentiality, its rapid progress, should be the themes of the exulting patriot, or the political economist, rather than of the sentimental young lady, does not surprise me. New York, you say, appears to you like an oriental fair, 'to which all the nations of the earth have sent their representatives to bargain and to bustle.' You are disgusted with the vacuity, the flippancy, the superficial accomplishments, the idle competitions, the useless and wasteful expenditure, of the society in which you mingle.

"But there are, my dear Gertrude, and I fear must be, sins and follies in every human condition. Ignorance and pretension, the petty jealousies of the rich of yesterday towards the rich of to-day, are evils necessarily incident to a state of society so fluctuating as

---

1 Disheartened.

that of New York. Where wealth is the only effective aristocracy; the dregs, of course, often rise to the surface. But New York has its cultivated and refined minds—its happy homes—the most elevated objects of pursuit—noble institutions—expansive charities, and whatever gives dignity and effect to life: and have *you* forgotten, Gertrude, that, 'unmeet nurse' as it may be 'for poetic child,'[1] it is the residence of a triumvirate of poets that would illustrate any land?[2]

> "It is I confess mortifying, that, in our country, where we ought
> 'To read the perfect ways of honor,
> 'And claim by these our greatness,'[3]

and not by any external nor accidental distinction—nor by being, in the noble language of Thurlow, 'the accident of an accident,'[4] there should be such an artificial construction of society—such perpetual discussions of relative *genteelness*—so much secret envy, and manifest contempt, and anxious aspiration after a name and place in fashionable society. We deplore this, but that it has its source in man's natural love of distinction, you and I must conclude, who have so often laughed over the six distinct ranks in our village of Clarenceville, so blending into each other, like the colors of the rainbow, that no common observer could tell where one ended and another began.

"One more criticism on your impressions, my dear child, and I have done. You have fallen into a common youthful error. You have formed your conclusions from individual and very limited experience. The prevailing cast of the society which Mrs. Layton courts and attracts, is such as you describe; but you must remember that the most exalted names in our land are occasionally found in the ranks of fashion, and I will not allow any society to be condemned *en masse*, where such persons are to be met, as Gerald Roscoe, Emilie Layton, and my Gertrude!

---

1 A play on lines from "The Lay of the Last Minstrel" (1805) by Scott.
2 Sedgwick's note in the 1849 edition: Of these three poets, Hillhouse [James A. Hillhouse, 1789-1841] has died, honored and lamented, Halleck has forsaken the heaven of invention for the prosaic labors of the ledger [as accountant for John Jacob Astor and other bankers] and Bryant still lives in honor amongst us, sinking every year deeper in the hearts of his countrymen.
3 Shakespeare's *Henry VIII* V.v.38-39.
4 Lord Edward Thurlow (English, 1732-1806), lawyer and politician.

"And this brings me to subjects far more interesting than any general speculations, and which I have purposely reserved till you should have dutifully read through all my prosing. I have by me a letter from Stephen Morley, Esq., announcing the appointment of my good friend Randolph, which Morley does not hesitate to ascribe to his (Morley's) 'desire to oblige Miss C. and her father.' Thereupon he founds a claim to a reciprocity of service; and after a formal declaration of his admiration of my daughter; he asks my consent to his addresses—and my *views as to settlements*. I have answered him by a simple reference of the whole affair to your arbitrement.

"You cannot for a moment have doubted what my reply would be to your first hasty and eloquent letter. It suffused my eyes with tears, and made my heart throb with the most delicious sensations. You seem to fear that I may deem your purpose rash—a 'dispro- portioned thought,'[1] and you tell me it was the inspiration of the moment. My beloved Gertrude, it was a noble inspiration, worthy of that heart that never yet 'affected eminence nor wealth.'[2] You say, and truly, that 'an unwilling marriage is the worst slavery—the indulgence of strong and innocent affections beyond all price.' My child, your purpose has my entire approbation, and you shall have my thanks for any sacrifices you may make to extricate Emilie. My only regret will be, my dear Gertrude, that you, who have so just an estimate of property—so fixed and operative a resolution to de- vote it to its noblest and most effective purposes, should transfer it to the hands of profligates and spend-thrifts. But we must solace ourselves with the reflection that Providence has so wisely regu- lated human affairs, that there is not so much left to individual discretion as we, in our vain glory, are apt to imagine. The money that we often regard as wasted, is put into rapid circulation, and soon goes to compensate the industry and ingenuity of the artisan and tradesman. It is sometimes as consoling to know our own impotence, as at others to feel our moral power.

"My tenderest love to my sweet little friend Emilie—my bless- ing to you, my beloved child. God be with you, and strengthen every benevolent feeling, and virtuous purpose.

"Most affectionately,
"Your father,
"C. CLARENCE.

---

1 Shakespeare's *Hamlet* I.iii.59-60: "give thy thoughts no tongue, / Nor any disproportioned thought his act."
2 Shakespeare's *Henry VII* II.iii.29: "a woman's heart, which ever yet / Af- fected eminence, wealth, sovereignty."

"P. S. I beg you Gertrude, to dismiss your pique against Gerald Roscoe—you will oblige me in this—I have been in fault, but I had no intention of implanting in your mind a permanent prejudice against him."

CHAPTER XII.

"We revoke not our purposes so readily."[1]
—BR.

WHEN Layton was left in the library by Gertrude, he had before him the necessary and difficult task of communicating to Pedrillo his final decision. The course of safety and true policy in this, as in every case, lay in the path of integrity. If Layton had, with the courage of a manly spirit, resolved not to shrink from the disclosure of his guilt, it is possible he might have averted Pedrillo's vengeance; but, alas! truth and simplicity are the helm and rudder first lost in the wreck of human virtue. Layton wrote half a dozen notes, and finally sealed and sent the following, in which he committed one of those fatal errors by which men seem so blindly and so often to prepare the net for their own destruction.

"My dear Pedrillo,—It is with infinite pain that I find myself compelled to announce to you, my daughter's unconquerable aversion to yield to your wishes, and her father's prayers and commands. It is in vain to contend longer. I have done every thing that the warmest friendship and the deepest and most heartily acknowledged obligations could exact from me. Her mother too has argued, pleaded, and remonstrated in vain. But, *console toi, mon ami*,[2] even Cæsar's fortunes yielded to fate, and there are others as young and as fair as my ungrateful girl, who will be proud to give you both heart and hand. You are too much of a philosopher to repine because the wind blows north, when you would have it south—shift your sails, and make for another port.

"As to our pecuniary relations—Fortune, the jade, has, thank Heaven, made a sudden turn in my favor, and I am in purse to the full amount of my debts to you. We will adjust these affairs by letter, or meet for the purpose, when and where you please.

---

1 From *The Two Foscari* (1821) by Byron.
2 Console yourself, my friend.

"My dear friend, I feel quite confident that the menace you threw out as to a certain mode of resenting a failure which, upon my honor, is no fault of mine, was uttered in a moment of *excitement*. You are, I am sure, far too generous, too honorable to betray a secret to the —— (here he made the conventional sign for the gaming club,) which would ruin me, without doing you the least possible good. Such *unmotived* cruelty men of your sense, Pedrillo, leave to fools.

"Believe me, with unfeigned regret that this can be the only relation between us, your sincere and unalterable *friend*,

"JASPER LAYTON."

Whatever Layton might have hoped from the servility of his note, from his assurances of confidence in Pedrillo's generosity, written as they were with so trembling a hand as to be almost illegible, he looked in vain for a reply. He remained at home, listening with feverish expectation to the ringing of the door-bell; a suffering worthy of a poet's inferno, in all cases of delay and final disappointment. There came oyster-men, and orange-men, and ashmen, servants with billets, boys with bills, (scores of them,) fine gentlemen, and fine ladies; but that for which his strained ear listened came not, and evening arrived without any response whatever. He then despatched a servant with a note, inquiring of Pedrillo if he had received the former one. The man returned with a verbal message, that the note had been received.

"Did you ask," demanded Layton, "if there were any answer?"

"I did, sir, and Mr. Pedrillo said if you wished an answer, he would give it to you this evening at the place mentioned in your note."

"The place—I mentioned no place—you have made some stupid mistake, John; go back and tell him I specified no place—stop—good Heaven!—yes it is—it must be *there* he means," and he snatched his hat and was rushing out of the house, when Flint opened the parlor-door and called out, "we are waiting for you, Mr. Layton."

"Waiting—for what?"

"Are you not going to the theatre with the ladies?"

"No, tell them I have an indispensable engagement;" and losing every other thought in one terrifying apprehension, he hastened to the secret rendezvous of the club. The accustomed party was assembled there, with the exception of Pedrillo; and Layton, after an anxious survey of the apartment, passed into an inner room. Pedrillo soon after entered, inquired for him, and joined him.

Layton essayed to speak in his usual tone of friendly recognition. Pedrillo made no reply for an instant, but looked at him with a diabolical expression of mingled scorn and malignity, and then going close to him, he said in a smothered voice, his teeth firmly set, and beginning with an oath too horrible to repeat.

"—— think ye to escape me?—'*unmotived* cruelty!' Have ye not paltered with me for months? Have ye not baited me on with hollow promises, finally, and at the very last, when you think I have no resource, to shake me off! '*Unmotived* cruelty'—have I not been a humble suitor at your daughter's door from day to day? have I not endured her coldness, her disdain, her shrinking from me, as if I were a loathsome pestilence—and this in the eye of gaping fools?—Have I not sat passively by, like a doating idiot, and seen her cheek change at the mention of Marion's name?—'*Unmotived* cruelty!' has not my purse saved you again and again from prison—my silence prevented your being kicked from these doors, and driven from society?"

"Pedrillo—Pedrillo!"

"Nay, I care not who hears me. By Heavens, Layton, I will speak in a voice that shall be heard by every man, woman, and child in the city; your proud name shall be a by-word, coupled with cheat—liar—"

"Pedrillo!"

"Away—the hour of reckoning has come—gentlemen," he cried, placing his hand on the door in the act of opening it. Layton pushed away his arm, and stood firmly against the door: "Hear me, Pedrillo," he said, "for one instant—you have no proof—I will deny your charges to my last breath—they will not believe your assertion against mine—I their fellow-citizen—you a foreigner—a Spaniard!"

"A Spaniard!" echoed Pedrillo; he paused for a moment, and a flash of infernal joy lit up his face; "my thanks to you—you have forgotten the confession of guilt in your morning's note? Think ye the *Spaniard's* word will be believed by your *fellow-citizens*, vouched by the accused's written, voluntary confession?"

Layton now, for the first time, felt the full and inevitable force of the power that was about to crush him. The blood forsook his cheeks and lips, his arms fell as if they were paralyzed, an aguish chill shook his whole frame, and he staggered back and sunk into a chair. No tortures of the rack could surpass those of the moments of silence and dread that followed. He was like one expecting the blow of the executioner, blind, and deaf to every sound but the horrible hissing in his ears, when the spell of acute torment was broken by Pedrillo's voice, whispering close to him, "It is not yet too late!"

Layton gasped for breath; he looked up to Pedrillo with a wild, vacant gaze, "I tell you," repeated his tormentor, glaring on him like a tiger who has his prey in his clutches, "I tell you it is not yet too late—the alarm word is not spoken, and you may yet leave this place with unsullied reputation, if"—

Large drops of sweat stood on Layton's temples. "If what?—speak, Pedrillo—my brain is on fire."

"I will speak—and remember, I speak for the *last* time—mark my words—I am no longer to be put off with pretexts, and duped with promises—Emilie must be mine without delay—you must accede to my terms—swear to obey my directions implicitly—not a breath for deliberation—yes or no?"

"Yes," was faintly articulated by the recreant father.

"Hold up your right hand then, and swear to obey my orders—precisely—hold up your right hand, I say—if," he added, with a scornful laugh, "if it be not palsied."

Layton held up his hand, and repeated after Pedrillo the most solemn form of adjuration. When this sacrilege was ended, Pedrillo said, "Come to my room to-morrow morning at ten o'clock. I shall have contrived and arranged the means to effect my purpose, and be ready to give you your instructions. Now, poor dog, go and join your fellows, and cheat and be cheated. You are not the only scoundrel, Layton, that passes along with a fair name; you are not the only one who feels the shame and the misery to consist not in the crime, but in the exposure!"

With this parting scoff, Pedrillo left his victim in an abyss of intolerable humiliation and anguish. He dared not look back; he could not look forward, and he madly rushed to the gaming-table, to seek in its excitements a temporary oblivion. Before he left it, he had pledged and lost the largest portion of that money which on the morning he had received from Gertrude Clarence for so sacred a purpose.

And this was the man who had so recently manifested, and really felt, generous instincts and kindly emotions. But what are instincts and emotions, compared with principles and habits? Those exhale in the fierce heat of temptation, while these move on in a uniform and irresistible current.

From the club, Pedrillo hastened to a scene of external gaiety which he felt to contrast frightfully with the wild disorder of the evil spirit, that was anticipating the judgment of Heaven, and was truly 'its own hell.' He knew that Mrs. Layton and her party were at the theatre. He ascertained the box they occupied, and gained admittance at a moment when his entrance attracted no attention, the audience being apparently absorbed in observing a spirited actress, who was going through an animated scene of a popular comedy. We said all were thus absorbed; but it was evident to Pedrillo's quick perception, that two individuals of Mrs. Layton's party were engaged in a little dramatic episode of their own, far more interesting to them than any counterfeit emotion.

Emilie Layton was seated beside Randolph Marion, simply dressed, without one of those costly ornaments, Pedrillo's favors, which she had recently worn in compliance with her mother's requisitions, and which, regarding them as the insignia of her slavery, she had cast off and spurned at the first moment of freedom. Nature's signs of another and willing thraldom now lent the most exquisite embellishment to her beautiful face.

The deep, speaking glow of her cheek—the smile that played over her half-parted lips—the dazzling ray that shot from beneath her eye-lids, consciously downcast, were the jewels that revealed her happy spirit. Marion, at short intervals, uttered brief sentences, perfectly inaudible to all ears but Emilie's; but, as every body knows, the atmosphere of lovers, like that of pure oxygen, gives a marvellous brilliancy and force, to all things visible and audible. In front of the lovers, and forgotten by them, but filling other eyes, sat Mrs. Layton, Miss Clarence, Miss Mayo, Major Daisy, and Mr. D. Flint—it was a proud moment for our friend Flint; he had reached the station for which he had long panted, as mortals covet the unattainable—he was perched on the very top-rung of fashion's ladder. He felt a secret delightful conviction, that he was to be naturalized, where he had been an alien. He *had* told his love—(the damask of Flint's ruddy cheek was not destined to feed concealment,) and he was received by Miss Clarence with something more than her usual kindness of manner. His innocent vanity knew not what this could mean, if it did not mean love; and with a brilliant perspective in his imagination, and seated between Miss Mayo and Miss Clarence, he looked like the king of the gods, all-complacent.

Suddenly it seemed that a 'change came o'er the spirit of his dream.'[1] His eye, as it rolled in friendly recognition from box to box, and glanced athwart the full pit, was suddenly arrested by the figure of a plain old man, whose position was nearly in the centre of the pit, his chin resting on his cane, and who was devouring the

---

1 From Byron's "The Dream," Part VI (1816).

play with the eagerness of a novice. This old man was—we must let the reader into the secret—*D*. Flint's father, and honored by his son with filial reverence; but never had the worthy son anticipated such a trial of his virtue, as encountering his father in such a scene. If the old man should see him, he knew he would force his way to him; would greet him in his homely phrase—would call him by that Christian name, so long, so studiously, and so successfully concealed.

Any where else, at any other moment, he would have overcome these shrinkings—but at this critical point in his destiny, in the presence of Miss Clarence, and Miss Mayo, aristocratic and exclusive by birth, fortune, and feeling—and to encounter too, the sarcastic observation of Mrs. Layton, who delighted to remind him that he had no rights within her circle—and Daisy's shrug, which at every approach of the vulgar looked the pharisaical prayer, 'God save us of the privileged order;'—it was all too formidable an array of circumstances, even for *D*. Flint's iron nerves, and for the first time in his life, he meditated a pretext and a retreat, and half-rose from his seat, but his honest soul revolted from the meanness, and he determined, with the resolution of a martyr, to maintain his position.

The second act closed, and the curtain fell, and the greater part of the audience rose, as usual. Flint (pardon him, gentle reader!) abruptly turned his back to the pit. He had scarcely effected this movement, when Miss Clarence said, "What a striking figure that old man is in the centre of the pit—he has a fine antique head—do you see him Miss Mayo?"

"Yes—a hero of the stamp of the Revolution, no doubt—probably one of the survivors of the Bunker-hill battle whom, as my tory uncle says, 'time multiplies like the wood of the true cross'."

Miss Mayo's random guess, had hit the mark. He was one of the valiant heroes of that day, still so 'freshly remembered,' and its story, the good old man had taught his son, and that son did now long to discharge his memory of its treasure; but he could far easier have fought his father's battles, than he could have spoken of them then; for Miss Clarence exclaimed, "the old man is forcing his way towards our box." Flint turned his head just enough to get an oblique glance at his father, who was eagerly intent on the box occupied by our party, but another object than Mr. D. Flint attracted him. His eye was fixed on Pedrillo, who stood alone with folded arms—a most conspicuous figure, resting his back against the door of the box. Flint had his own emotions to take care of, or he would have noticed the sudden change in Pedrillo's countenance, when his eye, turning from its intent gaze on Emilie, encountered the old man's—he tried to avert it, but it seemed spell-bound; in vain he tried 'to stiffen the sinews, and summon up the blood.'[1] The ghastly paleness of his cheek, and his livid lips, betrayed a thrilling, agonizing consciousness. Still, as if rivetted to the spot by a law of nature, he stood, while the stranger continued to approach, speaking to one and another, and pointing their attention to him, but evidently receiving no satisfactory reply. When the old man was near enough to be overheard by our party—"Will any one" he said, "tell me who that gentleman is?"

"Ha! ha! ha!" roared out a vulgar fellow, who had been amused at the stranger's extraordinary eagerness, "the old cock thinks he is crowing in his own barn-yard."

Nature had been warming and rising in Flint's honest bosom, and at this insult it overflowed. He leaped into the pit, with the spirit of Bunker-hill, and roughly pushing aside the offender with one arm, he stretched the other towards the old man, exclaiming in a breath, "impertinent rascal!" and "dear father, how are you?" His father started, as if waked from a dream, and grasping the extended hand, responded to the cordial greeting, "Duty! my son!—Lord bless you, Duty! how are you, my boy?" and he consummated the paternal benediction with a hearty kiss.

By this time all eyes were turned upon the father and son. Two or three loud laughs and a few cries of "encore!" were heard, but more honorable emotions prevailed, and generous sympathy with the simple demonstration of the true and pure affections of nature burst forth in a general clap.

The father was happily unconscious that he was the subject of observation. His interest had reverted to its first object, but when he turned his eye in quest of Pedrillo, he had vanished. *Duty*, amid better emotions, had a throbbing fear of degradation, till his startled ear caught Miss Clarence's voice, seconded by Miss Mayo, asking him to conduct his father to their box. Flint's glistening eyes and protracted smile expressed his sense of the goodness that seemed to set the seal to his fortune. He immediately conducted his father out of the pit. When they were alone, "Did you know," inquired the father, "the person who stood, with his arms folded, behind the ladies, that spoke to you?"

"Know him! yes, sir, perfectly well—his name is Pedrillo; he is a rich Spanish merchant from Cuba."

"Spanish!—from Cuba! do you know any thing more of him?"

---

1 Shakespeare's *Henry V* III.i.7.

"Yes, sir, all about him—but do not stop here, sir, you are trembling with the cold."

"Not with the cold," murmured the old man; "What else do you know of him, Duty?"

"Why, not much after all; I never liked the man—though I always thought he looked very much like you, sir."

"Do *you* think so, Duty?"

"Yes, sir, but pray come along father—Mr. Pedrillo is perfectly well known to our first merchants, and if you have any curiosity about him, I can find out, to-morrow, whatever you want to know."

"Well, well!" said the old man with a sigh, "proceed then, Duty;" and he followed his son, communicating to him as he went, that he had arrived in town that evening, and not finding him at his lodgings, and 'not feeling like going to sleep till he saw him, he had come to the theatre to while away the time.'

As they entered the box the young ladies, undaunted by Daisy's attempts at witty sarcasms, and Mrs. Layton's piquant raillery, gave the old gentleman the place his son had occupied between them, and in spite of a whisper to Gertrude from Mrs. Layton, that she had best, *en Minêrve*, crown *Duty's* father as Clairon crowned Voltaire,[1] she and her friend persisted in rendering him all the respect that the reverence of youth and fashion could pay to honorable old age. Flint revelled in the honest triumphs of a good heart and, it must be confessed, in an emotion destined to be less permanent.

'She has heard my name, she has seen my father, and never was she so kind and sociable,' thought he; and he felt that he had taken a bond of fate—had made assurance doubly sure.

Layton was punctual to his appointment, and at ten o'clock the following morning appeared at the City Hotel.

Pedrillo received him with the coolness and determined air of a man who has surveyed his battle-ground, accurately calculated his forces, and definitively arranged his plan—he had done so, and with the hardihood that scruples at no means to attain a long cherished object. He was driven to this desperation by the threatening aspect of his affairs. He had, a few days previous, received letters from a correspondent in the West Indies, informing him that his

---

1   Minerva is the Roman goddess of wisdom. Mademoiselle Clairon (French, 1723-1803) was among Voltaire's favorite actresses and performed in many of his plays. In October 1772, at her home, dressed as a priestess of Apollo, Clairon placed a laurel crown on Voltaire's bust and recited an ode by Marmontel in his honor.

position in the United States was no longer a safe one; that depositions were about to be forwarded to judicial officers here, proving his participation in a noted piratical affair, in which some of the noble young men of our navy had suffered. He well knew that justice would neither linger, nor be sparing in her retribution; dangers were accumulating. He had, on the preceding evening, at the theatre, encountered the eye that of all others he most dreaded to meet—the eye of the good old man, his father—for Pedrillo was, as our readers must long ago have discerned, the recreant son of the elder Flint—the brother of our sterling friend *Duty*—the same still successful villain who, at fourteen, committed a bold robbery, and a bloody deed, and fled from his father's roof, and his country's violated law. How such a scion should proceed from such a stock, we know not. It was one of those aberrations in the moral history of man, that we can no more account for, than for such physical monsters as the two-headed girl of Paris, or the Siamese boys.[1]

But, among Mr. Flint's neighbors there were of course some of those sage persons, who satisfy themselves with their solution of the riddles of life; and when little Isaac Flint, (for that was the vernacular appellation of the heroic Henriques Pedrillo,) a misdoer from the cradle, broke, for his sport, a whole brood of young turkies' legs; sewed up a pet gander's bill; or cut off a cow's tail; some of these sage expositors would shake their heads and say, 'Spare the rod and spoil the child.' Others would call to mind certain cruel deeds done by a maternal ancestor of Isaac, upon the poor Indians. We honestly confess we are not among those who believe they can, or who care to 'see through' every thing; we like, now and then, to indulge ourselves in clouds and mysteries, and when such an inexplicable wretch as Pedrillo is found in the bosom of an honest family, we are willing to confess, what the Scotch woman said of the fine sermon, we 'hae nae the presumption to comprehend it.'

Pedrillo was a child of fortune—eminently successful in his bold career. He spent profusely the wealth he had accumulated in his lawless adventures; but the caution of middle age began to steal on him with its experience, and preferring security to unlimited but

---

1 Ritta-Christina, l'Enfant Bicéphale, conjoined female twins with two torsos and heads, were exhibited in Paris in October 1829, dying in November 1829 at eight months. The Siamese boys are Eng and Chang Bunker (1811-74); they were examined and exhibited in Boston in 1829 and later settled in the US.

uncertain gains, he gradually withdrew from his bolder enterprises, and established a fair mercantile house in Cuba, and honorable commercial relations. Important money transactions recalled him to his native country. He had been absent twenty-five years, and he returned without a fear of meeting a familiar eye, or the belief that any eye could recognise in his person the rustic farmer boy. He was soon involved in intimate, and as it proved, fatal relations with the Laytons. Affairs had now worked to a point that admitted no farther temporizing.

Pedrillo dared not delay his departure a moment after Monday night. He had that all-conquering energy that finds stimulant in danger, and spur in difficulty. He was resolved, at whatever cost—there he had garnered up his soul—to possess himself of Emilie Layton. His pride, his revenge, all the passions of his nature, were now enlisted to effect this purpose. He had measured and weighed her father, and he believed that though he had not the hardihood to execute a bold deed, he might be used as an effective instrument. With this conviction, Pedrillo continued a plot, in which by a few master strokes, he meant to achieve the darling object, for which he had borne repeated disappointments, and months of irritating delay.

"You look pale and ill, this morning," he said, as Layton, ghastly and haggard, and with averted eye, strode up and down the apartment. "'Fortune, the jade,' showed you her other face last night, I understand. She has relieved you of a goodly portion of the load of her favors, you were so anxious to transfer to me yesterday morning—hey, my friend?"

"I came hither on business," replied Layton, impatient under the scoff he dared not resent.

"Yes, sir—you did come here on business; and do it with what appetite you may, it must be done, and done quickly. You have assured me that it is in vain for you to contend openly with the inclinations of your daughter. I believe you. You have weak nerves, Layton." Layton, for the first time, raised his eye to the speaker's face. "I repeat it—you have weak nerves. You could easier order a surgeon to amputate a limb for your child, than yourself extract a sliver from her finger."

"I am not here to be analyzed, sir."

"You are here for any purpose, to which I choose to apply you—you are henceforth an instrument—a tool—yes, a tool, to be worked by my hand." Layton's cheek reddened, and the veins in his forehead swelled almost to bursting, but he remained silent, stricken with the sense of the abject state to which he had sunken.

"Listen to me," continued Pedrillo, "while I communicate my plan. The grand masquerade, at the Park theatre, is to be on Monday evening. Your virtuous public is putting off the mask of hypocrisy, and putting on other masks. Miss Clarence, the saint! does not go to the masquerade—conscientious scruples, no doubt, ha! ha! *Tant mieux*,[1] she is disposed of. Miss Emilie too, purposes to remain at home, *tête-à-tête* with her *acknowledged* lover, Did I not see them together at the theatre?—I wanted but that to give vigor to my purpose. Mrs. Layton *does* go to the masquerade, with——I know not who—a scene of fine facilities for ladies of her temper!"

"What has all this to do with——"

"With my plans? Be patient my friend, and I will tell you. The Juno, in which I *must* sail for Cuba, lies in the bay, a few hundred yards from Whitehall-wharf. The ship is, in all respects, subject to my orders. She sails at 12 o'clock, on Monday night. You are to induce Miss Emilie to accompany you to the masquerade. I think your influence, or authority, or both, are equal to this achievement. There we meet. You are soon obliged to leave the assembly, on any pretext you choose—I leave that to your own ingenuity. You ask me to attend Miss Emilie home; a carriage, previously ordered, will be at the door; we will drive to the wharf. My boat, well-managed, awaits us there—a few pulls brings us to the ship, and once aboard, I am master of my destiny."

"But, good Heaven, Pedrillo! you have made no provision for the marriage?"

"Oh, the marriage!—the marriage!" replied Pedrillo, tauntingly, and smiling, as well he might, at the importance Layton affixed to a rite, when he was violating the first law of nature. "The marriage, my dear sir, that shall be solemnized, if not on consecrated ground, and by book and bell,[2] yet with all lawful ceremony. You have the surest pledge for this—the only pledge on which a man of sense relies. It is my *interest* to *marry* Miss Layton.

"Layton, 'there is a time for all things,'—you see I remember a few of the pious lessons conned in my childhood; I have given enough of life to transient *liaisons;* you understand me Layton? and having decided to marry, what think you of showing to the world,

---

1 So much the better.
2 Pedrillo indicates that though the marriage may not take place in a church (on consecrated ground) or with the traditional Christian elements of book (Bible) and bell (church bells), it will still be legally binding. He soon promises the additional performance of the religious sacrament of marriage by a Catholic priest.

a wife, young, lovely, and beautiful? An Emilie Layton? Layton is a name well known in the West Indies—a proud *unsullied* name."

Layton's eye fell from Pedrillo's exulting countenance. His blood curdled. He asked faintly, "where the marriage ceremony was to be performed?"

"On board the ship—we have a Catholic priest, who is going out to Cuba. He is well known to the Catholic Bishop, who will solve any doubts you may entertain. But why any doubts? have I not been willing—willing! most anxious to have the ceremony performed under your own roof, and in your auspicious presence. Would I not now—you know I would, Layton—glory in leading your daughter to the altar, before the assembled universe? Have I not been foiled in all my honorable efforts? Has not my patience been tired, exhausted, and am I not driven, and by your imbecility, to this last desperate resource?

"Take courage, man—it may seem bad, but it is not so. I promise you a letter from the Narrows, signed by Emilie's own hand, attesting that the priest has done his duty, and that I have provided every luxury for her that love could devise, or money purchase. My man, Denis, has already taken my orders to an all-knowing French woman to provide a lady's complete wardrobe. She has a carte-blanche[1] as to expense; and farther, for I would quiet your paternal qualms—I am not more than half devil, Layton—there is a plot within a plot, in this drama of ours. Denis has followed his master's suit, and has long had a penchant for your wife's pretty maid, Justine. Love has been kinder to the man, than to the master. Justine returns his passion, and but for her old parents, would follow him to the world's end—such fools are women, young and old, in their loves. In sympathy with their tender passion, and to secure Justine's services for your daughter, I have promised to settle five hundred dollars on the old people. Justine has joyfully acceded to my terms. She enters into all my plans, *con amore*.[2] She resents my wrongs; for *she* thinks—on my soul she does, Layton, that I have been falsely dealt by. Still drooping, man! do you any longer doubt my devotion to Miss Emilie's comfort—and happiness! if she will but be happy in the way I prescribe?"

Layton was in truth somewhat solaced by these details, as a man in a dungeon turns to the least glimmering of light, and he parted from Pedrillo more tranquilly than he met him, after having arranged the costumes in which they were to meet; Emilie

---

1 Free hand.
2 With love (Italian).

in a blue domino,[1] her father in black, and Pedrillo, (who never forgot the decoration of his fine person,) in the dress of a Spanish cavalier, with three white ostrich feathers attached to his hat by a diamond cross.

The days that intervened till the masquerade were marked with unqualified misery to Layton. He rode about the environs of the city like a half-frantic man, or shut himself within a solitary apartment of a tavern. He avoided his acquaintance, he shrunk from every human being; but most of all he dreaded to encounter his wronged child, and his noble benefactress, whose trust he had so basely betrayed. 'But for that last fatal loss,' he said and repeated to himself, 'I would confess all, and abide the consequences.' And he honestly thought so. Men often fancy, if circumstances were a little differently moulded, they should have the courage to do right. 'If it were I alone,' thought Layton, 'that had to meet ruin—but it is not—Emilie—all my children must suffer with me, all must suffer remediless ruin! And yet to be a party in this plot against my child—I—her father, her natural guardian! But, after all, if it be a plot, it is to effect an object to which she once assented—which I have avowed—which the world has approved, which mothers and daughters have envied. Life is a lottery, Emilie might marry Marion; but what does he promise more than I did, when her mother stood exulting with me at the altar? The poor child must endure a little disappointment, a little misery—yes, *misery* it must be! and she may return to us rid of this wretch, and with countless wealth—but if she dies of a broken heart!— well, well, I am too far in to escape. That horrible violation of Miss Clarence's trust, I must make her believe I paid the money to Pedrillo, he will not be here to contradict it; he must be loaded with the obloquy of the whole business. Emilie's husband! but his love, his disappointment, and his Spanish nature will be reckoned in his favor.'

Thus reasoning and confuting his own reasonings, thus vainly endeavouring to stifle a voice that is never stifled, Layton passed the interval till Monday evening.

---

1   A generic masquerade costume featuring two colors in a diamond pattern.

CHAPTER XIII.

"He has discovered my design, and I
"Remain a pinch'd thing; yea, a very trick
"For them to play at will."
WINTER'S TALE.[1]

THE purveyors of the amusements of our city took advantage of
the interval between the extinction of an old law, and the framing
of a new one, to get up masquerades in all the places of public
resort.[2] Laudable pains were taken by the manager of the Park-
theatre to conciliate that portion of society which, suspicious of
every doubtful form of pleasure, was expected to frown on that,
which had been already condemned by the public censors on the
ground of its affording facilities to the vicious. Gentlemen of the
first respectability and fashion were selected as managers, and
the maskers were not permitted to enter the assembly without
first unmasking to one of these gentlemen. The boxes were to be
filled by the more sedate, or fastidious, or timid, who chose to be
stationary spectators of the gaieties of the evening. The presence
of a multitude of well known observers, was expected to operate as an effective check to all tendencies to extravagance in the
maskers.

Mrs. Layton had arranged a party for the masquerade. Her spirits were excited by the approach of a form of pleasure unknown in
this country, save in some private circles, where very limited numbers and thorough mutual acquaintance had precluded the genius and artifices of invention. Her imagination was filled with the
romantic incidents that novelists and dramatists have conjured up
on this propitious arena, and she selected her character and meditated her part with the fresh interest of a girl of seventeen. She
was to personate the Sybil.[3] The character suited her genius and

---

1 Shakespeare's *The Winter's Tale* II.i.50-52.
2 Periodically from 1810 through 1821, the Common Council of the City
   of New York issued ordinances forbidding inn or tavern keepers from
   hosting masquerade balls. In 1829, when several theaters conducted
   masquerade balls (see Appendix C4), the Common Council petitioned
   the New York State Legislature to pass a broader statute forbidding
   masquerades and imposing a stiff financial penalty, which the Legislature
   did on 25 April 1829. Some continued to conduct masquerades, however,
   paying the fine out of the proceeds of the event.
3 Female prophet in Greek mythology, typically portrayed as a very old
   woman.

her figure, and she said, that 'inspiration, like herself, was of no particular age.' Her dress was a black velvet, so happily designed by her own exquisite taste, and executed by the felicitous art of a French dress-maker, as to avoid the grandmother and dowager aspect of velvet; to retain the grace without the form of the reigning fashion, and, in short, to appear sufficiently classic and imaginative for the Sybil of poetry. A few laurel leaves were arranged with a wild fantastic grace in the folds of her black hair; and over her face, instead of a mask, she wore a richly wrought white lace veil, which obscured without concealing her fine features, and falling over her right shoulder, formed a profuse and beautiful drapery. She was writing the last sentences of Fate on embossed cards, which she purposed to place between ivory tablets and distribute as sybilline leaves,[1] when Gertrude entered her apartment, and, after an involuntary tribute to the beautiful personification before her, asked leave, to Mrs. Layton's utter amazement, to accompany her to the masquerade.

"My leave!" exclaimed Mrs. Layton, "your going will gratify me beyond expression. My dear—my—no, not capricious—my *mutable* Gertrude; forgive me, but I am so charmed to see you waking from the rustic reveries of Clarenceville; if you stay with me three months longer, you will become quite imperfect and—interesting. But tell me, seriously, what has so suddenly reversed your decision against the masquerade?"

"Stronger motives for going than I had for declining to go."

"But, my immaculate friend, I thought your principles were against it."

"I did not say so."

"Oh, no, Gertrude, you are not so green, thank Heaven, as to make a formal profession of principles on trifling occasions; you only compel us to infer them from your actions."

"Thank you, but I am afraid this moral pantomime, this expression of principles by actions, like other pantomimes, owes half its significance to the observer; however, I am content it should do so, if your interpretation be but as favorable to-morrow as to-day." There was something in the intonation of Miss Clarence's voice, and in the expression of her half averted eye, that indicated more meaning than met the ear.

Mrs. Layton cast a penetrating glance at her, "You talk riddles, Gertrude, but I have no time to read them now. I presume

---

1   As if these were pages from the Sybilline Books, a collection of prophecies attributed to the sybil of Cumae (Italy).

Emilie has not changed her mind too? She prefers a *tête-à-tête* with Marion?"

"Certainly, to *all* other pleasures."

"She is right—happy child! these are the rose-tinted hours of love to her; the sands of time are 'diamond sparks' now; what will they be when, like her poor mother, it is near 'twice ten *tedious* years since married she has been?'—heigho!"

"What will they be! diamond sparks still, I trust. Emilie has done all that mortal can do to make them run brightly to the last—well placed a true love."

"Bless me, Gertrude, you speak *con amore*. I am a believer in love too, but not in *love matches*; however, though I have not been consulted in the affair, I have no objection to the transfer of her engagement. I confess I do not comprehend it. It is all Layton's affair. I assume no responsibility about my children, and Layton has made no communication to me but of the bare unexplained fact. Indeed I have not seen him since; he has come home late at night, and gone to his own room. How he has contrived to satisfy Pedrillo I cannot conceive, but I am told he was to sail to-day; he certainly was distractedly fond of Emilie—and so determined— it *is* a mysterious business; however I shall rest satisfied without making any inquiries. The rule of my philosophy is short and un-erring, 'Whatever is, is best.'"[1]

"Provided, Mrs. Layton, we cannot by our efforts make it bet-ter; but, pardon me, I forgot that my moralizing was limited to action—a difficult sort of *lay-preaching*. Promise me," concluded Gertrude, kissing Mrs. Layton, with an affectionateness of manner that brought to that lady's mind the first days of their intercourse, "promise me that you will remember your motto to-morrow, '*Whatever is, is best.*'"

"Certainly, my dear girl, to-morrow and for ever."

'What can she mean?' thought she, as Gertrude left her, 'by these dark intimations?—nothing, after all, I'll answer for it—poor thing, her imagination is so excited by this masquerade—for a woman of her education she is surprisingly raw in some things— she thinks, no doubt, she is about to commit a monstrous sin: what cowards women are made by such preciseness!'

Timidity of conscience is a defence that Providence has set about human virtue, and those who are willing to part with one of its securities, have not felt sufficiently either its worth or its frailty.

---

1   From Pope's *An Essay on Man*, Epistle I (1733-34): "And spite of Pride, in erring Reason's spite, / One truth is clear, Whatever is, is right."

Miss Clarence selected a black domino, the dress that would be most common, and therefore least conspicuous, and a mask similar to those generally worn, of pasteboard and crape—an effectual skreen. A floor had been extended from the stage over the pit; and on first entering on this immense area, thronged with representatives of all ages of the world, and of every condition of society, she was nearly overwhelmed with the timidity which a delicate woman, herself disguised, would naturally feel in a scene of such fantastic novelty. But she was sustained by the consciousness of a secret purpose that was worth effort and sacrifice, and she was soon tranquillized by the order that prevailed amidst confusion. There was a general and obvious consciousness of a new and awkward position; and with the exception of practised foreigners, and a few native geniuses, like Mrs. Layton, there was a prevailing shyness and tameness, that indicated that masquerading was as little adapted to our society as tropical plants to our cold soil.

"Let us step aside from the crowd," said our Sybil to her most incongruous attendant, Major Daisy, in the character of a French Count of the old school. "I see some persons here who have promised to join me as soon as they find me out. Gertrude, do you really expect to remain incognitia?"

"Certainly—you surely have not misunderstood me?" she replied earnestly, for at that moment she saw that Roscoe, in his ordinary costume, and without a mask, was approaching them.

"Then, *mon cher Comte*,[1] you have only to forget that our friend bears the name of Clarence; a burden," she added, accommodating her voice to the Major's ear alone, "from which you, as well as some others, would gladly relieve her."

"Oh, madame!" responded the delighted Count, "vous avez vraiment l'esprit de la divination!"[2]

"And, Gertrude, you are the unknown, l'inconnue mysterieuse,[3] Count."

"A relation of the mighty unknown," exclaimed the Major, forgetting his Countship, and speaking in character—"a *genteel* family!"

"Pardon me, Count; if I am to be ingrafted on that stock, I shall disdain the distinctions of your citizens' drawing-room—genteel! the mighty unknown takes precedence of all gentility, of nobility, of royalty, in all loyal hearts."

---

1 My dear Count.
2 You really have a talent for fortune-telling!
3 A mysterious, unknown person.

"And in my sybilline office I predict," said Mrs. Layton, "that he will be remembered when kings and potentates and all the boasts of heraldry are forgotten."

"And has the Sybil no kind prediction for one who has always done homage to her inspiration?" asked Roscoe, who now joined them, and as he spoke, reverently raised the folds of Mrs. Layton's veil to his lips.

"The Sybil is, even to her favorites, but the minister of Fate. Take what she decrees," replied Mrs. Layton, holding high her ivory tablets, and dropping a card from between them. It fell within the ample folds of the sleeve of Miss Clarence's domino. She extricated it, and gave it to Roscoe, saying as she did so, "This from the oracle, and may its spiritual counsel or stop, or spur you."

Roscoe started, electrified by the unexpected voice, but recovering instantly his self-possession, he replied, in a low tone, "The only oracle that can 'or stop, or spur me,'[1] is veiled in more than sybilline mystery."

"Lisez votre destinée, Monsieur,"[2] cried the Major, whose feeble attempts to support his character were limited to the painful effort of constructing a few French sentences.

"No, it shall be read by our priestess," said the Sybil, taking the card from Roscoe's hand, and placing it in Gertrude's; "why does our votary thus gaze at us?" she continued, interpreting the confused and inquiring glance that Roscoe cast, first on Gertrude, then on herself; "is he offended by finding the Sybil attended by a priestess not found on classic records—proceed, my priestess, there are few in this assembly who will detect the modern interpolation."

Gertrude glanced her eye over the card, and read the sentence aloud, feeling as if her burning cheek might, even through her mask, betray her private interpretation.

Your course is well nigh run,
Your prize is almost won,
And the treasure of your bridal day,
Will prove the treasure once cast away.

"Dark enough for Delphos!"[3] exclaimed Roscoe—"treasure once cast away! Heaven knows that the good woman commended

---

1 Shakespeare's *The Winter's Tale* II.i.186-88: "Now from the oracle / They will bring all, whose spiritual counsel had / Shall stop or spur me."

2 Read your fate, sir.

3 Delphos, the location of the oracle of Delphi in Greek tradition.

in scripture did not more earnestly seek her lost penny[1] than I have sought the only treasure that ever shall be 'the treasure of my bridal day'—he would have said, but it was a truth too seriously felt to be lightly uttered—he faltered, and then laughingly added, "Oh, it is a lying oracle!"

"Our favors contemned!" exclaimed the Sybil, "the destinies have misdirected them," and snatching the card from Gertrude, she shuffled it in with the rest, and again elevating the tablets, she dispersed the leaves among the crowd, that, attracted by her conspicuous figure, and lofty pretensions, had gathered about her. "There they go," she said, "full of pretty answers!—such as might indeed 'have been got from an acquaintance with Goldsmith's wives.'"[2]

Roscoe held up the tablet, before Gertrude's eyes, which he had caught in the general scramble—"It is the same!" he exclaimed, "there is a fate in this which the future shall expound for me," and with the deferential air of a devotee, he placed it in his bosom. Gertrude's heart was throbbing with the sweetest emotions, when a touch from Mrs. Layton, directed her attention to an object of sufficient interest to command her thoughts, even at that moment.

"Is not that Pedrillo?" she whispered, "that Spanish Knight, with three white ostrich feathers in his cap."

"He certainly looks like Pedrillo," replied Gertrude in a tremulous voice—"but can he be here? the ship sailed to-day—Emilie read the advertisement in the evening paper."

"That may be—cleared perhaps—but this is certainly Pedrillo. Observe—no one else would have so well arranged a Spanish costume. I always told you his taste was exquisite—it is he, beyond a doubt—that brilliant cross identifies him, he once showed it to me—there is not another such in the country. How he hovers about us—he has one of my leaves—poor fellow!—I should like to know his luck. Sir Knight," she added, raising her voice "if the destinies are but obedient to the Sybil's will, thy fate has been fortunate."

The Knight bowed, haughtily enough for a Castilian, but vouchsafed no other reply. "There are horribly portentous predictions among them," continued Mrs. Layton. "I would not outrage his feelings. On what pretext shall we ask to see it?—not to translate it into Spanish, for I see that African princes, Indian chiefs,

---

1 Reference to the Parable of the Lost Coin, Luke 15.8-10.

2 Shakespeare's *As You Like It* III.ii.267-69, as Jaques refers to the "pretty answers" that can be found in romantic verses (inscribed in gold rings).

blind girls, deaf and dumb, all have a gift to read my prophetic words—do aid me, Gertrude."

"My mistress commands me, Sir Knight," said Gertrude, "to read aloud your fate." He gave her his card, first passing his finger emphatically across the last line, and she read as follows—*'Dangers beset thee—vengeance pursues thee—blood is in thy path,*

> *Listen, stranger, to this prophecy of mine,*
> *but fear not,*
> *The blood's another's—the victory is thine!*

"Oh, my most tragic flight!" exclaimed the Sybil, really alarmed at the possible interpretation of her random prediction. "Indeed, Sir Knight, I designed that for my friend, the Count here, or some other carpet hero, who never encounters a worse danger than an east wind, nor a more fearful vengeance than a lady's frown."

"*Pardonnez ma Sybille,*" exclaimed the Count, "*J'ai mon sort et j'en suis tres content,—ecoutez.*"[1]

> "*Hope flatters—fortune smiles—success awaits thee.*
> *Then, linger not—the secret NOW disclose*
> *The fair adored will not thy love oppose.*"

The Major's imagination was for once carried captive. The prophecy elevated him far above his native region of prudence; and availing himself of an opportunity, which was afforded by the company falling into ranks and promenading to the music, he actually *committed* himself, and in unambiguous words made an offer, in the full meaning of that technical term. He had thrown the die that had remained in his tremulous hand for the twenty years that he had fluttered about the successive Cynthias of the minute; the belles and heiresses, who had fallen into the oblivion of wives and mothers, without the boast of an offer from the wary Major. Not Camillus, when he cast his sword into the scale—not Cæsar, when he passed the Rubicon—not all the *signers,* when they penned their immortal autographs,[2] felt their souls dilate

---

1 Forgive my Sybil ... I have my fate and I am very happy with it—listen.

2 Marcus Furius Camillus (c. 446-365 BCE), often referred to as the Second Founder of Rome; Julius Cæsar (100-44 BCE), Roman statesman whose decision to cross the river Rubicon (recalled in the well-known phrase 'the die is cast') in 49 BCE led to his invasion of Italy and the creation of the Roman Empire; the signers of the American Declaration of Independence in 1776.

with such a mighty swell, as Major Daisy, when he thus boldly encountered the possibility of a refusal. What then was his surprise, to find that Miss Clarence did not, in the slightest degree, partake his agitation—that she listened to him, much as one listens to a teller of dreams! That her feelings were evidently deeply absorbed in some other subject; and that when obliged to reply to him, she treated his declaration *en badinage*[1] as a dramatic part of the masquerade; and finally, when compelled to answer his reiterated protestations seriously, she dismissed them as the tame and wearisome tale of every hour.

The poor Major! caught in the very net he had so long, so well escaped; and treated, after all, as game not worth catching! His heart burned within him, his head swam, and he stepped short and high, when he was relieved by Roscoe's approach—and stammering out, 'my dear sir, I have an engagement—be good enough to take my place.' He resigned his position to one who produced as sudden a change in Gertrude, as if she had been transported from the north pole to the equator.

Roscoe had lingered near Mrs. Layton, to avail himself of the permission, accorded by Gertrude in their last interview, and at the first instant he could obtain a private hearing, he said to her, "Tell me, I entreat you, the name of the lady who personates your priestess."

Mrs. Layton, determined to maintain her character, and sport with the eager curiosity betrayed in Roscoe's tremulous voice, (she did not suspect how much deeper was the feeling than curiosity,) replied, "Do you, presumptuous mortal, inquire my priestess' name, when you have so long disdained to join the troop of pilgrims to her shrine—neglected to lay a single offering on her altar!"

Roscoe assured her—and she could not doubt it—that he was serious; but the Sybil was obstinate, and he, impatient of the spell, which he began to despair of ever breaking, left her and joined Gertrude.

Roscoe certainly did not, like the Major, 'make an offer,' nor did he talk of love in any of the prescribed or accepted terms. But there is a freemasonry[2] in love—it has its hidden meaning; and we should despair—if we were bold enough to repeat the short and low sentences exchanged by our lovers—we should despair of making them intelligible to the uninitiated. They would, in all

---

1 Lightheartedly.
2 Fraternal order or society with private or secret rituals, signs, and ceremonies shared only by its members.

simpleness, wonder what there was to cast so potent a spell over the scene, that it vanished from their senses—what to make Gertrude's cheeks burn, and her hands cold—to make Roscoe's heart throb in his manly bosom, and suffuse that eye whose lofty glance could thrill an assembly of his peers with tears as soft as ever trembled in a woman's eye. There was no declaration—no confession—but the dawning consciousness of being beloved—the first blissful moment of assurance—a moment for which there is not in all the experience of true love a counterpoise or equivalent.

The happy do not need observers, and we leave them, for those who demand our interest, and certainly deserve our sympathy.

Emilie Layton was sitting at home alone in the parlor, apparently quite absorbed in a book that lay before her, when the opening of the door quickened her pulses. She did not look up; the door was closed, and a moment of deep silence followed. It was her father who had entered, and for one moment he stood, heart-stricken, gazing on his destined victim. She was bending over her book, her brow resting on her hand, a hand that had the fresh dimpled beauty of childhood. The light of the astral lamp fell, as if it had been adjusted by a painter's art, on her golden hair, glowing cheek, and ivory throat; her beauty would have arrested the dullest éye, but it was more than her beauty that at that moment thrilled her father's soul. The gentle obedience of her life, her danger, her defencelessness—and he, her natural shield, made the instrument of her destruction. But it was too late to recede or to hesitate; any thing, he thought, would be more tolerable than the pang of the present moment, and, making a desperate effort, he said, in a loud voice, that broken and unnatural as it was, was evidently meant to be gay, "Emilie, my darling, I have a favor to ask of you—a frolic on foot—I want you to go to the masquerade with me." He threw a bundle on the table, "there is a domino and mask for you."

"But, papa!"

"No expostulation, if you please, the carriage is at the door; no one knows that we are going—we shall see without being seen, we will come away whenever you choose—in ten minutes, if you like—indeed I cannot stay longer. Do you hesitate? Emilie! it is extraordinary that you will refuse me this small request!"

"I do not refuse, papa," she replied, hastily throwing on the domino, while her voice, her whole person trembled, almost shivered with emotion. Layton hurried on his domino. Every motion was like that of an insane man. He opened the door, "Are you ready!—are you ready, Emilie?"

"Yes, quite ready."

Again he shut the door, turned to Emilie, and throwing his arms around her, he burst into tears, "Oh, my child, my child—promise me that you will never curse your father!"

"Curse you, papa!—Every day on my bended knees do I implore a blessing on you—and I will while I live—so help me, God—wherever I am, wherever you are"—

"Wherever I am!" echoed Layton, recoiling from her and striking his hands together, "I shall be—O Emilie, Emilie, pity me!".

"Pity you, papa! I do pity you from the bottom of my heart—you are not well—let me send away the carriage—we will not go to the masquerade, will we?"

"We *must*, Emilie," he replied, summoning his resolution. He feared he had already betrayed himself, and he added, pressing his hand to his forehead, "my head has been in a whirl—its going over now; I took an extra bottle of champaigne to-day, and my nerves are shattered of late. Throw on your shawl, my child, and let's be gone."

Emilie took a shawl that hung over her chair, her father snatched it from her and threw it across the room; "That's your mother's!" he exclaimed, "wear no memorial of your parents, Emilie. Oh, had your mother possessed one thousandth part of your goodness, I should never have been the wretch I am."

Emilie was impatient to end the frightful scene—"Here is a shawl of Gertrude, papa," she said; "I am ready now."

"Gertrude Clarence! she is an angel—but angels have not power to save, why should devils to destroy?"

Emilie made no further reply. She perceived that every word she uttered served but to increase the agitation it was meant to allay, and she quietly preceded her father to the carriage. Not another syllable was interchanged. The silence was unbroken, save by a sigh or groan from the miserable father, such as might have proceeded from a criminal going to execution, and as with him, 'time gallops withal,'[1] so it seemed to Layton, to impel him with inexorable speed into that scene where he was to seal his child's fate. The first and the only object he saw, when they entered the brilliant assembly, was the Spanish knight. *He* too, instantly caught a glimpse of the two persons he had awaited, with a restlessness and trepidation that he feared were betraying his secret purposes, even

---

1 Shakespeare's *As You Like It* III.ii.320, as Orlando and Rosalind discuss the movement of time—"galloping" at times, "ambling" at others, depending on the circumstances.

through his disguise, and making his way through the crowd, his towering plumes nodding above all heads, he approached them, and touching his hat to Layton, he placed himself at Emilie's side, and in a whisper told her that he had at the first glance recognised her. She made no reply, and they proceeded, with the tide that set that way, towards the stage. They passed a Mary of Scotland complaining to Queen Elizabeth, not of violated faith, but of a smoking kitchen-chimney; a Sappho bewailing, not the treachery of her lover, but the loss of a cook; Sweet Anne Page dancing with an Indian chief, both in Charraud's best style; and Sir Roger de Coverly mated with a sultana.[1] But these and all other incongruities were unnoticed by the trio. Emilie felt her father's step becoming more and more faltering, and as her arm, that was locked in his, pressed against his side, it seemed to her that his throbbing heart would leap from his bosom. He stopped as they approached that part of the stage where her mother retained her station, still the ruling spirit of the scene. Her spirits were wrought to the highest pitch by the success of her character—she kindled in the light of her own genius. Her sallies were caught and repeated by those who could comprehend them, and those who would fain appear to comprehend them—her brilliancy cast a ray of light even on the dullest and dimmest. Layton felt that there was something insulting in her careless gaiety and exultation at a moment when he was steeped to the very lips in misery. His mind was in that excited and bewildered state when demons seem to be its ministering spirits, when every wild unbidden thought presses with a supernatural force. He stood fixedly for an instant, his eyes glaring on his wife. She was in happy unconsciousness of his gaze. 'I could speak daggers to her,'[2] he thought—'and I will,' and letting fall Emilie's arm, he penetrated through the ranks that inclosed his wife, and said, in a voice she well knew, low and husky as it was, "One word of true prophecy for all thy lying inventions, Sybil. 'Walk in the light of your fires, and in the sparks ye have kindled, but this shall ye have—ye shall lie down in sorrow!'"[3]

---

1 Mary Queen of Scots and Elizabeth I were rivals for the English monarchy; Sweet Anne Page is a character in Shakespeare's *The Merry Wives of Windsor*; Sir Roger de Coverly is a country gentleman in Addison and Steele's *The Spectator* (1711); a Sultana is the wife or mistress of a Muslim ruler, usually Turkish.

2 Shakespeare's *Hamlet* III.ii.395, Hamlet speaking of his mother: "I will speak daggers to her, but use none."

3 Isaiah 50.11.

This sudden apparition, and these startling words so blenched Mrs. Layton's cheek, as to define precisely the limits of her rouge. She looked after the speaker, but he had rejoined his companions, and was lost in the general stream.

Emilie perceived, as her father resumed her arm, that he seemed lost and uncertain which way to turn his steps. "You are not well, papa," she whispered; "do let us leave this place as soon as possible."

"We shall leave it soon enough, my child."

The knight gave him a card; '*delay not*' was scrawled upon it. The words seemed to scorch him as he read them. He obeyed the mandate, and they retraced their steps towards the lobby. Suddenly Emilie slackened her pace, and then stopped. She dropped her pocket handkerchief. A lady who passed near picked it up, and without appearing even to look for its right possessor, tied it around her throat, and Emilie proceeded, unconscious of, or passively submitting to, the loss.

When they reached the lobby, "Surely, papa," said Emilie, faltering, "there is no occasion for Mr. Pedrillo to go further with us—his costume attracts attention."

"He must go home with you, Emilie," replied her father; "I am too ill to attend you—I must stop at a physician's, and have blood let—Pedrillo, look for a carriage." He uttered the premeditated words mechanically. They were scarcely audible; but Emilie, whatever might have been her reluctance, proceeded without any farther remonstrance. It would have been impossible to say which was most trembling, most agitated—father, or daughter. As he assisted her into the carriage, he retained her hand for a moment, and pressed it fervently to his lips. Emilie felt his tears gush over it, and springing forward, she kissed his hand tenderly, and mingled her tears with his. He groaned aloud. The knight's impatient foot was already on the step. The wretched father grasped his arm: "Pedrillo," he said, "God have mercy on your soul, as you are true to my poor child!"

"Amen!" was the only response, but never was a saint's prayer uttered with a deeper, more fervent, or more sincere emphasis. The carriage door was closed, the horses driven swiftly away, and Emilie sank on the bosom of her companion, exclaiming, "Oh, Marion, Heaven will forgive my poor father!"

Marion, (for it was in truth Emilie's true love that personated the Spanish knight,) Marion soothed her with every suggestion that tenderness could supply. While they are disencumbering themselves of every trace of the masquerade, and putting on their travelling cloaks, hats, &c., previously provided—while the carriage halts in one of the cross-streets leading to Powles Hook, and while four good steeds are being attached to it, we must return once more to the masquerade, and to Gertrude who, in obedience to the preconcerted signal of the dropped handkerchief, was hastening to follow her friend. Roscoe was still at Gertrude's side. We have been compelled to repeated recession, and long as it may appear since we left him at that enviable station, the time seemed to him short as a blissful dream, when Gertrude said, "Mr. Roscoe, I must put your generous faith to one more proof—I promise it shall be the last. Will you attend me to my place of destination?"

Roscoe's faith was for a moment disturbed, and he frankly expressed his distrust. "You did not surely come here alone?"

"No, I certainly did not; but I do not see the person on whom I relied to attend me, and I must go alone if you hesitate—my engagements will not permit me one moment's delay."

"Pardon me," he said, offering his arm.

"I do pardon you," she replied, taking it, "though I perceive you are but half assured." He answered nothing till they had left the house, and made their way through the rabble of hackmen, and idlers that surrounded the door. "Is this haste necessary?" he then asked, checking their hurried pace; "has it any object but to end this brief interview, and to leave me in the ignorance which I can no longer endure, and which, permit me to say, after your promise at our last interview, you ought no longer to protract?"

"My haste is essential, Mr. Roscoe, and believe me, it has no reference to you."

Roscoe's pride was wounded. "Forgive my presumption. I certainly ought not to have imagined that you, who have shown such utter indifference to my wishes—such an entire want of confidence in me, should have any farther reference to me, than as the instrument of your convenience."

"Mr. Roscoe!"—there was a treacherous tremulousness in Gertrude's voice. After pausing for an instant, she proceeded, "You are unkind and unjust to me—you have not claimed the performance of my promise. I am at this moment giving you the strongest proof of my confidence—making you privy and accessory to a hazardous elopement."

"An elopement!" exclaimed Roscoe, aghast.

"Yes," replied Gertrude, smiling; "an elopement—of which I am a zealous aider and abettor, and an humble attendant of my principals to Virginia, our ultimate destination."

"To Virginia! Then I now claim the fulfilment of your promise." Roscoe paused, and Gertrude was as anxious to pronounce the word that would dispel the mystery, as Roscoe could be to hear it; but it seemed to her like the word of doom, and while it hovered unspoken on her trembling lips, Roscoe continued, "I beseech you to end this tormenting suspense, which I flattered myself the chances of every day would terminate. Have I not endured it long enough—patiently enough? For Heaven's sake, do not walk at this furious rate—if you knew what efforts my deference to your wishes has cost me, you would not hesitate. I care not what you disclose—my interest in you is independent of all circumstances and persons other than yourself—I was proud—fastidious, it may be. There was a time when I should have shrunk from the disclosure of a vulgar or obscure name—or a name allied however remotely to dishonor; but now, truly I care not for any of these things—my faith, my hope, my love, centres in you alone."

Notwithstanding the intense interest with which Gertrude listened, and notwithstanding Roscoe's earnest remonstrance, she had not slackened her speed; and she now saw a carriage awaiting her at a few paces from her, and Marion, who had descried her, advancing hastily. She had just time to falter out a hasty reply to his last words—"Then is there an end of all motive to further concealment," when Marion exclaimed, "For mercy's sake, make haste, my dear Miss Clarence!"

"Miss Clarence!" exclaimed Roscoe—"Gertrude Clarence?"

"Yes, Gertrude Clarence—but not a *'prize lady.'*"

Roscoe was dumb for an instant, (seconds were now precious,) overpowered with thick-coming thoughts—surprise at this solution of the mystery, and amazement at his own stupidity—such as is felt in all inferior riddles—that he had not before discovered the solution—recollections, anticipations, fears, and hopes were thronging, and all concentrated in that one moment.

They were already at the carriage-door—Emilie had exclaimed joyfully, "Oh Gertrude, you've come!" and Roscoe had recovered his self-possession sufficiently to say to Marion, "Get in first, if you please—I have one word to say to—Miss Clarence."

"But a single word, I entreat," replied Marion; "there is no time to lose."

"In one word then," whispered Roscoe; "may I follow you?"

Gertrude uttered that precious monosyllable, worth in some cases the whole English language besides, and sprang into the carriage, but not till Roscoe had pressed her hand to his lips, and breathed out a "God bless you"—the shortest and best of all benedictions.

Marion was drawing up the blind, when Emilie stopped him, while she entreated Roscoe, who stood as if he were transfixed beside the carriage, to return to the masquerade, and attend her mother home, but on no account to betray his knowledge of their departure.

Roscoe promised. The blind was again drawn up, and the carriage hastily driven to a boat in waiting, which conveyed them without any delay to Powles Hook, whence they proceeded on their southern route.

CHAPTER XIV.

"Il me semble qu'il y a des friponneries si heureuses que tout le monde les pardonne."[1]
VOLTAIRE.

PEDRILLO deviated from his best policy when he communicated the secret of his conspiracy to his man Denis, and permitted him to extend it to Justine.

Denis, it is true, was a well tried tool of his master, who had never been betrayed into infidelity by any impulses or meltings of nature. But Justine was of a softer temper—a woman, with a woman's sympathies and affections. All these Denis had artfully enlisted in his master's cause, by making her believe they were only righting the wrongs of true love, and inflicting on Miss Emilie the penalty of her broken faith. The present violence being thus adjusted in Justine's feminine scales, her imagination was easily seduced by the brilliant perspective of honors and wealth that awaited her young lady, and of which she, the satellite and lesser light, would partake in liberal measure.

Her conscience was thus made tolerably quiet, but she had another anxiety that she could not so easily put to rest. She had, as has been seen, secured a sum for her parents which was more than an equivalent for the avails of her services; but she loved the old people with a true, filial love, and though, as she said and repeated to herself a thousand times, 'it was according to the course of

---

1   "It seems to me that some pranks (or escapades) are so fortuitous that the whole world forgives them." From *Dialogues et entretiens philosophiques* (1784). Voltaire wrote "adroites" (skillful), not "heureuses."

nature to leave father and mother, and cleave to the husband,'[1] yet it was most unnatural and brutish to quit them, and perhaps for ever, without their consent and blessing. She revolved this in her mind, till it was filled with sad misgivings and superstitious presages; and at last, to quiet her heart, she stole to her mother, and poured all its secrets into her bosom.

Her painful but affectionate confidence—nothing melts a woman's heart like a voluntary confidence—her confessed and true love for Denis—was there ever woman, young or old, who had not a chord to vibrate to the 'ringing of the true metal?'—her disclosure of her lover's and his master's almost incredible liberality all swayed the mother to a passive acquiescence in Justine's wishes. She gave the asked consent, and the craved blessing, and promised to reconcile her father, who was old and in his dotage, to her departure.

Success and happiness had a common effect. Justine became communicative to excess. At first, she had only sketched the outlines of the conspiracy—she now went on to detail all, to the minutest particulars, including in these the magnificent dress Mr. Pedrillo was to wear to the masquerade, and even the name of the humble artisan who was to be its fabricator.

Justine's mother listened to this plot with a strong and natural curiosity, and in her interest in its contrivance and result, and in her daughter's part in the drama, she lost every other consideration. But solitary reflection has a marvellous efficacy in adjusting the balance of justice; and when left alone, a sense of Miss Layton's violated rights dawned upon her—and being an upright and kind-hearted creature, she found that her previous knowledge of the affair was a participation in its guilt, that was like to prove an intolerable burden to her conscience. What was to be done? She was pledged to Justine—she had given her consent—that she might retract; but she had given her blessing—that was an appeal to Heaven; and according to her simple faith, as she afterwards expressed it to Gertrude, 'what was once sent up there, could not be taken back again.' She knew Miss Clarence, and was bound to her by ties of gratitude; and after much painful deliberation, she determined to obtain a private interview with her, and disclose the whole affair. This she immediately effected; first binding Miss Clarence, by a solemn promise, that whatever measures were taken to counteract the plot, they should not be such as would

---

1 Paraphrase of Genesis 2.24: "Therefore a man leaves his father and his mother and cleaves to his wife, and they become one flesh."

prevent Justine's peaceable departure with her lover, nor, if possible to avoid it, such as would publicly disgrace Pedrillo.

Miss Clarence listened to the tale with horror. That Pedrillo, a man unfettered by principle, without ties or responsibilities to the country, and stimulated by love, disappointment, and resentment, should contrive this abduction, did not surprise her; but that Emilie's father should be an accessory to the crime, implied a degree of iniquity beyond her belief. A little reflection, however, convinced her that the tale 'was o'er true.' She recollected expressions that had escaped Layton, which indicated that he was in Pedrillo's power, in a more alarming sense than would be implied by pecuniary obligations. The old woman's story explained his absenting himself from the house since her memorable interview with him in the library, and accounted for his wild and haggard appearance on the only occasion on which she had since seen him, and when he had studiously avoided her. Her own good sense, and preference of straight forward proceedings, would have led her at once to disclose her knowledge of the affair to all the parties concerned, and to counsel Emilie to give Marion, without delay, a legal right to protect her. But she was hampered by her promise to the old woman; and knowing that Pedrillo was under the inevitable necessity of leaving the country on Monday night, she hoped it was possible, as it certainly was most desirable, so to manage his relations with Layton, that there should be no explosion between them. She determined to communicate with Marion, assured that she might trust to his zeal whatever plan they adopted to secure safety to Emilie. Marion came at her summons, and never did two gray-headed counsellors deliberate more cautiously on the means to preserve a nation, than they on the best plan to be adopted; but they were many years from gray hairs, and it was not strange that a little romance should have mingled in their project.

They agreed that Layton must no longer be allowed the custody of his daughter, and Marion eloquently pleaded his right to assume the trust, and urged various and cogent reasons in favor of conveying Emilie to his mother's dignified protection. This might be effected, if Miss Clarence would give the sanction of her presence to their elopement. Gertrude's heart, at this moment, clung to New York; but she sacrificed unhesitatingly her own inclinations, and acquiesced cordially in his proposition.

After discussing and dismissing various plans, it was at last decided that Marion should employ the person who already had Pedrillo's order, to make for him a fac simile of the dress directed by Pedrillo; that farther, this person should be induced, by an adequate reward, to delay sending home Pedrillo's dress an hour beyond the stipulated time. It would perhaps be more accurate to say, that the punctuality to Marion was paid for—the breach of that virtue being in the common course of things, and therefore not liable to awaken Pedrillo's suspicions.

The precious hour thus secured was to allow the parties time enough to meet at the masquerade, and to escape from it far beyond (as they, presumptuously trusted) any further pursuit or annoyance from Pedrillo. They would fain have hit upon some scheme that would have saved the miserable parent from proceeding to an overt act in this guilty combination, but this seemed the only one by which Emilie's safety could be compatible with his preservation from the fatal consequences of a rupture with Pedrillo. Every particular was arranged before a disclosure was made to Emilie.

As soon as she recovered from her first shock of grief, and alarm, she remonstrated. Anxious as she was to escape from the toils set for her, she shrunk from being even the passive instrument of dyeing her father more deeply in sin. To the last, she continued unwilling and irresolute, and finally, and notwithstanding her lover's previous and earnest injunctions, when she saw her father's struggles, her tender heart was melted; and like all timid animals, feeling her courage rise in extremity of danger, she had, as has been seen, entreated him not to go to the masquerade, nobly willing to encounter danger herself, to save her parent from crime. But whichever way he turned, there was no possible redemption for him, and he pursued the path marked out by his evil genius to his own destruction.

After he had parted from his child, as his agonized conscience truly whispered, *for ever*, he experienced for a little time a horrible species of relief. The last and worst act was done. Resistance was over. Like the angels expelled from Heaven, he no longer contended with good spirits; he was no longer solicited by the pleadings of nature—the voice of God. A sort of torpor stole over him, and scarcely conscious of any motion of his will or body, he turned his steps towards his old haunt at the club-room. A disordered countenance was no novelty there, and attracted no attention. His associates were engaged in a game of desperate chances. He joined them. Fortune smiled upon him, but he was far beyond her influence. He looked upon the monstrous winnings he was accumulating, with the glazed unnoticing eye with which a man, walking in his sleep, regards outward objects; but the sleeper awakened on the brink of a precipice hanging over an unfathomable abyss, would not more suddenly have changed his aspect, than did Layton; his dull eye flashed, his cheeks became crimson and livid in an instant, as the door opened, and Pedrillo appeared before him, the same Spanish knight, as he believed, to whom he had one hour before resigned his daughter. Layton started up and grasped Pedrillo's arm, and would have said, "Where is she?" but the words choked him. Pedrillo shook him off as if he were a reptile. He staggered back and leaned against the wall, while Pedrillo, with the coolness of a savage who can torture and be tortured without a sign of emotion, turned to the gamblers, whose interest in their game was for the moment suspended, and detailed to them with clearness and precision the history of his relations with Layton, from their first meeting to this moment. Layton stood with his eyes fixed, motionless, almost senseless. He did not hear the but half-smothered execrations of his associates, when they were told how he had duped and defrauded them. That tale, that exposure—so dreaded—avoided at such horrible cost, fell now unheeded as household words. He did not hear the outcries at his parental treachery. He stood like a man upon a wreck, deaf to the last groans and struggles of the sinking ship; but as that man might strain his eye after a little boat in which he had embarked his child, so did his soul cling to that one treasure that might still ride out the storm that was engulfing himself. He made no denial, no protestation, no appeal; he was perfectly silent, till Pedrillo stated that Layton had finally crowned all his other treacheries with perfidy to him. "I deny it," he exclaimed, "by all that's holy, I deny it—I gave her into his possession—God help her as I speak the truth!—where is she?—in Heaven's name, Pedrillo, tell me where she is?"

Pedrillo's passions now burst forth with tenfold fury for his previous calmness. He exhausted every name of infamy, every form of anathema upon Layton, "Tell you where she is!" he concluded, "did I not, after waiting an eternity for my cursed tailor, go to the masquerade, and look and wait in vain for you?—did I not then go to your house, and receive from your servants the tale you had prepared? I returned to the masquerade and again sought you, in vain. I spoke to your wife—she professed ignorance of every thing; she dared to sport, and laugh at my demands; but I have spoken a word in her ear that has ended her sport for ever. I understand ye—you believed that *at the last* you might deceive me with impunity. You flattered yourself that I could not stay in the country after to-night—but I will stay—I will have revenge, if I perish in the fire I kindle."

Layton was at first confounded and bewildered by the appearance of Pedrillo. He firmly believed that Emilie was in his power, for that he had the testimony of his senses. He was confused by the horror of some new and unthought of form of misery or dishonor to his daughter; and it was not till after Pedrillo's repeated declarations that the truth stole upon him. "I too have been deceived!" he exclaimed, and added, in a faltering voice, "thank God!—thank God!" He attempted to raise his hand to his throbbing head, but his mind and body were exhausted. He had no strength to resist a new emotion, and he sunk under it, and fell lifeless at Pedrillo's feet.

Pedrillo spurned him as if he were a dead dog, and without replying to the exclamations that burst from every tongue, he rushed out of the house, and returned to Mrs. Layton's.

He found Mrs. Layton in the parlor, stretched on the sofa, in violent hysterics. Roscoe, who had attended her home, and whom she had entreated not to leave her, was walking up and down the room, meditating, as it might be, for such reflections are natural to a man in his position, on the singular channels in which some women's sensibilities flow; or, we rather suspect, if it could be known, and might be told, that he was thinking no more of Mrs. Layton nor of her concerns, than if she belonged to another planet.

At the sound of Pedrillo's footsteps she started from her women, who were chafing her temples and hands, and taking up an open letter that lay beside her, she threw it to him, saying, with a terrified look, "Read that, Mr. Pedrillo—you will then be convinced that I have had no concern in this unhappy affair."

The letter was from Emilie, and contained a brief communication of her intentions, and an explanation of the reasons for her clandestine departure. She had left the letter with one of the maids, with an express order that it should not be given to her mother till the next day. The girl was terrified by her mistress's nervous convulsions, and fancying that she must die if she had not present relief, and hoping the letter might prove the panacea, she produced it. The hysterics continued, for they were caused by anxieties more immediately selfish than any thing that concerned her child.

Pedrillo glanced his eye over the letter—"On the southern road"—he murmured, "by Heaven, I'll follow them!" He rushed out of the house, reinvigorated by a new purpose, which he conceived and executed with the rapidity of a man accustomed to the sudden vicissitudes of a desperate life. His men, men of proof, were still awaiting him at their assigned post. He selected the two cleverest and most daring, and mounting them and himself upon the three fleetest and strongest horses to be procured, he crossed the ferry to Powles Hook, and followed on the track of our travellers. They were two or three hours ahead of him, but he calculated rightly that after the first stage they would have no apprehensions of being pursued, and would either proceed leisurely, or stop for the night.

Pedrillo's companions did not at all relish their partnership in this wild affair. Their passions were not stimulated, nor their judgments obscured by any personal interest, and they saw clearly the rashness and folly of the enterprise. But they dared not speak out boldly. "What, Captain," asked one of them, "is your plan, if we overtake these runaways? this is no country for our trade. It will be an awkward business. Have you thought how we are to manage?"

"Yes; I have thought of every thing."

"That we have to traverse a settled country, and pass a ferry?"

"Yes; and if the country were settled with legions of devils, and the ferry led to the infernal regions, it should not stop me—listen to my plan.

"We shall probably overtake them on the road—one of you can do with a drivelling, unarmed coach-man—if there is time, and convenient place, bind him to a tree—if not, despatch him, we have no time to waste. The fellow in the carriage will make a stout resistance, but short—he is not likely to be armed, such precautions are rare, and rarely needed in this country. When he is done for"—Pedrillo paused, 'I will not,' he thought, 'give her this excuse for hating me,'—"No, my men; if it can be helped, we will shed no blood; I think ye have no appetite for that—bind *him* too,—maim him, if necessary, to secure us from pursuit."

"And is there not an extra lady to be disposed of?"

"Yes; we must take her with us."

"But, is it prudent to encumber our flying retreat with any superfluous baggage?"

"She will not encumber us—we must go in the carriage. If we leave her, she will release the men, and contrive some means to overcome us at last, for she is as ingenious as the devil."

"Well, we shall have a merry company of them, if we ever get to our good ship again. We left the priest tying Denis to a neat little damsel he brought on board this evening. But the carriage, captain; how are we to navigate a land vessel?"

This questioning and demurring was quite new to Pedrillo, used to absolute command, and implicit obedience, and he began to grow restive under it; but he prudently smothered his rising wrath, and replied, "I am something more than a mere seaman—I can manage four or six in hand, as well as the ropes of a ship. I shall put on the coachman's coat, and mount the box. And more, since you are terrified with the spectre of a ferry—know that we shall not retrace our steps, but strike across to Perth Amboy; I have ordered the boat to come through the Kills and meet us there—are you content?"

"If we were sure not to find the horses jaded?"

"And if we do! have we not here three first rates, that we could drive to Philadelphia before we should be overtaken?"

"But three are not four, captain."

"The devil, man! do you think to stop me with straws? shall we not find one of all their four, sea-worthy?"

"Well then, captain, if we overhaul them on the road, in a solitary place, before day-light, we may capture them; but supposing they are hauled up, in a snug harbor, where there are perhaps twice or thrice our number of men to aid them; will you not then tack about?"

"No, by my soul! if they are protected by a regiment of men and devils, I will not tack about—I have staked my life on this die."

"But we have not ours," muttered one of the men.

"Then stop, both of ye," cried Pedrillo, reining in his horse. They halted theirs, and he rode in front of them. "Go back," he said, "but not to the ship; you share neither danger nor spoil with me more—I promised ye, and you know I never yet have broke my faith to you—I promised ye more gold than your souls are worth—but go—seek another service, and a more generous master. I can do my work alone—a thousand cowards could not help me. I feel the strength of twenty good men in my right arm—come Triton." His little dog leaped up at his call, and received a caress. "My brave Triton! I have still one faithful follower. Let them go— better alone, than with those who fear to follow us."

He rode forward; the men fell into earnest debate; they had, at bottom, a superstitious faith in Pedrillo's invincibility. The first act of cowardice is as painful to men of daring, as an act of courage to a coward; timid as they proved in a land-service, they could not endure the thought of returning no more to the exciting dangers, and merry revels of their good ship; the reward, the gold glittered as they were relaxing their grasp of it; and finally, they spurred on their horses, overtook Pedrillo, and stammering out their apologies, they assured him they would 'do or die' in his service. He received their proffers rather as a favor to them, than important to himself; but he understood his art too well, not to keep their courage up to the sticking point, by fixing their eyes on the success and reward of their enterprise.

They had travelled more than three hours; had passed the road that strikes from the main route to Amboy, and were not very far from Brunswick, when Pedrillo began to manifest great anxiety. Their dangers multiplied, every mile they receded from Amboy. The moon was rising. He looked at his watch. "It is four o'clock;" he said, "in two hours we shall have day-light; spur on your horses, my men; our fate must be decided before the morning—ha! stop! Is not that a carriage standing before an inn?" They strained their eyes to define the distant object, and slowly approaching, they all pronounced it to be a carriage. "Were the horses attached to it?" was the next query; they were not.

"By my soul!" said Pedrillo, "I believe we have them!—softly, my men, we'll dismount and reconnoitre—here is a ruined shed, we will leave our horses here. We must approach cautiously—there are lights glimmering about the tavern—I will precede you a few yards. I can ascertain at a glance, if the persons whom I seek are here. If you hear me whistle, join me instantly—obey whatever order I shall give you—be up to your own mark, my good fellows—I ask no more."

Pedrillo slowly proceeded. In his eagerness he had forgotten that his little spaniel who, as usual, followed him, might betray him by the tinkling of his bells, and he took him in his arms, and kept his hand on them. Many a scene of danger and blood had he encountered without a variation of his pulse—many a peril imminent and desperate, without a shrinking or foreboding—but now his stout heart throbbed like a coward's—he felt that it was the moment of fate to him; almost unconsciously he slackened his pace, and midway between his companions and the inn he stopped. The fretted vault of heaven hung over him in its clear and inexpressible beauty. The moon was unobscured. If there be a *religious* light, it is that she casts over the hushed earth. Not a sound broke the all-pervading stillness. The sleep of winter reigned over nature; and yet to Pedrillo's startled conscience there was in this deep silence a loud accusing voice; on the beautiful arch of Heaven a hand-writing against him. "I am a wretch," he murmured, "an outcast—a solitary vagrant on earth, working mischief to the only being I love—and loved myself by none." The little spaniel, as if in intelligent reply to his master's words, reared his head from his bosom, and laid it fondly to his cheek—the tears gushed from Pedrillo's eye, the spontaneous response of nature to the touch of true affection. "*You* love me, Triton—poor fellow! if I perish, one creature on God's earth will cry over the moulds that cover me." The dog whimpered. He understood the feeling, if not the words, expressed in the broken tones of his master's voice—"hush, Triton, hush—we are both turning drivellers—our work waits for us;" and repressing his gracious feeling, he pressed on to the execution of his diabolical purpose.

As soon as he was near enough to the house accurately to distinguish objects, he perceived that the inn was a small edifice, which could only supply accommodation to very few persons, and therefore that he had no reason to apprehend the opposition of numbers; and on approaching nearer, he saw the figures of two females, or rather their shadows, defined on the slight curtains that obscured the windows of a small upper apartment, which was lighted by a brilliant pine fire. These persons might be, he was sure, after a moment's intense observation, they were, Emilie Layton and Miss Clarence. The room beneath was lighted too; he drew near one of its windows, and then all uncertainty ended, for there sat Marion before a comfortable fire, the relics of a supper on a table behind him, and he lost in a lover's reveries. His face expressed the glowing satisfaction of a man who has just secured his dearest object in life. A little blue silk hood of Emilie, and a pink silk handkerchief, that Pedrillo had often seen tied around her throat, hung over a chair beside her lover. Marion took the hood in his hand, held it before him, looked at it fondly, turned it round and round, rolled the strings over his finger, laid it down—took up the pink handkerchief—kissed it—folded it most accurately— kissed it again, and laid it next his heart. Young men will forgive him, and old men too, if they remember the fantastic manifestations of their youthful tenderness—but so did not Pedrillo—he wanted but this to stimulate his jealousy, and all his fearful passions to the overt act.

Our travellers had arrived at the inn, after a rapid and incessant drive, about an hour before. Marion believed they were beyond the least chance of pursuit, and fearful the ladies would be exhausted by fatigue, he had decided to stop for a few hours' repose. The inn was kept by a widow and her daughters, whose reluctance to be disturbed at so unseasonable an hour, was overcome by an extraordinary compensation, and the assurance, in answer to their objection that the only man in the establishment was absent, that the coachman would perform all the services the horses required. Accordingly, he did so; and after doing justice to a cold spare-rib the maidens set before him, and whetting their curiosity, in regard to the travellers, to the keenest edge by his oracular answers to their queries, he retired, to the only lodging that could be afforded him, in the hay-loft over his horses.

The ladies withdrew to their apartment, after first talking over their plan for the next day; the probable hour of their arrival at Philadelphia; and whether, as Marion urged, Emilie should permit him to lead her to the altar there, or as Emilie wished, and Gertrude counselled, the marriage should be deferred till their arrival at his mother's.

Marion was obliged to content himself with a rocking-chair in the parlor, as the only other unoccupied apartment was a little bed-room, to which there was no access but through the ladies' apartment.

When Gertrude and Emilie were in their own room, they seated themselves to warm their feet, and curl their hair; offices that heroines perform in common with baser metal. Gertrude had her own treasure of sweet recollections, and bright hopes, and for a moment she forgot there was any shade over Emilie's destiny. Poor Emilie sat looking intently in the fire, abstracted, and anxious. "Why so sad?" said Gertrude, kissing her.

Emilie dropped her head on her friend's lap, and burst into tears. "Oh Gertrude, I have such a load at my heart!"

"But why, now when we are beyond all danger—and you have been so tranquil and cheerful till now?"

"I know it, Gertrude; but when I am with Randolph, the present moment seems all enough and for me—I do not think of any thing absent, or past, or to come."

"And your friend has no such power over you?"

"Forgive me, dearest Gertrude—you are the very best friend in the world, and you whose friendship is so much stronger than any one's else, when you come to feel what love is, then you will understand me—I am sure I can't explain it. But now I am away from Randolph, my thoughts turn back to my poor father—to his distracted look—and at the last he was so tender to me. He must have been desperately involved with Pedrillo, or he never would have consented to sacrifice me. And my mother! Only think, Gertrude, how gay she was! how little she thought of what the morrow might bring to her! Oh Gertrude, I know——I know that evil and sorrow are before me—Hark! did you not hear a whistle?"

"Pshaw!—no, Emilie—you can fancy you hear any sound when your imagination is excited."

Emilie did not listen to Gertrude; her head was advanced like a startled fawn's—her hand on Gertrude's arm. She pressed it.

"There—again—hush——low tinkling bells like Triton's." She started to her feet——"It is Pedrillo!"

"Gracious God, save us!" screamed Gertrude, and springing to the door, she turned the key, and secured a momentary protection. The sound of the bells had been immediately succeeded by the bursting open of the entry-door, and a loud, rapid command from Pedrillo to his men, to seize Marion, who had heard the previous sounds, and was advancing to the door.

Three women, from the kitchen, rushed into the entry. Pedrillo presented a pistol, and they fled like scared pigeons. At a step he mounted the stairs, and while he was standing beating against the door, Gertrude forced Emilie, who was nearly lifeless, into the inner room, and bade her turn the lock, which she had just time to do before Pedrillo burst into the apartment. His eye glanced wildly around. "Where is she?" he exclaimed; and instantly he felt that his question was answered by Gertrude's erect figure standing like a statue, as pale and as fixed, against the door of the inner apartment. Pedrillo was struck by her lofty glance and determined air. He had never coped with heroism in such a shape, and he shrunk as he would not have done from an armed enemy. But the homage was momentary. "Suffer me to pass, Miss Clarence," he said, "compel me not to further violence."

"I would prevent you from further violence—have you forgotten every thing gentlemanly, manly, that you dare, like a common ruffian, to force yourself into our apartment?"

"I did not come here to reason or palter with you, Gertrude Clarence. I came here to right my wrongs—to have revenge for treachery; stand back, I command you, on peril of your life!"

"I will not move one inch, till you promise me"—

"Promise you!" he cried, interrupting her with a scornful shout; "do you think me a child, or fool, to be resisted by a woman!" and holding her off with one arm, he thrust his shoulder against the door, and burst it open with a single effort. Emilie was on her knees, her hands clasped, and her eyes fixed. He seized her arm. "Traitress! I have you now, and for ever!" Her hands relaxed, her arms fell, and every sign of life vanished. Gertrude received her lifeless form in her arms. "Monster! you have killed her," she shrieked.

Pedrillo laid his hand on her heart. "It beats," he said, "she will recover presently. Holloa there! my men! find the coachman instantly—order him to put to the horses; if he resists, put your pistols to his head—no delay!"

The sound of the contest below with Marion had just ceased. Surprised and unarmed as he was, he had made a brave resistance. The men, according to Pedrillo's order, had forborne to fire on him. He opposed their weapons with such implements of defence as the apartment supplied; and though repeatedly wounded, and drenched in blood, he had forced his way to the stair-case, when a new uproar broke out. Pedrillo's last command to his men was answered by the discharge of two pistols, and the instant appearance of Roscoe before him.

Pedrillo drew a dirk, and sprang towards him. Roscoe was well armed, and they met in desperate encounter. But the strife was unequal. What was Roscoe, who had never handled any weapon but the guarded foil, and that in the holiday exercise of the fencing-school, against an adversary practised and accomplished in the use of every mortal weapon, and accustomed to sudden assaults and desperate defences? Roscoe fought, it is true, with the impulse of a good cause—and so have many others, brave and noble, fought and fell. But he fought in a presence that was inspiration. His eye had met Gertrude's—had met her glance of tenderness, horror, and dread. She still supported Emilie in her arms, Emilie looking like a victim to be avenged, rather than a living creature to be saved. Pedrillo made repeated thrusts, vigorous and skilful. Roscoe parried them all; neither gained any perceptible advantage, till by a sudden turn Pedrillo disarmed him. Gertrude's eye fell, and she uttered a cry that pierced Roscoe's soul. Again she looked, and Pedrillo too was disarmed, and they had grappled. Another instant, and Pedrillo was conscious that Roscoe was gaining the ascendancy. "Here, my men!" he cried.

"There are more here!" was the answer.

"Ha!—stab them—shoot them down—spare none!" A death-cry and a heavy fall immediately followed.

"Randolph is killed!" shrieked Gertrude. The name, the words, roused Emilie like one awakened from the dead. She opened her eyes, gazed wildly around, clasped her arms around Gertrude's neck, and hid her face on her bosom. Roscoe's eye involuntarily turned towards them. Pedrillo profited by this impulse of treacherous tenderness, extricated his right arm, and drew a Spanish knife from beneath his vest—another breath, and he would have buried it in Roscoe's bosom, but his arm was palsied; drops of sweat started on his forehead, the blood in his swollen veins curdled, his crimson face changed to a livid paleness, for at that instant his father—his father, wounded and pressed by one of his men, fell across the threshold of the door. The ruffian stepped back to give force to a blow he was aiming with the muzzle of his pistol, at the old man's head, when Pedrillo shouted—"hold! stop! on your life do not harm him!"

Roscoe saw the sudden change, and felt that Pedrillo had become as impotent as a sick child in his grasp. He released him. Pedrillo staggered towards his accomplice. The fellow stared at him, as if the curse of Heaven were visible on his pallid brow. "Where is your comrade?" demanded Pedrillo.

"Dead!"

"Fly then, to Amboy. Tell our good fellows that I died no coward death. Tell them I fell by the hand of a brave man."—He plunged the knife into his own bosom, and fell at his father's feet. The man did not wait to see the issue, but unopposed, obeyed his master's last command.

The younger Flint was of the rescuing party, and had done his part bravely. When Pedrillo gave the command to shoot down the assailants, one of the ruffians aimed his pistol at the old man. Flint struck the wretch's arm. The pistol went off; but the bullet, instead of reaching its destined aim, passed through his comrade's head. The poor creature, in his dying agony extended his arms, clasped Flint and fell with him; Flint under, and nearly strangled in his death-grasp. As soon as he could extricate himself, he flew up stairs.

The work was done there. His father, regardless of his own slight wound, was assisting Roscoe to remove Pedrillo to the bed. There they laid him. His eyes were closed, and he appeared senseless. They tried in vain to staunch his wound. His little dog jumped on the bed, whimpered, cried most piteously, and alternately looked in his master's face and licked his wound.

The old man reverently clasped his hands, "Oh God," he ejaculated, "have mercy on his soul!—Forgive him, who has had no mercy on himself!" He paused, laid his hand on Pedrillo's brow, already covered with the dews of death. "Oh, my son, my son!" he continued, "would that I had died for thee! Through grace, I am ready to meet my Judge; I have an honest account to render; poor fellow, you've a fearful reckoning—robbery and murder, on land, and on sea!—Oh, God have mercy on you!"

"Father of mercies!" exclaimed the younger Flint, whose senses, till now, had been confounded, "this is not Isaac——is it?"

"Even so, Duty. I did not mean you should have known it, but I forgot myself. It is a grievous task to see a son and brother sinking into the grave with such a load of guilt upon him." The old man again clasped his hands, and raised his eyes in silent prayer.

Pedrillo unclosed his eyes, glared wildly around, then fixed them on his father, and murmured faintly, "it is too late!"

At this manifestation of life from his master, the little spaniel became louder and more earnest in his expressions of love and distress. "Poor fellow!—poor Triton!" said Pedrillo. "Will some of you, for the love of Heaven, give me a sharp pen-knife?—there is a chord that I would loosen." Young Flint opened his knife, and gave it to him. "Hold up your head, my poor fellow,"—he continued to Triton. The dog fixed his eye on his master's, and stretched his head towards him, and Pedrillo, with a sudden convulsive effort, drew the knife under his ear, and separated the carotid artery. The animal gasped, extended his tongue to lick his master's hand, and expired.

Exclamations of horror and pity burst forth. Pedrillo replied to them, with a ghastly smile, and stroking the dog, "poor Triton," he said, "you shall never be kicked nor caressed by another master—bury us in the same grave, if ye would do grace to the only prayer of a dying man."

"The only prayer!—oh, my son, my son!" cried the old man, "now—now while you have reason and breath—now implore your Maker's forgiveness!"

"And what good would it do? Is not the decree written against me, 'ye shall be judged according to your deeds?'[1] Can I restore innocence to the tempted?—can I give back the spoils to the spoiled?—can I fill again the veins of the murdered?—Oh no." His voice became choked and hollow, his features ghastly and distorted. "One word to you, sir," he continued to his father, but father he did not call him, his lips did not attempt that sacred name. "In my pocket-book are papers that will acquaint you with my affairs—you will have countless gold."

"Gold!—poor creature! I do not want it—God forbid I should ever touch your ill-gotten gold!"

"Build hospitals and churches, then—they may—hereafter—get my soul out of torment—some good men say so—but now, when revenge and hate, and passions I have not breath to name, are raging within me"—he laid his father's hand over his fluttering heart—"when hell is here, oh, how shall I escape!"

The convulsions of death spread through his frame. In his fearful struggle, he rose almost erect, and the last involuntary prayer of helpless man, burst from lips, that one moment before, refused to utter it—"Oh God! mercy! mercy!"

---

1 Reference to Romans 2.6 and Revelations 20.12.

CHAPTER XV.

"Do not hurry your finishing! Allow us some glimpses of that terra incognita—a heroine's establishment."
A YOUNG LADY'S UNPUBLISHED LETTERS.

WE were glad to drop the curtain over a scene, that we would fain spare friends and foes—the death-bed of the wicked—the saddest spectacle of human life.

Little remains to be told to those who may have graced us with their company thus far in our narrative, or to those who disdaining our chase of humble game, have just opened our book to be in at the death.

Roscoe, it may be remembered, was at Mrs. Layton's, and heard Pedrillo's declaration that he would follow the fugitive. He resolved to follow likewise. If Pedrillo really carried his mad threat into execution, he should be near to afford assistance. In any event he should be near to—Gertrude Clarence. He first went to Flint's lodgings. Flint, as he knew, would be a willing auxiliary, and in case of need a fearless and efficient one. He found our good-natured friend for once in ill-humor. He had relinquished the masquerade, a spectacle that his curiosity burned to witness, for the superior pleasure of passing the evening *tête-à-tête* with Miss Clarence. Even Flint, under the influence of the 'tricksy spirit,'[1] grew a little sentimental and shy of observation. But, lo! when after having made his toilet with unusual elaborateness, he went to Mrs. Layton's, he was told Miss Clarence was not at home. 'The course of true love never did run smooth,'[2] thought Flint, as he retraced his way sulkily to his lodging, and there he sat down to listen, with an indifference quite foreign to his lively spirit, to his father's tales of elder times. These were suddenly broken off by Roscoe's entrance.

Roscoe briefly explained his errand. Flint was all alive to the enterprise. "How fortunate you came for *me*," he whispered to Roscoe; "don't mention it—it is not proper to be told yet—I am as good as engaged to Miss Clarence."

Roscoe started; the shock was momentary, he smiled at his own credulity, and said mentally, 'My self-complacent, sanguine friend; as good as engaged—far better, *not* engaged.'

As they were departing Roscoe perceived that the elder Flint had armed himself with a bludgeon, and intended joining them.

---

1 Ariel in Shakespeare's *The Tempest*.
2 Shakespeare's *A Midsummer Night's Dream* I.i.134.

Roscoe remonstrated. The old man took him aside, and communicated his secret reasons. Roscoe feared they might be retarded by this addition to their party, but he could not refuse his assent. His fears however were groundless. The old man's energetic habits and excited feeling enabled him, though not so well mounted, to keep up with his companions; and such was the rapidity of their pursuit, that when Pedrillo dismounted, they were not a mile behind him.

Roscoe, as may be imagined, had not remained idly gazing on the dying man, while Gertrude needed his assistance. She and Emilie were conveyed to another apartment, where the women attended them with such restoratives as the house afforded, but these were not probably so efficient as the assurance—for Emilie had recovered her consciousness—that their lovers were near them and in safety.

Marion's wounds, though they witnessed that he had proved himself a true knight in the contest, were not alarming; and measures were immediately taken for the return of all parties to town, and for avoiding, as far as possible, publicity of the painful circumstances of the past night.

A coroner's inquest was summoned to sit on the body of Pedrillo. Previous to presenting the facts of the case, Roscoe inquired of the elder Flint if he meant to persevere in the resolution he had declared to his dying son. He replied that he did. "Had you not better," suggested Roscoe, "defer your ultimate decision; it will be perfectly easy to establish your claim to the property—after more deliberation your feelings may change?"

"For that very reason, my young friend, I choose to make my decision now. I have made it a rule, and it has carried me safe so far, to obey the first decision of conscience; you may reason and tamper with it, and soften it down; but take it at its word, its first bold honest word. It makes me shudder to think even of handling the poor creature's money; and I do not want it"—the old man shook his head emphatically, "I do not want it, Mr. Roscoe; my children are all good livers, and they are not brought up, excepting Duty, to be gentlemen, and the money would spoil them for any thing else. And for myself, what *could* money do for me? But may be make me *uneasy*. My journey of life is almost ended—I have more than enough to pay my expenses by the way; and would a store of wealth render me any more welcome at my *Father's mansion*? though it might make me far less willing to get there. My mind is fixed, Mr. Roscoe."

"I honor your decision, sir, and the reasons for it; but why not, as the unhappy man suggested, apply his property to charitable uses?"

"No, no, Mr. Roscoe, no; I have thought of that, but I should be ashamed to offer to the Lord what I won't soil my own hands with. What, think you, is the *spiritual* meaning of the command, that the sacrifice should be 'without spot or blemish, or any such thing.'[1] Can the fruits of such misdoings, as caused that poor fellow's last agony, be an acceptable gift for the altar of God?

"We condemn the Romanists,[2] because some among them fancy their sins may be redeemed—their souls bought out of purgatory by gifts to the church and the poor. But how much better are we, who encourage the living sinner by sanctifying the dead? There is a deep mischief in this, Mr. Roscoe, and often have I pondered on it. The rich man who fares sumptuously every day, and shuts his eye upon his starving brother; the miser that hoards his treasure even from himself; the Heaven-forsaken wretch who murders and spoils; all have their hours of misgiving, their lonely night-watches, when thoughts of death and the judgment to come harrow their souls. And how do they still the clamors of conscience? Is it not by the promise that at some *future* time—at the worst, when they come to die, they will give all to their Maker. But let their gift perish with them, and let the offering to the Lord be the fruits of an honest and obedient life. These he requires, and these are a sweet incense to Him."

Roscoe heartily expressed his admiration of the old man's sentiments. A blush that would have graced sixteen tinged his cheek as he replied, "you speak from your heart, Mr. Roscoe, I believe, but I am not clear that I deserve all you say. I, like other men, act from my feelings, and afterwards think of the reasons to bear me out. I have my own pride, and it would break my heart to own that self-murderer was my son. He was a boy when he left my roof, and he is forgotten. I am proud of my name. He was the only dishonest man, as far as I can learn, that ever answered to it."

"One more suggestion, sir," said Roscoe, "and I have done. Do your son's sentiments accord with yours?"

"Duty's? Perfectly—perfectly. An honest, independent, manly boy, is Duty. As is his name, so is he."

Their sturdy integrity, their good sense, and nice perception of true honor, secured to both father and son Roscoe's friendship for life.

So many of the facts as were essential to their verdict, were disclosed to the jury of inquest, and no more. Pedrillo's last request

---

1 Reference to 2 Peter 3.14.
2 Roman Catholics.

was respected. Triton was buried at his feet. The elder Flint remained with the body till the funeral rites were performed. Not one of the few assistants who officiated suspected the bitter feelings with which the old man bent over the grave that enclosed his first-born.

In consequence of Marion's wounds, the party was compelled to return to town by slow stages, and did not arrive till the third day after they had left it. They found Mrs. Layton's house in the greatest confusion. Layton had been brought home in a state of insensibility. When he recovered his consciousness, he dismissed his attendants, and locked his door. The servants had made repeated applications for admission, but no answer had been returned, and not a sound had proceeded from the apartment.

Mrs. Layton had shut herself in her own room, had denied access to all but her own maid, and had forbidden the servants to apply to her for orders on any subject.

In this state of affairs, our fugitives were received. Roscoe had at once a foreboding of the real condition of Layton, which he intimated to Gertrude in a whisper, and then ordered one of the servants to attend him to his master's apartment. After knocking and calling in vain, they forced open the door. Layton's body was lying on the floor; his spirit had gone to render up its dread account. An empty phial lay beside him, and a pencil and piece of paper, on which he had scrawled, 'Forgive me, my children—God have mercy on my soul!'

On examination, his affairs were found in the most disarranged condition. About half the certificates of stock, which Miss Clarence had transferred to him, were in his pocket-book, within an envelope, on which was written, 'The enclosed to be delivered to Miss Clarence, to whom, though bearing my name, they really belong.' Miss Clarence, on being applied to, declined to assume any farther control of the property than to vest it in the hands of trustees, for Mr. Layton's children, with a stipulation that a portion of the income should be at the disposition of his widow.

The grave interposed its shield at a fortunate moment for poor Layton. His gaming associates were not without a certain sense of honor which bound them to preserve inviolate the secrets of their club; and Pedrillo's disclosure was never made public. Thus Emilie was sheltered from a knowledge of her father's disgrace; and though she sorrowed long and bitterly, she had every solace that love and friendship could supply.

Our friend Duty was gradually awakened to the real state of his matrimonial prospects. He had a genuine admiration for Miss

Clarence, and the extinction of his o'er-grasping hopes was a serious shock to him. For the first time in his life, his sparkling eyes were dimmed with sentimental tears; but he was not of a temper to break his heart in a love affair, and gradually such little consolations insinuated themselves into his mind, as that 'Miss Clarence was probably in love with Gerald Roscoe before she ever saw him'—'That as Fate had so ordered it, that he could not himself obtain her, he would rather see her the wife of Roscoe, than of any other man on earth'—'That next in value to her love was her cordial friendship'—and finally, 'That if, as he verily believed, Gertrude Clarence had no equal, why should he not set about looking out for a *second best?*'

We do not know that we can conclude more satisfactorily, than by two authentic letters from the principal personages of our narrative, the one written during the summer following the last events we have recorded, and the other some months later, when time had matured and somewhat mellowed the feelings we have described. Both were addressed to Miss Marion—the first from Emilie.

"To Miss Marion.

"*Clarenceville, June, 18—.*
"My dear *sister*—Last Tuesday evening invested me with the right to address you by this endearing name; but no rights can add to the gratitude and affection your Emilie has long borne to you.

"We were to have had a private wedding—Gertrude desired it, and I, particularly on account of my mourning; but Mr. Clarence said there should be no sign of sadness on so joyful an occasion as the union of four loving and true hearts, and that the pleasure of a wedding festival to Gertrude's country friends, was worth some sacrifice on our parts; and so we consented—could we help it?—to his wishes. The doors were thrown open, and all Clarenceville was present, old and young, rich and poor, to see their friend, benefactress, and queen, united to a man whom they confess to be worthy of her.

"Before we went into the drawing-room, we were all, (by all I mean Gertrude, and Mr. Roscoe, and his mother—a celestial woman, Augusta—and Randolph, and myself,) we were all in the library. Mr. Clarence came in with his hands full of papers. 'You must forgive me, my young friends,' he said, 'for remembering, at this interesting moment, your worldly concerns—you, I presume, have entirely forgotten them. You and I, my dear Gerald, in pecuniary affairs, are hence forth equal partners.' He put into Mr.

Roscoe's hands papers which transferred to him the half of his fortune. Roscoe looked a little disconcerted; but he soon recovered himself, and replied, in his own frank and pleasant manner, 'This gift, sir,' and he kissed Gertrude's hand, 'has exhausted my gratitude; I cannot even make a return of words for an inferior proof of your generosity.'

"'Generosity! my dear fellow,' said Mr. Clarence, 'you know not with what joy I devolve half the burden and responsibility of my wealth upon you—with what gratitude I regard the benign Providence that has granted the dearest wish of my heart, in giving me a friend on whom I may repose this trust.'

"'As a trust then, sir,' replied Roscoe, 'I receive it, and, by the grace of God, I will never dishonor your confidence.'

"Randolph afterwards said, that this was a manner of giving and receiving, becoming rational and elevated beings, and he could not but contrast it with the usual quarrels about settlements—with the jealousy and parsimony towards sons-in-law on the one side, and on the other, the anxious reckoning of the father's wealth, and calculation of the chances of his life. For my part, dear Augusta, I did not think, I only *felt*, and had I not reason? for at the next moment Mr. Clarence turned to me—'And you, my little Emilie, my other child,' he said, 'I am to give you away too—it would be a shame to give you empty-handed, though Marion looks as if he felt now, and would for ever,

'That kindness, sweet kindness, in the fond, sparkling e'e,
'Has lustre outshining the diamond to me.'[1]

"'Does not the verse run so? my memory may halt, but not my love, for,' he added, giving me a check for twenty thousand dollars, 'you, Emilie, like the youngest daughters in fairy tales, have the best portion, for such in my opinion is a mere competence.'

"I did not say one word. I threw my arms around his neck, and he kissed off my tears. I thought of my poor father—God forgive me for comparing him with Mr. Clarence at that moment.

"My letter would exceed all bounds, if I were to give you half the particulars of the evening. The drawing-rooms were hung with wreaths of flowers. The gardener had not spared his finest plants; the lawn was illuminated with colored lamps, and a band of music was placed on the piazza. The children were merry and noisy, but the rest of the company were thoughtful—they felt that the

---

1 From "Yon Wild Mossy Mountain" (1786) by Burns.

wedding was a prelude to parting with Gertrude; and she is so beloved and honored here! 'Not a creature ever crossed your path,' said one of her old friends to her, 'but was the better or the happier for it.' Do you not believe, my dear sister, that the duties she has so well performed have risen as incense to Heaven, to descend again in blessings on her new home?[1]

"Randolph, saucy fellow! has just bent over my shoulder, and read my letter. 'Not one word of your husband!' he says. Oh Augusta, men do not seem to know that we are not forward to express what we feel most deeply. I am no great writer, to be sure; but if I were equal to you, or Gertrude, I could not find language to express what I feel for my husband.[2] 'There, Mr. Randolph, read that, if you like.'

"You do not yet know how much Gertrude has done for us. Poor mama was too much depressed to make any exertion. Gertrude wished her to take a small house, and devote herself to the education of my sisters. You know mama is very accomplished, but she said she had a natural antipathy to instruction—her mind would prey upon itself, &c. &c. So it was decided that my brothers should be sent to a boarding-school in Massachusetts, and my sisters should live with me. Randolph and I both begged mama to make our house hers, but she preferred a boarding-house, and she has a room at Madame Pignot's, beautifully arranged. I was glad to see she could interest herself in this.

---

1 In the 1849 edition, Sedgwick inserts the following paragraph at this point: Dear Gertrude! When first I knew her, I did not think her handsome, and now I do not think she is beautiful; but the thoughts that beam from her eyes, and the kind words that drop from her lips, the true jewels of the fairy tale, infuse into her face the very essence of beauty. There is light—happiness in every look and movement. Good people tell us we must not expect happiness in this life—they know, I suppose; but I am sure that content and cheerfulness, two smiling cherubs, will always hover round her. How can it be otherwise? She has every thing without and within—she has secured the infinite blessing of Gerald Roscoe's affection. She has escaped the perils of *a fortune*. To her mind it is rather sadly associated with the trials of her life, and she holds it, and all that she possesses, her husband's love, her own faculties, meekly, and as a trust from her Father in Heaven.

2 In the 1849 edition, Sedgwick adds to this sentence: ... I could not find language to express what I feel for my husband, what I expect from married life, shared with him whom I love and honor will all my heart, and therefore found it very easy to promise to obey him!——

"My tenderest love to your and *my* mother. Tell her, that but for some sad, sad recollections, I should be perfectly happy. But was not my morning fearfully clouded? God grant that my future life may prove that the gracious influences of Heaven were distilled from that dark cloud, and then, my dear sister, I shall not be unworthy of my happy destiny, and of that illustrious name, which I now for the first time sign.

"Yours truly,
"EMILIE *MARION*."[1]

"To Miss Marion.
"*New York, Feb. 18—*.
"My dear friend—You conclude your last letter with a request that I will write you a 'womanish epistle, full of feminine details; such as, what house I live in, how it is furnished and garnished, whom I visit, &c. &c.' I have quoted the passage, that if I answer it *à la lettre*, you may remember that you called forth my egotism. Mr. Roscoe was so fortunate as to be able to repurchase his father's house, a fine old family mansion, not far from our beautiful battery, and commanding a view of our animated bay, which, if equalled, we the untravelled believe is not surpassed, by the happiest combinations of land and water on this fair earth. The house is somewhat old-fashioned, but we have given it the most modern and convenient arrangement of which it was susceptible, without an entire and therefore, as we think, sacrilegious alteration.

"Is it altogether our misfortune, or in some degree our fault, that we have so few transmitted homes? As far as this is the result of the equal partition of estates in our country, and in our city, particularly, of the influx of population and the fluctuation of fortune, we cannot help it; but, certainly as far as it is our own fault, we should lament and correct it. Have we not a passion for change and novelty? Whence comes, in this city, our most pernicious and prevailing custom of an annual remove? the terrors of 'May day,' when the household gods seem changed into demons, and 'domestic happiness' to be no longer, as the poet makes it, exempt from the general wreck of Adam's fall. You are a phrenologist, my dear Augusta—is the bump of locality found on the American skull?

"I have known a father's house abandoned, because the apartments could not be made to communicate by folding-doors! or

---

1 Sedgwick ends the 1849 edition at this point, omitting entirely the letter from Gertrude to Augusta Marion that closes the 1830 and this edition.

perhaps the ceilings were a foot too low! those ceilings that have echoed the merry shout of childhood, the glad welcome, the farewell blessing, and the loud, home, heartfelt laugh. Our home should be loved as the ancient Jew loved Jerusalem—as he loved his temple—the 'holy and the beautiful house' he so tenderly lamented. It is the temple of the domestic affections; the altar on which the freest and most beautiful gifts are laid; the spot that, with all its accumulating associations, its holy spell of sacred recollections and sweet hopes, has no parallel on earth. My dear Augusta, I forbear—I perceive I am running into sentiment on this subject, and I have already said quite enough to convince you that I am satisfied with my location.

"Our furniture is the next topic on your list. I shall give you the principle on which we have proceeded; this is not quite so *womanish* as details, but those I defer for your own observation. We have not emulated the glittering and sumptuous drawing-rooms of our wealthy citizens, and we have carefully avoided (I have often seen this disparity) a bare and sordid aspect in the upper apartments. All our sacrifices have been to the household worthies who preside over hospitality; our lodging-rooms have their contiguous dressing-rooms, are warmed by heated air, and each story has its bathing-room.

"Our library is a fine apartment on the second floor. The rebuking genius of economy has not presumed to pass its threshold. It is richly furnished with the classics in English, French, German, Italian, and Spanish, and all of the best editions. No diamond type[1] to wear out young eyes, and vex old ones. The books are accompanied by their appropriate auxiliaries, globes, maps, atlases, prints, &c. The room is decorated with a few busts of those who are regarded in all enlightened countries as the noblest personifications of genius, Dante, Cervantes, Fenelon, Shakespeare, and Bacon.[2] One fine portrait is placed in the most conspicuous position over the fire-place—the *hearth-stone*—as emblematic of the right of the original to preside over the charities and felicities of home, as well as to be the ruling spirit of an apartment consecrated to the Muses. Whose is it? do you ask, Augusta? Whose should it be but his, who is *par excellence*[3] the genius of the age, the

---

1 A very small size of print type.
2 Dante Alighieri; Miguel de Cervantes (Spanish, 1547-1616); François de Salignac de la Mothe-Fénelon (French, 1651-1715); William Shakespeare; Francis Bacon.
3 Above all.

benefactor of our homes?—who by his enchantments has fraught more hours with pure and profitable pleasure than any writer of any age;—who has lighted up the dim eye of sickness—who has rejuvenated the old, awakened in them, the sleeping sympathies and affections of their youth, and filled

'Each blank in faithless memory's void;'[1]

who has unfolded the ample page of knowledge to the boy, and made his pulse throb with generous purpose and high aspiration—who has kindled in all our hearts a loyal, a more than loyal, a filial love; so that we all

'Do stand on tiptoe when his name is named.'[2]

Praise and glory on his head! Long—long may it tower above his fellows, and at last, when reverently laid beside the dust of his fathers, be honored and wept.

"How shall I descend, dear Augusta, from such a theme to the appointed topics of my letter—curtains and carpets, plate and china? I cannot—take it for granted, that the whole concern is in tolerable taste—that we, in our embellishments have selected those that develope and elevate the taste, and are its enduring gratifications—that we have *par exêmple*[3] some fine statuary, and beautifully sculptured Italian vases. Gerald has applied to Leslie[4] for a pair of his exquisite cabinet pictures. I trust the suspicion that he is reluctant to send his productions to this country, is unfounded; for though we are not yet rich enough to afford patronage to the fine arts, we are not without the capacity to admire and be improved by them; and it seems to me, that an artist should be proud to lay the fruits of his genius on the altar of that country, where it was first developed, even though the sacrifice should be unappreciated.

"Poor Seton! his Trenton-picture hangs in my own room, an affecting memorial of his genius and misfortunes—an altar-piece, that calls forth sacred recollections and hopes. To Seton, I owe

---

1 From Scott's "The Lay of the Last Minstrel." The portrait is of Scott.
2 Shakespeare's *Henry V* IV.iii.41-42: "He that outlives this day, and comes safe home, / Will stand a-tiptoe when this day is nam'd."
3 For example (French).
4 Charles Robert Leslie (1794-1859), painter born in England to American parents, who spent his childhood in Philadelphia but emigrated to England to study painting and settled there.

all the taste I may have in the fine arts, and probably much of the lively interest I feel in our native artists—an interest of which I have not been sparing in my demonstrations, for I have family portraits by our masters in that department, Copley, Stuart, Sully, &c., a variety of illustrations of our own scenery by our rising artists, and a beautiful picture of our sweet Emilie by Ingham, an American by adoption[1]—the painter has grouped her younger sisters gracefully about her, and with his usual eminent success, has transfused the soft and living tints of youth and beauty to the canvass, has shown his unequalled skill in drapery, and imparted such sparkling and living lustre to the eyes, that you could almost believe he had stolen Prometheus' fire,[2] and that the spirit beamed from its 'throne of light.'

"Dear Emilie! she deserves to personify the virtues of an elder sister. With beauty that is never seen without being admired, she avoids observation, and seems to have no ambition beyond that of performing well and quietly her domestic duties—a woman's gentle and best ambition, is it not? Your brother certainly thinks so, for he still regards her (and will always, I doubt not) with the intense devotion of one, who, through much tribulation, has obtained an unparalleled treasure.

"Poor Mrs. Layton is a prey to ennui. The death of her husband, and its frightful circumstances, for a while appalled her. She went regularly to church, and frequented evening lectures, and seemed to be undergoing a transformation, not uncommon, from a woman of the world to a devotee; but it proved a fever heat, not the gentle salutary warmth of religion, and it has passed away. Our highest moralists tell us never to despair of humanity, and we should not; but when were all-engrossing selfishness, frivolous habits, and a thirst for admiration and coquetry, indulged for thirty years; when were they cured but by the hard necessities of age? Thank Heaven, our country is not a theatre for such women as Mrs. Layton. She is isolated and fettered by our tame domestic habits—as much out of place as a jewel on a yeoman's finger, or a syllabub[3] on his table. She might have run a more brilliant career

---

1   Painters John Singleton Copley (American, 1738-1815); Gilbert Stuart (American, 1755-1828), specializing in portraits; Thomas Sully (English-born American, 1783-1872), specializing in portraits; Charles Cromwell Ingham (Irish-born American, 1796-1863), specializing in portraits, including one of Catharine Maria Sedgwick.

2   According to Greek mythology, Prometheus stole the sacred fire from the gods and gave it to humankind.

3   Traditional English dessert made of cream and wine.

in the more polished, and more corrupt circles of Europe, but *to be suspected*, is as fatal to an American woman, as it could have been to Cæsar's wife.[1]

"I am eagerly listening for the voice of spring, for you know, at the first gushing of the waters, at the very first passage of the steam-boats, you are to be with us. I expect to surprise you, who have received your impressions of New York society, from my distorted views of it while I was at Mrs. Layton's, with the delightful circles we assemble at our own house. In a city of the multifarious character of New York, it is a difficult art to select our society, a most critical navigation to steer clear of offending acquaintance you do not want, and to secure without forwardness, those you covet. However, the good to be obtained, fine society, the very first of social, intellectual luxuries, is worth effort. Fortunately for us, our position gives us the privilege of selection, and we make it without reference to any thing but the character of our guests. Those meet under our roof, who never meet elsewhere—persons of the first fashion, professional laborious toilers, and the secluded men of genius.

"Julia Mayo is our *prima donna*; but among all my female friends, and there are several talented in divers ways, not one is more fascinating to me, than Angelique Abéille, a little French girl, whose history I will some day tell you. She plays and sings exquisitely, and is the charm of our musical parties.

"Do not imagine, my dear friend, that I have be come a devotee to society, even though it be of the most elevated and attractive character. No, I am too rich in my own private blessings—in the character and affections of my husband—in the society of Gerald's admirable mother, and that of my dear father, to be in any danger of forgetting that the family circle is the inner temple, where our highest gifts and best affections must be consecrated, and will be rewarded. And in all my prosperity, it is my earnest desire and purpose, to preserve my mind from undue elation—to perform the serious unostentatious duties of a Christian woman—to walk humbly with my God.

"My letter has ended seriously, my dear Augusta; but how could I cast my eye over the whole of my prosperous condition,

---

1   The second wife of Julius Cæsar, Pompeia was suspected of adultery, for which Cæsar divorced her, stating that his wife "must be above any suspicion." Suspicions of Mrs. Layton's character or behavior could also have destroyed her social position, as the efforts to protect the Layton family's reputation, before and after Layton's death, suggest.

without serious thoughts of the responsibilities, the uncertainties; and the brevity of life?—without an emotion of deep gratitude to Him, who has given me wealth, and saved me from its perils, and who has enriched me with that, far better, and best of all earthly blessings, the affections of one, on whose truth and virtue I may repose without fear of any change—because I know *they* will not change.

"Am I boasting to my single friend? no—who shall dare to boast to one, who gives such grace and loveliness to singleness?— whose virtues do not need the highest stimulants and rewards; for that the *highest* belongs to *married* life, you must forgive me for believing, since I am (and always affectionately your friend,)

"GERTRUDE *ROSCOE*."

THE END.

Appendix A: The American Novel of Manners and Transatlantic Literary Culture

1. From William Cullen Bryant's Review of *Redwood*, *The North American Review* 20 (April 1825): 245-72

[Poet William Cullen Bryant (1794-1898) was a classmate of Catharine Sedgwick's brother Charles at Williams College. Bryant moved to the Berkshires in 1820 to practice law in Great Barrington. In 1824, Catharine's brothers Henry and Robert invited him to visit New York and to consider his professional prospects there. In May 1825, he moved to New York to become editor of the *New-York Review* and *Athenaeum Magazine*. In 1826, he became assistant editor of the *New-York Evening Post*, of which he later became editor in chief and publisher. We have omitted most of Bryant's analysis of the plot and characters of *Redwood*, reproducing instead his general comments on American manners as subject matter for fiction.]

This is a story of domestic life, the portraiture of what passes by our firesides and in our streets, in the calm of the country, and amidst a prosperous and well ordered community. The writer ... has not availed herself of the more obvious and abundant sources of interest, which would naturally suggest themselves to the author of a fictitious history, the scene of which should be laid in the United States. She has not gone back to the infancy of our country, to set before us the fearless and hardy men, who made the first lodgment in its vast forests, men in whose characters is to be found the favorite material of the novelist, great virtues mingled with many errors, the strange land to which they had come, and its unknown dangers, and the savage tribes by whom they were surrounded, to whose kindness they owed so much, and from whose enmity they suffered so severely. Nor does the thread of her narrative lead us through those early feuds between the different colonies of North America, who brought with them and kept alive, in their settlements, the animosities of the nations from whom they proceeded, and, in the midst of all their hardships and sufferings, contended about the division of the wilderness, with a fierceness and an obstinacy exasperated by the difference in the characters of those who composed them. Nor has the writer made any use of the incidents of our great national struggle for independence, at once so calamitous and so glorious, the time of splendid virtues and great sufferings, the war which separated friends, and divided families, and revived the half laid spirit of bloodshed in the uncivilised races about us, and called to our shores so many military adventurers to fight under the standard of Britain, and so many generous volunteers in the cause of humanity and liberty to combat under ours. She has passed by all these periods and situations, so tempting to the writer of fictitious history, so pregnant with interest and teeming with adventure, to make a more hazardous experiment of her powers.[1] She has come down to the very days in which we live, to quiet times and familiar manners, and has laid the scene of her narrative in the most ancient and tranquil parts of the country; presenting us not merely with the picture of what she has imagined, but with the copy of what she has observed....

On more than one occasion, we have already given somewhat at large our opinion of the fertility of our country, and its history, in the materials of romance. If our reasonings needed any support from successful examples of that kind of writing, as a single fact is worth a volume of ingenious theorising, we have had the triumph of seeing them confirmed beyond all controversy, by the works of a popular American author, who has shown the literary world into what beautiful creations those materials may be wrought.[2] In like manner, we look upon the specimen before us as a conclusive argument, that the writers of works of fiction, of which the scene is laid in familiar and domestic life, have a rich and varied field before them in the United States. Indeed, the opinion on this subject, which, till lately, prevailed pretty extensively among us, that works of this kind, descriptive of the manners of our countrymen, could not succeed, never seemed to us to rest on a very solid foundation. It was rather a sweeping inference drawn from the fact, that no highly meritorious work of the kind had appeared, and the most satisfactory and comfortable way of accounting for this, was to assert, that no such could be written. But it is not always safe to predict what a writer of genius will make of a given subject....Who then will undertake to say, that the hand of genius may not pencil off a few scenes, acted in our own vast country, and amidst our large population, that shall interest and delight the world?

It is a native writer only that must or can do this. It is he that must show how the infinite diversities of human character are yet further varied, by causes that exist in our own country, exhibit our peculiar modes of thinking and action, and mark the effect of these upon individual

---

1   Sedgwick soon took on just such historical subjects in her first short story, "The Catholic Iroquois" (1825), in *Hope Leslie* (1827), *The Linwoods* (1835), and several more short stories.

2   By 1824, James Fenimore Cooper had published several popular American historical romances, *The Spy* (1821), *The Pioneers* (1823), and *The Pilot* (1823).

fortunes and happiness. A foreigner is manifestly incompetent to the task; his observation would rest only upon the more general and obvious traits of our national character, a thousand delicate shades of manner would escape his notice, many interesting peculiarities would never come to his knowledge, and many more he would misapprehend. It is only on his native soil, that the author of such works can feel himself on safe and firm ground, that he can move confidently and fearlessly, and put forth the whole strength of his powers without risk of failure. His delineations of character and action, if executed with ability, will have a raciness and freshness about them, which will attest their fidelity, the secret charm, which belongs to truth and nature, and with which even the finest genius cannot invest a system, of adscititious and imaginary manners. It is this quality, which recommends them powerfully to the sympathy and interest even of those, who are unacquainted with the original from which they are drawn, and makes such pictures from such hands so delightful and captivating to the foreigner. By superadding, to the novelty of the manners described, the interest of a narrative, they create a sort of illusion, which places him in the midst of the country where the action of the piece is going on. He beholds the scenery of a distant land, hears its inhabitants conversing about their own concerns in their own dialect, finds himself in the bosom of its families, is made the depository of their secrets, and the observer of their fortunes, and becomes an inmate of their firesides without stirring from his own. Thus it is that American novels are eagerly read in Great Britain, and novels descriptive of English and Scottish manners as eagerly read in America.

It has been objected, that the habits of our countrymen are too active and practical; that they are too universally and continually engrossed by the cares and occupations of business to have leisure for that intrigue, those plottings and counterplottings, which are necessary to give a sufficient degree of action and eventfulness to the novel of real life. It is said that we need for this purpose a class of men, whose condition in life places them above the necessity of active exertion, and who are driven to the practice of intrigue, because they have nothing else to do. It remains, however, to be proved that any considerable portion of this ingredient is necessary in the composition of a successful novel. To require that it should be made up of nothing better than the manœuvres of those, whose only employment is to glitter at places of public resort, to follow a perpetual round of amusements, and to form plans to outshine, thwart, and vex each other, is confining the writer to a narrow and most barren circle. It is requiring an undue proportion of heartlessness, selfishness, and vice in his pictures of society. It is compelling him to go out of the wholesome atmosphere of those classes, where the passions and affections have their most salutary and natural play, and employ his observations on that where they are most perverted, sophisticated, and corrupt. But will it be seriously contended, that he can have no other resource but the rivalries and machinations of the idle, the frivolous, and the dissolute, to keep the reader from yawning over his pictures? Will it be urged that no striking and interesting incidents can come to pass without their miserable aid? If our country be not the country of intrigue, it is at least the country of enterprise; and nowhere are the great objects that worthily interest the passions, and call forth the exertions of men, pursued with more devotion and perseverance....

[I]f the writer of fictitious history does not find all the variety he wishes in the various kinds of our population, descended, in different parts of our country, from ancestors of different nations, and yet preserving innumerable and indubitable tokens of their origin, if the freedom with which every man is suffered to take his own way, in all things not affecting the peace and good order of society, does not furnish him with a sufficient diversity of characters, employments, and modes of life, he has yet other resources. He may bring into his plots men, whose characters and manners were formed by the institutions and modes of society in the nations beyond the Atlantic, and he may describe them faithfully, as things which he has observed and studied. If he is not satisfied with indigenous virtue, he may take for the model of his characters men of whom the old world is not worthy, and whom it has cast out from its bosom. If domestic villany be not dark enough for his pictures, here are fugitives from the justice of Europe come to prowl in America. If the coxcombs of our own country are not sufficiently exquisite, affected, and absurd, here are plenty of silken fops from the capitals of foreign kingdoms. If he finds himself in need of a class of men more stupid and degraded, than are to be found among the natives of the United States, here are crowds of the wretched peasantry of Great Britain and Germany, flying for refuge from intolerable suffering, in every vessel that comes to our shores. Hither also resort numbers of that order of men who, in foreign countries, are called the middling class, the most valuable part of the communities they leave, to enjoy a moderate affluence, where the abuses and exactions of a distempered system of government cannot reach them, to degrade them to the condition of the peasantry....

The peculiarities in the manners and character of our countrymen, have too long been connected with ideas merely low and ludicrous. We complain of our English neighbors for holding them up as objects simply ridiculous and laughable, but it is by no means certain that we have not encouraged them by our example. It is time, however, that they were redeemed from these gross and degrading associations. It is time that they should be mentioned, as they deserve to be, with something else than a sneer, and that a feeling of respect should mingle with the smile they occasion. We are happy to see the author of this work connecting them, as we find them connected in real life, with much that is ennobling and elevated, with traits of sagacity, benevolence, moral courage and magnanimity. These are qualities, which by no means impair any comic effect those peculiarities may have; they rather relieve and heighten it. They transform it from mere buffoonery to the finest humor. When this is done, something is done to exalt our national reputation abroad, and to improve our national character at home. It is also a sort of public benefit, to show what copious and valuable materials the private lives and daily habits of our countrymen offer to the writer of genius. It is as if one were to discover to us rich ores and gems lying in the common earth about us....

2. From the Correspondence of Rachel Mordecai Lazarus, Maria Edgeworth, and Catharine Sedgwick, 1824-27

[In 1815, Rachel Mordecai (later Lazarus) (1788-1838), a young Jewish schoolteacher from South Carolina, wrote to Anglo-Irish novelist Maria Edgeworth (1768-1849) to protest Edgeworth's stereotypical depictions of Jews in her fiction. Their correspondence lasted for decades. Catharine Sedgwick and her fiction became the subject of comment in their correspondence in the mid-1820s, and Lazarus acted as an intermediary between Sedgwick and Edgeworth, conveying Edgeworth's sharp critique of Sedgwick's depiction of manners, fashion, and British characters in her fiction.[1]]

Lazarus to Edgeworth, 21 October 1824

When I had last the pleasure of addressing you,[2] I mentioned "Redwood" an American novel which had then just appeared; ere this you have probably seen the work, perhaps received a copy from the author, yet I cannot deny myself the pleasure of presenting a book which merits the high encomium of being worthy the acceptance of Miss Edgeworth. I have read it with great pleasure and think that for purity of style, lively and accurate description, and correct delineation as well as originality of character, it deserves to be ranked among the first rate novels of the day. The characteristic difference between the manners of the Southern and Eastern states is happily and not too glaringly marked;

---

1   The correspondence between Lazarus and Edgeworth is excerpted from Edgar E. MacDonald, *The Education of the Heart: The Correspondence of Rachel Mordecai Lazarus and Maria Edgeworth* (Chapel Hill: U of North Carolina P, 1977). Lazarus's manuscript letter to CMS is found in the Catharine Maria Sedgwick Papers (CMS Papers), II.1.6, Massachusetts Historical Society, Boston.

2   In a letter dated 17 July 1824.

we are enabled to discern, not compelled to observe it. In justice to Virginia I must however remark that the slave picture is coloured far beyond what reality would authorise.[1] The condition of our slaves both in this and the sister states is far less miserable than that of the poorer classes of white people. They are comfortably maintained and with very few exceptions kindly treated. So long as the benefits of education are denied them, their state must be abject, and the necessity of retaining them is by all admitted to be an evil tho' at present an unavoidable one; but their usually cheerful demeanor argues well for the humanity of their masters....

Edgeworth to Lazarus, 2 May 1825

Redwood has entertained us very much. I am so much flattered by the manner in which my writings are alluded to in this book that I can hardly suppose I am [an] unprejudiced judge. But it appears to me a work of superior talent, far greater than even the New England tale gave me reason to expect. The character of Aunt Deborah is first rate, in Scott's best manner yet not an imitation of Scott.[2] It is to America what Scott's characters are to Scotland, valuable as original pictures with enough of individual peculiarity to be interesting and to give the feeling of reality and life as portraits, sufficient also of general characteristics to give them the philosophical merit of pourtraying a class. It is of great consequence to sketch and record such characters in America because in another half century they will have passed away and it would require more than the power of the master genius to raise them from the dead. Because your America is not like Scotland a land of traditions, it has little influence over our minds by early associations, great by actual curiosity. The present not the past must therefore be the American writer's domain. If you have any means of communication with this author I wish you could convey to her this idea if you think it just. There is another bit of advice I should wish to give; tho' it may not be palatable it may be salutary. It is to attempt European character only sparingly. There are a vast host of English critics with eyes and stings sharpened by competition and rivalry and party spirit who will detect the slightest deviation from truth in the drawing or even from fashion in the appearance of such characters. Unfavorable and unjust deductions would thence be drawn even against the truth and merit of

---

1   The Redwood family of the novel's title is from Virginia, and Mr. Redwood early in the novel tells the story of an abused slave, Africk.

2   Deborah Lenox, an unconventional spinster who speaks in Yankee dialect, was a favorite of readers. Edgeworth likely thought she resembled Jeanie Deans, a rustic unmarried Scotswoman in Walter Scott's *The Heart of Midlothian* (1818).

the American characters. The shades of fashion in minute particulars which it is almost impossible for a transatlantic writer to catch, evanescent as they are, influence irremediably London opinions. Many an inferior judgment will pass sentence in the higher London circles, sentence of *vulgarity*, equivalent to sentence of death on Redwood because one female character which aims at being fashionable is open to the criticism of "every prating she."

Lazarus to Sedgwick, 16 July 1826

Madam,

It is not without some degree of diffidence that I prepare to address the intelligent & deservedly celebrated author of "Redwood," a work which secondary to no novel of even the present day, is acknowledged with pride on this side of the Atlantick, & read with delight on the other. But it is not to add my mite to the general expression of applause that I have taken the liberty, the praise of an unknown individual, however warm & sincere, could be of little value, & would not excuse the vanity implied in deeming it of sufficient importance to be thus expressed, or authorise the presumption of a self-introduction to the notice of Miss Sedgwick. For several years past, it has been my happiness to be honoured by a correspondence with Miss Edgeworth, it is her sentiments that I am desirous to convey, & to Miss Edgeworth, whose talents & whose worth, beyond encomium, are highly prized by Miss Sedgwick as by me, I may safely trust to plead my apology.

Immediately after the publication of "Redwood," I sent this distinguished & excellent lady a copy, & long since received a letter from her, alluding to one previously written, in which her opinion of that work had been expressed. This letter by some ill fortune, was detained first in London, & then in Philadelphia & tho' bearing a date May 2d 1825, only reached me last week. I copy from it this paragraph.—[Lazarus copied the relevant paragraph from Edgeworth's letter here.] I will not apologise for the length of this quotation because I do not think that any part of it will be otherwise than acceptable. Miss E is a warm & candid admirer of merit in American, as in English literature, & it is delightful to those who prize her character as a woman even more if possible than her talents as an author, to remark her perfect freedom from all the envy & littleness of authorship: evidenced by her readiness in discerning, & her warmth in commending merit wherever it appears. I cannot close this letter without expressing a hope that Miss S will persevere in her useful & admirable labours, & contribute still further to enrich our native literature—permit me also to solicit that in the rank of her warmest admirers she will be pleased to place

her very obedient Servant
R Lazaraus[1]

Lazarus to Edgeworth, 6 January 1827

I mentioned in my last[2] that I had written to Miss Sedgwick and made an extract from your letter, to which the following is her reply: "The sentiments expressed by Miss Edgeworth, which you have so kindly transmitted to me, are among the best rewards of past exertion, and cherished as they will be, I trust they may give an impulse to future efforts. I need such encouragements, for I often feel depressed by a just sense of vast inferiority, both of natural and acquired power, to a multitude of those who are devoting their talents to the amusement and instruction of the reading world. I am much impressed with the just-ness of Miss Edgeworth's remarks, in relation to the happiest subjects for American novel-writers. Some of my most intelligent friends op-pose this opinion and maintain that there are peculiarities in our early history, which furnish the best materials for the fabric of a romance. There may be, but it requires the touch of a magician to body forth the shadows of the past, while an inferior artist may copy living and visible forms." Miss Sedgwick sent me with this letter "The Deformed Boy," her last publication; it is a pathetick little story, founded on fact, and related with a touching simplicity of style. It was written for the benefit of a Benevolent Society....[3]

3. From Catharine Sedgwick's Journal Describing Society at Saratoga Springs (1827)[4]

[Catharine Sedgwick irregularly kept a journal. The following excerpt is an account of a summer trip to the fashionable resort of Saratoga Springs, New York, in 1827. This was not Sedgwick's first trip to the

---

1   A note in Sedgwick's hand appears on the letter: Mrs Rebecca Lazarus—July 16 1826—This letter contains an abstract from Miss Edgeworth—her opinion of Redwood—Mrs L is the lady who wrote the remonstrance to Miss Edge-worth which induced that lady to write the Tale designed as an amende honor-able to the Jews.
2   A letter dated 20 July 1826.
3 . Sedgwick's children's tale *The Deformed Boy* was published under the auspices of the Publishing Fund, a Boston Unitarian enterprise, in 1826.
4   CMS Papers, I.11.6. A brief fragment of this entry appears in Mary Kelley, ed., *The Power of Her Sympathy: The Autobiography and Journal of Catharine Sedgwick* (Boston: Massachusetts Historical Society, 1993), 118-19.

resort, which figures in her second novel, *Redwood* (1824), but one can see her testing out her abilities to describe fashionable society in America, the primary milieu of *Clarence*.]

On July 23d I left home in company with George & Susan Pomeroy, Theodore & his wife, for Saratoga. Sister Frances was with us as far as Albany.[1] The day was pleasant and our party cheerful—no shadow over us but the recollection of the sorrow we had left behind, and the necessity of returning our dear Sister to her desolate home—a home without love is worse than a body without a soul—it is a body possessed by an evil spirit. My friend Susan L was to have met me at Albany but did not arrive till Tuesday night. The detention was amply compensated by passing a day with my Sister—imparting some pleasure to her, and enjoying communion with her bright, submissive & social spirit....

Wednesday 5 am we left Albany. George & Susan (the rest of the party having preceeded us) in company with Mr McIlvaine (cashier of the US bank at Philadelphia)[2] and his sisters, all well-informed amiable people, passing through this beautiful country for the first time & disposed to observe & enjoy. What a feast God has prepared in nature for his creatures. Let them be but true Epicureans, their appetite cultivated for the best food! A bright dewy morning. What a breakfast for a spirit that spiritually discerneth!

Our companions were kindly disposed and a little disposition to sacrifice to their gratification won their good will. We dined at Ballston,[3] and arrived at Saratoga at 5 O'clock.... We remained at Saratoga till Monday morning. Even at this short distance of time (19 August) I have scarcely an impression remaining of all the characters that figured on that gay scene. There were maneuvering mothers, playing their daughters like puppets, and pretty daughters who perfectly understood all the turns of the mazy dance and needed no aid from the mothers. But on the whole even in our most fashionable society there is very little of the debasing arts, the heartlessness, and depravity of the same class as described in England. The young are not naturally mercenary, and I rather think not often ambitious—they are too thoughtless and careless of the future. The artificial distinctions and wants of life have not the

---

1   Catharine's sister Eliza married Thaddeus Pomeroy of Stockbridge. Susan and George Pomeroy were Eliza's relatives by marriage. Catharine's brother Theodore Sedgwick II also lived in Stockbridge with his wife Susan Livingston Ridley Sedgwick. Sister Frances Watson (married to the abusive Ebenezer Watson) resided in Albany.

2   William McIlvaine was cashier of the Second National Bank of the United States in Philadelphia from 1826 to 1832.

3   Ballston Spa, a resort north of Albany on the road to Saratoga.

same arbitrary power here they have in Europe, and the habits of business in our country, and our comparatively simple mode of life, leave to few the necessity of fortunate matrimonial arrangements.

I was introduced to multitudes at the Springs who paid this compliment to what they deemed my literary success. It would be difficult for me, even in this quiet retirement where vanity is stripped of its illusion to balance justly the advantages and disadvantages of the little notoriety I have attained. I have prayed earnestly, and earnestly endeavored to escape the intoxication of flattery. I am aware that it is perfectly empty—that half who administer to my vanity do it to gratify their own. I sometimes perceive an honest heart-felt emotion and I am touched by it, as when a lovely woman said to me "I thought when I saw you I must embrace you." I do not disguise from myself that I feel a pleasure in being able to command a high station wherever I go, and that I often enjoy the power of being able to gratify others by notice and attentions. But I feel deeply the disadvantage of what my sweet modest Charles[1] calls 'Lafayette-ism'[2] on a very humble scale being the quest and profession of the public and being obliged to fritter away in general transient courtesies time and thought and feeling. I am conscious that what distinction I have attained is greatly owing to the paucity of our literature, and I have another powerful preservative against undue self complacency in the consciousness that whatever talent I have shown is the original gift of God—that it is not my own and has not been improved by industry and careful cultivation as it should—that I have more cause to mourn over what I have not done than to exult in what I have done—more cause for humility than for pride.

But to return to Saratoga, our own party was rich in gifts and graces. Judge Howe[3] with his good sense unaffected manners and benignant temper, S with her fine sagacious mind, ready wit, disdain of folly & of fools, my sweet gentle Sue, George with his sunshine face and temper, and always the gentleman, Theo. with his downright good sense, and his pretty wife, unaffected and amiable—Among all that I saw I hardly retain a distinct impression of an individual—The great distinctions, tall & short, old & young were nearly all that appeared on the surface....

I intended to have kept up my journal during my absence, but the heat and inconvenience and noise of my room which was a partnership

---

1 Catharine Sedgwick's brother Charles.
2 Marie Joseph Paul Yves Roche Gilbert du Motier, Marquis de Lafayette (French, 1757-1834), volunteered to serve the American Revolution as a general. He returned to tour the US in 1824, to tremendous acclaim and popularity.
3 Likely Samuel Howe (1785-1828), founder of a law school in Northampton, Massachusetts, and Robert Sedgwick's classmate at Williams College.

concern prevented my doing any thing more than write a few letters. At Lake George[1] I roomed alone, and was not occupied with Susan L's exciting conversation. Saratoga had changed its character during our absence[.] There are now so many objects for our tourists that they remain but a short time at the Springs. We had a splendid ball on Friday night, a great show of fine faces, fine dancing, fine dresses and fine jewels. Mrs Grimes as usual out-figured every body else, but her dress was in bad taste and well described by the remark that she looked like the Tawny Emblem of America on the Maps.[2] Little Signora Mecci [?] with her Maracobo[3] feathers her round arms and youthful face quite eclipsed her. Then there was a Greek Lion, a Lady of Scio who spoke all the languages of Babel and with her Grecian turban and French cher ami[4] attracted a good deal of attention.

I was introduced to her but as I perceived nothing engaging about her I felt less reluctance to distrust her pretension than I otherwise should. Mrs Henderson, dressed in white and decorated with diamonds suited my taste, and there were some very pretty young girls, graceful and elegant and simple. To these girls was (or should have been) addressed the serenade that waked us all in the middle of the night. "Arise arise Lady" was sung to the guitar by one of the finest voices in the world which I fancied to proceed from some love struck cavalier. I tried in vain to catch a glimpse of him from our window, but he was concealed behind one of the large wood-trimmed wreathed columns of the piazza. To my utter dismay I learned in the morning that the musician was a strapping son of Africa hired to pour out this amatory effusion! Oh spirits of Cavaliers & Troubadours where are ye!

On the whole I think an observation of our Country-people even at the Springs would lead to favorable conclusions. It is obvious that the greatest part of those who resort there are our people of fortune, our idlers, our Fainéants,[5] and yet you neither see nor hear much excess of any kind. There is a little whisper of scandal but very low and with few objects. Even manœuvering that conventional vice of fashionable society is rare. The lawlessness of beauty, the flippancies of coxcombry, the presumptions of ignorance, the impertinence of vulgarity, the conceits of pretension & the pride of wealth, are almost unknown. The equality

---

1 Yet another resort area, north of Saratoga.
2 Since the early days of European exploration, maps of America often featured an illustration of a female Native American figure, styled as a "queen" or "princess."
3 Marabou.
4 The Greek island of Scio was the site of an 1822 massacre in the war for Greek independence. Cher ami: dear friend.
5 Do-nothings.

of fortune, & still more of education in this country produces an even surface, at least to the eye of the casual observer. Like the physical aspect of our land which has no Castles, parks, or pleasure grounds but seems at the first glance of the eye to have an equal & moderate cultivation, a close observer will perceive that these are as marked degrees as obtain elsewhere, but the extremes are not so distant.

August 4 we left Congress Hall,[1] and the next hours (if indeed our memory survived that long) were forgotten.... The waves engulph an object and no trace of it is left on the surface of the water ...[2] I am satisfied that this time has not been lost to me, for I am far from thinking that the most useful intellectual acquisitions are made in the closet. During my fortnight absence I read DeVere, Wieland & some articles in the NA.[3] We came to Albany on Saturday, and were there disappointed in our promised conveyance to Lebanon,[4] & obliged to wait till Sunday Morn'g. I never felt more pained by the violation of the sacred day, and I hope I shall not again unnecessarily yield to the temptation of this using it.

At Albany we had parted with our delightful companions S & G, but we were happy to the end. At Lebanon we met many of our S[5] acquaintances, and I became quite 'pane e cacio'[6] with a Pennsylvania party, two beautiful sisters. I have seen a great many Philadelphians this summer, all (with one exception) sensible, unaffected & amiable in their manners, but not one distingue—to use the cant word—and not one approaching the dawn of that illumination which in certain parts of our country is the perfect day. Monday 6 August I parted from Mr Howe, and came to Lenox in the Post-coach, and had pure happiness from the sweet welcome at Charles'. Monday night came home, Mr Appleton here.[7] On Wednesday evening Mrs Griffith[8] & Eustatia arrived & went to the tavern, but the next morning after breakfast came

---

1   The main hotel at Saratoga Springs.

2   Both ellipses original.

3   Edward de Vere, 17th Earl of Oxford (English, 1550-1604), was a poet and playwright. *Wieland* (1798) is a novel by Charles Brockden Brown (American, 1771-1810). NA is the *North American Review*, a quarterly magazine founded in 1815.

4   The Shaker community at New Lebanon, New York.

5   Saratoga.

6   Literally, "bread and cheese" (Italian), as in "hand in glove," close companions.

7   Charles Sedgwick lived in Lenox, Massachusetts, not far from Stockbridge. Nathan Appleton, a Boston merchant, summered in the Berkshires, and his daughter Frances (who later married the poet Henry Wadsworth Longfellow) was an intimate friend of CMS's.

8   CMS's friend the naturalist and fiction writer Mary Griffith, visiting from Philadelphia.

here, her arrival excited much needless alarm, but happily, her delightful social qualities soon dissipated, & those who had taken up wrong opinions and prejudices had them all charmed away by the presence of the good spirit. On Friday afternoon I went to Lebanon with her, and remained till Monday, when my dear kind brother C carried me to Lenox—one of the most beautiful days that ever shone—returned to L Monday Eve'g & found all the family assembled at the Doctor's [?] where we passed a pleasant Eve'g. Since then till now (22 August) have been quiet at home.

4. Correspondence between Captain Basil Hall and Catharine Sedgwick (1827)[1]

[Accompanied by his wife Margaret and young daughter, Basil Hall (1788-1844), a British naval officer and travel writer, met the Sedgwick family in Stockbridge in 1827 during a tour of the United States and Canada undertaken as preparation for writing a travel book. Hall read *Hope Leslie*, Sedgwick's then recently-published historical novel about seventeenth-century Massachusetts, and as he was preparing to leave Stockbridge, he wrote a letter to her "correcting" the language and morality of the novel. Sedgwick responded with a vigorous defense of the American idiom and the morality of her fiction.]

Private
Stockbridge 2 Oct. 1827
Tuesday Evening

Dear Madam,

It is quite needless to say how much I regret not having the pleasure of again meeting you. I wished to have spoken to you of one or two points respecting matters in this country, which are not of a nature to bear written expression—& therefore must keep cold till we meet. I am almost afraid that I may already have talked rather too much on such subjects; but I was anxious to have your opinions, & thought it but fair that I should set an example of frankness. In travelling, one is obliged to incur some risk of giving offence—because there is not time for the establishment of that degree of acquaintanceship which enables the parties respectively to understand how far they may safely trust one another. In general, after a little time, one learns to detect the incipient symptoms of displeasure when a disagreeable topic is touched upon—& the dangerous ground may be avoided, accordingly—but, as

---

1 CMS Papers, II.1.7 and I.1.11.

I said, this can be done only in conversation & not in writing—which makes me the more regret that I should have missed—& just missed an opportunity so fertile as I believe in all the good things which I am in quest of. But this must pass for the present. Your brother, however, has asked me to give my opinion upon some few particulars respecting your works, which he assures me you will not be displeased with. I am aware of this being delicate ground—but I have also strong internal evidence which induces me to think that it may be safely gone over. If not—I can offer nothing in excuse. I have no doubt that you will write many more admirable books, & my wish, (naturally I hope), is to see your popularity turned to the best account in the history of letters—& this I conceive can only be accomplished by a resolute determination on your part to adhere to the best standards both as to taste & to mere expression. The staple commodities of imagination & knowledge of the human heart you possess, evidently, in abundance—I had almost said superabundance—but I don't use that word, as it might look like disapprobation, which is very far indeed from my thoughts. What I mean is, simply, that you seem to me, to have the means before you of doing anything you like, in one of the noblest paths of human genius. But it is precisely an account of your eminence, as to power, over us, that I am anxious to see that distinction rightly exercised—& as I cannot but believe that it is your true wish to glean hints from every quarter, I venture with the most unfeigned respect, to request to you, to avoid what, in the opinion of the best authorities is calculated to lessen the pleasure as well as the utility of your labours.

I had intended, when I began this letter, to have confined my observations to a few expressions which I conceive are not in use in England—& which would certainly hurt the credit of any author both in America & in England among good judges. But I am tempted to trespass a little further than I had at first purposed.—I would suggest, then, that it would be more agreeable to every class of your readers—to women as well as to men, to avoid the introduction of persons, or of scenes, or of circumstances which would not bear to be introduced into conversation in good company, without raising a blush—or exciting horror. I merely name Rosa—the drunken boat's crew—& the surgical details at amputation of the Indian girl's arm.[1] On the same principle all oaths & all vulgarisms—however characteristic—or however subdued by dashes (d—n for instance) are to be shunned as ut-

---

1   Characters and events in Sedgwick's *Hope Leslie*. Rosa cross-dresses as a male page to follow Sir Philip Gardiner, her former lover. A drunken boat crew threatens the virtue of white heroine Hope Leslie, while Native American heroine Magawisca loses her arm at her father's hands when she prevents his execution of Everell Fletcher.

terly repugnant to good taste—& as eminently hurtful to that delicacy of touch which belongs to finished works of art. It signifies nothing that high authorities may be quoted—you may be certain that even Sir Walter Scott is universally blamed by every person of good feeling & taste for his slightest departures from delicacy. I pray you to excuse this strong manner of speaking—but I wish, most earnestly, to convince you that all such methods of exciting interest are illegitimate—& such as a writer of genius ought to disdain.

I shall now mention the verbal points to which I conceive you may usefully direct your attention. But before I do so, I beg to mention that I consider myself quite as much a foreigner as you are, when the question is English composition. I am Scotch by birth & have therefore been obliged to study these particulars & so conscious are almost all scotchmen of their danger that they rarely go to press without subjecting their proofs to an English friend's eye. For my part, I never write a line for the Public without giving it the advantage of such scrutiny—& I invariably—& without the slightest mercy or remorse, expunge every doubtful phrase or word—or turn of expression (no matter how strong) that is not pure English in the opinion of the present judges—that is to say—which is not justified by the best usage at this moment—whatever old authorities may say to the contrary.

P.S. Wed. Morn. 3rd Oct. Last night after writing the above I thought it might be as well to take the opinion of my friends in this house & I read it aloud to the company—consisting of all the family but Mr. Ashburner.[1] There was a vehement exclamation against its being sent to you, by all except Sarah, who said you would like it—& subsequently all the party came into the measure except Ann—Mrs Hall was very doubtful. Upon this I resolved to destroy my critical lucubrations but gave them a respite at the desire of the company till Mr. Ashburner should be consulted. Accordingly, this morning he is zealous for the letter being sent to you—but this opinion he has given without hearing it read. I shall now, therefore, read it to him, & then, if he still thinks it should go forward, you shall have it—upon the solemn engagement on your part that it shall not be shown to any other person whatsoever.

Mr. Ashburner has just heard the above letter & he says it *must* go on to you—so I shall incur the risk (not of your displeasure—for that I feel I shall not receive)—but of giving you pain. For my own literary part I never care for the pain of a cure—& as I hope you will believe—that I

---

1 The Ashburner family (British immigrants to America via India) were neighbors of the Sedgwicks in Stockbridge, and the Halls were staying the night in their home. Indian-born Sarah Morgan Ashburner (1812-56) married Catharine's nephew Theodore Sedgwick III in 1835.

can have no motive in this matter but the advancement of your reputation & the good of letters—I shall make no further apologies.

I shall take advantage of the first leisure moments I have to make you a list of which I conceive to be errors in English composition—In the meantime I note underneath some which I observed in Hope Leslie although, in truth, I was carried along so swiftly by the high interest of the story, that I had but little time to notice these spots in the sun.

P. 94 Jeopard—this verb is not in use in England. Why not say endanger?

P. 139 Factory for manufactory—is very vulgar in England tho' general here.

P. 203 Variant—for various is a word I never heard before—it is very ugly & certainly not in use now.

P. 206 "The now thriving colony"—a clumsy form of expression. Put out the now, or say the colony which is now thriving.

P. 211 Located—a very disagreeable word which I grieve to say we are adopting from you—I beseech you to interpose your authority to stop its use.

P. 238 You talk of disinterested patriotism as being a rare virtue. I do not think it is so. Do you? If not, why not keep above the commonplace cant upon this occasion. There is as much public as private virtue extant I well believe—in England—& I trust here too. But you know better than I do.

P. 240 "To remark on" is very low English: The expression should be "To call his attention to"—or something else—but not as it stands certainly.

P. 244 The use of the word "Sir" by a Lady to a gentleman is indicative in England, of the worst possible style of breeding. I know it is used here—but it is very offensive to our ears.

P. 244 A *piece of meat* is also general here—but not at all in England except in very low company so say a bit—a slice—some—a little

P. 261 *To reciprocate* in the sense you mean it—is surely American & extremely disagreeable to English ears. Why not use the pleasant expression to interchange—or some other is good use.

Again, My Dear Madam, I must entreat you to forgive all this freedom & to believe that I am induced to risk appearing very intrusive in consequence of the good I know you can do if you set about it in the true spirit—

Yours most affectionately
Basil Hall

Stockbridge 6 Novr 1827

Dear Sir,

I should have acknowledged your favor much earlier but for the occurrence of a severe domestic calamity since your departure which has prevented my writing at all. I make this apology to you lest you should infer from my delay that I felt any thing but pleasure at the frankness which heralded your letter to me. Literary occupation is rather a pastime than a profession with me. I make no pretensions to infallibility & have no cause to feel any thing but gratitude at strictures which might annoy a regular bred & pains-taking author—If therefore I question your correctness in some particulars you must impute my defence not to an irritated and despicable vanity but to that universal instinct that opposes the shield to the weapon—or rather for I would not use an expression that could possibly imply I had perverted your hints, obviously given with a sole and generous reference to my good, into an attack—or rather then as the patient arrests the surgeon's hand when he fancies he has mistaken a healthy for a diseased part——a mere arrogant fancy it may be after all——

You say that "all oaths & all vulgarisms, *however characteristic* or however subdued by dashes are to be shunned as utterly repugnant to good taste." I agree with you that oaths are to be avoided as far as possible—they offend both against principle and taste. But the question seems to me to be whether in describing human life you are to exclude the majority of human beings—the vulgar—the class that by their accidental connection with the refined & susceptible afford the brightest light & the deepest shades of the picture. In describing this class (however painful the necessity) you must, if you would preserve a vrai-semblance[1] allow them to speak their vernacular language. It comes to this then that I must either exclude the Boats-crew or I must introduce such offensive words as I only allow myself to amelioration of through dashes that usage supplies, for I presume no sailor dispenses with oaths, save the crew of some exemplary member of the Bible and Tract societies, or perchance the men who have the good fortune to be commanded by an accomplished & refined *Port Captain of the British Navy.*[2]

Your hint as to indelicacy exemplified by an allusion to my poor unfortunate Rosa implies a fault the description of which must to a lady be both awkward & painful. There appears to me to be an obvious distinction between such an introduction of certain topics as shall excite the passions, & such as shall have a tendency to subdue them.

---

1 Appearance of truth.
2 Hall was a British naval officer.

A delicate woman would naturally shrink from being seen with a volume of Moore's poems or Byron's Don Juan in her hand,[1] or with that libel on human nature contained in the vulgar & indecent pages of Almacks,[2] but who but a prude would shun the contemplation of the *penitent* Magdalen!——One word more on this topic at the risk of being tedious to you. I should not have the presumption to plead Sir W.S. in my behalf if you had not yourself included him in your criticisms. You may take this liberty for you have the happiness to call him your Countryman and friend, but to me who am attached to him by a tie common to all the reading part of our race, the tie of benefaction, to me he appears above all law. Would not your principle limit his illimitable powers? Would you not circumscribe that expansive circle that embraces within its dominion human character under every variety of form, in its original graceful proportions, in its various deviations and in all the deformities of accidental circumstances. Is it not by the free use of this liberty that he commands the springs of all our feelings, that

> "All passions in our frame of clay
> Come thronging at his call"[3]

Is it not the abuse of this liberty that has banished Fielding & Smollet[4] from good society. If your scrupulous doctrine had obtained—If artists had admitted to their studios none but well-behaved, well dressed gentlemen & ladies where would have been the Apollo, the Venus, & the Laocoon![5]

To some of your verbal criticisms you will allow me to reply to without suspecting me of arrogance or petulance. I am aware that 'jeopard' is a rarity, though I believe sometimes still used by good authorities, but is our language so rich that we can allow a word to become obsolete for which there is no exact replacement? Is not jeopard a stronger word than

---

1 Thomas Moore (Irish, 1779-1852), poet, best known for *Lalla Rookh: An Orientalist Romance* (1827); *Don Juan* (1819-24) was also thought risqué.

2 Almack's, an exclusive mixed-gender social club in London, was mentioned frequently in so-called "silver fork" novels about London high society, including *Almack's* by Marianne Spencer Hudson (1827).

3 Lines from Fitz-Greene Halleck's "To a Rose, Brought from near Alloway Kirk, in Ayrshire, in the Autumn of 1822," in homage to Robert Burns, in *Alnwick Castle with Other Poems* (1827).

4 Henry Fielding (English, 1707-54), author of *Tom Jones* (1794), and Tobias George Smollett (Scottish, 1721-71), author of *Humphry Clinker* (1771), both comic and often bawdy picaresque novels.

5 Apollo (Greek god of the sun and of male beauty), Venus (Roman goddess of love and beauty), and Laocoön (priest of Apollo) were the subjects of famous nude sculptures.

'endanger.' I would apply the same justification to the phrase 'to remark on.' If 'not in use now' as Johnson[1] says or 'not in use in England' as you say should it not be used by those whose philosophy teaches them to prefer the expression of a certain sense to an exact obedience to the pedantry of the schools? "The use of the word sir" you say, "by a lady to a gentleman is indicative in England of the worst possible breeding." In England it may be, but not in America, and I am describing American manners, & must be allowed to claim for my own country as I would for France or any other civilized and polite nation a right to independent and peculiar manners. We do not admit that we are governed by English standards & surely is there anything in the usage of such a term that does not belong to mere conventional politeness, if it has any thing intrinsic the use is to be preferred to the omission as it is expressive of deference or respect. But I am content to rest on my first ground. The term may be now going out of use in our fashionable circles, but 20 years ago a lady who should have omitted it would have been deemed guilty of a gross pertness, & *Hope Leslie* in her day would certainly for such an offence have been banished from Governor Winthrop's parlor.[2] Indeed I believe she might with more safety have set a witch free than have uttered *No* without the gentle addition of *Sir*——"A piece of meat is" you say "general here, but not at all in England except in very low company." Again I must plead our Independence of English rules. There is certainly no more intrinsic propriety in saying a *bit* or a *slice* than a piece. However I have no pertinacious attachment to piece and as *piece* or *slice* would equally remind one of Capt H's kind interposition in my behalf—*slice* it shall be in a future Edition.[3] 'To reciprocate' you say 'is purely American—extremely disagreeable to English ears—why not use the pleasant expression of interchange' "To reciprocate' says Johnson 'to act interchangeably." Does not the Lexicographer justify my use & I prefer the word reciprocate as the most precise. Two persons are necessary to an interchange—one may reciprocate.

'You talk of disinterested patriotism' you say 'as being a rare virtue I do not think so—do you?'—Certainly I do not, and am greatly obliged to you for suggesting to me the expulsion of a sentiment untrue and most unworthy of an American—A native of a Country settled by men whose patriotism was identified with every other virtue, whose home & country had no existence separate from the enjoyment of perfect civil

---

1   Samuel Johnson (English, 1709-84) published *A Dictionary of the English Language* in 1755.

2   John Winthrop (1588-1649), founding Governor of the Massachusetts Bay Colony, is a character in *Hope Leslie*.

3   CMS did not carry out this promised change: the offending "piece of turkey" remains. *Hope Leslie* (New York: Harper & Brothers, 1842), I:217.

& religious freedom—All my historic recollection should have saved me from penning such a sentence, & I crave pardon of Washington and his coadjutors, the high and the humble, a glorious company and numerous enough were they the only disinterested patriots to make it a libel on our race to call that noble virtue *rare*. I must have written that "common place cant" under the pressure of some recent disappointment that set in a strong light the infirmity of personal virtue surrounded by political temptation. I must just have been reading certain speeches in *favor* of the tariff.[1] I hope you will not imagine from what I have written that I am childish enough to shrink in your own happy phrase from the 'pain of a cure,' on the contrary I gratefully acquiesce in some of your remarks and am more obliged than I have the power within these circumscribed limits to express to you. I trust you will not disappoint the expectation you have authorized of farther light & aid from you, should you find me an improveable subject you will not I am sure regret the pains a farther exercise of your spirit & benevolence may cost you——&c &c——[2]

5. From Basil Hall, *Travels in North America, In the Years 1827 and 1828* (Philadelphia: Carey, Lea and Carey, 1829), 30–31, 68–69, 253–54, 255–60

[The American reprinting of Hall's travel book (first published in London) caused a sensation. The character Edmund Stuart in *Clarence* is a lampoon of Hall, and the following excerpts show Hall expressing in print the same kinds of opinions that his fictional counterpart expresses about the defects of American culture. He critiques the effects of American inheritance law, and he does not describe the beauties of Trenton Falls, the location of a key scene in *Clarence*, preferring instead to describe the establishment serving liquor near it and the crudity of American tourists. The latter portion also documents Hall's visit to Stockbridge and his meeting Sedgwick.]

The lands on the left bank of the Hudson, for a considerable distance above New York, were formerly held by great proprietors, and chiefly by the Livingston family; but the abolition of entails, and the repeal of the

---

1 Protective tariffs on imported manufactured goods were a key point of conflict between the Jacksonian Democrats and the Whigs in the run-up to the US presidential election of 1828. Sedgwick is reacting against the pro-tariff Whig position.
2 As the closing of the letter makes clear, it is a draft. The final version sent to Hall (if, indeed, she sent it) has not been located.

law of primogeniture,[1] has already broken it down into small portions. Our host, at the time of our visit, possessed only a third of the property held by his immediate predecessor, while the manor of Livingston, an extensive and fertile district farther up the river, formerly owned by one person, is now divided into forty or fifty parcels, belonging to as many different proprietors; so that where half-a-dozen landlords once lived, as many hundreds may now be counted. And as these new possessors clear away and cultivate the soil at a great rate, the population goes on swelling rapidly, though we were told not by any means so fast as it does in the wild regions of the west. This comparative tardiness may possibly be caused by some lingerings of the old aristocratical feeling; though it is mixed up curiously enough with the modern ideas of the equal division of property, the universality of electoral suffrage, equality of popular rights and privileges, and all the other transatlantic devices for the improvement of society. Every thing indeed that we saw in these districts, not actually under the plough, wore an air of premature and hopeless decay; the ancient manor-houses were allowed to fall to pieces; the trees of the parks and pleasure-grounds were all untended; the rank grass was thickly matted along with weeds over the walks; and the old pictures were fast going to ruin under the joint influence of mould and indifference. It cannot, indeed, now be otherwise, for the moment the proprietor dies, his land is equally divided amongst his children; and by thus falling into many hands, no one has the means, if he had the inclination, to keep up the ancient state of things. The practical effect of this, as we saw every where exemplified, was to render the actual possessors utterly careless of those tasteful refinements above alluded to. By law, indeed, any man in America may leave his property to whom he pleases, or he may even entail it, exactly as in England, upon persons living at the time; yet the general sentiment of the public is so decidedly against such unequal distributions, that in practice such a thing very rarely if ever takes place. Consequently there is no check to this deteriorating process, which is rapidly reducing that portion of the country to the same level in respect to property, with those recently settled districts where entails and the rights of primogeniture never did exist, and are hardly known even by name; or if spoken of at all, it is with the utmost contempt and horror....

On the 18th of June we reached Utica, a town recently built, and standing near the canal.[2] From thence we made an excursion to Trenton Falls, which are well worth seeing; but as I am not so sure of their

---

1 Legal practices restricting inheritance of land to lineal descendants and to first-born sons, respectively.
2 A town in New York state on the Erie Canal.

being equally acceptable in description, I shall pass them by; though I should by no means recommend travellers to follow such an example....

A large party of tourists whom we encountered at Trenton Falls, in returning from a walk; which in any other country would, I am sure, have furnished conversation for hours afterward, and the gossip arising out of which would have been thought by far the best part of the fun, said not one word about the day's excursion, but sat down to dinner as sad and silent as if we had lost one of our companions over the cliff— a fatal accident, by the way, which did occur to another party only a few days afterwards. The sole occupation that elicited any thing like animation, during the whole ramble, was reading in the album—which, like all albums, was filled with the flattest trash that human dulness, inspired by compulsion, can produce. The said album was placed in a sort of shed, near the prettiest part of the falls, in what is denominated a bar, Anglicè, a tap, or grog-shop. These odious places, truth bids me say, stared us in the face every where; and that no one should mistake, the letters B, A, R, were written up most conspicuously.... In all countries such things are, undoubtedly, to be found, and too often, I grant, in similar places; and I should most certainly not have made these remarks, but for their unusual profusion in America, and the important part which ardent spirits appear to act in almost every scene ...

I felt a particular degree of interest in revisiting the interior of this part of the country, from a desire to compare the state of rural and also longer settled society, with that which I had now become pretty familiar with in the cities, and in the more recently peopled, bustling part of the States.... Whenever I spoke with disapprobation of the incessant high fever in which all the world seemed to be kept by the Presidential election,—or when I cast any reflections upon the mischievous practical effects of universal suffrage and annual Parliaments, in bringing into the Legislatures of the States ignorant and incompetent persons, to the exclusion of the ablest and most experienced,—or when I spoke of the limited nature of the information possessed by the great majority of all the persons I had yet met with, and of the difficulty I had hitherto found in carrying their ideas out of money-making, electioneering, and other local channels,—in short, when I did not think every thing in America perfect, or not so good as I had been accustomed to see in other countries, in correspondent situations, I was always told that I had fallen into bad hands—that I had been accidentally or wilfully misled by the people I had been amongst—or that I had unfortunately gone to such and such a town at the wrong moment.

From hearing these assertions so frequently repeated, I really began to hope that I had been deceived, especially as these optimists told me to wait till I had seen the people of the interior, out of the reach of the contaminating influence of cities, steam-boats, and stage-coaches. "Go to our flourishing villages, sir," they said, "and talk to our farmers; there you will see our character—there you will find the high-minded and intelligent citizens of our country."

I said I would do so with all my heart. And I kept my word. Nor did I go about the inquiry with any unwillingness to find things as they were represented to me; but, on the contrary, in all these researches I most anxiously endeavoured to see things as the inhabitants wished me to see them; took every possible means of explaining the anomalies I saw, or thought I saw, in a pleasant way, and persevered in following the rule I have been guided by through life—to see every thing on its most favourable side....

During my residence near Stockbridge, I went frequently into the village, it being my pleasure as well as my business to get acquainted with as many of the inhabitants as I could. This was an easy task, as they were universally as kind and obliging as I had found their countrymen elsewhere. I had also opportunities of visiting the neighbouring country houses and farms, sometimes in company, and sometimes alone, upon which occasions I had the means of seeing, on every hand instances of that energy of character, and ardent perseverance for which the New Englanders are so deservedly distinguished....

Besides these numerous detailed examinations of the country society in Massachusetts, we had the frequent good fortune to meet the more wealthy class of the village residents at their own houses. Upon one of these occasions I was gratified in a very high degree by making acquaintance with the accomplished author of several admirable works of fancy—"Redwood," "Hope Leslie," and others, which I am happy to find have been republished, and are becoming more known in England; because, independently of that high and universal interest attaching to works of fiction in the hands of genius—wherever placed,—these novels possess another and very pleasing kind of merit, in the graphic truth with which the country in which the scenes are laid is described.

It was our peculiar good fortune, not only to converse with the author, but afterwards, under instructions which she chalked out for us, to visit some parts of the country best adapted for showing off the beauties of a New England autumn. Thus prepared, we carried this lady's books in our hands to the tops of the mountains of the New World, as the tourists to the Highlands of Scotland used to carry the Lady of the Lake,[1] to aid their taste in admiring Loch Katrine.

In the meantime, however, the picturesque was obliged to yield to scenes of another description, as the grand cattle show at Stockbridge,

---

1   A long poem by Walter Scott (published 1810) set in the picturesque Trossachs region of Scotland.

the fourth anniversary of the Agricultural Society, took place at the period of our visit.

The hiliarity of the meeting, however, was essentially injured by the heavy rain which fell during all the morning; a circumstance the more provoking, from its being the only unfavourable day which had occurred for some time. It was truly melancholy to see the poor people's best clothes and other finery destroyed, and all their amusements marred. The merry flutes were no longer merry, while the drums became soaked, and scarcely yielded a sound, though ever so well thumped. The gay flags, instead of waving over the heads of the lads and lasses of the neighbourhood, hung dripping down to the very mud. The bright muskets of the awkward but showy militia were speedily tarnished; and instead of the whole fields being speckled over with parties skipping to and fro, the inhabitants of the village and surrounding hamlets, cased in great-coats, or cowering under umbrellas, were huddled together, silent and dissatisfied. All was discomfort; and it made one feel cold and damp, even to look from the window at the drenched multitude....

Shortly after the ploughing match was ended, the day cleared up, and I expected to see some of that merriment set a-going which I had been taught to consider as the appropriate and almost necessary accompaniment to such a meeting. In particular I hoped to see the women tripping out of the houses and mixing gaily with the men. But no attempt of this kind was made, or once thought of; the whole proceedings, indeed, being strongly marked with that air of laborious effort which always accompanies unwonted amusements; and certainly I never fully understood before what was meant by making a toil of a pleasure. The Americans, who are a very grave people, keep few holidays; and whether it be cause or effect, I do not know, but they appear wofully ignorant of the difficult art of being gracefully idle,—of relaxing from toil, and leaving off business, for the more pleasing occupation of interchanging good and kindly offices, merely as such, without reference to pecuniary profit, or electioneering politics;—as if bodily and mental profit, the gaiety of the soul and the elasticity of limb, which spring out of habitual and innocent festivities, were not so much clear gain! On this occasion, at least, there was no attempt at amusement even when the day had improved, for the very instant the ploughing match was over, all the women trudged home, unattended; while the men crowded eagerly to the tavern, where, although I must allow there was nothing like drunkenness, or riot, or noise, there was a great destruction of ardent spirits.

As I found the smell of whiskey and the clouds of tobacco smoke not very pleasant, I took the opportunity of examining the domestic manufactures, laid out for public inspection in the Academy. The articles exposed showed greater skill than I had expected to find in this remote country place....

At one o'clock, the men were summoned to dinner in the tavern, by a loud bell, and we set down, to the number of about 150.... Dinner, as I have often said before, is a brief affair in America, a mere business to be got over, not a rational pleasure to be enjoyed; and we were soon called away, by sound of drum, to join the procession to the church, where an oration suitable to the day, was to be delivered. The company walked two and two, with the most formal and funeral solemnity, the women being kept carefully separated from the men. I was rather surprised when the gentleman with whom I was appointed to walk, took me to the very last, the tail of the line, which, at first, looked odd enough, as it was obvious, from a hundred other things, that they wished to treat strangers with all distinction. But in the rear I found also the clergyman and several other principal persons of the village. This arrangement, which reminded me of the etiquette at a naval funeral, I found was a device for giving us the first entry into the church, and consequently the choice of seats; for when the head of the column reached the church-door, a general halt took place, and a lane being formed by the gentlemen who had been walking side by side now facing one another, the two clergymen took off their hats, and advanced from the end of the line up the avenue formed by the double row of people.

I was invited to follow next, and, accompanied by my friend, moved along cap in hand. I observed, that as the clergymen passed, about one in ten of those who were in the line touched their hats. There did not seem to be any intentional rudeness on the part of the other nine, as the omission evidently arose from want of habitual politeness in such matters. In fact, the whole affair was a most amusing though rather clumsy compromise between the natural consequence which arises from wealth and station, and the nominal rights and privileges of that much talked of equality which belongs to a democracy. The dignity of the sovereign people, it will be observed, was duly maintained on this occasion by their being allowed the precedence in the line of march; while their subjects, or rather the subordinate sovereigns,—the rich or influential villagers—by means of the device I have described, were allowed the more solid advantage of good situations in the church. The ladies, still kept apart, had already occupied one side, while the other was allotted to the men.

An appropriate agricultural discourse was delivered after a hymn and a prayer....

Appendix B: Images of Trenton Falls

[This appendix reproduces images in circulation c. 1830 and c. 1849 portraying a key site in *Clarence*, the scenic Trenton Falls in northern New York state. The first, an engraving, appeared in a gift book in which Catharine Sedgwick's story "Modern Chivalry" also appeared. The second, a lithograph, also dates to the late 1820s and gives some idea of the power and danger of the falls. The third appeared as a title page engraving for the author's revised edition of *Clarence* in 1849, suggesting that Sedgwick's novel played a role in the ever-growing popularity of the falls as a tourist site.[1]]

---

1 For more on these images and the falls as a tourist site, see Paul D. Schweizer et al., *The Art of Trenton Falls, 1825-1900* (Muson-Williams-Proctor Institute, 1989).

1. G.B. Ellis, Engraver, after Thomas Doughty, *Trenton Falls*, from *The Atlantic Souvenir* (Philadelphia: H.C. Carey & I. Lea, 1827) (published late 1826). Courtesy American Antiquarian Society

2. Catherine Scollay, Lithograph, *Fifth View of Trenton Falls*, c. 1825-26. Courtesy American Antiquarian Society

3. After George Innes, Engraved Title Page of *Clarence*, **by C.M. Sedgwick (New York: Geo. P. Putnam, 1849). Courtesy University of Pennsylvania**

Appendix C: Images of New York City, c. 1830 and c. 1849

[*Clarence* begins with "Flavel" strolling through the throng on Broadway in lower Manhattan. In 1849, when Sedgwick was preparing her author's revised edition of the novel, she commented on the great changes in this street scene in the nearly twenty years since 1830. Three images below show Broadway c. 1830 and c. 1849.[1] The first image is of Bowling Green Park, at the Southern end of Broadway (the "foot"), and the view "up" Broadway (looking north). The second is from a park at Broadway and Fulton Streets, and the view is "down" Broadway (looking south). In the second image, St. Paul's Church is in the foreground on the right (the west side of Broadway), with Barnum's American Museum across the street on the left (the east side). The spire of Trinity Church at the intersection of Broadway and Wall Street is several blocks in the distance on the right. The Park Theatre can be seen indistinctly several buildings north of Trinity's spire. The third image is from a nearly identical perspective as the second and shows the great changes in Broadway in twenty years, including new buildings such as the large hotel in the foreground that obscures the spire of St. Paul's. The final image is a newspaper advertisement for the 3 March 1829, masquerade at the Park Theatre celebrating the inauguration of Andrew Jackson as President of the United States, which Sedgwick attended and which served as a model for the fictional masquerade in *Clarence*. New York City authorities considered masquerades a threat to social order, but in 1829 theaters briefly took advantage of a loophole in city ordinances to hold public masquerades. The advertisement describes elaborate regulations seeking to allay fears of disorder.]

---

1   For more on these images, see I.N. Phelps Stokes, *The Iconography of Manhattan Island*, vol. 3 (New York: Robert Dodd, 1918).

1. After J.H. Dakin, Engraved by Barnard & Dick, "Bowling Green, Broadway," in Theodore S. Fay, *Views in New York and Its Environs* (New York: Peabody & Co., 1831). Courtesy American Antiquarian Society

2. After J.H. Dakin, Engraved by Barnard & Dick, "Broadway from the Park," in Theodore S. Fay, *Views in New York and Its Environs* (New York: Peabody & Co., 1831). Courtesy American Antiquarian Society

3. After August Köllner, Lithography by Deroy, Printed by Cattier, "*Broad-way*" (New York & Paris: Goupil & Co., 1850). Courtesy American Antiquarian Society

4. Advertisement for the Masquerade from the *New-York Evening Post* (29 February 1829). Courtesy American Antiquarian Society

GRAND FANCY MASK'D BALL—The public is most respectfully informed that in consequence of the wishes of numerous persons the Fancy Ball advertised for the 3d March, will be changed to a Fancy Mask'd Ball, which will be given at the Park Theatre on Tuesday the 3d March,—on which occasion the whole of the Pit will be floored over, forming with the Stage an immense Ball Room of 180 feet. Fancy Dresses, if required, will be furnished to the gentlemen to the extent of the wardrobe of the Theatre; applications for which must be made at the Theatre prior to Saturday Feb'y. 28. Gentlemen and ladies without Fancy Dresses will be admitted. Refreshments will be furnished to the company. Tickets admitting one gentleman and two ladies, $5. Only 400 gentlemen's admissions, with a proportionate number of ladies will be issued. A strong police will be engaged and every exertion made to prevent inconvenience from the arrival and departure of the company. Applications for tickets to be made to either of the managers, or the names or directions of the persons applying to be left at the Box Office and tickets will be delivered to them on the following day.

Managers.

Charles M'Evers, Jr.   S. J. Mumford,
J. B. Nicholson, U. S. N.   E. D. Hunter,
William D. Henderson,   D. C. Pell.

RULES AND REGULATIONS.

The fronts of the lower boxes will be taken out and the seats appropriated to the use of the company assembled.

No mask will be admitted to the Ball Room till first recognized by the manager from whom he obtained his ticket.

Carriages setting down are to have their horses' heads up Chatham street, and taking up to head down Broadway. Gentlemen are requested to take the carriages provided by the managers only, on returning, to prevent confusion and delay.

The doors will be opened at half past 7, and dancing to commence precisely at half past 8.

No Tickets or Checks will be permitted under any pretence to be transferred.

Proper persons will be appointed to take charge of Hats, Cloaks, &c. under the direction of the managers.

All dresses required from the Theatre must be sent for on Monday, and returned again on Wednesday before 12 o'clock.   fe28

MASKS MAY BE HAD AT NO. 150 BROADWAY.   f273t*

MR. & MRS. SANTANGELO'S STUDY, No. 72 Murray-street.—*Terms*—Ladies are instructed four hours every morning, Saturdays excepted, at

Appendix D: Selected American and British Reviews of the 1830 Edition of Clarence

[*Clarence* did not receive as many American reviews as *Hope Leslie* (1827) had or as many as *The Linwoods* (1835) later would, but reviews were largely positive. The earliest was in Bryant's *New-York Evening Post*, just as the novel had issued from the press, and may have been written by Bryant himself. The most unambiguously positive review is from Sarah Josepha Hale's *Ladies' Magazine*, while the longest and most critical was penned anonymously for the *North American Review* by a recent Harvard graduate, George Stillman Hillard.[1] In excerpting these American reviews (items 1-4), we have retained comments about character, manners, place, and Sedgwick's reputation as an author, omitting plot summary, long quotations, and vague commentary on style.

Sedgwick's British agent, John Miller, arranged for the British publication of *Clarence* by Colburn & Bentley in London. Published in three volumes, the novel appeared weeks after the American edition and attracted mixed reviews in London periodicals (items 5-6).[2] Some British reviewers suspected that the name "Clarence" was a fraud designed to capitalize on the recent death of King George III and the ascension of his son the Duke of Clarence to the throne as King William IV. Some also dismissed the American culture represented in the novel as inferior and Sedgwick's literary technique as outmoded. *Colburn's New Monthly Magazine*, published by Sedgwick's British publisher, gave the longest and most positive review, although even this positive review "corrects" Sedgwick's American idiom, much as Basil Hall did in his letter to her about *Hope Leslie* (see Appendix A4)].

1. *New-York Evening Post* (14 June 1830)

CLARENCE, the new novel by Miss Sedgwick, we should think likely to be more popular than even the previous works of the author. The story is one of the present day; the scene of many of the incidents is

---

1 See William Cushing, *Index to the North American Review* (Boston: John Wilson, 1878) for the identities of anonymous contributors. Additional American reviews not included are *New York Spectator* (18 June 1830) and *New-York Mirror* 7.50 (19 June 1830): 394.

2 Additional British reviews not included are *Athenaeum* 144 (20 July 1830): 472, and 145 (August 30): 481-82 and *British Magazine* 2 (December 1830): 471.

laid in our own goodly city; and the pages of the work are not sparingly sprinkled with what are called—"touches at the times." Thus it possesses the interest which belongs to the topics of the day, in addition to the higher and permanent interest arising from the skilful delineation of human actions, passions, and manners. Those passages which relate to our own city—to its external aspect, its amusements, its fashionable society, and its modes of domestic life among various classes—are managed with great liveliness and ingenuity, and constitute one of the most attractive parts of the book. The character of Mrs. Layton, the accomplished, witty, sentimental, heartless, fashionable lady, is exceedingly well drawn and preserved; some of the subordinate characters, also, the moths that flutter in the sunshine of fashionable society, are faithfully copied from a class numerous enough among us. Several female personages are introduced, who perform a very important part in the story—Emily,[1] the daughter of Mrs. Layton, gentle, obedient, timid, and child-like; Miss Marion, somewhat of a wit and blue stocking; and Gertrude Clarence, the heroine, with no fault but a romantic generosity; all drawn by a pencil which is at home in the task. A part of the events of the story take place at Trenton Falls; and the wild, romantic shores of that cataract, with their perilous walks, are well chosen for the scene of accidents which partake of a similar character.

2. *American Monthly Magazine* 2.4 (July 1830): 280–84

MISS SEDGWICK'S book has produced a general surprise. Her novels, hitherto, though perfectly different in plot and characters, have been at the same level of beautiful and graphic, but not very exciting description. The great traits in them are singular unaffectedness, and truth to nature in its household forms. No pictures have ever been drawn of the people and manners of this country which compare with those of her novels for fidelity and fulness. It was a pleasant and somewhat soothing occupation to sit down to a chapter of Redwood or Hope Leslie....The work before us is quite of another character. Without abandoning the field, in the selection of which she has done credit both to her judgment and patriotism, the authoress has brought into her plot characters common enough in our country, but which, till now, have been drawn in their deepest colors, only in the scenes of the old world. The story is contrived with a dramatic power which, knowing as we do, the quiet history and pursuits of the authoress, somewhat astonishes us. Where should she have dreamed of a character like Pedrillo—an uncopied, powerful, yet most natural villain—as admirably and originally drawn

---

1 The reviewer, perhaps intentionally, gives this name its more ordinary spelling, rather than the vaguely French "Emilie" that Mrs. Layton gives to her daughter.

as if, like the Italian bandit, he had sat for the picture to his captive? The *denouement* of Pedrillo's history is a specimen of the finest dramatic invention. Much as you are startled at the discovery of his origin, you cannot but remember instances enough within your own circle, of unaccountable and seemingly unnatural wickedness, to sustain its probability. His whole history shows a depth of the study of the human heart, and a maturity of contrivance in the plot which are not at all common in a modern novel. The portrait of Layton is another most forcible sketch, though of a class more within the writer's observation. It is characterized by the same freshness and truth to the principles of human nature ... The dark villany of Pedrillo contrasted with the shrinking sensitiveness and exquisite mind of Louis Seton—and both so true! Mrs. Layton's heartless sensibility, and Gertrude's strong, but perfectly feminine qualities—and both so familiar to our commonest experience! The admirable traits, yet at the same time so different, of Roscoe and D. Flint! These are the characters in the book which are best drawn and most original, though Major Daisy and Harriet Upton and Mrs. Roscoe are delightful in their places....

3. *Ladies' Magazine and Literary Gazette* 3.7 (July 1830): 320-25

It is no longer necessary to preface the notice of a work of fiction we think deserving of praise, with an elaborate defence of novels. The merit of this species of writing, when combining its prerogative of *amusement* with the prouder boast it has acquired from many gifted pens of *instruction*, is pretty universally acknowledged. In this view of the subject, we may unhesitatingly place the author of "Clarence" as the first and best of American novelists; and consider her works as a public benefaction, as doing honor to her country and her sex. It is not a trifling good she has effected to prove, by her own success, that American characters, scenes, and circumstances of being, may be wrought into a romance, which shall be intensely interesting, and yet not foreign to our habits of life, or dangerously exciting to the passions. Novels will be read by our people, and the only way to prevent the re-publication of the vapid trash, or worse, the licentious overflowings of the English press, is to support generously with national pride, the efforts of our own talented writers.

Were we to attempt describing by *one word*, what we think the distinguishing charm and excellence of Miss Sedgwick's writings, we should say, *appropriateness*. Imagination and judgment, seem in her pure and regulated mind exactly to harmonize. She has a clear and direct manner of telling her story, which leaves an almost irresistible impression of its truth; and yet her fancy is so fertile, that none of our novel writers equal her in the involution of plot, in that gradual and as it were incidental unfolding of the web of destiny, she has so ingeniously and yet so simply wove. The plan of "Clarence" is evidently to display the characters that move in the rich and fashionable circles; but the author has judiciously introduced specimens of every class—portraying with consummate skill, and delicate wit, the lights and shades of our mingled society. We have too the gratification of finding contemporary genius receives its just appreciation from Miss Sedgwick. She has dared to make allusions to American poets and painters, and this circumstance, trifling as it may appear to some, we consider of much importance in influencing that taste for our own productions which must be proudly cherished before the talents of our gifted ones can be fully and successfully developed.

An abstract of this most interesting book, would be of much value to our magazine, yet we hardly think it fair thus to anticipate the effect of a first reading—though Clarence is a novel that will bear to be read and re-read. However, the portrait of the heroine, we are resolved, shall adorn our pages: we consider her one of those patterns of female excellence, which will influence the characters of our young ladies more than a hundred homilies on the virtues and graces....

4. George Stillman Hillard, *The North American Review* 32.70 (January 1831): 73-95

... Clarence is a tale of our own times, descriptive of the manners of the present day and of this country. An author who delineates events among which the reader himself might, without any violation of probability, have been an actor, has much to struggle against.... The spirit of sympathy makes us feel a keener interest in the adventures of characters who wear the same dress, dwell in the same land, speak the same language and are interested in the same subjects as ourselves—while on the other hand, the matter-of-fact air and garb of sober reality which the world now-a-days wears, precludes the possibility of romantic delusion; and the creative power is both limited in its materials and checked by severe laws in the employment of them....

In the second volume we are introduced into the gay world of New-York, and among the gilded swarm that enact the solemn farce of fashion; we breath the scented air of drawing-room, our eyes are dazzled with the glare of candelabras, and our ears are familiar with the language of *persiflage*,[1] and the shining counters that pass current in the *beau monde*[2] for the sterling coin of sense. Our author seizes and embodies with magic skill the fleeing colors and changing forms of fashionable society, and the tone and manner of those who regard

---

1   Banter, frivolous talk.
2   Social elite.

life as one long drawing-room, of the heartless and fascinating woman of the world, full of sentiment and devoid of virtue, of the curled fop, whose soul seems lost in the folds of his cravat, of honest and respectable vulgarity and of worthless refinement....

Our objections to [*Clarence*'s plot] are grounded on the opinion that it is unnatural and improbable, and that the author has attempted to do what the highest genius could not accomplish. To give a highly romantic interest to events occurring in our own prosaic age and country....

Extraordinary events are continually brought about by extraordinary occurrences, and our surprise is continually called forth by the happening of incidents, which we did not expect even a page or two before.... The events at Trenton Falls must, we fear, fall under the same censure. It is not a little singular, that all the principal personages should meet there by accident; and the moonlight scene is too much like one of Mrs. Radcliffe's wild creations,[1] to seem in keeping with a 'tale of our own times,' and our own sternly matter-of-fact country. Would a lady of Miss Clarence's delicacy be likely to stroll out alone at midnight in search of the rapturous, like some love-lorn Rosa Matilda,[2] and engage in conversation with a man to whom she was an utter stranger? How can we imagine that Louis Seton, dangerously ill, and an object of so much interest to a wealthy family, should be neglected to that degree that he could steal out from his room, and wander unobserved to the very brink of the cliff that overhangs the Fall? And how could his delicate frame, weakened by illness, survive the exposure to the chill night-air, the plunge into the water, and above all the exhaustion of the nervous system by the frenzy of excitement into which he was thrown? ...

The least efficient portions of the book are those in which the author has attempted to give a tragic grandeur to the workings of dark passions, and to thrill us with the fearful collision of guilty minds. To do this with success, requires not only a peculiar and masculine talent, but a familiarity with all the dark corners of the human heart, and a cool observation of the language and conduct of men, in such circumstances, and under such excitements, as no respectable woman has ever an opportunity of remarking. The most valuable and characteristic scenes are those in which the lash of playful satire is applied to the lesser foibles of life, and the unostentatious *home-bred* virtues are set forth and eulogised; for these are the traits which women have the most frequent opportunities of observing, and are the most skilful in catching and delineating....

---

1   Ann Radcliffe (English, 1764-1823), writer of Gothic novels.
2   Rosa Matilda, pseudonym of Charlotte Dacre (English, 1782-1841), writer of romances.

The author has gone through the high-ways and bye-ways of life and filled her sketch-book with copies of nature, and by decomposing and combining these anew, she has given us a great variety of characters, each of which has the distinctness of individuality and the fresh coloring of nature; and yet none of them, (as far as we know) are representatives of any living being. We feel in reading the book, that we have certainly seen this person and been acquainted with that one, but we cannot tell when or where, and in endeavoring to remember, we feel that puzzling sensation attendant upon the effort to recall the effaced images of a dream.... Miss Clarence is well defined by the author herself, as a 'heroine of the nineteenth century.' She has the strong sense, the quiet energy, the pure-toned felling, the absence of affectation, extravagance, and mawkish sentimentality, which would secure the highest esteem and admiration in real life, and which enable her to act with decision and success in situations where some young ladies we have read of would only have screamed and fainted away. When we were first introduced to her, we were afraid she was going to be one of those pattern-women, who never do any thing wrong, and who make the worst imaginable heroines, because we know that in whatever circumstances they may be placed, they will do and say exactly what is most proper; but we were refreshed by perceiving, on a little further acquaintance, that she could now and then commit an amiable indiscretion, and be hurried by her warm-hearted impulses out of the pale of rigid prudence....We regard her as quite superior to the hero, though he is a very fine fellow, spirited, high-minded, self-forgetting, and with 'all good grace to grace a gentleman.'[1] He richly deserves the happiness that falls to his lot, but he has not that charm of individuality which Miss Clarence so eminently possesses. He seems to be merely one of a species, a promising young man about town.... But the hero of a modern novel is always the least important personage in it, and all that is required of him is, that he should be young, handsome, and brave, bow gracefully, and speak good English.

Mrs. Layton is the most brilliant and effective character in the book, and the perfect success with which she is conceived and embodied, discovers no inconsiderable portion of genius and inventive power. From the first to the last, she is the same finished piece of art. She wears elegance like a mantle, and to be graceful and *recherchée*,[2] costs her no more effort than to move and breathe. Her conversation and letters are full of that sparkling originality, which arises from the union of wit in conceiving, and taste in expressing thoughts. She has made the art of pleasing a study, and has neglected nothing which may

---

1 Shakespeare's *The Two Gentlemen of Verona* II.iv.72.
2 Meticulous; also, in demand.

contribute to entire success. She can encourage the diffident, flatter the vain, amuse the grave, instruct the gay, and adapt herself so dexterously to the taste and opinions of all she talks with, as to make each one imagine himself an object of particular interest to her.... She is armed cap-a-pie[1] for the encounter of wits, and possesses every weapon requisite for the mimic jousts of a drawing-room, the sparkling repartee, the keen-edged, yet sheathed rebuke, the disguised compliment, the gay *bon mot*, the pensive sentiment. She can employ them all with the happiest effect, wound without seeming to wound, and charm we know not why. Yet with all this, she is deficient in every thing that makes a person truly respectable and praise-worthy. She has not a spark of genuine feeling nor a ray of genuine sense, and has not read one page of the true philosophy of life, that philosophy which feeds the mind with thoughts of beauty, and stamps upon the heart sweet images of love. She fears nothing but ridicule, and worships nothing but opinion. She bows to the golden calf of fashion, and neglecting the unchanging form of things, watches the shadows of the clouds that pass over them. She is so exquisitely selfish as to sacrifice the affections of others to her own tastes, and she would not hesitate to gratify her slightest whim, though at every step she crushed a human heart. This portrait is drawn with a master hand, and what is peculiarly excellent in it is, that in our admiration of her fine powers, we never cease to lament and pity their perversion. No young lady could ever wish to be like Mrs. Layton, and no one can read her history without learning from it a valuable lesson. We have heard many people express surprise, that the author should have made Gerald Roscoe, a young man of so much moral purity, (and the young have the least charity for the unprincipled,) so great an admirer of Mrs. Layton, especially as the latter was so little of a hypocrite, and so openly avowed her contempt for things which most people regard as sacred. But no one will object to this, who knows the amount of the influence exerted by a fascinating married woman upon a young imaginative mind, and how possible it is for the strongest and purest natures to be, like Tasso's hero, caught in the toils spared by an artful Armida.[2]

We do not think the character of Pedrillo a very successful effort ...

We close our imperfect notice by cordially recommending this novel to the reading public, and we would even beg those who, as a general rule, avoid works of modern fiction, to make an exception in this instance. We are proud of our distinguished countrywoman, and regard her works as an honor to our land.... We are grateful to her for the

---

1 Head to foot.
2 See p. 265, note 4. A portrait of Mrs. Layton in this character adorns the Layton home.

pleasure she has afforded us, and would beg her to continue her labors in the vineyard of American fiction.... She has but to look around her to find an ample field for the exercise of her talents;—she may find abundant food for speculation in the Protean forms which society assumes in our wide continent,—in the gay throngs that chase amusement from one watering-place to another, and in the lowly virtues that cluster round our farm-house hearts, and, like flowers that twine around the living rock, give beauty and fragrance to the hardest and coarsest forms of life. To the writer of fiction, whose *forte* is character-drawing, we know of no land like ours, whether we regard the extent of our territory, the variety of the stocks from which we sprung, the youthful and electric vigor with which the veins of our world are filled, and the unchecked freedom with which it is our unvalued privilege to act and think. The face of society has not by long attention been ground down to one uniform level, and vigorous and fantastic shoots of character are not nipped by the frost of hoary convention.... And as the harvest is plenty, so are the laborers few;—the materials of romance in the old world are waxing threadbare; but the charm of unworn freshness is here like morning-dew. We would call upon all the sons and daughters of genius to be up and doing, and we would entreat the author of Clarence in particular, to persevere in the course she has so successfully entered upon, for her own sake and her country's sake.

5. *The London Literary Gazette* 707 (7 August 1830): 507-08

THE title of this work gives us little idea of the contents, which are American entirely, and exclusively American, and evidently written by a native. As a novel, it has no striking characteristics; the plot is full of old-fashioned improbabilities and mysteries—the personages as beautiful and superexcellent on the one side, as they are detestable and wicked on the other. Mrs. Layton is a Transatlantic copy of Lady Delacourt;[1] only the desire of something of novelty in the delineation has occasioned an inconsistency not in Miss Edgeworth's model. But what attracts our attention to these pages is their national character....

There are some curious marks of ignorance as regards English customs and facts. The traveller, for example, is a little effusion of spleen: we are not aware that even one of our gastronomes would deem salad with fish any solecism either in taste or manners: the hat under the arm belongs to our grandfathers: *Sir* Benjamin West must thank these pages

---

1 The reviewer clearly intends to refer to Lady Delacour of Maria Edgeworth's *Belinda*.

for his title:[1] and there is not a little national partiality in stamping the heroine as perfect in her literary taste, because she prefers Bryant to Byron....[2]

6. *The Ladies Museum* (1 September 1830): 170

The arts by which the literary appetite of the public has been excited for the last few years, during which the market has, notwithstanding, many splendid exceptions, been deluged with a greater quantity of trash than issued from all the purveyors of literature of the previous half century, are becoming too notorious to succeed much longer. The price of modern novels, rendered enormous by the necessity of covering the expense of enormous puffing,[3] has long driven the majority of readers to the circulating libraries, but even the libraries will refuse to purchase them, when puffs, reviews, and title pages, are alike deceitful. Who would imagine that "Clarence, a Tale of our own Times," was an American story, and the hero, Clarence, a clerk in a Yankee insurance office? What must be the disappointment of those searchers for scandal and slander, who, seeing such a title, put forth, with the usual flourish of trumpets, from the *fashionable* purveyor of New Burlington Street,[4] would expect nothing less than royalty for a repast? This "Tale of our own Times" is altogether foreign, an American story written by an American lady, a Miss Sedgwick, in a style which was considered good fifty years ago.

7. *Colburn's New Monthly Magazine* 30 (September 1830): 366-67

An American novel, and by an American lady—the first female writer among the natives heard of here, we believe, and certainly the first who makes her *debut* under the auspices of a leading publisher. The story is entirely domestic, and one of civilized life,—speaking, of course, with reference to the backwoods. New York is the theatre, and the society of that capital of the Western world—the fashionables of the place— furnished the prototypes of the characters. The tale itself, though not without interest, and often very effectively told, is a matter of inferior consideration; for both incident and complication are of the stuff of

---

1 See p. 144, note 1.
2 American poet William Cullen Bryant to British poet George Gordon, Lord Byron.
3 Advertisement or publicity with exaggerated praise.
4 The location of the offices in London of Colburn and Bentley, Sedgwick's British publishers.

English romances; the real value of the production—and real value it really has—lies in the portraiture it exhibits of society under new forms and new influences. It supplies at least a specimen of the manners of what is regarded as *good* society in the first state of America; presented by one, whatever may be her own station, whose every page proves her to be an intelligent and cultivated person. The aristocracy of New York is one of money, not of rank or of family, and thus, apparently, more susceptible of a ready classification than the common European mixture of birth, wealth, and title. But practically it is not a whit more so. The exclusive spirit of the official and more opulent classes is as repelling, and, we were going to say, as inveterate, but certainly as determined, as in the oldest state of feudalism; and, on the other hand, the struggle of the *nouveaux riches* to cross the barrier, to the full as resolute, though not more successful. The scuffle and scramble wear sometimes a laughable aspect, because so much of the tumult looks like, and perhaps actually is, imitative, though much also is indisputably the mere effect of similar circumstances. Novelties with them are antiquities with us. Their first sets and castes are our seconds and thirds; and, of course, in the eyes of the fine and fastidious among us, excessively coarse and contemptible.

The production is genuine American, and peculiarities of the country peep out at every turn; not of mere idiom or illiterate coarseness— there is no *guessing, concluding,* or *calculating*—but of terms *established* by custom, and not yet superseded by fashionable imitation—thus, the drawing-room and boudoir are still the parlour, and a splendid bookseller's, a fashionable bookstore. We observe it announced as *new*, that the expression of *riding* in a carriage is vulgar—the correct, the only admissible phrase, is driving. Of course, riding and driving are just become shibboleths at New York, however ambiguous the new terms; for driving thus expresses two acts, and only by circumstances can it be known, whether a lady, when she talks of driving or taking a drive, actually drives herself, or is driven by her coachman. The ladies, the most refined, we observe, use a breadth of language that will not, by and by, we suppose, be more tolerated in New York than in London— "O my dear soul," cries one lady to another, where "My dear," would be as much as would escape from English lips. "I know a thing or two," says another—meaning that she had too much tact to commit such a blunder, &c. More gesticulation, or rather, a more undisciplined giving way to emotion, is indulged in—such as when, on the very slight occasion, a young lady covers her face with her hands to hide her embarrassment. Whatever want of refinement, however, may appear occasionally in phrases and gestures, there prevails a genuine reserve, and unartificial decorum, in matters of conduct and sentiment. Profligacy is not treated with levity.... The current literature of London and America is a common topic; but the coupling of Halleck and Bryant with

Moore and Byron,[1] as names equally well known and equally prized, sounds strangely on an Englishman's ear. The heroine is an admirable sketch—spirited, frank, active, and essentially lady-like; and indeed the tale, independently of all considerations of value, arising from faithful descriptions of living characters, as a novel, is worthy to class among the best of our own....

---

1   See p. 299, note 1.

Appendix E: The 1849 Author's Revised Edition of Clarence

[The revised edition of *Clarence* was designed to be part of a uniform edition of all of Sedgwick's works. Although this project was not fully realized (see Introduction), Sedgwick's publisher George Palmer Putnam advertised *Clarence* heavily, analogizing "Miss Sedgwick's Works" to his collected editions of Washington Irving and James Fenimore Cooper and foregrounding the special status of *Clarence* as a novel published in a new edition after being out of print for twenty years. Sedgwick herself reflected on the changes of two decades in her preface to the new edition, and reviewers, taking their cue from Putnam's advertisements, emphasized the distinction of *Clarence* as a part of Sedgwick's larger body of work.[1]]

---

1 Brief reviews also appeared in *Graham's Magazine* 36.1 (January 1850): 94 and *Holden's Dollar Magazine* 4.5 (November 1849): 700.

1. Advertisements for "Miss Sedgwick's Works" and *Clarence* (1849)

a. George P. Putnam, Advertisement for "Miss Sedgwick's Works," *The Literary World* (22 September 1849): 258. Courtesy American Antiquarian Society

MISS SEDGWICK'S WORKS.

An Edition uniform with Irving's Works and the early Works of Cooper.

WILL BE READY IN A FEW DAYS,

CLARENCE; OR TWENTY YEARS SINCE.

THE AUTHOR'S REVISED EDITION—Complete in One Volume. 12mo. Cloth, $1 25.

RECENTLY PUBLISHED,

THE MYTHOLOGICAL TEXT BOOK.

FIRST ABRIDGED EDITION.

GRECIAN AND ROMAN MYTHOLOGY.

By M. A. DWIGHT,

WITH A SERIES OF ILLUSTRATIONS.

FIRST ABRIDGED EDITION. 12MO. HALF BOUND, 75 CTS.

From Prof. Webster, Principal of the Free Academy.
"A valuable addition to our Elementary School Books, being written in good taste and with ability, and well adapted to popular instruction."

From President Woods, of Bowdoin College.
"The work is highly appreciated here, and means will be taken to recommend its use to our Students."

Prof. Tayler Lewis, of the University of New York.
"I have carefully examined the work on Ancient Mythology, and think it admirably adapted for use as a class book in any of our Schools, Academies, or Colleges, besides being a book of rich instruction and deep interest to the general reader."

From the Christian Alliance.
"It ought to lie upon the table of every Student, and would be useful in every family."

b. George P. Putnam, Advertisement for the Revised *Clarence*,
   The Literary World (13 October 1849): 325. Courtesy American
   Antiquarian Society

ALSO JUST PUBLISHED.

CLARENCE;

A Tale of our Own Times.

By Miss C. M. SEDGWICK.

Author's Revised Edition.

WITH ENGRAVED PORTRAIT AND VIGNETTE TITLE.

Complete in 1 vol. 12mo. $1 25.

"There is all through Clarence a happy feminine grace
which adds vastly to its interest and effect.

" Mr. Putnam has done well in adding the works of his
gifted countrywoman to his series of American authors.
The volume is uniform with the works of Irving and
Cooper, in the neatest style of execution."—*Lit. World.*

---

2. Sedgwick's Preface to *Clarence; or, A Tale of Our Own Times* (New York: G.P. Putnam, 1849)

A remark of Johnson's, based on a mean quality in human nature, is not true of my countrymen; they do NOT rate a living writer by his poorest production.[1] On the contrary, they have perhaps an undue partiality for native living writers, and therefore, I hope they will not think me guilty of presumption, or temerity, in republishing old works, forgotten perhaps by most of their readers. I am aware that novels are, for the most part, entitled only to an ephemeral interest, and that the amount which mine were so fortunate as to obtain at their first publication, was owing to the fact that but a few fellow-workers divided the favor of my countrymen with me. Since the "New-England Tale," my first unaspiring production, appeared, many gifted native writers have enriched our romantic literature. A new mine has been opened in the north. Frederika Bremer[2] has electrified us with a series of works that have the richness, and raciness of European literature, and the purity, and healthfulness of our own. Other northern lights have shone upon us. Almost every weekly steamer brings us from England a new novel, written by some man or woman of genius; and France sends out by scores romances, to stimulate anew the wearied and sated appetite.

I certainly do not expect that my home and artless products, can compete with these rich foreign fabrics. If they have no intrinsic and independent merit, they certainly are not worth republication, but if they have, it is an incident in their favor, that they relate to our own history and condition, while the English novels illustrate a very different stage of civilization from ours; and the French romances portray that which we trust ours will never reach. Of the first we may say "it ripes and ripes," of the last, "it rots and rots."[3]

Since there are publishers genuine enough to pay the tax imposed by a copyright,[4] I hope to find readers who will relish a book for its home atmosphere—who will have something of the feelings of him who

---

1 Paraphrase of Samuel Johnson's remark in his *Preface to Shakespeare* (1765): "While an authour [sic] is yet living we estimate his powers by his worst performance, and when he is dead we rate them by his best."

2 Novelist (Swedish, 1801-65). She and Sedgwick met on Bremer's 1849-51 visit to the US.

3 Reference to Shakespeare's *As You Like It* II.vii.26-27.

4 US copyright law did not require publishers to pay royalties to non-American authors. Thus American-authored books carried a "tax," the cost of payments to their authors.

said he would rather have a single apple from the garden of his father's house than all the fruits of France.[1]

I should be ungrateful to many old and kind friends, if I did not acknowledge that I have been in part persuaded to a republication, by their expressed desire to revive their old acquaintance with the books now out of print. I should not be true if I did not avow my wish to make acquaintance and friendship with the generation that has grown up since my novels were published—with the young, ardent, and generous, the great class of novel readers, in whose memory I may live for a little while after my contemporaries and myself shall have passed away.

The selection of *Clarence* as the first in the series of republication has been accidental. The others will follow at intervals, and the series will include the smaller works, written for the largest class of readers and for children.

3. Review from *The Christian Inquirer* 3.52 (6 October 1849): 2

This is the first volume of a collected edition of Miss Sedgwick's works, producing [*sic*] in a style of great elegance by Mr. Putnam—print, paper and illustration unexceptionable, as they should be for offering the writings of Miss Sedgwick to her countrymen, as an ornament to their libraries. In any form these books must find a place there, for we are all justly proud of them. No American who reads at all will need that we should commend this or any other volume of the series. Clarence is one of the earlier of Miss Sedgwick's novels—a domestic story, full of incident, and instinct with moral instruction, without preaching or pedantry. Truths insinuated are sometimes more potent than truths insisted on. It is the privilege of some spirits to be able to make the picturesque subsidiary to the holy—a power which entitles the novelist and the poet to take rank with the prophet. Those who study attentively the works of Miss Sedgwick, will find that while they have been fancying themselves only amused or charmed, they have been growing ashamed of selfishness, ashamed of unkindness, of vanity, of detraction, of parsimony, deceit, arrogance; ashamed of all that is evil, and in love with whatever is pure, lovely and of good report.

4. Review from *The Literary World* 5.140 (6 October 1849): 297

MISS SEDGWICK has been aptly instanced as an American writer whose success and popularity have not been the result of transatlantic favor, and whose reputation does not depend upon the *dicta* of foreign

---

1 From *The Wild Irish Boy* (1808) by novelist Charles Robert Maturin (Irish, 1782-1824).

critics, inasmuch as it was acquired at the first without their aid. Ever since her first entrance into the world of letters her literary productions have been mainly, in every sense of the word, American. Not only have the scenes and incidents of her works of fiction been drawn from the history of this country or its domestic manners, but her more directly useful and perhaps most praiseworthy efforts have all been in illustration of its social habits and tendencies. Besides this, there are perhaps none of our writers whose works in their spirit and style more completely reflect the prominent characteristics of the American mind. They are marked less by the refinements of highly cultivated taste and imagination than by a rigorous straightforwardness of purpose and a practical energy, of which the principal ingredient is that rare quality in authorship, good common sense.

We do not intend to be understood as limiting our praise of Miss Sedgwick's writings to their indigenous character, any more than we would convey the idea that Americanism by itself is their most satisfactory ingredient. We are not so anxious for the establishment of that "national literature" for which so many ardent appeals are advanced by annual orators and weekly essayists, as to desire its advance at the expense of principles of taste and judgment, which lie far behind the circumstances of locality or nationality. We are not disposed to make ourselves uncomfortable with American books any more than with American broadcloth, so long as better are to be had. It is no consolation in the midst of the stupidities of a trashy novel or an unreliable history, to be assured that it is the production of native talent. We have every reason to believe that in the department of authorship, as in every other branch of invention, we may compete successfully with the old world, but never with anything that deserves the name of success, so long as our literature is tested by any other rules than those which have determined long ago the merit and the value of works which are by common consent the ripest fruits of the literature of our language.

If, then, Miss Sedgwick's works came to us with no other recommendation than that which she modestly advances in her preface—their American origin, we should hardly recognise their claim. We should not be amongst the readers whom she "hopes to find, who will relish a book for its *home* atmosphere—who will have something of the feelings of him who said he would rather have a single apple from the garden of his father's house than all the fruits of France." This is a proper and a commendable feeling within certain limits; but it would hardly be safe, even for Miss Sedgwick, secure though she be in the friendship and admiration of all American readers, to risk the permanency of her literary reputation upon the slender basis of its nationality.

We think, as we have already intimated, that it has a surer foundation—the foundation of good sense, active and enlightened sympathies, a genial warmth of sentiment, and an earnest energy of thought, ingredients which, while they would give the assurance of success to literary efforts of almost any description which taste or inclination might prompt, receive a higher impulse and a more satisfactory recompense when applied to advance the real and immediate interests of society, and to promote the culture of a *genuine* nationality.

CLARENCE is, we believe, one of Miss Sedgwick's earlier works. It is a domestic novel; one of a class which the modern improvements in fiction have rather elbowed out of popularity. It is called "A Tale of our own Times," but we outgrow our own recollection so fast in this country that its local descriptions and incidents have entirely lost their contemporary freshness. A description of Broadway some twenty years ago, in the first chapter, would hardly be recognised by a New Yorker; and the author is forced to introduce a note at the end of the chapter, apologizing for the air of antiquity which has unconsciously overgrown her subject. But the story is a good one. We remember reading it with interest, years ago, in a dingy two volume edition, and being very much interested in the fortunes of its characters. It is not one of those books which makes the reader wonder that it could ever have been written by a woman, for Miss Sedgwick, fortunately, has never allied herself to that class of authoresses who studiously ignore in their writings the Providence that has made them women. There is all through Clarence a happy feminine grace which adds vastly to its interest and effect.

Mr. Putnam has done well in adding the works of his gifted countrywoman to his series of American authors. The volume is uniform with the works of Irving and Cooper, in the neatest style of execution ...

Bibliography

Modern Editions of Catharine Sedgwick's Novels

Hope Leslie; Or, Early Times in the Massachusetts (1827). Ed. Carolyn Karcher. New York: Penguin, 1998. Ed. Mary Kelly. New Brunswick, NJ: Rutgers UP, 1987.

The Linwoods; or, "Sixty Years Since" in America (1835). Ed. Maria Karafilis. Hanover, NH: UP of New England, 2002.

A New-England Tale; or, Sketches of New-England Character and Manners (1822). Ed. Victoria L. Clements. New York: Oxford UP, 1995. Ed. Susan K. Harris. New York: Penguin, 2003.

Bibliographies of Sedgwick's Works

Blanck, Jacob, Virginia L. Smyers, and Michael Winship. "Catharine Maria Sedgwick, 1789-1867." In *Bibliography of American Literature*, vol. 7, 380-96. New Haven, CT: Yale UP, 1983. (books and short works in books only)

Damon-Bach, Lucinda L., Melissa J. Homestead, and Alison J. Roepsch, "Chronological Bibliography of the Works of Catharine Maria Sedgwick." In *Catharine Maria Sedgwick: Critical Perspectives*, 295-311. (includes magazine publications)

Sedgwick's Autobiography and Selections from Her Journals and Letters

Dewey, Mary E., ed. *Life and Letters of Catharine M. Sedgwick*. New York: Harper & Brothers, 1871.

Kelley, Mary, ed. *The Power of Her Sympathy: The Autobiography and Journal of Catharine Maria Sedgwick*. Boston: Massachusetts Historical Society, 1993.

Books about Sedgwick

Damon-Bach, Lucinda, and Victoria Clements, eds. *Catharine Maria Sedgwick: Critical Perspectives*. Boston: Northeastern UP, 2003.

Foster, Edward Halsey. *Catharine Sedgwick*. New York: Twayne, 1974.

Multi-figure Biographical Studies Featuring Sedgwick

Brooks, Gladys. *Three Wise Virgins*. New York: E.P. Dutton, 1957.

Cott, Nancy. *The Bonds of Womanhood: Woman's Sphere in New England, 1780-1835.* New Haven, CT: Yale UP, 1977.

Kelley, Mary. *Private Woman, Public Stage: Literary Domesticity in Nineteenth-Century America.* New York: Oxford UP, 1984. (Chapel Hill, NC: U of North Carolina P, 2002, with new preface)

Kenslea, Timothy. *The Sedgwicks in Love: Courtship, Engagement, and Marriage in the Early Republic.* Boston: Northeastern UP, 2006.

Mintz, Stephen. *A Prison of Expectations: The Family in Victorian Culture.* New York: Oxford UP, 1983.

Book Chapters and Journal Articles about Sedgwick

Short titles of Sedgwick's works treated are given parenthetically after a citation if the information is not clear in the citation.

Allen, Thomas, "Clockwork Nation: Modern Time, Moral Perfectionism and American Identity in Catharine Beecher and Henry Thoreau." *Journal of American Studies* 39.1 (April 2005): 65-86. (*Home*)

——. "Clockwork Nation." Chap. 3 in *A Republic in Time: Temporality and Social Imagination in Nineteenth-Century America.* Chapel Hill, NC: U of North Carolina P, 2008. (*Home*)

Arch, Stephen Carl. "Romancing the Puritans: American Historical Fiction in the 1820s." *ESQ* 39, 2 and 3 (1993): 107-32. (*Hope Leslie*)

Ashworth, Suzanne. "Invalid Insurrections: Intellect and Appetite in Catharine Maria Sedgwick's Biography of Lucretia Maria Davidson." *ATQ* 20.2 (June 2006): 419-47.

Avallone, Charlene. "Catharine Sedgwick and the Circles of New York." *Legacy* 23.2 (2006): 115-31. (*Clarence, Married or Single?*)

——. "Catharine Sedgwick's White Nation-Making: Historical Fiction and *The Linwoods.*" *ESQ* 55.2 (2009): 97-133.

——. "Women Reading Melville/Melville Reading Women." In *Melville and Women,* ed. Elizabeth Schultz and Haskell Springer, 41-59. Kent, OH: Kent State UP, 2006. ("The Country Cousin," *Linwoods*)

Baker, Dorothy Z. "'The story was in the gaps': Catharine Maria Sedgwick and Edith Wharton." Chap. 6 in *America's Gothic Fiction: The Legacy of Magnalia Christi Americana.* Columbus, OH: Ohio State UP, 2007. (*Hope Leslie*)

Balaam, Peter. "'Piazza to the North': Melville Reading Sedgwick." In *Melville and Women,* ed. Elizabeth Schultz and Haskell Springer, 60-81. Kent, OH: Kent State UP, 2006. (*New-England Tale*)

——. "Representing Grief, Mourning Representation: Melville's *Piazza Tales.*" Chap. 3 in *Misery's Mathematics: Mourning, Compensation and Reality in Antebellum American Literature.* New York: Routledge, 2009. (*New-England Tale*)

Barnes, Elizabeth. "Changing the Subject: Domestic Fictions of Self-Possession." Chap. 4 in *States of Sympathy: Seduction and Democracy in the American Novel*. New York: Columbia UP, 1997. (*New-England Tale*)

Bauermeister, Erica R. "*The Lamplighter, The Wide, Wide World*, and *Hope Leslie*: The Recipes for Nineteenth-Century American Women's Novels." *Legacy* 8.1 (Spring 1991): 17-28.

Baym, Nina. "Catharine Sedgwick and Other Early Novelists." Chap. 3 in *Woman's Fiction: A Guide to Novels by and about Women in America, 1820-70*. Ithaca: Cornell UP, 1978. (Urbana, IL: U of Illinois P, 1993, with new introduction) (*New-England Tale, Redwood, Clarence, Married or Single?*)

——. "How Men and Women Wrote Indian Stories." In *New Essays on The Last of the Mohicans*. ed. H. Daniel Peck, 67-86. New York: Cambridge UP, 1992. (revised as "Putting Women in Their Place: *The Last of the Mohicans* and Other Indian Stories," in *Feminism in American Literary History: Essays by Nina Baym*, 19-35. New Brunswick, NJ: Rutgers UP, 1992) (*Hope Leslie*)

——. "Imaginary Histories." Chap. 8 in *American Women Writers and the Work of History, 1790-1860*. New Brunswick, NJ: Rutgers UP, 1995. (*Hope Leslie, Linwoods*)

Bell, Michael D. "History and Romance Convention in Catharine Sedgwick's *Hope Leslie*." *American Quarterly* 22.2.1 (Summer 1970): 213-21.

Bellin, Joshua David. "Indian Conversions." Chap. 1 in *The Demon of the Continent: Indians and the Shaping of American Literature*. Philadelphia: U of Pennsylvania P, 2001. (*Hope Leslie*)

Birdsall, Richard D. "William Cullen Bryant and Catherine [sic] Sedgwick—Their Debt to Berkshire." *New England Quarterly* 28.3 (September 1955): 349-71.

Block, Shelley R., and Etta M. Madden. "Science in Catharine Maria Sedgwick's *Hope Leslie*." *Legacy* 20, 1-2 (2003): 22-37.

Brodhead, Richard. "Sparing the Rod: Discipline in Antebellum America." Chap. 1 in *Cultures of Letters: Scenes of Reading and Writing in Nineteenth-Century America*. Chicago: U of Chicago P, 1993. (*Home*)

Bromell, Nicholas Knowles. "Maternal Labor in the Work of Literary Domestics: Catharine Maria Sedgwick and Susan Warner." Chap. 7 in *By the Sweat of the Brow: Literature and Labor in Antebellum America*. Chicago: U of Chicago P, 1993. (*New-England Tale*)

Brown, Harry. "'The Horrid Alternative': Miscegenation and Madness in the Frontier Romance." *Journal of American & Comparative Cultures* 24.3 & 4 (2001): 137-51. (*Hope Leslie*)

Brusky, Sarah. "Beyond the Ending of Maternal Absence in *A New England-Tale, The Wide, Wide World*, and *St. Elmo*." *ESQ* 46.3 (2000): 149-76.

Buchanan, Daniel P. "Tares in the Wheat: Puritan Violence and Puritan Families in the Nineteenth-Century Liberal Imagination." *Religion and American Culture* 8.2 (1998): 205-36. (*New-England Tale, Hope Leslie*)

Buchenau, Barbara. "Comparativist Interpretations of the Frontier in Early American Fiction and Literary Historiography." *CLCWeb: Comparative Literature and Culture: A WWWeb Journal* 3.2 (June 2001). (*Hope Leslie*)

——. "'Wizards of the West?' How Americans Respond to Sir Walter Scott, the 'Wizard of the North.'" *James Fenimore Cooper: His Country and His Art* 11 (1997): 14-25. (*Hope Leslie*)

Buell, Lawrence. *New England Literary Culture: From Revolution through Renaissance*. Cambridge: Cambridge UP, 1986. (*New-England Tale* and *Hope Leslie* across several chapters)

Cagidemetrio, Alide. "A Plea for Fictional Histories and Old-Time 'Jewesses.'" In *The Invention of Ethnicity*, ed. Werner Sollors, 14-43. New York: Oxford UP, 1989. (*Hope Leslie*)

Castiglia, Christopher. "In Praise of Extra-Vagant Women: *Hope Leslie* and the Captivity Romance." *Legacy* 6.2 (Fall 1989): 3-16.

——. "A Hostage in the House: Domestic Captivity and Catharine Sedgwick's *Hope Leslie*." Chap. 6 in *Bound and Determined: Captivity, Culture Crossing, and White Womanhood, from Mary Rowlandson to Patty Hearst*. Chicago: U of Chicago P, 1996.

Cohoon, Lorinda B. "'A Just, a Useful Part': Lydia Huntley Sigourney and Catharine Maria Sedgwick's Contributions to *The Juvenile Miscellany* and *The Youth's Companion*." In *Enterprising Youth: Social Values and Acculturation in Nineteenth-Century American Children's Literature*, ed. Monika Elbert, 3-17. New York: Routledge, 2008.

Daly, Robert. "Reading Sedgwick Now: Empathy and Ethics in Early America." *Literature in the Early American Republic* 2 (2010): 131-52.

Dyer, Gary. "The Transatlantic Pocahontas." *Nineteenth-Century Contexts* 30.4 (December 2008): 301-22. (*Hope Leslie*)

Elsden, Annamaria Formichella. "'I Forgot Myself': Nation and Identity in Catharine Maria Sedgwick's Travel Writing." Chap. 1 in *Roman Fever: Domesticity and Nationalism in Nineteenth-Century American Women's Writing*. Columbus, OH: Ohio State UP, 2004. (*Letters from Abroad*)

Emerson, Amanda. "History, Memory, and the Echoes of Equivalence in Catharine Maria Sedgwick's *Hope Leslie*." *Legacy* 24.1 (2007): 24-49.

Fick, Thomas H. "Authentic Ghosts and Real Bodies: Negotiating Power in Nineteenth-Century Women's Ghost Stories." *South Atlantic Review* 64.2 (Spring 1999): 81-97. ("The Country Cousin")

——. "Catharine Sedgwick's 'Cacoethes Scribendi': Romance in Real Life." *Studies in Short Fiction* 27.4 (Fall 1990): 567-76.

Finger, Roland. "The Reassurance of Sororicide." *Pacific Coast Philology* 40 (2005): 117-37. (*Hope Leslie*)

Floyd, Janet. "Back into Memory Land? Quilts and the Problem of History." *Women's Studies* 37.1 (2008): 38-56. ("The Patch Work Quilt")

Foletta, Marshall. "'The dearest sacrifice': Catharine Maria Sedgwick and the Celibate Life." *American Nineteenth Century History* 8.1 (March 2007): 51-79.

Ford, Douglas. "Inscribing the 'Impartial Observer' in Sedgwick's *Hope Leslie*." *Legacy* 14.2 (1997): 81-92.

Garvey, T. Gregory. "Risking Reprisal: Catharine Sedgwick's *Hope Leslie* and the Legitimation of Public Action by Women." *ATQ* 8.4 (December 1994): 287-98.

Gassan, Richard H. "Skeptics." Chap. 9 in *The Birth of American Tourism: New York, the Hudson Valley, and American Culture, 1790-1830*. Amherst, MA: U of Massachusetts P, 2008. (*Travellers*)

Gee, Karen Richardson. "Women, Wilderness, and Liberty in Sedgwick's *Hope Leslie*." *Studies in the Humanities* 19.2 (1992): 161-70.

Gossett, Suzanne, and Barbara Ann Bardes. "Women and Political Power in the Republic: Two Early American Novels." *Legacy* 2.2 (1985): 13-30. (*Hope Leslie*)

———. "Two Visions of the Republic." Chap. 1 in *Declarations of Independence: Women and Political Power in Nineteenth Century American Fiction*. New Brunswick, NJ: Rutgers UP, 1990. (*Hope Leslie*)

Gould, Philip. "Catharine Sedgwick's Cosmopolitan Nation." *New England Quarterly* 78.2 (2005): 232-58. (*Linwoods*)

———. "Catharine Sedgwick's 'Recital' of the Pequot War." *American Literature* 66.4 (1994): 641-62. (*Hope Leslie*)

———. "Catharine Sedgwick's 'Recital' of the Pequot War" and "Refashioning the Republic: Gender, Ideology, and the Politics of Virtue in *Hobomok* and *Hope Leslie*." Chap. 2 and 3 in *Covenant and Republic: Historical Romance and the Politics of Puritanism*. Cambridge: Cambridge UP, 2006.

Harris, Susan K. "Preludes: The Early Didactic Novel: Narrative Control in *Charlotte Temple* and *A New-England Tale*." Chap. 1 in *19th-Century American Women's Novels: Interpretive Strategies*. Cambridge: Cambridge UP, 1990.

Higonnet, Margaret R. "Comparative Reading: Catharine M. Sedgwick's *Hope Leslie*." *Legacy* 15.1 (1998): 17-22.

Holly, Carol. "Nineteenth-Century Autobiographies of Affiliation: The Case of Catharine Sedgwick and Lucy Larcom." In *American Autobiography: Retrospect and Prospect*, ed. Paul John Eakin, 216-34. Madison, WI: U of Wisconsin P, 1991.

Homestead, Melissa J. "'Suited to the Market': Catharine Sedgwick, Female Authorship, and the Literary Property Debates, 1822-1842."

Chap. 2 in *American Women Authors and Literary Property, 1822-1869*. New York: Cambridge UP, 2005. (*New-England Tale, Clarence, Home*)

Insko, Jeffrey. "Anachronistic Imaginings: *Hope Leslie*'s Challenge to Historicism." *American Literary History* 16.2 (Summer 2004): 179-207.

——. "Passing Current: Electricity, Magnetism, and Historical Transmission in *The Linwoods*." *ESQ* 56.3 (2010): 293-326.

Kalayjian, Patricia Larson. "Cooper and Sedgwick: Rivalry or Respect?" *James Fenimore Cooper Society Miscellany* 4 (September 1993): 9-19.

——. "Revisioning America's (Literary) Past: Sedgwick's *Hope Leslie*." *NWSA Journal* 8.3 (Autumn 1996): 63-78.

Karafilis, Maria. "Catharine Maria Sedgwick's *Hope Leslie*: The Crisis between Ethical Political Action and US Literary Nationalism in the New Republic." *ATQ* 12.4 (December 1998): 327-44.

Kelley, Mary. "A Woman Alone: Catharine Maria Sedgwick's Spinsterhood in Nineteenth-Century America." *New England Quarterly* 51.2 (June 1978): 209-25.

——. "Negotiating a Self: The Autobiography and Journals of Catharine Maria Sedgwick." *New England Quarterly* 66.3 (September 1993): 366-98.

Krumrey, Diane. "On the Frontier of Natural Language with Eloquent Indians: *Hobomok* and *Hope Leslie*." In *The Image of the Frontier in Literature, the Media, and Society*, ed. Will Wright and Steven Kaplan, 261-65. Pueblo, CO: University of Southern Colorado, 1997.

LaMonaca, Maria. "'She Could Make a Cake As Well As Books ...': Catharine Sedgwick, Anna Jameson, and the Construction of the Domestic Intellectual." *Women's Writing* 2.3 (1995): 235-49. (*Means and Ends*)

Lewis, Paul. "'Lectures or a Little Charity': Poor Visits in Antebellum Literature and Culture." *New England Quarterly* 73.2 (2000): 246-74. (*Poor Rich Man*)

Loeffelholz, Mary. "Who Killed Lucretia Davidson? or, Poetry in the Domestic-Tutelary Complex." *Yale Journal of Criticism* 10.2 (1997): 271-93.

Lubovich, Maglina. "'Married or Single?': Catharine Maria Sedgwick on Old Maids, Wives, and Marriage." *Legacy* 25.1 (2008): 23-40. (*Hope Leslie*, "Old Maids," *Married or Single?*)

Luciano, Dana. "Evocations: The Romance of Indian Lament." Chap. 2 in *Arranging Grief: Sacred Time and the Body in Nineteenth-Century America*. New York: New York UP, 2007. (*Hope Leslie*)

——. "Voicing Removal: Mourning (as) History in *Hope Leslie*." *Western Humanities Review* 58.2 (2004): 48-67.

Matter-Seibel, Sabina. "Native Americans, Women, and the Culture of Nationalism in Lydia Maria Child and Catharine Maria Sedgwick." In *Early America Re-Explored: New Readings in Colonial, Early*

National, and Antebellum Culture, ed. Klaus Schmidt and Fritz Fleischmann, 411-40. New York: Peter Lang, 2000. (*Hope Leslie*)

McElwee, Joanna. "Rebels with Permission from Their Fathers: The Education of Saints and Insurgents in Catharine Maria Sedgwick's *Hope Leslie*." Chap. 4 in *The Nation Conceived: Learning, Education, and Nationhood in American Historical Novels of the 1820s*. Uppsala, Sweden: Uppsala University, 2005.

McKanan, Dan. "Wheat and Tares: The Liberal Encounter with Puritan Violence." Chap. 2 in *Identifying the Image of God: Radical Christians and Nonviolent Power in the Antebellum United States*. New York: Oxford UP, 2002. (*Hope Leslie, New-England Tale*)

McWilliams, Mark. "Distant Tables: Food and the Novel in Early America." *Early American Literature* 38.3 (2003): 365-93. (*Hope Leslie*)

Merish, Lori. "Gender, Domesticity, and Consumption in the 1830s: Caroline Kirkland, Catharine Sedgwick, and the Feminization of American Consumerism." Chap. 2 in *Sentimental Materialism: Gender, Commodity Culture and Nineteenth-Century American Literature*. Durham, NC: Duke UP, 2000. (*Home*)

Miller, Quentin. "'A Tyrannically Democratic Force': The Symbolic and Cultural Function of Clothing in Catharine Maria Sedgwick's *Hope Leslie*." *Legacy* 19.2 (2002): 121-36.

Mills, Rose M. "Reading *Hope Leslie* via Wollstonecraft: A Pedagogy for Sedgwick's Novel." *Journal of Kentucky Studies* 24 (2004): 110-16.

Milne, Gordon. "The Beginnings." Chap. 1 in *The Sense of Society: A History of the American Novel of Manners*. Rutherford, NJ: Fairleigh Dickinson UP, 1977. (*Clarence, Married or Single?*)

Mitchell, Domhnall. "Acts of Intercourse: 'Miscegenation' in Three 19th Century American Novels." *American Studies in Scandinavia* 27.2 (1995): 126-41. (*Hope Leslie*)

Nelson, Dana. "Sympathy as Strategy in Sedgwick's *Hope Leslie*." In *The Culture of Sentiment: Race, Gender, and Sentimentality in Nineteenth-Century America*, ed. Shirley Samuels, 191-202. New York: Oxford UP, 1992.

——. "W/Righting History: Sympathy as Strategy in *Hope Leslie* and *A Romance of the Republic*." Chap. 4 in *The Word in Black and White: Reading 'Race' in American Literature, 1638-1867*. New York: Oxford UP, 1992.

Ó Gallchoir, Clíona. "*Uncle Tom's Cabin* and the Irish National Tale." In *Transatlantic Stowe: Harriet Beecher Stowe and European Culture*, ed. Denise Kohn, et al., 24-45. Iowa City, IA: U of Iowa P, 2006. (*Redwood*)

Opfermann, Susanne. "Lydia Maria Child, James Fenimore Cooper, and Catharine Maria Sedgwick: A Dialogue on Race, Culture, and

Gender." In *Soft Canons: American Women Writers and Masculine Tradition*, ed. Karen Kilcup, 27-47. Iowa City, IA: U of Iowa P, 1999. (*Hope Leslie*)

Oshima, Yukiko. "Dreaming a Dream of Interracial Bonds: From *Hope Leslie* to *Moby-Dick*." In *Ungraspable Phantom: Essays on Moby-Dick*, ed. John Bryant et al., 238-51. Kent, OH: Kent State UP, 2006.

Ousley, Laurie. "The Business of Housekeeping: The Mistress, the Domestic, and the Construction of Class." *Legacy* 23.2 (2006): 132-47. (*Live and Let Live*)

Person, Leland S. "The American Eve: Miscegenation and a Feminist Frontier Fiction." *American Quarterly* 37.5 (1985): 668-85. (*Hope Leslie*)

Pratt, Lloyd. "Dialect Writing and Simultaneity in the American Historical Romance." *Differences* 13.3 (Fall 2002): 121-42. (*Hope Leslie*)

——. "'A Magnificent Fragment': Dialects of Time and the American Historical Romance." Chap. 2 in *Archives of American Time: Literature and Modernity in the Nineteenth Century*. Philadelphia: U of Pennsylvania P, 2010. (*Hope Leslie*)

Reynolds, David S. "Earth Above, Heaven Below." Chap. 2 in *Faith in Fiction: The Emergence of Religious Literature in America*. Cambridge, MA: Harvard UP, 1981. (novels, didactic novellas)

Robbins, Sarah. "Periodizing Authorship, Characterizing Genre: Catharine Maria Sedgwick's Benevolent Literacy Narratives." *American Literature* 76.1 (March 2004): 1-29. (*Live and Let Live, Boy of Mount Rhigi*)

——. "'The Future Good and Great of our Land': Republican Mothers, Female Authors, and Domesticated Literacy in Antebellum New England." *New England Quarterly* 75 (December 2002): 562-91. (*Love Token, Rich Poor Man, Facts and Fancies*)

——. "New England Authors and the Genre's Social Role" and "Cross-Class Teaching and Domesticated Instruction." Chap. 2 and 3 in *Managing Literacy, Mothering America: Women's Narratives on Reading and Writing in the Nineteenth Century*. Pittsburgh, PA: U of Pittsburgh P, 2004. (*Means and Ends, Stories for Young Persons*, "The Irish Girl")

Rosenthal, Debra J. "Race Mixture and the Representation of Indians in the United States and the Andes." Chap. 1 in *Race Mixture in Nineteenth-Century U.S. and Spanish American Fictions: Gender, Culture, and Nation Building*. Chapel Hill, NC: U of North Carolina P, 2004. (*Hope Leslie*)

Ross, Cheri Louise. "(Re)Writing the Frontier Romance: Catharine Maria Sedgwick's *Hope Leslie*." *College Language Association Journal* 39.3 (March 1996): 320-40.

Rust, Marion. "'Into the House of an Entire Stranger': Why Sentimental Doesn't Equal Domestic in Early American Fiction." *Early
American Literature* 37.2 (2002): 281-309. (*Hope Leslie*)

Ryan, Barbara. "The Family Work." Chap. 1 in *Love, Wages, Slavery: The
Literature of Servitude in the United States*. Urbana, IL: U of Illinois P,
2006. (*Hope Leslie, Linwoods, Live and Let Live*)

Ryan, Mary P. "From Patriarchal Household to Feminine Domesticity." Chap. 1 in *The Empire of the Mother: American Writing about Domesticity, 1830-1860*. New York: Haworth P, 1982. (*Live and Let Live,
Home*)

Samuels, Shirley. "The Family in the Novel: Cooper and the Domestic
Revolution." Chap. 3 in *Romances of the Republic: Women, The Family,
and Violence in The Literature of the Early American Nation*. New York:
Oxford UP, 1996. (*Linwoods*)

——. "Women, Blood, and Contract." *American Literary History* 20.1-2
(Spring-Summer 2008): 57-75. (*Hope Leslie*)

Sánchez, María Carla. "'Prayers in the Market Place': Women and Low
Culture in Catharine Sedgwick's 'Cacoethes Scribendi.'" *ATQ* 16.2
(June 2002): 101-13.

Scheiber, Andrew J. "Mastery and Majesty: Subject, Object, and the
Power of Authorship in Catharine Sedgwick's 'Cacoethes Scribendi.'" *ATQ* 10.1 (March 1996): 41-58.

Schneider, Bethany. "New England Tales: Catharine Sedgwick, Cather-
ine Brown, and the Dislocation of Indian Land." In *A Companion to
American Fiction, 1780-1865*, ed. Shirley Samuels, 353-64. Malden,
MA: Blackwell, 2007. (*New-England Tale*)

Schweitzer, Ivy. "The Ethical Horizon of American Friendship in Catharine Sedgwick's *Hope Leslie*." Chap. 5 in *Perfecting Friendship: Politics and Affiliation in Early American Literature*. Chapel Hill, NC: U
of North Carolina P, 2006.

——. "Imaginative Conjunctions on the Imperial 'Frontier': Catharine
Sedgwick Reads Mungo Park." In *Feminist Interventions in Early
American Studies*, 126-43. Tuscaloosa, AL: U of Alabama P, 2006.
(*Hope Leslie*)

Shields, Juliet. "Pedagogy in the Post-Colony: Documentary Didacticism and the 'Irish Problem.'" *Eighteenth-Century Novel* 6-7 (2009):
465-93. (*Redwood, Live and Let Live*, "The Irish Girl")

Simmons, Clare A. "*Hope Leslie, Marmion*, and the Displacement of
Romance." *ANQ: A Quarterly Journal of Short Articles, Notes, and Reviews* 17.1 (Winter 2004): 20-25.

Singley, Carol J. "Catharine Maria Sedgwick's *Hope Leslie*: Radical
Frontier Romance." In *Desert, Garden, Margin, Range: Literature on
the American Frontier*, 110-22. New York: Twayne, 1992. (reprinted

in *The (Other) American Tradition: Nineteenth-Century American Women Writers*, ed. Joyce Warren. New Brunswick, NJ: Rutgers UP, 1993)

Stadler, Gustavus. "Magawisca's Body of Knowledge: Nation-Building in *Hope Leslie*." *Yale Journal of Criticism* 12.1 (Spring 1999): 41-56.

Stearns, Bertha Monica. "Miss Sedgwick Observes Harriet Martineau." *New England Quarterly* 7.3 (September 1934): 533-41.

Steinberg, Stacy A. "'Unexpected and Inconvenient Notice': Domestic Entrapment and Servant Infidelity in *The Coopers* and *Live and Let Live*." *Legacy* 15.1 (1998): 85-91.

Stout, Janis P. *Sodoms in Eden: The City in American Fiction before 1860*. Westport, CT: Greenwood, 1976. (*Clarence*)

Strand, Amy Dunham. "Interpositions: *Hope Leslie*, Women's Petitions, and Historical Fiction in Jacksonian America." *Studies in American Fiction* 32.2 (Autumn 2004): 131-64.

———. "*Hope Leslie*, Women's Petitions, and Political Discourse in Jacksonian America." Chap. 1 in *Language, Gender, and Citizenship in American Literature, 1789-1919*. New York: Routledge, 2009.

Sweet, Nancy F. "Dissent and the Daughter in *A New England Tale* and *Hobomok*." *Legacy* 22.2 (2005): 107-25.

Szabo, Liz. "'Pleasure in an Illusion': Catharine Maria Sedgwick's *Hope Leslie*." In *The Image of the Frontier in Literature, the Media, and Society*, ed. Will Wright and Steven Kaplan, 275-82. Pueblo, CO: University of Southern Colorado, 1996.

Tawil, Ezra F. "Domestic Frontier Romance, or, How the Sentimental Heroine Became White." *Novel* 32.1 (Fall 1998): 99-124. (*Hope Leslie*)

———. "Domestic Frontier Romance, or, How the Sentimental Heroine Became White." Chap. 3 in *The Making of Racial Sentiment: Slavery and the Birth of the Frontier Romance*. Cambridge: Cambridge UP, 2006.

Templin, Mary. "'Dedicated to Works of Beneficence': Charity as Model for a Domesticated Economy in Antebellum Women's Panic Fiction." In *Our Sisters' Keepers: Nineteenth-Century Benevolence Literature by American Women*, 80-104. Tuscaloosa, AL: U of Alabama P, 2005. (*Poor Rich Man*)

Tuthill, Maureen. "Land and the Narrative Site in Sedgwick's *Hope Leslie*." *ATQ* 19.2 (June 2005): 95-113.

Van Dette, Emily. "'It Should Be a Family Thing': Family, Nation, and Republicanism in Catharine Maria Sedgwick's *A New-England Tale* and *The Linwoods*." *ATQ* 19.1 (March 2005): 51-74.

———. "'A Whole Perfect Thing': Sibling Bonds and Antislavery Politics in Harriet Beecher Stowe's *Dred*." *ATQ* 22.2 (2008): 415-32. (*Linwoods*)

Vásquez, Mark G. "'Your Sister Cannot Speak to You and Understand You As I Do': Native American Culture and Female Subjectivity in Lydia Maria Child and Catharine Maria Sedgwick." *ATQ* 15.3 (September 2001): 173-90. (*Hope Leslie*)

——. "'The Liberty of Substituting My Own Expressions': Women Writers, Revised Rhetorics, and the Paradoxes of Mediation." Chap. 3 in *Authority and Reform: Religious and Educational Discourses in Nineteenth-Century New England Literature*. Knoxville, TN: U of Tennessee P, 2003. (*New-England Tale, Hope Leslie*)

Wald, Priscilla. "Immigration and Assimilation in Nineteenth-Century US Women's Writing." In *The Cambridge Companion to Nineteenth-Century American Women's Writing*, ed. Dale M. Bauer and Philip Gould, 176-199. Cambridge: Cambridge UP, 2001. (*Hope Leslie*)

Wegener, Signe O. *James Fenimore Cooper versus the Cult of Domesticity: Progressive Themes of Femininity and Family in the Novels*. Jefferson, NC: McFarland, 2005. (*Hope Leslie*)

Weierman, Karen Woods. "Reading and Writing *Hope Leslie*: Catharine Maria Sedgwick's Indian 'Connections.'" *New England Quarterly* 75.3 (September 2002): 415-43.

——. "Remembering and Removing the Indian: Indian-White Marriages in Sedgwick, Cooper, and Child." Chap. 3 in *One Nation, One Blood: Interracial Marriage in American Fiction, Scandal, and Law*. Amherst, MA: U of Massachusetts P, 2005. (*Hope Leslie*)

West, Lisa. "The Nature of 'The Flourishing Village' in America: Prospects in Sedgwick's *Hope Leslie*." *Literature in the Early American Republic* 2 (2010): 103-29.

Wider, Sarah Ann. "In Search of an Audience: The Reader and Her Work." Chap. 3 in *Anna Tilden, Unitarian Culture, and the Problem of Self-Representation*. Athens, GA: U of Georgia P, 1997. (*Hope Leslie, Redwood*)

Yin, Joanna. "Calvinist Grace and Captivity in Trickster Narratives: Catharine Maria Sedgwick's *Hope Leslie*." *Studies in Puritan American Spirituality* 7 (2001): 183-212.

Zagarell, Sandra A. "Expanding 'America': Lydia Sigourney's *Sketch of Connecticut*, Catharine Sedgwick's *Hope Leslie*." *Tulsa Studies in Women's Literature* 6.2 (Fall 1987): 225-45.